TO:

with best
regards,

[signature]

FLAMES OF STRAW

*An Extraordinary Family Story Of Three
Men And The Women In Their Lives*

Andrew Zsigmond

authorHOUSE®

AuthorHouse™ UK Ltd.
500 Avebury Boulevard
Central Milton Keynes, MK9 2BE
www.authorhouse.co.uk
Phone: 08001974150

Although the author has used real events as a backdrop, the main characters featured in the novel are fictitional. All similrities with living persons are purely coincidental

©2010 Andrew Zsigmond. All rights reserved.

No part of this book may be reproduced, stored in a retrieval system, or transmitted by any means without the written permission of the author.

First published by AuthorHouse   3/3/2010

ISBN: 978-1-4389-4908-6 (sc)
ISBN: 978-1-4389-4909-3 (hc)

This book is printed on acid-free paper.

To Carol

With love for her encouragement,

and to all Readers, who enjoyed this private view of the XXth Century.

Flames of Straw tells the story of a Transylvanian-Hungarian family's turbulent life through the twentieth century in a novel of three books depicting three generations of the Zenta family up to its shattering conclusion on New Year's Day 2000.

In the course of a root-seeking trip from London to Transylvania, Adam accidentally stumbles upon information regarding his grandfather Titus' excommunication from the Church many years earlier. He begins an investigation in which he uncovers the astonishing history of the Zenta family.

During Titus Zenta's graduation from the Military Academy of Budapest he receives the Sword of Honour from the Emperor-King and meets the beautiful Hollywood actress Sarah Dombay. Titus becomes torn between the glamour of the capital and his service to the Austro-Hungarian Empire in World War One. It can only end in tragedy …

The story continues with Nicholas, who endures the Second World War under somewhat luckier stars – but his challenge comes from the retreating Germans from the Eastern Front. Anger and compassion drive him to dareing actions during the Holocaust, only for him to become the target of the communist secret police.

The Hungarian Revolution of 1956 forms the character of Adam, who, after his escape from Hungary following the anti-communist uprising, becomes a successful psychiatrist in London's fashionable Harley Street. His life is driven by his love of beautiful women, and as he becomes involved in the world of espionage and Eastern Bloc politics, can we hope for a happy ending?

1

Prologue

The burly Romanian frontier guard lieutenant replaced the black Bakelite telephone receiver. The Securitate control room had just reassured him that the car and its two occupants would have surveillance at 'Category A' level. He strolled back to the Jaguar XJS in the special lane and returned the passports with a lazy salute. Only then did he realise that once again he had ended up talking to the passenger. Damn these stupid English cars with right-hand drives, he thought. When will they ever join the rest of the world? His annoyance was obvious as he walked around the car once more. He had to get the driver to step out for the overhead spy cameras. A few more shots were required along the scheduled route for the Securitate agents.

'Just a final check of the boot,' he said. 'You don't mind, do you?'

'Of course not!'

The driver was in no position to mind anything. He got out of the car and opened the boot. After a brief search at the side next to the toolbox Adam pulled out a carton of two hundred Kent cigarettes, placing them on the top of the suitcases.

'Thank you, sir,' said the lieutenant, not caring a hoot that his act of bribery was being filmed by his colleagues. 'Have a good journey … I love your car! We don't get too many V12 Jags coming this way!'

Adam closed the boot and bounced back into his seat, just in time to observe the intense hatred on the face of the officer in his side mirror, but as he turned away from the cameras Adam thought he smiled for a split second.

'God, you do dislike each other! As nations, I mean,' whispered Gabrielle. Adam pulled away from the dreadful concrete frontier station, leaving the lane of ordinary tourists, by now five kilometres long, way behind. Miserable Trabants, Ladas and Dacias were breaking their backs under their loads, their occupants unable to hide their admiration for the elegance of the English car speeding away in the reserved lane.

'*Dislike*, Gabs, is not the word,' he said wryly. 'Perhaps *abhor* might get nearer to it … it's our Central European curse: hate thy neighbour; the twelfth commandment, especially applicable to Hungarians and Romanians.'

'You mean the eleventh being the usual one here too?' Asked Gabrielle with more than a teasing smile on her inviting lips.

'Precisely, and I mean it in every possible sense,' he said, putting his left index finger to his lips. The look on Gabrielle's face was of astonishment and surprise. Adam just knowingly nodded.

'Bang in a tape, darling, just for a while, because you will soon see nature playing a tune you will never forget.'

Lakme?

'Sure! The most underrated of operas,' muttered Adam, 'and you know, this version with Mado Robin recorded in the fifties is still the best, never mind Sutherland and Mesple.'

The winding road was virtually deserted, except for the odd TIR camion struggling uphill, suffering endlessly on the ten percent gradient. The silver-and-blue Jaguar hugged the bends with ease. The whisper of the 5.3-litre V12 engine did not disturb the 'flower duet' in the slightest. Gabrielle stretched in time with the music, her light khaki shirt generously unbuttoned in the heat, displaying a little more of her left breast than she intended. A few more turns and they were on the very top of the Transylvanian Alps.

'I must take a picture of this!' said Adam, pulling up to the luscious grass verge by the roadside. 'Just look at this scenery, darling, it puts Switzerland to shame!'

'No comparison,' whispered Gabrielle. 'Switzerland is cold and dramatic – this place seems warm, homely and inviting.'

'Just like your bosom,' he answered, and as they stood between the car and the deep valley below them, he gently slipped his hand into her half-unbuttoned shirt, her left breast more than filling his hand. She never wore a bra unless her dress demanded it and today it certainly did not.

'Are you sure it's all right here? You're so eager to christen your old homeland,' she teased.

'I just cannot wait, darling, just cannot wait.' He gently eased her down to the soft grass. Their lovemaking was not long, as it could hardly be in such circumstances. The music poured out of the car, enhancing their climaxes. The Act One love duet between the English officer and the Brahmin princess soared above their heads as he gently rolled off her to look into the perfect blue sky.

Lying there, smelling the grass, was a moment they would never forget. It was some time since they had made love in such a spontaneous way. After all, he was a fifty-year-old man, returning to his birthplace for the first time in some forty years, showing it to his wife; his second wife. She, twelve years younger, a quietly elegant woman and a beauty by any standards, very much wanted to be a part of this experience. They were a handsome couple who had much to offer each other. Their earlier affair had been followed by a seemingly perfect marriage. There they were like two teenagers, listening to their favourite music after an act of love, until the powerful scenery took them over once again. Adam looked into the deep blue sky, his Transylvanian sky.

'Gabs, look, down there!' Adam was pointing towards the bottom of the valley. The stream, a small bridge by the cottage – it all looked as idyllic as when it was first built hundreds of years ago, seemed still to be waiting for the return of the hillside shepherd and his small herd of sheep.

'Time has stood still here,' remarked Gabrielle.

'No. Time was made to stand still by the Romanian communists, the worst kind you can get,' he answered confidently. 'Thank God my father had the sense to drag us out of here in good time. I could so easily have been that shepherd in that valley,' Adam answered, meaning every word.

'Adam, why did you go suddenly quiet and put your finger to your lips in the car earlier?' Asked Gabrielle, frowning.

'Not a word of politics in the car, darling. You know when they asked us to step into their office at the frontier station, it was not because that greasy lieutenant wanted us to have a chance to stretch our legs. I'm certain they bugged our car.'

'Aren't you imagining that?'

'I only wish I was, I only wish … Let's go.' His mood changed. 'We have so much to do.'

As they returned to the road, the splendour of the King's Pass of the Transylvanian Alps opened up before them. The ancient forest closed in the rolling beauty of the mountains on the left, and the fertile valley hugging the River Kőrös on the right, as if in a frame. It was breathtaking. They were sorry to leave all this beauty behind, but scenic compensation was provided by the picturesque hamlets along the road. The pattern soon became obvious. A strict colour coding emerged for the villages of the two nations: the Magyars using the colours of red and green, the Wallachs preferring blue and yellow. Smaller towns displayed the legacy of communist 'industrial planning' – grey cement, and chemical plants blowing their obnoxious materials into the polluted sky. At the side of the cement works the roof tiles of the nearby houses had a good inch of grey white dust upon them. Only the local pathologist could possibly have known what the people's lungs must have looked like inside. Further along, new and larger chemical works tragically dominated the landscape. The colours of the rainbow were refracted by the fumes, which rose towards the sun, as if racing to be first through the hole in the ozone layer, ever enlarging it.

∽

When this plan was first whispered to Adam the changes in Hungary were well under way. The idea was initially a private one, involving a Romanian officer, half Hungarian by birth, who was willing to provide six rolls of microfilm. He had his reasons, but at that stage no one knew them.

Two members of the World Federation of Hungarian Freedom Fighters of the 1956 revolution met Adam at *The Gay Hussar*, the oldest surviving Hungarian restaurant in Soho, popular both with the left-wing English literati and members of the right-wing Hungarian émigré groups. Adam did agree, well before the Glenfiddich, that they were right. He also knew he was the obvious choice. The cover of a Harley Street doctor with the highest possible profile, on vacation to visit to his birthplace for his approaching fiftieth birthday, might even fool Gabrielle.

~

Well, it had; so far anyway. Having left the cement dust and the multicoloured fumes behind, the Jaguar cruised easily between the giant international lorries and the horse carts. One more turn to the top of the hill and Kolozsvár was spreading beneath the checkpoint used by the police to extract more Kent cigarettes from the hapless drivers. 'Cluj-Napoca – 2 km', read the signpost, in Romanian only. The Jaguar sailed past it into the city centre, where the architecture reflected the best Hungarian baroque of the last two centuries. Luckily it had been untouched by the war as the result of a clever piece of Romanian political trickery, ensuring that the principality stayed in their hands. The largest mounted statue in the world, that of King Matthias of Hungary, suddenly appeared, amazingly untouched, for the Romanians claimed some Wallach ancestry for him. In front of it stood the organiser of the trip, Adam's cousin, Andrew Székely, smartly turned out in his slightly shiny but well-pressed suit. Under his jacket a paisley-patterned gold waistcoat gave him a more dashing image in keeping with his extraordinary intellect. His pale blue eyes shone through his spectacles and his snowy hair (no longer the dark brown Adam remembered) was combed back off his face.

He had no idea of Adam's real reason for the visit, but he had organised the trip as the result of many telephone conversations. Too many perhaps, but that was '*The Gay Hussar Plan*': a very high-profile fact-finding tour attracting as much press and secret police attention as possible. That way the eventual brush-contact would not be spotted.

At the foot of the statue, the usual embraces followed. Adam hesitated for a moment before the second kiss on the cheeks. Thirty years in England had left its mark on him. He was no longer used to this Continental ritual, and neither did he like it, unless it involved women. The cousins were genuinely pleased to see each other. They had been close even when the elder doctor was just training to be a Catholic priest and the younger one was a little schoolboy in a Calvinist school. Adam had never forgotten their stroll together the day before his father packed the family on a train for the unknown.

'Gabs, would you like to jump into the back, please?' For several days this would be her routine, her bottom on one side, feet on the other, her shapely legs just about squeezing in. The rear seats of the sports car were definitely not meant for passengers, especially not women.

'To the flat – let's have a chat,' said Andrew.

The flat was in a multi-storey apartment block, but luckily at ground-floor level, part of the surrounding cement jungle. Inside, only the fine books, the occasional very valuable antique and a Reinhardt still life on the wall reflected the past glory of the family.

'Your wife is very beautiful, much warmer than her photographs. You know, I still have the one in *Vogue*, from all those years ago,' said the old Sekler. The good country wine came in profusion. Along with it, pieces of paper designed to keep the verbal side of the conversation politically non-controversial, as they knew that the telephone doubled as a listening device. Everybody's did. But Adam thought that it was stupid to be anodyne, so he let fly a few more innocent remarks about the 'socialist potholes on the roads, just like in Brent or Liverpool'. Gabrielle liked that and giggled – socialist city councils were her pet hates too.

After the dinner of grilled pork, paprika potatoes cooked in the traditional Transylvanian way and pickled dill cucumbers, cousin Andrew began to tire. He'd had to bribe and cajole for months to be able to provide this feast.

'We will drive to your birthplace tomorrow,' he declared, 'see how much you remember of it.'

'Well, don't expect too much, I was only eight when I was last there. But I do remember the church,' Adam added. 'Everybody remembers it, it was a true masterpiece of eleventh-century Transylvanian architecture with all those dead Zentas in the churchyard … quite something!'

The sofa was converted into a double bed for the visiting couple. Sleep came easily under the Reinhardt still life. It had been a long day.

'Coffee?' chirped cousin Andrew. It was 7 a.m. Well, coffee of sorts, much diluted with chicory. Nonetheless, it was warm and wet and went down well with the toast and jam – alas, no butter.

After about two hours' driving along the banks of the lazy River Maros, they arrived at the capital of Seklerland, Vásárhely, where the three of them checked into the Grand Hotel. Top-floor adjacent rooms were all prepared and duly bugged. Adam noticed an unsavoury-looking middle-aged lady, with sticky hair and shifty eyes, as she joined them in the lift, getting out one floor below them. He knew she would be the tail, as the commies often used inconspicuous women for the purpose. Such women having lost their libido, they considered them much more efficient; more meddlesome.

If proof of this was needed, it soon came. Adam had promised to lend his cousin his shoe-polishing kit. As he opened the bedroom door he caught the woman. She was holding her crude listening device against the door. Adam quickly grabbed it from her and dragged her along to the window at the end of the corridor. He was incensed.

'You will stop that right now, won't you, love?' he said menacingly. He opened the window and threw the device out. 'Next time you will follow it, understand?'

'I had to do it, I had to do it!' She screamed, as he let her go.

Cousin Andrew was astonished at the scene and murmured, 'Be careful Adam, this was just their first visit.' They went to eat.

The car, left outside the hotel, attracted a crowd of considerable size, young and old arguing about its bhp and other specifications. As often happens, one of the youngest ones corrected most of them. They were all fascinated by the right-hand drive, some considering it a great advance in motoring technology. By the time the three of them returned, the GB plate was missing, having become someone's souvenir.

The drive to the small village, some fifteen kilometres from town, did not take long, even on the winding road.

'Gabs, on the left, look, over there. Koronka. That was our vineyard.' Adam pointed.

'Quite right,' said the elder man. 'You do remember, don't you?'

'More than you think. You know, I was a very intelligent child before all this rot set in.' They looked at each other, smiling.

The hamlet suddenly burst upon them. The fences and woodwork were all in red and green, the right colours. As they left the large oak trees behind, the spire of the church became visible.

'I turn left here.' Adam's voice became a little excited. Down to the next right turn, then a lovely grassy lane led to the magnificent church, surrounded by a high whitewashed wall. They walked through a smaller version of a Sekler gate; a very richly carved wooden structure with a small roof giving homes to birds of all sorts. The pastor, as arranged, was there to welcome the Western visitors. He showed them around inside the church with great pride.

'The second pew on the left belonged to your family ... still does, I suppose,' said the young pastor in good English. 'We have a treasure here.' He unfolded an old Hungarian regimental flag. 'Your grandfather brought it back from the First World War.'

Gabrielle busied herself with the camera, taking a picture of Adam holding the flag, then other shots galore. Adam would be mad should she miss an important one. Oh, my sentimental husband, she thought.

'You must see the bell,' said the pastor. 'King Matthias gave it to us.'

This is pure enchantment, thought Gabrielle as they climbed the tower. The ancient bell next to her husband in the top of the steeple was not the usual kind of picture she took on holidays. 'Pull your head back a little ... that's good, hold it!' The churchyard came next. The pastor withdrew.

'Andrew, you won't be needing me there.' Turning to Adam, he continued, 'He knows more about this place than anyone.'

'Well, let me walk you around,' said the older doctor.

A section of the courtyard was clearly intended for the Zenta family. 'Uncle Charles ... heard of him. Peter, Alexander ... my God! Two-metre obelisks for all of them?' wondered the visitor. 'They were either really rich or it just became a habit no one dared to break,' he murmured.

'The latter, I bet,' was Gabrielle's reply.

'Where is Titus, our grandfather?'

The cousin hesitated a little before answering curtly, 'Surely you know about that.'

'No, I don't – what do you mean?'

'You mean your father never told you?' Andrew asked in amazement.

'No. Anyway, he and I spent the last thirty years in different countries.'

'Titus and our grandmother, Kathleen, are buried over there.' Andrew pointed over the churchyard wall. The couple turned together in the direction of his pointing arm. 'Are you sure you don't know?' Andrew asked again.

As they walked out through the church gate, all they could see was undulating grazing land with two small humps on it, surrounded by some trees.

'I must see that!' Adam was already walking towards the trees, some two hundred yards away in deep grass, full of the prettiest of wild flowers. When they got there, they were standing in front of twelve plum trees in the shape of a perfect horseshoe, with the opening facing away from the church.

'They were buried here,' Andrew said softly.

A Sekler, with features of Attila the Hun, was scything the grass near by.

'Can I borrow your scythe, sir?' Adam said as he approached him. 'I want to clear that bit, between the trees.'

'You should really leave that place alone. No one has bothered to do anything there for decades,' warned the man, who had the most lived-in of faces. 'It won't bring you any luck you know!'

By then, scythe in hand, Adam was already cutting the grass. Having done nothing like this for years it took him a little while to get the action going: right hand dragged back, holding the little crossbar in the middle of the shaft, pulling downwards and across, keeping his eyes on the bundle of grass he intended to cut with the yard-long, curved, medieval blade. A primitive golf swing, he thought, though with a straightened blade the contraption was more often used in peasant revolts. The area he cleared soon revealed two parallel mounds; they could only have been graves.

'Stand behind them, amongst the trees,' demanded Gabrielle for the camera. 'Hold it, point to the blade.'

Adam did as he was told. Suddenly his left hand caught the cutting edge of the upturned sharpened scythe. He didn't feel much until Gabrielle, looking through the lens of the camera, shouted, 'Adam, you're bleeding!'

Adam looked at his left thumb. A good gash along it, bleeding profusely on to the left mound. Titus' grave.

'Blood binding,' murmured the peasant.

'Rubbish!' retorted Adam, covering his bleeding thumb with his handkerchief. 'Just a little accident, that's all.'

Turning to his cousin he said softly, 'Enough of these dark hints. What really happened here?'

'Can I just say … that Titus was a bit of a lad. Like the rest of the family, I suppose. Women are in our blood, you know.'

'You mean adultery is!' Gabrielle added for good measure.

'Well, he had an affair with the pastor's wife. Finding it out, the wronged vicar was not particularly forgiving, as Calvinists often are not, so he promptly excommunicated him, denying him sacred ground for his burial. The family, impoverished by then, buried him on the last piece of land they still owned. They put the twelve trees around it. One for every person who attended the pastor-less funeral. Not many years later, our grandmother, Kathleen, demanding to be with him after her death, followed him there. And then, *they were just forgotten.*'

Book One

2

TITUS

The Royal and Imperial Army Officers' Academy of the Austro-Hungarian Empire was once again preparing for its graduation day in the southern suburbs of Pest. The union of the cities of Buda and Pest, with the construction of the Chain Bridge by the Scottish Clark cousins, was a wonder and less than fifty years old. The Danube was still blue and the graduates of the academy were donning their blue tunics for the parade. The exhilaration and expectation on their faces was as obvious as it was well deserved. Four years of arduous work completed, they were not to know that more than half of them would perish on the Italian front at Doberdo in the Great War.

To boost the diminishing standing of the House of Habsburg, caused by the erratic behaviour of its lesser royals, this year Emperor and King Franz Joseph was going to take the salute himself. The ascendancy of the Hungarian half of the dual monarchy was by now well established and within the Kingdom of Hungary, the Principality of Transylvania was enjoying its third golden age.

This year's ceremony was to have something new. Quietly copied from Sandhurst in England, there was to be a Sword of Honour presentation to the top graduate. Nobody but the Regent Viceroy, Prince Joseph Habsburg of the Hungarian branch of the royal family (which never got on too well with the Austrian Habsburgs), knew about it. The principal, General Hubay, called upon the graduates to assemble on the parade ground. In a quick march from the four corners of the ground representing the four corners of the kingdom, the graduates suddenly appeared. In less than a minute they were standing in front of their king in a perfectly formed large square. The instructors stood before them with swords drawn. The Prince Regent welcomed the proud parents sitting on both sides of the main stand. Dropping his voice, he then welcomed the Commander in Chief, His Imperial and Royal Majesty Franz Joseph. The King stood in front of the platform. The ageing monarch still cut a fine figure in his light blue uniform, wearing only four medals, which made him positively underdressed in comparison to some of his generals, who looked more like peacocks. His sash, however, made all the difference: for royals it always meant much more than any decoration.

'Ladies and gentlemen,' he started in a low voice, 'my wife and I are here to conduct this ceremony for the first time.' The King continued in flowing Hungarian. He was very serious about languages, being fluent in many. More than that, he prided himself on being able to give an audience to any of his subjects in his or her mother tongue.

'The Queen', he turned to the beautiful Elizabeth, 'just remarked to me how smart you all look,' he said, provoking smiles all around. 'She is always happy to be here …' He wanted to continue, but he was interrupted by a loud 'hurrah' from the crowd. The parents joined in with hurrahs in profusion, for the Queen was the most popular person in the country. 'You have graduated in larger numbers then ever before, because there are clouds on the horizon and your country will need you: as soldiers and leaders. I am told, amongst you there is a graduate of distinction. I have a secret for him that none of you could possibly know. He is to receive from me this Sword of Honour.'

The King turned to his aide-de-camp, who took the sword from the table. As he lifted it, the strong sunshine hit the highly polished brass, which gleamed in all directions. The Queen, dressed in black velvet, touched it gently. The King raised it with two hands to shoulder level and turned to the general. The bemedalled portly man stepped forward and in a loud voice he commanded, 'Lieutenant Titus Zenta de Lemhény, five steps forward!' The surprised young man emerged with difficulty from within the second row of the left middle formation. As he shuffled sideways he received a few whispered 'well dones'. He couldn't recollect later how he managed to be standing before his general, but there he was, this strong young man just about six foot tall, his very dark brown hair combed straight back under his peaked hat. His small perky moustache was well trained to point slightly upwards. The piercing light blue eyes confirmed his Sekler origin, which was reflected in his accent too. There was just no way of 'educating' that out of him. He was proud to belong to the oldest of Hungarian tribes, which had settled at the foot of the Carpathians some fifteen hundred years before.

The King leaned forward and passed the sword to the overwhelmed young man, whispering a most welcome 'well done, my son'. Their gloved hands touched for a moment, which he would never forget. 'For King and country,' he answered sharply, and with two quick clips he fastened the sword to his belt. The general announced that Lieutenant Zenta would now take the oath on behalf of the graduates. The lieutenant was handed a paper with the words of the oath to read which he promptly folded and put into his pocket. 'Company, the loyal oath. *I – state your full name – swear by the God of Magyars, that I will serve my king loyally and faithfully …*' The new officers standing at attention with their right hands held up, palms forward in a two-fingered boy scout position, were repeating the words after him, promising to die for their country; a promise most of them sadly would have to keep.

After the oath they were marched away to the four corners of the parade ground, where they all received their swords and returned to the stand to line up behind the Royal Army Band, playing the *Rakóczi March* (after Bihari, Erkel, Berlioz and Liszt – for this most successful of marches had many parents). The colours were presented by the Queen, who also tied her personal sash to the flagpole. Approving fathers, looking at each other proudly, mothers and sweethearts wiping the occasional tear with the most elaborately embroidered handkerchiefs, completed the picture. The general nodded to the regimental sergeant major, the most influential man in the Academy, who now dismissed the new officers. They threw their hats into the air. The mingling started and the royal couple took part fully, talking to graduates and parents alike.

The fattened spit-roasted oxen was an impressive sight in the western corner of the ground, and the gentle cooking of the meat could be smelled for miles around. Just before the food was about to be served, the King and Queen slipped away, taking an 'English leave', as it is known on the Continent. Titus' parents missed the ceremony. The work on the estate was too much for Charles to leave in his manager's hands. He declared, 'I am harvesting this year for *his* future anyway. I can't be in two places at the same time.' Perhaps he knew that this was going to be one of his last harvests, an occasion much more important to him than a mere military ceremony. His estate manager could naturally handle the whole thing but Charles would never admit to that. Needless to say, the question of his wife going on such a long journey on her own by train simply did not arise. Secretly she too would rather have stayed away; after all, Titus would be spending his leave at home before taking his first posting.

Titus soon found himself talking to a group of ladies: mothers and other officers' sweethearts. They were all keen to see the sword, or that might just have been an excuse, he hoped. These were good times in the life of the nation, which were reflected in the mood and the fashion of both men and women. Colours, colours and more colours invaded the garments; men in smart tunics with tight-fitting trousers disappearing into their highly polished knee boots, braided at the top, some wearing their old regimental dress wear, clattering their swords as they dragged them along. The women were elegant and beautiful, with their exaggerated bosoms, thin waistlines and padded bottoms. Their hats were just sensational. This was definitely the age of milliners, one of the best-paid trades in the land, when even a country maid would not be seen in the street without a decent bonnet.

Titus was by now relaxed enough to respond to the attention he was so obviously given by the ladies. Like all men who enjoy the company of women he was basically shy with them, and naturally they found this most attractive. The combination of obvious innate strength and a dash of shyness only a few could resist. And today was not the day to resist anything.

The dinner was served in the dining hall, decorated specially for the event. Red, white and green bunting covered the austere ceiling, with the principal wall full of oil paintings of the most important kings from the nation's tragic past. The founder, St Steven, the great knightly monarch St László, followed by Béla III, who, having received Richard the Lionheart for the first ever state visit of an English monarch to Hungary, joined him in the third crusade. In the centre, two larger pictures of Louis the Great and, naturally, Matthias. The line-up was completed symmetrically by Charles-Robert, Zsigmond, the nation's last Holy Roman Emperor, and the current Franz Joseph.

The place of honour belonged to Titus, who looked every inch the part, by now changed into his mess uniform and wearing his graduation medal on his navy blue braided tunic. His lieutenant's star was shining on his collar as Venus shone outside for him.

They were fed royally. The spit-roasted ox was delicious and the Bull's Blood of Eger, slightly tannic for his taste, went down well with it. They drank to the King and to the health of the staff of the Academy, then to each other.

There followed a short concert by the military band in the gymnasium, which most of them considered a bit of a bore. It served the purpose, because they had to clean up the dining hall for the Graduation Ball.

By the time the dancing was due to start, spirits were high. The ball was opened with the formal Hungarian 'palotas', the ballet scene from Erkel's opera *László Hunyadi*, danced by the cadets with young ladies from the nearby girls' boarding school. A very difficult dance to do even half well, full of rhythmic movements and sudden half-turns. They made a very good job of it. The following Strauss waltz had to be the *Blue Danube* – after all, they were only a few hundred yards away from it. Titus took the wife of the general for his first dance, a rounded lady of about fifty or so, wearing a tasteless dark grey satin dress with dark pink belt and blue rosettes. He supposed it was the right thing to do. Titus was a determined dancer and the lady was no newcomer to waltzes. As they twirled around, many of the other older ladies wished they were in her place.

'Aren't you lonely on your own here, Lieutenant? It's a shame that you of all people don't have anyone with you today.' She smiled.

'Madam, it's the greatest day of my life and I'm very happy not having to share it with anyone,' he answered.

'You are very popular with the ladies here and quite a few asked me if there was anyone special in your life …' she probed, with yet another smile.

'Special? Why, no, but I suppose I do have a sweetheart of sorts back home in Transylvania,' Titus replied. 'We exchange the occasional letter, more like pen-pals, nothing more.'

As the waltz concluded, he returned the large lady to her table, kissed her gloved hand and thought, It's time for a drink with my friends. The bar was at the other end of the ballroom. As Titus was hurrying towards it, weaving amongst the dancers, he decided to bump into one of the couples he had noticed during the waltz, a very dark-eyed beauty dancing with one of the staff officers. Their eyes met for less than a fraction of a second. The contact was immediate. They both knew one of them had to do something about it. He offered his apologies. She recognised him from the ceremony. He knew nothing about her and this bothered him.

At the bar he asked some of his friends about the beauty. They were amazed at his ignorance.

'Fancy not knowing Sarah Dombay, the rising star of the Budapest stage. The papers were full of her Ophelia, not more than a week ago!' one of them offered.

'Isn't our staff officer lucky to accompany a lady like that?' He asked his friend Péter Vadas, pryingly. He was full of anticipation as he waited for his reply.

'Oh, the staff officer she is dancing with?' Asked Peter. 'Don't worry, I really think there is nothing between them,' he continued. 'Rumour has it that she just finished an affair with some newspaper chap and wanted a night out, nothing more. She uses him to escort her once in a while,' Peter concluded to the open-mouthed Titus.

'Do any of you know her well enough to introduce me?'

'Don't be a silly lad, how could we possibly know her?' Peter patted him on his back. 'We wish we did, but she lives in a different world.'

'All right, fellows, then I'll introduce you lot to her,' Titus snapped, and turned away.

At the next convenient break in the music he briskly walked up to the actress, bowed his head slightly and asked the question that would determine his future life. 'May I be so lucky as to have the earliest possible dance on your card, ma'am?'

'Ah, the man of the moment, Lieutenant Zenta.' Her smile was outrageous, and her eyes like black diamonds.

The answer was going to be obvious, Zenta thought, the easiest thing I've ever done.

Flames of Straw

'Now let me see ...' Sarah looked at her card. 'The general is next, and then I have three others. What time is it, Lieutenant? I see, nine thirty. Then I can give you the slow foxtrot at quarter past eleven. It's a new dance from England, do you know it?' Her smile was getting wider.

'Ma'am, you're giving me enough time to go away and learn it from scratch!' Titus said with obvious disappointment as he walked back to his friends, who were amused at his expense.

Some heavy drinking followed, whilst his friends teased him about the slow foxtrot, and others offered steps for it.

'Don't worry, lads, some more Dutch courage and I'll be all right,' he reassured them, with frequent glances at the gold watch his father had given him after his matriculation, listening to it just in case it had stopped.

Sarah's escorting staff officer joined them for a glass of champagne. Some of the graduates pulled themselves together into a lazy 'attention'.

'No need, no need,' he said, 'enjoy yourselves, officers, it's your night. I just came to say that you are a great bunch and it was a pleasure to teach you.'

'Kind of you to say so, sir,' answered Titus as he replenished his glass. 'We are grateful to you for making things so plain for us. With all this gun automation, the whole thing is more like an engineer's lot.'

'True, and the race for supremacy in this automation is truly on, now,' the colonel answered gloomily. 'I just hope we will not end up on the wrong side, as usual. But enough of this gloom and doom, just enjoy yourselves.' Turning to Titus he raised his voice. 'I believe you have a dance booked with my actress friend? She is a joy to dance with, very positive,' he added.

'She will have to be, for I haven't a clue what this foxtrot dance is all about.'

'Don't worry, my dear fellow.' The colonel left with a smile.

'Give me a shot of apricot pálinka murmured Titus. Peter obliged and Titus went off into his future.

The handsome officer and the beautiful young actress made a perfect couple on the dance floor. Some of the more elderly ladies even wiped away the odd tear with their lace handkerchiefs. The men, irrespective of their ages, would have given anything to be in his highly polished knee boots. Sarah managed to lead without making it obvious, or even noticeable. They could exchange only a few words, but they never lost eye contact, their faces reflecting in each other's pupils. The grip of their hands became stronger as they danced on, until it hurt.

'Ma'am, I wish I didn't have to be so direct, but there is no other way. I am running out of time ... I must see you again!'

'Well, you can always come and see me in *Hamlet*, at the New Theatre. We are doing it for another week,' she teased.

'No way am I going to listen to that twit of a prince even contemplating lying "between your fair maiden's thighs", no way!' Titus pulled back in mock jealousy. 'He would never get to the final sword fight.'

'Now, now, it's only a play, and anyway, he is not a twit. Actually he is quite an actor, you know.'

Over a drink at her table Titus continued to press her about a date. He would either get one now, or he would just have to wait outside the stage door and waste a lot of time.

'You said you'll be doing the Shakespeare for another week, then what?' he asked.

'Oh, then I'll be off on a tour with it to Kolozsvár in Transylvania, I think for a month,' she answered uncertainly.

'Now, that does sound interesting! I can join you.' Titus nearly jumped for joy. 'Tomorrow is Sunday, so I can't do anything, but first thing Monday morning I'll try to fix it.' He was getting more excited by the moment. 'We must speak about this, please suggest something.'

'Well, all right. I have a day off tomorrow too. Come to my flat for tea. Number two, Snake Street, second floor, at four thirty. You will see the nameplate. But I really must leave you now,' she added anxiously. A bow, a kiss on her gloved hand matching the most fashionable gown of the day, the gentlest click of his heels and he was off. Sarah's escort was just approaching. Titus nodded to him as he walked out of the room, straight to his quarters and bed. He lay there thinking and scheming for a while, until he realised that he had not kept his promise to introduce Sarah to his friends. To hell with it, he thought, he would have plenty of time to do that. He fell asleep.

Titus spent all next morning in the duty roster room of the Academy. Yes, they were all to be given two weeks' leave before posting, but there was still a lot of work to be done and they had to take turns. He had to use all his not inconsiderable charm to convince the staff major to agree to his request to coincide his leave with Sarah's tour. By 15.30 hours it was all arranged.

He found a hansom cab and jumped into it. 'Snake Street, number two, but stop at the first flower stand on the way,' he ordered. I must buy roses, he thought. No, don't be too hasty, it's not your style, he lectured himself. So he settled for a bunch of red and white carnations. A good tip to the driver and he was running up the staircase two or three steps at a time. On the second floor he soon found the familiar name: Dr L Dombay, Attorney at Law. Good grief, she lives with her parents, damn it, he thought. He cleared his throat, tugged his tunic straight and knocked on the door. A smartly dressed maid opened it. She was used to young men calling. She just looked at him and asked 'Who shall I say it is?'

'Lieutenant Zenta.'

A small silver tray was thrust at him from behind her back. 'Oh, the calling card!' Top left-hand tunic pocket, he thought. He placed his card on the tray with a smile. I must get this one on my side somehow. His smile widened. In the hall he saw a very smart forty-five-to-fiftyish, slightly greying lady approaching him.

'Lieutenant! How nice to see you.' She reached out with her right hand. Titus duly kissed it. 'What lovely flowers,' she continued. 'They wouldn't be for me, by any chance?' She smiled.

'Of course they are, ma'am, of course they are,' Titus answered with a slight pause, as he handed them over to her. I suppose this won't hurt in the long run, he thought.

'Come in, Lieutenant, Sarah will be with us in a second, she is running a little late as always,' she added in a lower tone. Titus was shown to the sofa in the stylishly furnished turn-of-the-century drawing room. He had just sat down when he heard the voice he was dying to hear.

'No, I am not always late!' Sarah entered in the best theatrical tradition. Her smile was even more captivating than he remembered from the ball. She wore an elegant olive-green day dress, figure-hugging, showing a good portion of her ankles.

'Please, Lieutenant, do sit down,' she continued, offering her hand for a kiss.

'Just look at these beautiful flowers the lieutenant has brought me,' her mother interrupted.

'Lovely indeed! You know, Mother, it's really amazing how it is always you who gets the flowers around here,' she quipped.

'Well, the early bird ...' her mother answered, walking towards the kitchen.

'It's really a very nice room.' Titus pointed to the oil painting over the baby grand. 'I suppose he is your father? There is a lot of resemblance. Will I be meeting him too?'

'Alas not. Poor Daddy died two years ago in a hunting accident,' replied Sarah. 'I do miss him so,' she added, holding back a tear.

'Oh, how dreadful, I am sorry,' he offered. 'I noticed on your doorplate that he was a lawyer?'

'The best!' She answered.

Her mother returned, followed by the maid, with lemon tea and cakes. The conversation about Sarah's father continued. Apparently he was a clever man all right, not only professionally, but as a shrewd player of the stock market too. It was obvious that he had left the family very comfortably off. Once the weak tea had been served, Sarah's mother left the room discreetly. Now there was a chance to talk. Titus got straight to the point.

'You know, your tour? Well, I managed to get leave for the first two weeks of it.'

'Isn't that wonderful. You really mean it?' Sarah paused. 'You are a very clever man' – and a determined one too, she thought.

'Any chance of my taking you out for dinner tonight as you're not working? Just a quiet place for a chat. We might as well plan now as I will not be able to see you for the rest of the week. Let me take you to the 100-Year-Old, we could walk it from here. It's a beautiful day.'

'Well, fine, but can we make it an early one, please – the rest of the week will be very hectic for me too,' replied Sarah.

'It's a deal. I am ready now,' said Titus.

'Well, well. At least I won't have to get changed, then,' she responded.

Her mother was duly informed of the sudden decision. To kill a little time they decided to take stroll on Váci Street. The stylish narrow street was just recently rebuilt, full of new shops and coffee houses, the latter providing a venue for revolutionaries, businessmen and courting couples alike. The aroma of the strong coffee escaped into the surrounding buildings and the superb inner courtyards between them. The street even boasted a new theatre, which, naturally, interested Sarah.

The handsome officer and everybody's favourite new actress made an immediate impact on the passers-by and heads turned to admire them. At the top of the street, they turned left to the Danube and walked back along the Korzó a wide area of paving between the river bank and the row of new hotels, reflecting the importance of the city and its confidence as the driving force of the dual monarchy. They soon reached the restaurant on the ground floor of the baroque building.

Titus slipped a one-crown note to the head waiter. He need not have done. The restaurant would be quite empty for some time yet. He pointed to a particular table in the corner and the 'Reserved' sign quickly disappeared from it. As the food was of no importance to either of them, they rushed their order to get some peace so that they could talk. With the help of a bottle of Greyfriars, a light white wine from the Lake Balaton region, they began to plan the trip. He might as well travel on the same train, they agreed. Sarah would be lodging at a theatre pension and Titus in a hotel, any hotel! They could lunch together and meet after performances.

There was more wine as they relaxed over the meal. Titus took her hand in his, for the first time really – not counting the dance and all those silly hand-kisses. He looked into her beautiful dark eyes. He was about to open his mouth to speak, but Sarah, one step ahead of him, placed her index finger across his lips and whispered: 'I love you too!'

The ensuing silence seemed to last like eternity itself. There was just nothing else to say. The casual observer would have noticed four hands welded together.

3

Journey

The frantic activity of the Western Railway Station, recently completed by Monsieur Eiffel, reflected the excitement of this new and important mode of transport. The huge roof, built not so long ago, covered a large area that was full of the wonderful smell of steam locomotives. And all those gorgeous noises they made! No wonder people visited the place, travelling or not. The elegance of the travellers blended in well with the new uniforms of the railway workers.

Amongst them all, the smart young officer with his batman walking behind him cut a fine figure. The double-breasted grey greatcoat allowed just a glimpse of the hilt of the sword. The batman placed his luggage on the rack of his first-class compartment and left after a quick salute.

'See you in two weeks' time, Jack,' the lieutenant called after him.

'Sir!' He replied.

The theatrical group was already settled two coaches behind his, which was especially reserved for them.

The guard blew his brand-new whistle and lifted his hand semaphore for the benefit of the engine driver. A skid, some puffing and panting and the train pulled out of the station, heading due east, leaving only the addictive smell of steam and coal behind.

Titus took off his greatcoat and put it on the hook by the window. His service sword went on the rack, behind his small travelling chest. He wasted no time and crossed the ornately decorated dining coach, which was being prepared for lunch by six busy waiters in perfectly pressed white linen coats, denoting their particular ranks. He got to the door of Sarah's coach, twirled his moustache, took a deep breath and opened the door. The troupe had their personal luggage in the first third of the coach. Fashionable suitcases and battered chests were everywhere. On one of the lower shelves he spotted two large matching items; medium brown, with repeating beige patterns involving the letters 'LV' and finished with lighter edging and cornering. As he tried to negotiate them he noticed the name tags: Miss Sarah Dombay. Who else would pay the earth for Louis Vuitton items – after all, he was only Napoleon's luggage maker – but at least they could stand up to even the fiercest of Russian winters.

Having reached the thespians he realised that they were all at least good colleagues, if not friends. He would definitely be the outsider on this trip. Sarah, at the far end of the carriage, was talking to an exceptionally statuesque middle-aged lady in navy blue, who was just removing an extra-large hat. She must be Gertrude, the Queen. Titus guessed right. The tall blond actor will be Hamlet, definitely. That was right too. With such effeminate gestures he wouldn't last ten minutes in the army, he thought. In the middle of the compartment sat a rather distinguished man of around fifty, with greying hair, wearing a dark grey striped suit, highlighted by a narrow maroon pocket kerchief. He must be in charge of them, one way or another. He could fit into the army, no problem, considered Titus. He was having great fun, assessing them from the military point of view. At last he managed to catch Sarah's eye. They lit up as she started to walk towards him. The dark green silk taffeta bodice fitted her tightly, only to relent from the hips down. The bustle carried the colours of her hat, which she placed on the rack before he arrived.

'Hello, darling, isn't this wonderful,' she stated rather than asked. They kissed cheeks and held hands.

'You look out of this world,' he said. She did.

This was the age of elegant travelling. The railway system had just been changed over to the wider tracks, catching up with western Europe. The stations were brand new and so was the rolling stock. It was a novel experience for everyone, and people responded by overdressing.

'Let's get the introductions out of the way.' Sarah pulled Titus by the hand. With a slight bow of his head, Titus offered his name to everyone in turn with his outstretched hand, rather than wait for Sarah to repeat it. When they got to the important-looking man in the striped suit, Sarah looked at him, then at Titus, and said, 'And this is Sir. He keeps us under control and pays us at the end of each week. Mr Joseph Orsen.'

'Nice to meet you, Lieutenant! We all know of you from Sarah.' Their firm handshake was followed by further introductions.

The train continued to puff and pant its way along the track until they reached the inconceivable speed of fifty-five miles per hour, which for them all was just another wonder of the age. As they left the rest of the city with its interminable building sites behind, the Great Hungarian Plain opened up before them. There were grazing fields as far as the eye could see, interrupted by the occasional 'nodding donkey'-style of peasant well, with troughs around for the large herds of horses. Farther along, there were cattle everywhere. The cowboys wore below-knee-length blue pleated kilts, with black riding boots. Their embroidered white shirts had the unique Magyar sleeves. White-braided black waistcoats and perky upturned brimmed hats with pampas grass stuck into the left side completed their striking wear. In addition, all shepherds on foot wore large sheepskin coats with exaggerated shoulders, fur facing out against the extreme cold of the night.

There was a hundred miles or so of this before they would reach the thousand-year-old Hungarian principality of Transylvania at the foot of the Carpathians. The two states, separate until their union in 1867, were now very much a firm part of the monarchy.

The troupe of actors and the soldier had just finished a good-humoured lunch of savoury Hortobágy pancake, followed by roasted pheasant, when the train started to take the one-in-ten gradient of the mountains. As the murderously strong black coffee arrived, they found themselves travelling through King's Pass. All eyes turned to the scenery. The drama of the flattest land in Europe, quite suddenly followed by the Transylvanian Alps, was breathtaking.

'This is far more beautiful than I ever thought. You are so lucky to have all this as your homeland,' Sarah said without turning around.

'The whole place is not as dramatic as this pass, you know. There is a lot of grazing and farming land on the estate,' Titus answered, gently holding her shoulders as she was looking through the window.

'You must tell me more about your estate,' she said, turning to him.

'I will, I will, but this is not the time, darling.' Holding her hands, he went on, 'I will tell you all, very soon.' Titus squeezed her hands gently.

'The King', as he liked to refer to himself after his role in the tragedy, butted in, 'Is there a decent casino in town, young man?'

'Indeed there is, an excellent one, at the Hotel Belvedere. The new American thing, "blackjack", is very popular and they have a few roulette tables too,' Titus reassured him.

'You seem to know your gambling!'

'What young officer does not? In Budapest a few of us used to have a go. The food was so much cheaper, and I do like roulette all right – in moderation, of course.' Titus smiled.

'You men are quite dreadful,' Sarah cut in. 'It's such a waste!'

By the time the train pulled into the station, elegance or not, the group had had enough of travelling. The men stood up and started to shake their stiffened legs, the ladies began to make repairs to their make-up; who knew who might see them on the platform?

They were taken straight to the National Theatre in horse-drawn cabs with several carts to carry the scenery and the theatrical props. Titus went along with them, saying his hotel was just around the corner and he could walk it from there. With the assurance of a 'host', Titus helped them down from the cabs, the bottom of his sword catching on the cobblestones.

'Hamlet' looked at him, thinking how awful it must be to have to wear that thing.

'Is this the one you just received?' He asked.

'Sadly, no. I too thought that I could have that one to wear, but alas not. It's for ceremonial occasions only. They would not even let me bring it to show my parents. This one is my service sword,' Titus explained.

'Mean things,' 'Hamlet' said, turning away.

At the theatre, they were all given a slip of paper with their accommodation address on it. Sarah showed hers to Titus.

'Do you know where this place is?'

'Sure, I'll drop you there on the way to my hotel.'

'The Belvedere, I suppose,' said Sarah, knowingly. 'Nice for some!'

The cab drive took them past the cathedral into a wide baroque street. As they gathered speed the newly shod hooves of the horses produced sparks on the perfectly laid cobblestones. They entered a narrow side street on the left and the driver pointed to a pleasant house, surrounded by chestnut trees.

'Number twenty-three, Officer?' Asked the cabby.

'Yes, my man.' Titus helped him with the luggage, walked to the door and pulled the bell chain, telling the driver to wait and take him to the hotel in a few minutes. The grin on the driver's face was noticeable; he was always assured of the next fare there.

The old lady opening the front door was delighted to see Sarah. 'Heard and read so much about you, my dear, I am looking forward to seeing you next week. I have just received my complimentary tickets from the theatre. Can I show you to your room?'

Completing her greeting, she quickly switched her glance from Sarah's eyes to her lips and smiled. Titus quietly noted that she was hard of hearing. The digs were certainly more than adequate: a large sitting room, nicely furnished with bed, bureau, oil lamp and sofa. Next door was the bathroom with a wood burner.

'I am afraid we will have to share the bathroom, but I promise I will not spend too much time in it.' The woman smiled again as she left the room. 'Sarah!' Titus reached out for her.

She came nearer and they embraced for the first time. Titus looked into her large dark eyes and held her more firmly as they kissed. Oh, how they kissed.

'No, darling, not here, not now, I'm sure the landlady is just outside.' Sarah pulled back.

'I am certain she is,' Titus muttered. What he would have liked to say was, who the hell cared?

'Now, my love, let me rest tonight, I'm so tired and we have a rehearsal in the morning, Why don't you come along at least to the end of it?' begged Sarah.

'I'll be there.' Titus kissed her on her lips, more tenderly, walked swiftly to the waiting cab and disappeared behind the chestnut trees.

The mayhem at the end of the drama was well under way when Titus arrived at the theatre. He was wearing casual civilian morning clothes of brown tweed plus-fours and a smart trilby, reflecting his status as a country gentleman. He sat down quietly halfway along the middle aisle and watched the rest of the play, which he considered very well done, especially 'Hamlet', who gave an excellent account of the moody Danish prince.

'I have the rest of the week off, until the Saturday opening,' Sarah said, running to him to kiss him on his cheek. 'They have a lot of problems with the set. I also have a new understudy, a local girl. She will need the rest of the rehearsals.'

'Wonderful! Get ready and I'll take you to the estate to meet my parents,' he answered excitedly. 'Let's go back to your lodgings.'

He hurriedly packed some clothes for the short trip, leaving his uniform in the hotel, telegraphed his father, picked up Sarah and they were soon back at the railway station for the afternoon train to Vásárhely, where the line terminated.

How different this journey was, with just the two of them in the first-class compartment. They could indulge in a little private conversation for the first time since the restaurant. Sitting opposite each other, they held hands and their eyes never lost contact. They talked of Titus' family this time. The Zentas were large landowners with several farms on thousands of acres. Gregory Zenta had been ennobled by King Steven Bocskai in 1604. The family had also produced physicians, lawyers and civil servants of all sorts, but there was always a line of army officers to serve King and country. The estate had never been broken down by ongoing inheritance, because it was entailed on the eldest son, who took on the responsibility of compensating the others with loans, mortgages and earnings, all settled by previous agreements. The occasional sale of land was always a commercial decision and the proceeds were used for modernisation. This is how Charles and Helen, the quiet, loving couple who thought the world of their only son, ended up still owning virtually the whole of the land, the vineyards and the priceless herds.

'But you don't have any brothers or sisters, so what will happen now with your army career just starting?' Sarah asked perceptively.

'Well, therein lies the problem. I am determined to have a military career. Anyway, Father is doing well enough at the moment, but who knows?' Titus answered thoughtfully.

When they got off the train, the liveried family coach was there waiting for them. The four greys looked in perfect condition and raring to go, with Michael the family factotum in his smart black-braided coat in attendance, holding a long whip. He saluted Titus and grinned.

'Welcome home, sir – it's been a long time.'

'Too long, Michael, too long.' Titus shook his hand warmly and introduced Sarah. He added, 'Let's have some fun, darling. Why don't we sit up front and drive the horses, and let Michael be comfortable in the coach with the luggage?'

'Really?'

'Yes!' Michael was not at all pleased with the idea. 'The two rear ones are new, sir, you are not used to them,' he tried.

'Don't worry, Michael, I'll handle them.' Titus sounded absolutely certain. With some difficulty due to Sarah's long dress, they settled on the driver's sheepskin-covered bench and Titus cracked the whip. The horses started with a jerk, but soon settled. Titus and horses got on well together. He had been handling horses one way or another ever since his childhood. As they drove through town, once again heads turned, and some even nodded. They could not see the person in the coach, but they knew who it was, and that was what mattered. Those who recognised Titus waved, which further embarrassed poor Michael. When they turned on to the road leading out of town, Titus asked Sarah to take her hat off.

'I'll put them through their paces a bit.'

The rest of the journey took place on family land. Cornfields, vineyards, followed by fields, turned into meadows along the River Nyárád, with the road winding alongside the river, as best it could. The dust cloud they created behind them was a quarter of a mile long. It was difficult to say whether it was the horses or the passengers who loved the trip most. The tree-lined drive bent gently to the left and the manor came into sight. They turned into it and everything suddenly darkened in the shadows of the tall poplar trees.

'Do slow down a little, please,' Sarah said to the excited driver, 'I would like to put my hat back on.' As he did the manor came into view. It had classic lines and a Doric portico. Titus turned to Sarah.

'Look, they are outside, waiting for you.' He pointed ahead with his whip. Sarah was not the sort of person who normally worried about meeting people, but this was different. She had butterflies in her tummy.

As the coach came to a halt, the horses started to shuffle about as if asking for more. Michael got out of the coach. Titus jumped down, leaving Sarah behind for a moment. He ran to his mother. His long embrace was followed by him kissing her hand, then he turned to his father, embracing him.

'Please come and meet Miss Sarah Dombay.' He pulled them along.

Sarah was still perched on the driver's bench. Titus helped her down. She straightened her clothes and was about to say something when Charles stepped forward.

'It is an honour to have you here, ma'am.'

'Do call her Sarah, Father, it won't be long before we'll be engaged,' Titus teased.

'What?' exclaimed an astonished actress. 'Your son is a terrible tease, sir. We will be doing nothing of the sort. You know, so far we have only danced together on one occasion.'

'That could be changed, no problem,' added Titus, feeling more and more confident on his home ground.

'Well, at least his silliness has broken the ice, my dear.' Helen reached out with both hands. 'Let us go inside, Michael will follow with your luggage.' They entered the hall, which was cool and austere. On the main wall was an oil painting of the bearded King Steven Bocskai, wearing his famous hat, a simple folded item with braiding on its upturned edge, which was soon adopted by the whole nation – over the years, various versions of it were to be used by schools and the army. Below it were his framed Royal Letters Patent to Gregory Zenta, scrolled on dogskin . All the furniture in the house was over two hundred years old and of the simplest style. The impression it created was of brown, brown and more brown.

Sarah was taken to her room in the west wing, which contained a four-poster bed, a large wardrobe, a chest, a bureau with chair and a marble basin with a jug. All brown. Titus' room was in the east wing, very similar except that it had an ordinary divan-style bed. Brown.

The maid helped Sarah with her unpacking while Titus ran downstairs to have a word with his mother.

'What is all this about getting engaged? To an actress?' She confronted him gloomily.

'Well, Mother, it was a joke, of course!' He kissed her again on both cheeks. 'But I do admit I am very much in love with her, from head to toe. That's all.'

'Poor Kathleen would be terribly upset if she knew,' Helen replied.

'Mother, I am not even going to see her whilst we are here. Anyway, she was only a childhood sweetheart, she might be in love with someone else by now.'

'You know that's not true,' Helen concluded.

Charles entered the dark drawing room. 'I have not managed to congratulate you yet, my son,' he said, stretching out his right hand.

'What, for Sarah?'

'No, you fool, although I must say she is quite something. For the sword!' He grinned with undisguised pride.

They embraced warmly, patting each other's shoulders. Sarah walked in.

'You did tell me to dress for riding, didn't you?'

'I did, I did.'

'She is absolutely gorgeous,' Helen whispered to Charles.

'Yes, it worries me,' was his curt answer.

Michael came through, with hat in hand, reporting to Titus. 'Your black devil and the chestnut mare are ready, sir.'

'Are you sure you don't want a side-saddle, Sarah?' Titus teased.

'No thank you, even my mother has stopped using that,' she retorted.

'Follow me!'

If I can, she thought. First they rode past the stables, then the poultry farm. The geese were the size of turkeys, fattened up for the foie-gras, some of which was even exported to France. The machinery section, with the latest innovations for farming, followed. The farm hands and peasants just smiled, lifting their hats as they rode past. There were many 'welcome home' shouts from all directions. There was no doubt, Titus was popular with them. Some of the women started whispering amongst themselves. Titus suddenly realised that he was not going to get away with Kathleen not finding out about all this. More outhouses were passed until Titus shouted, 'Hold your breath, darling, here comes the piggery!'

They sped through as fast as they could. There must have been a thousand of them. Suddenly the meadow opened up again. Sheep were everywhere, then cattle by the River Nyárád, which was full of tasty trout, Titus' favourite fish.

'Up that hill!' Titus pointed to the right. 'Race you to the edge of the forest,' he yelled.

Before Sarah was sure of the direction, he was a quarter of the way along. He had dismounted and regained his breath by the time Sarah arrived.

'You're horrible, you never gave me a chance. This isn't the army, you know!' she complained.

'Let's ride along here,' Titus pointed to the track between the forest and the meadow, 'for another mile or so.' He let Sarah overtake him now and again.

'We are nearly in Koronka now; that's where the vineyard is. I am sure we will find a glass of wine.'

'This is very thirsty work. I have not ridden for two years and that was just around the park in Pest.' People still referred to Buda and Pest separately, ignoring their union.

The pebble road between the vineyards was as straight as an arrow, with peasants weeding the vines on the hillside. At the end of the road stood a large press-house, a good-looking peasant building, set into the hillside. Leading from it deep into the hill were cellars containing hundreds and hundreds of barrels of wine of all ages. Upstairs it had a comfortable set of rooms, like an apartment. The large stove sat reassuringly in the corner, next to the sofa. In front of it a long wooden balcony, carved in the Sekler Transylvanian tradition, was big enough to sit thirty people for drinks. Much of the decoration was of local ceramics. The view was incomparable, right down to the river and beyond.

The cool, fresh red wine was brought up for them in an earthenware jug, straight from the barrel. A large plate of cold meats and fruit followed, served to them on the shaded balcony. Titus went straight for the home-made peasant sausages. Sarah picked a little of this and a little of that in figure-conscious fashion, but thankfully, as far as Titus was concerned, she was not too shy with the wine.

'Sitting here, I never want to see a city again,' she started. 'Just listen to the birds. It's so idyllic.'

'Yes, darling, I always find it difficult to leave this place.'

Titus held her hands and pulled her nearer to him. They kissed for the second time, but they both knew this was going to be different. Titus eased her back from the balcony to the cool, dark room with the inviting sofa. As in the restaurant, Sarah stopped Titus talking, and whispered to him breathlessly, 'Take me, darling.'

Titus responded without words, only with tender and loving passion, which enveloped them for the next hour. The dusk met them still lying on the sofa. The birds had stopped singing. It was quiet, very quiet.

~

Sarah changed for dinner. Home customs allowed Titus to stay in his riding clothes. He just washed and shaved. The meal started awkwardly; Titus didn't even attempt to break the ice again – he could not stop himself thinking about the afternoon.

'How often do you have to read a part like Ophelia to learn it?' Charles asked.

Sarah was delighted at the question. 'This might sound conceited, but only once, if I can look at the page long enough afterwards.' Titus thought she was joking.

'I know all the parts in my scenes and sometimes I prompt the others,' she continued.

'What I could do with a memory like that!' Titus sighed.

'Well, you can't be all that bad, coming top of the class,' replied Sarah.

'Yes, but it's all down to hard slogging in my case, nothing comes easily for me – well, nearly nothing.' He changed his mind, still thinking of the afternoon.

They glanced at each other occasionally, but it became obvious that they both felt more than a little guilty.

After the dinner of green bean soup and Sekler goulash, followed by the aptly named pudding of Emperor's morsels, naturally all Titus' favourites, they went to sit on the dimly lit veranda for a cognac. The older couple soon left on some pretence or other to give them a little privacy.

'Darling, I am the happiest man in the world.' Titus savoured every word as he spoke. 'I will come to your room as soon as they go to bed.'

Sarah smiled. 'Are you sure it's safe? You mustn't embarrass me.' She became more serious.

'Of course I won't, just leave it to me,' Titus tried to reassure her.

It was a little after eleven o'clock when a gentle push opened Sarah's door, which she had left slightly ajar after retiring.

Titus wore tightly fitting trousers, lightweight shoes and a blouson shirt. Sarah wore nothing. She was, once again, one step ahead of him. Titus could not wait. He grabbed her without a kiss and carried her to the four-poster. They were in perfect tune with each other, for this was what their minds wanted, the same kind of pleasure – the rough kind.

The following two days measured up to all their expectations. These were happy days for their country and the national confidence was visible everywhere. Good trading created a wealth the nation had never enjoyed before, the arts flourished and the politics were stable. The actual reunion of the kingdom with its favourite principality had been the culmination of the aspiration of all Magyars. The neighbouring Romania was given a German king. Hungary was ruled by an Austrian one, an excellent monarch from the house of Habsburg, Franz Joseph. By patience and hard work he eventually managed to eliminate the bitterness caused by the crushing of the 1848 revolution, with the help of two hundred thousand Russians Cossacks. Transylvania did have her particular problems; the numerical increase of Romanians – or the Wallachs, as the Seklers preferred to call them – was an obvious one. They had come over the borders for many centuries, good-natured people, expert shepherds, and they were welcome. They settled in enclaves, and with an ever-increasing flow of followers, they established domination in these areas. Their very enterprising government in Bucharest provided them with cheap money and thus with strong purchasing power. This enabled them to buy land whenever there was a chance. The indigenous Hungarian population resented this, but they were convinced they could handle the problem, as they had done over the centuries, with supercilious arrogance.

The Zenta family fitted into this picture perfectly. They were the leading lights of the community and that was that. As far as they were concerned, they were invincible. Titus and Sarah were good manifestations of this arrogance, both breaking with tradition. In the past, an only son had never left the land for a career in the army; neither was it considered proper before for a young lady of upper-middle-class background to step on to the stage. In this little gem of God's creation, Transylvania, Titus and Sarah were like happy children for the next two days.

The afternoon before their return to town they were relaxing on the veranda when the screams of a young woman broke their solitude. A young girl of sixteen ran up to them. She was desperately miserable, dressed in simple but immaculate clothes. She ran past all of them and stood before Sarah, looked at her for a moment and declared proudly, 'Titus is mine, you will never have him. We have been engaged since I was twelve!' Then her head spun a little and she whispered in an unstable voice, 'Please don't take him away from me,' and collapsed in a quivering heap at Sarah's feet.

Helen rushed to her and tried to stand her up. With Charles' help she took her into the living room. Kathleen was still in great distress and her painful cries of 'don't take him away from me' could be heard for some time.

Titus responded to Sarah's questioning look. 'It was a childhood romance, darling. The "engagement" took place on the playground with a piece of string knotted on the top for the diamond. Nothing! I just don't understand her, it's not like her at all.'

'We women are much more affected by promises men make, you know that.'

'I love her like a little sister, I would never hurt her, never!'

The episode was to play on their minds for a long, long time; indeed, for ever.

His parents returned, first Helen, followed by Charles.

'She is fast asleep,' his mother said compassionately. 'The poor thing is totally exhausted, she must have run all the way here from her home in the neighbouring village. Someone teased her mercilessly about your visit.'

She turned to Titus. 'Let us forget all about it, we will take her home later.' She smiled, but her heart was not in it.

Charles beckoned Titus to his study, whilst the women had their coffee.

'How serious is this affair, Titus?' He asked plainly.

'Very serious indeed, Father, I do intend to marry her, eventually,' Titus answered, straight faced.

The conversation that followed was a typical one between a wise and concerned father and his serious but young son. Charles impressed upon him that he must take into account the eventual fate of the estate, the fact that there was no sibling to take over from him when the time came and, worse, that any posting for Titus would take him farther away from the family seat. Charles was also worried about the silly behaviour of Kaiser William in Germany, which he thought would do no good to anybody.

Titus for his part kept emphasising Charles' relatively young age and the political wisdom of Prime Minister Tisza, which would surely guarantee that the monarchy would not support 'Silly Billy'. As far as he and Sarah were concerned, theirs was a modern love match, both of them with different, difficult and strong careers. He reassured his father that they were in no hurry, so there was nothing to worry about. When they returned, the two women had just finished their coffee.

'Well, it's time to go.' Titus clapped his hands.

'Michael has packed everything and is waiting for you inside the coach looking very miserable,' said his mother sorrowfully.

'He needn't worry, I'll let him drive this time.'

Michael was delighted at regaining his rightful position. Titus and his parents kissed goodbye and the young couple settled inside the coach. Michael cracked the whip and the four thoroughbreds took up the command. A few waves of hands, and all one could see was a cloud of dust rising on the tree-lined road.

'God knows what will become of them,' Charles remarked to Helen.

'Nothing good, I fear,' was her thoughtful reply. She wiped her tears and Charles' too.

In the coach the young couple's mood was exactly the opposite. Alone again, they felt confident. Being no longer interested in the scenery, they just held hands and talked. In the back of their minds somewhere there was another person, Kathleen.

'Really, darling, please forget that childish episode.' Titus looked Sarah in the eye. 'It is so upsetting after the wonderful time we have had.'

Sarah squeezed his hand. 'She was silly, wasn't she?'

'You must be an awesome threat to her, you know that? She must have been devastated when those women went to her with their gossiping.' Titus shook his head, knowing he had to change the subject.

'Well, we have the rest of the day here and on the train later.' Titus put his arm around her shoulders. 'I really don't know much about you, other than you lost your father, not so long ago.'

Sarah was delighted to be given such a chance to talk about herself, but in reality there wasn't much to say. She admitted to having had a 'charmed life', a very good education, excelling in languages and drama. Ever since she was a very young girl and saw Mrs Déry, the legendary stage actress, she knew it was acting she wanted to do. After her education was completed, there being no formal drama teaching in the country, she had private lessons from retired actors.

The power of Sarah's memory had impressed one of her teachers, who was still playing elderly women and who, a year earlier, had dragged her to an audition for the part of Eve in Madách's *The Tragedy of Man*. Sarah did not get the part right away, but became the understudy to the star of the time. This actress rather liked to drink champagne late at night and on one occasion the spiral staircase from her dressing room became a little difficult for her to negotiate and she broke her ankle in a stumble. The accident gave Sarah the chance to establish herself.

The announcement that a perfectly unknown young actress was to take over one of the major female roles created some anger and hissing from the audience. However, her appearance in the 'paradise scene' caused the male section of the public to concentrate on the very difficult reasoning of the play as never before, and the female section to look at their escorts' faces with astonishment. Scantily clad – like an Eve should be – with her long brown hair covering her shapely breasts, her large dark eyes set in the most perfect of oval faces, it was little wonder that the men of the capital suddenly became great appreciators of this giant Hungarian Gothic drama. The critics, trying to ignore all this, raved about her 'delivery', which 'more than matched that of the still missing star'. The latter, conveniently, took a long time to recover from her fracture, which in turn enabled her to drink a lot more champagne, so everybody was happy.

'Wonderful! And you never looked back?'

'No, as I said, it's been too easy really, but I am sure I will have to pay for it along the way some time.'

Sarah and Titus said goodbye to Michael at the station. Titus slipped a ten-crown note to him. He was most reluctant to take it, but Titus' look convinced him.

They boarded the train and settled straight into the diner, continuing their conversation. He wanted to bring up the subject of her affair with the journalist but had no idea how to without seeming unchivalrous, so he decided to let it pass for the moment. But what if she won't mention it at all? he wondered. Sarah was similarly preoccupied with the subject, and Sarah, being Sarah, ordered her meal, fixed her gaze on Titus' light blue eyes and said, 'There is something I must tell you,' just when Titus was about to dismiss the whole thing. 'Darling, you know, don't you, that you were not the first man in my life.'

'Naturally!' Titus replied, trying to sound nonchalant. He twirled the tips of his moustache uncomfortably to conceal his inner burning. 'But may I hope I was the second?' He asked with a forced smile.

'You were most certainly that,' Sarah answered with vague innocence. 'And you know, now being with you, I can hardly remember Ivan – so much for the famous first experience.'

'Who was he?'

'The critic who wrote all those lovely things about my debut, but the pig made sure that what followed was leaked to his journalist friends. It took me quite some time to realise his game. It seemed strange that they were always at the places we were escaping to. You know, I never liked him really, but as a young girl, very naive, I was convinced that it was the thing young actresses were supposed to do.'

Titus was getting quietly incinerated within.

'When I found out that he had engineered the stories into the gossip columns, I told him to go. And you know, to my surprise, he never complained, he just walked away. That was when I attached myself to Alexander, your staff officer, who is just a very dear family friend. He escorted me patiently wherever I wanted to go. The rest you know.' Her head dropped gently. 'Talking about all this has made me feel quite ill.' Sarah pushed her plate away.

Titus wanted to say something, but his mind went blank and an awful silence followed.

'Would you like to taste your wine, sir?' The waiter's words came as welcome relief.

Titus nodded, and when the wine waiter left he reached out for Sarah's hands, buried them in his and whispered, 'I adore you.' Their first awkward moment was over; the second and final one was yet to come.

Sarah was a great success on the opening night. Her performance was more mature. Many of her lines were clearly directed to the second box on the left, where Titus sat proudly. After the opening performance, the customary party reflected the success. The cast were complimenting one another the way only actors can. There was no shortage of adjectives; even the local wine was praised. The mood was perfect and the director talked of future and grander projects. Every major town was building new and larger theatres, there was no shortage of work.

Titus was accepted by the troupe and, according to Sarah, 'Hamlet' was accepting him more than the others. When she teased him with this his answer was, 'Just put him in my platoon, we would soon make a man out of him.' Titus took Sarah back to her lodgings. Having sent the cab away, he walked around the chestnut trees to the back of the house. The ground-floor window presented no problem to him. Their passion was tender and satisfying, without a worry in the world. At around 5 a.m. he climbed out of the window and walked back to the hotel briskly. It was past midday when the bellboy knocked on his door. Titus let him in to find a note on a small silver salver being pushed towards him. He rubbed his eyes, took the note and threw some coins on the tray. He opened the folded and sealed piece of paper.

> *By Special Messenger, from His Imperial and Royal Majesty's Ministry of War, to Lieutenant Titus Zenta, who is commanded to report for his posting to the Garrison of Pécs, at 09.00, within 48 hours of the receipt of this order.*

The signature was indecipherable.

Without hesitation Titus packed his luggage, put on his uniform, adjusted his sword under his greatcoat and checked out of the Hotel Belvedere. As he left he looked around, and suddenly felt unhappy that he and Sarah had never managed to dine in the beautiful new restaurant, which was rated one of the best in the land. When he arrived at Sarah's digs in his uniform, she was unprepared and astonished to see him.

'Darling, I have been commanded to be in Pécs by the day after tomorrow. Luckily, I do have a train to catch, in good time, so there is no problem. I am here only to say that I love you desperately and I'll contact you as soon as you are back in Budapest.'

'Oh, Titus, please don't make it too long,' Sarah answered yearningly. Their parting kiss was full of foreboding. It reflected the uncertainty of the sudden change of their plans. Titus drew her to him again. The second kiss was better prepared and she was more relaxed in his arms. Her lips became softer. They both realised how very much in love they were, and it brought Titus a feeling of commitment he had never experienced before.

4

Barracks

When Titus arrived in Budapest it was very late and he was tired. He had no time to go to bed, only to wash and change his shirt. His batman, already informed that he was leaving, had all his things packed. On the top of the chest he placed his Sword of Honour, his name already engraved on the top of the blade. He looked at it, patted his name gently and took it to the duty officer. Titus saluted and reported that he was about to leave for his posting. He asked the officer to take charge of the sword and return it to the Commander General. The captain accepted it, they shook hands and saluted. Titus did a smart about-turn. He was never to see the sword again. In the green army coach which was ready and waiting for him he left the Academy, where he had spent so many happy days and which would forever be an affectionate memory for him, much more then any alma mater. The coach took him to the Southern Railway Station, where he caught the overnight sleeper of the first generation of railway hardware, noisy and uncomfortable.

He drifted in and out of sleep all night. His thoughts were everywhere, but always returned to Sarah. He was very much in love and naturally worried about sustaining the relationship, which now had to overcome some one hundred and fifty miles distance between them. He thought too that young officers were awarded minimum leave and even less salary, but also considered that the latter problem would be much helped by his stipend from the estate. He tried to chase these successive ideas out of his mind with little success. Just when he felt himself sinking into sleep, Sarah confronted him again and, gazing at her lovely oval face, he wanted to touch her silken skin. When he saw her dark eyes he was no longer keen to chase away the vision. He knew he had to, so he tried to remember the embarrassing episode with Kathleen, thinking that the stupid child should have known better. He could not win. He felt cold and buttoned his greatcoat higher. Then he saw Kathleen's innocent face, her fainting before Sarah and again he heard her cry of 'don't take him away from me!' Anger came over him. How dare she? I must put her in her place. Just wait until I return home … it must never happen again. His parents' concerned faces on his leaving were the last image before he mercifully fell asleep.

When he next woke up the train was just about to outflank the green Mecsek mountains on the left, with foliage of all shapes and colours spiced with more than a little Mediterranean flavour. The train had to take a sharp turn to the left to approach the unique city. This caused the wheels to screech, and Titus realised that was it, as far as sleeping was concerned. He shaved in the cold water that was provided in a jug in the toilet. When he was finished he put a little pomade on his hair and his moustache, forming it into shape. The train came to a halt just outside the main railway station that was being rebuilt to welcome the impending arrival of the wide-gauge system.

The regimental cab was waiting for him and he was sped away to the west side of Pécs, without seeing the famous city centre he had heard so much about.

'Good grief!' Titus said to the driver. 'A complete mosque, with a minaret. All we need is the muezzin to call the faithful,' he joked.

'Sir, there is an even bigger mosque facing Mecca right in the main square. It's being converted into a Catholic parish church.'

This place must have really suffered in the hundred and fifty years of Ottoman rule, he thought, but at least they have left *some* goodies behind. They finally reached the barracks. He got out of the cab and saw a young private saluting him. 'Private John Bakó, your batman, at your service, sir!' the strong lad with a broad Transdanubian accent introduced himself.

Titus gave John his first command. 'Take me to the commanding officer, before we get to my quarters.'

'Very well, sir, his office is on the way.' He picked up the baggage.

Five minutes before his allocated time Titus knocked on the door of the chief.

'Lieutenant Titus Zenta de Lemhény begs to report for duty, sir,' Titus said curtly, standing to attention.

The colonel hardly looked up, offering his left hand for Titus' papers to avoid the handshake. Titus handed over his letter of assignation and saluted again.

'Heard of you, Lieutenant, welcome to the real world.' There was no welcome in his tone at all. 'There are only two decent-looking actresses here and they are both spoken for,' he continued.

'Sir!?' Titus pulled back his head in resentment.

'Just to make sure you won't bother them I am posting you to look after the Serbs, a truly wonderful bunch of savages. Don't turn your back on them unless you want to collect an instant selection of penknives. You've heard of them?'

'Yessir.' Titus tried to maintain an even tone.

'You'll be leaving first thing in the morning to relieve Lieutenant ... whatever his name is, and will patrol the border with a platoon strength of reprobates. You see, I don't expose my best men to the sort of dangers the Serbs can dish out.' He paused, hiding behind his thick spectacles. 'So there is no need for you to unpack. You will be grateful to me one day for this. I'm giving you a chance to prove yourself!'

'Is that all, sir?'

'Yes, Lieutenant.' The colonel shuffled some papers on his desk. 'See you in the mess tonight.'

Titus saluted again, did as noisy an about-turn as he could and left the command room.

In his quarters he was fuming as he wondered what the matter was with his commanding officer, swearing he would never be like that with his men, never! He decided to spend the next few hours touring the base, thinking he might as well get to know the place he wouldn't get to see again for a while. John showed him around and he did not like what he saw. Everybody was apathetic; the attitude of the colonel was mirrored in every facet of the base. Returning to his room, he rested a little then shaved and dressed for dinner. On entering the mess he approached the bar and introduced himself. A captain patted him on the back.

'I can see from your expression that you have met our colonel,' said the captain. 'Every new posting entering this place wears the same face after having talked with him. Mind you, his bite is even worse than his bark, especially if you react to his bait.'

'Isn't he a bit too old to be a colonel?' Titus ventured.

The captain smiled. 'You've got it, he keeps being passed over because of his leftist views,' he replied.

Titus returned his smile. 'I knew he had problems. Thanks for that, Captain, I appreciate it.'

The door guard yelled 'Attention!' They placed their drinks on the bar and pulled themselves together, though not too much. The colonel walked in, took off his hat and somehow managed an insincere smile.

'Continue, officers; don't let me interrupt your drinking. You do that so well.' They all turned away in barely concealed disgust. He was wearing just one medal, a 'service medal', on his tunic. You've really been pushed aside, thought Titus.

The colonel had a plum brandy brought to him and moved to the window, where another lieutenant was gazing out.

'Are you the mess-duty officer here this week?' He asked. 'Call them to order,' he continued as he emptied his glass, 'and get the new chap to propose the toast, if we must have one.'

The duty officer called out the usual 'Gentlemen, take your places for dinner'.

Titus held off to see where he was being placed. It was the second table, halfway down. The officer continued, as was the established custom before they touched the food, or anything else, 'Gentlemen, remain upstanding for the loyal toast, which will be proposed for the first time by our new comrade-in-arms, Lieutenant Titus Zenta de Lemhény.' Titus raised his glass of earthy local red wine, turned towards the painting of the King and with the happiest possible expression on his face said, 'To his Imperial and Royal Majesty Franz Joseph.'

'To his health!' came the reply of the officers, loud and clear. The colonel's lips never moved.

They settled into their dinner, lentil soup followed by mutton stew, all washed down by more red wine. Titus chatted for a while and then, referring to his posting for the morning, excused himself and returned to his room. This time he slept well. The only dream he had was a short one; incomprehensible, noisy, ending in a great flash. The next thing he knew was his batman waking him up, bringing the hot water for shaving and his clean shirt. He washed himself down to the waist with great gusto. Titus was looking forward to his posting without apprehension, knowing he had a hard job to do, but also knowing he had been well trained for it.

Arriving in the courtyard, he saw two horses and a mule with his campaign chest on it.

'I beg to report, sir, that …' the private started, but Titus interrupted.

'No need for that, John, unless there are higher-ranking officers present.'

'Yessir.'

～

The plan was to go east to Komló then south-east to Mohács, where he would change and spend the night in a local inn. Next day through Croatia, right to the Serbian border, with two horse changes.

Passing through the wonderful sloping main square, he saw the large mosque being restored. The crescent moon had a chunky gold cross arising from it. Next to it stood the proud Hotel Nádor, famous for its kitchen. Would he ever be able to sample it? He wondered. At the bottom of the square they were erecting a ceramic and porcelain well, presented to the city by its famous son, Vilmos Zsolnay, whose invention of metallic paint glazing was his best-kept secret. He specially excelled with his 'eosin', a green-gold-blue mixture, which won him the first prize at the Paris World Exhibition.

The journey took Titus past the field of Mohács, where in 1526 Louis II and his army were conclusively defeated by the force of Suleiman the Magnificent, plunging the nation into a 150-year-long catastrophe and destroying it as a major European power. Gazing at the field, he was convinced that, generally speaking, his was the age that had the best chance to redeem this power, after the agreement with Austria, and he was destined to have a personal part to play in it.

In Baja they were given accommodation at the garrison station. Titus dined with the officers and noticed how much better the atmosphere

Flames of Straw

was here, commanded as they were by a captain only a few years older than himself. It was an early-to-bed situation if he was to keep to his exhausting schedule. At the crack of dawn they were off again. The next night they spent at a roadside inn.

It was easy to find his garrison HQ, a large square of a building, flying the flag. As Titus rode through the arched gate the duty sergeant shouted, 'Attention!' Hearing this, the second lieutenant buttoned up his tunic and ran towards him. He saluted as Titus dismounted his tired horse and 'begged to report' that he was willing to relinquish the command of Brod, looking as if he meant it all right.

The two officers were walking across the large courtyard, which was full of buzzing personnel. It had very large stables on the left, next to the ammunition depot.

'You really must have done something awful to get this posting,' Paul, the second lieutenant, said, looking at Titus' face.

'I cannot think what. I feel the colonel just didn't like my report from the Academy and wanted me out of his way. I don't mind it at all, it looks very exciting here,' he answered thoughtfully.

'It certainly is that. Wait until I put you in the picture,' said Paul. 'But first, let us get you settled in.'

Titus was pleasantly surprised at the more than adequate room. It was fairly spacious with good washing facilities and a large bathtub. In his excitement, he forgot about being tired. He changed into a clean uniform and found Paul still waiting outside.

The two men entered the office; whitewashed walls, well enough furnished, with a picture of the King on the wall behind the desk. They busied themselves with the administration of the handing over of the command, Titus being asked to sign here and sign there; they completed matters within an hour and Paul invited him to be shown around.

They inspected everything there was to inspect and Titus found most things in perfect order. He liked Paul for his honesty and for playing down the effectiveness of his command. After the two ensigns arrived Paul suggested dinner in what must have been the smallest mess room in the kingdom. They talked about the difficulty of controlling the frontier and the virtually permanent provocation by the Serbs, who always had a score to settle with someone, and since the occupation and annexation of Bosnia-Herzegovina it was now the turn of the

Hungarians. After the meal the ensigns excused themselves. Titus had another drink with Paul, who then also declared that he had to go to pack.

Titus went to his room and lay on his bed, thinking of Sarah and their few days together. It all felt as if it had happened years ago. He sank into deep sleep.

He was still lying on his bed, fully clad, when the outside activity woke him up. Rather grateful for the noise, he jumped up and went for a bath. Morning parade was imminent. Paul was on the parade ground when he walked out. The two second lieutenants joined the sergeant major, who was about to call them to order. Titus' arrival prompted him to cry out, 'Parade formation, attention!' The hundred and fifty men of the company hustled into shape, the bugle sounded the morning call and a corporal placed the flag on the rope of the pole. Two side drums sounded a hearty ripple; there were some more bugle tunes and the red, white and green horizontal tricolour flew in the early morning breeze. Paul stepped forward and told them that this was the last time he was addressing them. He seemed to be the only person pleased about this. Then he introduced Titus, with rank and full name, who in turn stepped forward.

'Men of the Eighth Company of the Second Pécs Infantry Regiment, I find it a great honour indeed to take over this excellent command. I intend to change very little, if anything, here, for I find everything in great shape. All I will ask of you is that you continue to serve King and country on this important frontier station, as you have been: diligently and with honour. Our unfriendly southern neighbour, Serbia, is restless, but we will not allow her to provoke us. With your calm but confident behaviour you will show that we are ready for them, should they lose their heads. I wish you all good morning.'

The sergeant took over to read the 'Order of the Day' and the day's deployments and dismissed the company.

Paul's horse was ready, with his batman in attendance. He shook Titus by the hand, mounted and rode out of the courtyard in a manner that indicated that it was not a moment too soon for him.

Titus decided to take the sergeant's patrol, to familiarise himself with his section of the frontier. They started off near the town at the crossroads where two sets of swing bars controlled the very occasional traffic. From there the border disappeared into the woods, going through fields and bisecting rivers. It was regularly violated by smugglers, Gypsies and even visitors from one village to another. Nobody really minded; the guards just chased them back. The real problem was when someone used them as an excuse for a little crossfire practice.

At a nearby point the River Száva disappeared into a swamp-like marshland. As the bulrushes provided good cover it was fairly easy to cross over by boat. Titus realised that this was a vulnerable point. That day it was all quiet.

After dinner, he sat at his desk to write a letter to Sarah. He decided to comply with the enlisted men's regulation of one letter per fortnight. The messenger was due to go the next day. He described his present lot to her, his first day as a serving officer of his small command, the mixed Croat/Hungarian town of Brod, and listed the problems he might face there. He concluded with ardent messages of love:

> *Our happiness was too short. This gives me the resolve to see my posting through and to be near you once more. It will be easy, for you are forever in my mind's eye. I see your beautiful face constantly and pray to God this will guide me back into your loving arms.*
>
> *Your ever-adoring Titus.*

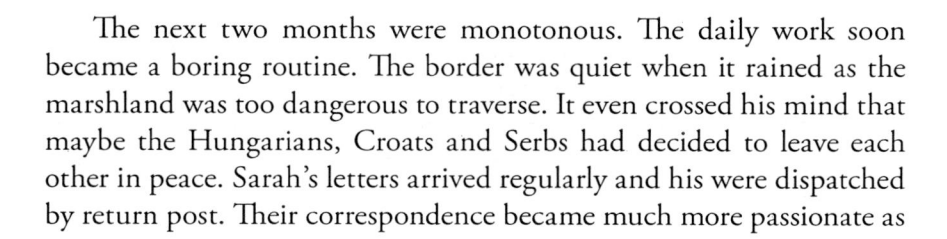

The next two months were monotonous. The daily work soon became a boring routine. The border was quiet when it rained as the marshland was too dangerous to traverse. It even crossed his mind that maybe the Hungarians, Croats and Serbs had decided to leave each other in peace. Sarah's letters arrived regularly and his were dispatched by return post. Their correspondence became much more passionate as time went by. His bodily need of her increased until it was unbearable, and he wondered how bad it was for her.

~

The century was only a few months old when one of his scouts went up to his sergeant and asked to see the lieutenant. The three of them met in Titus' office. The intentionally scruffy Croatian had just arrived back from his spying on a neighbouring village.

'Beg to report, sir, there is going to be a lot of trouble at Sebce, because of the wedding on Friday,' he started with great excitement.

'Trouble at a wedding? Come on, we are not going to get involved in that!' The scout 'begged to report' that this was no ordinary wedding. A Croatian boy had fallen in love with a Serbian girl at her village fair. They had been seeing each other regularly and their love blossomed. The lad had turned up at her parents' home and asked for her hand in marriage, at which point her older brothers ran him out of the village. The perky lass would not give up and she was duly locked up by the family. The lad decided to plan his marriage just the same, reassuring his parents that there would definitely be a bride on the big day.

He then hatched his plan to steal her, which worked perfectly. He rowed across the Száva in a borrowed postman's uniform, while her menfolk were working in the fields. She persuaded her mother to let her speak to the strange postman. Not much later they were rowing back to his horse, which he'd left on the north shore of the river. The girl's family had to find out who the courting lad was by beating the truth out of the real postman. Now they were coming for her.

Titus wanted to turn away, but the spy wouldn't let him. 'Beg to report, sir, they are coming armed with everything they could lay their hands on,' he concluded hurriedly.

Titus called his two second lieutenants and got a map out. 'The most likely point they will choose for crossing is here, just at the edge of the marshland. It will give them good camouflage, but it will do the same for us too. That's where we will be waiting for them.' The others nodded.

'We will only confront them and ask them to return. When they see us they will go away. Agreed?'

The others weren't so sure.

He cancelled all leave before the evening lowering of the flag and addressed the men briefly.

'Men, according to our intelligence report, there is a possibility of a border incident on Friday. I want you to prepare yourselves, to project your strength by your determination. Tonight's usual outing to the drinking dens of town is cancelled.'

This was greeted by a few disgruntled murmurs from those with a fixed assignation.

'After all, we don't want a word to slip out inadvertently, do we?' He continued, 'You will have your suppers and will get to your dormitories. In two hours' time I will inspect you personally, to make sure you're not playing cards or doing other ungodly things. Understood?' He raised his voice.

'Yessir,' they replied in unison.

'Any questions?' Titus asked, not expecting a reply.

A corporal stepped forward. 'Lieutenant, sir. I have been asked to be at a wedding of a Croatian friend of mine, at noon tomorrow. As I had leave, I accepted. He rather counts on me being there, sir.'

'With a little luck you will be! Dismiss!'

∼

At the morning parade at 07.00 hours, he reminded the men of their duty to defend their section of the border. He divided two platoons into three groups. Two smaller ones for his deputies and a larger central one for himself with the sergeant major. They left eighty-five men behind when they marched out of the barracks, four of them on horseback, and the men on foot with their newly issued Styer Mannlichers, the best rifle of the day. Four carts followed them. Through the small town they sang marches, mainly their favourite one, *The Copper Cannon of Aaron Gabor*. It helped them with the fast pace Titus had ordered. At the far end of town they fell into their prearranged grouping and went three different ways, with no more singing. They took up their well-camouflaged places, but it was difficult to stay hidden in their blue uniforms with strong coloured markings. By 10.00 hours bayonets were fixed, just in time.

The thirty or so Serb youths, some of them still drunk from the previous night's 'planning' of the escapade, arrived at 10.45 hours. Having hidden their boats in the marshes on the left flank, they crept across some river dunes into the edge of the bush land. From his vantage point Titus realised that they had all sorts of simple but effective weapons: straightened scythes, hatchets, pitchforks, twelve-bore shotguns, older rifles and a good few handguns too.

He whispered to his trumpeter to sound 'encircle', and he started off the bouncy ditty with great gusto. Titus commanded, 'Hold your fire. Follow, now!' The men burst out to confront the rabble. Noticing this, the eldest brother, who was obviously still drunk, cried out, 'Kill the Magyar bastards!' With their makeshift armoury they started striking out at the soldiers. One of them raised his shotgun and fired at a private from point-blank range, killing him instantly.

Titus, still confident that they could round them up, ordered, 'Hold your fire!' again. He rode his horse into the group, lashing away with his sword, trying to single out the one with the shotgun. He felt himself being pulled off the horse from his other side. Turning around quickly, he slashed the man across his face. The severed artery squirted blood on to his boots. The men were in hand-to-hand combat, using their bayonets against the more effective and lighter pitchforks. Titus had no choice now. 'Commence fire!' he yelled repeatedly. Whilst looking around to see his command being observed, he found himself facing one of the younger brothers aiming a handgun at him. The brother pulled the trigger, hitting him in the left shoulder. There was no pain but he soon noticed the blood oozing through the hole in his blue tunic. Before the man could reload, he aimed his pistol, hitting him in the face. The sudden appearance of a large hole in the middle of the man's head made Titus cringe. The Serbs threw themselves on the ground and fired back. On their right flank some of them took a soldier who had fallen earlier, and started to pull him into the sand dunes. Titus yanked his horse to the left and rode towards them. A man suddenly appeared from the bush and aimed at his horse, hitting it straight in the heart. Titus managed to direct his fall on him. Using his weight, he pushed the Serb's face into the sand and kept it there until the body felt limp. He then aimed at the other Serb, who was about to finish off the unconscious soldier with his hatchet. He too fell as the large blade was about to come down.

The pain in his shoulder was by now excruciating. Titus transferred the pistol to his left hand and with his right he dragged the private to safety. The mayhem around him was complete; hand-to-hand fighting with these bizarre weapons causing terrific injuries. The cries of 'attack' were interspersed only with the moans of the wounded. Sand, mud and blood were everywhere, and the crisp fresh air of a half an hour ago was now full of the foul odour of gunpowder. With the help of the outer flanks the resistance of the rabble ended. Titus returned to the original vantage point. He saw the horse of one of his deputies passing by without its rider from the direction of the melee. Looking for him, he noticed some of the Serbs by the river stringing him up on a tree by his boots, in readiness for the ritual of genital atrocities. He jumped on his horse and rode straight to them. In his reloaded pistol, he had six shots left, and he had his sword. He did not start firing until the last moment. A middle-aged man was directing the activities. Probably the bride's father.

'We will show you what we do to Catholic bastards!' he yelled towards Titus. Titus decided to go for him. Riding down the steep riverbank, he fired his gun. A large wound appeared in the middle of the man's chest, the impact throwing him back on to a dune. One of his cohorts appeared on Titus' blind side and with a six-foot loading pitchfork he caught his left thigh, giving him a good four-inch gash. Titus turned again and shot him in the throat. The man went down and gurgled for some time, until he bled to death. The right wing arrived in time to help Titus cut down the unconscious second lieutenant from the tree. The skirmish was effectively over. Some of the Serbs got into their boats and made for the other side of the river under a hail of fire.

The death toll included twelve Serbs; two severely wounded and left behind, one of them being the younger brother of the bride. Titus' unit suffered serious losses too: four dead and six wounded. He himself was not in the best of condition, with a good-sized hole in his left shoulder and a wide gash along his thigh, both bleeding steadily. They were all placed on the carts, Titus with the two Serbs swearing revenge. One of his second lieutenants took charge of their return to barracks.

As they alighted Titus was approached by the corporal with the wedding invitation. 'Well, you have probably missed the wedding, but you can go to the "knees up". Off you go, but change into a clean uniform, and not a word about what happened.' Titus sounded in agony.

The village doctor arrived to see to the casualties. He patched them up, but looked worried when he examined Titus. He sutured the leg wound and bandaged it, but when he looked at his shoulder he started to shake his head.

'The bullet blew off the end of your biceps and a good portion of your deltoid.' he started clinically. 'It's a surgical job, so you're going back to Pécs, my lad,' he continued simply, but strongly enough to preclude any argument.

'Good God, so soon?' Titus sighed.

When the doctor left, Titus wrote a short letter to Sarah, begging her to visit him. Once the letter had been placed in the military mail he felt much better. Unbeknown to him it also accompanied a commendation for him from his two sub lieutenants and his sergeant, trying to bypass the colonel. The cart was ready to take him, as well as one of his privates and a Serb, who were also considered in need of surgical attention. They set off for the military hospital in Pécs under heavy armed escort. It took them three changes of horses and the best part of four days to get there. The long journey gave him an excellent opportunity to think about his future, and Sarah. All his conclusions were gloomy, but he would not give up. He went over the same scenario again and again. In the end he decided that he was not unhappy at being injured.

The cart pulled up in the leafy courtyard of the hospital. He dragged himself off somehow, but could hardly move for the pain and stiffness. Refusing the stretcher and pointing the porters in the direction of the Serb, he murmured, 'Get him on it; he needs it more than I do, the poor bastard. He has a huge hole in his stomach; I don't think he'll make it.'

The young lieutenant surgeon looked at Titus' wounds and complimented the repair on his thigh, but when he saw his shoulder, he too shook his head.

'Yes, the muscle has completely gone and it has pulled back into the upper arm.' He continued, 'We will have to fish it out and suture it back. I'll do it right away,' he concluded sternly. As he turned away he murmured to his assistant, 'I hope it's not infected.'

Titus changed into a nightshirt and walked into a whitewashed room where he lay down on the oak table. The smell of carbolic lotion was bad enough, but the cleansing process was much worse. The pain was so severe that before he could do anything about it he yelled out loud enough to be heard on the other side of the courtyard. The anaesthesia in its most rudimentary form had to be administered earlier than the surgeon would have liked, but at least it gave him relief. The operating surgeon explored the wound and managed to hook back the escaped biceps muscle. It was badly twisted and he had to sew it back over the humerus and the coracoid process to the minuscule stump of a tendon. He suddenly realised that his patient was a rarity of less than one in ten who had a very small third head to this muscle. In his patient it wound around the brachial artery, certainly saving that, and subsequently his life, when it was severed by the bullet. The repair to the deltoid muscle was relatively easier. There were not many important details to worry about there. The bandaging was heavy, covering all his shoulder and most of his chest.

The young officer was taken to his assigned room, which would be his home for the next month. His left arm was raised and suspended from a hook on the ceiling. When he finally came around all he felt was an almighty headache, until he realised the position of his injured arm. Then he started to worry about the future mobility of the joint and the nerve supply to the area. A frank chat with the surgeon did little to reassure him.

On Saturday afternoon he answered yet another knock on his door with a loud 'Come in!' He paid no attention to the gentle opening of the door and the first thing he saw was a dainty shoe with the slenderest of ankles rising from it. When he looked up and saw Sarah standing in the door frame he jerked and wrenched his arm. The scream that followed began with a painful yell and ended in a shout of delight.

Sarah ran to the bed, knelt by it and held his head in her delicate hands. His right arm pulled her to him. Their kiss was eager, their two heads rolling to and fro to feel each other's faces and ending in a union of their lips, motionless. Endless in time and emotion, neither of them wanted it to stop, but Sarah, still holding his head in her hands, pushed it back gently on to the white linen army-issue pillow.

'What have they done to you, my darling?' she asked, knowing the answer as she looked at his bandages and his arm dangling in midair. 'How awful for you! How long do you have to endure this?' She could not stop herself asking questions.

Titus just grinned from ear to ear. 'I don't care! I am just so glad that you're here. Nothing will bother me now.' His voice became stronger with every word. 'I felt so miserable, not getting a reply from you, darling,' he added.

'Well, I just thought I would surprise you instead.' She smiled.

'What a surprise! Oh, let me kiss you again!' he begged. She let him, and they kissed again, again and again.

Titus insisted that Sarah should start the talking. Sitting at his bedside, Sarah told him of the great success of *Hamlet* and how she had now been given the part of Nina in Chekhov's *The Seagull*.

'That's the one with the long monologue for you, isn't it?' he interrupted.

'Yes, darling, I have just learned it on the way here, on the train, and can deliver it in two different ways, depending how the mood takes me on the night. Have you ever seen it?'

'No, I haven't. But I learned about it in school.'

'Well, you soon will see it, even if I have to drag you from here to Budapest.'

'You won't have to drag me; I'll walk if I have to.' He thought of his thigh. 'Well, perhaps not,' he said, pointing to the bandaging. 'I'll take the train, I think.'

'What is that?' Sarah asked in amazement, gesturing to his bandaged thigh.

'A gash by a scythe or sickle or something. The doctor says that it is no problem. Carry on …'

Sarah did, explaining how the theatre was changing constantly and how in a little village on the western coast of America they were talking of moving pictures. This left Titus totally baffled.

Quietly burning inside, he had to steer the conversation to men. 'Have you been out lately?' he asked clumsily.

Sarah was ahead of him. 'Of course, all the time! The producer tells me I must be seen everywhere and, you know, he *produces* all sorts of escorts for me. You would die if you saw some of them. There is one in particular who, I'm sure, would much rather be out with you, but he too does as he's told. The handsomest of ballet dancers, who only talks of art, music and dancing. Actually we have a very good time together. I introduced him to our Hamlet recently and haven't heard of him since.' She giggled. 'Good old Mr Orsen – you know, the impresario – he comes in handy for the odd date, and in some restaurants I have a regular table for my friends. So life is jolly good right now. Only you are missing from it to make it perfect, and I do intend to have you in it too. But now you really have to tell me about all this.' Sarah circled her hand around the bandages and the pulley.

Titus gave a very concise description of what happened: the roots of the problem, the three nations involved, the peasant wedding that acted as trigger and the border skirmish which nearly killed him, playing down his personal part in it. 'Well I am beginning to understand what Bismarck meant when he said something to the effect that the smallest stupidity can start a world war … if it happens in the Balkans,' he ended on a more serious note.

They ate stuffed cabbage and drank a good local wine for dinner, served up in the hospital room, and talked about more mundane things. Holding her right hand, he caressed it tenderly. He was not an ill man medically speaking and was yearning for her body in a more fulfilling way. In bed, prostrate, all he could do with his one functioning hand was to gently touch her breasts through her white lace blouse. They kissed again and again, which made matters worse for both of them. In their thoughts they were making love, but the physical restrictions were too much to overcome. Titus eased Sarah's hand under the bedsheet and she was willing to search for him.

Their eyes met for a moment. Sarah looked at him questioningly. The silence was total. The corridor was quiet. Sarah lifted the sheet and moved her head down his body. He gasped.

―

'Have you had a report from Lieutenant Zenta about the incident in Brod yet?' The Inspector General asked the commandant.

'Not yet, he is just recovering from an operation,' the commandant answered, looking at his desk.

'Surely his second lieutenants should have produced something by now. Where are they?'

'Well, actually, they gave me something …' He hesitated. 'Not a proper report, they called it a … er, a commendation.'

'Let's have it, Colonel!' Came the firm demand.

After further hesitation the colonel drew it out from the depths of his drawer, where he had intended it to stay for ever, and reluctantly handed it over to the inspector.

He stood by the window and started to read it, becoming more and more excited. 'Extraordinary!' He turned to the colonel. 'This should have been forwarded immediately. Why the delay?' he demanded of him, staring into his eyes.

'Inspector General, I am no believer in this sort of personal heroism nonsense. It's the enlisted working-class men who should matter,' he said, trying to make his ideological point.

'Precisely! What he did was for two of his men, working class or not. Take me to him right away!' He marched out of the command room.

Sarah was making some strong black coffee, a custom left over from the Ottoman occupation which had become a national habit, when the two men walked in. The Inspector General could not believe his eyes.

'Miss Dombay? What a pleasure! Oh, well, you two know each other? I am General Pataky.' He clicked his heels and kissed her offered hand. Seeing her with Titus, he decided to show his authority to the full.

'*Captain* Zenta,' he started, emphasising the rank. 'Having just read this commendation,' he waved it in his hand, 'I want to congratulate you for the way you handled a very sensitive matter and for your leadership in the field. I hereby promote you to captain, subject to approval by the Ministry of War.' He smiled, knowing he had never been refused a promotion. 'And I am also submitting that you should be decorated with the Cross of Fire, Second Class,' he concluded, twirling his moustache between his fingers and looking around as if awaiting applause. As the general shook Titus by the hand the colonel stood immobile with shock. The actress started clapping and the wounded officer lifted his head up and responded with the usual 'For King and Country! Sir!' loud and clear.

The colonel excused himself and left; the general turned to Sarah. 'Could I have a cup of coffee too, it smells wonderful,' he asked with mock shyness.

'Naturally, General,' Sarah replied with a similar mocking curtsy.

They chatted whilst sipping the good black brew. The general, realising that Sarah had come only for a short stay, offered to take her to the railway station for her return journey. Then, changing his mind, he quickly decided to cut his visit short and return to Budapest with her the next day. When he did eventually leave the room to complete the remainder of his business, Sarah and Titus burst into childish laughter.

'Do you know something,' Titus laughed, 'I feel terrible. That was like a scene from a second-rate operetta, and furthermore, the idea of the "gong" was just to make an impression on you!'

'Yes, he certainly perked up when he recognised me. I'm sure that with a word in his ear I could get you the "first class" one tomorrow on the train, if you want me to?'

'Sarah, you are a dreadful tease. You know you're very lucky I can't reach you. But if you do manage it, just tell him to post it.'

'Anyway, *Captain*!' Sarah bowed. 'What does this promotion mean?'

'I really don't know, but one thing is sure, the pay is going to be better,' he joked. 'And I hope they will take me away from the Serbs.' This was not a joke.

His batman knocked on the door and brought the four stars in on a salver. Sarah decided to sew them on his tunic, two on each side next to the existing two. 'Now you'll dictate me a letter for your parents, right?'

'Right!'

Dear Mother and Father,

Dad, if you only knew who is writing this letter on my behalf, you would not believe it and would never let it leave your hands ...

He went on to describe what had happened to him up to a few moments earlier and signed it,

With fondest love to you both, your son

Titus (Captain) (Sarah's darling lapdog).

There were tears in both their eyes when it came time to say their goodbyes. It was once again soft touches and tenderness and then Sarah walked out of his room to the waiting cab. The general, waiting in it, was convinced this was the luckiest day of his life.

The following weeks saw Titus recovering well. The dressing on his leg came off first, leaving a nasty indentation and a taut linear scar on it. The shoulder was different. When the arm was taken off the pulley, it stayed frozen in position. It took considerable professional expertise from the doctor to get the joint moving again, causing Titus more than enough agony.

'We won't get very far like this,' his surgeon friend added. 'I must send you to Harkány for some mud baths, they are most therapeutic.'

In the nearby spa town Titus had a wonderful time. The attendants were very obliging, putting him through a punishing routine of mud packing and sulphur baths. This loosened up his shoulder a great deal, but a quarter of the movement was still lost.

~

The passion of Sarah and Titus continued in their correspondence. They were most intelligent users of words. Titus had never realised before how powerful letters could be and how strong a feeling he could describe with the simplest of phrases. Sarah's career meanwhile went from strength to strength. She was rapidly becoming a legend in her youth, her fame nearly reaching the seemingly impossible level of that of her idol, Mrs Déry. The queue of fans before her stage door included university students, officers, princelings and gigolos. She was totally in command, handling them all.

As Titus' physical recovery continued it became plain that it would not be a complete one. The left biceps and some of the pectoral muscle fibres had healed quite well, but were still weak, and, as far as movement was concerned, he knew that the arm would remain merely a withered passenger. He tried every suggestion, exercise and any other ideas people came up with, but after a while no further improvement was attainable. At this point he had to take a transfer to Budapest, where he could be physically examined by the top specialists of the Military Medical Board, who, after several days of intensive evaluation, came to the unanimous decision that Captain Titus Zenta could no longer continue as a serving officer and recommended either cessation of his commission or a staff posting.

Titus was devastated. Being set on a professional army career, only to be told, practically at the outset, that it was all over, was too much for him. The Sword of Honour seemed a million years ago. Told to make a decision 'by the end of the week', he wandered on to the streets aimlessly and subconsciously headed towards Sarah's apartment. She knew nothing about his visit to the Board, and when she opened the door on that late autumn afternoon, it was no dashing officer she saw, but a glassy-eyed man about to collapse in confusion.

Sarah, realising that something was dreadfully wrong with her man, helped him in. Titus did not even make an effort to kiss her; he just walked in, sat down and looked towards the window, at the setting sun shining through the lace curtains, throwing its mesmerising patterns all over the flat. Sarah sent the maid for a brandy and went to fetch her mother from her bedroom. When the three women arrived back, they found Titus slumped on the couch, asleep. She considered calling for a doctor, but he was obviously in such good physical shape that she decided to wait. They took off his greatcoat and sword, opened the top of his tunic, removed his boots and put his feet up for more comfort.

As his sleep did not seem to lighten, Sarah left for the theatre when the coach called. When she returned home after eleven o'clock, Titus was still in a deep sleep, breathing slowly, but regularly. She sat down on an easy chair to watch over him and after a while she herself succumbed to her tiredness. It was not until the dawn sunshine started to break through the other window, throwing shadows in the opposite direction, that he first grunted, waking Sarah. Within seconds he was totally recovered from his cataleptic shock, nursing a nasty headache and feeling totally embarrassed.

'What …? Where …? What am I doing here?' he mumbled quietly in a hesitant voice. 'What happened to me?!' He jumped up.

'Nothing, darling, just sit down, I will tell you in a minute.' Sarah tried to sound assured. Only then did she realise that she had no idea why he was there or what in fact had happened. 'Have a sip of this brandy,' she continued, offering the glass she had poured out the night before.

'My head is bursting,' Titus said in a daze. 'What is happening to me?' he asked again.

'You will tell us soon,' Sarah answered calmly.

The events of the previous day started to return to him, and as they did, the severity of his headache lessened. He felt sick for a while but the brandy did the trick and after the third sip he felt much better but more ashamed.

'Now I will call a doctor,' she offered, observing his reaction intensely.

'No, please, darling, I know what happened … it was the shock of it all.' He tried to pull himself together, twirling his moustache, standing up, straightening his uniform.

'The shock of what?' She asked him.

Titus related the story of the Board's decision to Sarah. It shocked her too. Now she understood. For a man who always considered himself way above average in every sense, to be told that he was finished in his mid-twenties was a devastating experience, certainly enough to send him into his trance. Sarah, with her usual positive approach, made the decision for him.

'What's wrong with being a staff officer?' she stated, rather than asked. 'You will move up here and we can start looking for that diamond ring tomorrow, unless you did not mean your proposal!' she teased.

'Oh, darling, of course I meant it – I love you so much.' Titus was all hers in his submission.

5

Budapest

Titus informed the Ministry of War of his decision to take their most generous offer of a staff officer's post. He went out and bought a Mont Blanc fountain pen, saying that if he had to do a pen-pushing, roster-making, logistic-juggling job, he might as well do it with the best. To show that he too could be positive he went along to Váci Street's very best jeweller; Gronstein & Sons, and bought a diamond-and-sapphire ring, all alone. Then he booked a table at the Gellért Hotel, where he was going to stay until the end of the month, and invited Sarah for dinner.

The Gypsies were seducing the ladies of the restaurant with the sonorous sound of their new song, '*There is only one girl in the whole wide world*', when Titus, looking very smart in his new dress uniform and wearing the three stars of a captain on his high collar, stood up from the table and went on one knee by the potted palm tree next to Sarah and opened the box containing the ring.

'I hope you won't make me take this back. It is so much like you. Ever since I spotted it in the shop window, I could not take my eyes off its sparkle.' Sarah, struggling with the tears in her eyes, just shook her head. 'No, you will not take it back, ever.'

The marvellous cuisine paled into insignificance and neither of them noticed the bouquet of the excellent wine. Titus, longing for her, whispered, 'Darling, could you please stay with me here tonight?' but in his heart he knew the answer.

'How could I? Tonight you will drive me home and just kiss me goodbye. We must wait.' Neither of them understood why.

By the end of the month Titus had found himself a flat two blocks away from Sarah's. The small cul-de-sac concealed the entrance well enough for Sarah's occasional visit.

As a glamorous couple they were miles ahead of any other. They were seen at the right places, expensive places, especially at the centre of society life, the newly opened New York coffee house, built in contemporary style, with such lavishness that it would have befitted an opera house. It was certainly larger than some of the royal palaces of the Continent. Full as it was of art nouveau design, winding columns and deco finish, some considered it the ultimate in avant-garde and thus totally tasteless. Sarah liked it, so it was included in their circuit. Titus preferred the odd trip to the casino. He never used public transport and cabbing it everywhere was a strain on his finances. For him standards were there to be raised, not lowered, as he often explained to Sarah. The poor salary of a captain had to be supplemented by a generous stipend from the estate manager in Transylvania.

Naturally Sarah never noticed any of this. In her world young and beautiful actresses were always lavishly entertained, but usually by older and more established men, not by contemporaries. There had to be the odd present of jewellery. Titus wanted to give and Sarah was delighted to receive. The casino was a different thing. Sarah's objections were not because Titus lost money. She was more concerned with the late nights, especially when she had early rehearsals the next morning. Titus had a simple rule by now; when fortune smiled on him, he spent the winnings on the good things of life, and when he was hard up, he wrote a letter to the estate manager.

At work he settled into his new routine of dealing with mountains of paperwork. Nobody spared the new boy. His brain was one of the sharpest in the army and he excelled himself in logistics, which he actually found fascinating. Contrasting with the increasing mess he made of his private finances, his work for the army was impeccable. Everyone else hated logistics, so they were happy to let him get on with it. He received the promised decoration during the New Year's Day ceremony. His smart salute completely masked the severity of his hangover.

The telegram announcing his father's sudden death arrived two days later.

He ran all the way to Sarah's flat with it. When he entered the flat ashen faced, Sarah read the lengthy telegram. 'How could this happen?'

'Father had this terrible habit of adjusting the horses' reins whilst driving the coach, though we forever warned him not to do it. His coach must have hit a pothole or something and he slipped under the wheels. I telephoned the farm manager, who said the coach was half a mile down the road when they found him. His neck was broken,' he said, lowering his head.

'Oh, darling, I am so sorry. Please let me come and help you to pack.' Sarah took his arm.

'I am off to the ministry to ask for leave. I'll need at least a month to sort things out.'

They hurried along the street, arms linked as was the custom of engaged couples. This time they resented the recognition of their adoring public; they were full of their private thoughts. Titus left her at the door of his flat, kissing her gently on the cheek and quickening his pace for the further mile to the ministry. His commanding officer was naturally very understanding. Most of his men came from similar backgrounds and understood how these things happened. Titus was granted his request of a month off to bury his father and to make some arrangements for the smooth continuation of the family business.

On his arrival at the railway station Michael, dressed in black, greeted him. Titus opened the carriage door; he did not feel like driving. Sitting alone in the coach that killed his father gave him more time to reflect as they were driving through the estate. He was disturbed by the conclusion he arrived at. With tears in his eyes he ran to his mother, whom he adored so much. They clung to each other without a word. She, being desperate in her grief, took strength from his solid, reassuring support. The images in their minds were legion, past, present and future. He knew he would soon have to answer some serious questions. They had tea on the balcony where, not so long ago, the four of them were interrupted by Kathleen. This time the conversation was pure family trivia, neither of them being ready to address the real problem of the future.

The funeral was a grand affair in every sense. The multitude of villagers turned up in their Sunday black, filling the back of the ancient church. Michael drove the horse-drawn hearse, surrounded by 'hussars of death', as the locals called the pall-bearers because of their black-braided uniforms and tall feathered hats, six men on either side of the hearse. Titus in his ceremonial uniform walked to the church and joined his mother in the second row, leaving the first pew unoccupied. Traditionally this was reserved for visiting clergy, and was soon filled by ministers of the surrounding towns. The coffin was on the right-hand side of the pulpit.

Titus hardly noticed that Kathleen had sat down beside him, having left her parents in the row behind, with the rest of the Zenta family.

The young pastor, with a strong Calvinist oration, emphasised the great loss to the family, the community and the nation. Kathleen took Titus' hand and squeezed it, indicating her support. Titus turned towards her with a faint smile, patting her hand before withdrawing his.

Outside, more villagers filled the churchyard, and some of them even spilled over on to the little hill on the right. The strains of the last psalm died away and the coffin was taken to the left side of the churchyard. The vicar blessed it as it was lowered into the grave, which was sealed in minutes. A nine-foot obelisk, engraved in similar fashion to the surrounding Zenta ones, the first being that of Gregory from the seventeenth century, was placed on it by the six pall-bearers with a very clever device of ropes and pulleys. Another blessing and they filled some twenty carriages to return to the manor for the reception. Titus took charge of the event and shook hands with the men offering condolences. Helen quietly disappeared to start her year of mourning, which meant total seclusion from public view. Wherever Titus went Kathleen followed closely, more often than not holding on to his right arm. Her innocent support was totally natural and hardly noticeable.

During the next three weeks Titus took stock of his property and decided that he had far too much grazing land. With his manager, and after a fair amount of bargaining, he sold ten thousand acres to a Romanian boyar, a minor baronet, two villages away. Friends and family objected strongly to the deal. His uncle Philip was particularly vociferous about the wisdom of selling to a Romanian, even if his price was better. To him it was a matter of principle. 'You don't sell your own country to a foreigner settled here.' He was not alone in thinking that there was a grand Romanian strategy to buy up Hungarian land with very cheap money loaned by the Bucharest government. He put it to Titus plainly. 'They are buying up the province for annexation, don't you see?' Titus thought this ridiculous, reminding his uncle that the empire was one of the four greatest powers in Europe and nothing could possibly happen to it. 'They can't pack up the land in sacks and take it back with them.'

The boyar turned up with the cash, a suitcase full of it, and handed it over to Titus with noticeable disdain. He left without the customary handshake, which did not bother Titus at all. He loathed shaking hands with them anyway. He placed the suitcase amongst his luggage, which was to go to Budapest with him, in spite of repeated objections from the manager. It was not to last him very long.

The intimate farewell with his mother once again showed their closeness. He commented on her recent loss of weight, which was very worrying, but understandable in the circumstances. As at his arrival, they clung together with few words but real love. He demanded that she should try to eat properly, which she promised to do, provided that he wrote to her regularly. He turned around to walk back to the coach and saw Kathleen standing by the horses. Her fresh face and large blue eyes contrasted with the figure-hugging black dress. As always in the past she made him smile. He kissed both her cheeks, cupping her head in his hands. She did not attempt to kiss him, just lowered her head and whispered, 'I'll wait for you, however long it takes.'

'Don't, little one. I might never come back,' Titus whispered back.

'I know you will. The Gypsy fortune teller told me so, only yesterday,' she said loudly as he stepped into the coach.

He waved to her and then towards the balcony. All the two women could see was a trail of dust rising into the early morning sky as Titus disappeared in the distant valley.

~

Sarah was waiting for him on the platform of the Western Railway Station, being pestered by the new hobby of 'autograph hunting', when she noticed Titus followed by a porter with his luggage. She ran breathlessly towards him as fast as her long dress allowed her, holding her hat firmly on her head with one hand. They embraced to the delight of the crowd, and then he kissed her gloved hand. Arms linked tightly, they walked to the cab and disappeared into the ever-increasing traffic of horse-drawn trams and cabs.

The light rain reminded them autumn would not be too far away.

'You need not wear black to mourn my father, you know, even if it does suit you.' Titus smiled.

'But I most certainly will. In public anyway. It would not be proper otherwise,' Sarah answered more seriously.

Titus kissed her ever more impatiently. His apartment was still two miles away. When they arrived he pulled Sarah to him, looked into her eyes and glanced towards the bed. Sarah's face turned serious for a moment, then she smiled. Her eyes sparkled as she began to unbutton her dress.

~

He took to Sarah's hedonistic lifestyle with complete ease, even considered it idyllic. The pre-Christmas parties, theatre events and the Grand Military Ball, financed by the suitcase, came and went like images of another world, unreal, but all consuming. All too good.

~

Helen died the day after Christmas, early in the evening. The day before, she had distributed her presents to every family on the estate. As tradition demanded they had lined up in front of the manor, dressed in their finest winter clothes, high boots and heavy furs. This was her first appearance since the funeral of Charles. The procession started with the estate manager, followed by the men in charge of the various enterprises: vineyard, stables, cattle, pig-yards, poultry and grain. They were followed by their wives and their exceptionally well-behaved children. The long line ended with the shepherds and all the simple hands who made the estate the best in the principality.

Although Helen coped rather well for a while, some of the womenfolk soon started whispering to each other about how pale she looked, and how thin, and that she must be starving herself. She said goodbye to the manager and his family and went to her room. Feeling her end was close, Helen took Charles' silver-framed photograph from the side table and sat down in her favourite armchair. She held the picture close to her chest and, as she sighed and smiled, her wafer-thin heart broke with ease.

The telegram arrived the next day. Titus and Sarah had hardly recovered from the Christmas celebration at her mother's flat when the postman knocked.

'It's for Captain Zenta,' he said. 'I tried first to deliver it to his apartment, but there was no reply. A neighbour said he might be here,' the man went on, explaining to the maid.

'I am the captain,' said Titus, coming along the hall, expecting it to be a message from the ministry. When he realised the uniformed man was in fact from the post office, he knew instinctively what had happened. He gave the man a small tip and turned away.

'I dare not open this, Sarah,' he said fearfully, 'I just dare not.'

But open it he did. He had read only the first sentence when the splitting headache hit him. He held the back of his head with both hands and softly sighed to himself. 'And I only wrote to her once!'

Titus and the two women sat in the tasteful living room looking at each other gloomily.

'This is the end,' Titus muttered. 'Darling, give me your best notepaper, I am resigning my commission.'

'Are you sure, my love, please don't be too hasty,' Sarah begged him.

'I have no choice now. I'm in a pen-pushing job already, so it's not as if I'll ever be in command of anything important again.' His headache was getting more severe but his mind was becoming clearer. 'The land is waiting for me, so many livelihoods depend on me. I must go.'

His resignation letter was brief and to the point:

Respected Minister General,

The loss of both my parents in a relatively short time leaves me, the only surviving member of the family, with no alternative but to resign His Majesty's commission. I respectfully request you to grant me reserve officer status at your discretion.

I remain respectfully yours, sir,

Cpt. Titus Zenta de Lemhény

Titus delivered the letter personally to the Minister for War, who was already informed of the facts.

'I am sorry to lose you. So is the Logistics Department,' he started, walking towards Titus, who stood at rigid attention. 'Please accept my condolences, Captain. I wish you Godspeed. Your request for reserve status is approved as from now,' the portly minister concluded.

His goodbye to Sarah was swift. He asked her not to see him off at the station, wanting to slip out of the capital quietly. She agreed that it was the right thing to do.

Once the steam train had left the station, Titus cowered in a corner seat, hoping that nobody would join him.

The mounting anxiety within him was becoming unbearable. Two funerals in less than a year and the second being his mother's, whom he loved so much and who never showed anything but devotion and affection towards him, gnawed at his conscience. And all those letters he never wrote! She was the only person who knew his vulnerability and his many weaknesses under the stylish if overpowering uniform. She knew that he would need the support of a single-minded woman. Noticing Sarah's strength and determination, she welcomed her, reluctantly. Although she never considered Titus' character as flighty, she knew he was not at his best when things did not go his way.

Sitting on the train, Titus was gazing out of the window, without seeing anything. There were no thoughts left in his mind. None.

The guard, asking to see his ticket, woke him up from his sleepless daydream. He fumbled in his pockets, having no idea where he had put it. The guard eventually helped him out, pointing to the small shelf with the ashtray. This is enough! Titus thought to himself. Get on with it and pull yourself together! He was becoming irate with his own behaviour. He tried to concentrate again. I will take stock, settle down and wait for Sarah's next break. We will decide on a date and have the greatest wedding Transylvania ever saw. There are no financial problems, but there is the matter of the distance to Budapest. No! I'll buy a flat there – with these new trains distance is no problem! Sarah liked the manor and the theatres of Kolozsvár and Vásárhely. It all sounded so simple, but deep down he wasn't quite so sure. A few seconds later his mood changed completely; to hell with the lot! I will sell out. Why not? It has been done before. Yes, sell the lot and invest in industry. That's the way forward. The stock market. Damn these pretty pine trees and valleys. Damn Gregory Zenta and his 1604 mentality; these are modern times, we must adapt. Battling with his thoughts this way he did not have to consider the hundreds of familiar faces that would be looking at him on his arrival at the manor.

The funeral was less dramatic than Charles' eleven months earlier, with family and close relatives only. The exception was, naturally, Kathleen. She came along and attached herself to Titus again. Although he had always been very close to his mother he had not one tear in his eyes. The hurt he felt was deeper and the sorrow much more intimate, much more personal.

His next few days were spent busying himself with the manager. There was much to catch up with, a lot of new details to learn. The last time he had been around the estate to show it to Sarah it had all looked so rosy. Now it was becoming hard work. Whether or not he was to sell he still had to know what he possessed, what was profitable and what was a millstone around the neck of the property. They went along piecemeal and, logistics being his forte, he soon came to understand his position.

The evenings were a different matter altogether. His loneliness was suffocating. Having not lived in the house since he was old enough to go to the Bolyai High School as a boarder, he found it quite awesome. His memories of it had always been happy and active. Now all he had were endless nights and unclear thoughts, and he was incapable of tolerating them. He decided to discipline himself to write to Sarah each and every night. The letters soon became a diary of events, and they were dispatched to Budapest twice weekly.

Sarah was naturally delighted. Never before had she received such attention. Titus had a powerful pen, not too ornate, unlike his contemporaries. As Sarah's visit had been relatively recent she could understand Titus' problems very clearly. From his description of developments she even managed to give him advice, such as how to get into the new silk business. He most certainly had enough mulberry trees growing around the manor and along the roads. Titus was delighted with her interest, and started to press her about the visit she had promised at his departure. Sarah had agreed quite readily, but it would have to wait until a suitable break in her performances. But he could wait no longer and he wrote once again.

> *I must come to you, darling. I can no longer recall your face in the lonely nights. I have forgotten the feel of your embrace and the taste of your kisses. This place is becoming intolerable without you. I must come to you!*

Just before the heavy workload of spring he decided to take off for a week. He went to the Gellért Hotel. Sarah promised to join him after the performances of *Romeo and Juliet* at the National.

Titus ate his dinner alone and, while sipping his brandy, he was disturbed by the gentle stirrings and clapping coming from the tables nearer the entrance, heralding Sarah's arrival. He got up from his seat, pushing it slowly back, and moved toward her. He reached out, gently kissing her hand and then her cheeks.

'You look gorgeous, darling,' he whispered.

'Oh, Titus, I have missed you so much. My body aches for you.' They left immediately.

Their enforced separation showed in the searching expressions of their faces. Whenever their eyes met their breathing became deeper and faster. Back in his room, the physical declaration of their love had to be immediate. Sarah's hand slipped low. Titus was totally ready for her. The urge to get unbound from their intricate clothing was like sheer panic. They could hardly cope with the innumerable buttons of her tightly fitting dress and his new waistcoat, as they fell on the bed. They started their lovemaking nearly fully clothed. It was not until two hours later they found themselves naked in each other's arms.

'Do you remember Mr Orsen on the train to Transylvania?' Sarah opened new ground in their post-coital calm.

'You mean the older chap, who had the unenviable task of producing *Hamlet* out of that rabble? Of course. Why?'

'Well, he has just visited America. He met some producers there who came back with him and he is throwing a party on Saturday. We are invited. Would you like to go?'

'Of course, why not?' Titus agreed readily. 'Never refuse an invitation from an influential man, nor even a general for that matter. Mind you, the latter never throw parties anyway.'

Titus spent the rest of the week with his tailor, whom he pressed for a new dress suit by Saturday. He then contacted his stockbroker and some industrialists. The evenings were centred around the theatre and dining. By Friday he was convinced that selling out was his best option. On Friday night Sarah was free and her mother invited them to dine with her at home. This gave Titus a good opportunity to talk freely about their future. He considered their engagement based on the strongest possible emotion. He was certainly ready to talk of marriage, which they both wanted. As the conversation progressed, a realisation emerged between them; it was not what they were hoping for. The diversity of their professions and the distance that would separate them created a deep gap, which could only be bridged by their youth, their great love and their exuberance.

'I can really sell out and become an investor, you know,' Titus interjected.

'I know you don't really want that,' Sarah tried to reassure him.

'You're right,' he said, 'I couldn't possibly sell it all, but I could certainly trim down some of it. For the age we live in, the whole thing is too diverse, too complicated. With some sensible pruning I could come to live in town,' he added. 'I could support your career here, though I do fear that being a young and married star does not sound good for your public. You would disappoint too many of those chaps at the stage door,' he jested.

'Ah! Back-pedalling, are we?' Sarah teased.

'No, no. Never.' Titus held up his hands.

Sarah's mother had, most uncharacteristically, not interfered so far, but when she did, she sounded quite pragmatic.

'You must have a long engagement. The way the two of you behave, there is no hurry anyway.' Turning to Titus she continued, 'You should buy a flat here and stop wasting all that money staying in the Gellért.' It all sounded so sensible.

Their decision was duly postponed and in the end they were both happy with that. Neither of them knew what the next twenty-four hours were about to bring.

༜

Mr Orsen's party was very much a showbiz affair, held in the grand drawing room of his home, with a large caucus of visiting Americans in deep conversation with the host, their stomachs having been anaesthetised with the customary glass of pálinka. Stars of stage and opera were present in abundance. Unusually for a so-called private party there was also an equally large press presence. Grudgingly dressed in black tie as the invitation demanded, they looked conspicuous amongst the natural glitter of the stars and would-be stars, all there to impress. The whole gathering was well primed for something unusual to happen.

Sarah and Titus arrived soon after ten o'clock. Their host took them straight over to the Americans for introduction. As soon as they left, the producers turned to each other, murmuring excitedly. A new starlet of the operetta stage, showing the deepest décolletage of the decade, was buzzing about the guests, trying to entice the oldest one with her rudimentary English. He just looked far too busy to take the bait. The host gently moved her on and clinked his wineglass with a spoon. The band played a long and loud chord. All attention was suddenly focused on him.

'We are very happy, indeed privileged, to have amongst us six gentlemen from the United States of America tonight. They have already travelled the continent and, having been in our city for the past few weeks, have seen all the shows and plays we have to offer. Ladies and gentlemen, I would like you to welcome Mr Oscar Goldrhein, the head of Inter-Continental Studios of Hollywood, who would like to say a few words.'

There was a little polite clapping whilst the two men changed places.

The revered producer removed his monocle. 'Gracious host, ladies and gentlemen. May I say right away how impressed we have been with the theatrical scene of your wonderful capital city. The variety and depth of the activity here are second to none, and the beauty of the ladies is as astonishing as it is extensive. Perhaps you would allow us to try to take just one of them away from you. Inter-Continental Studios are currently involved in new projects involving ever-longer movies. My director has even called them "epics". You've all seen our male star, Randolph Capolto, but we have decided to widen our horizons to find his leading lady; a new face that is instantly distinguishable from the Anglo-Saxon or Latin stereotypes. I realise the way I am going to conclude these few words is unusual, but the studio has decided that in order to gain maximum publicity we will break new ground. To ensure this publicity for us, and indeed for the person we have chosen, we will take the risk of making this announcement in public, here, tonight. Ladies and gentlemen, we would like to ask Miss Sarah Dombay to join us at Inter-Continental Studios in Hollywood for the film version of *The Bedouin Sheikh*.'

A loud gasp took over the room like a tempest flattening a meadow.

The powerful drama of the announcement by Mr Goldrhein was not wasted. The ladies present responded with sighs of varying loudness, the men looked at each other in disbelief. Mr Orsen started clapping.

Sarah stood motionless in the middle of the glittering room, as the others started to move away from her involuntarily. Titus at first could not believe the words, but realisation that he had just lost his love and perhaps much more immediately cleared his mind. He turned to her, bent close to her ear and whispered, 'It's your decision, darling.'

With over a hundred faces turning intently towards Sarah, she had to respond.

'You cannot seriously expect me to answer you here and now. I am honoured to be considered for such an important part, with such a big star as Mr Capolto – what actress would not be? I do want to take up your offer, but in my personal life there are two other people I very much want to consult. One of them is here.' She moved a few steps and pulled Titus closer to her. 'The other one is my mother. And, I may add, I would like to consult the National Theatre.'

'That's no problem!' the manager of the National shouted good-humouredly from the surprised crowd.

'So if I may talk to my fiancé and my mother, I will give you a private answer tomorrow afternoon.' Sarah smiled at Mr Goldrhein. He was captivated. 'I understand you will be leaving for the United States the day after tomorrow,' she added.

The producer nodded. She stepped forward to offer a handshake. By the time Sarah had finished with them all them Titus was at the back of the room. It took her a few moments to notice him and catch up with him on the balcony.

'Darling, you are not cross, are you?' she asked with an ever more appealing look in her eyes.

'No, Sarah, I'm not cross. Far from it. I have had a revelation. I just realised that I am in your way. No, more than that. For the sake of your career, I have to let you go,' Titus answered quietly, with his eyes slowly filling up with tears.

'And I thought I could count on your support! But not a bit of it! You're just feeling sorry for yourself. Titus, this is a chance in a million, no more than that … you could come and join me! Don't do this! Titus, please … please.' Her voice faded away.

'No, Sarah, my mind, if I have any left, is made up. I am letting you go.' He moved nearer to her and reached out to take her head in his trembling hands.

'Darling, let me kiss you, perhaps for the last time.' Sarah pulled back slightly. 'Please let me kiss you!'

Sarah pulled farther back 'No! If you're so intent on going, then go! Here, take your ring.' She took off the sparkling diamond-and-sapphire ring and handed it to Titus, trying to hold back her tears.

Titus was in rage; he took the ring and threw it against the wall of the balcony with such force that it spun back into the darkness below.

'To hell with it!' His voice was like a clarion.

Sarah stared into the darkness outside in astonishment and turned. She threw her head back haughtily and walked slowly back into the room. Titus stood frozen to the spot. He hesitated for a moment, trying to compose himself, then took a deep breath, twirled his black moustache with his thumbs and index fingers and began to walk towards the hall. By the time he had collected his cloak and ordered a cab, Sarah was back in the drawing room, tapping Mr Orsen on his shoulder.

'Would you announce me, please?' She commanded with conviction. Her eyes were still moist when she stood in front of the orchestra, which played another long chord to attract attention.

'Mr Goldrhein, can I just say …' She gulped. 'Can I just say that I am delighted with your offer and I'm ready to leave as soon as my contract allows me.' She could no longer keep her tears back, and when she started to cry, the guests without exception took them to be tears of joy and burst into loud applause.

Titus was marching down the path to his cab when in the clear moonlight something glinted. He bent down to the shining object to find the dented ring. He picked it up and caressed it in his hands. 'Come with me,' he addressed it silently. 'You and I've made it easier for Sarah. She must never know. It's best this way. It's best, even if it will kill me.' With tears pouring from his eyes he kissed the ring and placed it in his waistcoat pocket.

6

Wedding

Dusk was gathering when Titus arrived on his estate. He asked for a light snack, to which he curtly added the demand for a demijohn of kadarka, his favourite, alas stupefyingly strong, local red wine that he consumed in record time. He added to it a couple of extra large brandies. Throughout the whole evening his mind was devoid of any thought or idea. He stared into space and felt an occasional pain hitting him from the nape of the neck to the crown of his head. He fell on his bed, semiconscious.

The next morning and for many more afterwards he was violently sick, for, much as he liked his brandy, he could not tolerate it. He went on like this for some time until, after an exceptionally heavy night of oblivion, he once again woke up with such a violent headache and subsequent vomiting that Michael decided to go for the town doctor.

The well-dressed, middle-aged medic quickly assessed the situation. It was not too difficult; the smell of alcohol was obvious, both in the room and on his patient. He examined him closely and sat at his bedside. As he turned to look at him, he noticed the damaged ring on the bedside table next to the oil lamp.

'Titus, my son, you of all people,' he began, as his patient's head turned slowly away from him. 'Look at me. I delivered you into this world and have known you all your life. I know about you and Sarah Dombay, everybody does. I am not going to let you drink yourself into an early grave. You had a rough time with the death of your parents, but you have too important a job to do in this part of the world to act like this.'

Titus started to listen, his eyes still gazing into nowhere.

'Ideally you should spend a couple of weeks at a spa, like Szováta, without alcohol, but unfortunately, at this time of the year, you're needed here. So, dare I say it, stop feeling sorry for yourself.' The physician cringed to himself as the words he so hated to use left his lips, but at least they hit home, as would a military command.

Titus looked at him, got out of bed, dressed, shook him by the hand and asked the maid to bring him a mug of ice-cold milk.

'It will not happen again,' he said, humbled.

In less than an hour he was in his riding breeches, boots and his short sheepskin riding coat, looking for the estate manager.

The next few weeks brought about the most feverish and productive activity of his life. He was keen to reduce his territory and sold all his grazing land; a good decision, according to the manager. The money from the sale was invested in the booming stock market of Budapest. This boom, mainly in the engineering industry, promised favourable returns, and he concentrated his efforts on that. Sadly, as usual more than half of his buyers were once again Romanians. They were very keen on buying more and more land. The remainder of the estate now consisted of flat arable fields and hillside vineyards, all close to and accessible from the manor. He had the house redecorated, keeping the imposing parts original and brown, but the living areas became livelier and more colourful. Some of the basic furniture went too and he replaced it with finer items from the Regency period that was so fashionable in England.

His fine horses fell into two categories; the working ones, as agriculture still demanded a lot of those, and a smaller stable of thoroughbreds for personal use and racing. His black stallion was still his favourite for dashing around. It could cope with any terrain easily, galloped well, but above all it was a graceful jumper, and Titus knew how to put it to the test.

The setting sun of early spring picked out Titus riding his horse on the crest of the hill, reins clasped in his right hand as the left shoulder still gave him occasional trouble. He heard a brass band playing in the village across the meadow. He was curious for a moment and decided to follow the strains of the music.

The Feast of St Agatha was in full swing. He was pleased to see the simple merrymaking of the villagers. The carousels and stands were full of colourful people engaging in their annual fun. In the square in front of the church the army band was playing in competition with the Gypsies, who were fiddling away around the cimbalom in the inn. The wine was flowing freely and he decided to have some. His welcome was both genuine and reverential. He appreciated this as many of his farm workers and casual labourers were there enjoying themselves. Titus wandered around the tables, clinking glasses here and there until he noticed one of the young peasant girls serving the wine. She was around sixteen or perhaps less. Her buxom figure was well displayed in her red felt waistcoat, laced only halfway up. A heavily pleated black skirt with small red roses on it swung around on her ample bottom as she twisted and turned around the tables, a white apron completing her outfit. Pretty now, he thought, but she will lose that figure after a couple of children. But it was now that mattered.

Piroska was well aware of Titus' glances, which over the course of some drinks progressed from appreciation to sheer lust. Liking his good looks and placing his jug of wine before him, she bent down just enough to show more of her bosom. To his pleasure she stayed in that position whilst she wiped the table clean, looking him straight in the eye. Titus responded by patting her on the back of her knee, then he started to move his hand up between her thighs. She giggled and spun away, whispering quietly in his ear, 'Later, my lord, later.' He had another drink and gave his moustache a twirl.

Titus did not care much for the idea of 'later', but poured some more wine from the pottery jug into the small matching tumbler and drank away with his peasants. He suddenly noticed Piroska waving to him from the doorway. Evidently she was of the same mind. His wine disappeared quickly down his throat and he followed her outside, where the dusk was closing in rapidly. He caught up with her at the back of the inn, where he had left his horse. The girl knew her way about the courtyard and beckoned him to the side stable. Titus took her voluptuous body, holding her tightly. As he pushed her bodice down her large youthful breasts fell free easily. He buried his head between them whist she rolled her chest from side to side. Piroska was biting his lips excitedly. She stopped and leaned backwards provocatively.

'You want cunt, my lord, don't you?' There was no alternative word in the vocabulary of even the prettiest of peasant girls.

The startled Titus almost pulled away, but realised that this was no Budapest and Piroska was no Sarah.

'Yes, love, I do want cunt.' He lifted her tightly pleated skirt.

The suddenness of it all, the unusual circumstances, and also the time that had lapsed since Sarah, so excited Titus that they did not spend much time in the straw. Although Piroska was no virgin and had known about sex from the age of twelve, she had no knowledge of orgasm. She was to find out all about that later. She stood up and let her skirt fall back into place, wriggling her bottom. She put her white apron back on and pushed her breasts into the pretty waistcoat. In no time she was back in the courtyard, on her way home. She had to be home early. Her parents were very strict about that. Cantering his way to the manor, Titus was in a much happier frame of mind. He chuckled to himself as he recalled her crude yet very innocent ways. In his mind he repeated her question in the barn. This was indeed a different world, a world he hardly knew. Arriving home, he had supper, drank some more wine and fell fast asleep.

~

Easter arrived and Kathleen appeared fresh from finishing school for her six-week break. Only then did she learn of Titus' return to the estate. Her parents had kept this news from her quite successfully. Her mother and father had a smallholding; they were comfortable, but by no means rich. Kathleen's private schooling fees at the well-secluded college in the middle of the Carpathians more or less absorbed their money.

The day before Good Friday she rode over on horseback to see Titus. She eventually found him stripped to the waist, washing himself in a water trough. He had just inspected a silo and was covered in dust from head to foot.

Titus smiled when he saw her getting off her horse. Kathleen ran to him and kissed him on both cheeks, remarking on the nasty scar over his left shoulder. Her eyes moved on to the gold necklace he was wearing, strung through a dented oval engagement ring. The beautiful stones glittered in the sunshine.

'What is that, Titus?' She asked timidly.

'Oh, Kathleen it's nothing, really nothing. It's my unlucky talisman. I must wear it all the time, otherwise I might get lucky and that wouldn't do,' he said, teasing her as usual.

'Stop it, Titus, it's Sarah's ring, isn't it?' Kathleen knew what she was talking about. 'No matter, she's gone to America. I read it in the papers. She will never come back,' she stated assuredly.

Titus put on his shirt and invited her to complete the rounds of the estate with him. She leapt on her lovely grey mare and followed Titus slowly along the dust track. They were talking of her completing her studies in the summer when Kathleen, turning to Titus, said, 'Then, I think we should get married.'

'Yes, Kathleen, we should,' he answered quietly. The matter was not discussed further.

Blaming each other for the break-up of their relationship, Sarah and Titus did not correspond. The going of their separate ways was final. Titus naturally had plenty of chances to read about her in the newspapers, which were in abundance now thanks to the new American rolling presses. Whenever he saw her picture or her name printed in a headline, he just turned the page stubbornly with a choking heart.

Kathleen's parents invited Titus for dinner on Easter Monday, and after the usual niceties the subject naturally turned to the wedding. Titus was delighted that it was going to be a fairly small affair of just two hundred and fifty people or so. For the reception he offered the manor house, the ground floor of which was just about big enough to accommodate that number. The coaches and horses of the estate could handle the transport. Everything was agreed and they drank to it. Kathleen's father toasted the young couple and announced that the dowry would be a motor car, a 1905 Vauxhall open sport model, a marvel of its age. Titus was naturally delighted as he was already toying with the idea of buying something like that and the present was without doubt a most generous one.

For the next few days they saw each other every day. Kathleen was an absolute delight. Her sparkling personality blossomed into maturity, now that she had got her man. They rode and walked, planning their lives together, yet there was not much to plan for beyond their wedding. Their lives were mapped out for them already: they were to live the fairly unexciting life of the provincial, well-to-do gentry or minor nobility of stable past and present. At this time the uncertainty of the future never occurred to them.

Their love was extremely tender and, thanks to Kathleen, it was definitely 'very proper'. Their kissing was passionate, without being lustful. Walking along, they would link arms or hold hands that brushed their bodies. Kathleen was totally fulfilled now that Titus was hers in their impending marriage. She never ever doubted this, and she did not dare to want more. Titus was too wounded to demand anything. This was comfortable for him and he was willing to wait and see what time had in store for them.

When Kathleen returned to her finishing school for the last time, Titus reverted to his previous way of life without hesitation. Piroska's appointment to the household was announced. He was still excited with her simple peasant coquetry. She knew all about the wedding plans and helped willingly with arrangements. Jealousy never entered her mind.

The date of the wedding was fixed for the last Saturday of May. Titus asked Peter Vadas, his friend of long ago, who was still stationed in the Pécs garrison, to be his best man. Peter was delighted. Titus was his hero. He arrived a week before the event. The rest of the week they spent in inns and vineyards. This constituted the traditional 'farewell to the lad', when the groom was dragged around the places of his past, as if he were going to spend the rest of his life on the moon. Peter was most impressed with the Imperial restaurant in Vásárhely and he considered the wild boar steak the best he had ever tasted – little wonder, as some of them had been shot less than fifty miles from the restaurant table.

The week was to culminate in the manor on Friday night. Piroska was in charge of recruiting more servants for the occasion. She even managed to get some Romanian peasant girls from the next village to join them. The all-night light-hearted frolicking could be heard for miles – the Gypsies made sure of that. The wine flowed, the girls were pretty and Titus had all the pickings. When he was woken up by Piroska, she had to chase two Romanian girls out of his bed.

'Home you go, bitches! I hope you'll all get pregnant!' was her blunt manner of dispersing them. The 'bitches' just laughed and, by the time Titus was out of his bathtub, they were well gone and order was restored.

Titus and Peter were at the entrance of the church well before eleven. They wore dress uniforms, with swords. The small church was once again full to overflowing. The second row, the Zenta pews, was this time occupied by Kathleen's family. The first row was left unoccupied. Kathleen and her retinue of school friends arrived in coaches. She looked natural, yet stunning. Her wedding dress was intentionally ten years out of date, just pre-turn-of-the-century style, with exaggerated bust and hip lines. It had heavy white brocade with an abundance of lace and a three-yard train, which was held by two pageboys. The bridesmaids wore a simpler version of the same dress in the same colour. Blue flowers were selected to go with the uniforms of the men.

True to Magyar custom, Titus took his bride's arm and walked her up to the waiting pastor.

The young pastor celebrated their union with a simple Calvinist ceremony, emphasising the wrath of God, should anything go intentionally wrong. 'All marriages are made in Heaven. No sinners may interfere with such a union, which is blessed by the Lord himself, for he will expel the creators of the original sin from his house.' His gestures from the pulpit were exaggerated and menacing.

The pastor walked down from the pulpit to bless the couple, his eyes piercing theirs. Titus considered the whole thing a little bizarre and Kathleen nearly burst into a giggle. She was certain of her side of the bargain and knew that no one could possibly take Titus from her. Titus wasn't quite so sure.

The peasants outside the ancient church were anxiously awaiting the emergence of the young couple. Right in the front line was Piroska, jumping up and down with anticipation, much to the delight of the young lads, who could not take their eyes off her voluptuous bosom. Twelve soldiers summoned by Peter from the local garrison formed the guard of honour. The sergeant gave the command to present arms. The men jumped to attention, with arms in front of their chests and chins pointing up and inwards. Inside, the couple began their exit together. The organist struggled with the Rakóczi March, reminding Titus of his graduation ceremony not so long ago. Appearing at the church door, they faced the sun, which showered them with light, showing off the somewhat over-elaborate design of Kathleen's gown, Titus looking every bit the romantic hero of a novel. They faced the strong sun like two brave eagles.

At the church gate the promised wedding present was waiting, engine purring. The beautiful yellow open Vauxhall gleamed in the sunshine to the delight of all the children from the nearby villages. Kathleen settled herself into the soft black leather passenger seat, the high backrest framing her white dress perfectly. Titus unbuckled his sword and passed it to Peter, who then placed it behind them. The crowd showered rice upon them. He depressed the clutch pedal twice and engaged gear. The car responded with ease, leading the procession of coaches back to the manor.

The tables in the living rooms were laid with the most magnificent display of food, offering venison, trussed pheasants and chickens, several roast piglets and goulash with scented dill pickles. In the large courtyard the spit-roasting oxen sent tantalising smells downwind. Barrels of delicious red wine were placed around, inviting everyone to drink.

The Gypsies played by the large well and the children in their Sunday best were darting about, running into staff and guests alike and receiving the odd clip round the ear for it. The main hall, ready for the family to receive their friends, was lavishly decorated with wild flowers from the valley, for the merriment to follow.

When the smiling couple appeared at the gate, they were received by the estate manager and his wife. Titus clicked back his sword and they took their place for the only formality of the day. They received Kathleen's parents, who were totally overcome by all this, their faces glowing and blushing. Kathleen was right after all, they thought. She had vowed she would marry Titus. Then came a little mingling with the local gentry, all of them overdoing the customary 'best behaviour' reserved for such an important social occasion. Eventually they took their seats and the wedding feast was served. The newlyweds were flanked by Kathleen's parents with her very proud father at her side. On Titus' left sat the pastor's wife and her husband, who proceeded to say grace, once again calling for the Almighty to protect this and all marriages.

When he had concluded, Peter stood to read the only telegram, which he had managed to keep secret so far: *'Thinking of you both on your happy day. Signed: Sarah Dombay, Hollywood, California, USA.'*

'That is very nice of her,' said Kathleen, turning towards Titus.

'No, not at all nice and totally unnecessary,' he replied dryly.

As custom dictated, before the meal toasts were proposed. Kathleen's father, in a few but to him poignant words, wished the couple well – like young birds, they had to leave their parents' nest to build their own for their future. Titus thought it a little banal but nodded his head at the right places. The old man went on to describe the virtues of chastity, trying to reassure himself, as he was most worried about the fact that he was giving away a virgin bride. No father ever liked to do that; somehow it just did not feel right.

The late afternoon was just about turning into the most beautiful evening when the dinner was served. Outside the merrymaking was totally different;, the steaming-hot oxen and good wine were making their mark. By now the older and younger generations were totally segregated. Within each there was another segregation of sexes. The girls wore their colourful folk dresses of embroidered white blouses, richly coloured waistcoats, heavily pleated skirts of varying colours and stiff little white aprons round their waists. They had on blue or red leather boots with matching tiara-shaped bonnets. The lads dressed uniformly in their unique Sekler costumes: black riding boots, white skin-tight braided trousers, white shirts and black braided waistcoats left deliberately unfastened. Their small black hats, with a bunch of feathery grass in the band and tilted to one side, completed their outfits. The boys were drinking and the girls were giggling, all knowing full well that at a decent village wedding not only the bride would get laid.

The large Gypsy band was doing its best to warm up the crowd, starting with the more '*lento*' end of their repertoire. The fierce Csárdás, the fierce rhythmic national dance of all Magyars, would come later. Inside, the more serious part of the wedding was going well. The wine loosened their choking clothes, their tongues and even their actions. Titus felt contact from the pastor's wife's foot upon his own underneath their table. He put it down to it being accidental. The second time there was no mistake about it. Titus looked into Nina's piercing eyes and saw nothing but exciting invitation. Taken aback, he pulled away his foot and turned towards his bride. Her eyes were full of admiration and happiness. The contrast could not have been greater. Being conscious of Nina's eyes, he tried to console himself with the innocence of Kathleen's, yet he knew full well that now there was no escaping Nina. Thankfully, Peter stood up to announce the first dance. Titus took Kathleen's hand and walked out to the courtyard, which was illuminated by hundreds of colourful lanterns swinging gently in the early evening breeze. The Gypsies, seeing them emerging from the house, abruptly ended their song about the 'acacia-tree-lined road', played a loud chord and, when the couple reached the middle of the courtyard, began the waltz 'Oh how we danced on the night we were wed …' Titus held Kathleen assuredly as they danced around and glided over the yard. The people started clapping as they passed and joined in – first Kathleen's parents, then the relatives, in strict order of seniority, followed by the guests.

The waltz was followed by the slower variety, known to them as English waltzes. When these had been played it was time to 'buy the bride'. Peter came forward and patted Titus on the right shoulder. He looked at his best man, who threw a hundred-crown note in a large woven peasant basket and took his bride from him, for a new, more ferocious dance. Titus walked back to the crowd. During each number the same thing happened three times. The male members of the family, the guests and the staff all placed notes in the basket until it was overflowing. Eventually they were all dancing on money strewn on the floor, and lots of it.

Kathleen was well prepared for this. She knew the custom. It all had to do with stamina, and it would go on for an hour or so. Normally the enormous amount of money collected at a wedding such as this went to the young couple, but the two of them had decided long before that they would use the money to found the 'Zenta Orphanage'. This encouraged Kathleen to look for the next dancer, and she even took on the youngest of village lads with their pennies.

When it was all over Titus took the floor again for the final Csárdás. The couple, Titus in his dress uniform and his conservatively dressed bride, looked truly magnificent in this natural setting. The dancing couples, the smell of the roast oxen, the unrelenting music and the splendid lanterns produced an atmosphere of great happiness for everyone. It was an expression of the stability of the landed gentry; solid, still feudalistic yet all-involving and thus nearly egalitarian. The event belonged to all of them and yet they all knew their places within it.

As the night progressed and inhibitions started to fall away the rustic frolicking began in earnest. The well-lit courtyard made the surrounding areas appear greatly darker. The scent of the acacias was more pungent in the stillness of the night and this was all welcomed by the younger generation. It was easy to slip away for a cuddle, or more. Kathleen and Titus decided to take the 'English leave'. On their way out Titus beckoned Peter, whispered something in his ear and pointed to Piroska, giving him a gentle push, setting him off in her direction.

'I heard that! You're incorrigible,' remarked Kathleen.

'Well, he'll have a better time there than with your school friends for sure, and you know full well that the best man must have some fun too.' He smiled, ushering her gently to the master bedroom, which had not been used since his parents' death.

The virgin bride certainly took no urging. As Titus placed his sword on the side chest, unbuttoned the interminable buttons of his tunic and managed to pull off his knee boots with his father's 'boot-puller', Kathleen had slipped off her stiff underskirts. The commotion outside would go on for the next three days, wedding couple or no wedding couple. They closed the shutters and the merrymaking outside became an acceptable background noise. Titus took her silken hand and started to walk her towards the bed.

For a moment his thoughts shifted to Sarah. As he stood by the bed the lavender-washed linen reminded him of previous delights. He was trying to chase the flashbacks from his mind when he felt Kathleen's dainty hand tugging him to attract his attention. Titus saw the wide-open pleading blue eyes, expressing a mixture of pleasure, uncertainty and even a little fear. They lay on the bed next to each other, still holding hands. Kathleen turned towards him and kissed the scar on his shoulder. This innocent gesture melted Titus' thoughts away. Sarah was gone. Titus turned to her and she lifted her head to await his kiss. When he took her there was just the softest of sighs to be heard.

~

The gleaming car was packed by mid-morning. Michael and a very sleepy Piroska had done a good job. The heavy brown pigskin suitcase was in the back, ready for the honeymoon trip that had been arranged to include the Szováta resort again. One week in the Star Hotel was to be followed by a trip into the Carpathians on the new road cut into the proud mountains. Winding around the Pin rock like a snake on a tree and showing a glimpse of itself now and then, it confronted the traveller with uncertainty right to the crest, which had been the natural frontier of the kingdom for over a thousand years.

Titus and Kathleen did not talk too much, they never would, yet there was a contentment between them that was obvious and comfortable. Their silence was occasionally interrupted when they glanced at each other, or by Titus pointing to some site of interest along the road, such as the 'Killer Lake', formed less than a century ago when the mighty mountains suddenly moved in front of the very eyes of the frightened villagers, drowning many of them in the newly formed lake. The survivors gave it its morbid name before the cartographers had their chance.

'Have you not seen it before?' Titus asked as he pulled up by the lakeside.

'No, but Papa used to talk about it. It makes me shiver to see the tops of hundreds of pine trees trapped in the lake sticking out like some pagan symbols of the dead.'

Titus restarted the engine with a roar. Another hour's drive and they had arrived. Their hotel was an old converted castle. Its special attraction was the nearby dense forest, the largest breeding ground for wild boar in the principality. They would hunt from early the next morning.

～

The shoot was well organised and Kathleen insisted on being part of it. They set out with twelve rifles and about fifty young beaters, who had to be fit enough to climb trees should a more self-respecting boar decide to charge. The hunters would have to look after a number of these lads, for it was not unusual for a decent boar to overturn a medium-sized tree with one of them on it. Titus ordered his wife not to leave his side and rightly so, as they soon found themselves in the thick of things.

It was a large hog, threatened by some of the beaters, which decided to take no more of the noise they created and began to charge at one of the youngsters. The gigantic black animal snorted and snuffled ferociously as he attacked.

'Here he comes!' One the young men cried out. Titus turned, pushing Kathleen behind a large tree. The magnificent animal surged towards the beaters like a runaway steam engine. When it saw its intended prey it leapt into the air with enormous strength; Titus fired his Purdey twice. Momentum kept the ton of flesh going and it landed as dead weight on the young beater's legs, breaking one of them instantly. The poor lad screamed out in agony until the others managed to lift the beast off him while dark blood poured out of the neck of the animal. Kathleen comforted the injured man until two others carried him back to the road and lifted him on to the cart.

Further cries of 'Here he comes!' Were heard from the left. By the time Titus and a local hunter had arrived, the female was digging at the roots of the pine tree. Halfway up it another youth was shouting for attention. He knew that in two more minutes the tree would fall. The experienced huntsman raised his gun to his shoulder and took out the boar cleanly, saving the beater's bacon. By midday the hunt was over, with beasts lying in abundance around the carts; the young injured man was still groaning on one of them.

'I'll have the head of that one stuffed for the hall,' Titus said proudly.

'The rest will go to the smoke house!' Kathleen declared with similar excitement.

The remainder of their honeymoon was equally unusual. They stayed at mountain huts, hunted deer – Kathleen winning her first trophy – or just enjoyed the magnificent views, whichever way they looked.

Their last weekend took them back to town to the Grand Hotel in Vásárhely to quietly wind down. The general elegance of the hotel, with its own palm court ensemble, was the pride of the capital of Seklerland, the province within the principality. The residents were enjoying the ambience and the management was convinced that no other hotel like it existed in the land. Perhaps they were right. The consortium that owned it, in which Titus had a ten per cent holding, spared no effort, or expense. Chandeliers from Vienna and furniture from Paris were testimony to this. The total elegance culminated naturally in the restaurant, where Titus had reserved the best bay-window table for their stay. The manager was only too happy to grant the influential groom his wish.

For the last two days they walked about the town, looking at the developing main shopping square. Kathleen's attention was easily attracted by the new shops springing up everywhere. She specially favoured the Italian shoe shop. After her spending spree he had to drag her away to the Castle Hill overlooking the inner city, to his favourite inn, the Golden Bull, to sample the new imported beers from Bavaria. The honeymoon was going well; they were together in every sense of the word. The mobility brought about by the car enabled them to travel as well as relax. When they finally returned to the manor on Monday they felt as if they had been away for a year.

Titus, invigorated after the idyllic fortnight, threw himself into more reorganisation. There was little doubt that the estate had to change further. At the height of the power of the dual monarchy there was a glut of farm produce and experts agreed that industry and commerce were the intelligent way forward. Within months he had sold further thousands of acres to a boyar.

His broker in Budapest was pleased with his purchases in both heavy and light industries of the day, such as railway rolling-stock manufacturing and electrical equipment production. The estate was virtually wound down to a large vineyard and some animal husbandry for the local market.

At the end of the month Kathleen told the delighted Titus that she was pregnant. Her pregnancy was totally uneventful, and she gave birth to a strapping lad whom they called Nicholas after her grandfather. At the latter stage of the pregnancy Titus started once more to rely on the favours of Piroska, who was still running the household for them. She knew her place in the pecking order of life, knew what was expected of her and got on with it. It created no friction at all with her mistress, whom she much admired. This arrangement was as old as the hills that surrounded them.

Nicholas was followed by Rose some four years later. She was born on the day when the heir to the throne, the unpopular Archduke Franz Ferdinand, and his even more unpopular wife, were slain by the bullets of Gavrilo Princip in Sarajevo.

The date was 28 June 1914.

7

War one

Titus, realising that war was inevitable, sat down at his desk and wrote a letter to the Ministry of War offering his services and requesting a new medical appraisal for active duty. Luckily his letter was opened by his ex-deputy, now in charge, who summoned him straight away to the Royal Military Hospital.

The manor was decorated with bunting and the staff was lined up, waving their flags, patriots to the core. Even Kathleen was wearing a rosette of the red, white and green tricolour. Her hair was wound in a bun and she wore a simple black velvet dress, which was to become her favourite.

Titus was most happy to be back in uniform, which, to his surprise, still fitted him rather well. When he looked into the mirror only the first suggestion of greying at his temples proved that it was not a short leave he'd taken from his beloved army. He was pleased with what he saw. He lifted his fingers to his moustache and gave it a majestic twirl.

He kissed Kathleen and the children, shook hands with the manager, gave Piroska a friendly pinch on her face and went back to Kathleen to kiss her hand. Then he turned to Nicholas again and gave him a hug. He picked him up and threw him into the air, catching him on the way down. It was a game they both loved. He got into his car, taking the manager with him so that it could be brought back from the station. He started the engine, engaged first gear and looked back once to see Kathleen waving her little flag. The rising dust of the road marked the end of his five years back on the estate.

Titus sat motionless in the railway coach, his thoughts wandering. What would Budapest be like now? Would they take him back into active service? Thankfully he did not have to worry about his family. They were all in very good hands.

~

The medical took up the best part of the morning. He was poked and prodded by specialists, as is their wont, the doctors mumbling to one another in a strange language of their own from behind their spectacles. They eventually declared him fit and he nodded his head in agreement. Then the surgeon asked him to lift his right arm, which he did with ease.

'Lift the left one now,' the surgeon ordered.

'What for?' Asked Titus, questioning the command.

'I would like you to,' came the curt answer.

Titus managed to raise it to just above the horizontal and saw the medical colonel shaking his head.

'It's not quite enough, is it?' He stated more than asked.

'Look here, sir, it is plenty,' Titus started with a worried look, which changed to anger as he spoke. 'I can point "forward" with my right arm, move my soldiers to "ground" with my left. The only time I would need both my arms pointing upwards is if I surrendered, and I don't intend to do that against those bloody Serbs!'

The other medics began to chuckle to themselves in admiration and convinced the surgeon to ignore the poor performance of the left shoulder. By the time all his details had been processed the ultimatum to Serbia had expired and the eagerly awaited war began, to 'punish them quickly and effectively' for the murder of the royal couple. The government tragically ignored two factors; the arduous Serbian terrain and the fact that Serbs had a mighty friend in 'Cousin Russia'.

Titus started to learn all there was to know about the Serbian campaign and joined his new posting as infantry battalion commander of his old Pécs regiment. He felt totally at home with the command and often wondered how on earth he had managed without it for so long.

Once a week he wrote to Kathleen and the children. The campaign itself went without a hitch, for his fighting took place on fairly flat terrain on the left bank of the River Danube. In spite of the fierce opposition they gained territory and took villages and towns by the dozen. Naturally, he reported back, and these victories were very highly regarded at HQ, which credited the success to his leadership. High Command was so impressed that he was relieved and transferred to the new and more important Italian front.

His new campaign also started well, but this front was very different and after a few months it turned into a war of attrition between the imperial forces and the Entente. The most unacceptable facets of modern warfare were all in evidence – dirty trenches, poor equipment and both intentionally and unintentionally uncertain leadership, all of which added up to poor morale. Titus was incapable of understanding that for some officers the new and strange socialist ideology was more important than the defence of the country.

The Italian spring offensive, with substantial help from her allies, came with full force, but once again it petered out. The opposing forces fought desperately for the territory surrounding the Doberdo plateau time and time again; pounding by the heaviest 38cm chubby mortars with their enormously destructive shells day after day and the appearance of the largest tanks ever produced did not make the simple foot soldier obsolete. It was the fourth time they were attempting to take the hill-farming area on the Alpine side of the beautiful Isonzo valley with the large arched bridge spanning the river when Titus once again had to give the command, 'Fix bayonets!'

His judgement was correct. The lull gave an excellent opportunity for the attack after the hillside had been saturated with artillery fire.

'Men, we will take it again and this time we will keep it! We have the reinforcements to back us up and that important height will stay ours!' Titus yelled. He drew his sword and took his pistol in his left hand.

'Follow me, men. For King and Country!'

After the initial bayonet charge and close combat the Italians stopped fighting and surrendered in droves. He found out only later that their morale was even lower than that of his own men. He took the hilltop more quickly than on the previous occasions. The raised flag was immediately noticed by the Italian artillery and the shelling started all over again. Titus had taken up his binoculars to try to find the origin of the bombardment to send word back to his heavy guns when there was a terrific explosion. An Italian shell hit one of the ammunition depots their withdrawal had left behind. The incredible force threw him against a rock and a trickle of crimson blood showed the spot where shrapnel had entered his skull. The first-aiders started working on the unconscious man, realising that he needed immediate surgery. The khaki ambulance with the large Red Cross on its side was soon on the site and the young surgeon, feeling the exposed end of the metal fragment with his fingertip, gave the order to the driver, 'All the way to Trieste!' The driver knew that he meant the large military hospital there and that he was to get there fast.

~

Titus regained consciousness three days later, looking into the face of Sarah. 'If I'm dreaming I must not wake up, but oh, God, please let me live this dream,' he thought. He rubbed his eyes and opened them again and again. The face was still there. He mustered up all his strength and touched the blurred vision. Yes, it was that face he knew so well! Her bonnet with the Red Cross on it came in to focus, then her uniform, her arms and her hand on his opened shirt, holding the battered engagement ring on the gold chain around his neck.

'You should not be left alone, you know,' she said, squeezing his hand.

'Oh, I feel such a fool, being in bandages again for you.' He spoke like a little boy apologising for doing something wrong. 'I have so much to tell you. My God, this head of mine is killing me.' The pain was returning in no uncertain way.

'Have a look at the shrapnel they dug out of you.' Sarah held up a twisted piece of metal about half an inch long. 'No wonder you have a headache. You just about survived this, but I was willing you on, the way I perform these miracles in my Hollywood films. Dead easy!'

The days of convalescence gave them time to talk and think. The hospital had previously been a palace with the most beautifully set-out garden. The first few days they just walked about. Sarah told Titus that, having made a dozen or so silent films, mainly comedies, she decided to end the frivolity and volunteered her services as a troop entertainer cum nurse. When she heard that a Major Zenta had been admitted, she demanded to be placed with him and during the next three days, whilst he was unconscious, she'd learned of his bravery.

On the other hand Titus knew *nothing* of her. He had intentionally not followed her career since they'd left Budapest.

'Tell me about him?' Titus pointed to the gold band on her wedding finger. There was a little tremor in his voice.

'Do you really want to know?' Sarah replied, nervously, just as she used to. They walked through the flowering magnolia trees and sat down on a bench. 'I married the impresario who signed me up at that party. He had been very good to me, Titus, and after two films I proposed to him. I needed some security, but he is still in Hollywood and I am here with you.' Her words were ominous. She took Titus' hand. 'Titus, I think a lot of him, but I am always thinking of you too. I don't know if I love him or not, and right now this is the best way. He and I do not even agree as to the reasons for this war, but you are my patient and I will nurse you back to good health and return you to your family.' Titus was in no state to argue.

'Listen, we are entertaining some of the troops in a theatre in Trieste on Saturday. I can get you a front-row seat. Do you think you're up to a little noise?' She asked mischievously.

'If you make the noise, definitely. But what sort of noise? Those men don't want a recital of classics,' he quizzed.

'You'll be amazed what I learned in America! You have to be all things to all producers there,' Sarah answered knowingly.

~

Titus felt like a complete idiot sitting in the front row, dressed in his khaki overcoat with a large white dressing wrapped around his head like a turban, having to respond to shouts of 'get your hat off!' from behind. His gestures back were expressive if impolite.

The Light Cavalry overture by Suppé was followed by two comedians, novelty acts and various turn-of-the-century evergreens. Then came Lehár operetta duets with the artists wearing far too much make-up. Then a pianist. Then a violinist. It went on and on, until the funny compère, a variety artist himself, announced the star attraction.

'The celebrated Hollywood film star, now back with us working as our nurse, and you may be just lucky enough to be looked after by her – Miss Sarah Dombay, with an act from the American Wild West!'

Titus had never seen this Sarah on the stage before, in a gun-slinging, singing act incorporating 'John Brown's Body ', 'The Battle Hymn of the (still neutral) Republic', and other similar numbers. The demand for more was followed by a tap-dancing routine, totally new for the audience, ending with the arrival of the chorus girls and a ferocious can-can. Titus could not believe his eyes, nor his ears for that matter. Sarah had quite a good voice for rhythmic tunes of no consequence and carried her audience with her. The ovation she received was overwhelming and very informal. Not the type she used to get at the National Theatre at all.

Show over, Titus walked her back to the hostel. In the corridor he was about to ask Sarah to kiss him goodnight when she grabbed his arm.

'This is no time for any decent nurse to leave her patient unattended for a whole night.' Her big brown eyes, set in the loveliest of oval faces, flashed invitingly at him. She turned and walked towards her room.

Titus followed her and the door closed quietly behind them.

∽

Some weeks later Titus was called to his CO, who started to read the cable he'd received. *'I, General Árpád Sipos, Divisional Commander, hereby confirm your promotion to full colonel, and you will receive the decoration of the Order of the Cross of Fire with Swords.'*

Titus hardly had his new rank on his lapel when he had to face the medical board for what was to be the last time. They all knew what the outcome was to be, for Sarah had prepared her patient well. During the examination the young surgeon who had taken the shrapnel out of his head had warned him of possible future complications: lapses of memory or consciousness, changes of mood and personality, even fits affecting certain areas of his body. Then the chairman read out the report that simply stated that in the interests of the army, but above all in his own interests, he was to be most honourably discharged. Titus saluted and walked out of the room without response. The waiting Sarah took his arm and they started to walk down the corridor. His steps began to quicken towards the railing and he bent over it to be violently sick. He considered it to be the result of the events of the morning. Sarah believed it to have some connection with his head wound.

They said a tearful goodbye. Tears of friendship rather than those of love, a friendship that could only come to those who had once been lovers.

～

The long and lonely railway journey back to Hungary was very different from that which had brought him into the army. The national tricolour, the bunting and the cheering crowds at the stations en route were replaced by subversive posters, red flags and demonstrating mobs. Titus' blood was at boiling point when he arrived at Pécs to change to a civilian train. He had a few hours and decided to take a walk to the city centre, perhaps to say goodbye to it. He admired the Zsolnay statue and the brilliant eosin ceramic well and was about to continue his walk to the square when he heard the noise of a crowd from a side street.

The procession was a relatively small one as far as anti-war demonstrations went. Led by men in black leather coats, some of the workers from the local tobacco factory carried the red flags of impending revolutions. They were shouting 'End the imperialist war' and 'Form a communist government'. Titus was astonished to see that the leader of the march was none other than his first CO in Pécs.

The bespectacled little Bolshevik noticed Titus in the doorway and shouted towards him, 'Down with this war of yours! Down with the aristocracy! Long live Lenin and the revolution!'

Titus stepped forward. 'I've heard of you, you cashiered communist. So this is what has become of you. You cowardly traitor!'

'Your time has gone, ours is just arriving, and we will hunt you down even in deepest Transylvania!' The man growled.

'And what's wrong with right now? Are you afraid?' Titus leaned closer menacingly.

The would-be revolutionary lowered his red flag to use the brass tip on the top of the rod as a spear and started his run towards Titus. His momentary hesitation gave Titus enough time to take his pistol from his holster and aim for the chest. The ex-soldier realised he had made a mistake, and tried to jump away. The shot aimed at his chest hit him in the side of the neck, severing his carotid artery immediately. He fell on to the kerbside and, as his heart contracted, the bright red blood that tried to supply his sickened brain with oxygen squirted rhythmically at Titus' feet. Realising that he might be in danger from the others, Titus pointed the gun just above their heads. 'For God's sake stop! You have nothing in common with this mad dog. Away with you.' To add weight to his words he fired the rest of the magazine above their heads. The marchers, most of whose hearts were elsewhere, reconsidered their revolutionary zeal and folded their flags for another day.

~

The episode played on Titus' mind as he journeyed home, and by the time he got out of his car at the manor he was in deep depression. The sight of Kathleen and Nicholas waiting at the gate brought temporary relief and he smiled. He kissed his wife tenderly and threw Nicholas playfully into the air. His son's fall was quicker than he had anticipated, and he just managed to catch him. 'Hey, what happened here, you've really grown since I last saw you, and I think we'd better stop this game! Right? You're just too big for me now.'

During the family dinner his gloom became palpable. Kathleen, sensing his depression, did not want to burden him further with the problems of the estate. Next morning the manager came to him early to tell him the bad news concerning the past year. The virtual collapse of the agricultural market had not affected them too badly, but animal husbandry, which was by now their main activity, was sadly similarly unprofitable. They had to cut back further and rely on the vineyard, but nowadays there was not too much to celebrate and sales were dropping. The industrial upset he had observed on his way home had affected the value of his shareholdings and this, in turn, had reduced his earnings by some thirty per cent. It was bad news on all fronts, including the military one. Admiral Horthy's minor victory against the British Home Fleet with the cruiser *Navarra* in the Adriatic blockade was the only good news in many months.

~

Parliamentary elections were suspended during the war, but the death of the local MP gave Titus the idea of standing for Parliament. The thought of being in the capital, giving him a chance to look after his stocks better, appealed to him. And, who knows, Sarah might be there too.

His campaign was a short one. Once word got around that Colonel Titus Zenta was running in the colours of the conservative Independence Party, the opposition put up only a token candidate. It took him only a few appearances at public meetings and even fewer social functions organised by Kathleen to be elected with a seventy per cent majority.

Kathleen went with him to see him take his seat in the magnificent Gothic Parliament building, on the Pest side of the River Danube. Based very much on the Palace of Westminster, but with the added advantage of being designed solely for the purpose, it was the last relic of the thousand-year-old kingdom. Titus had the good fortune to deliver his maiden speech within the week. He chose the subject of 'Greater integration of minority nations into the dual monarchy'. Right as he was, his idea was much too late.

The death of the old Emperor sank the nation into such depths of depression that there was very little response in the House when the ageing Prime Minister invited the parliamentarians to declare the usual 'The King is dead, long live the King!' Yet the coronation of Charles IV in Matthias' Church in the Castle of Buda was still a very momentous act, even if the close observer could see that after the act of crowning the Holy Crown of St Steven nearly slipped off the King's head. A bad omen. Standing next to the young King, his queen, Zita, and Crown Prince Otto appeared to offer a stable enough setting.

Yet there was general unease and Titus felt it acutely. He said to Kathleen that he feared for the young and vulnerable monarch. His instinct was to do everything in his power to sustain the system and he became more and more active in Parliament. He warned the left of the House not to bring about a national catastrophe by disrupting the functioning of Parliament, for they were playing into the hands of the surrounding countries, which were all hell bent on establishing nothing but their ethnic states. This at the expense of the multinational monarchy that, although it had problems, was still the best way to run the Danube valley.

The total collapse of both the eastern and western fronts and the following announcement of the armistice brought about the cessation of all normal activities in the capital. The ominous news from Russia of Lenin's putsch, which was to give the word 'revolution' a bad name for the next forty years, brought personal problems for Titus. The establishment of the Soviet state further reduced the value of his stocks, which only four years earlier had seemed invincible. The hysterical reaction by the Hungarian left, led by the renegade aristocrat Karolyi, brought the Bolsheviks into power in Budapest, to the delight of the surrounding nations. Overnight all Titus' holdings and industrial earnings disappeared, totally. The temporary occupation of Budapest by looting and scavenging Romanian troops was the final blow for Titus. He just about managed to slip back home with Kathleen, to be reunited with Nicholas and Rose, who had been looked after by a most competent English governess. His joy was short lived.

~

The Entente powers setting the principles of the Treaty of Versailles in 1920 were pondering how to produce lasting peace on the continent of Europe. President Wilson, M. Clemenceau and Mr Lloyd George had no personal knowledge of the countries of middle Europe. Their crazed advisers were redrawing frontiers, which defied human reason, a thousand years of civilised history and even God's geography. The protocol of Trianon confirmed the loss of two-thirds of the territory of Hungary, placing five million Hungarians into the four surrounding countries just outside her new and painful frontier. It tragically divided towns, separated land from supporting farm buildings, split families in neighbouring villages and, most banally, divided a hapless peasant from his outside toilet. Then the 'grand peacemakers' opened a bottle of champagne, or two.

8

End one

The political loss of Transylvania to the Romanians compounded Titus' loss of personal fortune. He started to complain of recurrent headaches of increasing severity and bouts of excessive melancholy followed by a state of hopelessness. But what bothered him and his family most was his feeling of inadequacy. He started to drink heavily again, which made him euphoric, and from time to time he would talk of being able to 'take on the world again'. Nicholas and Rose were sent to boarding school in Vásárhely. Kathleen had not cherished the idea and became very withdrawn. As a regular churchgoer she begged Titus to join her for the services. He went along reluctantly to hear the stern pastor, who was a year younger than him, still preaching the wrath of God. He could not, however, escape the vicar's wife's new advances. The sight of this spectacular-looking lady with a strong, sculpted face, severely dressed in high-necked blouses, or wearing neckbands, sending him the strongest signs, hit him like a bolt of arrows. The possibility of resisting her did occur to him for a moment, but in his present mood there was not much point in resisting anything. And Kathleen just looked away.

Their first meeting was a coincidence; she was walking her dog, a long-haired black puli, and Titus was driving past in his rapidly ageing open-top yellow Vauxhall. To stop and greet her was not at all remarkable; it was part of the social graces still observed by 'society'. The conversation was, alas, an altogether different thing. She took no time; a week on Friday she had a pretext to visit relatives and conceivably stay overnight. Titus needed no excuse. He would stay in town after a visit to the new Romanian National Commercial Investment Bank.

'See you at the Grand,' he said.

Their lust was obvious, noticeable and natural. Titus took Nina's hand to walk her into the chandeliered restaurant to the bay window. The string quartet burst into a Gypsy song; *'The Night of Dark Eyes'*. Heads turned to look at them, conscious of the obvious scene they were creating, but neither of them minded. The gentry never did. The pastor's wife should have.

The dinner went well and the wine was good.

The following torrid love scene in the bedroom belonged more to the farmyard than to the boudoir. Had there been an observer, rape would have been the obvious description. Her consent was in her eyes, not in her actions. Their tour de force continued until the early hours.

Next morning, Titus drove home like a fiend, his head splitting. The powerful car tore along the poor-quality roads at great speed through the surrounding villages, leaving in his wake a dozen or more dead chickens and other poultry. At home his depression got the better of him again. In addition to the melancholy, this time he was full of shame. Yet he knew that he needed to see Nina again. The occasional pastoral visit by her husband gave her a chance to meet Titus. These were supplemented by 'visits to the ailing aunt' in town.

Their trips became regular events.

Titus' personality change could not have come at a worse time. The cloud around his aching head blurred the very obvious collapse of his world around him. Yet the news from Hungary became better. The Nationalists, under the command of Admiral Horthy, took it upon themselves to rid the nation of mob rule by a dozen Bolsheviks who had plunged the country into mayhem. This produced the occasional longer lucid period in him. He wanted to fight again, and tried to offer his services to the Admiral surreptitiously, but he was now trapped in the Romanian state. The boyar, with whom he had had business dealings in the past, became regional governor, and on taking office in town he addressed the crowd, first in Romanian, then in equally perfect Hungarian.

'This is the most glorious day in the history of Romania and Transylvania, when the two finally unite, to establish a greater and grander Romania for the glory of the world!' He paused for the applause that never came. The crowd's silence was total. He picked up the Romanian flag of blue, yellow and red – a hasty copy of the French tricolour – and continued. 'From now on this is the banner we serve. This one, have a good look at it. For if I see the Magyar rag in anyone's hand again there will be no mercy!' The boyar pointed in several directions among the crowd. 'Yes; now we are all subjects of His Majesty King Charles II of Greater Romania, and don't you forget it! My men will remove everything Magyar or Sekler from this city. By tomorrow you will learn new street names. Romanian ones. You'd better start now.

'*Treasce Regele!* Hail to the King!'

Titus and Kathleen could not tolerate his words any longer, and with a defiant gesture they walked away from the front of the crowd. They got in their car and Kathleen, grasping her head, burst into tears. Titus raged with anger. This was the man to whom he had sold more than half of his family estate, he kept thinking. By the time they arrived home his head had started pulsating again. When he got out of the car he was confronted by a Romanian sentry. Titus, being fluent in Romanian, addressed the soldier in no uncertain terms. 'Away with you, Wallach dog. Now!' The simple peasant soldier just pointed to the portico of the manor, where the Romanian flag was being put up.

'Boyar Toca's order. He will be using your house as his HQ until peace is established in this province,' he said sheepishly.

'Like hell he will!' Titus tried to push him away, but Kathleen took his arm, trying to constrain him.

'It's no use, Titus. Look, they are everywhere.' She spoke in a forced whisper. 'We must wait until the boyar arrives.'

The noise of the approaching cars on the tree-lined causeway was soon heard in the crisp winter morning air. The first things Titus noticed were the troop carriers flying the large, brand-new Romanian flags. The boyar's car pulled up. He got out and went straight up to Titus. 'I have authorisation from our High Command to use this house, which is no longer part of its surrounding estate anyway, for the next three months as our posting. Please make arrangements to move immediately,' he started in a fairly low key.

'This is outrageous, Boyar! This manor is our home. It is not a hotel that you are requisitioning,' Titus tried.

'Consider yourself lucky. Had *your* Bolsheviks got here first they would just have confiscated it, and probably would have strung the lot of you up as well. This way you are in the civilised hands of Romanians, who will show you how a province like this should be run. The ownership of this land is once again back in the hands of those who had it two thousand years ago.' He pushed Titus gently aside and walked up to the front door, then turned around and concluded, 'Naturally, you may appeal to Bucharest. It is your right as a Romanian subject.'

Piroska brought the children out of the house, clutching their tiny hands. They were most unusually quiet. The eight-year-old Nicholas more or less understood what was happening, but little Rose, not realising the tragedy of the situation, just wanted to go back to her room to fetch her toys.

The picturesque cottage, which was about a mile and a half away but significantly in sight of the manor high on the hill, belonged to a different world. 'Rustic and basic' was how Kathleen had described it. The following week the servants helped to move the most essential of their belongings, but Titus insisted on leaving important items behind, to give the futile impression that he was not giving up the manor for good.

The 'three months' passed, time and time again. Within a year the Zenta family was officially told that moving back to the manor was out of the question. New legislation precluded the placing of real estate out of the ownership of its surrounding land support. He was offered some compensation based on 'market value', but there was no market.

Under pressure, Titus went to work. He bought a larger cottage nearer to the vineyard, which was by now his only property. The household was run by Piroska and some others. Old Michael became his number two and with his help 'Koronka Wine' became an efficient business, supplying not only local demand but some of the international market too. After Christmas, the children went back to boarding school, which was religiously based and thus luckily not disbanded by the

Romanians. They did, however, introduce compulsory learning of the less-than-two-hundred-year-old Latin-based Romanian language, by all accounts a wonderful creation, to all schools. This included its literature too, but as there was not too much of that anyway, nobody minded.

***

The news of the Wall Street collapse hit Titus severely. His shareholding, which was gradually improving, once again disappeared. He could pay off his promissory notes only by selling his cherished Vauxhall. When the dealer collected the car it marked the end of an era, for they both knew that he would not be able to cope much longer with such devastating personal losses.

For a while he reverted to using his coaches, both the two-wheeler and the liveried ones. He also took to riding again to the vineyard and even to town. He still liked to call at the Golden Bull, which by now had a new Romanian head waiter. In the mid-twenties he could still arrive on horseback wearing his breeches and riding boots and not look out of place. All his old outfits still fitted him perfectly.

At the beginning of the year he went to pay Nicholas' school fees at the boarding school opposite the Golden Bull. The restaurant had an excellent kitchen and he decided to lunch there with Nicholas. Appearing in the hall, he was about to be seated by one of the regular waiters when the head waiter, hearing the two men talking to each other in Hungarian, intervened with a curt Romanian 'good afternoon'. Titus decided to ignore him and continued to talk to the young waiter in a language they had always used. He was about to take his regular table for luncheon and asked the man to show Nicholas to the table as soon as he arrived from the Bolyai High School across the square.

The head waiter got to the table first and quickly placed a 'Reserved' sign on it, telling Titus that he could not be accommodated on this occasion. Clenching his teeth, Titus turned to the man and in perfect Romanian explained to him that he had never in his life had to make a reservation here before and, besides, there were plenty of tables unoccupied. Young Nicholas arrived at the restaurant to see his father outraged to a degree he would never forget. Titus took the sign and placed it firmly in the head waiter's top pocket. He had turned to his teenage son to greet him with his usual hug when he felt the man's hand on his shoulder. Titus' hand moved down towards his boot and he drew out his horsewhip, lashing the startled head waiter across the neck. 'Get out of my way, you Wallach dog! How dare you treat us like this?'

As other men appeared, Titus suddenly realised that the confrontation had been deliberately engineered.

'Well now. So this is the new management, I see.' As the other men eyed him menacingly he took his son's hand and, turning away, walked out of the courtyard. He turned to Nicholas and said, 'Let's teach these dogs a lesson,' his tone by now one of equal proportions of anger and mischief. He mounted his horse and told his son to follow him. The black stallion hesitated at the steps and received a little encouragement from his spurs.

He entered the hall and rode straight into the restaurant, to the natural consternation of the guests.

'Ladies and gentlemen, please forgive me for the coming inconvenience, but I have decided it is time to rearrange the furniture here. Please do continue your lunch.' He bent his head in a mock bow.

Titus rode his horse into the middle of the room and jolted the reins downwards. The well-trained stallion kicked out, toppling the nearest table behind him. A little to the left another went down, and then another to the right, until all unoccupied tables were scattered all over the place. As the majority of the guests were Hungarian he received a rousing round of applause, some stating to their partners that this was the way a horse should be ridden. Titus apologised to them for the inconvenience again, then he hooked up his whip to the chandelier. He bowed, sweeping his right arm down in front of him. The chandelier crashed to the ground obligingly. He rode back to the corridor and pinned the astonished head waiter against the wall with his whip. 'Titus Zenta de Lemhény at your service, please do send me the bill.' Nicholas was old enough to enjoy the magnificent spectacle his father presented. He was full of admiration. 'Father, that was terrific!' The boy beamed. 'That will teach them a lesson, won't it.'

Titus dismounted and led the horse on one side and his son on the other across the leafy square to the best boarding school in the province.

'Do you think they will give us a little lunch in the canteen?' He asked his proud son, the back of his head splitting with pain.

~

It was a month before he could ride again. His head ached ominously, and he had also developed some flashing visual disturbances. This led to his next and perhaps his heaviest drinking bout, which lasted a week. The perplexed Kathleen could no longer influence his actions. Ignored, and perhaps sensing the impending catastrophe, she totally withdrew into herself. Titus, having entered another manic phase, thought of Nina and decided it was time for another clandestine night at the Grand.

He chose to use his two-wheeler coach and picked up the startled Nina at her place of alibi. As Titus and Nina drove through the main square, the cinema hoarding opposite the hotel showed a familiar face. *The Burning Flower*, starring Sarah Dombay, it declared.

'The gods are smiling on you again,' Nina started. 'Perhaps we should go and see Sarah's film first, then you could have me for dessert. Would you like that?'

Titus found himself holding the back of his head as the throbbing headache started again. 'Let's book in first, then we will see,' he answered calmly. They walked into the elegant suite overlooking the square. The giant cinema hoarding could be seen clearly over the top of the trees. He went to the bathroom, stripped to the waist and shaved carefully around his ever-curling moustache. He could not take his mind off the large picture of the beautiful face he knew so well. Having wiped himself, he walked out of the bathroom. His half-naked body belied his fifty-five years; strong, trim, with a scar around the left shoulder and some wasting of the muscles around it. He held the occipital region of his head and walked out on to the balcony for fresh air. As the dusk gathered a floodlight was shone on to the hoarding. He was exactly level with the most beautiful face he had ever known. The large dark eyes mesmerised him.

He held his head between his hands and stared at Sarah's lips. They seemed to move to say, 'I love you too.' He gripped the crooked engagement ring still hanging around his neck and crashed to the cement floor.

∼

Nina screamed hysterically for the hotel doctor. When he arrived the old physician recognised whom he was attending. He felt his neck for a pulse. There was none. He looked at Nina with disdain and closed Titus's eyelids.

The post-mortem showed a massive subarachnoid haemorrhage from a burst berry aneurysm at the base of his skull. The coroner declared death from 'natural causes'.

The vicar thundered from the pulpit, denouncing the temptation of evil and all those who succumbed to it. 'The victim must be forgiven.' He looked at Nina in the front row on the women's side, dressed in black with her head bowed. 'But the evil must be exorcised!' He shouted with both arms raised pointing towards the door. 'The knight of the Devil will not receive this church's sacrament, nor a place in its garden amongst his more honourable ancestors.'

Kathleen stood up from the second row, the traditional pews of the Zentas, and walked towards the main door with pride and dignity.

A week later Kathleen's uncle said farewell to Titus with the simplest possible service on a small hillside opposite the church. There were only twelve people present, including Kathleen, the children, old Michael and Piroska.

From the bell tower of the church Nina waved a handkerchief as the coffin was lowered into the lonely hillside grave.

Book Two

9

NICHOLAS

Nicholas was devastated by the macabre funeral service. He had always idolised his father and understood how his personal and financial collapse had occurred in such a relatively short time. His happy childhood, followed by the harsher years at college, was now destroyed by Titus's death. He had another year to qualify as an agronomist, which he intended to complete come what may.

He adored his mother. He often heard the family discuss her gentle but possessive nature and her total dedication to his father, which initially he did not quite comprehend. Now he understood, realising that there had to be a special bond between a most charismatic man like his father and the quietest, most dedicated mother, who wanted only one possession in her life: his father.

He and sister Rose grew up in a family whose fortunes had declined in front of their very eyes, yet neither of them had heard a harsh word between their parents.

These were the thoughts in his mind in the coach on the way home. Naturally, he appointed himself head of the family. Old Michael would continue to run the remaining estate until he qualified. Piroska and his mother would look after the household and Rose would go to boarding school. Things were reasonably clear in his mind.

They had dinner together. For the first time the young head of the family took Titus' seat. Nicholas was a truly handsome young man. Titus' stronger features had been smoothed down by Kathleen, producing an oval face with less of the Sekler cheekbones. The piercing pale blue eyes remained, as did the dark brown hair, neatly parted in the current Hollywood style. His moustache was somewhat fuller than those belonging to the idols of his age. A good six feet tall, he had slightly bowed legs that he put down to horse riding at an early age. This pleased him, as he thought they looked rather good with the breeches and riding boots which he liked to wear. He was a charismatic young man. Certainly the young ladies of the inter-school dances where he accounted well for himself in the 'Black Bottom' and the 'Charleston' thought so.

Although academically average, in fact a bit of a struggler, he had inherited a sharp enough brain from his father, which manifested itself in quick repartee and dealings, splendid bluffing, and even practical jokes. But above all it was his sense of humour which made him very popular with his friends. Not for Nicholas the struggle in the library. 'My bum is not big enough for that!' He used to declare to his friends. Nicholas' last year at the college was a real drag, which could not pass fast enough for him. He lived from one dance floor to another, ever perfecting his Charleston. When he eventually did receive his agricultural management diploma he swore he would never enter another academic establishment, unless there was a dance going on in it.

At his graduation ball he was introduced to a tall, willowy-looking girl from a nearby college, a contemporary of his, who wore her dark straight brown hair in a loose bob. Irene had those typical, slightly exaggerated Sekler cheekbones and transparent blue eyes. Definitely a member of my tribe, he thought. She could certainly dance, blurring the thousands of fringes all over her fashionably beige dress through the twists and turns of modern dancing. She told him she lived in the next county, some thirty miles away, and was visiting a friend in town, having matriculated there two years previously. There was no particular rapport between them and neither were they looking for any. But they were compatible dancers together, always such a relief when starting off with a new partner. Nicholas soon forgot her name, but always remembered the tall, fashionably dressed girl who had danced so well.

The slow small-gauge train jogging along the Nyárád valley in the morning sunshine of the early summer gave him time to reflect. With his diploma in his case he was looking forward to taking over the running of the estate – or what was left of it – from the rapidly ageing

Michael, and he was hoping to manage other nearby farms too, given a chance. His mind turned to his much-loved mother, and like a child he started rehearsing opening phrases for their moment of meeting. They had not seen each other since his father's funeral.

The small railway station was on the far side of the river and the bridge leading to their house was a good mile away, adding considerable distance to his walk home. For a moment he considered walking across the weir built of wood, covered with twigs. He used that short cut regularly, but he was worried about carrying his luggage across it. While gazing over to the other bank he heard a coach pull up behind him. Turning around, he saw old Michael struggling down from the driver's perch.

'Michael, my friend, I thought you were ill and couldn't make it!' The two men clasped each other's hands affectionately. 'How good to see you,' he added.

'It's only my joints, sir, they do get a bit difficult now and then,' Michael answered, rubbing his knees.

'Is Rose at home?'

'Ah, sir, that was going to be a surprise for you, now you've ruined it all.' He smiled.

'Don't worry, old pal, I'll pretend not to know anything.'

The large cottage with its steep red roof looked beautiful in the early summer glow. As they approached it he could see his mother on the veranda. Nicholas jumped down from the coach and ran towards her. He threw his arms around her waist, picked her up and spun her around, kissing her fondly on her cheeks. All the lovely words he had thought to say to her were forgotten in the tenderness of the moment. He showed off his diploma and gave her a present of a silver brooch.

'Mother, thank God Rose is not around, I had no money left to buy her anything.' He winked at her.

'Then you are in big trouble because I'm here all right.' The voice came from the lounge as Rose came running out.

'Well, such is life, but if you look into the top of that bag, you might just find a little something.' Nicholas smiled.

The pretty teenager in her flowery summer dress soon found the box. The wrapping was off in seconds. 'New liqueur chocolates!' She gasped. 'Wonderful! Thanks, brother, but they will ruin my figure.' She giggled.

'What figure, you mosquito?' He gave her a big brotherly hug and kissed her. 'It's time you started eating, they will never make an opera singer out of you looking like that.'

Kathleen had a meal waiting for him; she had dressed in plain black, as she had done since the death of Titus. Her dresses were made of rich satins and velvets, with added black lace. At dinner Nicholas took Titus' seat for the second time with his mother on his right and Rose on his left. Michael and Piroska, now the voluptuous mother of three, also joined them for their first meal together. The consommé with vermicelli strips and roast duckling cooked by Kathleen were designed to please Nicholas. He tasted the wine and smiled, flashing his perfect, brilliant white teeth.

'Michael, we will bring this Riesling up to Rhineland standard in a couple of seasons,' he said with great satisfaction.

They enjoyed the hearty meal, which was completed by the special custard cake for which his mother had become famous on the estate and which was his particular favourite.

Next morning the siblings went horse riding together. It was Rose who challenged Nicholas. She knew she was good but she found Nicholas outstanding in every discipline. The ride took them near the old manor where the boyar now lived with his large family. Rose pulled up her horse and looked longingly. Tears filled her eyes, and Nicholas swore that one day he would retrieve it.

Within the week his call-up papers had arrived. Owing to his studies he had so far been exempted from Romanian national service, but they had caught up with him. He was to report to regional command in forty-eight hours.

It was peacetime in the region so Nicholas felt neither endangered nor threatened by his enlisting, but it took him some time to come to terms with being a Romanian soldier of all things. He packed his colourful 'call-up chest', a large wooden box heavily decorated with flowers, Nicholas' adorned by red tulips with green leaves on a white background, the national flowers and colours of Hungary, made especially just to ram the point home.

The receiving sergeant shouted, 'You there, you, the tall one with the moustache, come here! You're tall enough for the Guards, aren't you?' It was more a statement than a question. 'Can you ride a horse?'

Nicholas' ears pricked up; even the Romanian army might be tolerable on horseback. 'Yes, sir, I can ride to any standards,' he answered confidently.

'Any standards, eh? All right, over there.' The sergeant pointed to a corner of the large room, where a tall guy was already loafing and leaning about on everything he could. Another four were selected, two of them Seklers, the rest Wallachs. They were measured up, given uniforms and under an escorting corporal sent to the capital. The barracks of the Royal Guards in Bucharest was the best in the land. King Charles II of the Hohenzollern family had a passion for his horses, almost as much as for his mistresses.

The training held nothing for Nicholas, he was past all that. The only thing he could learn from it was formation riding, and even that was only a matter of control. Their uniform was a watered-down version of that of the guards of Napoleon III. In this new kingdom everything was a French imitation. It was their way of saying thank you to France, the midwife to the birth of this enlarged land. Nicholas was more than a little self-conscious wearing the high-booted red and blue uniform and often wondered what Titus would have made of it. But times had changed. With French flair and help Bucharest was developing to a unique parkland design; wide avenues meeting in the shape of a star, presenting a large triumphal arch that could not have come from anywhere but Paris. The new monarchy was popular and the state itself felt strong – only a few years earlier, no Hungarian would have been drafted into the guards, especially a Sekler. Being fluent in Romanian, alas with a Sekler brogue, Nicholas used to say that he was not the only one at court with an accent. The King himself had a pronounced German one. Nicholas conversed easily with the courtiers, particularly with the ladies-in-waiting. The odd walk in one of the parks with them on his day off was the height of his romantic life, until Antonietta appeared on the scene. Daughter of a boyar, she had qualified as a nursery nurse and was called upon to serve in the royal family as a nanny. They first met in the park. The royal crest on the side of the large black perambulator containing the latest addition to the family made it easy for the handsome guardsman to approach her. She was trying to overcome the restraints of her strict upbringing and he was more than ready to meet the obviously ripe and very beautiful girl, dressed according to the latest Paris fashion. Antonietta was all Romanian, with thick black hair, dark eyes and a figure second to none. A beauty of her bloodline without a doubt. The Wallachs south of the Carpathians were an exceptionally good-looking race, in the dark Mediterranean mould. The mixture of Slav, Turk and Latin produced an even face of good features. With the fashionable new make-ups coming from Paris in abundance the result was so stunning that even some of the army officers were inclined to use a little of it.

Antonietta fell for Nicholas in the biggest possible way. She arranged all her pram pushing for days he was off duty, and Nicholas in turn tried to get allocated household duties rather than state ones. His accommodation in the barracks precluded any private meeting for the two of them, but Antonietta had her own small apartment in a block for the higher-grade staff. It had to be there. It would not be easy.

Their break came on a Saturday. He had a day off and the royal family was weekending away, taking another nanny. With other staff also on board the royal train, Nicholas took his chance. He walked into the household apartments situated in the right wing at the very rear of the palace. With the family being away security was not too strictly observed. Wearing his uniform and producing a few assured salutes, he was soon knocking on her door.

Antonietta was wearing a nearly see-through negligee, designed to barely hold her breasts together, producing a most inviting cleavage. He gazed at her like a child who had just seen his first Christmas tree. His eyes caught the suggestion of the black triangle through the fine silk. He moved closer, looked at her long black hair, which hung down to her slender waist, then at those dark brown eyes; oh, those eyes! They were an invitation to bliss. Antonietta looked at Nicholas – one of the best-looking guards in the household, who was even noticed by the Queen herself. Nicholas had no previous serious sexual experience other than a quick smooch after a school dance, and he was keen, very keen, to put this behind him.

Nicholas visited her apartment whenever his duty roster permitted, which was nowhere near as often as he would have liked. Their relationship always retained an element of inexperienced fun and laughter. Love was the only entertainment they, as underlings, had in the stifling Prussian-style court life. His next posting was luckily to the palace for interior duty. It involved wearing an even more ornate if clumsy uniform, with a very low-hanging sword, which was ultimately to end his service with the Romanian royal family.

It was Crown Prince Michael's birthday and the usual extravagantly large party was thrown to honour the young teenager. He was a considerate and intelligent adolescent, with great charisma and fairness, all good qualifications for a king-to-be. But that day was his birthday and he let go. The heir to the Romanian throne naturally filled the private rooms with his friends. The fancy dress and mask party was going well when a chase started involving some of the lads. The guards on duty at various points along the corridors created perfect totems to skid around and to use as turning poles on the highly polished parquet floor.

Nicholas was targeted for the next chase and received several kicks to his boots and sword sheath. During the next round, when one of the boys stood on his perfectly polished boot, he decided that he had had enough of the brats' activities, and with his left hand he delivered a glancing blow to the top of the head of one of them. The youngster took immediate objection and removed his mask. To his astonishment, it was the young prince, whose friends began laughing at him uproariously. Unfortunately, the incident had been observed by a malicious lackey who decided it was a good time to teach the Sekler guard a lesson. He insisted on taking the young prince to the captain of the guards, demanding that the incident be fully reported

Nicholas was immediately arrested and charged with royal insult, a charge just below that of treason. His court-martial was arranged to be held within the week. The King himself took a great interest in the matter, to a degree that the newspapers started to publish ridiculous stories. The small and quite insignificant incident was blown into a national issue and everyone debated the untouchability of the royal family.

The prosecuting colonel demanded a long prison sentence, so Nicholas had to take his defence much more seriously than he had envisaged. Firstly, he had to find an officer who was willing to defend him. It was the visiting Antonietta who came up with the idea of asking the quiet administrative secretary of the Guards, Major Joseph Grunnfeld, a Jewish officer, himself from Transylvania, to help him. A qualified lawyer, Grunnfeld was sympathetic to Nicholas' plight.

He came to see Nicholas, who looked most miserable without sword, epaulets and belt, sitting alone in his minuscule cell.

'Man, you were an absolute idiot! How on earth could you hit out at that lot and find the prince's head?' He maintained a more serious air than he truly felt about the matter, secretly seeing the funny side of it.

'But, sir, they were dragging me about whilst I was trying to stand to attention. I didn't mind that so much, but when one of them stood on my boot I just lost my temper. I didn't hit him hard at all,' he attempted to explain.

'Hard or not is not the point, Zenta. Even His Majesty wants to come to your court-martial and, because you are a Sekler, the press is out for your blood too. We will have to be very careful,' Grunnfeld concluded more worriedly.

'Anything you say, Major, anything.' Nicholas was extremely concerned, envisaging a long prison sentence.

'Well, I will work out a general plan for your defence.' The major sounded a little more reassuring. 'We *must* stick to the truth and not let them get a political angle on it in any shape or form, otherwise we stand no chance at all.'

~

The court-martial was held in the main lecture theatre of the Military Academy. The royal arms on the wall behind the panel of officers and the flag of a new and proud nation signified the attendance of the King. The heavy oak tables of the two advocates were placed opposite each other but with many more officers of significance on the side of the prosecution. The defence consisted of Nicholas, the major and a lieutenant clerk. Three generals as acting judges were seated at the large carved-top centre table, but below them two significantly large gilt chairs were placed for His Majesty and the Crown Prince.

According to royal protocol, first to take their place had to be the defence, then came the prosecution followed by the three judges. They all stood for the royal entrance. The King and Prince wore uniforms of blue and red with gold sashes and the inevitable low-slung swords.

The presiding judge called the court to order. The opening statement was read out by the lowest-ranking prosecution officer, exaggerating the severity of the blow, not mentioning the masks they were wearing and referring to the accused as a Sekler recruit who took his opportunity to insult the beloved 'Family of the Nation'.

Nicholas slumped back in his chair and received a noticeable prod in his ribs from the major's elbow.

The first witness, the lackey, further exaggerated the prosecution's claims, adding that he had seen the glee in the Sekler's face when he delivered the blow, 'virtually flooring' the 'Heir to the Sacred Romanian Throne'. At this stage everyone noticed that the young Prince was wriggling uncomfortably on his far-too-large chair. The press and public were clearly divided. The former, in anticipation of a good headline, were nodding with satisfaction. The public, including the family and staff, Antonietta amongst them, were certainly not so sure. They knew the accused well enough.

The major quietly objected to the opening statement and refuted any malice, either personal or political, and called on his defendant, whom he described as one of the most loyal servants in the palace, to stand up. With his clever questioning he extracted statements from Nicholas as to his devotion to royal duty and love of the Crown Prince, adding that the best defenders of the minorities in Romania were the Romanian royal family themselves, who had demanded their inclusion in the Royal Guards. It would hardly be in his interests to insult them. The King nodded with satisfaction, a point not lost on the major. Alas, he was not allowed to call the Prince as witness.

Addressing the judges in his summing up, Grunnfeld played the loyalty card once more, both his own as a Jew and that of Nicholas as a Sekler.

During his summing up the King quietly asked his son. 'Did he really "floor you", Michael?'

The young Prince was most indignant in his denial: 'I didn't feel anything, it was nothing, I don't understand,' he replied with considerable embarrassment.

The King took a piece of paper out of his pocket and scribbled six words on it, 'Guilty, but only to be discharged', and handed it over to the presiding judge, who read it with great disappointment but resignation.

The judge showed the note to his two colleagues. This way they did not have to listen too intently to the winding-up speech of the major.

The royals left the courtroom before the sentence was read out after the shortest deliberation three Romanian judges had ever made. The presiding general commanded all to stand and declared, 'In the name of His Majesty King Charles II of Greater Romania and his heir Prince Michael, it is the considered verdict of this court-martial that the defendant, Nicholas Zenta, is guilty of royal insult. He is to be dishonourably discharged with immediate effect.'

Nicholas, now realising that he was a free man, shook the hand of the major. As far as he was concerned he was going home tomorrow. If that was not a victory, what was?

Honour was well served by the King's decision. The blow to the Prince's head was punished, but the man could take off his foreign uniform and walk free from a foreign court. The only sad face in court was that of Antonietta's. At the conclusion of the trial her first and most innocent lover waved to her; she sighed and they never saw each other again.

Nicholas decided to take the earliest train out of Bucharest to avoid the press. At the railway station with his army chest, he just had enough time to buy the morning papers before his departure.

All but one reported his case with sympathy. The exception was the official organ of the newly formed Iron Guard, a vicious fascist organisation emerging in support of right-wing movements all over Europe, which carried a headline about a 'JEWISH-ROYAL CONSPIRACY', warning the former of persecution and threatening the latter with overthrow, and demanding the immediate cashiering of the defending Jewish officer.

10

Work

Nicholas' return home to his mother was, if anything, even sweeter than his homecoming after leaving college. He was back in less than a year instead of the expected three, which as far as he was concerned was a bonus in itself. The fact that he'd clouted the Romanian Crown Prince, which he forever had to play down, made him a local hero. A true 'son of Titus', a 'Wallach basher'. That was really something amongst the minority Hungarians. His reputation grew and he obtained good management jobs in addition to managing his mother's vineyard.

The whole family was devastated by Michael's sudden death. The old faithful had died in excruciating agony after injuring himself with some farming tool and developing lockjaw. The villagers turned out in droves for the funeral of this most popular and much-loved man. Nicholas was particularly upset, for he had lost a kind of father figure whom he loved and with whom he had been looking forward to working.

From his various appointments he received good earnings and he lived well. He had his horses and he rode a lot. The great depression was clearly on its way out and the Romanian government was eager to present this as their success in economic management, 'after a millennium of Hungarian misrule'. Nonetheless, there was some consolidation both in political life and in economic management. Romania was doing her best to exploit this to the full. Socially there was Vásárhely to visit for excellent theatre and cinema. He knew all about his father's affair with Sarah Dombay, and perhaps for this reason he was attracted to her films and would never miss one. But neither did he boast to his mother about seeing them, though she probably would not have minded anyway. She had now passed that phase of her life.

He had a good baritone voice that he let fly in the local choir, and he played the violin rather well whenever he was given a chance in the local inns and restaurants. He liked to take over once in a while from the lead Gypsy violinist to play one of his favourite songs. His style was excellent and this didn't go unnoticed by the admiring female clientele. His light blue eyes and exceptional good looks, which more than outshone those of his father, coupled with good dress sense and the ability to play a popular instrument to a high standard, attracted the attention of everybody. He did like a drink, or more than one, but it was mainly wine. Politically he stood right of centre in the Zenta mould, hating everything Romanian and being totally convinced that Transylvania's annexation by them was only temporary. Unlike his father, and perhaps learning from his mistakes in business, he would deal only with Hungarians. A man at ease with administration and with an above-average flair for leadership and risk-taking of the bluffing kind, he was an optimist whose handsome smile would open many doors and hearts for him.

His sister Rose was now a very pretty teenager, with a promising mezzo-soprano voice, whose dream it was to be the greatest Carmen ever. She attended the singing section of the Vásárhely Musical Academy and was making good progress.

Kathleen was still wearing her favourite black but always in an imaginative and inventive way, still talking little but constantly aware of everything that was happening around her. She was liked by everybody except for the vicar and his wife Nina. They lived near by. The pastor was still preaching eternal retribution and Nina was still 'visiting auntie'. No one knew the object of her current affections.

Kathleen's main problem was that of finding a place where she could worship in peace. Although in principle she could have continued to attend the pastor's services, she chose not to sit in the traditional second row of the Zentas; it would prove far too embarrassing for her. The alternative became another village, Iszló, some fifteen miles away across the Koronka hills in the next valley. This was no particular problem while Michael was alive to drive her there, but since his death she had had to organise her monthly trips well in advance. There, the pastor and his wife were more than kind to her and she got to know them well. They had a large family with a boy at law school and three girls, the youngest of them being Irene.

The vicar was a dour looking man, befitting the position he held, with a 'full set beard' that would not have looked out of place on the captain of a ship. His wife was a kindly woman, totally preoccupied with looking after the three girls, who were all still living at home. Not an easy task. They indulged in plenty of energetic activity as they waited for the 'right man', or rather their knight on a white charger.

On the first occasion when Nicholas escorted his mother to church he naturally caused some excitement amongst them. He immediately noticed the twenty-year-old Irene, the youngest of the three girls, and recalled the night of the college dance. But this was a very different meeting. Early eye contact aroused a healthy interest between them and when, during dinner, he asked her to pass him one of the platters, their fingers touched for a split second, the contact completing an electric circuit of a thousand volts for Irene. She was in love with Nicholas. Irene would recollect much later that she had kept asking for things to be passed to her just to have the feeling repeated. The stroll in the garden, later, was a quiet episode. It took a while before they held hands as they walked around the flower beds and the perfumed, fully blossomed cherry trees. They talked little, and what they talked of was pure, innocent trivia.

Irene was a very tall, willowy girl with clear olive skin, perhaps a shade too thin, but that was what the latest fashion demanded and she was always keen to follow the trends of the fashion pages. Her oval face and her high cheekbones were like a Modigliani painting, exquisitely expressing her Sekler ancestry. Her beauty was completed by her very dark hair worn short. Whilst they walked in the garden and orchard, Nicholas reminisced about the occasion when they had danced together.

'I so wanted to dance with you when I saw you doing the Charleston – your movements were mesmerising.'

'And I thought it was me you found irresistible, ha!' She answered, teasing him.

'Maybe not at the time, but I do now.' He raised his eyebrows and with a broad smile squeezed her hand gently.

'What changed, then, Nicholas?'

'Well, I suppose I have. At that time I was looking at your hands and feet – now I am looking at your beautiful face, and you.' He was quietly pleased with his answer, enough to bravely put his arm around her shoulder, but Irene wriggled out of the way like a youthful snake.

'My sisters will be watching. You mustn't,' she whispered.

Nicholas pulled back in mock servility and bowed. Lifting his head, he noticed two large oak trees at the bottom of the garden at the end of the trellis. He took her hand again and steered their walk in that direction.

'Look at that huge owl there, he is looking at us too,' he said hurriedly.

'What? I can't stand them!' she exclaimed, jumping back. 'They're awful creatures.'

As she pulled back he moved sideways and spun her around to the large trunk of the tree, out of sight of any would-be observer. He kissed her in haste, but then relaxed his grip, only to find Irene holding herself in her captive position. Their second kiss was a softer, more lingering and passionate one, with their bodies closely pressed together.

'That was a dreadful trick, Nicholas Zenta. There was no owl there at all.' Nicholas looked teasingly at her and smiled.

When they emerged from behind the tree a few minutes later the grip of their hands was much firmer, so much more determined, their fingernails gently pressing into each other's skin. The walk had to come to an end sometime, however, much as they wanted to prolong it. It would not have been proper otherwise. The situation was fraught with the convention of the 'respectability' of the family.

∽

With his day-to-day work and the distance between them their courtship was a laborious one. He had to steal time, jump on his horse and ride the undulating hills to see Irene just for a few minutes, usually chaperoned, overheard or watched by the various members of the family. Their only physical contact being the greeting kisses on their cheeks and the fleeting touch of hands, Irene still experiencing the electricity of their first touch at the dinner not so long before.

On Irene's birthday Nicholas hired a full Gypsy band to serenade her under her bedroom window, as was the custom. They set off; he on his horse and the band piled on a cart following behind. They slowly crossed the hills and by nightfall they were assembled below her window. '*The night of dark eyes*', a favourite of Titus, was the first sonorous number to be struck up by the leader of the band. Inside the house full of girls there might have been some momentary dispute as to who might be the subject of the serenade, but as it was Irene's birthday they all looked to her. In the garden Nicholas beckoned the band to stand under Irene's window, but instead they moved into the main flower bed, destroying it in the process. Never mind, I'll send someone over and have it fixed tomorrow, he thought.

All seemed to go well. Irene placed a candle in the window, indicating her acceptance of the serenade. She was well aware of who was behind this very romantic gesture. At this point Nicholas should have called off the Gypsies, but being a man of impetuous excesses he decided he would rather like to sing and asked the band to play '*I'd like to gather all lilies on a May night*', a sentimental little number, but that was a little too much for the vicar. He glared out of his window and, seeing the band standing in the middle of his favourite flower patch, yelled out, 'Nicholas Zenta! I'll have you hung, drawn and quartered if you don't repair that flower bed immediately, you hear me? Immediately!' Before Nicholas could say a word, he angrily slammed his window shut.

The Gypsies stared directly at Nicholas, who then paid the leader; leaving him standing on the spot, they headed back to their cart. 'Well, my lad, you have work to do,' Nicholas muttered to himself, rolling up his sleeves. Thankfully the garden shed by the first oak tree was open and he started to repair the damage in earnest. Irene, peeping out between her curtains, saw Nicholas in his white shirt and riding boots digging away in the clear, warm and rather inviting moonlight. He patched things up the best he could, stealing a few flowers from some of the other beds to replace the ones destroyed. Irene, feeling very sorry for him working away on his own, leaned out of the window and whispered, 'Shall I come and help you?'

'Oh, my love, if only you would.' He opened his arms pleadingly and smiled widely.

'I am not really sure I should, you have been drinking,' Irene whispered. 'Am I safe with you?' she asked, awaiting his reassurance.

'Oh, please, Irene, I need help with this broken rose stem in the middle of the flower bed, it's had it,' he begged.

Irene put a wrap over her lace-topped linen nightshirt and came down through the back door. 'Don't you even think of touching me,' she whispered assertively. 'I know my sisters will be watching us.'

'I won't, my love, I won't,' he promised.

The pastor looked out of his window again and saw the two of them digging away. He turned to his wife in bed and said, 'Huh! That will teach them.'

She sat up and wondered, 'Are you sure they are all right out there together in the middle of the night alone?'

'Of course! They know we are watching them, they will be fine.' He smirked to himself, went back to bed and fell fast asleep.

In the warm moonlit garden the two would-be lovers found it difficult to control themselves. They had worked for nearly an hour and it occurred to Nicholas that ruining the flower beds was the best thing he had ever done.

'What should we do with this broken rose?' He asked.

'I'll dig it up, and you fetch another one from the church garden, by the wall. They have planted some there and nobody is going to miss one,' Irene whispered.

Nicholas was off like lightning, jumping over the stone wall only to return a minute later holding the little potted tree.

'Oh, a yellow one, how lovely. It is my favourite colour of rose,' she said with genuine delight. They planted it gently in the middle of the flower bed and Irene stepped back admiringly. 'When I look out of my bedroom window from now on it will always remind me of you and this evening. You are quite a man, Nicholas Zenta,' she said, wagging her index finger at him.

Irene and Nicholas, very satisfied with the result of their efforts, returned things to the shed. Resting his hands on the back of his hips, Nicholas stretched his back and groaned. The long moonlit shadows followed them as they entered the small outhouse. The door closed behind them.

They were not to emerge until much, much later.

∽

The following Sunday Nicholas insisted on going to church with his mother. Immediately after the service, dragging her along, he approached the pastor. Looking him straight in the eye, he asked for Irene's hand in marriage, and to everyone's surprise he received a reassuring embrace from him. He took the simple engagement ring from his pocket and slipped the diamond on to the astonished Irene's finger. Turning to the family, he announced that the wedding was to be planned for the following year.

He felt that his choice was a certainly splendid one, for Irene was a sensitive, caring and very beautiful girl, good hearted and well educated. An avid reader of literature as well as trivia, she more than compensated for his more narrow education and unpredictable moments. She was impressed by his impish sense of humour and even more by his exceptional looks. The film-star-like smile and the flashing pale blue eyes always warned, indeed promised, that the unexpected might happen at any time. Not too keen on his occasional drinking bouts, she was convinced that she would be more than able to handle him with her ability to calm and conciliate.

∽

As they walked back to the vicarage on the cypress-lined lane, their shoulders touching, they were as convinced of their future together as any betrothed couple could ever be. Back at the house the family was very happy and full of smiles, the kind that one reserves for occasions when something agreeable and comfortable is happening. Nicholas, sensing this, kept responding with mischief, at one point trying to walk his fiancée of a few minutes into the ditch beside the lane by leaning against her. But she, noticing his trick at the last possible second, gave him a sharp dig in the side. They were very happy.

Seated next to each other at the family lunch later, much as they would have liked to display affection, a vicarage Sunday lunch was hardly the place. Their knees may have touched for a split second, which to them was a source of extreme pleasure, but that was it. After dinner Irene's father toasted the couple and asked the Lord to bless their lives.

'An important family occasion like an engagement must be marked socially,' he said. 'We will mark it with a garden party for the two of you on the second Saturday after Lent.' The young couple were very pleased with this idea. That's not too long off, they thought, it will be a memorable occasion.

As the weeks passed by they both looked forward to their Sunday meeting in church, which at least gave them a chance to look at each other longingly. Nicholas worked every God-given hour to save as much as he could. He sold wine and traded horses with great effect. His intuitive appreciation of the main chance got him good offers and his charismatic smile helped to conclude the deals.

~

Charles Szábó was a few years younger than Nicholas, his best friend and drinking partner and a theology student at Vásárhely about to complete his studies and become ordained as a pastor in the Reformed faith. A round-faced, jovial character, he had put on some weight owing to the generosity of his flock. Whenever he had some free time he accompanied Nicholas to the market and even helped him with the bargaining. They usually ended up in an inn, drinking away some of the profits. He was a very positive person, and his support and help would make sure that Nicholas would make his fortune in time for the wedding.

The end of Lent was getting ever nearer, and Nicholas was doing rather well with his deals. He took particular pleasure in making a good profit from the boyar's men, for his hatred of Romanians was no less than his father's. His usual saying was that the Romanians made the best shepherds and the best whores, which summed up his philosophy vis-à-vis the temporary occupiers of his land. The theft of Transylvania was very painful for the whole of Hungary, but much more so for the two million Magyars and Seklers trapped in the once proud principality. The Romanian occupation was now in its twelfth year and well consolidated. The government had removed most outward signs that might have suggested that the province had ever been Hungarian. Town and street names and memorial plaques had all disappeared long ago. Alas, they could not do much with the most original style of architecture, both in towns and especially in the hamlets. These structures still proudly testified their origins, like the Sekler gates, richly carved wooden structures with ornate roofs, declaring to the visitor that he was about to enter a Sekler's home.

A week before the engagement party Nicholas' activities became even more frenzied. He wanted to buy an expensive diamond-and-sapphire brooch in the shape of a panther for Irene, a fashion introduced by Mrs Wallis Simpson in England. The young ladies of the age talked of nothing else, so it was an easy decision for him to make.

He was buying and selling horses at such speed that he could hardly remember which stock belonged to him. Only two days before, in one deal, he had made more money than he could handle. It was definitely time for celebration.

Irene's family was preparing for the big party, which was to include a buffet with spit-roasted wild boar, a Gypsy band and a small jazz band to provide the modern dancing Irene loved so much. Meanwhile, Nicholas and Charles were collecting the outstanding money from dealers and farmers on their way to the Grand Hotel in Vásárhely, where they decided to spend the night before the event.

The sun was just about to dip behind the ornate spire of the town hall, spraying its evening rays in all directions off the iridescent glazed ceramic tiles, when the two young men dismounted their horses at the side of the hotel, which still had a facility for such transport in spite of the ever-increasing motor traffic. The groom took the horses away to the stable and a young man dressed in uniform livery carried their leather bags into the hall. The two men took charge of the saddlebags that, in the case of Nicholas, contained a large amount of money. They checked in and Nicholas told his friend to take care of his luggage as he had to get to the jeweller's to buy the brooch immediately.

Mr Kohn was just about to pull the shutters down on his shop window, full of sparkling fire and light, when Nicholas turned up. They greeted each other as old friends. The old jeweller used to supply Titus' much greater demands in the past.

'I thought you would call for the panther in the morning, Nicholas,' he said in a very heavy Yiddish accent, smiling.

'No, no. I don't want to do anything in the morning. I just want to get to Iszló. Come on, how much, then?' He smiled too.

'Well, didn't we agree on twenty-five thousand leis?'

'We certainly did not, you old rascal!' Nicholas answered in mock anger. 'It was more like fifteen thousand.'

'Never, you good-for-nothing son of a great man. Your father would have never pulled a trick like that! He just used to pay up. Huh.'

'Well, he had plenty of dough. I'm much poorer!' After a short silence Nicholas said, 'Come on, let's settle on twenty thousand. It's a good deal!'

'Oh, all right, you scoundrel; I wouldn't do this for anybody else. Keep quiet. I'll be finished if this sort of dealing gets out!' Kohn winked.

'Of course I will, and just think, you'll have my business for ever, how's that?' He promised.

Kohn rolled his eyes towards the ceiling and said nothing.

The panther carefully wrapped, Nicholas was soon back at the hotel to change out of his breeches and boots into a safari-style linen suit for the night out with Charles.

They were in a gregarious mood, spruced up for a drink in the cocktail bar, which soon became four or five. They dined in great style, drinking the best wine and plenty of it. When they got to the brandy stage Nicholas decided it was time to show his young friend the Golden Bull. He had never forgotten Titus' romp with his horse in the restaurant and started to relate the story of twelve years ago to Charles. They walked down the hotel steps; the cinema lights on the other side of the road lit up the beautiful face of a very elegant, mature lady with big brown eyes. The sign below the face proudly stated: 'Sarah Dombay, in the new Hungarian production of *The Cottage and the Palace*.'

Nicholas tugged on Charles' arm and pointed towards the hoarding.

'You know, I was nearly *her* son!?' He said with pride.

'What do you mean, you idiot. Give you a couple of drinks and you start talking gibberish.' He pulled his arm away.

'Seriously, my father nearly married her, but luckily for her she went off to Hollywood instead.' Nicholas laughed. 'It's quite a tale, I'll tell you in the Bull.' And tell he did, whilst the Gypsies played and the wine flowed.

'Irene does not know the half of it and my mother keeps telling me to be quiet when I get to the excommunication. I suppose one should. It's a bit delicate.' He took another flask of wine and poured again. Some of the local horse traders sent them more and the two just kept drinking. The band played and continued to play, while the occasional hundred-lei note was weaved into the leader's bow by the two men.

The early hours found them dreadfully drunk and full of devilment. Charles came up with the 'great idea' of serenading a girl whom he hardly knew and didn't even like that much. The Gypsies, never ones to refuse money and a bit of fun, naturally agreed, and besides, Nicholas would never say no to a bit of serenading.

The procession cutting diagonally across the main square in the warm moonlit night in the total absence of traffic would have looked bizarre to the casual observer, but there was no one there to observe. The two drunks were followed by the band, who would take advantage of their inebriation. They stood outside the house. Charles was not even sure of the window. He took pot luck – and missed.

This would-be vicar croaked away with great gusto while the band tried to keep up with him. His friend offered to help and received an instant rebuff to mind his own business. This was not *his* serenade. In anticipation of even greater tips the Gypsies, forming a semicircle around the cimbalom, had started to play a more furious number, when an irate woman with a head full of metal curling pins leaned out of the window.

'You useless bunch of layabouts!!! There is no Margaret here, but I'll give you "recognition", if that's what you're after!' With that, she opened the window fully and emptied the contents of her chamber pot on top of them, most of the urine landing on the head of the lead violin. The

Gypsy began a tirade of curses to the effect that all her pigs and chickens should die of some dreadful lurgy before the summer.

They realised that it was time to stop. After suitable bartering they paid the band and the procession started off in the opposite direction. The two of them went back to the Grand and asked for a nine o'clock call.

The knock on the door was acknowledged with loud grunts and the porter went about his duties, happy that he had done his job. It was the chambermaid who found the two partially clad drunks still fast asleep and snoring away, well past midday. At the vicarage the garden party was fully prepared and about to start.

As the guests arrived, everyone was quite convinced that at any minute Nicholas would appear on his horse. But he was still some four hours away. Reality hit Nicholas hard. He tried to arouse Charles in the next room, losing more valuable minutes.

'I'm off to Iszló, pay my bill and follow me as soon as you can!' he yelled in panic as he ran off to the stable. His heart rate was around 120 when he leapt on to his calm grey mare, which was totally oblivious to his problem. With his thighs tightly gripping the girdle of the three-year-old, he shot out of the courtyard to join the busy road, which by now was full of cars. Dodging between them, he found the country road, knowing that he would be at least three hours late.

~

Irene sensed that something was terribly wrong, whilst the others pretended to be calm around her, saying 'any minute …', but the tension soon engulfed all of them and heads kept turning in her direction, then towards the gate, then back to Irene. Two hours later Irene's father decided that there was no point in pretending that all was well and called for the attention of the guests.

'With the passing of the hours the family and I have become concerned about Irene's fiancé.' He swallowed hard and continued. 'This was to be a happy occasion but it has become marred and we feel that we cannot continue. Nicholas has possibly had an accident, but it is unlikely, because his friend Charles, who is with him, would have informed us,' he continued. As he talked, Irene became more anxious, especially when she noticed her sisters whispering to each other expressively. 'As I was saying,' he went on, 'there will be no engagement party, but there is plenty of food and drink, so please enjoy yourselves and we will find out what has gone wrong.' The precise-minded vicar gestured his guests towards the food tables.

Irene just stood on the veranda in total confusion and despair. A practical joke was the first thing she thought of, but that had to be dismissed. Two men on two horses could not have had an accident. Drinking never entered her mind. In her Unitarian upbringing drinking on that scale was unimaginable. So he must have forgotten, as simple as that! She thought for a moment. No, Charles would have reminded him. There were no other options. She considered crying for the sake of effect but dismissed that immediately. She was too strong to disappear into her room and lock herself in. No, this was not the way to behave. She decided to join the others picking at the food, and noticed her parents walking away towards their bedroom.

It was nearly an hour later when Nicholas was spotted on the horizon, riding towards the house like a man possessed. With more than half of the guests gone by then, Irene stood at the top of the veranda steps, where Nicholas could easily see her in her cherry-red party frock. He was a hundred yards or so away when the other rider came into distant and dusty view. The poor horse was barely alive when Nicholas dismounted. He ran towards Irene, dusting himself down, looked up to catch her sad eyes, and murmured, 'Sorry, Irene, my love. I got very drunk last night and did not wake in the morning. Please forgive me, if you can.' His voice faded away and he lowered his head.

The few remaining eyes were focused on Irene, who could think only of forgiveness, although her eyes demanded retribution.

'In my heart I would like to forgive you, but in my head I cannot. I am deeply hurt by your action, especially for the sake of my family, who suffered more than I waiting for you. So you were drunk! We don't know what that means in our house.' Now genuine tears appeared in her lovely eyes, and she wanted to conclude the whole charade. 'Please go away, I will never see you again. Take your ring, I don't want it.' She removed it from her finger and shoved it at the pitiful man, who was standing a few steps below her. He turned slowly away and started his lonely walk back to the exhausted horse, held by the ashen-faced Charles.

Irene's parents reappeared and the vicar put his gentle hand on Irene's shoulder to lead her back into the house.

'Well said, my love, I was willing those words to your lips from behind you. You've made the right decision, so now let's forget all about it.'

Irene's soft cry suddenly became uncontrollable sobbing.

The garden was deserted except for Kathleen, who was standing alone in her customary black. She felt a strange chill come over her as her knees buckled and she fainted on to the soft lawn.

~

Nicholas was hardly sober for a week, in spite of Charles' protestations. He, quite rightly, considered the loss of Irene an absolute disaster that had to be drowned in wine. After months of brooding it was Charles who decided that his friend needed a good talking to.

'You give in too easily! Why don't you go to church on Sunday to see her? Just do something! Everyone says that she still loves you and she is just waiting for you. After all, whose fault was it?'

When Nicholas first suggested to Kathleen that they should go to church again she was aghast. 'I can't, I am too ashamed to go there! I will just have to pray alone. The vicar here looks away from me because of your father and now you do this to me. No!' She was adamant.

'Mother, it is not the same. They want you back in Iszló. Ask Charles Szábó. Please let us go back on Sunday. Please,' he pleaded earnestly.

Kathleen struggled with her pride and her principles and eventually gave in. Nicholas decided that a complete change of image was a necessity so that he would be taken seriously after what had happened and, as business was good, he bought himself a car. Not for him a flamboyant sporting model – a saloon was more suitable, so he opted for a dark blue Morris Standard, dependable and elegant. He especially liked the long bonnet stretching in front of the windscreen with the small, square British Union Flag, denoting its origin, at the apex. On Sunday morning, he was ready to drive over the two hills. When he entered the small mountain church with his mother on his arm, the silence was palpable. He placed Kathleen in the pews reserved for widows, all of them naturally dressed in black. He walked over to the balcony and settled in the front row near the organ. It would give him a perfect view of Irene. He caught her eye; she turned away instantly but within a minute she gazed back towards him. There was no bitterness in her look at all and she was responding to the pleading look in his eyes. The vicar's sermon was about reconciliation, yet they both knew they would have to wait some time for that. It had something to do with 'standards'.

Nicholas was attending an agronomists' meeting in Vásárhely when through the window he noticed Irene on the other side of the street walking towards the railway station. He jumped out of his chair and darted out of the room, to everyone's surprise. As he tore across the street, dodging the cars, he shouted her name. Before she could locate the source, he was standing before her.

'Irene, please don't spurn me,' he started, panting. She stood still. 'I have not had a drop to drink for months,' he continued with slight exaggeration.

Irene's heart felt no desire for revenge and she thought he was far too good looking to lose, so what was the point?

'You are a bad man, Nicholas, a very bad man.' She accepted his outstretched hand, which squeezed hers so tightly. He gently pulled her to him and held her in a close embrace. As their heads touched their tears mingled. He walked her to the railway station to catch her mountain train. As she climbed into the carriage Irene called to him.

'See you on Sunday!'

His face was full of delight until he suddenly remembered that it was still only Tuesday. When he arrived home he could not contain himself.

'Mother, guess what!' He picked her up in the kitchen and swung her around until her hair came undone.

'You fool. Look what you've done,' she said, trying to sound angry.

'Mother, I've seen Irene again and all seems well between us – I think she'll have me back!' He skipped away like a five-year-old.

Back at his office he picked up the telephone and wound the bell handle. The brand-new exchange soon connected him to the vicarage.

'Sir, it's Nicholas Zenta speaking.' His voice came out a little high pitched and he was annoyed with that.

'Hello, Nicholas, are you well?' Came the friendly reply.

'Very well, sir.' He tried to deepen his voice a little. 'May I come to see you for a few minutes?'

The pastor agreed. He had no vengeance in his heart; in fact he liked Nicholas very much. He rather thought that his waywardness was more than compensated for by his total honesty and charm, the former meaning more to him than anything.

Next day at the appointed time of ten in the morning Nicholas climbed out of his car in front of the vicarage office, this time smartly dressed in his tweed suit. He was let in by Irene's youngest sister, who on seeing him nearly jumped out of her dress.

'Your father is expecting me.' He kissed her lightly on the cheek and walked passed her towards the study. As he entered he was received by the man of the house, who was smiling through his beard.

'I am pleased the two of you are reconciled. I spoke to Irene after your call and we agreed that we should forget about the whole unfortunate incident, even if you were dreadfully irresponsible. I feel sure that it will not happen again.' He looked up at him from under his bushy eyebrows.

'No, sir! I've learned a hard lesson.' Nicholas was delighted that he did not have to deliver the speech of apology that he had rehearsed. Feeling on top of the world and without any further ado, he got into his gleaming car and drove to work.

The formal reconciliation came after the next Sunday service. After lunch he decided that the engagement celebration would have to wait until the spring. He had a lot of work to do and wanted to make some more money, a lot of money, before going ahead with their plans. Everyone considered this a little too cautious, but he was adamant. This time everything would be done properly.

During the next few months he spent all his time either in his car or in the saddle. From deals to sales, from markets to transport firms, he was wheeling and dealing on an ever-increasing scale. Money was accumulating nicely. He managed to see Irene for the odd few moments, but only when there was actually some business to be done in her vicinity. She thought he was overdoing 'being diligent' and decided to take him to task about it.

'Nicholas, no doubt this way we will have a house, furniture and money, but by the time the wedding day comes I will have forgotten whom I'm marrying.'

'Well, in that case don't you think we ought to start with getting engaged?' he replied, reminding her of that particular and still-outstanding event.

'Indeed I do! You will not leave this place until we have agreed on a date,' she demanded.

'Right!' He took out his pocket diary and looked at her. 'What about the first Sunday after Lent,' he suggested.

'Nicholas, that's the anniversary of the day you didn't turn up,' she pointed out in amazement.

'Correction, I was only late.' He grinned sheepishly at her.

'Late and drunk, to be precise,' she mocked. 'But we won't talk about that.'

～

Their continuing courtship left a lot to be desired. Her geographical isolation and the fact that her strait-laced family were not part of Nicholas' social circle meant that there could be no clandestine meetings, only Sunday strolls arm in arm which convention allowed. Nicholas was longing desperately for another night of rearranging the garden and kept giving a knowing nod towards the shed, which Irene tried hard to ignore. He definitely did not have the courage to arrange another serenade.

The summer Red Cross Ball in Vásárhely was the first occasion they were given a chance to spend a whole evening together, but even then they were constantly watched by friends and relatives. An arrangement had been made for them; they would spend the night in Julius' flat. Irene's only brother had married some years before and, as a very successful solicitor, he had a family apartment in the very heart of the city in Roses Square.

They danced the night away in the ballroom of the Continental Hotel, a less famous place than the old-fashioned Grand but with a better ballroom. Hungarians and Romanians seemed to mix easily on the dance floor but their tables were well separated. The cabaret was carefully arranged to be bilingual. 'If only every day could be a Red Cross Ball day,' some may have thought – justifiably. At one o'clock, the carriages and taxis started to arrive. Nicholas and Irene departed to Julius' flat and sat down to discuss the usual post-social-events taboos, politics and religion, sex not being on the totally open agenda yet. After a few brandies Julius and his wife had the good sense to give them some privacy. Irene and Nicholas walked out on to the balcony under the beautiful moonlit sky. They held on to each other, exchanging kisses and caresses and longing for more, much more.

Christmas seemed to come and go quickly, but at least it gave them the opportunity to make their plans for the engagement party – mark two. He still had the panther brooch.

New Year's Day was regarded as the start of the hunting season in Transylvania and Nicholas was not only keen but an excellent shot. He teamed up with Charles and Julius for the shooting. However depreciated the family fortunes became, nobody was ever willing to give up the old way of life. So they made the pretence of being the gentry amongst the ever-increasing number of Romanians, most of whom could still be hired to act as beaters. They hunted for large and small game with reasonable success. It helped to fill the larder for the hard winter to come.

~

The beginning of the thirties saw an increase in the activities of the Iron Guard in the province. Modelled on the 'Brownshirts' of Nazi Germany, these thugs came from the lowest strata of Romanian life. Vociferous, uneducated, dastardly bullies sprung up initially in the capital, Bucharest. They organised sorties against Jewish business, property and later individuals, whose intellectual or business performance they could not match in any seam of private life. Their actions became more vicious, and when they first started trouble in Vásárhely they produced total consternation amongst both communities. Nicholas truly hated them. Jews had lived in the province since the beginning of the twelfth century in their own inimitable way and complemented the community well, although never really assimilating into it. Now they were threatened by the Wallach nationalism from south of the old border and these upstarts who, like the Iron Guard, had infiltrated the province from Bucharest in the past few years. Nicholas had very little political credo but hated dishonesty and unfairness. This new phenomenon was totally alien to him and it conditioned his political thinking for the rest of his life. The power base of the Iron Guard was that of simple prejudice, although in their Romanian ethnic mix they could hardly imagine that they were Aryans or something equally nonsensical. Nicholas decided to fight them. His decision was made easier by the Guard also declaring its intention to rid the land of the Magyars after they had finished with the Jews.

The small diversions like fishing and hunting were as pleasant as they were transitory. Then came work, even if it was on the boyar's estate. He tried to put out of his mind the fact that, not so long ago, it had belonged to his family. Nicholas was more pragmatic about this than Titus would ever have been, but nonetheless it hurt.

Spring arrived and with it the date of the new engagement party. The guests at the last one all naturally wanted to be there. There was to be no party the night before for Nicholas this time. He was just to drive over for the midday reception. Charles was adamant that he would make his own way there and Kathleen went over two days before to help with the preparing of the food. Nicholas woke early and prepared for the short journey in his gleaming Standard. He drove into the hills, casting long shadows in the beautiful morning sun. The distance was much less than that covered the previous year, and this time he had plenty of time. The main road from Vásárhely crossed the track at a point called 'Maidens' Well', famous for the suicides of many young girls who found themselves pregnant with an unwanted child. According to legend, the first one was pushed in by an angry father who did not want his daughter to give birth to a Wallach shepherd's offspring, but later victims just ended their own lives rather than face the wrath of the family. Carrying their unborn, they jumped into the large cold well to a dreadful death. Thankfully, as time passed, the well became less and less used for this gruesome purpose.

As he approached the fateful spot, Nicholas could see a horse-drawn cart with four people on board being chased by two riders wearing the black-shirted uniform of the Iron Guard. His blood boiled. They were in territory where no Romanians lived at all. He pulled up his car at the crossroads to ensure that the cart would have to stop. The occupants were Jewish and the driver had a look of horror on his face. Nicholas got out and confronted one of the riders as to what they were up to. Knowing the answer, he was prepared and was ready to pounce.

'We are chasing these filthy Jews out of Vásárhely,' the younger one said proudly.

'Well, as you are now on my land, you need go no further,' Nicholas started quite calmly, but he was quickly interrupted by the same youngster.

'Get out of my way! We are going to chase them out of the county.' He tried to start up the horses with his whip but Nicholas was faster. He spun around, grabbing the rider's jackbooted leg and at the same time kicking into the loin of the poor horse. The unsuspecting animal yelped, throwing its hind legs upwards. The young man fell to the ground, where the next kick landed squarely in his face. A trickle of blood appeared in his right eye.

'You've blinded me, you Sekler bastard!' The man yelled, throwing his hands up to his eyes.

The other rider threw himself off his horse on to Nicholas' back. The fight became very dirty. Punches missed and landed, some follow-up kicks were aimed at groins. As the younger one was still worried about his eye, the fight went on until the two began to tire. Nicholas was slowly gaining the upper hand and head-butted his opponent, breaking his nose. The sudden squirt of blood frightened the man, who staggered backwards, falling into the deep, rocky ditch.

'Watch out, Nicholas!' Yelled the bewildered driver.

Nicholas, surprised to hear his name, turned to look at him. The younger man took his chance and pounced on his back. The warning worked, as Nicholas leaned forward as far as he could to throw his attacker over his head. The man landed at his feet. He dived at him, taking his head in a lock. Nicholas' menacing finger appeared in front of his left eye.

'If you want to keep this one, you stop right now! Understand?' His voice left no doubt that he intended to carry out his threat.

The man spread his hands out in surrender and Nicholas pushed his head into the dirt.

The two men dragged themselves up and gathered their horses, swearing revenge as they rode back towards the town.

'God has brought you to us, Mr Zenta, let me look at your face,' said the lady sitting at the back of the cart. She climbed down and started to clean him up, revealing a thumping black eye and a cut over his cheekbone. His clothes were torn and covered in dust. The driver walked over to him and said, 'Thank you very much, Nicholas.'

'You know me?' Nicholas asked. He looked closely at the bearded face. 'Major Grunnfeld? God, whatever happened to you?' He asked incredulously.

'I'm afraid I was cashiered out of the army for being a Jew. We were all thrown out, and nicely settled in town until now. You see, I have been practising as a solicitor and had just won a case against these men.' He pointed towards the two galloping away. 'They demanded that we get out of town and "go to dig muck".'

Nicholas was dusting himself down. He took his watch from his waistcoat pocket and gasped. 'My Lord! I am in trouble again! Listen, take my keys and go to my house. Let yourselves in and I'll be back as soon as I can,' he said, hurriedly pointing towards the village.

'Are you sure? You're bringing trouble on yourself, you know. They will come back with more of them.' Grunnfeld was genuinely concerned.

'Don't worry, I'll handle that when the time comes. Find Piroska, she is an old servant. She will help you once she sees the keys.'

∽

The vicarage was, if anything, even fuller than a year before, and when the appointed time came and there was no fiancé to be announced, the consternation of the invited people began to resemble that of a beehive just before discharging a new queen bee and her followers. There was only one person who kept her composure. Even for her it was very hard, and she had to resist the temptation to run away and lock herself up in her room. The minutes passed like hours. The critical looks and shrugging shoulders dominated the scene. Nobody dared to look towards Irene.

It was well past one o'clock when Nicholas' car appeared on the horizon, still a good five minutes away. But at least he was coming.

When he got out of the driver's seat his dishevelled state was the first thing the guests noticed, but when he turned around to display a well-beaten-up face, everyone gasped.

Looking serious and taking no notice of the crowd, he ran up to the veranda, took hold of Irene's hand and, looking into her eyes, quietly asked her to follow him. Now the silence was deafening and the mood changed. Nicholas' ever-smiling face looked like that of a battered statue. Pulling Irene behind him, he took centre stage and started to speak, without answering her question, 'Whatever happened to you?'

'Parents, ladies and gentlemen, friends,' he began. 'I must apologise to you for my lateness once again. This time I'm afraid my delay was caused by the unexpected intrusion of the Iron Guard. As you can see, I look a mess.' He allowed himself a faint smile. 'Today I had a chance to repay a debt to a man who, not so many years ago, saved me from a very heavy prison sentence.' In a few concise phrases he described the events, understating the way he had dispatched the two thugs. Irene looked him in the face and knew better. He turned to her and concluded, 'Now, my love, let us announce the date of our wedding, but, before we do, may I give you this and ask you again to forgive what happened last year.' He took the little box from his inside pocket and opened it. The high sun struck the panther's stone eyes just as in reality the jungle light would reflect in the proud animal's piercing eyes. The guests gasped with admiration as he pinned it on her graceful chiffon dress, as close to her heart as he dared put it.

The vicar moved nearer and patted him on the back, uttering a quiet 'Well done, son'. He shook his hand firmly and held Irene's tightly. They began to mingle amongst the excited guests, and within minutes the previous year's vagabond had become today's hero. The party had now turned into an instant success, and this gave the young couple their chance to slip away for a stroll in the garden. Nicholas could not resist dragging her towards the shed, but he received a sharp elbow in his side for his effort.

'Don't be bad,' she whispered.

'I only wish I could be!' He responded quietly.

Later in the afternoon Nicholas bade farewell and took his mother's arm, walking her to his car for the return journey. He knew there was a bewildered family waiting for him at home.

Ageing Piroska had settled the Grunnfelds into one of the spare cottages on the farm. They were rather quiet and felt desperate. The small boy was still shaking and crying, his mother doing her best to comfort him. The teenage girl was quietly absorbing everything around her. The grey-bearded father was contemplating the next move but answers were not forthcoming.

When Nicholas arrived, somewhat cleaned up, he shook Grunnfeld firmly by the hand and as they started to talk the story slowly emerged. Having been cashiered out of the Romanian army when the government undertook to purge all Jews, he quietly settled in Vásárhely and joined a small firm of attorneys. In this capacity he had defended a young man who was accused of murdering a postmaster in a robbery, set up by the Iron Guard to boost their coffers. He exposed the 'framing' of the youngster and the instigators received lengthy jail sentences.

Their fellow yobs, swearing revenge, began making the lives of the Grunnfeld family a misery with constant harassment. To compound the problem the Iron Guard received official recognition as a 'political movement' and started recruiting from the lower strata of society. When they felt powerful enough they began to undermine the very existence of the Jews.

'But this cannot be tolerated! We have all been living together and doing business together for six hundred years. Who are these scum to tell us to stop it now? We must do something to protect you all.' Nicholas was outraged.

'No, Nicholas, it's no use. We have tried everything and in the end were given twenty-four hours to pack our essentials. We still have some valuables that they hadn't noticed us pack. It would be best for us if we were to settle in a quiet village and buy a shop. It's far too dangerous for us to stay in the city.' Grunnfeld had tears in his eyes and had described their situation so emotionally that Nicholas could not believe his ears. He had heard of some of the unsavoury things going on in Bucharest during the past year, but had never imagined their extent.

'I know just the place for you, outside Régen; you know, the German-Saxon town. There is a quiet village near by. I manage some farms around it. I'll take you there, the trading post needs someone like you. Tonight you will all stay here and in the morning we will leave.'

Nicholas left the family a little more reassured as he walked out of the lounge to his office and the telephone. True to his word, they were on their way at the crack of dawn, Nicholas driving his Morris Standard a little way ahead of the family in their horse-drawn cart. The beautiful teenager could hardly take her eyes off 'their saviour' whenever they had to stop their strange procession. By mid-afternoon they had arrived at the trading post, which was too impressive a name for a motley collection of shops, blacksmiths and a livestock auctioning ring. The Grunnfelds were relieved to find a small but decent house with an empty room next to it. Its previous owners had belonged to a Hungarian cooperative called appropriately 'Ants'. The Romanians had closed it down. From the house the Grunnfelds could see a small manor-type building on top of the hill, earmarked for the new Zenta residence.

～

The coming year brought nothing but hard work for Nicholas, occasionally punctuated by seeing Irene. The venues were usually the houses of friends and relatives, all fairly well organised. Irene did not like riding, so that excuse to meet was out of the question. But there were the mountains everywhere and they beckoned them, constantly. They were had been starved of physical love ever since their only encounter in the garden shed. The whole episode was rapidly becoming a vague memory. So he became extremely excited when he told Irene of his new hobby: fell-walking.

As they laced up their brand-new boots they both knew the true reason behind their outdoor pursuit; food in rucksacks on their backs, off they went. Nicholas was looking well turned out in the new fashion of plus-fours and matching jacket, while Irene wore a long flared woollen skirt with every possible matching accessory. Even their hats looked the part. Nicholas' trilby sported a bunch of needlegrass secured with an edelweiss carved from ivory, Irene's had a chiffon scarf tied around the hatband and pulled under her chin in a loose bow. They looked as if they were ready for a safari. Their first walk took them along the banks of the River Nyárád, up to the top of the meadow and to the edge of the wood, where many years before Titus and Sarah had ridden after their arrival. It was soon one o'clock; picnic time. They unpacked their rucksacks and out came the food and wine. They had settled in a clearing at the edge of the wood. Ahead of them they could see the whole valley, a view that had so impressed Sarah many years before.

They did not eat much as their longing for one another soon made them lose their appetite and their intention to picnic. Nicholas took her hand and Irene responded with a trembling kiss. A gentle, lingering kiss.

Irene reached her arms out and pulled him closer to her. Their lovemaking was tender and quiet.

They giggled like children all the way back to the vicarage. The vicar smiled to himself when he noticed how clean their boots were, even though they boasted about the length and difficulty of their walk. From that moment the words 'long walks' held a private meaning for them. These regular walks continued and they always returned with sparkling boots. The vicar began to worry.

With the house ready there was no need to delay the wedding any longer. Nicholas became a hero of sorts around the trading post as he presented more and more business through his contacts. The plans were in place for the midsummer wedding. The only condition Irene insisted on was that Nicholas and his best man, Charles Szábó, should spend the eve of the nuptials at the house of her best friend, right next door. There were to be no accidents this time. And there were none. The two of them arrived, according to Sekler custom, just a minute before the ceremony. The pastor and Charles were waiting for them.

The simple Unitarian service demanded faithfulness and, as neither of them could imagine anything else, their vows did not unduly tax them. The reception was a pleasant enough affair. The well-kept vicarage garden framed by large oaks made it an ideal setting in the shadow of the ancient church. The presents were plentiful and more extravagant than they had expected. A modern art deco canary-yellow bedroom suite from brother Julius was useful, but the one gift that took their breath away was the seven-branch solid silver candelabra, with the Star of David at the base. Its simple message read 'Remember us by this', and was signed 'The ever-grateful Grunnfeld family.' As soon as Irene saw it she went to find them. They were sitting in a corner of the garden talking to some of the guests who were not so prejudiced against Jews, for sadly even well-meaning people had started to succumb to the ever-increasing anti-Semitic propaganda. Times were changing.

The guests drank to the health and happiness of the couple, who then left. They climbed into the Standard to drive to the Grand for their overnight stay, before catching the train that would take them to the Black Sea holiday resort of Constanca the following morning. Two weeks after their return, Irene announced that she was pregnant.

~

The birth of Adam, a good-sized lad of eight pounds, two ounces, in the canary-yellow bed was greeted with unanimous approval. Unfortunately the celebration was short lived for next morning Irene started to develop a fever, which rose hour by hour. Only the midwife knew what was happening and tried to contain the puerperal fever with tepid washes. It was to be of no avail. Irene's temperature kept rising and the headaches started. Next morning her pelvis and lower abdomen were griping her with ever-increasing pain. The midwife called the doctor, who did not have to dwell too long on the diagnosis.

'Nicholas, your wife is going to die of septicaemia if she does not receive the right treatment. I shall telephone the pharmacist in Vásárhely, who will prepare some arsenic injections for me. Go and get them. Now!'

Nicholas did not need further prompting. Within minutes he was in his car and on his way. His mind, which always focused on the positive side of life, became gloomy. The light-hearted approach that was such a distinct aspect of his personality was gone and he was left in a state of devastation and disdain he was not to experience again for many years. He knew only he and the speed of his car could save the life of his wife. He drove along in the middle of the narrow gravel road and, like everybody else, he found the recent change from left- to right-hand driving confusing. Only the fact that cars were so sparse saved the country from total chaos.

When Nicholas returned with the package for the doctor he found Irene in delirium. He did not even look at the crying child lying in the ornate brass cot. He just did not want to look at him.

The dangerous medication produced some improvement and a further dose twelve hours later consolidated this slight progress. The physician changed the next phase of the treatment to salicylic acid, and by the end of the third day the fever had started to subside. The tepid sponging brought the temperature to near normal and on the fifth day Irene opened her eyes and asked to see the baby. Nicholas picked up his son and placed him on the pillow next to his wife. The baby was quiet for a change. Irene cuddled him with tears in her eyes and whispered, 'My beautiful boy ... you know you nearly killed me.'

'He would not have survived you,' Nicholas added quietly, and bent down to kiss them both.

11

LIBERATION

After a long campaign the Nationalist government, ably led by the traditionalist Regent Admiral Horthy, set about regaining at least some of the lost Hungarian territories. The artificial borders set by the Treaty of Trianon had painfully trapped three million Hungarians on the wrong sides. Horthy's main problem was that the regional decision-makers in the persons of Hitler and Mussolini were a new and dangerous breed. His view was that it was better to deal with the Devil himself than not to deal with anybody. In the short term this philosophy bore some of the fruit he so much wanted for his decimated nation, but sadly it tainted his impeccable reputation. The first and second Vienna Diktats redrew the borders once again and most Hungarians found themselves back in the country in which they so longed to be.

When the sudden news came that Northern Transylvania was to be returned to Hungary, Nicholas was in the perfect place. Having deep knowledge of the territory and being of the right background he was the obvious choice to be appointed as district administrator. His first job was to plan the actual takeover and the triumphal entry of the Regent leading his army into Vásárhely. The crowd was expecting him to arrive on his white stallion but a cloudburst made the cobbled stone roads somewhat dangerous for the ageing Regent on his horse, so Nicholas advised the commanding general to use his black open personnel carrier. Rain or not, the warlord had to be seen.

The main square was lavishly decorated by Nicholas and his crew. The red, white and green tricolour with the national arms topped by St

Steven's Crown was much in evidence behind the main podium. Plants and garlands in the same colours flanked the stand of the dignitaries. Nicholas had the five-year-old Adam dressed in a child's version of an army uniform. His cap sported a proud small white goose feather. The khaki tunic, buttoned tightly, was held in with a belt and the trousers fitted perfectly into the tiny riding boots. When gently prodded by Irene he was to go forward and greet the Regent Admiral and the First Lady of the Nation as they were seated together in the front row for the grand ceremony.

It all went well. They arrived to tumultuous applause and took their seats on the podium. A young girl dressed in traditional folk wear of white pleated skirt, heavily embroidered blouse, waistcoat and tiara-shaped headdress stepped forward and curtsied before Madame Horthy and presented her with a bouquet of flowers. As she retreated Adam received the encouraging push, stepped forward and walked up to the Regent, who was sitting on one of the magnificently carved chairs. He stood up, revealing his worn but still handsome features. Wearing his old admiral's uniform with white naval peaked cap, epaulettes and his medals, including the large shield of his own Order of the Valiant, he cut an impressive figure. When he noticed the small boy coming towards him he stepped down from the stand, picked him up and held him high for the cheering crowd.

'There is a little patriot if I've ever seen one!' He said in his gravelly voice. There was another burst of applause when Adam ran back to Irene for her hug.

After the welcoming speeches Horthy made his reply, not a stone's throw from the Grand Hotel, the place of so many past Zenta escapades, now once again in Hungarian hands. He called for peaceful coexistence with the Transylvanian Romanians, who were given immediate citizenship in the now enlarged Kingdom of Hungary. The speech was followed by a most impressive military parade, including all branches of the defence forces. The heavy artillery and mortars were followed by tanks, personnel carriers and various regiments marching with short thudding steps, their arms held firmly by their sides, in total contrast to the German and Russian goose-steps, as if they were trying to make a point.

The ceremony completed, the Zentas made their way home, with Adam constantly asking whether he had done well. He was repeatedly reassured, and the experience never left the mind of the five-year-old. The following day Nicholas took up his appointment and started to wind up his agricultural management. The neighbouring Romanian majority ignored the whole transition and carried on with their daily chores. All they noticed was the change of flag on the official buildings and, once again, it was back to the thousand-year-old Magyar and Sekler place names. As far as the Hungarians were concerned the event was one of great historical importance, but sadly some of them reacted in the only way a millennium of rule had taught them – with supercilious superiority. Nicholas could quite easily have been one of these had it not been for the moderating influence of his level-headed wife. She even managed to convince him not to join any of the political parties that were springing up everywhere. Other members of the family, alas, had no such wise counsel.

Two days after the liberation the now rapidly ageing Kathleen, elated by the events, began feeling unwell and called for the ever-faithful Piroska. By the time she arrived, Kathleen had just tied her white hair into her usual bun, and suddenly she became ashen. She asked to be seated in her favourite easy chair. Piroska, who was only one year younger but in perfect health, helped her mistress and made her feel comfortable.

'Piroska, dear, could you please give me Titus' picture?' She pointed to the silver-framed photograph on the mantelpiece. In it a very serious Titus was wearing his graduation uniform with the Sword of Honour.

'Certainly, madam,' Piroska answered quietly, and took the photograph with glazed eyes. She gently handed it to Kathleen, who held the heavy picture and looked at it for a moment. Her frail hands began to tremble under the weight of the silver frame. She wanted to clutch the picture to her chest, but was unable to hang on to it, and her weighty treasure slipped out of her weak hands and crashed to the ground, shattering the glass. Kathleen stared at it for a moment and bent forward to try to pick up the pieces. Her knees buckled underneath her as she fell to the ground on to the proud photograph – lifeless.

Three days later Irene's father conducted a short Unitarian funeral service for the family on the hillside overlooking the village and the church. Her coffin was lowered next to Titus' in the still-unmarked grave. The twelve small plum trees in a semicircle around the grave were soon to produce their first fruit.

～

Unlike his father Titus, who had sent him to boarding school as soon as he was old enough, Nicholas decided that his family should live together. Holding Irene in high regard, he ceded Adam's education to her. She knew the teachers of the local schools and considered them excellent, thus Adam went to a school where they were taught in both languages – Hungarian for all subjects, with more than adequate emphasis on the one-thousand-year history of the nation, and Romanian, purely to enable him to exert his will over the Wallachs in case they did not understand the language of the state. This consideration reflected the mainstream thinking of the day perfectly.

Life at the village trading post just outside the Saxon town of Régen had decidedly taken a turn for the better. With the Hungarian political takeover offices, schools and services had to be established in haste and this gave an excellent opportunity to earn good money. Nicholas collaborated with Grunnfeld to their mutual advantage.

Nicholas wanted to do more and so, in addition to running the district's administration, he took over the leadership of the Volunteer Guard, an army reserve organisation, at the rank of major. This gave him the chance to wear a uniform. It also gave him some insight into the function of the gendarmerie and the military, although his brief was to train cadets gathered from all high schools. The twice-weekly meetings and weekend work consisted mainly of square-bashing and target practice with their 0.22 rifles. One of the back rooms of the Zentas' new home was full of these weapons, and more: it was also Nicholas' personal armoury. Adam was absolutely fascinated by it. Nicholas sold the last remaining acres of the old Zenta estate and thus ended over four hundred years' connection with the life of the gentry. Happily, he did keep a sizeable vineyard and in his spare time he concentrated on winemaking. It was his one and only hobby. The produce was of excellent quality, to his and Charles Szabó's delight.

After selling off enough to pay his taxes the rest was consumed by his social circle, consisting of the professionals, clergy and ex-gentry.

∼

The declaration of war on the Soviet Union hit the Transylvanian communities very hard. More than the rest of the nation, as they knew that only a win by the Axis powers of Germany, Italy and Japan would keep the enlarged Hungary together. As their problems were in the East, their basic concern was not the survival of democracy, as in the West, but avoidance of communism, of which they had received such a good dose back in 1919. Because of its unfortunate geographic position the nation became the most unwilling ally of Germany. It had to make a tragic choice between Bolshevism and Nazism; a Hobson's choice if ever there was one. They knew the former from tragic experience, leading to the break-up of the country. The latter was a new concept and so far it had helped in the reunification of all Hungarians. Stalin or Hitler? It had to be the latter – a pragmatic choice at the time but proving to be a totally tragic one within five years.

The Zentas were never great fans of anything German, and Nicholas intuitively sensed the catastrophic outcome of the political situation. He felt safe in his position of authority, which exempted him from call-up. Naturally, the Romanians knew that it would need only a small political mistake by Hungary to enable them to regain northern Transylvania, although they were even more committed German allies through their German royal family. They started to organise themselves. Small units of desperadoes led by ruthless fanatics sprang up in the mountain regions. These created problems for the new administration with guerrilla warfare resulting in the destruction of Hungarian property and acts of terrorism against political figures. They had the tacit approval of the Bucharest government.

∼

Flames of Straw

Young Adam soon made his mark; he was a bright child, much adored by his mother and loved by his father. He was intelligent without being bookish and excelled in school. Life at home in the large house with enormous gardens and the nearby mountains, full of wolves, bears and boars, excited him. His nanny, Sylvia, a Romanian girl, perfected his second language. She was pretty if somewhat plump with a round face and a well-endowed figure. Irene spoke no Romanian and Sylvia's Hungarian was rudimentary. It often fell to Adam to translate for them. He was fascinated by the arrival of his baby sister Kathleen and, by now eight years old, was not satisfied by the explanation that 'the stork brought her'. Sylvia offered more and he was all ears. He was about to receive his first lesson in 'village biology'.

She took out her large bosoms from her folk-wear blouse. Adam, astonished, was allowed to touch them. This excited the sixteen-year-old maiden. Taking her clothes off completely was natural enough for her but a revelation to the young boy. He could not believe his eyes, particularly when he was encouraged to touch her. To his surprise he felt strange and warm. Liking the feeling more and more, he became comfortable with the naked woman. The breasts and the wholesomeness of the female shape became fixed in his mind and the image created would often recur to him. His sexuality was thoroughly established. He would ask her to show her large breasts again and again, or to lift her skirt, which she did with innocent abandon. The only reservation she created in the child's mind was his assessment of the female sexual organ, which he considered woefully inadequate, at least from the urinary point of view.

∽

Adam was walking home from school when three Romanian lads accosted him. They knew who Nicholas was and they also knew about the ammunition in the back room. Adam wondered how they knew this; perhaps it was through Sylvia. One pengő for a bullet was an extremely good price and he thought that there was easy money to be made here. And who would notice twenty bullets missing from the chest? Adam provided the ammunition and they parted with the money. He promised them more. The next day he walked into the store and bought a child-size yet exceptionally powerful crossbow. This is something. Everybody will envy me for this, he rightly thought. The boy could not get home fast enough. In the garden he took aim at the large elm tree and delivered the nail-like arrow bang into the middle of the trunk. He did it twice more, with similar precision, and decided to show it to his mother.

Bursting into the lounge, he found Irene sitting in a chair breastfeeding Kathleen.

He took aim and shouted, 'Look at this mum!'

As he released the trigger the steel bolt travelled through the air with horrendous energy, just passing the baby's head and hitting the wall. It was still vibrating there when Irene, realising the closeness of a fatal accident, demanded to know the origin of the lethal weapon. Adam, stunned by the event, offered the cowardly explanation that he had borrowed it to show off his expertise to some friends.

Incredibly the whole incident was forgotten until some weeks later when the Romanian lads approached him again. They wanted a hundred bullets. Adam, agreeing, went to work on the problem. Just on the other side of the garden fence, next to a small woodland area, stood a large twenty-foot-tall haystack with a ladder leaning conveniently against it. This was to become his den. He was quickly on top of it, making a shelter with some old blankets. The bullets were placed in an old rag on the top. He was rather proud of his work and was looking forward to all that money he was going to make the following week. The electric storm came first. On Friday night the Zentas were giving a dinner party. They were about to settle down to eat when the first thunder was heard in the distance. This was a common enough occurrence at the foot of the Carpathians so no one took much notice. Halfway through the hot and tasty chicken soup, lightning, attracted by the metal on the top of it, hit the haystack square on. The fire started to devour the hay and within seconds the first bullet had exploded. The others quickly followed one by one.

Nicholas, convinced that they were targets of a terrorist attack under cover of the storm, shouted for everybody to take shelter, and ran to his desk, pulling out his Luger. Gazing through the window, he noticed the burning haystack with bullets firing out in all directions, looking like an impromptu if inexplicable fireworks display. Adam came into the dining room and stood silently by the door, attracting the attention of his father.

'Do you know anything about that?' Nicholas pointed to the fire.

'Well, Father, er, I was playing with some bullets. I must have left some up there,' came the uncertain reply.

'Oh, I see. And just how many bullets have you left up there? They are still exploding.'

'I suppose about a hundred.' Adam's reply was hardly audible.

'A hundred? What? Are you crazy? Just come with me, young man, I want to talk to you!' He was marched off by his ear to the study for the interrogation.

The extraction of the whole truth did not take too long.

'A gunrunner at the age of eight! I see. What are we coming to?' were the only words Irene and the guests heard before Adam's screaming started. The ensuing beating was to stay in his memory for the rest of his life. Next day Nicholas rounded up the rest of the would-be guerrillas. They also received a good beating and were duly locked up. At that stage Nicholas still believed in Hungarian supremacy. His position provided him with the title 'honourable' and he demanded respect for it from all. If a Romanian inadvertently dropped it he would even receive a slap across the face for his omission. Irene and even Adam objected to this as it was such a sharp contrast to his usual easy-going nature. 'They must be kept in their places,' he used to say when he was questioned by Irene, who rightly described it as 'atavistic behaviour' and put it down as a 'manifestation of his stock', and Titus.

The time to reflect upon his position came after the announcement of the defeat of the 2nd Hungarian Army by the overwhelming power of the Russians at the bend of the River Don. He turned away from the wireless to look at Irene.

'Well, darling, it seems our time in Transylvania is up, unless of course a miracle happens.'

'Are you serious?' She questioned him.

'Deadly serious. Look, the Germans have lost virtually every battle since Stalingrad. Our army is wiped out. We won't be able to defend Hungary at the Carpathians. As soon as the Russians arrive Romania will change sides to make sure that they get north Transylvania back. It can't happen any other way,' he explained.

'My God! You are right. Should I start making preparations to leave?' She asked worriedly.

'Yes, darling. We still have a few months but it's never too early to get ready. There's so much to do.' Nicholas' head dropped slightly and his voice faded as he finished the sentence.

~

The desperate shifting of the government in Budapest to the far right was the next piece of bad news. Regent Horthy could not stop the further tightening of the *'numerus clausus'*, the anti-Jewish legislation demanded by the Nazis to limit their higher-education opportunities.

Nicholas' secretary brought in his mail. Everything was opened and stacked as usual except for one envelope which had a red band around it, marked 'Confidential'. He thought he would start with that one to get it out of the way. The rambling letter from the Ministry of the Interior demanded a list of all Jews in his administrative area, in three categories: fully Jewish families, partly Jewish families and christened Jewish families.

His first thought was of the Grunnfelds. It won't happen to them. I won't let it happen to them!

The letter went on about collecting the families in category one immediately and transporting them under gendarme escort to a ghetto being set up in Vásárhely, for further forwarding to the west. There was no time to waste. He stared at the piece of paper in front of him, utterly shocked. To make his visit to the Grunnfelds look less official, Nicholas took Adam along with him on the Friday evening. The family were about to settle for their weekly ritual of the Sabbath meal. The silver candelabrum was already lit when Nicholas knocked on the door.

'What brings you here, my friend?' The astonished Grunnfeld asked with a welcoming smile. 'Come in, please. Hello, Adam, how nice to see you too. We are just about to eat our chicken noodle soup, please join us.'

'Thank you, no, I'm afraid we cannot. But I need to speak to you for a moment, I am the bearer of bad news, Major.' An old habit, he always does that, Nicholas thought. He was shown to the dining room, full of the aroma of the delicious dinner about to be served. The family congregated around him while he spoke of the letter he had received and what awful news it was for them. The whole family stood in disbelief. All, that is, except for Joseph. He turned to his wife, who had murmured about the soup getting cold. 'Forget my dinner, Ruby, dear. I must talk to Nicholas seriously.'

Grunnfeld said prayers and left the table hurriedly. The two men went to a back room just behind the trading area which he used as his office. Adam stayed with the family to have some of the delicious soup.

'Fortunately, I may be able to help here so please don't despair,' Nicholas started quite optimistically.

'Take care, you must not endanger yourself,' Grunnfeld responded.

'Yes. One thing at a time,' Nicholas started stoically. 'We will begin with Ruth, she will be the easiest to conceal. Our maid, Sylvia, got married recently, and as she speaks perfect Romanian Ruth could act as our new Romanian nanny for a while, then I might even switch her to being our daughter. I'll get the papers made out for her.' He was becoming more enthusiastic.

'You want to break up my family, Nicholas!' Grunnfeld was aghast.

'No, Joseph. Not break up, just break into two, for a while. Listen to me. There is no other way!' He grabbed Grunnfeld's arm. 'It will only be for a short while and you'll be able to get together again as a family when this damned war is over.' Nicholas tried to sound reassuring. 'Right now you and Ruby will have to disappear – as if you had never existed,' he continued. 'Now, where were we? Ruth to us, Aaron to Irene's parents. Not even those thugs would bother a vicarage and nothing would point that way anyhow. That just leaves the two of you. I've been racking my brains about it. I know you both speak Spanish and that will help. We will have to get you out of the country. Fiume or Trieste, there are plenty of neutral ships there. First of all that beard has to come off.'

'Yes, of course.' Grunnfeld's whisper was hardly audible. 'Now, if you'll please let me have my meal with my family I will tell them of your plan. When do we start?'

'Tomorrow,' Nicholas answered, nodding his head. 'It's the end of the week and people's minds are on other things. This will give us a head start.'

The two men gloomily returned to the dining room, where the rest of the family were laughing happily. Nicholas dragged Adam away. Grunnfeld took his place at the head of the table and took the wine for kiddush and the food for Hamotsi.

The two Zentas were only at the end of the path when they heard Ruby's heartbreaking cry. Adam looked at his father, whose face showed no emotion at all.

Having talked the matter over with Irene after dinner he realised that what he was planning was a total violation of his oath of office and, should he be found out, he and his family would also end up deported. During the weekend he had the Grunnfeld family photographed. Two of each member and each wearing different clothing, in front of different backgrounds. He made new sets of identity documents, using old ink and old-fashioned pens, and stamped them with his circular seal. Then he proceeded to dirty them here and there, spilling a little coffee on one and putting the cup on the corner of the other to mark it. They were then placed on the veranda for a few hours of sunshine and during the evening taken into the oven for a few minutes to make them buckle and curl. He was very satisfied with the result. Aaron became a distant cousin whose parents had perished in the Vásárhely bombings and was now farmed out, like so many others. Ruth made an easy transition into a Romanian peasant girl. Irene was convinced she would put on a perfect show.

When Nicholas returned to the Grunnfelds' on Sunday with Irene he hardly recognised his old friend. Clean shaven, he looked much more like the major in Bucharest he had known all those years ago; only his eyes were different. They were sad and desperate and ready to burst into tears. Ruby just wandered about in the little house in a daze or nightmare, placing things aimlessly to postpone their separation. Nicholas knew he had to lift their spirits.

'The quicker we act, the better. You told me about your Spanish honeymoon and all those trips absorbing the architecture of the Andalusian cities; you both speak the language well so I have turned you into Spaniards. Over here on a trip, you have lost your passports and it is in my power to give you a letter of passage, a sort of travel document, until you get back home. Here it is. Not perfect, but I did have to issue a genuine one recently and it worked all right. So let us hope it works again, for both our sakes. Try if possible to get to Fiume on the Adriatic or whatever they call it now, Rieka, I think. There are plenty of ships there. The children will be safe with us. I'll bluff them through anything.' He tried to sound as convincing as he could. 'You do understand everything, don't you?'

Grunnfeld certainly did, but his wife, by now dressed for travel, was still unsure.

'Could we not take the children with the letters? At least we would all be together,' Ruby tried again. Joseph looked at Nicholas knowingly.

'No, Ruby. It would look too obvious. They are safer with us. Nobody will suspect *me* of anything, especially if I am in uniform.' He tried to make light of it. 'And in any case I don't want you to look like a family in flight. We will all meet again after the war. Now it's time for you to go.'

He went out to his car, but nobody followed him. The close-knit family just could not bring themselves to say goodbye to each other. They were reduced to a crying mass clinging hopelessly to their father.

Irene went over to Aaron and Ruth and Nicholas started up the car to take their parents to the small-gauge railway station at Remete.

∽

'Can I go to visit Grandmother with Aaron?' Adam asked Nicholas as they were preparing to turn Aaron into an evacuee.

'Why not! You can come for the trip, but that's all. No chatting to anyone,' Nicholas said, trying to be as hasty as possible. He considered little Aaron the weakest link in the plan.

Nicholas' petrol coupons had all been used that month so they had to go by the narrow-gauge train from the station. This was a happier trip and the boys occupied themselves with playing the game of guessing the name of the next station.

When they arrived at the small picturesque railway station by the River Nyárád the little bus used to take people into the hamlet on the hillside was not to be seen.

'Another puncture,' yawned the guard. 'It will take him ages.'

'You couldn't fix a lift for us?' Nicholas asked the uninterested man.

'No, sir. You'll just have to walk it.' He turned away.

The twig weir was right behind the station; the more than considerable short cut was a little more substantial than its name suggested. Built of tree trunks and covered with heavy branches and intertwined twigs, it was a functional if noisy piece of village engineering. Nicholas was in no mood to walk all the way down to the bridge and back, nearly two miles. Pondering by the weir, he turned to call to Aaron to carry him across.

'Aaron, we must find a new name for you. What do they call your grandfathers?'

'One is Isaac and the other one is Peter,' the boy answered.

'Well Péter! Péter Zöldmezei. Yes, good! It will translate your name from Greenfield. You won't forget that, will you?'

'Péter?' Adam interjected, giggling. 'That's the name of the village idiot in Iszló, we can't call him that!'

'Another word out of you, boy, and there will be trouble!' Nicholas' voice was sterner now, quietening Adam.

Nicholas picked up Aaron first and stepped on to the twigs and planks. They made a dreadful sound as the twigs twisted under their weight and the whole contraption felt as if it would give way imminently. Then he returned for the suitcases.

'Follow me, son,' he said to Adam, turning towards the river to walk the planks again.

'You're not going to carry me?' Adam asked, aghast.

'Correct first time. Now get on with it – and hurry, I don't want to be here all day,' Nicholas continued.

Adam placed his foot on the nearest plank of wood on top of the twigs, which shifted a little to the side. He pulled his foot back fearfully. The noise of the rushing water and the twigs falling freely to the lower section of the weir was truly terrifying. Adam's second attempt was only a little more certain, and after a few more steps he proceeded on all fours. That worked well enough for a while, but when the gap between the planks widened he had to stand up again to step on to the next one. Nicholas was watching out of the corner of his eye as Adam passed the halfway mark.

'Father … Please … Help!' he yelled, tears flowing down his face. Nicholas took pity on him and went back. He picked Adam up and put him on his shoulder. With Adam sitting up there, swinging from left to right, the extra weight exaggerated the motion of the twigs under his feet, and by the time they had crossed the river his son's fear of water was engrained in his developing psyche.

Aaron was safely delivered to Iszló. The vicar reassured Nicholas that all would be well with little Peter as there was another town evacuee, a four-year-old girl, about to be taken in by them. The whole thing would look much more natural. Adam took Aaron to play in the back yard. The animals were still an attraction and there were plenty of them: geese, ducks, guinea fowl of all sizes and, at the bottom of the garden, some prize turkeys. They started to chase them all over the place until Adam was attacked by a very proud cock turkey protecting his noisy hens and fledglings. He came towards Adam like a steam engine. Adam turned on his heel as fast as he could, but not fast enough. The large fearless cock was fed up with the aggravation and took a good chunk out of Adam's calf. It just wasn't his day, and he still had to face the weir on the way back, after tea.

∼

Spring 1944 brought about the massive German retreat from the Eastern Front. It interested Adam, and he started to plot the positions of the armies on his school maps. He soon became conversant with the personalities and the armoury of the war. Radio news, distorted as it was, provided some information, and he learned that 'tactical withdrawal' meant another lost battle for the Germans. The locals would never forget the spectacle of the daily procession of the huge convoys of interminable lorries, Homag combat vehicles, personnel carriers, and tanks, Panthers, Tigers and PZKW IVs, heading due west, interrupted by miles and miles of Cossack and Ukrainian refugees fleeing the wrath of Stalin.

Whenever Irene's parents visited Adam would go and play with Aaron on the side of the main road the Germans were using for their retreat. They had counted endless tanks together with just about every size of artillery. They even knew how many types of mobile kitchens they were pulling back from the front. On one particular occasion, as they crossed the road between the fairly fast vehicles, Aaron misjudged the speed of an oncoming lorry as he tried to follow his friend. Irene was looking through the window, just in time to see her young charge disappearing under a large Mercedes lorry. Adam yelled out and his high-pitched voice was luckily heard by a lieutenant, who immediately ordered the retreating procession to a screeching halt. The officer dived under the large machine to drag out the frightened boy. Only a trickle of blood running down on to Aaron's face from his earlobe gave any indication of his terrifying experience. He was more hurt by the potassium permanganate solution Irene used to disinfect the cut. The German was never to find out that he just saved the life of a little Jewish boy. Perhaps he would not have cared – to him he was just a curious little lad in trouble. Following the incident, Irene issued new rules as to how to continue the traffic spotting.

Nicholas' work became more difficult by the day. The Romanians, whose mother country had predictably switched over to the Soviet side, became virtually impossible for the administrator to handle, and were openly threatening the physical future of the Zenta family. He realised that their remaining time in Transylvania was limited and decided to take a week off from his work. He took his enlarged family to a spa hotel in Szováta, which he loved. The week by the shores of Lake Bear would give them a chance to think things out and make a few decisions about the future. It turned out to be a holiday they would never forget. During the idyllic week the war seemed as if it were taking place on another planet, even though it was closing in on the other side of the Carpathians. Irene and Nicholas were blissfully happy floating on the very saturated salty lake. Ruth in her bathing costume looked very pretty. She was happily contented and could hardly take her eyes off her hero, Nicholas. Young Adam was wondering how would she compare with the naked Sylvia, but unfortunately he had to be content with climbing trees. And there were plenty. He was, after all, only nine.

Onlookers would not have noticed much out of the ordinary. Those who were not perishing on the Eastern Front still had a fairly good life. It was too easy to forget the misery of the army and the ever-increasing persecution of the Jews whilst in the comfort of an hotel, but Ruth and Aaron were a permanent reminder for the Zentas. Ruth had slipped into the role of au pair with the relative ease of a teenager and had become a good friend to Irene, but could never take her eyes off dashing Nicholas. It was a strange mixture of admiration of his authority and a healthy teenage fancy for a very handsome man.

The break gave the parents a good chance to plan the future, although initially they were doing their best to avoid talking about it, for a while at least. On the fifth day Nicholas was relaxing, floating on the lake again, when he heard a commotion around the hotel entrance. He did a quick backflip to turn towards the lakeside. Wiping the salty water from his eyes, he noticed Irene walking towards him in her flowery swimming costume and a cape thrown loosely over her shoulder.

'Two German cars with some officers have arrived and are creating havoc with the management. I think they want to requisition the hotel,' she said in amazement.

'I must see that,' said Nicholas excitedly, pulling on his towelling robe.

The old hotel manager looked pleased to see the younger man coming towards him.

The major and captain were adamant.

'The hotel must be emptied by tomorrow midday at the latest. I am taking it over on behalf of the Wehrmacht and General Dorff.' The blond jackbooted young major was tapping the reception desk with his horsewhip with every word to make his point crystal clear.

Nicholas walked in, extended family following close behind him. Why not have a good argument, he thought, staring the young officer confidently in the eye.

'Herr Major, I am a paying guest here and I still have another two days to spend with my family. You can't just boot us out.' Deep down he knew the major could do anything he wanted.

'*Mein Herr*, this is absolutely no concern of yours. We are in a middle of a tactical withdrawal and we need this hotel as our HQ.' The major turned to look at Nicholas.

'That's a euphemism for another rout, isn't it?' Nicholas said calmly.

'Nicholas, please, don't!' Irene whispered fearfully.

'Well, now, what have we got here? A military strategist in swimming trunks, eh? I see.' The major moved closer, menacingly tapping the top of his boot with the whip. 'And why aren't you fighting in *your* army anyway?'

That's a good question, Nicholas thought. 'Well, because someone has to feed you out there and I've got that job. And wasn't I lucky not to be at the bend of the River Don with my comrades of the Second Army, because they're still waiting for your help and here you are,: "tactically withdrawing".'

The major could hardly contain himself. 'Another word from you and I'll finish you off here and now!' He unbuttoned his gun holster.

Irene had also had enough of the argumentative Nicholas. 'Leave the major alone, he has a difficult job to do.' She stood between the two men and pushed her husband away. Deep down both men were happy she had intervened, the major because he was dog tired and Nicholas because he was wondering how the hell to get himself out of the hole he'd dug. He turned around and ushered Irene and the family towards the staircase.

Back in their room the very upset Irene gave him a well-deserved dressing-down for his crass stupidity. 'I know you like to play games, Nicholas. However, you not only endangered yourself but us too, and what about Ruth!!' she shouted, stamping her feet in frustration.

'Well, it doesn't hurt to bring the *Übermensch* down to earth once in a while, but I suppose you're right. It felt good, though,' he argued on. 'Anyway, this is it now; we are leaving first thing in the morning. You might as well start packing.'

The light breakfast they ate before leaving was still reminiscent of the good old days of peace and contentment. The early morning sun shone gently through the window, providing a warm glow. The scene belonged to a world that was to end very soon. The battle-grey uniforms at the other breakfast tables were evidence of that.

Outside, Nicholas' pride and joy, the black Standard, was packed ready for departure. He seated his family in the car, placing Adam on the front passenger seat next to him. He was about to get in when the major appeared suddenly.

'I thought that might belong to you' he said, sporting his freshly polished boots.

His batman did good work there, Nicholas thought, looking at his feet.

'Why, what's wrong with it?' Said Nicholas in amazement.

'Don't you know that it is strictly forbidden to display the flag of an enemy of the Reich?' The officer pointed to the small enamel Union flag on top of the bonnet.

'What? You're worried about that?' Nicholas could not believe what he had just heard. 'It just denotes the origin of its excellent engineering.'

'That is the very reason I am confiscating it!' The major unbuttoned his holster again.

Before the astonished Nicholas could say another word he was surrounded by a number of the major's men, some opening the doors. Irene begged Nicholas not to argue.

'Perhaps you haven't heard this morning's news, Zenta,' the major continued, Luger in hand. 'Your country has been occupied by the Wehrmacht, with immediate effect. We have full powers to do as we want and the first thing I want to do is to get rid of this.' He raised his gun, aimed at the small flag and pulled the trigger. The colourful enamel shattered to pieces. Nicholas was held by two privates; the others helped the family out and unloaded the luggage.

The date was 19 March 1944.

∼

The summer of 1944 was spent in preparation for leaving Transylvania for Hungary. Irene was slaughtering chickens, roasting them and storing the pieces in large containers of lard to preserve them. She did the same with pork and veal. The journey had to be delayed time and time again. Nicholas was needed in his office to sign further requisitioning papers for the ever-retreating German army. The rout continued all summer, with miles of war vehicles and foot soldiers tired to death, walking relentlessly to the next stand somewhere only to be defeated by an overwhelming force once more. Then came the Don Cossacks and their families in their pathetic carts, drawn by horses barely more than skeletons. The people in them had not seen food for days; they were utterly destitute. Old folk, women and children begged along the road. Their men had thrown in their lot with the advancing Germans years ago, mistakenly considering them liberators. War over, they were all sent back by the victorious powers to meet Stalin's retribution. None of them survived two years.

For Adam the retreat continued to provide a basic military education. He was conversant with all war paraphernalia, divisional signs and armoury. He continued to update his school maps from the radio news, and when he accidentally found the BBC Hungarian Service, illegal or not, he began to get a fairly accurate picture of what was happening. Nicholas listened with him and they often argued as to what some snippet of information meant. One thing they both agreed on – Germany's situation was hopeless and that, in turn, meant so was their own. The armoury was rolling westwards incessantly and Nicholas thought that with so much hardware they ought to be able to stage a 'Hitlergrad' somewhere, but as time passed he talked more and more about the fact that all they were doing was antagonising the world – the Allied powers as much as their last remaining friend, Hungary.

In attack the Magyars supported them, fearing the giant Soviet state with more than good reason. The Germans did look all powerful, Teutonic and proud. It was not too difficult for the ordinary Hungarian, for whom the Allies were a million miles away, to offer their country as an avenue through which to destroy Bolshevism, which was alien to their bones.

In retreat, they soon realised that Germany presented Hungary with the biggest problem in her tragic history. The army was still fighting and getting more involved, as they now had to defend their actual borders, but the thinking population started to see that the cause was lost, pure and simple. Nicholas knew that the partition of Transylvania would be reversed and, as an administrator who was not averse to slapping the face of the odd Wallach who refused to touch his hat quickly enough, his life would definitely be threatened. The only way out was to pack and go – fast. Irene and Nicholas had talked about the matter many times before, but new developments added urgency to the move. Irene was her usual pragmatic self; she did not need convincing. Her only demand was that the Grunnfeld children had to be included. They, in turn, were more than happy as they thought it meant getting nearer to their parents, wherever they were. Adam was the clear winner; a long train journey with all those armies to see along the way was sheer heaven, never mind the delay in going back to school. Nicholas received his official transfer to Budapest and set about making new identities for Ruth and Aaron. It was the least of his problems as he had everything at hand. The only way he could go wrong was if someone reported or denounced him. The odd Romanian might just do that. It was unlikely, though, as they all acted as if they had been on the Allied side since day one of the war.

The beautiful teenager and the broody young boy had to become members of the family. The evacuation procedures were strict about that. Irene's dark looks helped a little, and she came up with the idea of dyeing her hair exactly the same black as Ruth's. The rest was Nicholas' problem. He got on with it, and the two identity certificates took less than a day's work.

The family went to say goodbye to Irene's parents. Irene, her mother and sisters tried to keep their emotions under some control. It was impossible. They clung to each other crying. Nicholas tried to persuade Irene's dear brother, Julius, to leave too, but he was adamant and would not hear of it. The pastor blessed the extended family and prayed for them, the best he could. At the railway station, after the kisses and handshakes, they somehow knew that they would never see each other again.

When the telephone rang in Nicholas' office the next day the message from the Ministry of the Interior was simple; the last train to take civilians out of Vásárhely was to leave on 3 September 1944. It would be followed by a purely military one a week later and the evacuation of Transylvania would be complete. This gave them five days.

Irene spent the next day weeping as she chose the last few items to take.

'Will we ever come back, Mum?' Adam asked her.

His mother gave him a cuddle. Her eyes were full of tears and she just said, 'I hate leaving our lovely warm house with the winter coming so soon.' Adam took that to be a 'No' and buried his head in her bosom, comforted by the warmth of her body.

Next day they were still busy packing boxes and chests and carrying them outside when a large mountain owl landed on the silver birch tree. Nicholas was busy burning papers in his office and Irene became absolutely hysterical. In Transylvanian folklore the poor bird is regarded as the bringer of death, and Irene was in no mood for any message of demise.

'Adam! Bring that rifle, you know, the little one!' she shouted. Adam knew it was the 0.22 she wanted.

Irene loaded a single bullet, aimed and pulled the trigger. Some leaves fell to the ground but the large bird flew away towards the dark and gloomy mountains.

'This is a bad omen! One of us will die, soon!' She said, just audibly.

When Adam told the returning Nicholas what had happened, to his great surprise his father just looked at him and nodded in agreement.

'Yes, son, it is true. One of us is in great danger. Let's hope it's not you!' He smiled and ruffled his son's short-cropped hair.

The day before their departure Nicholas decided to talk the problems through with everybody. The important thing was to act as one. To mingle and play together, to mention the others as one would talk about parents and siblings. In order to integrate the two strangers Adam was told to walk and sit with Ruth and Aaron to play with little Kathleen as much as possible. They had supper together, and whilst the children were gathering things they considered indispensable for the future, Irene dragged her husband to the veranda.

'Bring a glass of wine, darling,' she started. 'Can I tell you something?'

'Of course, my love.' It must be very private, Nicholas rightly thought as he walked to the dimly lit veranda, bringing two glasses of wine. 'Cheers!'

'Cheers, darling.' Irene sipped a little of her wine. 'I have something important to tell you, please don't be angry.' She paused for a moment, composing herself. 'I am two months pregnant.' She turned her eyes towards the ground.

'But that's wonderful! Absolutely wonderful.' Nicholas' handsome face was full of genuine joy.

Irene could hardly believe her ears. 'You don't mind, just now?' she asked in amazement.

'Mind? Sweetheart, how could I?' Nicholas was totally reassuring and he smiled widely again.

Irene moved closer to embrace him. 'Is anything ever too much for you? You are without a doubt the kindest man in the world and, damn it, the handsomest. Let me kiss you!'

Next morning they packed a cart; three changes of clothing for each, the rest all food.

They were to spend their last night in Transylvania in Vásárhely with the Székelys, cousins whose family included a young man who was about to be ordained as a priest. Cousin Andrew, wearing his regulation theological college long navy blue coat, was the first to greet them.

'Nicholas, may I take Adam for a walk in town? It's such a lovely day,' he asked most respectfully.

'Of course. This may be the last time he will ever get to see it.' Nicholas' answer sounded gloomier than he meant it to be.

They went off to visit the castle and then the two large cathedrals built by the Romanians opposite each other in Széchenyi Square. From there they went into the Palace of Culture. Built in ornate Hungarian secessionist style, covered with a complicated pattern of Zsolnay tiles from Pécs, it contained a concert hall, a theatre and an art gallery. Andrew showed Adam everything; they spent most of the afternoon in the picture gallery, which had a good selection of the classics.

As they came out the Palace, the Grand Hotel loomed high on the other side of the road.

'This is where our grandfather Titus died.' Andrew pointed to the third-floor window.

'Nobody ever talks about him much,' Adam commented.

'No. He is kept such a secret,' said the priest-to-be. 'I aim to find out everything about him. I'll let you know all one day.'

'Promise?'

'Sure!' He took the boy's hand and they started to walk home.

~

The night passed quickly. Irene and Nicholas sat in the garden with their hosts and opened another bottle of wine. They ignored yet another Allied air raid, which turned out to be just a flight to somewhere else. The nearby railway line became busy very early. The airport on the other side, no more than a mile away, started off its daily activity at first light. The Russians were coming. They would be followed by the Romanians soon.

God help those who decided to stay.

12

War two

The late autumn dew lay heavy on the lawn and bowed the branches of the small trees. The family and their guests started to wake. Nicholas rounded up his youngsters and cousin Andrew.

'You lot, come with me to the airport. Want to see some planes taking off?' Naturally the answer was in the affirmative; even Andrew wasn't too old for that. They caught the bus at the bottom of the road. On arrival the strong military presence was a testimony to the chaos caused by the sudden need for evacuation. The place was teeming with soldiers of both nations and grey-suited civil servants. The planes, Junkers and Dorniers, were taking off and landing by the minute, trying to salvage whatever they could. But what fascinated the boys were the Messerschmitts and the Stukas – the agility and fast turn of the former and the terrifying noise when dive-bombing of the latter, as they had so often seen on movie newsreels.

The gusts of wind created by the innumerable propellers were throwing Adam and Aaron about the observation platform, to their great delight. Adam, being the most knowledgeable plane spotter, amazed his elder cousin, who, being a future priest, had no particular inclination to learn too much about these machines of destruction.

Nicholas reported to his contact. He handed over some sensitive documents and in return received his new orders.

'You do have a uniform, I take it?' The man in charge of the civilian evacuation asked.

'Naturally. I am a major on the reserve list,' Nicholas answered confidently.

'What reserve list? I thought they had all been called up!' The man, who had two days' growth of beard, looked up.

'Not me, sir. I have been spared to look after a predominantly Romanian district in the Régen area,' he explained.

'Dreadful lot! I congratulate you for surviving it.' The man sized Nicholas up above his half-moon spectacles. 'So you can handle difficult people. Good!' He picked up his phone and asked the operator to connect him to a Colonel Benkő.

'Hello, Colonel, Erdős here. I've just heard the sad news that your chap in charge of the train tomorrow has been taken ill. Yes. Then you will be pleased because I've found a replacement for you who's listed on it anyway. No. He is a reservist major. Aha. I've just said that to him. Anyway, he's here with me. Shall I send him over? Very well!'

'You heard that, Zenta. Will you pop over to Hangar B and report to Colonel Benkő? He'll put you in the picture.' He offered a handshake, which Nicholas grabbed with enthusiasm.

Over in Hangar B the conversation continued where the phone call had finished.

'Good morning, Colonel, Nicholas Zenta at your service.' He stretched out his right hand.

The two men shook hands and, as the colonel was in no mood to waste time, he started to brief Nicholas.

'I either provide a man to take charge of the train, or the Germans take it over. So you are it as far as I'm concerned. Get into uniform and get yourself over to the railway station. Here are your papers. Please sign here for the "special cargo". Good luck, Major. The rest of us will be following you on the last military train in two days' time.'

Nicholas went back to the platform to collect the children and then caught the bus back to the Székelys' house.

Irene was ready and Ruth was very excited – the children loved the commotion. The impending departure meant different things to different people but, by the time the two battered old taxis arrived, they had all settled down. Nicholas was attired in his virtually unused uniform to say farewell to his cousin and his family. Ruth was mesmerised by him and kept looking at him with undisguised admiration.

Tears in the women's eyes, a few waves from the taxis and they turned the corner to the main road.

The railway station was a microcosm of what was happening in the rest of the country; uniforms, noise, confusion and arguments. The compelling smell of the steam engines was the only connection with the normality of the past. Every member of this new family, however small they were, took charge of their own case or bag of clothing. Four porters carried the two chests of food. Owing to the very heavy and most effective Allied and Russian bombing of the railway lines, no one knew how long the journey would take. Retreating trains were priority targets for the bombers along the single-track line. Platform 4 was the place of embarkation.

'There must be some mistake, Nicholas, this is a goods train,' the startled Irene said, turning to her uniformed husband, proudly wearing the rank of major for the first time in front of such a large public.

'No mistake, darling, I just didn't want to upset you with the details. The Germans confiscated all the carriages, this is all they've left us. The better news is that we have a whole cattle carriage to ourselves, it comes with the rank.' He pointed to the star on his lapel, smiling broadly.

'Nicholas Zenta, you are a most incorrigible man! You should have told me, I would not have put my best suit on, and this ridiculous hat can go as soon as we're on board.'

~

The German SS lieutenant in his Teutonic black uniform and well-polished boots yelled out. 'Clear the way! Move over!' He was followed by his sergeant and some Hungarian gendarmes escorting a long column of civilians. They were recently collected Jews of all ages, men and women, hanging on to each other in bewilderment, the six-pointed yellow stars of David on their chests. Some wore them with defiant pride, some tried to cover them with their scarves. The elder ones showed resignation. Some of the very young cried desperately.

Irene pulled Aaron closer to her.

The gendarmes parted the crowd and escorted them to the first two carriages. Fifty in each.

Nicholas could not resist a quip.

'Look at them, they're getting beaten on every front, they moan about manpower shortages, but there are plenty for dirty work like this.'

Irene cringed.

The lieutenant asked for Major Zenta and demanded a receipt for his 'special cargo'. Nicholas scribbled something on his piece of paper with obvious disgust. The sad procession was followed by other 'politically exposed' civilians selected for evacuation to escape lynching when the Romanians returned. They were given a little more room. Four families to each wagon, one family in each corner, at the end of the train. Between the two groups a wagon was packed full of paperwork and documents. The Zentas got the last carriage, the back of which had a makeshift door fitted to it. To Adam's total delight the train was given an anti-aircraft unit of eight elderly soldiers and a sergeant. This was the last item on the train, their only defence, but they also had to double up as guards for the first two wagons. Nicholas helped Irene up into the cattle truck. She decided to make a home out of it by placing some of their blankets on the floor. Their clothing and the food chests served as pillows to lean on or furniture to sit upon. They could hang other items on the hooks. There were plenty of them; the wagon had been used to carry carcasses in its previous existence. The four large sacks of straw would be their bedding. In one corner there was a bucket and a bowl with a jug for their bathroom. Irene hung up two blankets around it for some privacy. Nicholas turned up with a plank of wood and placed it on the two chests to make extra seating. Irene allocated the sleeping areas. The four children alongside each other, the boys and the girls sleeping head to toe. Irene came next and Nicholas next to her, near the door.

The final scene was more or less a tragicomedy, but following Nicholas' example they decided to see the humorous side of the situation. The two women looked at 'the room' and laughed. Aaron, quietly absorbing everything around him, went to the darkest corner to sit down. Adam was already busy talking to the soldiers through the open rear door and getting acquainted with their guns. He could hardly wait for the first Russian Yak 3 fighter plane to start strafing.

Flames of Straw

Nicholas walked down the platform and raised his hand to the guard, who in turn raised his hand semaphore. The driver pulled the forward lever and the engine puffed and panted. The large wheels, eager to grip the cold iron railway lines, skidded for a few seconds. More steam came from the valves and the regular beat of the large engine slowly started to develop, pulling the desperate train into an unknown future. When Nicholas' wagon arrived he jumped on to the last step of the train.

As the sad train pulled out Irene brought out some wine and offered a glass to Nicholas. From the open half-door on the back of the wagon they had a good view of the late autumn sky. Only the anti-aircraft gun interfered with a near-perfect view. Irene realised that Nicholas was being fully stimulated, which kept him on a high. She had to ask him to take stock.

'You know, you are a hero to our Jewish children, please watch them.'

'Of course, but why do you say that?' He had a sip of his wine.

'Well, neither of them can take their eyes off you. When you disappear, Aaron just looks at the spot where he last saw you until you return. And when you do return Ruth takes over and … well, it's very difficult for her … she is nineteen and you do look rather like one of the film stars she has seen. And now the cleanest uniform in the country. She has a crush on you of gigantic proportions.' Her voice went quiet.

'Darling, I understand what you mean and please don't worry about Ruth. At the moment she is suffering the pain of a young woman in love with the wrong person. She'll transfer her infatuation to some handsome young man very soon, I'm sure,' Nicholas said emphatically. 'But let me explain our situation. As you know, this is normally a four-hour journey, but the guards say it could take as much as a week. It is possible we will suffer a lot of Allied bombing and low aircraft attack. Repairs will have to be made to the railway lines and all military traffic will have priority. So, my darling, you should settle in, we could be here for a while.' He put his arm around her shoulder. 'My main worry is the hundred or so Jews in the first two wagons. All I have for them to eat is kitchen swill, at best. They are going to suffer terribly, some will certainly die.'

'You can't let that happen!' Irene's reaction was immediate.

'My darling, I will have to be very careful. This is a dangerous operation. When you hear me swear or call them names if there are others I have to impress, you must ignore it. I must appear "strong",' Nicholas explained.

'But you are strong, darling, you are, much stronger than you think.' Irene pressed her cheek to his and kissed him.

It was getting late, time to eat. They had enough food to last for some time. They had wine, Nicholas had made sure of that. There were going to be many long nights.

By the time they woke next morning Adam was already amongst the soldiers, who were coughing and spluttering in the smoke from the engine filling their open platform, where the centrepiece was the revolving anti-aircraft gun. The sergeant, knowing Adam was the son of the major in charge of the train, let him climb on to the gun seat, twirling it around. Adam decided that whatever the others might think of this journey, he was going to have fun.

The first day they made only a little progress. They were shunted into a siding at the first town to give way to a lot of military traffic, both German and Hungarian, the former loud and reasonably well organised, the latter left to their own devices. The horrendous sight of retreating Hungarian soldiers trying to jump on to open German trucks, expecting to be pulled up by their comrades-in-arms only to receive a rifle butt slammed on to their grasping fingers, was commonplace. Nicholas could hardly bear it without making a comment, which thankfully was drowned by the noise. Ruth helped with the daily chores of clothes washing and meal preparation, for Irene had just started to suffer from morning sickness. Aaron would have been happy to play Monopoly – throughout the journey he had been successful in finding partners – but Adam preferred to sit on top of the carriage and would only join in after dusk. They were allowed one hour by the oil lamp; the games had to be very short.

Breakfast consisted of chicory coffee and dry toast. This did not please the ever-demanding Adam in the slightest, and when he asked his mother why he had to have his toast dry he was curtly told to go and wet it in the bucket. The main meal was at midday, when they ate meat from the containers, sometimes warmed up over an iron grill on a small fire, with boiled potatoes cooked on the oil burner. The aroma of the meal was pleasant, spread far and tickled the taste buds of the soldiers on their mainly open platform just behind the Zenta wagon. When it came to the pork chops, the Grunnfeld children looked at each other and giggled.

'All right, *Mum,* it's veal again today, isn't it?'

'Of course, darlings, I know it's your favourite,' Irene replied, taking up the lightly disguised joke.

Aaron took to the idea more readily than Ruth, but after some soul-searching she too conformed and eventually the mock veal gained her grudging acceptance.

The train chugged along when given a chance; a mile or so forward, then a little back, then shoved into a siding for a longer wait. The successful air raids destroyed the direct line due west so the train had to be diverted north. This promised further delay. Being the lowest-priority train on a single-track line, they forever had to give way to the military traffic carrying the hardware of the Wehrmacht somewhere where it would be lined up 'in defence of the Fatherland'. To frustrate this retreat air attacks were daily occurrences and increased the need to shunt the train out of the way so that repair gangs could get to the damaged lines or derailed trains ahead of them.

Some of these gangs were the so-called Work Service, comprising mainly able-bodied Jewish youngsters or other 'undesirables' such as homosexuals, Gypsies or political prisoners, none of whom could be called up into the army. Understandably, their commitment to quick repairs was negligible and this constantly added to delays. The train often languished in the sidings, with Nicholas waiting for the next call to progress a few miserable miles. In the pleasant enough September weather, comfortable and still quite sunny, with the train stationary in the sidings, people would just get off the wagons, spread their blankets and picnic by the railway embankments, waiting for the three loud whistles from Nicholas or the driver giving notice of the impending restarting of the engine.

At stops such as these people would mingle and talk about their families and the homes they had just left behind. Irene often worried that one of her extended family would slip up with an ill-thought-out comment which would have been totally disastrous, resulting in the swift transfer of the Zenta family into one of the first two wagons, guarded by Nicholas' soldiers, which had none of the privileges of the others.

People, being what they were, moved forward as far as they were allowed to gaze in the direction of those poor unfortunates who accepted their miserable lot with such dignity. Yet all they could see was their sad faces, becoming ever more emaciated, pressed against the window bars, taking turns to gasp some fresh air. Their food was worse than atrocious; a thin, cold liquid with a few floating pieces of meat of the most dubious origin. The lucky ones found the odd potato or root vegetable. They would receive this gruel daily in large tin drums lifted up by the soldiers, to quickly disappear inside. From then no one knew what happened to it, ow it was distributed or indeed consumed. The drums were just handed down empty the next day. Once a day the guards opened the sliding doors and one person in each wagon was allowed to empty the buckets of excrement on to the embankment.

They would try to grab some weeds to clean the filthy receptacle as best they could, then return with it for a further day's use. They had no facilities for washing at all.

Sometimes Adam and Aaron would pretend to chase each other to get as near the two front wagons as the soldiers and their old sergeant would allow them, just to report back to the family. On return Aaron would cry; Ruth would even experience pangs of guilt, saying she too should be in the front wagons. Irene would spend hours with them in a quiet corner talking about some future reunion with their parents – one day.

Whenever the train stopped, and it did again and again, the men would emerge from inside the wagons and climb on top to look for a nearby farmhouse. If they saw one, they would run to it to try to buy some bread. Nicholas would even manage to get more wine, which he drank during the dark and long evenings with Irene or perhaps with his sergeant. Occasionally even the young lieutenant would get a glass, though Nicholas didn't like to encourage him too much after he noticed the lustful way he looked at Ruth.

They made a little more than a third of the distance in the first week. The chaos of retreat was total. As they came closer to the River Tisza and left the relative safety of the mountains behind, the air attacks increased both by day and night. One minute they would be chugging along at the breakneck speed of 20 mph, the next minute the siren would be sounded by the soldiers on the gun platform. Irene would have to drag Adam off the roof and give him a hug or a kiss and usher him inside. Theirs was a very special relationship, demonstrated frequently, but his pleading to let him see the Russian Yak fighters, or better still the larger Il 2 Sturmoviks, being shot down would fall on deaf ears, for the moment at least. The strafing would last for up to four runs until the Russian pilot would realise that his target was only a cattle train. Nicholas would tell the engine driver where to pull up, preferring a good bend, until it was all over. If they were caught in totally open space, all but the persons in the first two wagons would be ordered off the train to hide in the cornfields. The red stars on the side of the Yaks were easily visible; sometimes even the faces of the pilots could be seen. If the anti-aircraft guns had a good day shooting down a fighter there would be loud yells and applause, not least from the children. First the plane would jerk upwards from the momentum of the exploding shell, then it would stall briefly and dip left or right before plummeting down and hitting the ground, instantly producing an orange, red and black mushroom cloud. At other times, the machine gun would blow an oil pipe in the plane and the escaping oil would hit the pilot's face, blinding him long enough for disorientation to set in, the ensuing fireball leaving no doubt as to the outcome of his sortie.

After the 'all clear' Nicholas would check the engine for possible damage, while Adam rushed back to the soldiers to find out who the clever chap who grounded the planes was. Nicholas would fill a jug with red wine and present it to the lieutenant. By the time the train started again they would be well into the second verse of a rowdy song.

The night attacks, mainly by the RAF, were much more serious. The sound of the siren would be followed by hurried dressing and taking cover in the fields. Shivering on the moist dewy ground, the people would huddle together for warmth. The night attacks were much longer and the solitary searchlight next to the guns would do its best to find its intended prey.

Everyone hoped that the bombing would not hit the lines and cause more delays, but even if it missed the targets, some damage always resulted and had to be put right before the journey could be resumed. After such a night attack Nicholas wouldn't allow the driver to restart his engine until the repair gang had checked the lines ahead of them for damage. The gangs usually worked back from the next station along, and the train would wait until they arrived and gave the all clear.

With a diversion towards the north it took them two more days to arrive at the provincial town of Miskolc, well north-west and so nowhere near Budapest. At the outskirts of town the battered train was shunted into a forlorn siding again, out of the way of the 'more important traffic'.

Food supplies were getting low and would not last, unless progress dramatically improved, and with the Allied bombing becoming more intense there was little chance of that. Nicholas was well aware of the problem, which was much more severe in the case of the first two wagons. His soldiers had already removed four dead bodies at various stages of the journey and buried them under the embankments without any fuss. Three older folks could not take any more of the brutal conditions and one baby had died of diarrhoea after being fed the 'soup', which had been reduced both in quantity and strength until it was little more than dirty water.

The Mayor of Miskolc, also the garrison commander, was a fellow graduate of Nicholas called Alexander Great. Being a large chap he had soon acquired the nickname of Alexander *the* Great. Nicholas knew that the train would be stationary for days; he decided to look him up. He got Irene to clean his uniform and he put on a fresh shirt. And with his greatcoat he looked quite respectable.

At the town hall, which doubled as a very busy HQ, Nicholas waited for his turn and eventually entered Alexander's still quite sumptuous office. The friends, who had not seen one another for a long time, embraced with the usual Hungarian overenthusiasm.

'Well, Nicholas, I was just saying to myself, only a fool would stay in Transylvania to wait for the double clout of the Russians and the Romanians, but what are you doing here?' said Alexander, still shaking Nicholas' hand.

'Alex, I'm bringing the last civilian train over, closely followed by the last German one. We have been travelling in cattle wagons on a disused line just outside Miskolc and are fast running out of food. Could you let me have some from your stores?' Nicholas asked in a measured tone.

'Well, Nicholas, your train was overtaken by the German one half an hour ago. You are on a military line from the Eastern Front, so you and your train are strictly speaking in no man's land. You can do as you like, within reason,' said the big man, and Nicholas pricked up his ears. 'How many of you are there on that damned train?'

'Twenty-five soldiers and some two hundred and fifty civilians, including over ninety Jews. Alex, what do you think?'

'Jesus Christ! I can't handle all that!' Alexander looked Nicholas straight in the eye. 'We never had a food problem during this war but the Germans cleaned us out just last week. All we have left is some bread and a few sides of sheep.' He held up his hands in apologetic surrender.

'I'll take it!' Nicholas said quickly, before Alex could change his mind. Alexander picked up his telephone and called his secretary into the room.

'You know that sack of food the Germans left behind?' he asked. 'Oh, by the way, Clare, this is Major Zenta.' He pointed towards Nicholas, who smiled at the well-turned-out redhead in an over-ironed shiny two-piece suit.

'Yes, sir!' The secretary smiled back. 'It's still out at the end of the corridor. They were in too much of a hurry to come back for it,' she said, pointing towards the left of the door.

'You can have it, there is some good stuff in it, and Irene will be able to cook something with it. Now sit down for a moment, for God's sake.' Alexander pulled a chair over for him.

He went on to explain that the Waffen SS colonel was supposed to have taken the sack for himself, but having just received a telephone call ordering him to pull his men back in defence of the Reich, he had forgotten all about it. He was sure that the Germans' plan was to retreat as far as the west bank of the Danube, which was to form the front line in the defence of Germany.

'What about my train, then? They *have* now occupied us officially. To whom do I report?' Nicholas's mind was racing ahead of itself.

'To yourself, I suppose, so long as you don't get entangled with the Arrow Cross. The little fascists are getting more influential by the day.'

'Alex, we have very little time, let us do something that we can both be proud of after the war.' Nicholas got off his chair and leaned on his friend's desk with both arms.

With thoughts flashing through his head, and mindful that the man on the other side of the heavy oak desk was a professional soldier who would soon have to welcome Marshal Malinovsky at the entrance to his town, he went on to explain his position.

'I don't want to be under Russian control until we reach Budapest and I take up my transfer post there. The Russians are at the most only four days away. If they take me in uniform I'll be a POW at best, but back in civvies I stand a better chance. What I am trying to do is this; I'll let my fittest Jews go during the night. All you have to do is to promise me that should the matter get reported to you, you'll ignore it. Just don't send your reservists after them. How's that?' Nicholas demanded excitedly.

'What you are suggesting is very dangerous. What will the others, the Hungarians on the train, do? Some of them are bigger Jew haters than Himmler, and they could report you to the Nazis on arrival. Have you thought of that?' Alexander went on with his objections, but he did promise that he would not send anyone towards the oncoming Russian lines. He ended by whispering a name and an address into Nicholas' ear, which even his secretary could not hear. Nicholas repeatedly nodded his head.

His mind was made up; he knew that the chaos around him was playing right into his hands. The pretty redhead came back with a piece of paper about the release of some old sheep carcasses and bread. Alexander scribbled his signature on the bottom without reading the text and banged his circular rubber stamp next to it.

'Nick Zenta, you haven't changed a bit! I wish you luck – by God, you're going to need it.' The big man offered his hand. Nicholas shook it and smiled at both of them, but the smile was for his own benefit, the one he used when things were going his way.

Adam and Aaron were sitting in their very favourite spot on the roof of the wagon, looking at the guns, when the small green army truck arrived bringing Nicholas and the food. They called to Irene, who took charge of the sack of food and started unpacking it inside their wagon. Nicholas told the driver to pass along the train, and he handed over two loaves of bread and half a carcass of old and rather dried sheep to each wagon. The remainder would be given to the Jews in the first two wagons.

When his sergeant opened the bolted sliding doors, he and Nicholas were hit by the indescribable stench coming from inside. The people were clinging together; they were frightened and suspicious of uniformed men. He walked up to the first wagon and asked for Rabbi Elder.

'Come with me for a moment, Rabbi.' They wanted him out of earshot of the others. They walked away from the wagons and the soldiers. Nicholas continued, 'I have managed to get some extra food for us all. They are distributing some of it later. It's only old mutton, but it will fill our bellies.'

'It will be most welcome, Major, but I am sure that is not the only reason you have asked me to walk with you.' He looked at him through his small glasses, with a most penetrating gaze.

'No, of course it was not. I have a plan and with God's help I might be able to save at least some of your people,' Nicholas continued in a quieter voice.

The wise old Jew was not quite sure what he was hearing and looked at Nicholas questioningly. 'I hope, Major, that what you are saying is not just some cruel trick. We have had so many of those in the past months. Please do tell me what you mean,' he continued.

'Well, we have just been overtaken by the military train, so we are the last one on the line. There are no Germans behind us so we are virtually unsupervised. The only authority in town is a good friend of mine and the Russians are four days behind us. I am duty bound to take you to Budapest and I intend to do just that. This, however, does not mean that I cannot let some of you go. I can forge the numbers on my papers and could increase the number of your dead.'

'But some of them would not be able walk into town, they are that weak,' the rabbi responded with alarm.

'Precisely! So what I propose is to let all those fit people over ten and less than fifty years old walk into the cornfield tonight. They will have their mutton stew and that will have to last them until the Russians arrive.' Nicholas turned to the bearded man dressed in black. 'What do you think?'

'That could be nearly half of them; you will never get away with that!' The rabbi's eyes lit up. 'How are you going to do it?'

'I will have to push the train back to the well, to take on water. You will choose those who are fit enough to last for two days and two very cold nights in the cornfields, though the tall maize will give them some protection. Tell them of my plan and I'll be back as soon as darkness falls. God bless.' Nicholas turned and walked away.

'God bless *you*, Major,' the rabbi whispered quietly.

The evening was upon them before they knew it. At first the rabbi considered the selection virtually impossible, but when he looked around he realised that there would be fewer people able to last the long, cold nights in the open than he had first thought.

He consulted two cantors and the whispering began. At first nearly all of them wanted to go, which was not unnatural in their desperate circumstances. Common sense, however, soon prevailed, and the destitute became more rational.

A dozen or so women were chosen first; somehow they bore the physical tragedy of their people best. Then some lads were quietly selected, followed by four young couples who had no children and one couple with eight-year-old twins. The two cantors also wanted to go but the rabbi decided to stay behind. His wife was extremely weak and he feared she might not last another week; therefore his decision was as obvious as it was quick.

They ate the stinking mutton stew cooked up by some of the wives and the soldiers and boarded the wagons once again. To make Nicholas' work easier the thirty or so who would try to escape entered the second wagon.

The shunting restarted and Nicholas told the driver to push the train back into a remote siding. Standing by the engine driver, he stopped the train at a warehouse with an open field behind it. He chose the spot carefully, so as to block the line of vision from the third coach farther back. Only four metres separated the wagon from the building. Once they had crossed that, the warehouse would give them perfect cover as far as the fields behind.

When Nicholas told Irene what he was about to do she held her breath in awe, then she just looked at him with quiet admiration. Ruth's eyes were full of tears. Adam and Aaron became very excited and offered to help, which Nicholas declared unnecessary, thanking them anyway. Little Kathleen just played in quiet oblivion, cuddling her worn rag doll in the corner of the wagon.

~

Dusk fell and the escaping Hungarian families in the remainder of the wagons started to light their fires on the station side of the train. A few bricks, with charcoal in the middle topped with some makeshift iron grills, were their kitchens. A pot was placed on top containing a little meat or *kolbász*, the spicy Hungarian smoked sausage, or fish from the nearby River Tisza. The atmosphere was almost carnival-like, with the women busying themselves and the men discussing the latest developments of the war whilst fetching water from the railway station. The children, who were becoming scruffier by the day, played around the fires or, as in the case of Adam and Aaron, sat on the last wagon, empty now since the army had taken away the anti-aircraft unit. The flat surface became their playing ground, to the envy of the other children, who were now invited to join them. They could climb up to the platform with ease, stepping on a bolt here and another iron projection there. They were all looking forward to the train moving out to get a wider view of the countryside

Eight o'clock in the evening was the agreed time for Nicholas to open the wagon door adjacent to the warehouse. His few remaining soldiers were eating the mutton stew from their army-issue tin plates with the others. Nicholas went to the old sergeant and told him to go around and check the fires, as some of them looked positively dangerous.

The heavy iron bolt of the door shifted with not a little grinding and the selected people slipped out on to the platform and ran to the blind wall of the warehouse. From there the maize in the cornfield, nearly five foot tall, gave them immediate and perfect cover. In only a few seconds they had all disappeared. Nicholas looked back only to see a sobbing young mother handing her dead child to two young men.

'Can we bury him in the field?' One of them whispered to Nicholas. 'She has two more children to look after, she can't come with us.'

Nicholas nodded, snapped the bolt back and walked to one of the cantors, who was standing by the edge of the cornfield.

'God bless you, Major, please look after the others. Some are very near to death.'

'On your way now. From tomorrow you will be able to hear the artillery. When you do, lie low for two days. By then this siding will be full of Russians and their tanks.' He smiled. 'You could also ask them to slow down a bit. We want to get away, you see,' he added, his brilliant teeth flashing in the dark as he patted the cantor on his shoulder. The man took his ten-year-old son's hand and disappeared into the maize field like a ghost through a brick wall. The rustle of the overripe, large brown leaves died away as it absorbed the few selected members of God's chosen people.

Nicholas jumped over the wagon coupling just in time to meet the returning sergeant, who begged to report that 'all fires were under control' and invited him into the last wagon for a glass of wine.

―

The train departed very early next morning. Having been overtaken by the military one it was in the last slot of the Hungarian evacuation from Transylvania. The Zenta family could be forgiven for thinking that the whole thing was rather ominous. This phase of the journey lasted only as far as the town of Eger. When they pulled up at the station, Nicholas, with an ulterior motive, tried to find out the length of their projected stay at the station. The stationmaster's office was run by the old master himself, a pot-bellied man with a handlebar moustache, and his young daughter.

'You will be lucky to be out of here before dusk, Major,' answered the old man. This suited Nicholas well. He told Irene that whilst the food situation might be all right, the state of affairs concerning wine certainly was not, and where else could this be so perfectly remedied than the home town of Bull's Blood itself. Irene took no particular notice as Nicholas was forever running around and doing things she knew very little about. Soon after he disappeared through the station the shunting started once more; a little forward and a lot more back followed by even more stationary periods, so no one noticed yet another jerk forward. They were a good five miles out of town when Irene asked her son whether he knew where his father was.

'No,' the boy answered. 'He might be with the engine driver,' he offered, without looking up from his maps.

Sadly he was not. The unscheduled and, for a change, early departure had left him in the middle of the town looking for the best wine bargain. When he eventually returned to the station, with a demijohn of the strong red wine and a smaller Szamorodni dry for Irene, he anxiously confronted the old stationmaster. The poor man made a few excuses to the effect that what did he expect, there was a slot for the train and he had to let it go. He was holding on to his moustache as if someone might take it from him and Nicholas felt like doing exactly that.

He had to think fast. Car, horse and cart – how on earth could he catch up with his train? The mechanical rout of the Wehrmacht was by now absolute. The sorry remains of the Hungarian army had all but withdrawn to defend the capital. The roads were empty, the train had gone and the Russians were around the corner.

The young lad riding his Raleigh 'The Best' towards him was more than a little concerned when the major stopped him.

'How much is that bike of yours worth?' Nicholas demanded.

'Why?' The boy asked, looking worried.

'Just tell me, lad, how much?'

'My father paid forty pengős for it before last Christmas.'

'Well, it's your lucky day. Here is fifty for it, let's have it.'

He pushed a fifty-pengő note into the startled boy's hand, and before he could object to the sudden sale of his most precious possession, Nicholas was pedalling away south-west on the deserted road.

'I'll leave it at the next railway station for you,' he shouted back. Get your father to bring you over to fetch it. He can have the wine too!' That really hurt, but he had no choice. Knowing that the demijohns were too heavy for his handlebar and would impede his progress, he left them at the roadside.

Amidst the tired autumn scenery the train to nowhere was still puffing and panting like an asthmatic old man hoping to make it to the next tobacco shop. The heavy artillery fire announced Marshal Malinovsky's intention of moving up the line; he was delighted at the prospect of bringing his tanks to the Great Hungarian Plain, which was ideal terrain for swift advance. Farther south Marshal Tolbuchin was ready to cross the Danube.

Nicholas, still on the bicycle, had been pedalling almost non-stop for two days. He was desperately worried because he knew that as the train got nearer to Budapest it would be subjected to more air attacks and it now had no anti-aircraft gun on the rear wagon.

On the morning of the third day he caught sight of the train. The great puffs of grey engine smoke were tantalisingly visible on the horizon and for the first time he was praying for some trouble to stop it. It came in the shape of three Russian Yaks. Ahead of the attack they decided on a little strafing again. The engine driver stopped at the side of a wood, some five hundred yards from the station at Emöd, as he edged the train towards the capital. Nicholas handed the bike to the stationmaster and told him that a boy of about fourteen might call for it from Eger. Arriving with three days' growth of beard and totally dishevelled, he leaped on to their wagon. Irene was glaring at him with anger and astonishment.

'My God, Nicholas, where have you been? We have been out of our minds with worry!'

Nicholas moved towards her with a disarming smile. Saying nothing, he put his arms around her ever-enlarging waist, rubbing his beard into her face playfully. She pushed him away, but gently, and being grateful for his safety, she placed her head on his dirty khaki tunic and began to sob uncontrollably.

'You know, darling, the saddest thing is that I had to leave all that lovely wine on the roadside,' he offered, trying to cheer up his wife.

She banged her fists on his chest and her cries softened.

Nicholas ran quickly to the engine driver, had a chat with him and looked at the map, then he went to the Jewish wagons. The space left after the escape made the condition of the remainder a little more comfortable. The rabbi, the only person with some authority left amongst them, informed him of another death – an old lady. She had been buried hastily in a nearby field. Nicholas took the ledger from the rabbi and made an alteration – it would help with the numbers later. The rabbi told him that another man would like to disappear during the coming night. Nicholas said he would come back if there was a chance. He had just returned to his wagon when two whistles were sounded, indicating imminent departure. The train pulled out lazily.

The ensuing night brought the worst air raid of the journey, now in its fourth week. The night bombers gave a bad trashing to the outskirts of Godollo, the next station for the aimless train. All except for the occupants of the first two wagons spent the two hours of the raid in the nearby fields, shivering and huddled together. The few remaining anti-aircraft units on the outskirts of town did their best without much success, and quite a few bombs scored direct hits along the railway line. The unfortunate penal units, euphemistically called the Work Services, had their work cut out the next morning. The damaged tracks took nearly two days to repair adequately for the train to pass along slowly, after which they blew the lines sky high to make them unserviceable for the Russians.

Two days later the train reached the military defence ring of the capital. Army activity became very apparent once more, and to the untrained eye the defences looked impressive. Some optimists even talked of a turning point to come. The terrain would have been perfect for a serious counter-attack, but since nearly eighty per cent of the German army existed only in the insane mind of the Führer, they had no chance to make anything of the opportunities geography so generously offered.

The Red Army addressed the German problem more seriously and slowed down their advance to regroup for the siege. This was a godsend for the Zenta family. They would be able to reach the capital. Nicholas feared for the Jewish deportees, as news of the Hungarian Arrow Cross atrocities against the Jews in Budapest indicated that they even surpassed those of their mentors, the SS. He was preoccupied with this as the train passed through a heavy ring of assembled armoury and headed for the engineering splendour of the Western Railway Station. When it pulled up under the arched structure of the ornate station, being the last train from the east and considering its cargo, there was not too much interest in it. This made Nicholas think.

The family alighted first, piling their few belongings on to the crowded platform. The still very elegant Budapest travellers turned away from them in disgust, rightly assuming the unkempt group of Transylvanian refugees to be totally flea ridden.

Nicholas had an early taste of things to come when two Arrow Cross men, a weak and weedy-looking officer with his underling, a rather stocky chap with a round face and short-cropped hair, walked straight up to him and arrogantly asked for the padlock keys for the Jewish wagons.

'You will naturally show me your authorisation, won't you? Because if you haven't got any you might as well be on your way.' Nicholas' bluff was issued in a quiet and relaxed manner.

'There is no authorisation, and there is no need for any, we are commanded by our leader to round up all Jews,' the officer protested.

'Well now, then you do have a problem. These *are* all rounded up already and I *do* have papers to deliver them to the Central Ghetto and to nowhere else.' Nicholas unfolded the piece of paper he had concocted with Alexander Great and held it in front of the face of the little man with a look of disdain.

'You see, these are not your run-of-the-mill little Jew traders. There are academics and other experts amongst them, and my order is, if you care to read it, "To be handed over to the direct charge of Colonel Eichmann".' Got it?' He felt pleased with himself. 'Now if you want to be helpful, you can count them for me as they get off. Mind you, don't get too close, they stink to high heaven and are full of fleas and lice. You might even find the odd dead body in the back of the wagon. They have had no burials for the past three days. Watch the ones with sores on their faces, they might be infectious!'

The weedy man was perplexed. The last few arrivals had been bad enough, but this lot had spent four weeks on a train. He didn't really want to pursue the matter. Nicholas felt that he was at an advantage and told him that he needed a large lorry or two small ones.

'We have no lorries, you must know that. We just walk them, fast,' the man answered, whilst his fat companion stood back in wonderment.

'What do you mean, you have no lorries, you're wearing brand-new uniforms. How come transport is a problem? You know, we've had to spend the last year in one outfit,' Nicholas said, teasing them. 'Just go and get me some transport and let me get rid of these stinking Jews.'

The two marauding pigs went away, promising 'some sort of vehicle'. Nicholas turned around, his face creased in two with a smile. Irene stared at him and shook her head in disbelief; Ruth admired her hero, mesmerised by the man's blatant bluff.

Nicholas was now seriously worried about the Jewish wagons, and even more so about the deteriorating condition of the deportees. He went to see the stationmaster to explain his predicament.

The middle-aged man looked at Nicholas questioningly. 'You walk in here, in these appalling times, to tell me that you want to save some Jews? Do you understand what I'm saying? If I were to report you, you and your family would be deported with them. You know that, don't you?' He was sizing Nicholas up, not quite knowing what to make of him.

'Well, the answer to your question is *yes*, and I know you have a very good reason not to report me. I spoke to Alexander in Miskolc only last week. Besides, what's wrong with upsetting the SS?'

'All right, it's true, there is a good sprinkling of Jewish blood in me too, which I've managed to keep quiet until now.' The stationmaster began to open up. 'The only way you can save them is to take them to the Swedish Embassy. There is a young diplomat there, a second secretary, called Wallenberg. He is issuing some very impressive-looking "passes". It's a big bluff, but we are all hoping they'll work.'

Nicholas was excited at this information. He wanted nothing better than to be able to rub some German noses in the dirt. He still felt aggrieved about his car being confiscated; not the most noble of motivations, but he could not resist it.

Nicholas told the old sergeant and his ageing reservist guards to disembark the Jews before the arrival of the Gestapo. They all had to be helped down. Once on the platform they huddled together. Their smart clothes of four weeks earlier were by now mere rags, and the once bright six-pointed yellow stars were hardly distinguishable from the rest of their clothing.

Irene and the rest of her family passed them, hardly able to meet their tearful eyes. The Grunnfeld children could not even look at them, they just passed them by carrying their luggage. The rabbi recognised Irene. There was momentary eye contact and the bearded man looked towards the sky, as if thanking God. The Zentas settled into one of the guards' rooms, which was to be home until they received the accommodation address from the Ministry of the Interior. Nicholas was busy organising the escape of the remaining Jews. He had to think fast and work even faster.

'The Gestapo's last train from this station is about to leave for Galicia in Poland. They will eventually end up in a place called Auschwitz. It is on the platform on the far right-hand side, over there.' The stationmaster pointed through the dirty window. 'Your lot should really be transferred there.' The man sounded worried.

'Forget it! It's bloody chaos here. The lorry, let's have it.' Back to plan 'A', he thought. He started to hurry the man.

'It's arrived. Can you see it, over there. The green one parked in Theresa Ring Road.' He pointed in the opposite direction, through his front window.

'Perfect.' Nicholas grabbed his hand tightly, shook it and ran down the staircase to the platform.

He had a brief conversation with the rabbi and shouted out in a loud voice, 'All Jews follow me. Come on, come on, hurry up, I haven't got all day for you lot.' Pointing to two of the weakest he screamed, 'You two, move!' He tried to sound as unpleasant as he possibly could. The rabbi whispered into a couple of ears and the message was soon passed on to the others. Heads were raised and steps quickened. The old guards, equally exhausted, could hardly keep up with them. The few travelling civilians and the German and Hungarian army units just parted for the ragged people as they walked through the main gate, leaving Nicholas barking authoritative orders.

'Come on, you miserable Jews, on to that lorry there. Get on with it!' He yelled, but there was a smile in his eyes. He gave a hard push to one he knew well. The man stumbled a little more than the push warranted. That looked good, Nicholas thought.

Once on the lorry the guards took up their visible positions around the captives and Nicholas and the sergeant climbed into the cab. All along the Greater Ring Road he drove like a madman. When they arrived at the huge ornate iron gate of the Royal Swedish Embassy he noticed some more Arrow Cross thugs. Nicholas hooted loudly at them to move aside.

'Special delivery from Transylvania!' He shouted, uttering the words without thinking. He waved aside the guard, who, respecting his uniform, obeyed.

Nicholas told the guards to keep an eye on the Arrow Cross as he pushed the doorbell. A lower-ranking official opened the door and in the most broken Hungarian asked the officer what he could do for him.

'Major Nicholas Zenta de Lemhény for Mr Raul Wallenberg. Urgent.' He handed the startled man a rather crumpled Transylvanian calling card.

'Sorry, Officer, he is busy right now. Can I help?'

'I would have asked for you if you could, wouldn't I?' Nicholas replied, becoming impatient. He raised his voice. 'Please go and get him. Right away!' The man disappeared for about five minutes, but to Nicholas it seemed like an eternity. A tall, willowy man who looked rather like a German officer wearing civilian clothes appeared dressed in a striped navy blue double-breasted business suit and light blue tie. Nicholas looked him straight in the eye, seeing nothing but kindness. What a difference, he thought. Still within earshot of the guards and the thugs, he yelled back, 'Keep a close eye on those bloody Jews!' He grabbed the startled man's arm and hurriedly explained the situation as they stood outside the embassy door. Wallenberg was not too happy to talk to a Hungarian officer in uniform, but if Nicholas was anything, he was convincing.

'Get them all here into the courtyard quickly, I'll turn them into Swedish citizens within an hour, then you'll have to take them to one of our safe houses. I'll let you have the address,' the brave diplomat whispered. 'But can you control the Arrow Cross mob out there? They have been here for two days now.'

'Don't worry about them, sir,' said Nicholas, sounding a little overconfident. He went outside and proceeded to shout over the heads of the Jews, for everyone to hear. 'Get in here, you miserable lot. One by one. You – there – you're number one. You'll get your vaccination here and back in the lorry for the ghetto. Come on, move yourselves!' He pushed the first man in and a steady flow of people began to move up the staircase.

Wallenberg was as good as his word. An hour later they all held a piece of yellow paper with a blue cross on it, declaring the bearer to be the subject of the Kingdom of Sweden and protected by the Crown.

Nicholas reloaded them on to the lorry. This time Wallenberg joined them.

'Can you read this for me, please, I can't pronounce it.'

Nicholas looked at the address and turned to the driver. 'Üllői ut 4.'

The journey didn't take long. The sergeant pulled up on the wide street, outside an unassuming three-storey house with a fairly small oak door. Wallenberg opened it and offered his hand to Nicholas in farewell.

'I will open up the rooms, Major, just make sure they all get into the hall. You are a revelation. I have not often had help from an officer like you. Take care of yourself,' the tall man said quietly.

'Much more important that you do, sir!' Nicholas smiled, shook his hand and turned to the guards. 'Get them all in quickly, then we can all go home.' His argument was persuasive. At the very end of the long line, like a good shepherd, came the Rabbi.

'What a great man you are, Nicholas!' The bearded man whispered, grabbing his forearm, but trying to conceal any emotion. Nicholas acknowledged the old man with the faintest of smiles. He was still visible from the outside and had to be most careful. Two minutes later he slammed the large door shut and got into the lorry, starting off in the direction of the Western Railway Station. The road was fairly empty, quite ordered except for the occasional building smouldering from the previous night's bombing. He dropped his tired sergeant and guards off at their new barracks. The NCO began to wonder.

'Major, what if they ask us about the Jews?'

'Just tell them they are all on their way to Auschwitz.' He patted him on his shoulder and shook the hands of all his guards. 'Well done, men, very well done. One day you'll be proud of what you've done today. My thanks to you all.'

Nicholas parked the lorry on the side of the street next to the busy station. He walked through the entrance and noticed Adam outside the guard's room.

'Is your mother angry with me?' He looked to his son for reassurance.

'Very, but I told her not to be worrying about you and that you had everything under control.' Adam was ready to reassure his father. He reached for his hand and looked up at him in awe. They went up to the stationmaster and Nicholas gave the ignition key back to him.

'They're all in a Swedish safe-house. I hope that Wallenberg knows what he is doing.'

'Don't worry about him, he does,' the man replied, trying to keep the conversation short, nodding towards the connecting door. 'I don't want the lorry back, please take it away. You might as well run it until the diesel runs out. You won't be able to get more anyway.'

Nicholas was delighted. It solved the transport problem for his family for the next day. He dragged his son away from the maps on the wall and they walked back to the guard's room. Entering, he held up his hands in mock surrender. Irene just shook her head in disbelief again. Ruth was very obviously happy to see Nicholas. They ate some cold meat, drank chicory coffee and settled down on the floor for some sleep. It did not take the exhausted Nicholas too long to find oblivion for the night.

First thing in the morning he told the family to gather their things and go to the lorry. He drove to the Ministry of the Interior in the city centre. Parking his lorry by the sentry, he walked into the building to get the address of his new accommodation. When he returned he asked the sentry for directions.

'You see, over there, to the right-hand side of Gellért Hill. Can you see the red-brick house with the turret? Well, yours is right next to it.' The man pointed across the grey rolling Danube.

'Very good, my man. You can go home now, I'll find it!' Nicholas winked at the corporal.

Nicholas drove the van over to Buda across the graceful Elizabeth Bridge, full of heavy military traffic. At the foot of Gellért Hill – named after an eleventh-century monk who was hurled from it by his enemies tied to a wheel, for spreading the Christian message a little too vehemently – he turned left, and left again, into Orom Street. The red-brick building loomed high, just as the sentry had said, and right next to it was number 13, a beautiful but sadly deserted villa. The view below them to the river and the castle was breathtaking. Irene and Ruth started to take their pitiful belongings off the lorry. Nicholas fumbled for the keys. He opened the baroque-style solid iron gate and forgot the war, at least for a moment.

13

SIEGE

The ominous turn in the fortune of Budapest came with the Allied bombing when the late autumn rains had arrived, compounding the misery of the Pearl of the Danube. As civilian transport was virtually paralysed, food totally disappeared. Those with jewellery would willingly exchange an expensive piece for a loaf of bread. Burst sewers and dead horses left to rot created a stench so obnoxious that it lingered in the memories and nightmares of the survivors beyond the next disaster of their ever more miserable lives.

The Zenta family were luckier than most. When the Ministry of the Interior had arranged Nicholas' transfer some six months before he was simply given an address to find in Orom Street, 'just north of the Citadel', a large fortified structure on top of the hill overshadowing the still-famous Gellért Hotel. Titus old territory, he thought to himself. The ministry had done a good job. The house was on the hill facing one of the most spectacular sights in the city; Castle district was to the left with the mighty Danube flowing towards them. The Chain Bridge was in the middle of their view with Margaret Island, a large public park, to the top right and the beautiful neo-Gothic Parliament building on the Pest side. Through the tall leafless elm trees to the extreme right the graceful Elizabeth Bridge was still carrying the through traffic of the capital. The family's new home, a grand villa, stood on the right side of the road as they approached it, just two doors away from the large, dark, turreted red house of an ex-minister of finance. It was an ornate Romantic-style structure built of grey stone with rendering of similar colour between the slabs. The large windows, which were flanked by Ionic columns and protected by wrought-iron window bars, boasted the perfect view. Naturally, the Zentas were not told to whom it had belonged before, but the fact that the expensive antique furniture was still in place made Irene curious. 'No one would leave such a place voluntarily. Wealthy, perhaps merchant people – possibly Jewish.'

Aaron pointed to the front door frame. In a small oblique area of about two inches by half an inch the white paint was missing where the mezuzah had been ripped off. The small holes made by the nails were clearly visible. Irene put her arm comfortingly around Aaron, and gently pulled him to her chest. Nicholas was his usual reassuring self. 'We've survived this so far, we can't succumb now. Before I report for work we must find some food. The ration tickets are virtually worthless but the villages still have plenty. The well is full of water and that's most important. We will be fine.' Surviving the coming night's bombing was the only thought in their heads.

The deep rumbling noise coming from the west was hardly audible. A low E flat, the first note of Wagner's *The Ring*, announced the impending catastrophe. The noise became louder and higher pitched by the second, the bombers now becoming menacingly visible in the entire space between city and sky. The hundreds of Gloucesters, Halifaxes and Lancasters were approaching the enemy capital to destroy it. All they had to do was discharge their deadly cargo into the square marked out for them below. The dogs stopped barking and cats deserted their favourite streets and gardens. The city was quiet except for the ever-increasing boom of the planes.

The large searchlights came to life in quick succession, darting their columns of light towards the deafening noise. The anti-aircraft batteries were awaiting the first sightings in the brightly lit clear sky. The first one spotted looked like a fly caught in a small boy's torch. In a second there were hundreds more, like a plague of locusts. The batteries adjusted their sights and opened fire at the slowly approaching planes. First were the tracer bullets, then live ones criss-crossing the light beams, giving Adam the most amazing aerial display through the darkened window. Irene had absolutely no chance of dragging him away to the cellar.

The exploding flak with its puffs of smoke added to the visual effect when the bombs started to rain down into the inner city. With not a railway station or factory in sight, and with the Wehrmacht still out on the peripheries, strategic justification was non-existent. The relentless attack was to go on for another two hours and the ever-exploding bombs created several rising mountains of dust. Free of their murderous cargo, the bombers took a ninety-degree turn to the north and then continued this for a full 180 degrees, to head back to their bases, disappearing behind the hills of north Buda. The slow turn would make the larger planes very vulnerable to the ground fire that would hit many of them. When, in quick succession, four bombers crashed into the hills the male members of the Zenta family applauded. The order of the leading bomber's wing commander to 'return to base, route B' would be followed by that of a colonel on the ground. 'Cease fire and sound all clear.'

Nicholas told Adam to stop explaining to Aaron what was going on and go to bed immediately – or else!

Next morning the green army lorry was still outside the house, and although it was very low on diesel Nicholas decided to take a chance to get to the nearby village of Erd to buy or steal some food. Winter was upon them and the war was coming to combine with the cold to cause devastation. It was Irene who suggested that Ruth should help and go with him. The admiring teenager was delighted, and the two of them climbed into the cab. The two youngsters were somewhat peeved to be left out of the trip, but Irene wanted no nonsense out of Adam after the previous night and the well-behaved Aaron would not argue anyway.

The lorry started its journey downhill and turned left into the main road leading out of Buda, eventually turning south-west. It took them forty-five minutes to get into the village against the conflicting flow of German traffic. Nicholas parked the lorry near the main square and told Ruth to look after it whilst he went to rustle up some food.

Although the Germans had taken most of their livestock, wealthy peasant cottages still had plenty to sell for three times its normal price in cash or for gold. Having emptied the office safe in Transylvania before leaving, Nicholas had both, including some family Napoleonic coins.

With the instinct of a dealer, he knew which houses to approach and soon purchased what he wanted. Half a pig, mouth-watering sausages of all shapes, sizes and colours, lard, flour, dried fruit and compote. And naturally a couple of demijohns of good country wine. For every item he had to barter heavily, then, slapping hands, he smiled and told them to place the merchandise in front of their gates for collection. He walked back to the van and Ruth.

By dusk they were fully laden and ready for the return journey on the single-track dust road. As they approached the 'T' junction to rejoin the main road from the south, Nicholas noticed the stationary German traffic on it. He jammed the brakes on.

'We mustn't get near them or they'll take all of this, lorry included,' he said to Ruth hurriedly. 'Damn these idiots! Something has broken down and jammed the rest behind it. It will take hours.' He engaged reverse gear to back up, out of sight. Ruth stared at him, mesmerised.

A little back track amongst the leafless acacia trees provided them with good cover. Nicholas was restless as he jumped out of the driving seat. 'I'll go and take a look at what's happening!' He hardly turned his head as he set off towards the German column briskly. As he had thought, looking at them from a distance, the problem of the retreating Wehrmacht was a simple one. That good old workhorse, a Tiger tank, once driven in the North African campaign and now coming back from the Eastern Front with a fair mileage on it, had given up in the worst possible place where it had to climb over yet another narrow humpback bridge. The major leading the unit was desperate to get another tank in front of it to tow the dead tonnage away, but the canal banks were too steep to outflank it. The officers were busy studying their maps for a solution. Nicholas realised that it would take a good few hours to solve the problem. They needed another tank from farther back to outflank the whole column at the next bridge. There was nothing in front strong enough to do the job. The early winter darkness fell as he was walking back to the lorry, and he was cursing the Germans in his thoughts. They have been retreating from Stalingrad non-stop and can't even get that right! Some *Übermenschen*! By the time he got back he noticed a definite chill in the air and found a shivering Ruth in the dark and deserted cab. He turned on the engine to create a little warmth, but started to worry about the diesel, which was by now very low. The fuel gauge was not working. He checked the diesel level with a stick and it showed less than an inch and a half. He needed that to get home.

'Ruth, dear, we have to stay in this lorry for a few hours yet, perhaps even for the night. There is one blanket – you can have it. I'll find something in the back.' He jumped up into the lorry, emptied the potatoes on the surface and returned with the sack.

'You cannot cover yourself with that dirty sack,' Ruth said. 'The blanket is big enough for both of us.' She lifted it up to show him. 'You can roll up the sack to make a pillow,' she continued slowly.

The bench seat would have made a perfect bed for one but was very awkward for two. They tried every way to settle and after each attempt all Nicholas could hear was Ruth's shivering.

'We must huddle together, it's going to be a long night,' he said without a second thought as to what he was offering to the beautiful and infatuated teenager.

She moved closer to him along the seat and leaned against his shoulder. Nicholas smelt the innocent freshness of her face and felt the piercing look of her wide-open dark brown eyes. He put his arm around her slender waist and felt her body shudder and move a fraction nearer to his. He turned his head to see her face, but there was just darkness. Her heavy black hair smelt of soap and youth – and beauty. Her lips opened against his cheek. He turned towards them. She felt his bristling moustache and they kissed.

∼

As the lorry started off to rejoin the road in the early freezing morning, the guilty silence inside the driving cab was a total contrast to the noise the crows were making next to the them on the frosty field. Nicholas was trying to explain to himself how this had happened. His conscience was killing him, as he had never been given to adultery, but evidently he was not made of wood either. Ruth's hero worship of him had been obvious since the incident at the Maiden's Well, but since then he felt that he had become a surrogate father to her. There was no holding back the emotions of an ever-growing and ripening young girl, her adulation turning to adoration and desire with ease. For Ruth it was her first experience, which she would probably never be able to shut out of her mind. Would I ever want to? she wondered as she sat quietly next to Nicholas, hardly daring to look at him

The lorry approached the city. The nearer they got, the heavier the German traffic became, pulling back to the Buda hills from every possible direction. When they eventually turned into Orom Street the two lads were waiting for them. Irene and little Kathleen appeared and Nicholas started to unload the lorry.

Irene was quick to notice the change in Ruth. It was most unlike her not to look at Nicholas at all. Perhaps she is depressed after seeing those battle-grey uniforms, she thought.

When they had carried all the food into the house, young Adam went to the wireless set and shouted for his father.

'Dad! Quickly! Come here! They have just announced the Regent. He is going to speak in a minute.' The lad had been a great fan of the old man ever since he had lifted him up at the celebration in Vásárhely. He had relived the moment every time it was shown in newsreels or in documentary films. The sombre music that preceded his address ended and the wise, well-known voice of the head of state began his fateful speech. *'Fellow Hungarians. Every sober-minded man must realise that Germany has lost this war ...'* By now Irene and Nicholas were standing in front of the old-fashioned set, staring at it. Ruth was washing Kathleen.

'Wonderful – but far too late,' was Nicholas' considered comment. 'All that will happen now is that those Arrow Cross thugs will get into power and the bloodshed will worsen.' Sadly, he was right. They were just waiting in the wings to grab power and they did, within twenty-four hours. With their SS allies, they kidnapped the Regent's son, Nicholas junior, rolled him into a carpet and told the ageing head of state that if he ever wanted to see him again, he'd better go quietly. Their chief, Szálasi, had the audacity to swear in by St Steven's Holy Crown as the 'Leader of the Nation', pledging support to his paymasters.

The routed Germans continued their retreat, mainly into the Castle district, sticking to the outmoded belief that this area would somehow save them from the expert Russian artillery. It had exactly the opposite effect, serving them up on a plate to the Red Army. The gunners hardly had to aim to effect devastating destruction. The few remaining elite

Hungarian units joined forces with them. Their attitude was different. Only their leaders knew that their positions were untenable, but the Hungarian units were obsessed with defensive thinking – they were, after all, fighting to defend their capital city. Even when all was lost and the largest-ever horde of an army totally encircled them, they still fought back with outrageous valour. They would fight on to the last; the last hope of defence, the last bullet and the last man. From the villa in Orom Street Adam and Aaron were able to observe the whole fateful battle as from the best ringside seat. Looking downhill towards Pest, they could see the bridges majestically straddling the greying Danube in the clear November air and the fires from the previous night's shelling. For an even better, more enhanced view, they would climb on to one of the sheds on the opposite side of the street. On the first Sunday of the month they were about to take up their position when they heard an enormous explosion. They looked towards the heavy structure of Margaret Bridge, the farthest one from their observation point, to see a dust column rising on the Pest side. Full of early morning traffic and trams packed with people, the busy bridge seemed to rise towards the sky, only to fall back into the cold grey river. They could not hear the screams from where they were but could see the trams running into the angry depths. Even the boys realised that as the siege proper has not yet started this could not have been a strategic act. The Germans needed the bridge more than anyone! Was it a mistake? They were to learn that a German explosives expert who had wired up the bridge for possible destruction later had accidentally detonated it. The clumsy officer was summarily executed.

~

Nicholas could not delay reporting for work any longer and, when he did, as an administrator he was put in charge of overseeing the rounding up of the Jews and their placement in the ghetto. His area was around King Charles Street, and he had to complete his task in the first week of December. Even in these difficult days he managed to forge a few extra Swedish letters of safe conduct and lose a few of his charges at the new Wallenberg office at the city end of Üllői Street, the long straight avenue leading towards the airport of Ferihegy. What perplexed him most was not only the totally unnecessary brutality of the Arrow Cross thugs, but the sort of orders he was receiving from the puppet government. Three weeks before the beginning of the siege of the city he was told to change all Jewish-sounding street names. He changed only one of them and called it Titus Street. His father's flat used to be in number 50.

Christmas arrived and was celebrated, even in these difficult times. Nicholas took two large branches of the pine tree from the garden of the villa, tied them together and decorated what was the most crooked-looking Christmas tree with candles. Thankfully, there was no blackout that night. The six of them sat around it admiringly and sang 'Angel from Heaven', every Hungarian's favourite carol. Nicholas gave a bonbon to each of them and that was that.

On New Year's Day 1945 the Katyusha rockets, nicknamed by the population 'Stalin's Organs' for the whistling musical sound they made, announced the beginning of the long-expected siege of Budapest. Within seconds the outskirts of the large and already battered city were on fire. There was no more pretence. The outcome could no longer be doubted. The city would be conquered, lost or liberated according to one's belief. The Zentas were ambivalent about this. Positively Anglophile, they supported any attempt to leave the Axis to join the Allies. Even the last-ditch attempt by the ageing Regent on 15 October was welcomed, but along came the thuggery of the Arrow Cross with their demented, yet to some still charismatic, leader Szálasi, and all was lost. The road he chose was that of total ruination of the nation he pretended to lead. He constantly reminded the army of their oaths of service and by and large they kept it to the end, defending the city against the overwhelming might of the Russians and prolonging the pain for all. When their heavy artillery started to pound the Castle, which loomed grandly over the Danube below, Szálasi still issued orders to transfer Jews to the west. On 5 January, under rocket fire, Nicholas had to line up his Jews from Swedish safe houses in Pozsonyi Street to take them to the ghetto. By then there were five thousand of them, swelling the population of the ghetto to some sixty thousand. But at least they got there! To others under Arrow Cross command, this was an open invitation to decimate them further. Men were stood by the riverbank to be shot into the Danube and women stripped humiliatingly of all clothing before being pushed through the gates of the ghetto; little wonder that *they* considered themselves 'liberated' by the Russians on 16 January. Two days later all Pest would be seized, but the hills of Buda would take another month.

After he had transferred his last consignment, Nicholas bluffed his way home with ease through Arrow Cross guards, by now checking everyone's movements, and took off his uniform. He would lie low until the siege was over.

∼

As the battle for Buda began a retreating German colonel pointed to the ugly red-turreted villa that stood out from the harmony of the surrounding hill like a testimony to bad taste and ordered his driver to take him to it. He was not interested in its architecture, but he thought the turret would become an exceptionally useful observation point. His retinue followed him and he sent his number two in to find out who was living there. When he returned with the answer that the family had fled, considering it to be too exposed, and there was just an elderly couple there, ex-servants, he thought, the general in charge of reconnaissance issued orders to requisition it for one week and gave instructions to set up his radio station in the turret. Since the 'official' occupation in March 1944 they did not need to do any paperwork to take over premises. The old couple retreated to their quarters and the platoon-strength unit took over the rest of the house to provide reconnaissance and radio intelligence to the retreating army. The general told his lieutenant to go and find someone to cook for them. He didn't think the old couple were quite up to it. The lieutenant knocked on the door of the villa next door but one to the monstrosity. Adam answered. Not speaking German, he had called for his mother, who had had a good command of the language ever since her Carpathian finishing school. A deal was struck and Irene offered to go with him. When she later returned under the pretence of fetching some utensils, she went to the bedroom where Nicholas was having a nap.

'Nick!' Irene sounded excited. 'A German general, I think he said his name was Wengel, has moved into the red house and wants me to cook for them. I said it was all right.'

'Of course it's all right, but we must be careful. You all know the routine, it has worked so far, it will work a little longer. Ruth knows what to say, Aaron will be quiet, but I want you to send Adam to me, I must talk to him.' By then Nicholas was on his way down to the cellar, which doubled as a seldom-used air-raid shelter. He did not want to end up working for them and decided to continue to ' lie low for a while'.

Adam received his first 'briefing' in no uncertain terms. 'Now, your father is stuck on the east side of Pest, probably taken by the Russians. Don't overdo the familiarity with the soldiers and stop running across the road every time a shell explodes to check what's got blown up. Got it?'

Irene returned with Ruth and went straight into the kitchen to prepare what was to be the only meal of the day for the unit, who were by now well organised. When the two women served up the paprika stew there was general appreciation of their effort.

The general was *korrekt*; very matter of fact. 'You seem to have a large family in your villa. There's a small lad there, about ten. I saw him looking through the window. Why don't you bring him over with you tomorrow, he seems to be quite interested in what's going on. I'll be happy to show him around. I too have a family and a boy of his age – that is, if they've survived the bombing of Dresden,' he said with concern, staring into the distance despondently.

'He does not speak any German, *mein Herr*,' Irene said, trying to deter him.

'No matter, we will understand each other. I haven't seen my boy for three years now,' the general said, his voice trailing off.

Irene ran home as fast as her pregnancy allowed to tell Nicholas of the general's unusual request to see Adam.

'Send him down here, immediately,' was his stern reply.

Nicholas read the proverbial "Riot Act" to Adam once more and sent him off, now clutching his mother's hand with a bunch of papers under his arm. Adam shook the outstretched hand of the general, who asked one of his corporals, who had some sort of Hungarian background, to interpret for him.

'You seem to be very interested in what's going on around you, young man. What do you have there?' he asked, looking at Adam's package.

'My maps, Herr General, I thought you might like to see them.'

'Maps, eh? I thought civilians were not allowed to have them,' the general said in mock consternation.

'Well, I'm sorry, General Wengel, but they are only children's maps …' But before he could finish the sentence he felt the hand of the officer gently stroking his head.

'You know my name, do you? Interesting. Never mind. Tell me, how do you see our situation?' The general leaned back, crossed his arms and looked at Adam. According to Adam's 'briefing' their 'position was hopeless', as Marshal Tolbuchin and his immense land army had to be only a day's drive to the south and the north was well sealed up. Budaors had been taken the previous day and a large column of Russian tanks was about to cross the Danube north of Margaret Island, commanded by Marshal Malinovsky. The southern units would probably take the Citadel, right behind the turreted house, in two days. The bridges could not be held much longer either.

'Gloomy, eh?' The general asked, raising his eyebrows.

'Desperate, sir,' the lad answered seriously.

'Well then, why don't you come with me and I'll show you how to slow them down, on the eastern side at least.'

The general beckoned Adam to follow him, then he turned to his sergeant and snapped some orders. He put on his tin helmet, looking at the admiring Adam, and gave him his heavily gold-braided peaked cap, which sank to his ears immediately. The background noise of the permanent shelling and mortar fire, interrupted by the machine guns of the street fighting, became ever more deafening.

The loud commotion in the turret of the ugly red mansion and the two corporals holding handsets, shouting orders into them, made the general's head turn.

General Wengel and the young boy arrived at the far side of the road. The German cleared some of the branches of the trees out of the way as Adam walked under them to his favourite lookout spot by the shed. The thunderous explosion at the bottom of the hill made him jump. He saw the elegant Elizabeth Bridge rise at its Pest end, the graceful pillars collapsing in a heap. Two more explosions took out the long single span, and they could see Russians on the other side falling back with the force of the shock. The two unlikely observers walked a few yards to the left to a gap in the trees. Within a minute, they observed the similar collapse of the middle section of the Chain Bridge – the very symbol of the union between the two proud cities now lay in total ruin. Five minutes after they emerged from the red house all connections had been cut with the east side of the capital, as the other bridges followed suit. It made little difference to the main thrust of the Russians; they were approaching the Castle from the south-west, having already crossed the Danube much farther south.

When Irene and Ruth turned up the next day to start preparing for the day's meal they found the Germans packing their hardware to leave. The general told Irene that her services were no longer required and gave her a thousand pengős, far too much for the few meals she had cooked. He put on his helmet and gave Irene his gold-braided peaked cap.

'Give this to young Adam and tell him that I'm keeping his maps. Fair exchange, I think, eh? And by the way,' he turned to look at Ruth, 'your secret is safe with me!' The two women were gripped with terror by the revelation of the general, grabbing each other in a fearful embrace. Could their ruse, which had survived such a long and agonising journey, be exposed so close to safety? How had he discovered them? 'Oh, you don't need to worry, I've got a war to fight.' With that he got into his battered DKW Kugelwagen and gave orders to his company to set off for the Castle. He was going to fight his last battle there. Irene and Ruth almost collapsed in relief.

Irene gave Adam the cap and sent him down to the cellar to fetch his father. Four days later Adam spotted the first Russians at the bottom of the street, edging along gingerly. He called to his father, who then made sure that everybody got into the cellar – just in time, as within minutes a Russian was spraying the house with bullets from his sub-machine gun, leaving an ugly pattern of holes in the rendering and breaking the toilet window. The Russians had settled themselves in at the top end of the road encircling the Citadel, behind the house. That had to be taken first before they could concentrate on the Castle in front of them.

It took four days of very heavy fighting, throwing everything they had at the few remaining Germans in the fortification before the red banner could be hoisted on top of it. Their victory was celebrated in the usual way with extra rations of vodka. This spelled trouble for the poor women of the territory they had just taken. Marauding, drunken Russians visited houses looking for terrified women for a gang rape. If their menfolk objected to this raping of their wives, daughters or even mothers, they were quieted by a rifle butt in their faces or were shot on the spot. Many young girls were to die during these outrages, and many more would be mentally scarred for ever. The victorious soldiers would then ransack the houses, looking mainly for watches, and then drink the cologne that was lying about on the dressing tables in the bedrooms.

Nicholas was naturally aware of what was happening and it terrified him. Hoping that Irene's pregnancy might save her, he was more concerned about Ruth. She wouldn't stand a chance, so he decided that at least until the start of the next battle she had to be hidden. The whole family was involved in the urgent preparation of the back end of the large cellar. Nicholas dragged an old mattress down with some blankets and ordered Ruth to settle on it. He gave her a bucket to use as a toilet and ordered the poor girl to disappear behind some broken old garden furniture. Every possible piece of junk was piled in front of it to make the place as inaccessible as possible. She would have to stay there until some sort of order was established, or at least until the next battle took the soldiers away.

Thankfully the plan worked well. She was saved from the unwanted attentions of the drunken Russians, although a week in the cold and damp cellar took its toll on her health for some time to come.

The turreted house on the hillside overlooking the very area of the final battle yet to come attracted the attention of the Russian command too. An officer turned up with a couple of soldiers to assess the place. Nicholas spoke to him in his rudimentary Russian, telling him how the Germans had used the place not so many days before. They had left enough evidence to prove his point. The captain was impressed and told him that it would now be General Volkov who would take up residence there. Nicholas was pleased with his ploy, as the high-ranking officer would provide them with the best protection from his very own hordes. Adam was even more delighted, as he was convinced that his fun would continue with the new occupant. By the evening the large, round-faced general and his command were installed in the ugly mansion. He promptly sat down at the magnificent grand piano and burst into Mussorgsky's *'Promenade'* from his *'Pictures at an Exhibition'*. The strains of the music were a welcome contrast to the prevailing artillery and machine-gun fire, and Nicholas was quick to exploit the new situation. Next morning he presented himself to the music-loving general and offered Irene's services to cook him a 'welcoming Hungarian meal'. He would assist.

The general took to the family. He was an intelligent and kind man, a linguist, who would never miss a German radio broadcast. 'I get a better picture of what's going on than from ours,' he would say openly. He was immaculately dressed and demanded the same from his immediate retinue, including his 'political officer', who never seemed to be too far away.

After the third dinner that Nicholas and Irene had served up for the officers he felt in a strong enough position to bring up the problem of the poor, still incarcerated Ruth, and the horrendous stories of mass rapes during the short lull in the fighting. He came to the point, telling the general that the family had been sheltering two Jews, a small boy and a beautiful teenager, whom he had been hiding to avoid her being raped. In his answer the general was sympathetic and indicated that he knew of the problem of the drunk soldiers, but he added that this was a nasty war and he could not discipline the whole of the army. In any event, she could now come out of the cellar because the offensive on the Castle was to start in the morning. With the rest of Buda already taken, he envisaged less than two weeks' fighting, and the army would not have time to be raping anybody, at least until it was all over.

At four in the morning the family was woken up by the artillery fire, which announced the beginning of the last battle for the capital. This was followed by noisy, whistling rockets, criss-crossing all over the place. Some incendiary bullets started a fire in the Royal Palace, which turned the whole magnificent romantic building into a fireball, rendering it a pitiful skeleton within an hour. Adam, watching the destruction of the largest and arguably one of the finest palaces in the world, stared in total amazement from his vantage point right in front of the house. The orange-red flames on the top of Castle Hill reached the sky, its occupants evacuating the building, which had protected them from the slowly advancing thousands of Russians. He could just see them all regrouping outside the building – Germans and Hungarians, no friends of each other, but united in battle against the masses of Bolsheviks who were taking the ground from under their very feet, inch by inch. The end could not be far off. The building just behind and slightly north of the palace was the Ministry of Defence and was packed with ammunition.

General Volkov ordered his radio officer to instruct the artillery to concentrate the shelling on it. Adam saw the changing direction of the fire. The solid, thick-walled building held for a short while before an almighty explosion sent the roof in thousands of directions.

The confusion among the defending forces was exacerbated by the fire raging at Royal Palace. More soldiers ran out on to the plateau in front of it and grouped around the large equestrian statue of Prince Eugen of Savoy, the liberator of the city from Ottoman Turkish rule some two hundred and fifty years before. He could be of no help now.

Just below them, at the foot of the hill, the Russians were gathering for the final assault in ever-increasing strength. The taking of the Castle would be their task. Full of vodka, their source of Dutch courage, they were raring to go. General Volkov was to direct the southern and part of the eastern attack from his turret. He could see Adam sitting at the side of the road with his legs dangling down the hill, ignoring his mother's umpteenth demand to come back into the house. Irene decided that it was time for some fatherly intervention, and told Nicholas to bring the boy in. He had started to walk in Adam's direction when he noticed a Russian soldier running towards him dangling a set of binoculars. The startled Nicholas just watched while the powerful Zeiss Ikon equipment was placed around his son's neck to allow him to observe the battle in the raw. Adam looked towards the turret and saw the general nodding to him. Nicholas saw no point in trying to bring him back now as he was having such a 'good war'. He just told the poor worrying Irene to 'let him watch history in the making'.

Through the heavy binoculars the boy could see the gathering Russians on three sides of the hill, his best view being to the Buda side of the totally destroyed Chain Bridge, where they were starting to walk up the winding pathway. Some of them had opted for the short cut and started to climb up by the tracks of the now bombed-out funicular. He could see the German and Hungarian machine guns aimed at them, holding their fire until the order was given; this came just five minutes later. The three guns opened up in unison, decimating the attackers. The next wave of infantry was to follow within minutes, then the third, fourth … and the tenth. The carnage was complete, the corpses strewn everywhere, making the work of the next wave of attacking soldiers even more difficult.

Turning his head towards the battle in the north-west section, where a tank battle was causing a rout in the Russian advance, Adam observed the Hungarian retreat towards the John Hospital and to his amazement he saw a young boy just a few years older than himself dressed in a Hungarian military cadet uniform zigzagging across the rubble and between the burned-out war machines with a small package under his arm, which he passed on to an officer some distance away. The brave little messenger in his early teens appeared to be quite an expert in finding cover when he needed it. His running made a lifelong impression on Adam, and he would have given anything to be in his uniform. He sighed and had to be content with his lot; just to observe the great siege, perhaps the least-sung-about episode of the war.

The defence against the Russians was to last until they had run out of ammunition, which happened the next day. When the last bullet was fired, they sat down amongst their guns and waited for certain death. When the Russians appeared on top of the plateau they were in no mood to take prisoners, they just gunned them down where they sat on the cobblestones. Swinging his binoculars to the left, Adam saw a group of Jews being herded along the western road towards the Castle by a gang of Arrow Cross thugs. A motorcyclist drew up and spoke to their leader. A few minutes later all the Jews were gunned down on the spot. Amazingly, they still had ammunition for these atrocities, although not for fighting. Nicholas was to find out later that the victims were the patients and medical staff of Maros Street Jewish Hospital. With this act the despicable thugs achieved the total extermination of all the Jewry of Buda.

Part of the Castle had been taken, the rest was soon to follow, and by 13 February the whole of the city was in Russian hands. The raping and looting restarted in earnest and lasted for many weeks.

General Volkov, in a more civilised mood, sat down at the Steinway and played Prokofiev's Seventh Piano Sonata as his celebration. He asked whether he could take Adam in his personal car to visit his friend, tank commander Colonel Vasiliev. Nicholas agreed and the boy went away with the general. At the western foot of the hill, where he had seen the cadet, some thirty T-34s lined the side of the road. The colonel saluted the general and invited him to inspect some of the devastation. They climbed on to the gun turret, sitting Adam in front of it. The powerful engine was started up. The driver held the left transmission still, allowing the right one to move forward. They were soon in the middle of the road, driving towards the total carnage that was once the proud Castle of Buda. The turret just managed to hold the two men but it was awkward for Adam, who, by now, had slipped down to ride on the 700mm gun, smiling at the officers in appreciation. From that moment, and in spite of the devastation, the boy considered the war a source of fun. As the tank entered the Western Gate the horror of it all faced them. Dead bodies in the hardly recognisable army uniforms of Hungary, Germany and Russia lay everywhere. Rotting horses alongside them were confirmation, if it were needed, of what had been happening in the last few months.

～

When the general's car turned left into Orom Street they saw some strange soldiers, drunk and staggering around the house. Aaron was running out of the house screaming. He grabbed hold of the general's sleeve and pointed to the open gate. Volkov, sensing something unusual, started walking towards the open front door, closely followed by Adam. In the hall, two soldiers were holding on to Nicholas, his face bleeding badly, while another two had pinned the six-months-pregnant Irene to the marble floor, her floral-printed front-buttoning dress torn to shreds. The general wasted no time. He took his service revolver and shot into the ceiling. The soldiers' mayhem was instantly transformed into total silence. Then he turned towards the one who had his trousers pushed down to his knees and shot into his thigh, shattering the femur. The man yelled in agony. The general shouted a few words of command and the soldiers let go of Nicholas, who ran to Irene, picking her up from the floor. Ruth opened the kitchen door and put her head out fearfully. She saw the soldiers scrambling down the stone steps, dragging the screaming beast along with them.

General Volkov put his revolver into his dark brown leather holster and walked back to the red house. A few minutes later some fierce chords of Rachmaninov were heard by the Zentas.

14

PEACE

The new Provisional Government of Hungary eventually established itself in the battered Parliament building and began rebuilding some sort of nation from the ashes. Its composition was a curious mixture of adherents to the old regime, some democrats trying to establish a new and more modern country, and the communists, who had arrived on the back of the tanks from Moscow. The former subconsciously knew that they stood no chance, the centrist democrats were convinced that they were the primary choice of the country, and only the communists knew that in the not-so-long run they would prevail. They were acquainted with the real secrets of the disgusting Yalta Agreement, which cast the land into the Soviet sphere of interest.

Nicholas' activities in saving so many Jews had become common knowledge amongst those who mattered. The just-right-of-centre Smallholders Party wanted a presidential candidate and he became one of their main choices. Nicholas was not well known to some of the old hands but the younger members of the party, being conscious of the necessity of Jewish support in the future, wanted him above everyone else. When the decrepit black Mercedes and the rickety Skoda arrived at Orom Street at the beginning of March in the late afternoon, Ruth was sweeping the curving stone steps of the villa.

'Is this the residence of Nicholas Zenta?' Asked the man in the ill-fitting dark grey suit.

'Yes, he's in the garden behind the house,' said the now totally self-assured dark beauty. As a gesture she was wearing the Star of David for a few days, having hidden it for the past two years.

The man walked to the back of the house to find Nicholas. 'Zenta, my pleasure.' Nicholas offered his hand to the strangers.

'A delegation from the Smallholders. May we come in and talk with you, sir?'

'Of course! How can I possibly help you?' Nicholas asked.

The serious-looking men walked into the splendid villa, took off their hats and coats and entered the spacious lounge. They made themselves comfortable in the leather armchairs, their leader lighting his chubby pipe. In the anteroom next door Adam could hear every word clearly.

'Mr Zenta, by all accounts you appear to be a very special person and a very brave one,' the man started without hesitation. 'My party, and I hope it's your party too, is enjoying the widest support in the land. We must make sure that Hungary takes a turn towards democracy and we need a charismatic head to be put forward for the presidency, which will be elected by the Parliament we control. I might as well be totally open with you. You are our number-one choice because you are a model Hungarian and you did not get tainted as a Nazi sympathiser during the war. The other one is Zoltán Tildy. Please do us the honour and let us put your name forward as our candidate.' The grey-haired man took two puffs from his pipe in quick succession, blowing great gusts of smoke into the air.

'Gentlemen, I don't believe what I am hearing. If you, all of you, did not look so serious I would think it was a joke. You do me a great honour even to consider me, and believe you me, that is very kind, but I know myself more than you do and I do know that I am not the man to be your presidential candidate. Besides, I happen to think that the Reverend Tildy would be the perfect choice. I would personally like to support him.'

The serious men from the Smallholders Party continued to try to persuade him to reconsider, but Nicholas became more dismissive of the whole idea.

'As a matter of fact I have to present myself at the Ministry of the Interior first thing in the morning. I hear that they have some designs on me as a Chief Constable for one of the counties. I think that's more in my line.' He stood up and shook hands with the serious gentlemen.

The cars had hardly turned right at the bottom of the street when Adam ran to him.

'Dad! They wanted you to be President and you said no! Why?' He asked excitedly.

'Adam, now listen to me! Not a word about this to anyone – I mean friends or strangers. This meeting here tonight must stay a family secret. Promise.' Nicholas glared at his son.

'But why, Dad? Why?' The boy nagged.

'Adam, I don't want to hear one more word about it. Come, let's go and eat, I'm hungry.' He ruffled his son's hair.

The dinner conversation was about the visitors. Everybody offered an opinion. Irene – very much against the idea; Ruth – undecided, but mainly against it. Adam and Aaron were very disappointed not to be moving into the presidential villa. Kathleen was asleep.

∽

Next morning Nicholas was duly appointed Chief Constable of the southern county of Baranya and told to move to Pécs as soon as possible. As the family possessed absolutely nothing other than their well-worn clothes, he was very sincere when he told the new minister that the family could leave at a moment's notice. He received half of his first month's salary in advance and a letter of passage for the rail journey. On a separate piece of paper there was a hastily typed address; the new Zenta home, number 3, Flower Street. Just as he had in Budapest, he wondered for a moment about its previous owner, then shrugged his shoulders. Who might be living in his house in Transylvania now? Some Romanian, no doubt. So it didn't really matter, did it?

∽

The small stone-and-brick villa on the slopes of the Mecsek mountain, just a twenty-minute walk north of the city centre, , alas uphill, was in every way perfect for them. Built in the style of the twenties it had lovely modern features and facilities and yet it retained some romantic ideas too, like a honey-coloured stone wall on one side of the dining room encircling the inviting fireplace and a very large semicircular covered patio overlooking the city. Right in the middle of the view below them was the Romanesque cathedral with four spires.

He soon found out that the previous owners, a businessman and his family, were on a western tour when the war broke out. They had not been heard of since, so the police had requisitioned the house pending their return. The villa was fully furnished with a combination of modern and antique furniture. With only a nominal rent to pay the Zenta family suddenly found themselves living in more than acceptable circumstances. Nicholas had his army uniform cleaned and wore it for work. From his advance Irene bought some fabric to fill the gaping inadequacies in everybody's wardrobe, just before she was admitted to No. 1 Obstetrics Clinic. Within a week Anna, weighing six and a half pounds, better than the average war baby's size, entered the world – a beautiful baby with blue eyes and noticeably Hungarian features.

The next few years promised a stable life in the new democracy. Zoltán Tildy was duly elected President. Nicholas was much teased about it within the family, who called him Mr President, at least when out of earshot of strangers. Nicholas immersed himself in his new work. He had to recruit police personnel, change some of the organisational procedures, introduce new techniques, set up new departments and even take part in the work of a national committee set up to design the new uniforms. This he enjoyed immensely, and he brought home various sketches of designs night after night. Naturally, Irene and Ruth had been instrumental in choosing the one he eventually recommended, which was finally accepted by the Ministry of the Interior. It was quite an inspired hybrid, a virtual copy of the British bobby's outfit, including tie and helmet, except for the colour. They decided on medium grey. Another small difference was the tailoring of the trousers, which fitted inside the ankle boots with a strap under the soles of the feet; a concession to muddy side streets. He received a commemorative medal and a handsome cash prize for it.

In June 1945 Nicholas was sitting behind his desk, walled in by paperwork, when his middle-aged and extremely loyal and hard-working secretary called him on the intercom. She announced that an American major from the US Control Commission, a small token organisation set up by the Yalta Agreement to run parallel with the huge one of the Soviet Union in Budapest, was on the telephone.

'Is that Major Zenta?' A vaguely familiar voice enquired.

'It is he. To whom am I speaking?' Nicholas asked in turn.

'Nicholas, this is Joseph Grunnfeld, Major Joseph Grunnfeld, or to be absolutely correct, Joseph *Greenfield*. I Anglicised my name,' the excited voice explained.

'Well, how about that! Just at the time when your children were about to become Zenta de Lemhény,' Nicholas joked.

'I know you better than to believe that, Nicholas Zenta – how are they?'

'Why don't you get on the express train and see them tonight? Is Ruby with you?'

'No. She is on an ocean liner from America. They flew me over in a Liberator. I am here to make sure that you get some decent democracy, at long last. I am acting as legal adviser to the Commission,' Joseph explained. 'And you are right, Nicholas, I'll do just that. I should be with you for dinner. What's your address?'

Nicholas telephoned Irene and told her to expect a surprise guest for dinner, but maintained that she did not know him. In the hope that she would keep away from pork he tried to be a little diplomatic in suggesting she get some veal in because he knew the guest loved *pörkölt*, the spicy Hungarian ragout.

Joseph arrived on the late afternoon express from Budapest and queued for a taxi, only to be told that the county police station was actually only a hundred yards away, across the road. His American uniform with its beige, light coat created a stir in the provincial railway terminal. He picked up his brown leather overnight bag and started the short walk. When he asked the sentry standing outside the heavy wooden gate to be directed to 'his chief', the man on duty saluted and said, 'First floor, Major, right in the middle – you can't miss it.' Within a minute the two majors were in a friendly embrace.

'Before you say anything, Nicholas,' Greenfield pulled his crisp linen handkerchief, monogrammed *J.G.*, out of his beige trouser pocket to blow his nose and wipe his eyes, 'can I just say '

'No, Joseph, please, please don't say anything. It's all over, thank God. Let me take you to your children.'

Greenfield dropped his head to his chest for a moment, then placed both his hands on Nicholas' shoulders. 'Zenta, you are one hell of a fellow. I cannot think of anyone who could have pulled off your blatant bluff. I've heard about the way you delivered a truckload of my people to Üllői Street, brushing aside the Arrow Cross.'

'Come on, Joseph, don't let's talk about it! I was lucky with them, that's all.' Nicholas walked to the corner of the room and put on his overcoat.

The two men walked into the courtyard of the large police station, past the cells full of muggers and drunks, to the small black Skoda saloon, where the driver was already waiting for them. He saluted smartly and opened the rear door for the American.

'Home, sir?' The corporal asked Nicholas, who just nodded to him.

'I know it's only been a year, but you do look very different in your American uniform. They will be in for the surprise of their lives.'

The early summer evening found the Zenta family on the large semicircular patio. They could see the black car pulling up and the two men in uniform getting out. There was nothing unusual in Nicholas bringing someone for supper. As the two men walked along the pebbled path, the stones under their feet shifted noisily. Through the thick distorting glass of the front door Ruth could see only the outline of the two peaked caps. She opened the door and said 'Hello' to Nicholas. She directed her glance to the unusual uniform, ignoring the face of the man now standing right before her. She was about to turn away when the familiar voice said, 'Hello, Ruth, darling, hello.'

Ruth raised her face towards him and met the dark eyes of the stranger, who had taken off his peaked cap. The scream could have been heard throughout their half of the city.

'Daddy! Daddy! Aarooooon! Come here right away! Oh, Daddy!' Ruth melted into her father's arms, sobbing uncontrollably.

'Let me look at you, darling, I had forgotten how beautiful you were.' Joseph's arms were shaking.

Aaron ran in, followed by the inevitable Adam.

'Daddy, hello! Where's Mother? Is she all right?' The boy threw his arms around his father, burying his face amongst the brass buttons of the brown tunic. Then Irene greeted him enthusiastically. Finally, Adam offered his hand, but he too received a demonstrative cuddle. Kathleen, not really understanding the commotion, continued playing with her toys. Anna woke and started crying. Order had to be re-established, and only Joseph could do that, by standing to protect Nicholas from the two women who were about to lynch him for keeping such a secret.

'This sort of thing could give one a heart attack!' said Irene, trying to reach her husband. 'You should have told me who you were bringing.'

'Surely you never expected me to do that?' He smiled as he was drew back from Ruth and Irene. 'All right, all right, I'm sorry, let's have a drink, all of us.'

They settled on the patio and Nicholas opened a bottle of Törley *sec*, the Hungarian *méthode champenoise*. Joseph cuddled his children with tears in his eyes whilst Irene prepared the glasses. Then he stood up, raising his full glass, and simply declared, 'To a truly great Hungarian and the beloved Zenta family, who saved us all!'

The embarrassed Nicholas quite rightly saw no point in trying to stop his guest proposing the toast, which echoed repeatedly into the early evening. When they eventually managed to sit down to the veal ragout, Aaron, ever so proud to see *his* father in uniform, confidently declared that on this occasion at least they were not eating 'pretend veal'. The evening belonged to the Greenfields. First it was Aaron, then Ruth, who talked about the experiences of the past year. Naturally, the train journey and the siege of Buda featured highly in their stories. Joseph had no chance to talk until they had emptied their heads of their overflowing memories, ever returning to 'when Nicholas did this' or 'when Nicholas did that'. Their favourite was the opening of the wagon door for less than a minute near the warehouse, allowing the escape of the fittest. Eventually they had to be stopped by Irene reminding them that their father also had a story to tell.

And what a story it turned out to be.

The taxi taking the 'Spanish couple' to Vásárhely railway station gave Joseph the last private chance to strengthen Ruby's resolve to go through with the scheme; a difficult and harrowing decision for a mother of a close-knit Jewish family, made momentarily worse when the driver decided to take a short cut, passing the house they had rented until the Iron Guard turned up and they had to leave. She opened her mouth to gasp, but Joseph, knowing what was coming, transformed her cry into a deep gurgle with the palm of his hand. The driver, mistaking the episode for a muffled cry of fear, offered to slow down in anticipation of a better tip. Joseph said, *'Gracias, señor,'* and whispered a Yiddish encouragement into Ruby's ears. The taxi driver helped the porter to pack the luggage on to his battered handcart and received his tip. He smartly clicked his heels and threw his right arm out int a Fascist salute. *'Viva España, Viva el Caudillo!'*

His loud appreciation of the few extra pengős attracted the attention of the duty policeman. Thinking he too could be a beneficiary of similar gratitude, he gave the travelling documents the most cursory examination and added a *'Viva Franco!'* For good measure.

The train journey took them five hours and they arrived at the Western Railway Station in Budapest. The taxi ride to the Duna Hotel was swift and uneventful. The Spaniards were very much liked as a nation in Hungary, therefore it would take a very determined person to harass one. There was no reason to doubt anything about the stylish couple who were so friendly to the reception staff, tipped well, and gave nobody much trouble.

Next morning, the second stage of their journey was planned to take them to Graz in southern Austria. This was part of the Reich, and thus it was to be a more difficult trip. The train would take them to Vienna, where they would have to change. After leaving Hungary, the whole trip would be amongst Germans, with large numbers of military personnel moving to and fro. Ruby, worrying about her children, naturally became gloomy from time to time, but Joseph would notice and remind her that they were a travelling couple and a very happy one at that. With Hungary being under official German occupation all travel papers were cleared on embarkation at the Eastern Railway Station. The railway guard was happy with the tickets and reminded them about the change of stations in Vienna. The man standing next to him wasn't so sure.

'What happened to your passports, señor?' He asked with a piercing look.

'Some Gypsies stole my briefcase in Transylvania, and the authorities there gave ...'

'Ah, in Siebenburgen!' the man interrupted, using the German name of the principality. 'Yes, it's full of them, but what was the nature of your visit there?' He looked at Joseph again.

'I was reporting the most well-arranged tactical withdrawal in the history of warfare. Most impressive, I must say.' 'José Gomez' smiled. 'My card, sir.' He handed it to the Gestapo man. 'It started as a holiday. We got stuck in the mountains, but I managed to get through to my editor who told me to send some dispatches.'

'*El País*, eh? Influential newspaper, a bit too neutral for our liking.' The man looked at Grunnfeld again.

'We have to be, but you know full well where our heart lies! In any case, I've just finished an article about the Spanish Volunteer Division, I'm taking it to Vienna for dispatch.'

'Very good, very good.' The secret policeman took his wallet from his inside pocket and placed the calling card next to some counterfeit dollars before waving them through.

The well-dressed foreigners settled into the first-class coach in a bench-seat compartment with an older Hungarian couple already sitting at the corridor side. The elderly man offered the Grunnfelds the window seat in broken German. His 'wife did not like to sit by it', he said. Great, Joseph thought, less chance to converse.

The train pulled out of the station and Joseph noticed a man with a wide-brimmed hat jumping on to the steps of the last coach. A split second later and he would have missed it.

Leaving the hills of Buda behind them, they travelled virtually due west. Ruby looked at her husband anxiously. He started to speak in Spanish to her so as to prevent her from using any other language during the course of the trip. The older couple certainly looked baffled but Joseph now had the chance to explain to Ruby what he had just seen out of the window. He told her to expect some sort of a trap and not to react to anything. He decided to go to the toilet, the farthest one towards the end of the train. He hadn't gone too far when he saw the Gestapo man in the company of a black-uniformed SS thug and an Hungarian gendarme checking papers in the third-class coach. He turned around and hurried back to his compartment.

The three men moved slowly through the masses of people amongst the wooden seats of the third-class coach, trying to trap escaping Jews. Their trick was simple, but effective. The gendarme would go ahead, look at the papers of the travellers and report to the two Germans. If they suspected somebody of trying to pretend not to be a Hungarian, the gendarme would say something to shock and the other two would watch the reaction like hawks. Ruby and Joseph were looking out of their window when the gendarme arrived, brushing his cockerel-feathered black hat against the top of the door frame. He saluted the passengers and asked for their papers, politely. The old couple handed over their passports and the Gestapo man, just out of sight, nodded approval. Then Grunnfeld handed over his letter of passage. Seeing it in the hands of the gendarme, the Gestapo man indicated to him to test this one. The gendarme moved out of sight and the two Germans moved into the door frame to look at the Spanish couple. Grunnfeld was gazing out of the window when a large warehouse came into view and the darkened background showed a reflection of the two men in the window. Noticing this, Joseph squeezed Ruby's hand, which he was holding. The gendarme shouted loudly, 'Arrest that Jew there, quick!' The elderly couple's heads turned towards the door in unison. The Spanish ones kept looking at the rolling countryside.

The Gestapo man's face grimaced in frustration; he had to be satisfied – for the moment.

The change of stations in Vienna was uneventful. The taxi ride reacquainted them with the city they were so fond of. Compared to Budapest, here one could hardly believe there was a war going on. The Ring was untouched by the ravages of war and the people were as elegant as ever, still reflecting the old cliché that in Vienna no one dresses out of season, or out of place. Fortunately, the equally well-dressed Grunnfelds blended to perfection.

The train to Klagenfurt was a smaller, more local one, without the bustle of the international express full of locals returning from shopping in Vienna. Dressed fashionably, the Grunnfelds became more obvious, especially as they were speaking in Spanish. Joseph still had to keep telling Ruby to smile and be more cheerful once in a while. The mountain scenery soon became breathtaking. The proud overspill of Tyrol and the Semmering Pass and the fact that there was no obvious Gestapo activity relaxed the couple for the moment. They could almost be what they were pretending to be, just ordinary travellers.

Klagenfurt was a bustling yet small city of southern Austria. Introspective and insular, the people here had little in common with the crazed corporal who was running – and in their opinion losing – the war for them.

Here, the Grunnfelds had to change on to the Italian train that was to take them to Udine, through the frontier crossing of Tarvisio. Axis allies in the war or not, both sides were keen to assert themselves and controlled the station with eagerness. Trains from both nations alternated on the single-track line. The travellers were a cross-section of the geography of the terrain – Alpine shepherds and peasants, soldiers, policemen, *carabinieri* and many deserters. All of the latter were Italians. The frontier guards were keen to catch escapers but they concentrated on men of possible call-up age.

The Germans, of course, were still obsessed with catching Jews. They had had a spate of them during the early spring, most of them fit young men on the run. When the Grunnfelds presented their well-used travelling documents, printed by Nicholas in the back room of his office, they were taken aback and concentrated on the legality of the papers themselves, rather than the people they pertained to. When they checked with their superiors the answer was that they were acceptable documents. This happened once again at the German post and they then passed over to the Italian side. Once there, the Italian guard suggested that the Spanish consulate in Trieste would issue them with new passports.

José Gomez naturally agreed with him and thanked the soldier for the idea. When the train eventually started off in the direction of Udine the couple on the run were visibly relieved. Whatever could happen to them now that they were in Latin jurisdiction of muddled carelessness and bribability?

Udine was a beautiful, well-kept town in a valley tucked into the foot of the Alps. It was full of fair-haired Italians with less of the extrovert mannerisms one would attribute to their more southern brethren. In the covered walkways, supported by magnificent columns, the Grunnfelds could mingle with the rest who, up till now, had had no taste of the war. The shops were reasonably stocked and the coffee contained much less chicory than in the rest of Europe.

Joseph enquired about travel possibilities to Trieste, only to be told that there weren't any. Mussolini may have made the Italian trains run on time but he clearly forgot about Udine. He was eventually told to try at the post office. They had somebody going there regularly who might be able to help. The somebody turned out to be a fellow who took the mail there on a motorbike. Whilst Ruby was sipping her coffee, Joseph walked over to the post office, worrying about the journey to the port. The man behind the desk took more than a passing interest in the fairly affluent-looking traveller, reassuring him that he need not to worry. He had a motorbike with a large sidecar, even a hood in case of rain. After all, they were near the Adriatic sea. Hearing this, Joseph became interested, and when he opened his wallet and showed some Swiss francs he knew that a bargain could be struck.

By mid-afternoon they had strapped the suitcase on the back of the sidecar and placed the smaller items around Ruby's legs. With Joseph as pillion on the Moto Guzzi, they set off south towards the distant sea.

After about four hours of dusty motorcycle riding Trieste suddenly came into view. They still had to turn off the main road to call into some hamlet to deliver an item or two. Eventually the driver managed to get them to the port and they alighted outside the harbour master's ornate cream-coloured office building. They had to dust themselves down. Standing on the pavement, Joseph spotted a cast-iron bench about thirty yards from the entrance and carried their suitcase to it, telling Ruby to wait there for him.

In the large office with the biggest cheese plant ever in the corner by the window, the harbour came into perfect view. He was relieved to see some boats with both Spanish and Portuguese flags. He needed a neutral ship. Most merchant carriers were only too willing to take a few fare-paying passengers. He was offered a Portuguese ship to Lisbon and two Spanish ones to Barcelona or Málaga. The harbour master was a little surprised to hear that a Spaniard preferred to go to Lisbon, but Joseph explained that there was an incident going on there between the British and German embassies over the washed-up body of an English officer, carrying possible classified material regarding invasion plans, and he wanted to report it. Besides, he added for good measure, the wife's folks lived in Cádiz and it was easier to get there from Lisbon than from Barcelona. The real reason was that the ship sailed later that day and there were more American ships in Lisbon than in any other port.

Ruby was delighted with the news. She had not been looking forward to speaking Spanish with the crew on a native ship.

On their arrival in the Portuguese capital, which was, at the time, the busiest civil port in the world, they got the taxi driver to take them to the American Embassy. In the taxi Ruby unpicked the lining of her fashionable satin hat to get at the other travelling documents that had been provided by Nicholas' simple press, describing them as US citizens. They were not going to fool mighty America with them, but they had to get past the Portuguese sentry before seeing the GI.

Having done so, they asked for political asylum, and within a week they were aboard a Panamanian ship on their way to New York.

On their arrival, the immigration officer, noticing Grunnfeld's name on the brand-new passports issued by the Lisbon Embassy, pressed the button beside his left knee, summoning the FBI agent from the other side of the harbour office. He introduced himself and asked the couple to follow him to start their debriefing immediately. Joseph put on a sparkling performance in four European languages. His knowledge of Romania and Hungary impressed his questioners. Ruby accounted for her side of the story equally well. Within a week Joseph was asked to join the OSS with the rank of major. Ruby was given an apartment in the Bronx and was introduced to other Eastern European Jews. She was not at all surprised when during their second weekend in America, Joseph told her that he was to fly to England. During their goodbye he whispered into her ear, 'I am going to get our children, Ruby.' She just nodded with tearful eyes. 'Please do, darling, bring them home.'

By then called Greenfield, Joseph worked as a strategist for commando groups. He ended up in Munich after the collapse of the Reich and worked tirelessly, at first as one of the American officers who interviewed and debriefed Admiral Horthy. The old man and his family made such an immediate impression on him that he was unhesitating when he declared that not only did Horthy have no charge to answer at the Nuremberg War Crimes Tribunal, but that he should be recommended to appear as an Allied witness. Later, when the ex-Regent and his family were allowed to settle in the lovely seaside town of Estoril, just north of Lisbon, he became one of his many Jewish benefactors, right until the end of the grand old man's life. When the American Control Commission was formed, Greenfield asked for a Budapest posting and had arrived in the capital a week earlier. It did not take him too long to find Nicholas Zenta in Pécs.

15

END TWO

When Joseph came to the end of his story none of them could believe the time. It was well into the early hours of the morning when Aaron asked yet another 'last question'. Quite rightly, he considered that after months of Adam it was *his* turn to gloat about *his* father, and nobody argued. Eventually, it fell to Irene to assert herself about it being time to head for bed.

The two men could not resist talking a little more politics and drinking some more wine from Villány.

'You know, I have only been here for a short time, but I am already full of bad vibes at what's happening.' Joseph's words startled Nicholas.

'What do you mean? For God's sake, we have a good chance to be a parliamentary democracy and with a right-of-centre government, it suits me fine,' Nicholas answered with genuine surprise.

'I really don't know how to say this. Something really nasty is brewing. No, I correct myself – it's being brewed! You know all those Muscovite communists led by Rákosi?' Joseph asked his startled host.

'Of course I know them, a nasty bunch of commies, but you know, few will vote for them – no chance!' Nicholas dismissed the idea with a gesture.

'Well, let me tell you that it is an open secret in the Control Commission that they are unstoppable. They will use quasi-constitutional means to get into power and that will be it. Look, Nicholas, believe me, Rákosi said it to my face at a reception.' Joseph lowered his head into his hands. 'But you know what upsets me most?' he asked. 'Over ninety per cent of their leaders are Jews! My people, Nicholas, do you understand?' He looked his friend in the eye.

'Thank God I didn't get involved in the politics of it all. We will be all right here in the provinces, we probably won't notice these changes.' Nicholas patted Joseph on his shoulder.

'Keep away from them, they are vile and awful people.' Joseph emphasised every word.

'Come on, I think it's time for bed for us too.' Nicholas put his arm around his friend's shoulder and showed him to his room.

~

The next day brought the tearful departure of the Greenfield family from Pécs. The Zentas settled into a period of day-to-day existence. Nicholas was busy at work, trying to make some sort of a police force with the limited resources he was given. Irene's life was serene and simple. She had always dreamed of becoming a lady of leisure, to read and perhaps even to write, yet she was lucky if she managed to put her feet up for a short while. She kept her slender figure well but her hair was greying rapidly, and because of the poor quality of hair dyes available, she decided not to do anything about that and left it to nature. Young Adam had to be happy with going to school and forgetting about army and air force hardware for the time being. It was algebra and Latin and plenty of homework, lots and lots of it. Kathleen was about to finish kindergarten and go to elementary school. She was a pretty little blonde with inquisitive eyes. Anna was happy just to pull every item on to the floor, no matter where others had put it before.

Winter came and Nicholas had to work late hours. Irene and the twelve-year-old Adam grew ever closer to each other in the long evenings. There was a lot of missed schooling to pick up and Irene's innate intelligence and good education were an invaluable help to Adam. They would talk very openly with no subject being barred, including the current love affair of the operetta soubrette of the local National Theatre, which happened to be featured in the daily newspapers. Then it was back to literature or, even worse, spelling. The school leaned towards the arts and humanities and demanded an inordinate amount of poetry recitation. Adam took to it with ease, learning by heart whilst walking up and down the room. He worked out a password for the two of them in the shape of a silly little rhyme: '*Where is the happiness, you might desire?*' The other one would have to answer: '*In a cosy room with you, working by the fire!*' It would haunt him later in his life.

Christmas Eve 1946 was a splendid one in every way, reflecting the harmonious life of a very contented family, full of hope for the future. In contrast with the year before there was once again a tall pine tree in the house, full of beautiful decorations and lots of proper presents underneath. As custom dictated, the tinkling of a bell declared the departure of the angels who had left the Christmas tree behind with all the presents on behalf of Baby Jesus. This was played out for the benefit of Kathleen mainly, but Adam loved the whole thing just as much. They would all enter the lounge together to savour the smell of the burning candles and the pine needles, a moment that would last for the whole year in the memory of the children. Presents were opened at midnight and they would stay up until the early hours.

Nicholas woke early on Christmas morning and reached out for Irene, who responded by turning towards him. They kissed and cuddled and made love – quietly, as Adam's room was right next to theirs. Adam was always aware of their lovemaking, which made him feel warm, happy and contented. Anyway, all he could think about was the pair of wooden ex-army-issue skis he had received for Christmas, courtesy of the police force storekeeper. The Mecsek mountain was just behind the house and the snow was good that year.

In the calming aftermath of their lovemaking, Nicholas was gently caressing Irene's right breast when his hand suddenly stopped. He went still for a moment, then moved his two middle fingers gently. Yes, he felt a lump, about three-quarters of an inch long. He gently withdrew his hand and looked at the ceiling.

'You felt it too?' Irene asked softly. 'It's been there about a month, I think.' She turned towards her husband to observe the look on his face. 'It's probably nothing, darling, but we'll have it checked out.'

The surgeon asked Irene to remove her blouse and bra and sit with her back straight. He was observing the contour of the two breasts, noticing a slight indentation of the upper outer quadrant on the right side. He asked her to lift her arms up, then lower them slowly, then he moved to stand behind her. Irene seated on a chair he lowered his hands and with the palm of his hand carefully examined the left breast, then the armpit, then the same on the right side, pinching the skin over the small but significant lump and noticing some adhesion to it.

'Well, Mrs Zenta, you do seem to have a lump in your breast, as you say.' He looked at her through his pince-nez. 'Having just had a child not so long ago, it could well be benign. In any event, we must operate. I propose to do it on my next list, this Friday.' He scribbled a note to himself.

'What would you propose to do, Doctor?' Irene asked apprehensively.

'Normally, we would keep you under ether whilst the histological examination is made, but we have a problem, so I will do an excision of the lump only.'

Irene was elated with the news; she was naturally concerned about the more radical surgery of mastectomy. She was delighted that they had only a 'problem', and she did not enquire as to what it was.

On Thursday evening Nicholas was working late and Irene was helping with Adam's homework. Her concentration wandered for a moment and she bent down to grab Adam as he lay on his stomach on the rug by the giant tile-covered fireplace.

'My darling boy, I know I am going to die soon,' she whispered. 'Remember the day back home when I fired at the owl and missed?' They all referred to Transylvania as 'home'. 'Well, the old saying that it would bring death is true, it will be my death!'

Adam was shocked by the outburst and thought it futile to argue with his mother. He got up to kneel in front of Irene and they embraced in a flood of tears. At that moment Kathleen entered the room and ran over to them both. She joined them in the embrace and started to cry without knowing the reason why.

Under the dreadful smell of the simple ether anaesthetic the surgeon once again felt the threatening lump and shook his head. He examined the armpit once more with more concentration, then the pits around the collarbone.

'There is nothing there,' he murmured to his assistant, 'we will do an extended lumpectomy.'

'Why not a radical mastectomy, sir?' The younger man asked, sounding assured.

'Well, I never do that in the absence of supraclavicular or axillary lymphatic involvement. Besides, I hate mutilating women.' He started to scrub up, knowing that he had not convinced his younger colleague.

The confident incision of the old surgeon followed the exact line of the breast, along its outer edge. He proceeded to dissect the skin and took away the area which, he felt, was adhering to the mass underneath. Taking a good portion of subcutaneous connective tissue, he worked his way around the lump, including some of the normal breast tissue around it. He took out the small mass and rolled it between his fingers, to feel its consistency, noticing the curiosity of his assistant.

'How does it feel, sir?'

'It is fairly hard and circumscribed. What do you think?' He handed the lump to his subordinate.

'Agree, sir, probably the scirrhus type – she stands a vague chance.'

'Suture up, please.' The surgeon gave his assistant the usual order and walked out of the theatre, taking his rubber gloves off along the way.

Nicholas was waiting for him in the anteroom.

'How did it go, Doctor?' He asked anxiously.

'Oh, very well, Major, very well. Your wife will make a complete recovery, very soon.' He tried to reassure what to him was just another worried husband.

'But what about the long term?' Nicholas was not quite satisfied with the answer.

'Well now, sadly, I cannot be too sure about that. The outcome of this disease is most unpredictable. The important thing was that I did not find any obvious glandular involvement. That gives us *some* hope.' The old surgeon shook his hand, signalling the end of the discussion.

Irene did 'make a complete recovery very soon'. Within a week she was at home performing household chores, looking after the family and being the inspiration behind Adam's homework. Her operation scar became slightly infected near the area where the lump had been nearest to the skin, and this did not please the younger surgeon who was looking after her follow-up. The family prospered, and by 1948 stability was totally evident in every sense of the word. They had a good middle-class status and the only cloud on the horizon was, naturally, the possible recurrence of Irene's disease. She was the least concerned, and much more interested in the progress of her children.

∼

A year and a half later Irene's cancer did recur. She was gardening when she felt the pain at the side of her breast. She ran to the bathroom to take a look. There was an area of redness in the scar with the smallest possible nodule on it; no larger than a freckle, but angry and threatening, like the wild flesh of keloid that may grow in an old wound. She felt her breast, as the surgeon had done, with the palm of her hand and, feeling a distinct lump underneath the nodule, she burst into tears. She knew immediately that this time she would have to have the dreaded mastectomy. The young surgeon, now in charge, did not hesitate.

'If I am to save your life, we must go ahead as soon as possible.' There was no doubt in his voice.

'Is there no other way?' Irene asked the inevitable question.

'There isn't. I will have to take away the whole of the breast tissue and most of the pectoralis muscle underneath, together with all the lymph nodes in the axilla and the supraclavicular region.' He pointed to her armpit and the area above the collarbone.

'Please do it, Doctor,' she said quietly, her eyes filling up with tears. She knew her fate.

The operation went according to plan. The talented young surgeon was satisfied with his work and next day he telephoned a friend of his in Budapest to arrange radiotherapy for Irene. Whilst she was supported by the hospital staff Irene coped well, but after being discharged her world seemed to turn upside down. Nicholas collected her and took her home in a taxi. She went to the bathroom and locked the door behind her. Gently, she took off her blouse and then the bandage and looked into the mirror. The sight of the long S-shaped scar covering the whole of her side hit her like a thunderbolt. It was too much for her and she cried out.

'God! What have you done to me!!' Irene ran into the bedroom and threw herself on the bed, sobbing uncontrollably.

Nicholas followed and tried his best to console her. His task was enormous. When someone like Irene, who was more than able to control the problems of her family, suddenly had to succumb to a life-threatening problem of her own she could only feel cheated and abandoned if not given the right type of support. Nicholas realised this instinctively and had to muster up his own innate resources. He had strength, which helped, honesty, which was useful, but he also had a very personal sense of humour, which he could use without being pretentious.

'I *am* ambidextrous, you know, all we have to do is to swap places in bed,' was his approach.

Irene, in a moment of self-pity, thought of slapping him, but seeing the genuine and compassionate smile widening on his handsome and mature face, she burst out laughing.

'So you won't leave me for that gorgeous young soubrette at the theatre, then?' She asked in mock girlish peevishness.

'No, darling, she was absolutely useless in bed,' he replied, pushing his luck and receiving a kick in the shin for it.

'Ouch, that hurt, I think revenge is in order here!' He felt an urgency come over him that had to be satisfied immediately. He pushed her gently on to the bed and made love to her in a manner that surprised Irene in its ferocity. She needed to be 'taken' in order to be reassured and Nicholas did not fail her. His love was little less than sheer force, which put the problem into the category of 'prospective', where it stayed for another year.

The insidious takeover of power by the communists lead by Rákosi became suddenly complete and absolute, just as Joseph Greenfield had forecast not so many years before. This affected Nicholas as a police chief more than anyone else. A circular arrived from the Ministry of the Interior informing him of the formation of the State Security Authority within the force. It also informed him that the new department would subsume the ordinary police, and this would include him. The new man in charge was named as Captain Schneider and, although he was of a lower rank and technically his number two, Nicholas would have to report to him. The language of the circular was also different from the previous ones. It talked of 'class struggle' against all 'reactionary forces' and 'agents of imperialism', which included the aristocracy, those who held high office before the war, the clergy and the 'kulaks', the better-off peasantry. It didn't take Nicholas too long to realise that his days were numbered. His stubborn honesty would never allow him to work with this 'Gestapo', as he immediately and not too originally called the new department. That evening he went into the officers' mess, a routine he followed every Friday, and that day he had one too many. He explained to his fellow officers what was about to happen to the force and he called it a 'dirty communist trick'. One of them went back into his office, picked up the telephone receiver and told the operator to put him through to Captain Schneider at the SSA at the Ministry of the Interior in Budapest.

Autumn was late but beautifully warm. The Mecsek mountain hung over their house like a multicoloured tapestry. The leaves turned every colour from purple to the lightest green, and as they fell to the ground in the light breeze they covered the narrow roads and tracks like a rich eastern carpet. Walking was a way of life in the mountains, a social event during which people would meet and still greet each other by touching or raising their hats. Nicholas was addicted to it, and he insisted that the family follow him, challenging and tiring out everyone, constantly. As a result of the physical activity Sunday dinner was quickly devoured by them all and the family went to bed early.

At 2 am on Monday morning three loud and aggressive knocks came on the Zentas' front door. Nicholas approached the oak door, tying the belt of his dressing gown. Through the porch window he noticed the outline of a stranger in a leather overcoat, with two others. Why knock so loud? He thought to himself. He opened the door and in the hand of the stranger in the shining leather coat and wide-brimmed hat he saw a revolver. Flanking him stood two men, one being a uniformed officer of his with whom he occasionally had a drink on Friday evenings and the other a civilian.

'Nicholas Zenta?' The man with the gun asked casually.

'I am. What's the problem?' For a moment Nicholas thought the whole thing was a joke or a mistake, but he caught the look in the deep-set eyes of the stranger and saw nothing but hatred.

'You are under arrest for statements against the people and on suspicion of espionage. Dress immediately and hand over your service revolver.' Nicholas turned around dazed and went back to the bedroom, where Irene herself was about to get out of bed. 'Darling, these men are here to arrest me. I think their leader is the Captain Schneider we have heard of. He looks very serious. I'll go and clear up his problem. Please don't get up, everything will be all right.'

Irene was not so sure about things turning out 'all right'. Rumours about nationwide 'purges' of 'class aliens' were rife. She quickly put on her dark blue white-flowered dressing gown.

Nicholas came down wearing uniform. He opened his dark brown revolver holster and handed over the gun he had never used since it was issued to him. Schneider took it from him and placed it in his coat pocket. Nicholas suddenly realised the seriousness of what was happening and he kissed Irene with passion. As their embrace unfolded the tips of their fingers touched and Irene felt that electric sensation of many years before. He started walking down the path. At the gate he looked back and smiled. He was never to see his wife alive again.

Book Three

16

A<small>DAM</small>

Nicholas was handcuffed and taken to his own HQ. The sentry saluted him as he was aggressively pushed out of his car. He acknowledged it with a faint smile and said, 'Hello, John, I don't think you will have to do that any more.' He was marched swiftly to one of his criminal interrogating cells, locked in and curtly told that his interrogation would commence at 11.00 hours. Having taken his tunic off, he lay on the stiff and narrow bed and fell asleep. He had to be awakened the following morning for a slice of stale bread and a brown sludge they called coffee. He washed and shaved in cold water and dressed before being ushered to his own office to meet Schneider.

He hardly recognised his own room; all had been changed during his weekend off. The antique maps of the city, the county and the country were gone and in their place photographs of the bald-headed communist dictator Rákosi were placed on the wall behind the desk, flanked on each side by Lenin and Stalin. Pointedly, the chair he had always used for interviewees was moved to the corner of the room and he was told to stand in front of his desk. Schneider walked in without a word. Fairly small in stature, he had dark brown greasy hair, held in place by some hair cream of the most dubious origin and smell. His round metal-framed spectacles rested on his large nose. He was wearing the brand-new uniform of the security force, now renamed State Security Authority; a slavish copy of the Red Army uniform in olive khaki. The Russian-style epaulets showed the rank of captain. He sat down on Nicholas' chair.

'State your name, please,' he demanded in a slimy, sweetish tone, without looking up.

'Major Nicholas Zenta de Lemhény, Captain,' Nicholas answered with more than a little mocking humour in his voice.

The captain's fist hit the desk so hard that the rubber stamps and other items on it flew off in all directions.

'Let's get a few things straight. You're an ex-major and as far as nobility titles are concerned, they no longer exist, so you are plain Nicholas Zenta. Understood?' He hit the desk again to make his point totally clear.

'If you say so,' Nicholas answered quietly.

'If you say so, Captain!' The man yelled.

'Sorry, Captain. You see, I'm not too familiar with the Russian epaulet rankings yet.'

'You will be, by Jove, you will be, I promise you!' Schneider bent to pick up the file with 'Zenta, Nicholas' printed in large letters on top. He opened it at the end and mustered a faint smile. 'The charges are that you have supplied highly confidential information to an American imperialist lackey and that you made public statements against the people and the Communist Party. Both these are treasonable offences. Everything is documented here in detail, you could save us all a lot of trouble by signing a confession.' Schneider beckoned Nicholas to come to the desk.

'Well now, Captain, until you opened that file there, I thought all this to be a bad joke. But it isn't, is it? Naturally, I am not going to sign anything. Furthermore, I want my solicitor here immediately.' Nicholas was playing for time.

'Zenta, let me be clear. I don't want you to be under any misapprehension about solicitors and bail – I'm sure you will be asking for that in a minute – because in this country they are all things of the past. You are a dirty traitor and an enemy of the people. You deserve nothing and you will get nothing! I give you a last chance to sign here.' He pointed to the bottom of the page. Nicholas shook his head.

The captain turned to one of Nicholas' constables, who was totally confused by what was happening before him. 'Take this pig from here and lock him up.' Then he turned to Nicholas. 'Zenta, your next interview will be different, very different!'

Nicholas was marched out of his office and back to the cell. His uniform was taken away from him and he was given a parcel of prison clothing.

'I am very sorry I have to do this to you, Major,' said the sergeant, locking the door behind him.

～

Irene and her children were totally bewildered after a second day passed with no message from Nicholas. That evening Irene, listening to the radio, heard the news of the arrest of Foreign Minister Rajk – the man who, until the recent reshuffle, had been in charge of establishing the SSA – the dreaded State Security Authority – as Minister of the Interior. Several other high-ranking officials and police chiefs were also named, amongst them her missing husband. She decided against saying anything to her children but she managed to sleep only a few hours during the night.

Next morning Irene was about to send Adam off to school when a car pulled up and a very official-looking gentleman walked up the path carrying a battered briefcase. He identified himself sheepishly as a messenger from the City Council. He fumbled in his briefcase and produced a document with a seal in the bottom right-hand corner. On the top the document proudly declared itself as an 'Order of Internal Deportation', giving the Zenta family seventy-two hours to move from the premises to the village of Jonk, in Tolna county, where accommodation would be provided for them. The reason given was simply that the family was 'class alien' and non-deserving of their present 'exalted status'. The poor man was dreadfully embarrassed, crumpling his hat whilst Irene was reading his 'important document'.

With tears in her eyes the bereft Irene ran into the house, shouting, 'Nicholas, where are you, where are you?' Adam, ready for school, looked at his distressed mother and took her hand gently.

'Mother, please, please don't worry, everything will be all right, I know it will.'

'I must speak to your father, he must be at the police station.' She ran frantically towards the telephone, but Adam stood blocking her way.

'You can't call him, Mother – the phone is dead – it's been cut off.'

At that moment the thirteen-year-old Adam took charge of the family. He threw his school satchel into the corner of the living room and brought his mother's hand up to his face. 'Let's start packing, Mummy, there's no point in arguing, we'll have to go. Father will find us when he's released, please don't worry. I'll take good care of you.'

She stared at her son. 'I know you will, my beautiful boy, I know you will.' She started crying uncontrollably.

~

The four of them got off the wooden-benched train at Jonk railway station and collected their miserable belongings from the guard's wagon – bedding tied in bundles, clothes in battered suitcases. The train puffed away from them as they stood in front of the rather smart village station. A railway worker, a sort of factotum of the small station, walked up to Irene as autumn leaves danced around in the gentle breeze. Irene started to shiver a little and took Anna's hand. The sun shone through the bulky grey clouds and Kathleen asked for an ice cream.

The guard could not have been friendlier. He reassured Irene about the impending arrival of the bus, which would be driven by the village beekeeper, and helped to carry their luggage to the bus stop, which was marked by a semaphore flag. The rickety bus announced its impending arrival with a lot of clatter. Having seen better days, the shaky old machine had been farmed out for the three-mile journey between the station and the centre of the village, with one stop at the outskirts. The driver, another nice chap, helped them to put the bundles and cases on to the rear end of the bus and the short but very slow journey towards a picturesque hill commenced. The simple dirt road wound around a meadow first and then it had to take the Letka Hill itself, square on. The beekeeper changed down to second gear and the old diesel engine coughed a few times as if it were trying to psych itself up before the big event. When it actually got going it seemed to travel more slowly than walking pace, and stopping and restarting was a major effort. It shuddered and shook before lurching into the next climb. The girls were enjoying the bus ride. Adam and Irene looked at each other and burst into a fit of giggling, to the surprise of the other passengers, who kept turning back to look at the family without a man.

It was the first laugh they had had since leaving their house in the Mecsek mountain, and they giggled even more with every groan of the bus. Mercifully, the summit came into view and for the descent into the village the driver switched off the engine to save the precious diesel. The speed downhill on the poor road surface gave all passengers a good shake-up and the items in the luggage holder a good chance to fall through the large holes in the nets. Their last belly laugh together continued until the bus pulled up, then they realised that they had no idea where they would spend the night. Irene went across the road to the small but important-looking house, on which the oval white shield showing the new communist emblem of a lot of wheat – everywhere –– and a hammer crowned with the alien red star stated that it was the village Council Hall. Luckily the chairman inside was an old-fashioned man who, having read the deportation document, felt a genuine sympathy for the broken family. As an ex-Justice of the Peace he had nothing but contempt for the new regime and wanted to help its first victims.

He explained that there was an empty building, not much more than a small cottage, near the village centre which they could take over, although having been abandoned by its previous owner, it was 'in a bit of a state'. But he would get the crier out tomorrow to let everybody know about the newcomers' plight. He was sure the people would respond and bring a few things for them. Meanwhile, tonight they'd better stay in the inn. Enquiring how Irene would make her living, he was told that her plan was to do needlework and sewing, but she needed a sewing machine.

Next morning the crier was rolling away on his side drum, walking along the streets of a village much larger than it had at first seemed. Stopping every few hundred yards, he yelled out as loud as he could that the new family without a man needed their help and the woman needed work. Their response was astonishing. The peasants arrived one by one, bringing so many things that by the end of the following day the mud-brick-built cottage had all the basic essentials, including a rickety old Singer sewing machine.

Settling into their new life lifted the gloom a little. There was much to do, such as registering Adam and Kathleen at the local school and making the cottage vaguely habitable. The four rooms were joined by an outside covered veranda. The two front ones had connecting doors; they decided these would be the living room and kitchen, which had a table and four chairs where they could eat.

The next room would sleep her and the girls. The last one, farthest back, contained Adam's bed, the sewing machine and washing facilities. With not much ventilation, this was soon christened by Irene as 'the cave of smells'. The outside toilet, a glorified latrine, stood proudly at the bottom of the garden. They spent the late autumn evenings in the front room, doing lessons, playing and above all wondering about Nicholas' fate.

Adam was way ahead of the other pupils at the school. Three years in Pécs had given him a head start in most subjects. He joined the Boy Scouts and soon became section leader, picking up arm badges in the various arts and crafts. He was heartbroken when the communists dissolved the movement and introduced the Russian-style Pioneers in its place. His interest turned to opera when he was given a chance to listen to some LPs, and he spent days replaying them time and time again. This way he learned the more popular ones by heart, and when he was given the opportunity to take them home, he astonished Irene with the depth of his knowledge. They would listen to a different one every dark winter evening, both dreaming that one day he would become a famous tenor.

~

Nicholas' second interview with Schneider came a week later. New personnel were deployed by the Ministry of the Interior, a different brand of thugs in the Gestapo mould. The ordinary policemen were moved to rooms at the back of the building and the new men took over the main part and the more prestigious offices. The largest cell was converted into the 'specialist interrogation room', a modern and sinister torture chamber.

When Nicholas was pushed again into his old office, Schneider was ready for him. This time his guards shoved him forcibly into an old chair.

'Are you Nicholas Zenta, the son of Titus of the same surname?' the man in the new uniform asked curtly.

'Before I answer any questions, Colonel, I demand to know what has happened to my family.' Nicholas' look searched for the officer's eyes, which were fixed on an old, very yellow newspaper headline.

'You are not in a position to demand anything, you class alien bastard!' Schneider's fist came down on his desk with a crash yet again. 'But I tell you, they have a better fate than they deserve, a better fate than my mother and I had. They happen to be in internal exile, in a village where they can rot for all I care,' he mumbled.

Nicholas was surprised how easy it was to get the answer out of his interrogator. He was relieved to know that they were at least safe, but he also knew that he would have to pray a price for it.

'Was your father Titus Zenta, who killed mine? 'The question came again, only in a fiercer tone.

'Yes, his name was Titus, but I know nothing about him killing your father.' Nicholas was astonished at what he was hearing.

'Well, I will have to expand your education.' Schneider picked up the old newspaper and walked over to Nicholas, unfolding it in front of his face. 'PATRIOTIC OFFICER KILLS EX-SUPERIOR. Would-be revolutionaries scatter as leader lies slain.'

The article was referring to an incident in the city when a wounded major travelling home shot a man leading a demonstration. The picture showed the man lying in a pool of blood, with a gaping wound at his neck. Next to him lay a broken pair of spectacles.

Nicholas felt a choking sensation coming over him and thought he would be sick. For a moment he felt sorry for Schneider, especially as he knew nothing about the incident. He looked up from the paper and found Schneider's eyes for a moment. They were full of hatred and desire for revenge. Nicholas wanted to respond in some conciliatory way, but Schneider delivered a humiliating slap on his left cheek.

'That's what I think of you reactionary bastards,' he yelled. 'Now sign your confession!'

'Schneider, for a moment I felt pity for you. I promise I know nothing about what happened, but that will not make an iota of difference as regards me signing anything. You might as well have it straight, I sign nothing. Nothing at all!' Nicholas pushed the paper away decisively.

'I'll make you beg to sign it, believe you me,' Schneider snarled. 'Take him downstairs to the Zenta suite.' He gave a mocking laugh, pretending to enjoy his own joke.

The two thickset guards picked Nicholas off the chair and marched him to the old-fashioned lift, digging their fingers into the soft flesh of his armpits. When they arrived in the cement-walled room they released him with a very painful pinch. Another, new officer presented Nicholas with the confession papers once more. Nicholas shook his head without a word. The officer nodded to the two guards. Their blows were heavy and accurate; they took turns to deliver blows, stopping just short of making him pass out. There were two on the face followed by one in the pit of the stomach, and he bent over in breathless agony. Another uppercut came from the other henchman. The officer waved the papers, holding a ballpoint in his hand. Nicholas grunted a 'no, never', and the routine recommenced as if choreographed. It was the uppercut which sent Nicholas staggering backwards, and when he slipped on his own blood his head crashed against the brick wall. The unconsciousness that followed enveloped him like a warm velvet cloud.

The bucket of cold water a few minutes later did not produce the usual coughing and spluttering. He remained in virtual coma for some six hours, after which he came to a little, just enough to start to vomit. He heard the two henchmen arguing about hitting him too hard. He looked towards them and saw a number of blurred figures where the two men stood. They turned him over, which virtually saved his life as he was about to inhale his gastric contents before passing out again.

The doctor came and questioned the guards. With his pencil torch he looked into Nicholas' pupils, which were very sluggish in responding to the light. The large blood clot on the back of the head confirmed the diagnosis of severe concussion. He indicated that the patient should be admitted to hospital for observation immediately, but was told that it was out of the question. He warned them not to hit him again, unless – of course – they wanted to kill him.

The physician's matter-of-fact delivery was a ploy to frighten the men. It actually worked for a while. They reported to Schneider, who was outraged, yelling at them that they were not up to the interrogation standard expected from the SSA and they'd better start practising their routine with the electrical apparatus.

When the two electrodes were placed upon him, one pinching him on the top of his foreskin and the other just behind his scrotum, he still had double vision and was quite significantly confused. Not in total control of his faculties, he could not anticipate the excruciating pain that gripped the lower part of his body when the lever was depressed. The current increased to twelve volts, giving him an electric shock that violated every sensory ending of his nervous system. His body, clad only in a shirt, arched in agony with every shock, only to fall back on to the wooden table where he was made to lie. Then the piece of paper appeared again – out of focus – before his eyes. He would shake his head. The now-expert torturer increased the amperage with the rheostat. His screams became louder with each completion of the circuit, until in one of the pauses the relaxation caused him to urinate violently over the whole machine, ending the session to accompaniment of the obscene swearing of the thugs.

For the night, they tied their semiconscious victim in a sitting position. They placed a stick below his bent knees and pulled his arms underneath it, locking the stick between the knees and the elbows, handcuffing his wrists at ankle level. They could now pick him up by the stick and place him in the middle of the cell. When he was first left in such a position, the initial discomfort was a dull ache. The pain increased as the circulation to his legs was cut off. Next morning a new officer appeared with the dreaded paper, promising instant relief from his agony. Well past the stage of knowing what the paper was all about, he instinctively shook his head, leaving the henchman no alternative but to report his own failure back to Schneider.

What days of torture failed to produce, a change of tactics achieved within minutes. Nicholas was taken to face Schneider in his office, where a comfortable chair and a forced smile awaited him. The security chief was desperate for success.

'Zenta, you're a foolish man, but I admire the way you have stood up to those brutes,' he started, pretending to have had nothing to do with what had gone on during the past few days.

Nicholas sat quietly rubbing his eyes; they just won't focus as they used to, he thought.

'Look, I'm sure you want to know what has happened to Irene and your family. It's only a few weeks but I can tell you that they seem to have settled well into their new lives.' He spoke like an old friend of the family.

'Where are they? How's Irene?' Nicholas glared at him in disgust.

'They're fine, just fine. They are living in a village called Jonk, in Tolna county. I have some photographs here. Would you like to see them?'

'Photographs, what photographs?' Nicholas leaped to his feet. Schneider pointed to a pile of photographs on his desk as he walked around it. He handed them over to Nicholas.

They were carefully arranged in some sort of order. The first one showed a small house and even smaller figures in front of it, looking away, unaware of being photographed. Nicholas rubbed his eyes again and walked nearer the window for more light. The next one showed the two girls; Kathleen seemed to be running around little Anna, who was sitting on a log. Then came Adam, dressed in Boy Scout uniform and the large Baden-Powell hat, carrying a wooden perch with a swallow carved on it. Finally a much thinner Irene, with her greying hair tied up in a bun – her favourite style – sitting behind a sewing machine.

'You bastard!!!' Nicholas' cry was as loud as and much more painful than any uttered during his torture sessions. He dropped the photographs and tried to lunge towards his adversary. The guards were ready. They jumped on him and pulled him back on to the chair.

'Now look here, Zenta, I have just about had enough of you!' Schneider's voice soared to its normal, sharper tone. 'You either sign, or I'll have them split up – the girls to an orphanage, the lad to a corrective school, and as far as your wife is concerned she might as well end her life as the village whore.' His fist came down on to his desk like a thunderbolt.

Nicholas stood up, walked deliberately to the old desk, picked up the ballpoint pen and signed on the dotted line; Major N. Zenta de Lemhény. He never looked at the content of the document.

His 'trial' was held before People's Court No. 2 in a secret session, lasting less than a day. The county prosecutor read the charges: the accused was an 'enemy of the people' who had collaborated with the Germans in the deportation of the Jewry of Transylvania. Then, following the war, he gave state secrets to an agent of American imperialism, one Major Joseph Greenfield of the US Army, who was subsequently declared *persona non grata* and given forty-eight hours to leave the territory of the Hungarian People's Republic. The charges ended by citing his 'seditious statements against the people' in the officers' mess in his HQ. Before sitting down the prosecutor demanded ten years' jail with hard labour. The defence lawyer agreed with everything the 'comrade prosecutor' had said and added that he 'could not think of any extenuating circumstances'. He thought five years would be a sufficient sentence. The three judges put their heads together and the one in the middle announced the sentence; 'two years' loss of liberty', which astounded everyone in court.

~

Irene read the short item about the sentencing of a provincial police chief as part of a wider purge 'to clear society of all reactionary forces of the past, and enable the nation to build a socialist world based on the most solid of all foundations, Marxism and Leninism under the leadership of the greatest Hungarian pupil of the glorious comrade Stalin, Matthias Rákosi.' The villagers now knew what, until now, they had only guessed. Their reaction was one of sympathy for the family without a man, and the menfolk raised their hats a little higher to Irene when they met her in the street.

Their everyday life concentrated on sheer survival. Irene took in as much sewing as she could fit in looking after Anna during the day. When Adam and Kathleen returned from school they had their main meal of the day, of whatever she could buy in the village shops. After dinner came homework and, in the case of Adam, more opera-listening until bedtime. By the age of fourteen he could hum a dozen operas from beginning to end.

The first Christmas letter from Nicholas gave the family another opportunity to shed tears for him, although he sounded quite cheerful. The heavily censored lines described only the lighter side of life in jail in Fehérvár, reassuring Irene that he was in exceptional company. 'Socially, one could not ask for more; my five cell mates are two barons, a count, an ex-MP and a High Court Judge, and the rest of the jail has more aristocrats than the Upper House used to have.' He omitted to tell of the mental cruelty and brutal weekly beatings they all suffered in the name of re-education.

The spring of 1951 brought the final catastrophe in their shattered lives. Irene noticed an angry red patch developing in her scar and, later in the same week, she experienced some difficulty in picking up small items around her sewing machine. A little puffiness in the fingers of her right hand made her unusually clumsy. None of the signs worried her initially, but the gentle swelling soon spread up her arm, which annoyed her enough to mention it to the village doctor at her next check-up. The look on the old and experienced physician's face was enough for Irene to know that the matter was very serious.

'Mrs Zenta, you know all there is to know about your illness and in a way it makes my job more difficult,' he said. 'Your tumour has recurred in a very aggressive way, blocking up the lymphatic circulation in your armpit, hence the swelling of your fingers and arm.'

Irene looked at the doctor and in her intelligent eyes he saw that panic was taking her over.

'I understand,' she said softly. 'Is there anything you can do to make me last until my husband's release? We are so alone and he has another year to serve … Please God, help us,' she whispered, as if in prayer.

He held her swollen arm. 'No one can stop this progression now, but when the time comes, I will be able to help you with the pain.'

'When will the time come?' She asked, with her voice now hardly audible.

'It will not be too long, Mrs Zenta, but you know I will always be here – do not hesitate to call.'

Irene put on her coat and hat. She looked elegant, even imposing, as she walked out of the surgery on to the main road, where so many hats were raised for her.

By the summer she had to refuse work. Her right arm became heavier and heavier, until it had to be put in a sling. She had lost weight steadily and her wound, now reopened, needing dressing at least twice a day. The doctor, true to his word, did his best, but bandages were in short supply and she had to hand-wash one set whilst wearing the other. With less work came less money and less food and with less food came more nights of weeping. Kathleen would wake up Adam in the next room and they would go and see what was happening to 'dear sweet Mummy'. The three of them would soon cry together in the frightening loneliness of the dark. Luckily, little Anna would sleep through the deep misery of their night. Unlike her two siblings she could not yet comprehend the impending catastrophe.

By the summer school break Irene's condition had deteriorated to such an extent that she could no longer work at all. She started to complain of a severe dull backache, which was soon diagnosed by the doctor as a metastatic tumour in her spinal column; a further indication of the terminal nature of her condition.

~

Nicholas, in the political wing of Fehérvár prison, was guarded by SSA thugs in the most violent way, along with all the other 'class aliens'. As his six-monthly letters to the family suggested his fellow inmates were all from the highest strata of pre-war society. The standard of conversation in the workshop or in the exercise yard attained academic heights, unfortunately way above his head. From Dante to Dumas, Shakespeare to Shaw or Bach to Bartók, everything was continually discussed, as if in an ever-running intellectual smorgasbord on a top-class cruise. This way the political prisoners could support each other mentally and, more importantly, they could have an esoteric conversation their guards could hardly comprehend.

Alas, a political correction institution like this necessarily entailed degrading and drastic physical violation too. The slightest dissent or even a dismissive look would attract regular beatings in the basement. The prisoner would hear his name yelled out along the corridor by the senior guard; just a simple surname and the order 'bring your towel!' These four words would implant instant fear in the mind of the subject, who would then be supported with words of encouragement and friendly pats on the shoulder from his cell mates, until the door opened. Then the prisoner would have to walk along the long corridors to the torture room, where he would receive a violent beating from the three guards. Some prisoners would choose to be dragged along, resisting, in the belief that this would sap the energy of the animal-like frenzied beaters.

Nicholas' assured attitude, and the fact that he was regarded as a 'renegade copper', provided him with ample opportunity to hear 'Zenta, bring your towel!' Having never fully recovered from the very first beating in Pécs, he was affected much more seriously. The initial damage had caused scarring in the angular gyrus area of his brain, which was microscopically enlarged with every new blow. These he had to endure by the dozen at every session of this brutal ritual. At first he just kept rubbing his eyes, but then he noticed visual hallucinations. He called these 'sheets of flame', some sort of moving lights, which must have originated from the injury to the back of his head when he hit the wall with such force in Pécs.

During the long and lonely nights, when he closed his eyes and wept on the wooden planks they called his bed, the flames would start to reappear. He wanted them to disappear so that he could find Irene's face, but as soon as he created an image of her the flames would immolate it with overwhelming ferocity. In the morning he would 'demand' a chance for Irene to visit him from the sergeant guard, only to be told, 'Zenta, bring your towel!' Once again. He was trapped, there was no way out and he had enough insight to realise that the thugs were breaking his spirit. He needed to see Irene to break the vicious circle of uncertainty and worry, but the system didn't allow visiting for anyone with a sentence as short as two years.

The high school language mistress, giving the newly compulsory Russian lessons, was the first person to notice the general deterioration in the condition of the Zenta children. It was just one week before the summer school break of 1950, when Nicholas still had another ten months to serve in prison. When she questioned Adam he told her frankly of the worsening of Irene's health. She decided to visit Irene on the pretext of asking her to do a little sewing. She found Adam helping to change the dressing on her chest in conditions which were very near to utter squalor. The language mistress, a war widow herself, offered to take Anna off Irene's hands. She could look after the little girl until the school holidays. Adam reassured his teacher that he had a job lined up for the vacation as a cowherd at the cooperative farm, starting the following week. He would get a few florins as well as dairy products for his work, so there would be no worry about food. He could also help with changing Irene's dressing and Kathleen could look after her whilst he was out in the fields. Anna's few belongings were packed in the battered old case and she walked away with the teacher after kissing 'sweet Mummy' goodbye. Irene, in a soft voice, thanked the lady she had never met before for her kindness and concern.

Adam spent the summer working in the fields surrounding the village. At dawn he would help Irene dress her ever nastier-looking wound, then he would turn up at the cooperative farm and take the twenty or so cows along a narrow, cool, tree-lined road, aptly named Walnut Meadow, to the surrounding fields. Using his whip to carry the linen bag containing his drink and food for the day and a book, he would go to collect his charges. He had a new book to read each day, and in between chapters he would fill his time by humming his operas. His favourite reads were *Ivanhoe*, *Robin Hood* and the Hungarian classic *The Stars of Eger*. Late afternoon would arrive much sooner than he had ever imagined and it would be time to usher his small herd back to the cooperative and to pick up his supply of food for the day – milk, cheese, butter and some meat, usually poultry or pork.

Arriving home, he would cuddle 'sweet Mummy' for a while, clean up the house and help to cook dinner. Adam needed to be her 'right hand', which was by now grossly swollen and permanently in a sling. He would cut up the meat and the vegetables for yet another stew. After dinner came the near-daily routine of washing Kathleen's clothes for next morning. They would dry instantly in the heat of the night. Sometimes he would surprise Irene by bringing Anna over for a few hours to play in the yard. Their days usually ended with fetching in the dried dressings from the line and rebandaging Irene's chest, where the angry wound seemed to grow by the day. Irene constantly thought of Nicholas and kept looking at the only photograph of the four of them, taken during their last autumn together in Pécs, in which he was still wearing his uniform with the single gold star of a major and looking very proud and handsome.

The late summer of 1950 was an exceptionally hot one and with it came all the problems of a landlocked country The worst was the flies, swarms of them. When they arrived the life of a cowherd boy at first just became miserable. Reading on top of the hill, overlooking the grazing field and his herd, became virtually impossible as the pests would not leave any man or beast alone. Wherever he tried to usher his cows the cloud of flies followed and, as reading was out of the question, he occupied his time by humming his favourite opera excerpts louder and louder until they became full-throated deliveries of arias, duets or even choruses. The odd peasant would yell across the hills, telling him to 'shut up', though he occasionally got encouragement from some elderly lady praising his adolescent yet ringing tenor. As 'shepherd boys' – usually playing their flutes – are fairly common devices for opera composers when depicting a rural scene or innate tranquillity, Adam was happy with his lot. He dreamed of becoming the new Caruso, or his favourite Hungarian tenor, Sárdy, and of joining Aunt Rose on the operatic stage, but for now the flies were his greatest concern. All he wanted was a little breeze or some rain to blow them away. As neither of those things had turned up by the end of the day he would, once again, take the cows back down the dirt roads to the farm, his chest inhaling the dust from their hooves and breathing the pungent smell of their manure.

One day the cooperative sent Adam to fetch butter for the village from a dairy some ten miles away. Not trusting his bike's rear wheel, he decided to take the day and walk. When he arrived at the dairy he was called into the manager's office, while they filled his satchel with the village's butter for the week. The stern-faced man sitting behind his desk knew him well and knew of the problems of the family.

'Adam, my boy, I have just had a telephone call from the chairman in Jonk. Your sister has called the doctor. Your mother has taken a turn for the worse. You'd better head straight back, it does not sound too good,' he informed Adam gravely.

'Thank you, sir, here's the money for the butter. I'll go back straight away.' He handed over the cash and went to the dispatch room for his school bag, then started running homeward in a panic. He could not bear the thought that Irene might be in danger and die before he could get home. There were fair-sized hills between the villages and a lot of running to do. His mind was racing, urging him to run faster and faster. Paths, side roads and short cuts approached him, one after the other, and he ran at them with increasing ferocity. He saw glimpses of the sun through the branches of trees and he lengthened his stride to step over the shadows of the branches, to get him home even quicker. His effort was virtually superhuman. He desperately wanted to help his mother, he wanted to be back with her. The more he tired the bigger breaths he took, thinking that the more it hurt him, the less pain would punish his mother, and for that he would endure whatever it took. After a while he became an automaton, running and breathing rhythmically to get himself back to the cottage, which he felt he should never have left. His determination sped him past everyone until he fell at the front door.

The doctor was still treating Irene's collapse when Kathleen noticed her unconscious brother. The hyperventilating boy was dragged to bed by the physician, who immediately noticed that his hands and fingers were showing signs of hysterically induced tetany. He tapped the side of Adam's face over the facial nerve. The muscles of his cheeks contracted. The doctor had now switched his attention to Adam and, removing a pillow case, he placed it over the boy's face, making him rebreathe his own exhalations. A few minutes later his respiration became more regular and he opened his eyes, only to face the wise old man's wrath.

'Adam, you will stay in bed for a day, otherwise you will burst your lungs. That's an order. You will do exactly as I say. We can't afford to have two sick people in this house, can we?' He turned back to Irene, not waiting for an answer. The following morning Irene quietly asked to be helped to the veranda. She wanted to feel the warmth of the early sunshine as she penned her last letter to Nicholas:

Dearest Nicholas,

I feel my life is slowly slipping away. It is far too exhausting to fight on, though there is still so much to do and to say. It has become impossible.

Our life together has not been without its difficulties, but didn't we also have so much fun! We have three wonderful children and they are a credit to us. Such fine young people. I do love them so very much.

Don't grieve too much for me, darling. Get on with your life when you return. Remember, our children will need a mother to take care of them.

With all my love, as always,

Irene

~

'Adam, darling, would you change my dressing for me, my wound is itching dreadfully – I could tear myself apart,' she whispered. Her paleness was upsetting Adam, who never heard her complaining this way before.

'Of course, "sweet Mummy". Turn over on to your left side and let me see.' Adam started to unwind the yards of gauze, to get at the lint covering the wound. When he saw the gaping hole in her flesh, which he knew well enough, he recoiled in disgust. Luckily Irene was facing in the other direction and was spared the horror in her son's eyes. He had to grab his neck to stop himself being sick. Irene's head slowly turned back and, seeing the expression on Adam's face fixed on her chest, she looked at her wound and screamed.

'Oh, no! Maggots!!! But God, I'm not dead yet!' She slid down her chair, looking into the bright sky, and fainted with the words, 'Dear God, why do you punish me so?'

Adam soon realised what had happened. In the casually washed lint and bandages a little of her flesh had attracted one of the millions of flies so common at this time of the year and it had laid its eggs on the dressing, which had been placed back on the wound. The agile and filthy little white maggots had begun eating her dead flesh, when she had noticed the itching. Adam screamed hysterically, grabbed the forceps he used to handle his better stamps with and started to remove the vile things one by one, throwing them in all directions. In the perfect light he was able to do a good job, but he saw at least one of them burrowing down towards the chest cavity. He dragged his mother into the room and ran to the doctor's house.

The old physician arrived with Adam just as Irene was about to regain consciousness. They stared at her wound as two more maggots appeared from within. The doctor removed them hastily. Later he agreed with Adam's theory as to how they got there, but the only treatment he could offer was intravenous morphine into her 'good arm' and, when it had taken effect, a general disinfection of the open area of the wound with a weak iodine solution. Adam knew well what that meant.

Irene, weak with exhaustion, thanked the doctor when he had finished rebandaging her with the new gauze. The room smelled of fresh iodine by the time Adam saw him to the door. Looking anguished, the doctor turned back.

'My son, do you think some of those dreadful things burrowed too deep to pull out?'

'Yes, Doctor, I do. I saw at least one disappearing at the beginning, unless it was the one you pulled out later,' Adam answered thoughtfully.

'Let's hope so. I have no penicillin left, but I could get some in for tomorrow. I'll be back. Goodbye!' He turned and walked hastily down the street.

He did return with an ampoule first thing in the morning and injected the new antibiotic into Irene's emaciated thigh. He took her pulse and felt her forehead. Shaking his head, he placed his large Bayer thermometer under her left armpit. It read 40.5 degrees Celsius, indicating a fever. By the evening her temperature had soared and a further dose of penicillin could not prevent the onset of pleurisy, perhaps as the result of the entry of the horrible maggot into her chest cavity. Fulminating bronchopneumonia mercifully followed, and three days later Irene slipped quietly away, as Adam held her hand. Kathleen was doing her homework in the other room.

Anna was skipping back from the shops with the language mistress. Nicholas had just heard the sergeant guard's voice yelling from the corridor: 'Zenta, bring your towel!'

The date was 1 September 1950. Adam was a few months short of being fifteen, but that day he became a man. No one had to close Irene's eyes; the coma had done that the day before. He bent down to kiss his mother's face, then her swollen hand. He slid quietly on to the knitted rug on the wooden floor next to his mother's bed and was racked by sobbing.

～

The chairman of the village council telephoned Fehérvár jail and found the governor in an unnaturally good mood.

'Oh, his missus died, eh?' He said in a low, emotionless voice. 'Well, he's only two weeks to go here. All right, I'll let him go early; one less bloody fascist for me to contend with.'

Nicholas, pale, with a bruised eye and some grazes on his high cheekbones, arrived in Jonk the day before the funeral. He had no money for the bus and nothing to carry so he decided to take in the fresh autumn air and walked across the Letka hill, straight into the village.

The first person he asked gave him directions to the cottage and he arrived just as Irene was being placed in the black-stained wooden coffin by the two peasant women who did this sort of thing. Adam knew nothing of the chairman's telephone call to the jail, nor of his father's release, so their reunion in the front room was more than emotional. After the tears were shed and Adam had explained that the girls had gone to stay with the schoolteacher, Nicholas asked his son to leave the room so he could spend a little time with Irene and say his goodbyes.

He bent over the coffin to kiss Irene's emaciated face. Then, kneeling beside the coffin, he fell into a deep, involuntary self-examination. In a monotonous, whispering voice he apologised for the past, for his drinking, and even for ending up in jail and deserting his family. He begged her for forgiveness.

'I have never been worthy of you, Irene, and I kneel beside you, once again too late. As for my past, I've already suffered my private hell during the last two years, and my sheets of flames tell me that I have no future. Our son is our future now. You've made a man out of him, Irene, a strong man, one who can cry. I'll cry with him for a while, then I will join you. Please forgive me, Irene, please, please do.' Nicholas stood up to pray as a Calvinist prays and asked his God to receive his wife and prepare a place for him.

The girls were brought home from the teacher's house and the family spent a night together for the first time in two years. There was little to eat but such a lot to say, so many questions to ask. Anna was sitting on her father's knee and staring at his much-worn face.

'What happened to your eye, Daddy? Why are you rubbing it?' She asked. Nicholas looked at Anna's little face and, searching for answers, he smiled.

'Well, little one, as I was walking home through the woods, there was this big, big eagle perched on a tree branch. I thought I would catch it for you. I jumped as high as I could, but I missed it by an inch. He flew off and the branch of the tree hit me in the face. Serves me right for trying to capture a bird at liberty.'

'But Adam says you must never capture birds!' Offered Kathleen.

'And he is right. Birds must be as free as we would like to be. Now come along, it's bedtime for you girls. Adam, where do they sleep?' He asked his son, but Kathleen leapt to her feet quicker.

'Can we sleep with you tonight, Papa?'.

'Of course you can,' He replied, feeling their need for comfort and reassurance, 'but only tonight, then back to your own beds – understood? Go and warm up the bed for me. I want to talk to Adam for a minute.' Nicholas patted Anna on her bottom on her way out.

'Good night, Papa, see you all tomorroooooow!' Anna skipped happily out of the dark and gloomy room.

'Don't forget your prayers!'

'No, I wooooon't. It's the funeral tomorroooooow! We must all praaaaaaay!'

'You just be quiet there!' Kathleen was outraged by her sister's behaviour, which at least brought a faint smile to the family's sad faces.

Nicholas at last had a chance to talk to his son alone. He put his hands on the lanky boy's shoulders.

'Was it awful for you all?' He asked quietly.

'You know, Dad, it wasn't all that bad until the very end. The whole village helped us. They used to call us the family without a man. The worst bit was Mother worrying about what was happening to you.' He lowered his head. 'Everyone in the village said that they beat political prisoners. I can see they beat you.'

'Adam,' he held his son's head affectionately between his hands, 'I will say this to you just once. No, they did not. They never touched me. I've had a fulfilling political re-education, that's all, do you understand?' Tears appeared in Nicholas' eyes as he emphasised his message to his son.

'I understand, Dad, nobody ever touched you!' Adam hugged his father.

'Well now.' Nicholas rubbed his eyes. 'I understand everything is arranged for tomorrow's funeral. How did that happen?'

'You have no idea how nice most of the people are around here. The doctor and the chairman arranged everything; we will have to pay them for the coffin but the hearse and the horses are free.'

The matter-of-fact way Adam was handling the problem, although he was clearly upset to the point of trembling, convinced Nicholas that his son had an inner strength he had never seen in him before. He ruffled his chestnut-brown wavy hair with tears in his eyes. He felt he had to change the subject.

'Any jobs going?' Nicholas wanted to sound eager for work.

'The woodcutting season is about to start, I'm sure the cooperative will take you on. Shall we cover the coffin?'

'Yes, Adam, let's do that.' The two men walked into the front room.

Just past midnight the rain started. It was as if a dam had burst. No thunder or lightning, only a sudden and relentless downpour from the sky, the sort of rain that could move hills and wash the soil away from the roots of the largest trees, sending them crashing down to the ground. Mud from the smallest hill slid down and filled the ditches, then covered the roads. Wet autumn leaves were flying around in the wind, sticking to anything in their way.

The pastor and the physician arrived for the walk to the cemetery. The Zenta family were waiting for the horse-drawn hearse, which duly arrived with two men and two elderly women, all in black. The rain became heavier and Nicholas told the girls that it would be better if they didn't come to the cemetery. The language mistress, in total agreement, offered to take them home for a few hours. Nicholas was to pick them up on the way back. He was grateful for her offer and he told the girls that this was for the best and to show gratitude for the lady's kindness.

Nicholas and Adam joined the two drivers and brought the coffin from the small parlour. Totally wet through, they set off in the warm but persistent rain. The pastor, in his pleated, embroidered black cloak and matching hat, was somewhat better protected than the other three and, although the cemetery was only a mile away, Adam soon started to worry about the short journey. He knew that the narrow winding road, usually such a pleasant lane, would be difficult for the black cart and whispered a warning to his father. There was little anyone could do. The two women started their well-established wailing routine and they introduced their new line about the family without a woman.

'That's ridiculous, Dad, tell them to stop it!' Adam whispered to his father in disgust.

Nicholas looked at his son first and, realising what Adam was referring to, he turned to the women.

'It's far too wet for you in this rain, my dears. Would you like to go home?' He asked the nearest one, trying to sound vaguely considerate.

The spurious tears disappeared immediately and they left, trudging back to the village ankle deep in the thick autumn mud. The cortège struggled up the wet road to the small cemetery, making little progress in spite of the frequent use of the whip by the driver. Behind them the few mourners were, by now, totally covered in sludge. Turning into the cemetery, the exhausted horses became unsettled. One of them tried to bolt and reared on to its hind legs. The other one became unnerved, and Nicholas realised that there was a great danger of the cart overturning. He left the others, ran in front of the horses and leapt up for the cart pole between them, dragging it down by pulling on the mouthpiece of the more unruly horse with all his weight. Disaster was averted by his quick action and the horses began to calm down. Adam could think only of the coffin rolling off the cart and stood there mesmerised by his father's timely intervention and the way he had taken charge of the family once again.

They stood staring at the graveside as the coffin was lowered into the clay grave, and Adam's thoughts started wandering to the impending residential school and all the work yet to come. He knew that every time he did his homework he would think of 'sweet Mummy' and himself sitting by the fire in Pécs – and their silly little rhyme.

Totally preoccupied as they were, deep in thoughts of the future, the rest of the funeral, the oratory of the pastor and the muddy walk home would never exist in the memory of either man. They would be astonished that all they could ever recall was the rain, the mud and one of the horses rearing up on its hind legs, screaming its agony at the sky.

17

Student

Although now only a woodfeller, Nicholas always changed into a smart suit for the evenings when he went to fetch Anna from Mistress Emilia. He still cut an extremely fine figure, and this ritual developed into full courtship over the months. Being widow and widower eased the formal part of establishing a relationship that, neither of them really wanted, was predestined to happen. The linchpins were the girls, who were longing for a more normal way of life, with a mummy and a daddy and preferably both at the same time. Adam, for his part, was just glad to see his father bothering to shave and change in the evenings before going to bring the girls home for a few hours. As he was one of her better students, Adam got on very well with Mistress Emilia, who was Mica to her friends. Small in stature, with dark brown hair, usually as short as she could get away with, she was 'interesting' rather than a beauty. From the point of view of his education her general knowledge and natural ability to convey it were a godsend to him. Their rapport, made during lessons in school, further eased the budding mature romance between his father and Emilia. The stage was set to formalise their fragmented situation, but as a woodcutter was still only a woodcutter, changes had to be made if Nicholas was to have a more permanent association with her.

The forced collectivisation of farms by the communist government gave Nicholas the last chance in his life to use his agronomist qualification. They needed someone with specialist training in agricultural management to start off the new cooperative farms, and although the last thing

Nicholas wanted was to 'help the commies' – as he put it – he was soon elected chairman of the Red Star Agricultural Cooperative Farm, which was somewhat better than being a woodcutter. The real bonus came from the fact that the enforced venture also included winemaking, and furthermore he was going to be allowed to buy his own – but smaller – private vineyard as an extra bonus. So, in a very short time, he was back in the hard grind and macho world of the farmer. His 'sheets of flame' continued to bother him, but he noticed the beneficial effect of alcohol on these. He was given a two-wheeled cart – a great luxury – and a splendid lively chestnut stallion named 'Cartwheel', a slight exaggeration of his habit of rolling exuberantly in the yard or field when not in harness. In his cart Nicholas could inspect the farms, the fields and the vineyards on the gentle slopes of the surrounding Transdanubia, as western Hungary is known. These inspections presented him with more than enough opportunity to sample the wines of the region and pálinka, the excellent but extremely potent hooch, distilled from the stems, seeds and skin left after the pressing of the grapes.

Despite these changes in his life, Adam was overjoyed with the news that he had got a place in the high school. The application form not only concerned itself with previous academic results, but had a strong emphasis on 'class origin' and father's occupation. The allocation of places was strictly controlled; 55 per cent went to children of working-class background, 35 per cent to the peasantry and only 10 per cent to the 'progressive intelligentsia'. When Nicholas, Emilia and Adam sat down to fill it in, they fell about with shrieks of laughter.

'What chance for the son of a baronet/political prisoner/'class alien'/imperialist agent, then?' Nicholas asked.

'Well, that is not the case, Comrade Zenta. This young man is the son of a peasant; his father is actually the chairman of an agricultural cooperative farm. What could be more important than that, when we are engaged in building our socialist future?' Adam bent over in a mock bow.

'Brilliantly stated, young Comrade Pioneer. So, we will answer the question of "class origin" with "peasant",' added Emilia, laughing.

'But what about this one here: "Reasons for wishing to engage in further education?" Nicholas rubbed his eyes in wonderment and looked towards Adam. 'Please pass that demijohn, son.'

'To be a worthy citizen of our people's republic, through serving our beloved leader, Comrade Matthias Rákosi, the greatest pupil of the glorious and even more beloved Generalissimo Stalin. Well?' Asked Adam.

'May he rot in hell,' Nicholas murmured as he poured himself another glass of red wine.

The application form was eventually completed and forwarded for his comments to the local party secretary, whose attitude was, 'Oh, anything for Zenta. I need him here, because if he leaves, the co-op could falter, and I know that would be the end of me.' So, at the end of the form, he added:

'There could be no better young comrade I could possibly recommend.' The county party secretary endorsed it similarly and the form finally arrived on the headmaster's desk.

~

Nicholas and Emilia were quietly married during the early summer, Adam acting as best man by proxy, as he was still too young to sign the register. Kathleen was delighted to be standing in the front row too and Anna burst into a skip around the room at the first possible opportunity, singing, 'Looovelly wddddding, looovely weddddding, there's a cake at home!' On the wall the pictures of Comrades Lenin and Stalin on the right, Messrs Marx and Engels on the left, looked serious. Rákosi, with his large bald head, on the middle wall, looked simply evil.

Summer gave Nicholas a chance to get his vineyard into shape and Adam decided to make some money by clearing tree branches from around telephone wires before going to boarding school; a well-paid job, but not without danger. With hatchet and handsaw slotted into a leather belt, the chosen student had to climb every tree whose branches had grown too near the wires and cut them back to lessen their interference. The work was paid by mileage and good money was not too difficult to make, provided the young chap could climb trees. Adam's Transylvanian training came in handy. He, being in charge, considered this work much more acceptable than last year's cow herding, and he could also sing his opera arias to his heart's content, provided the foreman wasn't around. The post office man in charge hated opera and could not imagine why a peasant lad would wish to be involved with that sort of 'foreign rubbish', when there were all those 'wonderfully soulful Magyar songs' about. He did, however, admit that in his young student there was an excellent tenor in the making.

Adam worked like a monkey, up and down trees of every shape and size. The acacias came bottom of his tree poll: full of vicious little thorns which tore his skin to pieces as he climbed them, they snapped more easily, and broken limbs amongst his fellow branch cutters were all too common. He saved his money well; after all, he wanted to look smart at the college and he knew that there was a girls' nursery school training college near by too. This spurred him on, and by the time autumn arrived he considered himself well turned out.

~

The headmaster of the college was a dyed-in-the-wool communist, a lapsed Catholic priest who had given up the cloth and had married a nun. He welcomed Adam to the college and paraded him before the others.

His arms in gesticulating wildly, impersonating a jerky windmill, the fat, bald man with the overlarge lips started, 'Your attention, boys. Quiet, please!' He continued, 'I want to introduce you to a new comrade.' He looked down at the application form the Zenta family had completed. 'Best marks in his previous school, yet he comes from peasant stock.' He looked up to see the reaction of the others. 'His father is the chairman of his local cooperative. You see, intelligence comes from ordinary working classes.'

Adam wanted to die on the spot.

'Adam, tell the assembly why you want further education.' He turned and looked at his new pupil proudly.

'Comrade Headmaster,' Adam started off his well-rehearsed statement. 'I want to be able to build socialism in our country and make it the envy of the world. For let there be no doubt, our cause is a just one and it will be victorious. I want to say this loud enough so that American imperialism will hear it even in the White House, in

Washington!' By now Adam was sinking into self-induced shame on the rostrum as he lifted his right fist in the communist salute and added the much-abused word 'Liberty!'

The applause from the reluctant students was loud enough. They had to clap rhythmically when someone said something as politically correct as Adam's gibberish clearly was. One idiot started yelling, 'Long live Rákosi!', which went on in unison for a while, then came the most elating moment, when another one shouted, 'Long live Stalin!' Well, this applause – according to socialist protocol – had to last even longer than that for the previous chant. Adam supposed that the boys did this to keep themselves away from classes as long as possible. The thought crossed his mind that only three years before they all used to pray together at the beginning of each day.

Halfway along the side of the hall two students leaning against the wall with fairly derisive smiles and hardly opening their mouths for the chanting of the 'Vivas' caught Adam's attention. Judging by their fresh clothing they must have been new boys too, but they knew each other, and that made all the difference to their apparently casual behaviour. He hoped it would not be too long before he would get to know them.

Adam walked into his half-full classroom. The housemaster, Dr Tóth – who held a PhD in German lang/lit – was sitting behind his desk on the podium, busying himself with his list of names. He walked up to the young man, who was – according to Emilia - the students' favourite, and coughed quietly. The gently greying and very handsome master looked up and recognised him from the assembly.

'Er ... you are Zenta, aren't you? Yes, you put on quite a confident show earlier on – well prepared, eh,' he stated, rather than asked.

Adam had very little idea how to get out of this predicament. 'Sir, I understand you know my stepmother, Emilia Vargha – now Zenta, of course,' was the best he could do.

The man put his pen down and looked at Adam again, in a very different way. 'Well, I heard she remarried recently. Zenta? That's a Transylvanian name, isn't it?'

'Yes, sir, although the town is now in Yugoslavia. My father was an administrator until the end of the war. We escaped on the last train,' he added hurriedly, with a look on his face which begged forgiveness for his assembly performance. Distrust ruled on such a scale that eye contact and innuendoes mattered more than words. The young student was desperate not to be labelled as one of the commies and the experienced master was afraid to be open with him.

'All right, that is enough for the moment. You will sit over there.' He pointed to a place next to a rather fat chap, right in front of the two cocky boys from the hall. They were just taking their places.

This is going to be a great start, Adam thought as he turned around to walk to his seat. He murmured some kind of introduction to his new bench mate, sat down and started to busy himself with his books. His neighbour's name was Gustáv, but he was told to call him Gusty – Gutsy, more likely, Adam thought, but this is no time to make enemies, especially not of the largest chap in the class.

The school had been a well-established, fee-paying, independent school until about two years before, when the commies nationalised the lot in the name of the proletariat and introduced Russian as the second language. Not so much the language of Pushkin or Tolstoy but rather that of Lenin and the greatest 'bee's knees' the world had seen, or would ever see, Stalin. His picture, dressed in the uniform of a generalissimo with his ancient acne spots carefully removed by the party photographer, was placed on the main wall, in a central position – naturally. Underneath the framed photograph, his most famous quotation was displayed for the benefit of all – 'WITH WAR, FOR PEACE!' A dialectical thought, if ever there was one, worthy of this greatest military genius, who used a gun only to rob a tsarist post coach or two, until he also realised that it came in handy to shoot the odd general – of his own Red Army, of course – just in case the poor fellow might think of usurping him. They were less likely to shoot back than, say, the Finnish or German ones.

The housemaster stood up to attract the attention of the class. He welcomed them all, 'collegiates', those who lived in and day boys. He got some fellows from the front of each row to distribute the curriculum for the year, the schedules of the classes and the names of the masters. It was all there for them, except for the names of the Russian language and literature masters. He went through each point one by one and announced that he was taking the Hungarian language and literature classes himself. The murmur of satisfaction from the class spoke well of his reputation as a 'no-nonsense, old-fashioned master', which simply meant that he was not a commie. Then he went on.

'Boys, you will have seen that our Russian-language colleague has not yet been appointed. No matter, I know the Cyrillic alphabet, so I will start those classes until someone arrives, which should not take too long.' He wanted to continue, but was interrupted by a spontaneous 'hurray' from the boys, the loudest noise coming from the benches behind Adam. Then suddenly the bald headmaster walked in and the class stood quietly.

'I am visiting the classes one by one to welcome you again. As I said in the assembly, you are specially selected to receive the best education our socialism-building nation can provide. Never forget what Comrade Lenin said: "Youth has but three duties: to learn, to learn and to learn." As you know, the best Hungarian pupil of the Soviet Union is our beloved Comrade Rákosi, who was an exemplary student in his youth, winning a prize at … at … well, one of his favourite subjects. You must follow his glorious path!' He stroked his bald head and directed a piercing look at one of the boys, who happened be his nephew, prompting him to start clapping. It was a miserable example of applause, but Adam joined in and looked at the housemaster, who was glancing out of the window with no intention of partaking in the ritual designed to frighten off any would-be aggressor with designs on the 'peace-loving socialist camp'.

With the headmaster leaving the classroom, house business was completed and the master declared that tomorrow's Hungarian literature lesson would include a rendering of Petőfi's *'At the End of September'*, and with a dismissive glance at the door he murmured, 'I am sure it must be one of the favourites of Comrade Rákosi too.' Derision was avoided when he added more loudly, 'Class dismissed!'

Kiss and Rácz, alias Louis and Andrew, were the first to stand and leave the classroom for the ten-minute break. Louis got straight to the point as they walked towards the freshly tarred wooden corridor.

'So you are a bit of a commie, then, Zenta?' He eyed him accusingly.

'Bollocks,' Adam answered his classmate, with equal disdain – taking a chance. 'If you believe that crap I gave the headmaster, you must be daft. I wasn't going to say that I was the son of a political prisoner coming here to start an anti-Bolshevik movement, was I?' He realised that he had just said words he had never heard his father use, but he had been very keen to put the matter straight ever since he had seen them standing in the hall.

'Sure, but wasn't it a bit extreme to say "shout loud enough to be heard in the White House"?' Asked Kiss.

'Perhaps it was. I have no idea how I came to say that. I just loved the rhetoric of it.' Adam smiled.

Rácz was more conciliatory. 'It was a stupid thing to say, but we'll overlook it this time.' He put his hand on Adam's shoulder.

'How come you two know each other so well?' Adam wanted to change the subject desperately.

'We were in the same primary school and both our fathers perished in the war. As our mothers work for a living we became "working class".' Rácz laughed. 'They are only fooling themselves. I'd like to bet there are no more than two commies in the whole class of thirty.'

'That's two too many!' Kiss was serious – he always was.

'Who are they?' Adam asked eagerly.

'Well, Kovács must be one – he's some sort of relative of the headmaster, the little squirt – and Palócz. I don't trust him either, he's always looking around, watching,' Kiss tried to sound informative.

'Don't be stupid,' Rácz interrupted, 'he's looking for some food that somebody might have left behind!'

'Hey, I've left some of my treasured Naples wafer biscuits in my drawer! They are like gold dust around these parts.' Adam turned and started to run back towards the classroom.

The dormitory was right across the barren quadrangle; a large square building, more like a Victorian prison than a college for the offspring of the wealthy. The founding fathers must have been great promoters of the spartan way of life, at least for their sons.

The boys were allocated rooms according to the years they belonged to, so the three managed to get beds next to one another along the middle of one side, Adam's bed being under the window facing the back street. Cliquing started right away and further swapping of beds took place, so that everyone was pleased. There were the footballers and ping-pong players, the latter activity encouraged by the school as a (cheap) socialist game in which the nation would ascend to ever greater heights, to the annoyance of the decadent West. And, of course, there were the gymnasts. Hungary was always strong on gymnasts, but now the party had decided that building muscle was second in importance only to building socialism and gave it ideological support.

~

The Monday morning assembly started boringly enough. The lower school were all in the front of the hall and the last four years stood around the wall or at the back. Not many noticed when the headmaster started his preamble about the formation of the 'Pioneer Corps', the communist youth movement introduced to replace the banned Boy Scouts. BP's movement was considered to be the thin edge of the imperialist wedge and a dire threat to budding minds wanting to absorb the great teachings of the last century's bearded philosopher, which he had developed in the British Museum, of all places. No matter, it had to be done … The headmaster waffled on for a while, explaining that a corps had been set up and that the biology master would be in charge from the staff side, but they needed a student leader too.

'Adam Zenta!!!' Franci cried out with a broad smile. 'We want Adam Zenta!' Adam was about to lunge at his friend but Franci, being prepared, ducked out of the way very neatly.

'What a good idea,' the headmaster continued. 'I must say I had an older boy in mind, but you're right, Járai, as a representative of the peasantry and a good young comrade, he will indeed be suitable. Come along, Zenta – any objections?' Naturally, there were none. Even the kindergarten children knew that they were not supposed to object to comrades who were higher up in the pecking order.

Kiss gave his friend a shove, whispering, 'Go on, do your bit of "shouting at the White House" – scare those imperialist dogs!'

Adam thought he would never make it to the rostrum as he took those first uncertain steps, but on he went somehow and soon realised that he was standing next to the headmaster again and was expected to say something.

'Thank you for making me Pioneer Leader for the school. I know it is my duty to do my best for you all and I will. I have good friends here, who are determined to help me.' He pointed towards the other three and continued, '… and with their help I cannot fail.' Adam leapt off the rostrum without any rhetoric or 'Liberty' salute and joined his friends, reassuring them that they would be sorry in due course.

Organising the Pioneers proved to be less of a problem than Adam first imagined. He waited for the next biology lesson and when it finished he went to see the master. The others were out in the quadrangle by then.

'Sir, I understand you are in charge of the Pioneers in the school. The headmaster told me to report to you, I've no idea why.' He tried to wriggle out of the job.

The lanky young master with a head of bushy fair hair looked around guardedly and, seeing no one near by, beckoned Adam closer by flexing his index finger repeatedly. 'I know your father; mine was a sergeant of his in Pécs,' he said quietly. 'He was also kicked out.'

Adam could hardly believe his ears.

'You have been a Boy Scout, haven't you?' The young master continued, still rather quietly.

'Yes, until it was abolished. I was platoon commander,' Adam answered enthusiastically.

'Well, let us make the best of the situation here. There's nothing we can do about the damned uniforms of navy shorts, white shirt and red kerchief ties – they will blend into nature, I don't say. But short of that we will run it like old times. What do you think?'

The astonished Adam swallowed hard and said nothing. His widening eyes told everything, and in them the young master could see his own image growing. They definitely understood each other. On the way to the parade ground Adam, shaking his head in amazement, thought that so far in his new school he had met only two commies; the headmaster and his scrawny little nephew. This in a country that was supposedly a rampant communist state with more red flags than bicycles.

The appointment of Mrs Emilia Zenta to the post of Russian language and literature mistress doubled the would-be friends of Adam, in spite of his insistence that he hardly knew his stepmother. Their name was the same and that was what mattered to them. It was fortuitous for her, though, as the presence of Adam with his two friends prevented the usual classroom diversions and indiscipline. Yet she had to overcome the natural and understandable hatred of the language she had to teach. The petite, rounded little lady was a formidable language mistress, totally in command of her subject, projecting her strong personality through piercing brown eyes which could pick up any dissent. Her problem was the political implications of teaching the greatest of Slavonic languages, which nobody damned well wanted nor cared about. Emilia needed every trick of the well-trained professional to overcome this contradiction, which she eventually did achieve with total honesty by bringing in Latin parallels whenever she could and pointing out similarities with the great Western languages wherever possible. Thus she ended up teaching a fair amount of those too, under the auspices of Russian language and literature.

As Adam's first senior year was coming to a close, the annual school dramatic production of a classic turned out to be *John the Valiant*; a hybrid operetta and folk play based on the poetry of Sándor Petőfi, the tragic hero of the 1848 revolution against Austrian rule – a choice which he instigated with his circle of friends. It had an inspired musical setting by the totally insignificant composer Kacsóh. The storyline was simple enough: Johnny the shepherd joins the army, sees the world and ends up fighting for the King of France (who is an idiot). His heroics lead to him being offered the princess (who is not too pretty) and half of the kingdom, but he would rather return to his village sweetheart, who – by now – has been driven to her death by her wicked stepmother. No matter; he throws a magic rose into an even more magic lake and out pops his sweetheart. All ends happily and Johnny the shepherd becomes John the Valiant Hero.

There was no contest for the part of John. In the final year of the school was a young man, Sándor Balogh, the idol of all students. An ex-Boy Scout leader (who still wore the badge under his coat lapel), he had a ringing tenor voice, which later filled opera houses in the best character roles right up to Britten's *Albert Herring*. Zenta, Rácz and Kiss got smaller parts, but what mattered to them was that they could actually be on the stage with Balogh and even hear an occasional daring anti-commie statement uttered from the great tenor's mouth. The girls were provided by the sister school and naturally they were all very pretty – at least in the eyes of the boys.

There was one in particular; Ilona, the lovely blonde daughter of the maths master. Adam and Louis made a beeline for her but after a creditable start by Adam, the favours of the freckle-faced and pigtailed beauty suddenly switched towards Kiss. This left a great hole in Zenta's ego. He was still massaging his broken heart weeks later.

The colourful show, full of national costumes and flags and with a good sprinkling of Magyar melodies, was a great success from every point of view. Within a few years Balogh was singing the title role in front of thousands in Budapest. The three lads couldn't contribute much musically as the sudden outpouring of testosterone into their youthful circulations was causing their voices to break. For the very same reason they were able to look at the girls from a different point of view. The warm, late spring evenings of the performances, some of them on open-air stages amongst the blossoming acacia and lilac trees, would invariably turn the minds of the participants to romance. Kiss had his freckled Ilona, Rácz soon found the generously proportioned Cini, but Zenta was still looking – and going back to the dormitories on his own whilst the other two had the privilege of walking their newly acquired girlfriends home first.

By the time school restarted Adam had been in love with at least three girls from the neighbourhood. Alas, none of them even considered responding to his consuming desires. Meanwhile the others, even the younger Franci, were visiting the households of their adolescent girlfriends and taking them for walks in romantically leafy Walnut Meadow – a narrow lane in a gorge, full of venues for a hidden kiss or cuddle. He was still looking in the mirror to squeeze yet another unsightly red or white spot straight on to it. His testosterone level was ever increasing and he speedily outgrew his friends. His dark brown hair was full of lustre, but the damned spots, like numerous erupting volcanoes, coupled with his tall and lanky stature precluded any feminine interest in him, except that of the mothers. They just loved him. Some even went so far as to admonish their daughters for not responding to the 'lovely Adam'. It just made matters worse, as no self-respecting chick wanted to have her boyfriend picked for her by mother, of all people.

Yet he went on trying. Adam joined the dance school, where girls were in abundance, as only a few lads bothered. More often than not, they danced with one another. The lessons were held in the gym, and the dance teacher was an ex- – actually a very ex – debutante. The music came crackling out of a phonograph that had seen better days, so Madam had some castanets to add rhythm to the 'good oldies'. The whole thing was semi-hush-hush, since social dancing was not exactly what young cadres should have been engaging in, but as the daughter of the local party secretary also attended, this potentially dangerous bourgeois activity was overlooked. He even sent along some Russian gramophone records, which after one attempt were quietly placed in a corner.

Adam became quite an accomplished dancer. He was good at the tango and foxtrot, average at the waltz but for some reason very good at the Viennese variety of it. Margit, herself a lanky creature, hit it off with him on the gym parquet but even she would not hear of a 'walk home'.

His first serious brush with the authorities started just after he finished working with the Pioneers. It began with cutting out red letters to make the usual slogans for the celebration of the 'Glorious October Revolution of 1917', falling on 7 November. The working classes never managed to understand the strict adherence to the date, just to comply with the change from one religious calendar to another; after all, weren't religions the 'opium of the people' anyway, as Lenin so scientifically observed? But theirs not to reason why, a month before the party secretaries, perhaps the most despised species in existence, came to assert themselves on the long-suffering populous. They drilled everybody in the art of spontaneous enthusiasm for the 'beloved date that changed the world'– 'for the worse', thought Adam. The scuffle between two boys from the lower forms was nothing unusual. Even comrade Pioneers let their hair down once in a while. The problem was that they started to throw gym shoes at each other. Adam was standing on the podium, just in front of the master's desk, enjoying their little diversion until one of the shoes appeared to head straight at him. He lunged out, dived to his right and punched it in midair, goalkeeper-style. He was proud of himself for a moment, certainly until he heard the scary sound of shattering glass. The diverted flight pattern of the shoe unfortunately caused it to land on the nose of the 'Greatest Teacher of Mankind', Stalin, making a mess of his generalissimo uniform. The classroom became as silent as the original's mausoleum in Red Square.

'You'd better report this to the head,' said his weasel of a nephew.

Adam turned to the shattered picture, which had duly fallen on to the wood-boarded floor, and ten thousand ideas of how to repair it quickly flashed through his mind. They were of no use.

'This is now a matter for the police!' the headmaster yelled at the roomful of Pioneers – his lips becoming more purple with each word. A sergeant was duly found.

'Who perpetrated this hideous crime?' He asked weightily.

Had there been a proverbial dropped pin it would have sounded like cannon fire.

'Well, I'll rephrase it. Who threw the shoe?' He stared into the classroom.

'Gusty' coughed and put his hand up. 'I threw it, Comrade Sergeant, but not at the picture ... er, I was aiming it at Adam Zenta,' he said in a voice that twice changed octaves in the course of the sentence.

'Which one of you is Zenta, then?' Asked the policeman, thrusting his thumbs into his leather belt.

'That's him, there!' The nephew pointed his finger straight at Adam.

'Well, what have you got to say for yourself, lad?' The uniformed man turned towards Zenta.

'Comrade Sergeant,' Adam started slowly, trying to work out what his next words would be. 'Yes, it was coming at me – I punched it away and it landed on his face.' He looked at the Great Leader, whose photograph was totally shattered, with a piece of glass sticking into his right eye.

'So you touched it last, did you?'

Adam nodded, and before he could say anything the policeman had put his hand on his shoulder. 'Come along, lad, we will continue this at the station.'

Adam was removed from the commotion, although Kiss tried to say something to the effect that it was not really his friend's fault.

The police station was only a block away from the school, but for Adam it took an eternity to reach it. Everybody turned their heads to see who was being taken there this time. Once they were inside, the sergeant's attitude changed.

'Listen, lad, you're in big trouble,' he offered much more sympathetically. 'I don't care a hoot about you smashing up Stalin pictures, but we have a man from the Ministry of the Interior here today and I know he will take a dim view of your activities, so just be bloody sorry, won't you?' He said, wagging his finger.

Adam's chin dropped towards the stone floor as he realised his predicament. It was not too long before the man in the brand-new trench coat burst into the room, walked up to Adam and slapped him across the face.

'How dare you call yourself a Pioneer leader?' He yelled at the top of his voice.

It took Adam a good few seconds to conclude a close observation of at least half of the Milky Way, and when his head stopped spinning, he received a similar slap, this time on his other cheek, sending him back to continue his studies in astronomy.

'I shall direct the comrade headmaster to dismiss you as Pioneer leader! Understood?' The man promised, the pitch of his voice rising exponentially. 'Comrade Sergeant! Lock him up for the night and make sure he gets no food.'

The sergeant, disgusted with what he saw, quietly removed Adam and locked him in a cell normally used for drunks. Its smell was pungent, a very strong mixture of urine and vomit, which served as a good nasal stimulant for Adam to regain his faculties. He sat in a corner, deep in thought, and began his one-night stint as a political prisoner. A few hours later the sergeant threw a bar of milk chocolate to him through the grille of the observation hole.

～

Returning to the college, Adam noticed the smiling Franci coming along the corridor. He already knew that Adam had been booted from his exalted position of top Pioneer and quickly informed him that 'the nephew' had taken over during the morning assembly. Adam even managed a smile about that. He had grown fed up with the ideological youth movement that had never offered him anything.

'So they slapped you around a bit, eh?' Franci enquired eagerly.

'You could say that, but it wasn't all that bad really.' Adam began to feel like a hero and continued walking briskly while his friend tried to keep up with him.

Word of his eighteen-hour incarceration got around the school and his prestige rose so high that even some of the girls wanted to know the details, which he, uncharacteristically, decided not to divulge; and certainly the one concerning the bar of milk chocolate that had come flying in through the observation slit. But the night in the cell did have an lasting effect on Adam. The commie regime had certainly had it as far as he was now concerned. He became more resolute and outspoken. The first casualty was his stepmother Emilia, to whom he said that he was 'not going to learn any more Russian lang/lit', and that was that. He went as far as to persuade her to give him clues as to what he would have to translate in front of the class the next day, to save her face. This method worked well enough most of the time, but on some occasions poor Emilia did get the order wrong and Adam would murmur to half the class, including Kiss and Rácz, that 'This was not the section we agreed on in the corridor!' Derision usually followed in their part of the class, like a mini political demonstration, with the Russian books frequently flying in the air.

~

A nation in despair can go as far as to invent heroes who may only live in the minds of the inventors. Such was Bálint Boda, or BB, who was supposedly a young man, strong and fearless, capable of doing untold damage to communists. Like his real counterpart Zorro, he too would leave his signature after some heroic deed, in his case 'BB'. A few of these appeared daubed on the walls of official buildings, and Kiss explained to Adam that it was some kind of anti-commie resistance logo. Adam's reaction was immediate.

'Why couldn't we be another BB, whether he exists or not?'

'You mean actually do something?' Louis asked.

'Jolly right I do – something really decent.' Adam grabbed his friend's arm.

'Any ideas?'

'Well, we have to work out something. Something that would really hurt them.' Adam was in deep thought as they walked towards the centre of town, when a 250cc Tatra motorcycle roared past. 'How about him? The party courier.' He nodded towards the smartest building in the main road, the large red banner declaring it to be the headquarters of the Hungarian Workers' Party, a dreadful pseudonym for what it really was – an organised exploiter of the working class. 'Why don't we take the bike off them? Let's have a look where he puts it!'

Kiss was a keen motorcyclist and had his own clapped-out 125cc version of the Czech Czetka motorbike. He liked Adam's suggestion. 'We could go down to Lake Balaton on it. I have a sort of girlfriend at Siófok and she must have friends. Who knows, even you might get lucky,' Louis teased Adam. Adam became even more interested in the idea of a trip to the largest lake in central Europe, which provided some hundred miles of holiday resorts and was known by the nation as the 'Hungarian Sea'. It had all the good things of life one could reasonably expect, so it should be fun, Adam thought – especially on a new and gleaming motorbike belonging to the party. The thought was irresistible, and they started to plan in detail. By the following Thursday they were ready and waiting for the return of the courier.

He duly arrived and yelled into the office that he was clocking off until Tuesday – even 'good comrades' took their weekend breaks seriously. The lads watching from the open chemistry-room window across the narrow road could easily observe the cadre placing the key into the tin box on the wall. They did not have to wait too long to see the secretary coming to lock the box and the door before he too left the office. Kiss and Zenta weren't worried about the two flimsy locks. They went to Adam's house to spend the night. Nicholas, slightly worse for drink, made a big fuss of the two boys and, having read their interim reports, which were impeccable, decided to take them to the local patisserie for some treats. While the lads turned their attention to the delicious cakes, he had another couple of shorts – a rum and a Pálinka – after which Adam had no difficulty in persuading him to let them go to the lake for the weekend, 'by train' – naturally. On their way back to the cottage he gave them the train fare and a hundred florins for pocket money; obviously the co-op farm had produced a good dividend that quarter. When they returned home, Emilia's dinner was waiting and they devoured the meal in the most convivial company, made even livelier by Kathleen and Anna. After dinner Emilia took to her piano and Nicholas sang some of the songs he used to serenade the young maidens of Transylvania with, many years earlier.

The first light of a steamy dawn welcomed the rucksacked lads as they walked stealthily from the Zentas' quiet cottage, along the banks of the narrow stream to the rear of the party HQ. They climbed over the fence and soon Kiss was giving Adam a leg-up so that he could break the window. They used a slice of bread with a good dollop of jam on it to keep the sound down but, even so, it cracked with a fair noise. A crowbar jerked the tin box off the wall and they had the keys in seconds. The gleaming Tatra looked most inviting, but they decided to push the motorbike along the bank of the stream for a while, before mounting it. Adam settled behind Louis and they were off well before daybreak.

Their arrival in Siófok, the largest town on the southern shore of the lake, was duly noted by all the young girls of the resort, who, it seemed, appreciated the wonderful machine. The weekend was a whirlwind of social experience for the boys; the first time away from home on a pleasure trip involving beach life, music and shows was a new way of life for the lads from the sticks. The girls were all there and they were beautiful! Adam could not take his eyes off the bikini-clad bodies littering the golden sand. The only difficulty was they hadn't noticed him much yet. Once the motorbike was parked their status symbol was no longer any help. Adam decided that the lot of a sixteen-year-old boy was decidedly a sad one. Even the twelve-year-old girls were looking only at the volleyball players performing by the lake. Louis's 'sort of girlfriend' also turned out to be a disappointment. Distinctly flat-chested and totally befreckled, she had a ten-year-old cousin who was not the sort of blind date Adam had envisaged and, having noticed a poster advertising a performance of Verdi's *Aida* in the open-air auditorium on Margaret Island in Budapest, he decided to turn to culture.

By now Louis considered the bike to be his and his alone, so Adam had to prise the keys from his friend. When he had succeeded, he took to the road like a dervish. Budapest was about an hour away and he arrived in good time for the Saturday night performance. He approached Margaret Island from the Buda embankment, and as the chill of the Danube wind hit his face he recalled the moment he had seen the bridge being accidentally blown up by the Nazis. He glanced to the right, towards Orom Street, but all he could see was the red-turreted villa with the trees. Halfway along the bridge he turned left on to the island, and the scent of the giant park full of spring flowers suddenly overwhelmed him. Adam reduced his speed and looked for the water tower. The ticket office was next to it. He parked the bike, managed to get a good ticket for the performance, looked up at the large clock on top of the entrance and decided that there was enough time for a stroll before the first violins would begin the short prelude to the grand work.

The enchanting park in the middle of the great river was just about to burst into full bloom. The late afternoon enhanced the scent from the flower beds and the trees lining the roads and the paths. Adam was delighted to be alone. He hummed the melodies he was soon to hear, which he had learned from the old Russian recordings. He bought himself a *virsli*, the Hungarian version of a frankfurter, an orange drink made locally from coal of all things – a great invention of the people's regime – and a vanilla ice cream. This had to do for his pre-theatre dinner. Having consumed them on the shore, he was the first to enter when the large walnut doors opened.

Adam could not take his eyes off the giant scenery on the stage, ready to play its part in Verdi's superlative achievement. The audience took their time arriving. Everybody was dressed in their best, mainly leftovers from pre-war days. The elegance of the women impressed Adam. Sitting in the aisle seat at the end of a row, he had a good view of the stage, which soon became dominated by Radames. The part of the young Egyptian general was sung by József Jovitczky, a mountain of man with voice to match his stature. Even in the quietly controlled *'Celeste Aida'* Adam realised that the tenor could easily be heard in the last rows and was amazed when, at the end, he went for and achieved an easy, if not a little too loud, top B flat. Adam had never heard it sung that way on his records but considered it perfectly justifiable in the context of this big voice in the open air.

The Aida of Livia Warga started in a more subdued way in her opening lines but by the time she had to show the struggle of her emotions in *'Ritorna vincitor'* the fragile princess had captivated her audience too.

For the second act's triumphal march the producer borrowed the one and only much-loved 'elephant of the nation' from the zoo. This wonderful female of the species also happened to be called Aida, was beautifully turned out in her leathers and clearly enjoyed herself on the stage. Whenever Radames or any other member of the cast sang her name she answered with a decent, albeit off-key, bellow.

Amonasro's appearance caused a great surprise. Adam knew that Alexander Sved was one of the greatest ever Hungarian Verdi baritones, that he had spent many years in the West and that this was his first post-war appearance in the role. He had not even had time to learn the libretto in Hungarian and rendered his part in the original Italian, with great effect. During the closing scene in the tomb, Radames, seeing Aida unexpectedly, calls her name, which was once again loud enough for the animal to hear. The elephant replied from somewhere backstage in her usual fashion and the tenor had to turn away from his audience to hide his smiles. The love of his life soon followed and they had to start their farewell to the world facing the papier-mâché cave for 'O *terra addio*'. When their last soft note stopped and Amneris, the jilted princess, offered her '*Pace*', wishing the lovers eternal peace, the elephant trumpeted her own note into the warm evening. Thus ended Adam's first great operatic experience. Within an hour and a half, at just past midnight, he was back in Siófok. The dancing in the Hall of Culture was still in full swing. Having sung his way back on the motorbike with every bit of *Aida* he could muster, he had lost his voice and couldn't even ask for a dance, never mind talk to girls. This settled his fate on the sidelines once again, whilst Kiss was twirled away by the beauties.

By the next morning with only a few florins left, which they needed for the two-stroke mixture, Adam and Kiss decided it was time to go home. The beautiful summer day was ideal for a motorcycle ride and Louis twisted the throttle fully open whenever he could. Being a water fanatic, he suggested a lunch break by the banks of the Kapos canal, a favourite place for all those 'socialist workers' who could not scrape together enough to be able to afford the lake. They'd hidden the motor amongst haystacks and presented themselves in swimming trunks. After they had devoured their last sandwiches, Kiss suggested a swim. Adam – remembering his problem with water – was not too keen, having been told by his father not to dare to get into the canal, which was notorious for its many swirling currents. The Red Army had damaged the canal base by fishing with hand grenades, an efficient way of collecting the dead carp from the surface of the green water, without having to spend hours on the banks with a rod in hand.

They plunged into the canal water. Kiss was, as talented in the water as in everything else, was a superb swimmer, and he tore past Adam, only to see the spinning eddies with the small funnel-like whirl in the middle. He thought himself well past his friend and cut to the right. Adam was too slow to move away and received a good kick in the nose from the stronger swimmer. He knew he was in trouble right away as, completely disoriented, he found himself swimming towards the bottom of the canal. His panic deepened as he inhaled water and started to swallow large quantities. No cliché can be truer than 'his whole life flashes past a drowning man's eyes'. Suddenly it all came back – childhood, Sylvia, his father's warning, everything, as he took in even more water. His last thoughts were how annoyed his father would be about the motorbike and the swim. One more mouthful of water and he mercifully lost consciousness. Kiss was still swimming away when he noticed people on the banks screaming and pointing somewhere behind him. When he turned and saw nobody, Louis panicked too. A young man of about twenty, realising the problem, dived in and caught up with the drowning Adam, but only just in time. Louis swam up-current and got to Adam and the two of them dragged the lifeless body to the canal bank. Placing Adam face down on the slope, the young man started to push the water out of his chest with the rhythmic pressure of his palms. Adam grunted and spouted water, pints of it. He came to nursing a splitting headache and a bruised and profusely bleeding nose. Then he thought again how annoyed Nicholas would be when all this got out. They were in a terrible mess. The near-drowning brought a lot of unwanted attention to the two, with people advising them how to get home, one even offering a lift on his cart to the bus stop. Louis quietly encouraged Adam to take the offer and to meet him behind the party HQ after nightfall.

By the time they got home, Nicholas had heard about the accident. His anger certainly did not disappoint Adam. Bruised nose or not, Adam received his greatest rollicking since the exploding bullets on the top of the haystack, the only difference being that there was no humiliating spanking. Sent to his 'cave of smells', he was told not to bother to come out until the next morning. But he had to get out, as there was no way Louis could push the bike along the stream path on his own. Adam was in deep thought when Emilia brought in some food for him. Mustering up all his charm, he even offered to learn some Russian and convinced his stepmother, whom he had started to call 'Mum', to help him with some piano-playing to distract Nicholas.

After dinner the chords of a Magyar song, *'Misty Dew On The Hills'* – one of Nicholas' favourites – invited him to sing along. It was time to sneak out of the windowless room. Down to the stream he ran, along to the waiting Louis.

'Right, let's push it up,' Adam whispered, but there was no way. The heavy motorbike, which they had managed to ease down two days before, was far too heavy to push up the steep slope.

'What about doing a Bálint Boda with it? I thought that was what you wanted to do,' suggested Louis.

'Right you are! Let's burn it!' Adam lowered his voice.

'What about their office?' Louis asked.

'Let's burn that as well,' Adam suggested dispassionately.

The short conversation was followed by ferocious activity. Adam went to the HQ office and came back with a dirty rag and a block of white chalk. Louis took the cap off the petrol tank and poured some mixture on to the rag. Then he shook the bike, spilling more of the contents over that. Adam ran to the shed and with the chalk wrote 'BB' on the door. He then ran back to the office and piled all the documents he could find in a heap on the floor. He could not open the wooden filing cabinet, so he dragged it near the pile of paper and lit it with the soaked rag. On his way out he noticed a neat Olivetti portable typewriter, which he took off the side table. By the time he got back to his friend, Louis was ready to set the bike alight. When this was done, they started to run in two different directions along the edge of the stream.

Louis ran all the way home to the next village. Adam's shorter run back to the 'cave' took only minutes. He crept in quietly just as Nicholas started on another tear-jerking song. He pushed the typewriter under his bed and opened a book. The sound of the fire engine passing the front of the cottage made him forget his headache.

The devastation they had caused at the party HQ was total. The commies simply did not know how to handle the arson. First they pretended that it was 'an electrical short', which did not account for the burned-out bike. After consultation with even commier commies, they released the frightening news that it was an 'unprovoked act by Anglo-American imperialist agents in the pay of the CIA, SIS or even the French DST'. The hunt for Bálint Boda was extended.

Kiss's uncle was a Roman Catholic priest in the next village. They offered to sell the typewriter to him and with the proceeds thereof they went to Pécs on a day trip. In one of the small shops on Süllői Street, the name of which had been changed from the original Franciscan Street to honour a commie cadre, they each bought a pair of thick rubber-soled shoes, just like those the Western Teddy boys had brought into fashion to complement their wide-shouldered, long jackets and drainpipe trousers.

The rest of the summer was spent performing compulsory 'social work'. This was a new and clever invention for making people work, not for the pittance they were normally paid but for less than that; for nothing, absolutely nothing at all. Rákosi and his communist cohorts were convinced that they had cracked it. How could the building of socialism fail when it was done for nothing?

Some years earlier, a comrade of the Ministry of Agriculture, returning from an enlightening and elevating visit to the Southern Republics of the Soviet Union (where traditionally the Russians were even more hated than in Hungary), decided that the collective farms should now grow cotton. Feeble objections from older experts, stating that although the landlocked temperature of the area might approach those of Kyrgyzstan and Uzbekistan, with the microclimate being so different the idea just might not be the best one for Transdanubia, were brushed aside. At Central Committee level the advisers were exposed as raving, ranting reactionaries and were sent to the dreaded Recsk concentration camp to re-educate themselves with some rock-breaking.

Nicholas arrived in his single-horse cab, given to him as his mode of transport as chairman of the co-op. He was shaking his head in disbelief when he was told to plant the little sticks from Tajikistan in the Red Star Cooperative Farm's acres, but having been 're-educated' at Fehérvár jail, he knew what to do, which was of course to follow with blind obedience. So, he stuck them in the fertile land of Transdanubia. Lo and behold, two years later the sticks grew into weedy, spiky, horrible little bushes and white blobs appeared on them. When Nicholas was told this was cotton he fell about laughing, went home, opened a bottle of wine and asked Emilia to play *'The Gentle Grave of My Mother'*, another of his favourite Magyar songs. This was really a time to cry, as when he had last seen a picture of a cotton plant in the Academy of Agriculture as a young agronomist student in Vásárhely, they had had blobs the size of Granny Smith apples. His were about the size of a knocked-about ping-pong ball.

The students were told to form themselves into 'socialist brigades for the great cotton-picking harvest' as the newsreels were going to broadcast the event for the breath-holding nation. The four of them, to feign determination and dynamism, called themselves 'The Brigade of Steel and Fire'. Kiss and Zenta, after their escapade with the bike and the party HQ, would naturally refer to themselves as 'Steal 'n' Fire'.

The actual picking of the miserable blobs was the nastiest work ever offered to a Magyar. Bending down for days, shoving your hand between the razor-sharp spikes to pull off the fluff of cotton, which was reluctant to leave its bud, was no panacea for anyone proud of his cuticles. The bleeding started within minutes. The swearing soon followed. For the second day, when the filming was going to take place, Járai turned up with his knitted winter gloves. They were all lined up for the cameras. The clapperboard clapped and the well-rehearsed 'action' commenced. The director kept yelling, 'Smile, will you smile! Keep smiling!!' The camera dollied around, zooming in and out. He picked on the handsome blond features of Járai and instructed him.

'Bend down – head up – look into the lens – smile – get up.' Járai was following the director's instructions meticulously when his knitted glove caught one of the spikes. As he leaned backwards the thread snagged and unravelled, and his finger appeared at the end of the line of wool pointing to the spot where it was attached to the stem. The director was not amused and told him so. 'You idiot – yes, you! You've just ruined reels of good work. What the hell are you doing with gloves on?'

'My hands are full of scabs, that's what.' He pulled the gloves off and showed them to the still-running cameras.

'Cut, you idiots, cut,' the director ordered his crew, who were by now laughing uncontrollably. 'You … you idiots.' He seemed to like the word, his finger now pointing at Andrew Rácz's ragbag of a brigade. 'Get the others and line them up over there,' he ordered, pointing to another part of the vast valley, where the little blobs looked a shade larger.

The cameras started purring away again. Nicholas wagged his finger at Adam, advising him to try to behave himself.

'Bend down – look into the lens – smile – get up!!!' The director of the great newsreel yelled his orders again. Then 'Enough! Enough of these idiots. Get me some girls now,' he ordered next.

'Can you get me one as well?' Kiss asked.

'You can piss off, you idiot, piss off!' The director shouted. 'I've had enough of you, idiots!'

Everyone turned up to see the Russian epic *Kirov*, not because they felt life would be a void without listening to every word the little apparatchik of Leningrad ever uttered in his mammoth speeches (that is until someone had the good sense to bump him off). No. They were to see the short news section concisely entitled 'Cotton Harvest in Tolna County – a new defeat for imperialism' during the interval – after the first three hours.

The little man in the title role went about his party business with great gusto and determination: in factories amongst smiling workers with showers of welding sparks, in fields amongst the happiest of peasants harvesting just about anything in their Sunday best, and even in a laboratory looking down into a microscope, with the plaque 'Zeiss Ikon' denoting its German origin carefully concealed by his thumb. Beside him, a professorial-looking chap benevolently smiled. Next, Sergei Mironovich Kirov was building a dam, the biggest ever. Then he came to the climax of the first half, and met Stalin himself. And when he was allowed to shake the hand of the Greatest Dam-Builder of them all, the audience was allowed to see – yes – a little tear welling in his overwhelmed eye. This was obviously an artistic device to make the second three hours totally irresistible for the expectant film watchers.

But now it was time to see the cotton-picking masterpiece. And masterpiece it was. Nobody could believe their eyes; the camera sweeping through a valley full of huge cotton buds tried to convey the importance of the message that was about to follow. The commentator was beside himself, with superlatives flying like kites. It took the watchers little time to catch on that these shots contained some distant sand dunes, which, of course, were to be found nowhere in the country. But then came the closer shots and the students started clapping as they recognised each other. When they saw their own smiling faces on the screen they could see very little of the plant and none of the miserable blobs. Once again the huge white buds appeared, like snowballs. It just didn't fit. Járai could not contain himself any longer, and when the film showed the large expanse of cotton fields yet again, he yelled into the dark room with a strong, mocking Russian accent: 'That's not here – that's bloody Uzbekistan!'

The cinema erupted in unbridled hilarity, and with the darkness providing more than a little extra courage they shouted things like 'Hey, Gutsy, how near are you to Tashkent?' and 'Zenta, where's your turban?' or *'Allah akhbar!'* The audience lost control and started banging on the wooden floorboards with their feet, drowning the commentary, until the news item came to a merciful conclusion.

The second half of *Kirov* lived up to expectations, totally. It was so boring that a few of the braver ones started to walk out under cover of the darkness, some whispering things like 'It's time to feed the chickens' or 'It's my turn to take the watch at the fire station'. Nobody dared to leave without an excuse. Certainly not the students, as the nephew was right in the middle of them. With many of the adults gone, some were swapping seats to get nearer to friends or the few girls in the college. Mercifully, with ten minutes to go, the story got to 1934 and along came a very sensible citizen of the Soviet Union. Without any further ado he shot the 'Great Man' stone dead. This caused a bit of a problem for the Greatest Leader of Progressive Mankind, so he decided to do the most befitting thing he could think of and renamed the Mariansky Opera and Ballet in his honour. The auspicious and world-renowned company, which had until now carried the name of its finest and most accomplished dancer and producer, was henceforward be known as 'The Kirov' after a dead party secretary whose feet had never worn anything more delicate than a pair of jackboots.

˜

Adam and his fellow fourth-formers were given one more grand opportunity to make their mark in the building of socialism. On 5 March 1953 the world learned that the Shining Light of the Proletariat, Generalissimo Iosif (Joe) Vissarionovich Dzhugashvili (better known to friend and foe as Stalin), was no more. On the first of the month, having got utterly drunk, he went to bed, and in the early hours of the morning a common-or-garden stroke did what millions would have given their right arms and left legs to do. It choked him. His frightened physicians – the few who had managed to survive his several purges of doctors – had placed a few leeches over the revered body and to their greatest surprise the appalling little sticky things did not cure the Boss. They did, however, give him a moment to open his eyes and raise his left arm towards them in a final curse. Fearing acute lead poisoning by being stood blindfold against a wall, or at least an unexpected sojourn in Siberia, they pondered for a while, or to be precise for two days, before one of them was pushed forward by his colleagues to advise the Politburo that they'd better find a new Great Leader. His empire, the self-titled 'Camp of Peace' in the world of the cold war, had not been forewarned of this possibility, but it came as no surprise to the average commie that the sun still rose the day after the announcement.

In Hungary bald Rákosi and his underlings were equally perplexed. They knew they had to mark the occasion with something supremely spectacular, but they were devoid of ideas. For the Great Teacher's seventieth birthday only two years before, they had sent a train full of gifts collected from every corner of the land. Organisations were plainly told to pull their fingers out and produce something really extraordinary for him and, of course, the poor things did their best. From knitted gloves and coat hangers to bicycles and trolley buses, they all donated an item. The eventual cost of the gifts was so enormous that it broke the current economic Three Year Plan and pushed the already impoverished nation to the verge of bankruptcy. For his seventy-first birthday they built the largest Stalin statue in the world, all sixty feet of it, naturally in a prime spot, having demolished an architectural gem of a church to provide the site for the monstrosity.

Now, bereft of ideas, Comrade Ernő Gerő, a particularly vicious sidekick to the bald wonder, came up with the idea of building a city to the glory of the Greatest Builder. And after prolonged heart-searching he came up with the earth-shatteringly imaginative name: Stalincity. When he stood up in the plenary meeting of the Central Committee of the Hungarian Workers' Party and presented the original idea in a two-and-a-half-hour dissertation of a speech, there were no dissenters. Rákosi did worry for a moment. The scheme could have been grand enough to usurp his own power, but pragmatic considerations had to come into play. In less than an hour a leading film actress, the pretty star of many folksy parts, was about to be delivered to his villa by his heavily curtained Zil limousine. He urged everyone to embrace the 'Idea of the Century'.

For Gerő there was only one small hurdle to overcome. There was not a penny in the kitty for this 'city'. But would any revolutionary hero of the proletariat be concerned by an irrelevance as insignificant as that? Certainly not! He would make the nation provide the labour for free, he said with great panache. Social work will build it, in the best Bolshevik tradition, and he looked to every student on vacation and every sweating worker with a Sunday off. This original and unique concept gave Rácz, Kiss, Járai and Zenta the chance to be part of the wonderful project. They, Gusty and the nephew, and all the others, were bundled into a lorry, taken to the site and told to 'get on with it!' Bricklaying did not feature too highly amongst their collective expertise but, an order being an order, in the pouring rain they began to slap a bit of cement between the broken bricks (intact ones were kept for the facings), and before you could say Bob's your uncle or Joe is your aunt, walls started to appear in cornfields by the Danube.

Stalincity, true to the name of the Greatest Steelman Ever, naturally had to have some 'steel' about it. Gerő and his comrades, not to be deterred by the fact that the country produced no iron ore anywhere near by and that there was no available spare electricity supply, went ahead with the creation of their unique scheme of building a giant steel manufacturing plant. Within weeks Gerő decided to come and see how Adam and Co. were getting on with things. The 'construction workers' were all told to put on their Sunday best because, naturally, a film crew would be there. At the allocated time, the rising dust signalled the arrival of the important party personnel. Seven black cars brought Comrade Gerő and his retinue of bodyguards to the building site. A Mercedes, bringing the instigator of the great idea, followed three Skodas from Czechoslovakia carrying apparatchiks and some security thugs. Another three two-stroke Wartburgs from the German Democratic Republic, similarly painted black, containing the lesser comrades from the local council with several more ape-like security yobs, completed the procession. Ernő Gerő, the man of the moment, sitting in the supreme comfort of his limousine, was the most renegade Jew, who had thrown his many-thousand-year-old historic religion to the wind and re-educated himself into the most vengeful, agnostic Bolshevik in Moscow. His vitriolic speeches were only preludes to his more ruthless activities as Minister of the People's Republic and, more importantly, a very highly regarded member of the Politburo. When he arrived to inspect Járai, Kiss, Nephew, Rácz and Zenta's structure, remarkably the heavens opened again. For some reason – and the annals of the party one day might tell us why – he was less warmly dressed than his well-turned-out underlings, who were wearing double-breasted leather coats. First he berated the early June rain, which by then was running down the underpants of the lads, and then he started to walk towards them. He got as far as Kiss, patted him on his soaking head for all the work he had done on the building site and smiled, just for the benefit of the cameras, which made sure that none of the SSA submachine-gun slingers were in the picture frame. When asked to do the same in front of a better backdrop he told the newscast director curtly to 'fuck off' and suddenly retreated to the Merc. The others didn't know how fast to follow their leader, but in a flash the whole inspection team disappeared in mud and rain.

Returning home, Andrew Rácz convinced Adam to be confirmed in the Reformed Church as an act of defiance. He made enough noise about it for all party secretaries to hear, the local one stating openly, 'Zenta has just blown his chance of further education.' He was wrong.

～

The year 1953 started well. After a few irrelevant Politburo changes, which seemed about as significant as a game of musical chairs in hell, the one that really mattered also took place. Everyone's favourite communist outcast, Imre Nagy, suddenly became prime minister. Nagy, although a Muscovite himself, had never forgotten his roots and became popular in 1945 as the minister of agriculture who embarked on a period of agrarian reforms through land distribution to the peasantry. His gesture sadly could not last long, because along came Rákosi and Co. and drove the lot of them into the disastrous collective farms. The Rákosi clique showed their displeasure to him personally by throwing him out of the Central Committee and later out of the party itself. Now, Nagy was suddenly invited to take over as premier and try to extricate the country from the mess they had so eagerly made. Nagy was patriot enough to accept the impossible task. He knew he had to create some preconditions before he could even think of doing anything, and he started off by opening the padlocks of the political prisons and of the notorious concentration camp of Recsk. This action opened his people's minds too and the country seemed to change overnight. Although it still looked like a red forest of stars and rags, there was a whiff of, if not overt freedom, certainly disguised liberty.

The social and cultural restrictions loosened at the very same time that Adam more or less became a man. He threw himself into reciting the poems of Hungarian romantics of the nineteenth century, and he particularly excelled at the revolutionary Petőfi. He would perform at the drop of a hat at any opportunity, from national holidays to cultural evenings. His voice had now settled into more manly tones, enough to start singing opera again, this time carefully selecting the arias he could best handle. Emilia greatly encouraged this with her piano accompaniment at home and at performances in the local Hall of Culture, a grand name given by the commies to a pre-war Tradesmen's Hall.

Adam's voice was steady and had a steely quality which made it ideal for Verdi and the realistic approach of Puccini and Leoncavallo, which was often called verismo. *'Di quella pira'* from *Il Trovatore* and *'Vesti la guibba'* from *I Pagliacci* would normally please the audience. But his greatest success was *'Hazám, hazám'* from *Bánk Bán*, an opera by the nineteenth-century Hungarian composer Erkel, arguably the most neglected composer in the world. Bánk Bán, the hero of the opera, is a historic figure, the Palatine of Hungary who struggles between love and country, thinking that by killing the Queen he might at least save his honour. Sadly he loses all: his beloved wife, his child and then his own mind. The second-act aria is similar in structure to Verdi's *'Celeste Aida'*, though composed decades before that great tester of tenors. With passion and drama well blended, the difficult piece ends with a B flat which Emilia transposed down by a full note, to save the young voice. The little concerts were successful enough for even some of the local girls to notice the changing features of the handsome young man. One of them was Annie.

A positively pretty newcomer from Budapest, Annie was not yet fifteen and lived with her very quiet mother, with no father in sight. As a million or so Hungarian soldiers had perished on the Eastern Front, this was not particularly unusual and no one would question such a situation. After all, people still did not boast too much about their husbands or fathers having been Russky-bashers a few years before. She was of average height, shapely, perhaps a little too shapely for her years, with thick, black, wiry hair which would just curl and curl until it reflected the confusion inside the head it covered. She would sit in the front row and clap until well after the others had ended their applause. Concert over, she would stay behind a little just to give Adam a chance to say hello. Having been given the brush-off by many of the girls in the past, he was only too delighted to see a very pretty face smiling at him for a change.

The spring evening, when the outburst of a billion or more buds changed the aroma of the air from sharpness and moisture to a mixture of velvet and chestnut, did what it was meant to do for a young lad desperate to feel himself at last a man. He noticed the curly hair and large eyes in the front row as he was singing *'Utam muzsikálva járom'* (My journey is music) from Lehár's operetta *The Wizard*. The top note was a comfortable G, which he blasted straight at the pretty girl in the white flowered dress. She started clapping before anyone realised the short aria Adam used for encores was over. In no time he had donned his flat school cap and was heading to the main exit, where Annie was already waiting. Rácz told Kiss to leave Zenta alone as this was not the night for burning down party headquarters. Adam was pleased when he was not challenged by them to go to the bridge in the middle of the village where they usually did their chatting sitting on the wall, waiting for the *Titanic* to pass under them in the foot-deep stream.

Adam's suggestion to Annie of going for a walk in Walnut Meadow was accepted quickly. Too quickly, it occurred to Adam for a moment. Having received enough 'noes' for similar suggestion in the past, he was relieved and started heading for the spot in the leafy crevasse where he always knew he would end up one day. He did wonder why Annie did not have to be at home after the concert like all the other girls. She had no father, that would definitely be one reason, but mothers were usually even more strict. Why not hers? He brushed these thoughts from his mind as they sat down on the still-warm grass and started to touch. Annie's mouth opened enough to invite a kiss and Adam leaned towards the cherry lips, which had a beautiful bluish hue against her lily-white face in the perfect moonlight. The first real kiss of his life was like an explosion of soft tenderness and burning desire. Annie could kiss! No tight-lipped teenage experimentation, hers was the kiss of a woman who knew how to use her lips and her tongue. Adam was confounded. He fondled her well-developed breasts as she lay on the grass and she helped him to remove her clothes. He felt aroused and was about to move on top of her very inviting body when he heard a noise behind him. The gentle whispering came from the right. Annie was oblivious but Adam turned his head, only to see three figures some twenty yards away; grown-up youths edging towards them. He jumped to his feet and yelled at them, as they started laughing loudly. Annie buttoned up her dress.

'I know a better place, on the way home,' she whispered.

'I wonder who they were?' Adam felt she knew them.

'Nobody, just peasant lads, I know them, they're harmless.' She took Adam's hand. 'You, Adam, I just can't resist. Come with me.'

Adam looked back. The three dark figures followed them until they reached the large farm buildings and then suddenly disappeared. She led him through a short cut, past a small building site that was a totally deserted mess of trenches and building materials. They started kissing again and Adam wished for the leafy aromatic meadow. Annie's kisses captured his mind and her invitation was direct.

'Take me, Adam,' she whispered.

Adam pinned her against the new wall, between a pile of fresh bricks and the battered cement mixer, which had seen better times, but certainly not a more important time for Adam.

~

The two met regularly because Annie 'just could not resist' Adam, which even he thought was an exaggeration. After a few similar occasions her sad story emerged as they walked through the meadow.

Apparently, whilst her father was fighting on the Russian front, her uncle moved in with her mother in the one-room home in 'Angel's Land', the most run-down slum on the outskirts of the capital. The three slept in one bed for years. When her uncle got drunk, which was more often than not, he would take her mother whilst she watched and cried quietly, knowing that one day it was going to be her turn. She was about ten years old when she was first brutalised, and for the next four years she had to take the abuse in exchange for her food. Her mother, not knowing what to do, chose to withdraw into herself until the matter came to the attention of the authorities, which solved the social problem with customary ease. Uncle, a Stakhanovite worker when sober and a 'good comrade', was told to 'cut it out', and mother and her fourteen-year-old were sent into 'internal exile'.

Annie was, not unnaturally, scarred for life. Her innocent developing psyche was destroyed by memories of unrelenting sexual experiences with her uncle, involving her mother and herself, and her reaction was to go for more. 'Nobody can damage me!' She would say if six peasant boys asked for her favours in turn, and she would see them off, one by one.

Adam became remarkably understanding. Initially taunted by his friends for going out with the 'village bike', he would often fight for her until he was absolutely sure that he had made his point and the teasing stopped.

Annie kept coming to the little concerts to hear Adam sing, and in his company she would be just like any other girlfriend, except the other girls would have nothing to do with her. A total outcast from her age group, she carried on in her sweet way; tender love in the meadows with Adam, then a volcanic binge of all-night sexual activity with the farmhands in and around the stables or behind the bowling alley, when she would offer herself to the team, and the opposition.

When Nicholas found out that Adam's Walnut Meadow activities involved Annie, he decided that a man-to-man chat was long overdue.

'You know that wretched girl you're knocking about with late at night is nothing but a whore?' He said, straight to the point.

'I'll tell you what she really is, Father; she is the sweetest girl for miles around and I won't let you talk about her like that!' Adam answered defensively, knowing there was more to come.

'Oh, I see! Do you know that "sweet girl" was laid by half a dozen of my farmhands last night?' Nicholas raised his voice.

'I do, Father, I do.' Adam held his head. 'She told me this afternoon. Father, she is sick, she can't help what she's doing when she's like that.' He was close to crying. 'I'm trying to help her, can't you see?'

'Well, lad, you're to stop "helping" her – instantly!'

'Dad, please listen to me. You know I won't "stop", as you put it, there's no way.' His voice was barely audible. 'You don't know what she has had to put up with ever since she was eight years old, do you?'

'As a matter of fact I do, we all know why they were deported here, I've seen their papers in the council secretary's office, and that makes all the difference. It is also stated on their file that she had to be treated for some sort of general infection which rendered her infertile. I bet she hasn't told you that! Don't you see, that's why she does not ask you all to wear protection! That's why she doesn't get pregnant!! You are in danger, son, please believe me.' He reached out for Adam's shoulders.

By now Adam was in tears. He felt as if a thunderbolt from Hell had hit him. He stepped away, then turned and ran out of the cottage living room, sobbing uncontrollably. He had to see Annie, quickly.

∽

Adam headed straight for the dilapidated small mud-brick cottage at the end of the village, which had been allocated to the two when they arrived. Annie was cleaning the windows, reaching them with ease without having to stand on any support. When she noticed the gloomy Adam, she dropped her wet cloth and ran to meet him.

'Hello, Adam, darling.' She kissed the air pointedly , before kissing him on the face. 'Something wrong?' She asked, her hands on her hips.

'A lot's wrong, Annie, an awful lot.' Adam swallowed. 'Everybody's saying all sorts of things about you, even my father.'

'I can handle that, don't worry – you said you could too,' she answered cheerily.

'None of us can "handle that". Anyway, what is "that" supposed to mean?' Adam was angry, tears still pouring from his eyes.

'Come in, Mother's at work.' She took the arm of the reluctant Adam, who noticed her voice becoming monotonous in tone, just like when she first told him of her past.

Adam entered the small house, which reminded him of the one they were given when his father was arrested, but this wasn't as tidy.

'Annie, were you out with those lads last night?' He asked softly, blowing his nose.

'No, that was the night before.'

'No, Annie, "that" was last night, you were with me the night before, remember?'

'Adam, no, I can't remember, they just called for me, I had to go.' Her voice sounded like that of a ghost.

Once inside, on Adam's insistence, she mumbled through her sad story again, but some new facts also emerged. A year before she had become pregnant in Angel's Land and her neighbour had performed some rudimentary abortion on her. The ensuing infection eventually affected all her pelvis, causing a fever so high that she passed out after a convulsion and regained consciousness only two days later. The subsequent damage was irreparable, seizing up all her pelvic organs, and the doctor gently told her that she would never fall pregnant again. As she was underage for the abortion the authorities were informed and, after a cursory investigation, they shrugged their shoulders and sent her away.

'But why do it with everybody, Annie? Why?' Adam pleaded.

'I only want to "do it" with you, but if somebody asks, I just have to. I can't say no! Do you love me? You do, don't you?'

'Of course I do, but I can't make love to you any more. What if I get infected?'

'You won't, it wasn't VD or anything like that – look at this.' Annie fumbled in a drawer and gave Adam her hospital discharge paper, which expounded about a staphylococcal pelvic infection. 'You see, I was infected by an instrument. I am not infectious now. Please don't stop loving me, not now!' She pleaded. He sat down and held his head in total confusion.

'Promise to stop doing it with all those lads. Promise!' He asked her softly.

'I promise,' was her unconvincing reply.

Adam got up from the wicker chair, stroked her heavy curls and began to walk out. 'I must go home, Annie. See you … soon.'

Two hours later, returning from work, her mother found Annie hanging from the main beam of the cottage.

The date was 30 April 1953.

18

Medic one

Adam's devastation was total. Having lost in his first girlfriend the person who taught him to kiss and love, this created an inner turmoil in him, resulting in him blaming himself for Annie's death by not taking her obvious cry for help more seriously and for involuntarily walking away when she was so desperately vulnerable. The fact that he was not much more than a child himself, and perhaps might not have been able to really alter events, had never occurred to him. He decided that he was to blame for Annie's death and he took his mental burden seriously.

His next attempt at singing was a disaster. Halfway through *La Bohème*'s 'Che gellida manina' his thoughts wandered to Annie's tiny frozen hands and he had to walk off the stage, swearing that he would never return. His friends did their best to drag him out of his depression, but there was a limit to what they could achieve with horseplay and other well-tried methods of adolescent psychotherapy. He was simply not ready to respond to anybody's social stimuli and withdrew into preparations for matriculation. For his A-level subjects he had decided to take Hungarian language and literature, chemistry, biology and history, considering the combination suitable both for his heart and his head. He started nurturing the idea of becoming a medical student at the medieval University of Pécs. His voice soon returned with extra timbre and width, persuading a small-time theatrical organiser – who called himself an impresario, naturally – to offer him operatic singing lessons. Adam went along with the idea, but he was less sure of a future on the grand stage. He was always suspicious of his own pitch. The voice was pure tenor all right, but he noticed that from G upwards every note sounded like a B flat or a top C, and he started to croak out on the C#s. This was no problem in concert standing by the piano, but in spite of reassurance that this was just part of his voice 'growing up', he realised that he could not, for ever, transpose a full note or more. Yet the little concerts were really successful. He would belt it out on Saturday nights, carefully avoiding looking towards the seat where Annie used to sit. His feeling of guilt just would not yield.

The pre-matriculation drama production was Gárdonyi's *The Wine*, a witty play about a brooding man who finds solace in drinking, and much of it, until rescued by a beautiful buxom widow. Adam was offered the lead. The production was a huge success and it was taken around the other villages and towns. He even got into the newspapers, getting very good notices and hailing a new talent for the stage.

His lonely success continued throughout the stages of matriculation, culminating in distinctions in his A-level subjects. At the 'Farewell to the School' ceremony the ever-enduring commie headmaster pinned the gold medal on Adam's chest and wished him 'every possible success in building socialism for Hungary'. Adam's feelings towards the old fool were not too kindly, but when their eyes met as they shook hands, to his surprise Adam suddenly felt a strange sympathy for the head. He was not quite sure why he felt this way until some years later, when he read the headmaster's handwritten report to the university praising him as 'a most genuine man'. Well, genuine or not, Adam was ready to find a girlfriend if he could, but he kept running into the pre-Annie problem over and over again. There was nobody more popular at the student functions, the girls were delighted to dance with him, but as soon as he suggested a walk in Walnut Meadow they slid out of his grip and walked away from him, smiling kindly. Annie's suicide was still in everybody's subconscious mind. Not once could he take a tiny hand in his and disappear amongst the perfumed and leafy paths as his friends did. So he just sang and danced away the summer as best he could, without the youthful affair he so much longed for.

Autumn found Adam totally ready for his new life as a medical student in Pécs. The heavy tan pigskin suitcase, which had once belonged to Titus, was packed to capacity, and it weighed a ton. It was designed for porters of trains and steamships who knew how to sling these things around, making the job look easy, and Adam could hardly lift it. Although nearing six feet tall, at eleven stone in weight he was a bit on the weedy side and Nicholas laughed at his feeble attempts to look comfortable with the classy luggage.

The whole family accompanied Adam to the small railway station. When the huge steam engine cleared the approaching bend and suddenly appeared, larger than life, puffing and panting like a black bull on the attack, tears of joy appeared in all their eyes. Nicholas helped Adam with the heavy suitcase and wished him good luck at the other end of his journey. Adam murmured something to the effect that it was going to be no problem at all, hardly believing it himself. He kissed his sisters and his stepmother's hand and finally his father. By the time he jumped up on the first step of the train it was gently pulling out, southbound. A quick wave and he was alone, realising that being a grown-up was going to be a lonely business.

Arriving at the much grander Pécs railway station, he somehow managed to drag the suitcase off and walked slowly towards the exit. On the other side of it he saw a few taxis, and without hesitation called one over. The two-stroke East German Wartburg pulled over to him and, as he settled into the back seat, he confidently ordered it to 6 Constitution Street, the digs he was going to share with Járai's elder brother Stefan, already a final-year medic.

Stefan was a stoic but nice chap. Adam knew him well and much revered him, the way only fresher medics can revere anybody even only a year ahead of them, never mind four years their senior and virtually qualified. He welcomed Adam and pointed to one of the carefully made beds, telling him that this was going to be his. He also handed him a piece of paper with the letterhead of the Medical School of Pécs, inviting Adam to register that same afternoon, before five, when he would be given his syllabus.

Adam looked at his watch and decided to leave his suitcase unpacked for the time being. He walked down to the bottom of the street to catch a tram. In service since the beginning of the century, the rickety old yellow rattlebox came along with a surprising amount of noise given that it had but two small coaches. He leaped on it, taking a seat by the window, and started to marvel at the beauty of the medieval city, whose original stone walls were still visible here and there. It took him up Franciscans' Street – still called such by all in spite of being renamed by the commies after one of their invented heroes – and amongst the small shops, nearly hitting the pavement, until it reached one of the many sidings. These were placed where the street was wide enough to allow another to pass in the opposite direction. More often than not there was a short wait and time to enjoy the sights of this wonderful small city, still undiscovered by the rest of the world. The bell would soon sound, announcing the impending commencement of the rest of the journey, as if it were an event not to be missed. The main, sloping square of the city at the foot of the Mecsek mountain was surrounded by the unforgettable baroque buildings of the town hall, the Nádor Hotel, the Louis the Great High School for boys and an ancient apothecary, which could rival any in the world. At the bottom of the square stood the unique well designed by the porcelain genius, Zsolnay, whose metallic green eosin-glazed structure was redirecting the low autumn sunshine on to the surrounding buildings. Adam felt he was in heaven, and there was yet more to come. The edifices of King Street became more ornate, more elegant, culminating in the sudden appearance of the National Theatre – rococo at its best, all details worked out to perfection, even the wrought iron appeared to be sculpted. The billowing balconies between the large framed windows that embellished the frontage only enhanced the crowning glory of it all, the large dome, appropriately topped by Eros, with more than a little resemblance to his Piccadilly Circus namesake of the same period. It occurred to Adam that all this was intentionally hidden from mankind, waiting for someone to come and hail it into universal glory.

By the time the tram had turned right at the end of King Street Adam knew that he and the romanticism of Pécs would get along very well. 48-er Square, named after the revolutionaries of 1848, was the turnabout for the tram, and on its right stood the imposing art deco building of the Medical and Law Schools, these being relatively new faculties of the ancient humanist- and arts-oriented university. Adam climbed the steps with just about the right feeling of apprehension and presented himself for registration to a chap who looked like a clerk, with a withered stump of a left arm.

'Good afternoon, Comrade Zenta,' he greeted Adam, hardly looking up from a file displaying the name Adam Zenta.

A right berk, Adam thought.

'Class origin?' He asked, now faintly looking at him.

'Peasant, sir,' Adam answered quietly.

'We call each other comrades here.' He was now looking Adam squarely in the face.

'Yes, of course, Comr …' Adam clipped off the end of the word.

'Well, here is your syllabus and your progress index, which will be signed by your professors after all tests, assessments or examinations. Your subjects in the first year will be biology, chemistry, physics, Marxism-Leninism, military studies and the language of progressive mankind – Russian.' The man mustered a faint smile.

After his tram journey through Pécs, which Adam thought to be a most classy city, the words brought him back to reality.

'Tomorrow morning, assembly in the Grand Aula for taking the Hippocratic Oath will be followed by your first lecture, inorganic chemistry, by Professor Cholnoky,' the man continued.

At least we don't have to kick off with the -isms Adam thought, turning on his heel as the short conversation ended.

Adam woke early the next morning. He thought of making an impression on his year-mates and dressed well. He put on his grey suit tailored for riding boots and considered himself quite dashing. The fact was that he looked like an anachronism, as if Titus had returned suddenly. By the time he got there the Grand Aula was full of freshers and many members of their proud families. All in dark matriculation suits, except for Adam, in his breeches, who certainly managed to stand out.

After the national anthem the dean of the faculty addressed them first, congratulating all on gaining entrance to this, the most difficult of all courses, and wishing them well for the next six years. As a word of warning he also mentioned that about a quarter of them would drop out in the years ahead. Then came the personnel manager cum party secretary, the man with the stumpy arm. Adam guessed what was coming and he was proven right. Stumpy, in a dry and lifeless voice, droned on for over forty minutes about the importance of the 'new man, building socialism for the nation' and about the necessity of 'vigilance, for the enemy that is never too far away'.

You are bloody right, mate, Adam thought. The meeting ended with the singing of the much hated *Internationale*. His lips never moved.

The ethos of being a first-year medic is probably less than zilch. With the exception of having to clean muddy boots, the fresher is expected to do anything required for anyone from the second year onwards. The structure perpetuated itself and needed no enforcing. All Adam could think of was that next year he would be in the second year and he could command attention from a lesser being, with the minute movement of an eyebrow.

There was only one exception to this rule – the Cultural Group. If one was lucky enough to be called to join it, well – all would be very different. They were the elite, who provided the shows for the long evenings of the students of all faculties. Adam just had to join, or rather to be called. He wasted no time and approached Stefan, his final-year flatmate. Although Stefan was not a member of the Group, in his coveted position he could pull strings, and for a significant number of heavy favours, including Adam playing Cupid for him, he pulled them. By Christmas Adam was in the Group, singing his arias. This was life as it should be lived. He was convinced that he had reached the pinnacle of his existence. Medicine *and* opera! What else could anyone want?

The organising leader of the Group was a fourth-year medic who was by any standards an amazing actor. As is so often the case, he looked upon singers with disdain. He knew he had to have some, but never considered them to be on a par with those who could make music by delivering prose, and above all that written by the English Bard. He would admit to Wagner being as near as damn it to the prosaic theatre, but he also knew that there was precious little chance of him producing anything like that for many a year. So, having to be content with doing students' shows, he grudgingly accepted Adam; 'A tenor? Isn't that a disease?' he said, quoting Toscanini, loosely.

The first show was planned for the end of the first semester, just before the Christmas break. The commies did try to change the name of Father Christmas to the Russian version of Father Winter, but Christmas it stayed. They could not get many takers for the chap carrying a hammer and sickle in each hand instead of the local chocolate, even if it was mostly chicory.

The show was a type of variety. Comedy, opera recitals, sketches and poetry, all mingled together in a very classy arrangement. Adam got an aria to sing just before the interval. He went for the safe Erkel's *Bánk Bán* second-act favourite and did very well. ZsaZsa, his year-mate, was very pleased, and after congratulating him she did not walk away. Good sign, he thought, and asked whether he could sit with her during the second part of the performance. She said she would be delighted.

The first item after the break was a satirical singing team called the 'Stop Trio'; a tenor, a baritone and a bass taking the mickey out of everything in sight. Under cover of being funny, they even had a go at the system itself. Adam loved it. Having seen them amongst the 150 freshers he knew them vaguely, and as soon as they were off the stage he went along with ZsaZsa, who, knowing the three better, brought them together immediately. The tenor of the group was not too dusty and everyone knew it, including the chap himself. He resigned on the spot and Adam was invited to take his place, with a rehearsal the next morning for an appearance on local radio. The accompanists were Nick on piano and George on drums. They knew their stuff, so all that was necessary was for Adam to learn his lines. They were to meet at the house of the baritone, László.

The show ended with Zoltán, the group leader, performing the 'Nose monologue' from *Cyrano de Bergerac*. He was unbelievable! He took over the stage and filled it with his presence. Every word he uttered had a life of its own. He mesmerised his audience into total submission with his enormous talent and created applause whenever he wanted by the raising of an eyebrow or the flick of a wrist, yet he never seemed to abuse his privilege. The show ended on a high note of applause for Zoltán, and Adam, like the gentleman he was, offered to walk ZsaZsa home. They talked about the results of the first semester and at the gate in front of a pleasant modern house Adam accepted her offer of a handshake. All he could think about was the next day and the recital.

Nick, the bass, was in charge of deciding how near the knuckle they could go, both socially and politically. László, also known as Spotty because of his freckles, knew every tune there was on earth, so he suggested the melody line. All Adam had to do was to slot in.

The main difference between them and any other aspiring trio of singers was that they used the best serious and classical tunes to convey banality or humour. The juxtaposition between the seriousness of the music and the stupidity of the lines was so vast that the listener had to tune in, as it were, otherwise he would be hopelessly left behind. The radio performance made them quite well known in town and they were sought after for appearances by various organisations. This, in turn, boosted their morale and, more importantly, put money in their pockets.

The idea of doing a 'Student Opera' lasting over an hour and using the same principles worked a treat. Naturally they had to find female students with good voices for the love duets. They chose one of the greatest of popular duets from the end of Act 1 of Puccini's *Madame Butterfly*, parodying the seduction of the innocent would-be geisha by the cad Lieutenant Pinkerton. Their version had the anatomy student hurriedly trying to get the female cadaver into bed while still lovingly dissecting her. His surprise would come when the half-dissected body stood up to agree with his proposition.

~

Adam found academia totally boring. When all students declared some interest in a particular subject and attached themselves to a department, he went for biology, to recreate Pavlov's experiments with his dogs. Only God knew why the white-bearded Russian biologist considered that we were all driven by conditional reflexes, or indeed why this was included in a medical curriculum, but counting saliva drops after varying electrical stimuli was thought to improve the character of the socialist man. By taking away a few drops here and adding some there, Adam completed the whole range of the experiments, perhaps the biggest plagiarism of all time, but none the less he received commendation for it signed by the departmental chief he befriended and countersigned by the man with the withered arm. He duly framed it and placed the thing in his toilet.

The biggest influence on Adam, as on the rest of the students, was the tall, thin, but totally captivating Don Quixotic professor of anatomy, John Szentágothai, known by all students as St John. An internationally known neuroanatomist, he was the best lecturer in the whole faculty and a member of the Scientific Academy, the country's highest scientific institution; perhaps the only man in the country who never used the word 'comrade' and got away with it. The students had to fight their way into the steeply raked Victorian lecture theatre when he was about to burst into a lecture. The moment before his entrance the auditorium would become totally silent with expectation, then the lanky man would virtually run in front of the lectern, pull a grotesque facial grimace at the students and declare, 'This was the result of an initial contraction of the *musculus levator labii superioris alaeque nasi*, followed by that of the *levator anguli oris* pulling, in turn, on the *orbicularis oris*, all supplied by *nervus facialis*.' The lecture 'The small muscles of the face and their actions' was the highlight of the year because he was able to personally demonstrate every one of them. Flexing each little muscle fibre in turn produced expressions any gargoyle would have been proud of; this coming from an extremely serious and much-respected man added to the fun of it all and naturally produced a number of very poor imitators for students' reviews. At the end, totally against prevailing custom, he would receive the only applause of the academic year.

∼

When ZsaZsa decided to go for Adam, she told him so in no uncertain terms, 'Adam, I was twenty years old last month and I am still a virgin. It won't do! I want to start a sex life. I want it with you, and I want it soon.'

'I am your man!' Adam exclaimed theatrically.

'The family owns a little press-house by the side of our vineyard. I had the keys copied.' ZsaZsa dangled the brand-new shiny keys on a ring, under Adam's nose. 'Saturday?'

'Saturday is fine. We can spend the whole afternoon there, perhaps.'

'And the night. I have an alibi!' She giggled, still ringing the keys.

~

Only ZsaZsa was more pleased than Adam, walking back hand in hand on the winding leafy roads of the Mecsek mountain on Sunday morning. Their act of love had closed the tragic chapter of little Annie for Adam and opened a new one, that of womanhood, for ZsaZsa. Neither of them professed any overwhelming love for each other; they were just pleased to be in each other's company. Adam liked the obvious class ZsaZsa exuded. She was a tall, willowy girl, perfectly proportioned, with a cherubic face and dark brown hair, cut fashionably short. She was the only daughter of a very famous surgeon and a most beautiful mother, whom Adam could hardly take his eyes off. They lived in an elegant family home and the two women wore clothes of great quality, not a situation he came across too often in post-Stalinist Hungary. Being totally dedicated to the bourgeois way of life he remembered as a child, he felt at home with them, and particularly enjoyed the formal afternoon teas ZsaZsa's mother served up so impeccably. Their friendly and rather giggly affair was soon exposed, at least as far as the mother was concerned. The problem was that mother and daughter sounded totally indistinguishable, even more so on the telephone. When Adam pushed the coin into the phone kiosk's slot and heard the 'hello', it never occurred to him that he was not speaking to his girlfriend.

'Darling, are you busy this afternoon?' He asked unhesitatingly.

'But why, Adam?' The voice started to tease, as was its habit.

'I want you to come over to the flat, Stefan is away today.' Adam twisted and turned inside the small kiosk, trying to block out the noise of the traffic outside.

'But why, Adam?'

'Now stop it, you hear, or I will tell you!' He raised his voice in fun.

'Do tell me, Adam,' she went on teasing.

'Well, I just want to screw you again, that's why,' Adam said in a smug voice. He had hardly finished the sentence when he heard a tapping on the kiosk. Turning suddenly, Adam saw ZsaZsa's smiling face pressed against the window. He banged down the receiver as fast as he could and opened the door ashen faced.

'And who are you chatting up on the telephone, my dear?' she asked cheekily.

Adam walked out of the kiosk in a state of terminal embarrassment.

'You know what, Zuz, you won't believe this – I just invited your mother over to the flat for a screw! I can't tell the difference between your voices and your mother just strung me along,' Adam attempted to explain.

'My God, Zany' – she used her own nickname for him which would soon be taken up by joint friends – 'that's awful – or is it? Ah, it's time she knew anyway!' ZsaZsa changed her mind halfway through her response.

'It's all right for you, but I daren't face her. And what about your father?'

'Now that's different. He would be terribly upset. He won't find out. It's a shame, though, because he forever teases Mother that you're after her, really.' Her voice became mischievous again. 'Anyway, what was her answer?'

'Well, her answer was that she did not want to upstage you.' Eh!?

'Is that so? Well, I'll just have to prove you both wrong, won't I?' She grimaced. 'Come along, Zany, I just happened to read some filthy Western magazines about oral sex. See if it impresses you.'

It did.

As the first year came to an end the People's Army calling papers arrived for every male student. They had to report to the Military Department of the university to pick up their railway vouchers and present themselves a week later at the barracks in Tata, a smallish town in Northern Hungary. The system wanted to make sure that corruption would not set in amongst the youth during the usual old-fashioned lazy summer vacation, and decided to do away with the decadent thing. Instead they would provide some character-building square-bashing.

The large white barracks was situated at the north end of the town, and when Spotty (aka László), Adam and Nick jumped off the army lorry that had brought them from the railway station suddenly all they could smell was lime, whitewash and carbolic. Spotty turned to the others and said, 'I feel a Soldiers' Opera coming on, don't you?'

They were issued with the Russian-style uniform of khaki folding caps, shirt uppers held at the waist by the standard leather belt, breeches and knee-length black boots. All smelling of disinfectant. The terribly smart sergeant major lined them up haphazardly and welcomed them with an impeccably thought-out address;

'Listen to me, you bloody good-for-nothing scientists! I was about to take my family on holiday when I was told to come here to turn you scum into men. So I am not in a good mood right now – in fact I am bloody fuming! So if any of you bastards even think of outsmarting me in any way, let him be told here and now that he stands no fucking chance at all. Understood?'

The company of medics looked at each other in stony silence.

'I want a bloody answer - understood?' He yelled even louder.

'Yeah – yes – aye,' was heard here and there but that was not enough for the SM.

' "Yes, Comrade Sergeant Major, it is understood" is the bloody answer. Now I want to hear it from the top of your voices!'

After the third attempt he was vaguely satisfied with the volume and he continued.

'The highlight of today is that, before anything else, you receive your jabs; typhoid, paratyphoid, cholera, yellow fever and God knows what other crap all rolled into one. It's you bloody professors who worked it all out, so don't blame us! You see the building with the red cross over there? Well, that's the place. It is manned by a bunch of failed medics who I don't suppose like you lot too much. So get over there, and I want to see you all back here after lunch! Good day, comrades!'

'I can't hear your bloody answers! Good day, comrades!!!'

What followed was sheer torture that no one was ever to forget. The feltchers, as the unqualified chaps in the dirty white coats were known, lined them up four at a time, with shirts off for access to the right pectoralis muscle. The ten-millilitre syringe with the fifteen-gauge needle was brandished about menacingly until it was the turn of the next poor victim. The muscle was grabbed between fingers and thumb until it hurt and with the other hand the thick needle was sunk slowly and painfully into the flesh. As the muscle was released, the dubious content of the huge syringe was slowly injected, creating almost intolerable pain as the thick liquid expanded inside the tender muscle fibres. George Garami, the handsome curly-headed drummer of the Stop Trio, was the first one to pass out after the inoculation. He was soon followed by others. The rest just moaned and groaned with tears in their eyes, rubbing their wounded chest muscles. When they reassembled on the parade ground, they were only a pale shadow of the confident mass of young students of an hour or so before.

'Are there any musicians amongst you, you dreadful weaklings?' The SM started off again.

Nick the pianist and George the drummer, sensing some easy option, raised their hands with natural hesitation, not hearing Adam's loud whisper of 'Don't do it!'

'Well now, you two suckers,' the SM continued with obvious delight, 'since the barracks has been redecorated for you professors the pianoforte will have to be carried back to the entertainment room from its temporary housing in the store block, over there.' He pointed to a building in the farthest corner. 'You may display your musical talents by carting it over wearing full kit – on the double!!!' He yelled.

Whilst the rest were allocated dormitories the musical duo reappeared at the door of the warehouse and proceeded to carry the weighty upright across the square, stopping once in a while to rub their aching chests, bruised by the inoculation, and trying to ignore the odd remark from some of the others, like 'Give us a tune, Nick!'

The first three weeks were sheer hell; square-bashing, forced marches of fifty miles in full kit plus arms, in the landlocked heat of Hungary, interrupted only by running around obstacle courses or scrubbing toilets with toothbrushes. The material for the Soldiers' Opera was building up fast.

The company commander was a nice enough second lieutenant, who'd recently graduated from the Frunze Military Academy of the

Soviet Union. Regarding himself as somewhat above the NCOs, he eventually gave permission for a show on the last Saturday, four days before their discharge. A few rehearsals in the late evenings produced a performance that outshone the students' one with ease. Forced marches to the 'Triumphant March' from Act 2 of *Aida* were as obvious a choice as many others. Adam got the star billing in Verdi's *Il Trovatore*, singing a cursing adaptation of the '*Stretta*' whilst cleaning the overflowing toilets. The whole thing ended with the 'Slave's Chorus' from *Nabucco*, emphasising that the students were to leave for home whilst the NCOs would have to stay in the dreadful barracks. Naturally, they were not too impressed with this particular interpretation of events and immediately cancelled Sunday privileges in favour of yet another forced march in the sweltering sun. They were demobbed the following week and a few of them, including Adam, received the grand rank of lance corporal of the Hungarian People's Army.

For the short remainder of the summer vacation Adam was back with Nicholas and the family. The girls were growing up beautifully and the three siblings, to everyone's delight, got on well together. The girls were very proud of their big brother, soon to be a second-year medic, and he loved them dearly. Nicholas was still called the President at home, continued to manage the co-op farm, but also spent a lot of time in his vineyard and with some of his friends in the local pub, the Chestnut Tree. His concentration had much deteriorated since the days of 'Zenta, get your towel' in Fehérvár, and although he had retained his sense of humour, he had become ever more dependent on alcohol. This bothered Adam a great deal and he decided to talk to his father about it, only to be told that it was none of his business. As there had never been an issue of contention between the two men Adam was determined to make his point, only to be rebuffed time and time again. Next time he caught his father sober and alone in the house, after a three-day binge, he came straight to the point.

'Your behaviour over the past few days has been totally disgusting, Father!'

'It has, has it? And why is that, Adam?' Nicholas asked quietly.

'You are the talk of the village and it is not nice for us to hear that "Zenta is drunk out of his mind again" wherever we go.'

'I drink my own wine and pálinka and I do not owe a penny to anyone and my work gets done, so who's harmed if I drink a little too much?' His explanation was offered in subdued voice.

'That is just the point, Dad, we are all harmed by it, the whole family, can't you see? What have we done to be stigmatised as the family of the drunk Zenta?' Adam pressed his father.

'Enough of your insolence, young man. I have a bad headache and I will not tolerate any more of it from you, so let's stop now before it's too late.' Nicholas turned away.

'Father, ever since you came out of prison you have not been the same. We know what happened to you there, but that was so long ago. Why are you being so weak?' Adam walked around him and stood barring his way to the door.

'Adam, you know nothing, nothing at all, and you are beginning to make me very angry – get out of my way!' Nicholas raised his voice angrily for the first time.

'No, I won't! I have not finished yet. You are a very lucky man to have been given a second chance to live a decent family life, so why are you are destroying it with your drunkenness, why? I think you're downright offensive!' Adam looked piercingly into his father's eyes.

Nicholas grabbed his son's shirt and, shaking him, slapped his face.

'I suppose you will hit me back in your righteousness – well, go on, this weak man can take it!'

'No, Father, I won't, because in the long run that slap of yours will hurt you more than mine ever would.' Adam walked quietly to his room, recalling the very different beating he had received after selling the bullets to the Romanians in Transylvania.

Nicholas sat down, put his heavy head between his hands and started sobbing quietly. A few moments later he stood up, brought his fist down on to the heavy wooden table and yelled, 'My God, why have you created me to be so weak!'

Adam's second year in medical school saw him assert himself as a more confident student in preparing for the big exams of physiology, biochemistry and anatomy. At the same time they were receiving ever better notices with the Stop Trio. To improve his voice he joined the Philharmonic Choir's tenor section and immersed himself in Handel's *Samson*, Mozart's Requiem and Beethoven's Ninth. They all had good, substantial tenor parts and the soaring top notes, when the tenors tried to outsing each other, were always good fun.

With ZsaZsa he was seen in the numerous fashionable coffee bars of the city centre and the student pubs, especially the Elephant, not far from his digs. Theirs was an existence in total contradiction to the one so readily recommended by the state. In ZsaZsa's house he found the elegant, stylish way of life he longed for; liqueurs and confectioneries served at teatime, when everyone made a special effort to look smart, especially the mother, who, since the telephonic mistaken identity, not only understood her daughter's relationship with the smart young man but was actually very proud of it. The wise father did what wise fathers do in these circumstances; he retired into his favourite corner, sat in his rocking chair and read the most watered-down communist newspaper he could find. Some of what he read suddenly interested him.

The headlines and the editorials were once again full of the official party lines of anti-Western imperialism, and on the home front praise for the factories and farms that had produced over ten times their norm. But tucked away in small corners they also contained news of the formation of small groups of intellectuals, especially writers, poets and playwrights, who discussed the issues of the day, naturally in the context of the nation's socialist development.

The XX Congress of the Communist (Bolshevik) Party of the Soviet Union was given the prominence an earth-shattering event like that should receive, just like the other nineteen before it. To start with, one sixth of the world's population, which was in the most envious position of flying the red flag on every street corner, did not take the blindest bit of notice. They had heard it all before, ad nauseam. But when the porky general secretary, the ex-peasant and later political commissar Nikita Khrushchev, stood on the rostrum to denounce – in the vaguest possible way – the former glorious leader of the goddam universe, Generalissimo Iosif Vissarionovich Stalin (Dzhugashvili) himself, well, the progressive intelligentsia perked its collective ears up.

'Something might change,' some of the bravest were heard whispering to not too large an audience.

As the Kremlinologists were anxiously concentrating on their Richter recorders, the only bang they may have heard was that of Rákosi smashing his ornamental paperweight into hundreds of pieces in his office, crying out to his shivering underlings, 'All this will change bloody nothing here!!!' Back in official power after the short-lived liberalisation of Imre Nagy, the small, corpulent Rákosi and his despicable lieutenant Ernő Gerő were going to carry on as if nothing had happened.

~

The exams in the major subjects of pre-clinical medicine came at the end of the second year. Adam obtained good passes. He was especially pleased to have the signature of his Professor of Anatomy, Szentágothai, on his pass-book.

The year ended with the summer ball held in the annexe of the magnificent National Theatre. This was a large and prestigious event. The girls came in frills and the young men in their brand-new dark suits. Many of them wore bow ties, the nearest they could get to suggesting formal black-tie wear, still very much frowned on by the powers to be. The ball opened with the freshers struggling with their version of a minuet. The midnight cabaret star attraction was the Stop Trio, naturally. By popular demand they performed an act they considered below their usual standard, but the audience liked it immensely, so to their great surprise they had to present it once more. The whole thing was based on the irrefutable fact that the authorities that ran every state outlet just could not handle the decision-making that went with it. The title was 'On the Move Again'. A bad enough one, the boys thought. It parodied the fact that the butcher's shop had become an art salon or the greengrocer an espresso bar overnight, by the authority of party officials making deals amongst themselves. Set, as usual, to very serious music, the pedestrian plot depicted officialdom at its worst and it ended by describing some recent unpopular moves within the faculty itself.

The gummy-handed administrator from the Personnel Department was amongst the audience and he did not laugh. Not once. The fate of the trio was sealed in his mind; he was going to make sure that they lived up to their name and … stopped now.

After the show the trio disappeared to the bars with girlfriends and fellow students, who, patting them on the back, congratulated them for 'going farther than ever' with their criticism of the regime. George the drummer, an exceptionally good-looking lad with the prettiest girl-friend, Éva, decided to add to the sedition by inviting some of them to his flat to listen to the still-banned *'Rhapsody in Blue'*. This was an offer nobody could refuse. They all poured into the small square by the theatre and started to walk up the Mecsek mountain, passing the Hotel Nádor on the right and the converted mosque on the left. George's flat (something of a euphemism) was a large basement room just about big enough for everybody to sit wherever they could. Éva served murderously strong black coffee and the opening bars of the 'Rhapsody' filled the room. To everyone's surprise it was not the much-coveted Gershwin/Whiteman recording but a new one by the Hungarian piano virtuoso Cziffra, himself a victim of SSA atrocities, who during his interrogation had his fingers savagely beaten. In the thawing years of the Nagy premiership he was released and allowed to make the recording, but when baldy Rákosi came back, he banned its distribution. This act ensured the success of the recording through the black market and made Cziffra an even bigger hero.

'Once again!' demanded the pianist Nick, and once again the vinyl started spinning, showing off the natural virtuosity of the young man whose 'Pour La Mérite' was yet to come. The philharmonic dawn performance of nature outside the bedsit was in full rubato when Spotty decided it was time to call it a day, saying, 'See you in the army barracks next week.'

Standing on the parade ground again, the sergeant major asked for a volunteer 'with good handwriting'. The well-considered response after the previous year's experience was total silence. The second and more demanding order produced a deafening void and stony-faced staring into nowhere that even the Chinese Terracotta Army would have been proud of. The NCO could naturally not give up and bellowed out once more, 'Can none of you fucking doctors write?' It was time to act, and the student behind Adam gave him a gentle shove, propelling him forward. 'Aha, at last we have a scribbler! Your name?' The sergeant major yelled.

'Lance corporal Adam Zenta, Comrade Sergeant Major!' Adam introduced himself in a monotone.

'You are one lucky man, my boy,' came the NCO's garbled and surprising response. 'You are company secretary as from now, exempt from all military training for the duration of your stay here, with promotion to full corporal rank. You will compile all duty schedules for these cowardly shits, understood?'

'Understood, Comrade Sergeant Major, understood!!!' Adam responded with glee.

He was quick to realise what his promotion and appointment meant. His own office next to the company commandant would give him all the privileges of a pen-pusher doing duty rosters and guard allocations. He settled down to work without delay to arrange the rosters for the first week. The chap who had pushed him forward was put on kitchen guard, a highly coveted position because of possible access to the food out of turn.

By the time he returned to the sleeping quarters to meet the others, who were already dog tired after a day of square-bashing, he had more 'friends' than he ever imagined, all reminding him of past favours and giving promises for the future. He was all powerful and took great delight in telling them that he would 'naturally do his best'.

The commanding lieutenant had a passion for popular medicine. He wanted to know everything about how his body functioned, especially in the sexual department. Adam rolled off loads of simplified explanations for him and in turn received yet more privileges, such as being allowed to remove his uniform in the sweltering landlocked temperatures of thirty-five degrees. Sitting in his office wearing Russian knee boots, swimming trunks, sunglasses and tin helmet, he made a ridiculous sight. Still, he was very comfortable as he waved to the others passing in formation with full kit for yet another forced march. As Adam put his feet up and shoved a few papers around whilst 'minding the shop', the rest of the students had to endure the most horrendous exercise. George the drummer, being one of the smaller ones and at the end of the line-up, was given the outdated and extremely heavy Maxim machine gun to pull, which he managed for a little while. When they eventually lined up for a mock frontal attack they had to cross a meadow with a crevasse. For the left flank it was not much more than a few steps down and a few up, but at George's end it was quite an obstacle, with a long drop into the crevasse and a steep climb out of it. He had just started to lower the huge mass of metal into the gorge in front of him when one of the sub lieutenants yelled, 'You there, get a move on!!!'

'I'm doing my best, Comrade Sub-Lieutenant, but it's bloody heavy, you know,' George called back, trying to sound amicable.

'Not bloody good enough, you little shit,' the sub-lieutenant shouted.

'Well, if you want it to get down faster, I can do it,' George answered angrily, letting the cumbersome machine go. By the time gravity had propelled it to the bottom of the steep drop it was a useless tangled mess of shapeless metal.

'You will suffer for this, you Jewish git!' Yelled the outraged sub lieutenant. 'I'll have you court-martialled. Arrest him!' He ordered the nearest two medics.

'Come on, Lieutenant, he didn't mean it,' pleaded Nick. 'It slipped out of his hands.'

'Quiet, or you'll go with him,' the sub lieutenant said, pointing his finger right into George's face, and he shouted again. 'Arrest him!'

When they returned to barracks Adam could not believe his eyes. George Garami was at the end of the procession, flanked by two soldiers. He ran out, still 'undressed' down to his secretarial basics, and the sub lieutenant yelled at him, 'Zenta, prepare court-martial papers against

Lance Corporal George Garami. I'll be in the office to list charges in five minutes.' He was still livid.

I have five minutes, Adam thought, and he wasn't going to waste one of them. He jumped into his uniform as quickly as he could and knocked on the commandant's door.

It took him just a couple of minutes to promise the lieutenant the most detailed lecture on ejaculation in return for not pressing charges. As a result poor George was placed on latrine duty for the rest of his stay with the People's Army. He was allowed to leave the barracks only for the final concert. This was to take place in the town's Cultural Hall. All officers, town dignitaries (who were basically glorified commie secretaries) and their families were present. The lads were given two full days to present a patriotic show. The satirical nonsense of the trio was not considered appropriate and was duly banned, so it was back to recitals and singing. Adam did his Erkel aria and decided to finish off on a light-hearted note, singing Lehár's *'You are my heart's delight'*.

With his uniform still virtually brand new he looked very smart and his top B flat worked well. The pretty seventeen-year-old sitting between the party secretary and his wife in the front row clapped enthusiastically. After the show there was a small party and Adam presented himself to her. They danced for a short while and then he suggested a stroll in the parkland next to the hall as an alternative to the stifling heat of the dance floor. Within minutes they were on the grass, making love. Adam thought to himself, Not bad at all – and I'll never see her again. Ah, to hell with it. They walked back to the hall.

19

REVOLUTION

By the time the students returned Stumpy and the Personnel Department were ready to deal with the trio; all they had to decide was how. The warped mind of the man soon invented a device, the Students' Parliament. In a caricature of the word that would rob it of its dignity, he would get a few commie students to denounce one of them in public. He was sure the others would quietly withdraw to the total state of silence so fervently advocated by the party. Stumpy picked on László, the very popular baritone of the trio. The grandson of a well-respected ex-mayor of the city and son of a member of the Military Knightly Order of the Valiant, invested by Regent Horthy, he fitted the bourgeois image perfectly.

When the broadsheet went up naming him as 'the enemy of the people' and inviting all comers to denounce him at the meeting of the 'Parliament' and demand his expulsion, the news spread around the campus like wildfire. Overnight, Spotty became totally friendless. Fellow students who had courted his attention only the day before crossed over to the other side of the street when he appeared. They would excuse themselves with, 'You know I like you, László, but it's more than my life is worth and I don't want to be sent down with you. I'm sure you understand.' All the fun of being a third-year medic disappeared. With the loathed Rákosi back in power the country reverted from the enlightened days of Imre Nagy to 'fighting the imperialists and their local lackeys through our glorious class struggle'. László was considered one of these lackeys. Adam was the only one who would walk with him or sit next to him at lectures for the week leading up to his 'trial'. His defiance was an expression of his romantic ideals of what he considered real friendship, coupled with his total hatred of anything communist. He just had to take a chance.

When the two of them walked into the large lecture theatre of the Department of Chemistry it was filled to capacity. They sat down in the front row. László turned to Adam and whispered, 'You'd better be quiet, just say nothing, or I'll definitely be kicked out.'

'Are you sure, Spotty? Someone will have to or you're finished,' Adam tried.

'Someone, yes, but not you!' László insisted quite rightly. 'Just sit with me. That will be fine.'

Adam was about to insist when the side door burst open and in walked Stumpy in the company of the student secretary of the party, a four-foot-six, round-faced final-year medic whose head appeared too big for his thin body. They sat down facing the sea of anxious faces.

Stumpy, whom the students rightly considered a moral cripple, opened the disgusting proceedings. 'Comrades, we are gathered here to rid ourselves of a class alien who is infecting our faculty by his very presence amongst us! A remnant of our inglorious past, he is hell bent on destroying the society of the proletariat. He chooses the weapon of humour to ridicule what is so sacred for the majority of us, the building of socialism for our people. He must not succeed. He will not succeed!' He paused and looked up, waiting for the applause.

Fewer than twenty people out of several hundred made a miserable attempt to clap, but he went on regardless. 'I would now like to ask the comrade secretary of the students' party organisation to start the denunciation.' He looked smug as he sat down.

The gnome stood up and walked to the lectern, where he presented an utterly ridiculous picture, as only part of his large head was visible over the top of it. Some could not resist a quiet chuckle as the head turned this way or the other like a puppet at the fair. The ethically stillborn party secretary presented a vitriolic attack on László and his 'clique', which brought a different dimension to the laughable charade.

His charges ranged from László living the lifestyle of the decadent bourgeoisie, dressing like a teddy boy with far too narrow trousers and large turn-ups, to abandoning Bartók and Kodály for the cacophony of

American jazz and Gershwin. Serious enough charges, he maintained, to expel him once and for all. Then he invited students from the floor to concur with him. To everyone's great surprise a fellow year-mate who worked in the same group as László stood up, and a worried sigh went up. Surely not, Adam thought wrongly. Without once looking towards the front row, this fellow stated that he clearly remembered an occasion when László kept on talking during the singing of the *Internationale* (every commie's favourite tune – ever). Now that was a serious charge! Adam and László looked at each other and nearly burst into laughter, but yet another nincompoop started up and recounted that he was told the accused never addressed anybody as 'comrade', which must clearly mean that he wasn't a 'progressive intellectual'. Things were going well for the gnome – his charges were sticking.

Then another hand went up and, to the further surprise of them all, it belonged to a well-respected colossus of a peasant boy; the son of a farmer, he was given a chance to become a doctor and he took his chance seriously. His face was a study in 'terminal acne' but he had a frame and shoulders that told everybody that he was the weightlifting champion of the university. The two in the front were flabbergasted that he should join in. He was just not that sort, they thought.

The shrewd peasant lad began slowly. 'Comrades, we have heard very serious charges levelled against László here and let me say right away, they are all true! Yes they are!' The silence was deafening. 'This sort of behaviour is clearly intolerable in a people's democracy and an example must be made.' The look on the students' faces reflected their disbelief. 'I propose a motion which, should you all accept it, would deal with this matter here and now, once and for all. All those who are in favour of giving László the Ultimate Disciplinary Warning, raise your hands!' He looked around, encouraging everybody by moving his bushy eyebrows up and down.

'Ultimate Disciplinary Warning!!!' The cries went up everywhere as they all realised this was the only way to stop László being expelled.

The two on the podium were hardly happy with the events as they wanted László to be sent down, but they had little choice. Adam also jumped up and demanded the UDW, and so did the pianist and the others. By the time they had finished and the lecture theatre had quietened down, Stumpy and the gnome were gone and Spotty was safe, at least for the time being.

Next morning the notice was duly posted to the effect that László had been given unanimous UDW by the Personnel Department of the Faculty of Medicine, and a week later a further notice appeared, accusing Adam and Nicholas (the bass of the trio) of unacceptable behaviour, setting the date of 22 October 1956 for the next Students' Parliament.

This time Stumpy and the Gnome were not going to be hijacked by a clever, acne-ridden medic.

~

Adam and Nick were hardly counting the days for their turn to be the target of rotten eggs and tomatoes thrown by the commies. In fact they were feeling utterly depressed. Once again, gone were the relatively easy-going days a student would rightly expect from his university years, and they found themselves back in the times of the *Kirov*-type films, cotton-picking and jerry-building Stalincity. And now they could be kicked out, to boot. Generally, in the country, anger and frustration were thick in the air, for people had smelt freedom for a short while and they liked it. Liked it enough to dare to at least moan to each other about it. Some formed discussion groups, like the Petőfi Circle – named after the revolutionary poet of 1848 – in Budapest to talk about introducing a little freedom to an utterly totalitarian system. They felt that further oppression could not work in a country where the gutter element governed over a sophisticated and cultured nation. Somehow they wanted to square the political circle.

The students of Pécs University were utterly shocked and confused by the resurgence of this moral terror and intellectual genocide. The sparkle had left them, the smile had gone, and greyness started to prevail all around them as their appointed day drew ever nearer.

On the morning of 22nd October 1956 the nearly twenty-one-year-old Adam dressed in his best well-cut navy blue suit, white shirt and his favourite white-spotted navy tie. He had always considered this outfit lucky, ever since his matriculation, which had gone so well. The sun was beating down, belying the date, as the Indian summer asserted itself with long shadows, making the city look even more romantic. By the time he got on the tram he was so hot that he felt like taking his tie off, but he admonished himself. If this was to be his last day as a medic he might as well spend it in style, he thought, bringing a wry smile to his face. As the tram thudded along the rickety old lines he took pleasure in looking at the gems of the city's architecture, especially his favourite, the National Theatre. The nearer he got to the Medical School, the calmer he became. Two lectures and a tutorial separated him from his impending ordeal in the company of the very calm-minded Nick. The lectures came and went without him taking in a word of them. The pathology tutorial was more difficult for the rest of the group, who had to relate to Adam's presence one way or the other. He noticed the student who had spoken against László. He and his girlfriend had positioned themselves farthest away from him. Judas was counting his silver.

～

By two o'clock the lecture theatre was full to bursting with students still pouring in. All the medics were naturally there, but no one had expected such a large turnout from the law and arts faculties. As they had spilled out into the corridors and beyond, the organisers had to abandon the idea of an indoor meeting and suggested the quadrangle. Stumpy and the gnome looked at each other and their expression suggested an element of fear. Adam, who was sitting next to Nick, elbowed him in the side and whispered, 'Look, what do you think, they actually look scared, don't they?' Nick raised his eyebrows and smiled in bewilderment. They stood up and started to walk to the quadrangle.

Feeling strength in their numbers, the nearly two thousand students burst into spontaneous applause on seeing the two of them appearing through the side door. A very popular final-year medic appeared and climbed on to the hastily erected wooden platform. He held up his hands to attract attention.

'Dear boys and girls,' he started seriously, instead of the customary 'Dear comrades', and his choice of words signalled that something fundamentally historic was about to happen.

'We have been summoned here once again to be part of this disgusting spectacle they call a Students' Parliament. Well, I have a message for them all. After eight years of their version, we shall give them a real parliament, so, dear parliamentarians, this gathering belongs to you now. No more show trials for daring to think differently, no more class struggle, no more dialectical materialism and definitely no more Marxism-Leninism! They all belong to an alien empire from which we are going to dissociate ourselves from this moment on. So let us hear your real demands, demands as regards both this alma mater and the government in the capital. I will be the speaker of this parliament, where you may all make your points. As far as I myself am concerned, I do have a demand. Mine is multi-party democracy! Do you agree?' He spread his arms out in front of him, gesturing to the crowd.

'We agree, we agree,' they shouted from all corners of the quadrangle.

'Yes! Multi-party democracy, including the detested communists, just to show we're fair – any more demands?' He looked into the crowd.

'Freedom for Cardinal Mindszenti!' A timid student whispered just loud enough for someone next to him to yell out, 'Liberate Mindszenti!'

Nobody wanted to argue against this demand. The 'Conscience of the Nation', he had been incarcerated after a show trial in the most hideous circumstances, which included the parading of lewd, nude women in front of him during his interrogation in an attempt to break his determined spirit.

'Remove the communist emblem from our glorious flag!' Someone else shouted.

'Disband the SSA!!!' Cried another.

'Ruskies out!' Came from a law student, which was then taken up by the others, rhythmically bawling, 'Ruskies out! Ruskies out!! The cacophony of over a thousand voices reverberated around the walls of the quadrangle and ascended into the sky, stopping the traffic of the main street just in front of them.

'This is terrific!' Adam turned to László and Nicholas. 'We must record this for posterity.'

'What do you mean?' Nicholas looked at his friend.

'Why not hijack the university weekly and print an "extraordinary edition!" Come on, what about it?' Adam pleaded with his friends, and shook Nick by the shoulders. 'We could …'

'You mean us, the Stop Trio, printing the paper?' László stared at his friend with more than a little incredulity.

'Yes, I mean exactly that!' Adam did not wait for the answer but ran up on to the platform. The crowd of well over a thousand people had expanded to include passers-by from the nearby cigarette factory as the workers ended their shift.

'Fellow citizens, student friends, ladies and gentlemen.' Adam's last two words sounded like an anachronism, as nobody had dared to use them for the past eight years. 'What is happening here today is too momentous in the history of our country and this city to go unrecorded. The three of us' (he did not need to say who the three were) 'have just taken over the student newspaper, *The University of Pécs*, and will print an extraordinary edition to mark this event.' His voice grew louder. 'We want your demands listed and articles from you all, to fill six pages. So let's get on with it – you'll find us in the editorial office in the Faculty of Law.' He was about to step back when he heard a well-known but dreamy type of lad who was training to be a schoolmaster shouting towards him, using the palms of his hands capped around his mouth as a megaphone: 'Can I write a poem?'

'Of course you can, Dennis.' Adam smiled widely. 'May this autumn day be a new spring for the nation!' he added, in a mock-poetic mood.

Adam stepped down and a popular year-mate appeared behind him to speak. Charles Peter, known as Charleypeter, or simply CP, was ready. Over the past hours he had been quietly jotting down the demands of the speakers and by now he had sixteen of them. The crowd burst into applause at seeing him on the rostrum. He raised his hands and waved a piece of paper at them, asking for silence, then read them out carefully, one by one, to the delight of the crowd, which cheered every demand in turn. The main ones being:

The withdrawal of the Red Army from the territory of Hungary.

The immediate disbanding of the SSA (the secret police) and the arrest and trial of those involved in atrocities in the past.

The liberation of Cardinal Mindszenty.

Withdrawal from the Warsaw Treaty and a declaration of Hungarian neutrality.

A free general election, with the participation of all the political parties of 1945.

The rest of the demands covered the whole spectrum of everything they could think of; a larger pension for war widows, the disbanding of the classification system, the return of the Soviet-controlled uranium mines near the city, and many more. He read them with such clarity and gusto that everyone thought he had just invented them all. The applause he received after the sixteenth was so tumultuous that some even tried to lift him on their shoulders. CP was never going to be the same again. With the twenty-two demands – by the time he had finished – he had become a dedicated anti-communist and an advocate of the ideals of the day, when the platform belonged to him, if only for a few precious history-changing minutes.

When he left the platform Adam was waiting for him.

'Let's have them, CP, they are going on the front page with Kiss's poem, it's brilliant!' He snatched the pencilled sheets of paper out of his hands, and noticed that Dennis was still in a heaven of his own making.

Without waiting for his reaction, Adam dragged László and Nicholas to the editorial office situated in the Faculty of Law, urging them to start to make some sense of the various pieces of paper that had started to pile on the desk of the editor. The holder of the office to date had been the senior lecturer in Marxism-Leninism, who, sensing that his days were numbered, had the audacity to take the platform and address the students, whilst Adam settled into his chair.

The tall and extremely good-looking lecturer raked his wavy fair hair with his fingers and reassured everybody that his on-the-spot conversion to democracy by his own students was absolute and permanent. Living up to his reputation as a most eloquent man, or simply verbose, according to others on the staff, he went on to demand his own party 'to cease the outrageous wounding of the sense and sensibilities of this, our much-hurt nation'.

He fooled only a few, and after receiving the least applause of the evening, he did not even try to claim back his office from Adam, who was by now talking to some of the printers with the assuredness of someone who knew absolutely nothing about typography. Nevertheless, by midnight the skeleton of the intended paper was there, to the greatest surprise of the trio.

The elated crowd was reluctant to disperse, and the fifth-year speaker took to the platform yet again. He officially closed the Second Students' Parliament and asked the boys and girls to note the gathering of the secret police outside the gates.

'This meeting was undoubtedly the overture to further political changes and we must now look to the capital for leadership in the person of Imre Nagy. Only he can guide our movement to a successful conclusion.' Pointing to the bunch of leather-coated men, he added, 'Do not be provoked by them, they belong to the past. Give them no excuse to interfere with our way. Let's see what happens elsewhere, for something surely will. For those of you who thought that the past few hours were simply a sweet dream, I can only say buy our newspaper as soon as it's on the streets and you will be able to read every word you have heard here. And now, let us sing our national anthem.' The large and happy crowd burst into Erkel's inspired music to Kölcsey's 'Hymnus': *'God Bless the Hungarian, with Good Mood and Thy Bounty'*.

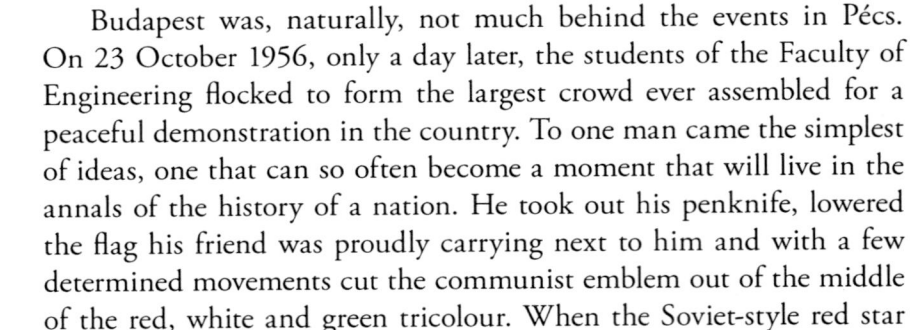

Budapest was, naturally, not much behind the events in Pécs. On 23 October 1956, only a day later, the students of the Faculty of Engineering flocked to form the largest crowd ever assembled for a peaceful demonstration in the country. To one man came the simplest of ideas, one that can so often become a moment that will live in the annals of the history of a nation. He took out his penknife, lowered the flag his friend was proudly carrying next to him and with a few determined movements cut the communist emblem out of the middle of the red, white and green tricolour. When the Soviet-style red star sitting on top of a bunch of wheat and a hammer fell to the ground, a cheer went up, and so the process, later known as the 'days of the falling stars', began. As the long procession moved on the hated red stars on top of official buildings, schools and factories were pulled down in ever-increasing numbers, to the delight of the watching populace, who became happy falling-star-gazers, mesmerised by this political version of an astronomical phenomenon.

Motivated by the events in the Polish city of Poznań not long before, the leaders of the demonstration wanted to record their sympathy with the only friendly Slav nation in Europe. They led the crowd to the statue of General Bem, a much-loved Polish soldier who was one of the most successful generals of the 1848 War of Independence, which had been cruelly suppressed by the Cossacks of Tsar Nicholas II. Full of symbolism, full of emotion and full of nationalistic fervour, the crowd was beginning to sense its strength, and needed only the slightest stimulus to change its mood. It came when the nation's favourite actor, Imre Sinkovits, stood up to recite the country's best-known poem, Petőfi's 'National Song', which had heralded the 1848 revolution against the Austrian empire. The first verse really summed it up:

> *Arise, Magyar, it's your country calling,*
>
> *Now is the moment, now or never.*
>
> *Shall we be slaves, shall we be free,*
>
> *That's the question, what's your answer?*

… and the crowd joined in the refrain, for everyone knew the poem by heart:

> *God of Magyars, we swear, we swear,*
>
> *We won't be slaves, any longer!*

From that moment events took an almost cataclysmic turn. Within a few hours the largest statue of Stalin in the world was pulled down by sheer force, leaving only Joe's boots on the plinth. The leaders of the initial and orderly demonstration lost control of the enormous crowd, which had split into two main groups. One headed to the radio station to demand the reading of their fourteen points and the other to the beautiful neo-Gothic Parliament by the side of the Danube, hoping that they might hear Imre Nagy speaking.

The SSA was ready for them at both places. They had positioned themselves inside the broadcasting building and on the roof of the House. The street in front of the Hungarian Radio Building was soon filled beyond its capacity by the crowd, which contained increasing numbers of ordinary workers. They were demanding the appearance of the ex-premier and interspersed their chants for him with rhythmic shouts of 'Ruskies out!' That was all the party hierarchy inside needed to hear. Someone ordered one of the three hundred SSA henchmen to open fire to frighten the crowd. It was a fatal mistake by the communists as the crowd might well have dispersed as darkness closed in. By half past nine in the evening the secret police were freely firing into the masses in a vain attempt to clear the street. The officials inside telephoned the nearby army barracks for help. When the units arrived it did not take them too long to appraise the situation and side with the insurgents. The armed phase of the revolution had begun.

In the building of the Central Committee of the party not much more than a pistol bullet flight away from the Parliament, the hated Ernő Gerő – that unhappy man of the wet day in Stalincity with Adam – put on his thick spectacles and dialled the Kremlin. He was reassured that the Soviet units stationed in Hungary were on full alert; they had already left their bases and between 2 and 3 am they would occupy the capital. The city, which had given them a rough enough time in the first months of 1945, was ready, and when they arrived again they got a reception the mighty and revered Red Army would never forget. The Hungarian forces were by now siding with the insurgents, and reinforced by students as young as ten years old and workers as old as great-grandfathers. They attacked the T34 tanks with bare hands, inferior firepower and Molotov cocktails, until they were totally annihilated. Their military leader emerged from the nearby tank division. The six-foot-six-inch Colonel Paul Maléter, soon to symbolise the new thinking in the army, was a hundred per cent behind the crowd that, alas, still lacked credible political leadership. This gap was to be filled by Imre Nagy again. Although he had been kicked out of the party after his premiership in 1953 he was now invited to the Central Committee building and was appointed to the same post. There was simply no other man in the land of similar stature and unblemished political past. His first utterances on radio amounted to little more than finding his feet in the melee, but as time passed he realised the historical significance of the moment and declared his colours, agreeing with most of the fourteen points broadcast on the waves of the now 'Free' Kossuth Radio.

Naturally, neither the Russians nor the SSA would give up after the first round, which they had lost so comprehensively. So on 25 October, 'Bloody Thursday' – for every self-respecting nation has this adjective placed before at least one day of the week – people began fraternising with the few Russian units they had not totally blown to bits and began to drape the tanks with the Hungarian flags. Once the Russians learned the real reason for their presence they were perfectly willing to give the demonstrators an escort to the Parliament, to listen to an address by Nagy. To add to the dramatic tension the radio started to play Beethoven's Egmont overture, which was repeated at every possible opportunity for the next few confused days. When they arrived at Kossuth Square some well-concealed Russian units, or perhaps even the SSA on the roofs of the adjacent government buildings, started to fire indiscriminately into the swirling crowd below; they killed 120 people in as many seconds. This action changed the attitude of the people from being dismissive of them – in the ecstasy of victory – to something they would much regret in the following few days. The secret police suddenly became know for what they really were, 'the murdering SSA', the 'people- killers', who would be hunted down by everyone who had a chance to take a rifle in his hands.

～

Meanwhile, back in Pécs, Adam was busy trying to put together the next edition of the weekly. He was quietly proud of the interviews he had managed get for it from the mayor of the city, the army commander-in-chief, Colonel Csikor, and especially the one from the manager of the National Theatre, Mr Katona. The manager told Adam that he would re launch the season with Erkel's *Bánk Bán*. I must start practising immediately, Adam thought. I might even audition for understudy of the lead tenor. On the way out he was already humming the Act 2 aria as he walked down the ornate winding staircase while the lift stood idly by, the inevitable 'Out of Order' notice on its door handle.

At the university offices the animated conversation was all about no food reaching the capital owing to the Russian ring of armour around the perimeter. There were a few well-established points where a van or a lorry might get through, but to feed over two and a half million mouths was a different problem, needing concerted action. They had to get out to the villages and get some help. Nick was ready to drive a van and shouted for Adam.

'Jump on quickly, I'll drop you at Birjád, where you can read out this notice to the peasants whilst I go on to the next village and do the same. I'll pick you up on the way back.' He shoved a piece of stencilled paper into his friend's hand. Adam understood the urgency and in no time they were on their way. He looked at the piece of paper.

'Just a minute, I wouldn't give half a loaf of last week's stale bread to anyone reading this to me, it's so anodyne. We must beef it up a bit.' He took his pen out of his jacket pocket and started to make alterations, adding emotive adjectives. The 'population' of Birjad became hard working and would part with their spare food as their patriotic duty to the brave freedom fighters who, although gloriously victorious, now lay besieged by the tyrannical Red Army. A few more well-placed, rather obvious and crude adjectives here and there and Adam was ready. He jumped off the van and ran into the office, demanding the village crier. When the man in knee boots, sheepskin coat and hat pulled his long pipe out of his mouth, Adam could see both of his teeth, even though they were on different sides of his mouth, one on his upper jaw dangling down on a long brown root and the other in the middle of the lower jaw, reaching upwards, with not a chance of meeting its mate.

'Get your side drum, mister, and roll on it like never before. Today I will be doing the crying. Come on now, we have no time to waste.' Adam gave the man a push as he tried to fasten the braided buttons on his coat.

The unlikely duo first stopped by a leafless oak tree opposite the hall. The man rolled his drum and heads started to appear from the cottages. Adam stood on the plank of wood that served as a resting place for the elders of the village and read the improved text pleading for foodstuff. He looked around for reactions. They came in abundance.

'Never understood half of them long words, son, but your heart must be in the right place. How about a couple of chickens?' Called an old peasant woman, grinning toothlessly at him. Is there no dentist in this godforsaken place? Adam thought.

'How about a couple of dozen eggs?' Shouted a young maid, dressed as a married woman, her head covered with a heavily hand-embroidered scarf. Worth a fortune, Adam thought, a whole winter's work is in that.

'We are very grateful for the eggs, but we do need more meat!' Adam shouted back.

'You can have this smoked ham,' a younger man bellowed, bringing a hind leg wrapped in white linen.

'Brilliant!' Adam yelled. 'Take them over there by the bus shelter, just outside the hall. My friend will be back in a minute with the van.' He moved along the muddy street and his companion started rolling the side drum again. By the time they had reached the next stop in front of the church, just below the large and now empty stork's nest built on the electricity pylon, they had been joined by a few children marching to the rhythm of the drum with military precision. Adam made a few more improvements to his text as the food poured in, now including bags of potatoes and the inevitable sacks of cabbages. After two more stops he decided to call it a day and waited for the van. The two were delighted with their haul, packed solidly in the van. The pianist knew the outskirts of the city better and headed for the tobacco factory, which one could smell for miles yet miss its gates with ease. As they unloaded into the receiving bay they were simply astonished. The mountain of food was begging to be taken to the hungry in Budapest. Tired, Nick decided to rest for a while in a quieter corner of the noisy factory and declared that he would be ready to leave in four hours. Adam went back to the office to see how things were coming along, only to find total chaos.

'Zenta!' A fourth-year law student yelled at the astonished Adam. 'Some commies or SSA were here last night and the bastards have destroyed all our typed scripts and stencil machines. There will be no newspaper out of this set-up for at least a week!'

Adam was speechless, with tears in his eyes. He started to pick pieces of paper off the dirty floor, trying to match his handwriting on them. It was useless. He tried to roll a piece of crumpled paper into the typewriter to rewrite some of the interviews from memory, but the old Olivetti had been kicked around by the previous night's visitors and refused to accept it. Adam decided to cross the large quadrangle to find his friends and tell them the bad news. He ran the hundred yards as fast as he could.

'Am I glad I see you,' shouted László, spotting the dazed Adam as he ran inside the dormitory building, which was doubling up as their brigade HQ. He handed Adam a National Guard arm tricolour and stuck a Second World War rifle in his hand. 'Come along, the other two are waiting in the courtyard, we have our own personnel carrier, so we must move quickly. There is a little arresting of commies to be done. I thought this would be right up your street!' He didn't wait for an answer, there was no need for one. Adam followed his friend, whose confidence was growing by the minute.

The army vehicle and the driver, a regular corporal, were waiting on the corner. The trio plus another year-mate, Zoltán, a quiet, big and burly chap, clambered on to the tail end of the open-back green carrier. Nicholas, the bass, started to speak quietly. 'I will be acting commander of this special unit whose orders are to arrest three of the most vicious commies in this city. I have a list here with some names and addresses.' He waved a piece of notepaper. 'We will have to find them and bring them into the police station. The first one is Major Nemes, the local chief of the secret police.'

'I know where he lives. Not too far from us in the new part of the town,' called Zoltán, lifting his rifle to draw more attention to himself.

'OK, Zoli, you instruct the corporal.' Nick sat down as the carrier pulled out of the cobblestoned courtyard.

'What if these chaps do not want to come?' Adam asked, thinking there might be an article in all this.

'We will just have to make them, won't we,' Nick returned, patting his awkward old-fashioned rifle.

'You mean to fire these things?' Asked László in amazement.

'Listen, lads, this is now actually a revolution.' Nick emphasised every word. 'There is no going back as it has its own momentum now and we are just tiny cogs in the whole thing.'

'You know something, chaps?' Adam's eyes swept around the four of them. 'We look quite an intimidating lot. With these trench-coat-style macs and wide-brimmed hats we could even call ourselves the "Stetson Hat Hit Squad". Now nobody in his right mind would dream of resisting such a ferocious-looking lot.' He too patted his rifle.

When the car pulled up at the first address, László went to the back entrance. Nicholas and Zoltán knocked at the front door of the new tenement building and Adam crossed to the other side of the road, cocked his rifle and aimed at one of the second-floor windows. He knew this sort of building well; Flat 8 had to be at the back.

The knock on the door was answered by the wanted man. Major Nemes was a colossus, but he was also a pragmatic policeman and decided not to argue with the loaded gun. 'I'll be back in a couple of days,' he shouted inside the house. 'Don't you worry.' He put on his coat, the size of a small tent, and climbed into the back of the carrier casually.

'So you are students and so-called revolutionaries?' Nemes said, turning to Adam.

'I don't think we are here to discuss what or who we are,' Adam replied quietly.

'Stop, you lousy dogs! Stop at once.' The cry became louder as a young woman ran out to the carrier and tried to get on it as the others were clambering up. 'Release my father at once! Don't you see, you're just as bad as him; you're doing the same as he was doing. You're no better; this is just going to go on and on. Stop, you dogs!' The fierce yet pretty woman wanted to carry on but the corporal stamped his foot hard on the accelerator.

'She's right, you know, I'll be back for you and the rest pretty soon. Pretty soon.' The major's voice became quieter and more thoughtful.

Adam looked at his cocked rifle and then his captive's fat and reddened face, wondering whether he was doing the right thing.

The city Communist Party secretary was more than surprised when Adam and László burst into his office while Nick stayed with Nemes and Zoli, minding the entrance to the building. Mr Molnár did his best to edge back to his desk but Adam spotted his intention and beat him to it.

'I'll have that, thank you!' He pulled out the heavy oak-panelled middle drawer and took the shining Beretta and a tin can of rounds from it, placing the gun in his coat pocket. The secretary didn't give them any more trouble. On climbing into the car he saw the major and he managed a wry smile, expressing his delight to be in 'such good company'. Adam quickly reassured him that 'it was to get even better, with a little luck', and told the driver to carry on to King Street.

The office of the county prosecutor was on the first floor of a building in a narrow street connecting King Street and the Apollo cinema. It was too narrow for the car to turn into, so they left it on the main road with Zoltán in charge of the two prisoners. Nicholas told Adam to cover the front door and the two of them walked into the office, startling two men who were busy burning papers in the large tiled hearth standing in the corner of the room.

'Prosecutor Schaffhauser?' Asked Nick, pointing his rifle.

'I am he,' the heavily bespectacled middle-aged man with a slight hunchback replied.

'And who would you be, sir? Nick asked the other.

'I am his deputy,' the younger man answered quietly, looking at the gun in the hand of the student.

'It must be our lucky day!' Nick exclaimed. 'Well, both of you, downstairs and into the car – quickly, gentlemen, very quickly.'

'Hey, lads, we got an extra one here, I'm sure they won't mind, will they?' László was pleased with the hour's work.

They all sat on the bench seats of the carrier, each prisoner alternating with one of the medics. Nemes once again broke the silence.

'In all seriousness, gentlemen, you're making a very big mistake.' He looked at Adam sitting opposite him. 'You would do yourselves a favour if you were to drop us at the edge of the city and then we could walk to the nearest Soviet unit. If you don't, we will hunt you down when they return.'

'Don't you think we are doing you an actual favour by locking you up safely? This crowd would lynch the lot of you if we were to tell them who you were!' Adam looked him straight in the eye. 'So, quiet please, and just consider yourselves lucky, that's all.'

'To the main police station, 48-er Square,' Nicholas ordered the corporal.

The drive took no more than five minutes. Nicholas showed his papers to the duty sergeant, who could not believe his eyes when he saw the four prisoners.

'You know, you're brave lads – I mean, taking these four on.' He shook his head from side to side. 'Two in each cell be OK?' He asked.

'Perfectly OK!' Nicholas answered.

The heavy metal doors opened and banged closed behind the four, giving hardly any time for the students to look inside the cold cells.

Adam took the keys and looked at his friends. 'Should we throw these away?' he asked with a mischievous smile.

⁓

By the time they had packed a large van full of food collected from the nearby villages it was nearly midday, perhaps a little late to set off for the capital, but the driver was still nowhere to be found. When he eventually turned up he was reeking of pálinka. Staggering into the courtyard with two days' growth of beard, he reassured them all that he was looking forward to doing his bit for the revolution and if he was given the chance he wouldn't mind kicking a few Russian arses as well.

Adam and Nicholas were to be the caretakers of the inebriated Steven's lorry and were in charge of the proper distribution of its cargo. Steven hugged them on arrival, declaring, to the students' surprise, that 'there has always been a strong bond between tobacco workers and future doctors and as a foreman it was his duty to maintain this important connection'. As he would have liked to have been an ambulance driver, things were working out just fine with this impending trip. But to further strengthen his medical involvement, he was also going to make absolutely sure that his five-year-old granddaughter would become a doctor, or, if that was not possible, at least 'a nurse in a very senior position'.

Rapport established, they set off on Highway 6, which originated in 48-er Square. They were soon passing the Zsolnay porcelain factory, now set to produce electricity pylon insulators for the People's State, rather than the magnificent items that had won first prize at the Paris

Exhibition. They soon entered the foothills of the Mecsek mountains, to descend on the north-eastern side, passing the viaduct. The road itself was good – in fact the only one built since the war – so once they reached the flat they could travel at the breakneck speed of fifty miles per hour. They passed the Szekszárd junction on the right and soon realised that most of the traffic was made up of similar lorries and vans, clearly carrying food for the capital. Like Adam and Nick, the accompanying men were wearing the red, white and green armbands of the National Guard; some were also flying the tricolour, naturally minus the communist badge, which had been cut out of the white band, leaving just a hole; very much the symbol of the uprising.

Steven took every possible gamble during the four-hour journey, recklessly overtaking farm machinery and animal-drawn carts in the poor visibility of the grey autumn afternoon. He insisted that there was 'nothing to worry about whilst the road is dry'. The two young men looked at each other disbelievingly. Yes, the road was dry, so to hell with worrying – drunk or not, the man behind the wheel seemed to know what he was doing.

Soon after reaching the Danube for the second time, at Dunaföldvár, a sleepy town on the banks of the river, Steven decided to 'overtake a few' and put his foot down. After a cart drawn by a rather emaciated horse and a tractor dragging a carrier full of sugar beet, there was just another van to overtake. As they pulled next to it Adam recognised the familiar van from the village. On its side the first two words of the 'Red Star Cooperative Farm' were hastily overpainted with the name Petőfi, indicating the fall of yet another star. He stood up a little, trying to get a better view of the occupants of the cab, and saw his father concentrating on the road ahead. He was oblivious of his son, who, by now, was waving frantically to catch his attention. Nicholas Zenta was also involved in the very same activity. He had collected and was driving a van full of food to Budapest when he had become aware of the other van overtaking him. He had murmured to his aide sitting next to him that had he still been a policeman he would have immediately arrested the driver. Suddenly his attention was drawn to a youth waving his hands. By the time he recognised Adam, the other van was pulling up alongside the now bare acacia trees.

'Father, Father!' Adam got off and threw his arms around the greying Nicholas. 'What are you doing here?'

'My darling boy, I knew you would be involved in all this.' He held his son's shoulders in both hands as tears appeared in the corners of his eyes.

'You bet I'm involved – up to my neck! I wish we had the time to tell you, but I will when it's all over.' Adam felt a rush of joy that he hadn't felt in months. 'Where are you heading?'

'Well now, I'm glad you've asked that, because to be honest we haven't got a clue.'

'No problem, just follow us. My friend Nick in the van has all the instructions we need. Apparently near Hey Square there is a depot of sorts for us, so long as we get there before eleven p.m. No time to waste!' Adam grabbed his father's hand and shook it heartily and the two men hurriedly walked back to their vans.

Now driving in tandem, the two dilapidated vans soon approached the small town of Ercsi, where to their great astonishment they saw an extremely large concentration of Red Army units in just about every side street, piece of waste ground and the drier fields. The two men looked at each other in disbelief; the best explanation they could agree on was that the Russians were 'having a little rest, before their total withdrawal'. But deep down they knew differently.

It was pitch dark and the depot was poorly lit. There were lorries and vans unloading their cargoes everywhere. Outside, the queue for the food was getting longer by the minute. The citizens of the capital placed unguarded wooden chests at various points of the long line of people into which men and women were placing their change and even their higher-denomination notes, in lieu of payment for the food. The sturdy chests were hastily marked: FOR RECONSTRUCTION!

Adam became intoxicated with the atmosphere and decided that it was time to take a second lone escapade in the big city. No open-air performance of *Aida* on Margaret Island this time, but instead a lesson in history was the overwhelming attraction. Thinking he'd better disappear before the others tried to change his mind, he told Nick of his decision and went over to his father, who was still unpacking live chickens in large wicker cages.

'Dad, I won't be going back tonight, I've got to know what's happening here, so God bless and good luck!' He wanted to make the parting as short as possible.

The two men embraced and Nicholas held his son close. 'Goodbye, son, please take care of yourself.'

'I will, don't you worry – love to everybody! Kisses for the girls!' Nicholas watched his son walk away.

The date was Thursday, 1 November 1956.

∽

Adam managed to get to his aunt's flat in Museum Ring Road, two blocks away from the famous Astoria Hotel. It was a few minutes before the midnight news on Free Kossuth Radio. Aunt Rose, the ex-opera singer, now firmly established as leading mezzo-soprano in the chorus of the State Opera House, and her much older husband were listening to the news summary. They welcomed Adam and dragged him to the wireless.

The news was as astonishing as it was fatal. The newscaster, who spoke in the most cultured Hungarian, had only a few days before said that he had lied on the air enough and had sworn that he would never do that sort of thing again. He started his news round. 'Prime Minister Imre Nagy, in a reshuffle of his ministers, has created an inner cabinet, excluding all those who were compromised by being members of previous administrations. In a diplomatic note to Dag Hammarskjöld, Secretary-General of the UNO, he has declared Hungarian neutrality and asked the organisation to guarantee the nation's new non-aligned status. In a separate note he also informed HE Ambassador Andropov of this decision. The ambassador has acknowledged it.'

'Game, set and match,' Aunt Rose exclaimed. Her husband who, would spend hours scanning the radio frequencies, was not so sure.

'Personally, I don't like what I hear on the BBC World Service. The English and the French are talking to the Israelis – that can only mean they are about to attack Nasser and take back the recently nationalised Suez Canal. They wouldn't otherwise involve the Jewish state! That lot'

– pointing his finger towards the east – 'won't put up with it. You can bet it will end in tears!'

'You are far too pessimistic, Kálmán,' said Rose as she started to make the bed for her nephew.

'But they are pouring in at Zátony. I spoke to a railway worker who saw endless trains carrying the latest tanks crossing the border.'

'I saw a ring of them around Budapest as we drove up,' Adam added quietly.

'Well, we shall all see. Right now we'll have a glass of warm milk and honey' – her standard nightcap to keep her voice steady – 'and go to bed.' Rose raised her hand, signalling the end of the discussion.

⁓

Adam could hardly wait to start his sightseeing tour the next morning. Ready to absorb the recent past and to be a part of the present, he put on his mackintosh and his wide-brimmed hat, walked out of the main atrium of the still-smart turn-of-the-century block and recoiled. The night before in the dark he had noticed the sorry state of the buildings, but in the light of the early sun casting long shadows, the city looked totally devastated. Some of the Molotov-cocktailed T34 tanks, 150mm self-propelled guns and armoured carriers were being dragged away from where they were obstructing the main road by workers of nearby factories, even though they were still on a general strike. The stench of burned bodies was very noticeable and some were still visible, lying in the gutters. The intense fire resulting from the Molotov cocktails blowing up the engines and fuel tanks had cindered the poor crews beyond even the vaguest chance of recognition. Bodies shrunk to the size of small children were visible on kerbsides, near blown-up vehicles. With the cobbled stones of the streets dug up to be used as barricades for the recent fight, and bullet holes of various sizes having peppered every building, the pearl of the Danube was, once again, in a sorry state.

He walked along to the nearby Sándor Bródy Street, to take a look at the Hungarian Radio Centre, which, until recently, had been affectionately dubbed the 'House of Lies'. There was not much to be seen, except for innumerable holes in the walls. A white banner over the main gate proudly declared the new name of the building. Free Magyar Radio! Well, it was to be that, at least for another day or so; meanwhile they played Beethoven's *Egmont* overture again and again.

Corvin Close came next, the site of the fiercest fighting around the cinema of the same name. It was now under the leadership of Gregory Pongrácz and his irrepressible family. The devastation was absolute, but strangely life had already restarted. Women were seen carrying bags, trying to find something, anything, for supper. With hardly a penny in their purses, they ignored the chests full of money, big 'paper money', marked FOR RECONSTRUCTION. A younger mother was dragging her scruffy twelve-year-old boy, yelling at him, 'Steve, enough is enough! Take that submachine gun back to the barracks, immediately!'

The inner city, a 'D'-shaped area flanked by the inner ring road and the Danube, was totally devastated. Broken glass from the romantic buildings mixed dangerously with the cobblestones and general rubble from their shell-ridden rendering. Wherever he looked, bullet holes were a testimony to the fight of only a week before. The green areas where the fallen had been hastily buried were marked by candles and little red, white and green flags, an honour given to those who had made the ultimate sacrifice. Organised groups were digging up the bodies for reburial in a more sacred place. The theme of their discussion was the same wherever Adam turned: 'The Ruskies have gone, we'll be all right, the workers are going back on Monday.' What could be simpler? he thought. But what about all those Russians he had seen on the outskirts of the city, only yesterday? And why weren't they at least facing east? That too had occurred to him, but he cleared it from his mind. They will go! They must – surely.

He passed the famous 100-Year Old restaurant where his grandfather had heard 'I love you too' from the most celebrated lips of his age. He walked to the railings of the embankment. His head involuntarily turned up and a little to the left. He wanted to see the end of Orom Street, from where he had observed the siege nearly twelve years before, but some trees were in the way and so he had to be satisfied with the sight of the ugly turreted red building. He lowered his head sadly and looked into the swollen grey Danube. 'Why do we have to be shot to bits by these bastards twice in a dozen years?' He murmured to himself.

Adam turned right and walked along the once famous embankment. The red marble obelisk, built to celebrate Russian heroes, which stood in front of the burned-out Gaiety concert hall, had mercifully been pulled down. It made him feel better. He even managed a faint smile. At the end of the embankment, the Parliament building came into view, a Gothic structure in the lightest of grey limestone, with its hundreds of small spires trying to climb towards the sky. The crowning dome in its geometric centre was reaching upwards in praise of a much-loved but now bygone age.

He walked through Parliament Square, admiring the majesty of the building itself. Having never been so close to it, he was surprised at how much of the royal ornamentation was still intact. Under the dome the full royal coat of arms was perfectly displayed. Adam could not help but notice the Transylvanian shield of seven turrets below black crow wings, with the ancient image of the sun and the crescent moon in its lower right-hand corner. The national flag was hanging from the balcony of the first floor. Adam remembered the radio commentator describing it a few days earlier, when Imre Nagy, the new prime minister, had first addressed the tumult in the square. It all seemed to be history now.

As he headed towards Margaret Bridge, the white square building of the Communist Party HQ came suddenly into view. He could just make out a commotion. A bunch of dark-suited Russians, unmistakably soldiers in civvies, were looking up and down the road like thieves in the night. As Adam got nearer he could see them lined up to form a human shield for the waiting black Zil limousine with the curtains drawn. Between the gaps he could just make out the shape of two overcoated men in large hats hurrying to the car. As soon as the door closed behind them the car started off and headed up to join the Large Ring Road, turning right. He did not realise at that time that he had observed another moment of history; the defection of the last two remaining communists of the National Government, János Kádár and Ferenc Münnich, taken by their masters to the east to commit one of the greatest treacheries of modern times by turning 'Muscovite Guiders' – a popular expression for those with power who smuggled or led in the enemy.

He crossed over the dull grey Danube on Margaret Bridge, recalling the performance of *Aida* six years earlier in the island's open-air theatre, and turned left into Bem Quay. Walking south, he soon arrived at the statue of General Bem, where the mood of the students had turned a peaceful demonstration into an uprising, without a single bullet being shot. The outstretched left hand of the freedom fighter from the previous century pointed towards the source of all the ills of this one, the white building of the Communist Party HQ.

By the time he had arrived at Adam Clark Square, squashed between the tunnel under the castle and the Chain Bridge built by Scottish engineers to unite the cities of Buda and Pest, Adam was exhausted. He decided that he had enough of his own history lesson; it was time to go and listen to more up-to-date news on the radio. He was about to turn on to the bridge when another commotion made him look towards High Street, which housed the building of the 'People's Court', the site of many show trials of the past, including that of Cardinal Mindszenti. Three freedom fighters wearing the tricolour armband of the National Guard and as many soldiers, fully armed, were escorting four exceptionally well-clad SSA officers in civvies. Remembering his own, similar activities a few days before in Pécs, he allowed himself another faint smile. Tired but at the same time emotionally elevated, he decided to head back to his aunt's flat.

∼

Meanwhile the attention of the political world at large was very much divided. Nagy's letter containing the Declaration of Hungarian Neutrality duly arrived at the UNO's New York palace and lay idly on the desk of a third-rate underling, whilst Secretary-General Dag Hammarskjöld, normally the most decent Scandinavian, busied himself with 'saving Egypt from the Anglo-French-Israeli aggression'. This was naturally reported to Moscow and thence to Ambassador Andropov in Budapest. The information circle complete, the latter decided that with the valuable time gained he could change the events everyone took for granted and picked up his red dial-less telephone.

'Comrade Khrushchev please, urgently – Andropov here!' He was curt with the soft-voiced secretary. 'Nikita Sergeievich? Yes, Yuri here from Budapest.' His voice turned most amenable. 'We have amassed an immense force in Hungary by now, just as comrade Marshal Zhukov has ordered.'

'They are to be withdrawn by fifteenth January. Isn't Comrade General Malinin negotiating it with their chap … what's his name, er, Maléter?' the First Secretary of the Communist (Bolshevik) Party of the USSR asked hurriedly.

'Yes, Comrade Nikita Sergeievich. That is the very reason I am calling you on the hotline. There is no need to withdraw.'

'No need to withdraw? Are you mad? Aren't they supposed to sign the articles tomorrow night?' The chairman scratched his bald head.

'Comrade Khrushchev, Imre Nagy has sent me yet another demand to withdraw and I assured him that we will do so, provided he will promise not to appeal to the UN. Having agreed, we are gaining invaluable time. Invaluable time! Whilst the West is busy with Suez we can retake Hungary in two days! Believe you me, Comrade Nikita Sergeievich, I can do it. I only need very little help!' The ambassador's thoughts were clearing in his mind by the second.

'What help is that?'

'Serov! Can you get him on the next plane? We control all the airports!'

'Why should you want the head of the KGB? This is not a secret police matter.'

'I trust him better than those guys in uniforms. We think alike. Anyway, I have just had two members of their government sent east, to Szolnok, a small town where we have a strong presence, to form a new Workers' and Peasants' Government.'

'I like that, Yuri, I like that! Good work, Yuri, very good work. Serov will depart within the hour. That will scare the shit out of them in Solny, or whatever they call it.' '

'Very well, Comrade First Secretary, just you leave the rest to me!'

'Very well, Andropov! *Do svidania!*' The smiling chairman said his goodbyes and put down the receiver.

'*Do svidania, tovarisch …*' Andropov heard the click. 'Comrade!!!' He slammed his receiver down with force. 'I have just saved world communism – and our face. That should be enough to make me chairman one day!' The suave ambassador mumbled to himself as he smoothed his perfectly cut grey hair and dusted down his immaculate navy suit.

At that moment he became third in the line to the office he considered intellectually already his.

~

After a hearty supper of pork chops in sauerkraut and cream sauce Adam and Aunt Rose's husband settled down to listen to the news. First the BBC World Service Hungarian broadcast, which was full of gloom and doom as things were not going too well with the Suez Canal. Even John Foster Dulles, the wise old American Secretary of State, had turned against the invasion, which was fast running out of any support, if it had ever had any in the first place. At the House of Commons in London the Labour Party was demanding the head of Prime Minister Sir Anthony Eden, a foreign affairs specialist if there ever was one. Having obtained further news of the Red Army pouring into Hungary, the announcer implied that there was no real chance for the Hungarian freedom fight.

In contrast the Free Hungarian Radio hardly mentioned Suez, which it considered a sideshow as far as matters Hungarian were concerned.

'Tomorrow, there will be a press conference in the Parliament building for the Western reporters. A senior member of the "inner cabinet" and Cardinal Mindszenty will give a national "proclamation" on this wavelength in the evening.' Perfectly normal things, the men thought, but Aunt Rose had seen enough last-minute drama on the floor of the State Opera to say that she didn't think things were ever that straightforward. They went to bed, where everyone had the right to dream his own version of the future.

On Saturday morning Adam went out to buy some of the many newspapers that had virtually flooded the streets. The communist *Free People* had been replaced by the similar-sounding *People's Freedom*, an old trick of the party from the days of illegality, when the rule was that old paper should change the name and do the same. But this one declared itself 'cleaned up' on its front page, offering 'categorical opposition to the criminal leadership of the Communist Party'. The organ of the Social Democrats, *The People's Voice*, assured the nation that the 'Socialist *Internationale* demands the withdrawal of the Soviet forces from Hungary'. The independent *Magyar Nation* stated, 'Every sober-minded, honest working man wants peace in the land.' The Conservative *Little Journal* led with the 'Government's new diplomatic notes to the Soviet Embassy'.

It took the two of them all morning to comb through the extremely informative papers, which left no subject untouched. One even reassured them that the acting profession would also return to work now that some of the trams were running. What really mattered was that by Monday morning everything would be operational and everyone would be working. Adam decided that he would catch the train home first thing Monday morning.

The midday news on the radio announced, 'A high-ranking Soviet Army delegation will visit the prime minister at 14.00 hours in his Parliament office.' With the frivolous cry of 'This I must see!!!' Adam put on his coat and hat and with a happy spring in his step started to walk down Kossuth Road. As the Parliament building came into view through the leafless trees he quickened his steps. By the time he had edged in front of the small and very good-humoured crowd the three black Zils were driving into the square past the prime minister's office. The reception was to be held in the ornate splendour of the Hunters Hall, the organisers' motto being 'anything at all, just get them out of the country asap – let them have all the trimmings!'

The seven smartly dressed generals alighted from the four limousines; some straightened their very long grey coats, one or two waved towards the silent and very still crowd. The leader of the delegation, General Malinin, got out last. The others waited patiently until he was ready and started their walk up the grey steps towards the main door, where General Maléter and Minister of State Erdei were standing anxiously.

Some two hours later they left with beaming smiles.

On the way back to the flat Adam bought the evening edition of the new and revolutionary *Magyar Independence* for the princely sum of sixty filler; it reported 'The Changed Government', assuring readers that 'The ministers of the days of bad memory have been sacked'. As a rider to the same article it published a factual-sounding statement describing that afternoon's meeting, adding that the discussions would continue at 8 pm.

Naturally they did. How could the leadership of a captive nation which had just won a little independence from the mighty Soviet Union refuse their invitation 'to conclude matters' at their HQ in Tököl? It was only a question of crossing 't's and dotting 'i's. Or was it just another ploy, to ensure that the withdrawal by 15 January 1957 would be conducted in a dignified manner, the idea being that there would be no victors and no vanquished? The Red Army would leave in a show of glory with red roses placed in their submachine guns, the unforgettable 'gimme guitars' of Second World War watch-collecting fame, given by the prettiest of Hungarian girls. The Magyars could handle that! They could have anything they wanted, so long as they bloody well left!

Whilst the Hungarian delegation, led by the six-and-a-half-foot General Maléter, was being driven to Tököl, Aunt Rose turned on the radio. It was playing the last few bars of some very solemn Chopin. Then the unmistakable voice of the announcer who had promised 'never to lie again' came on and with due reverence announced that Cardinal Mindszenti, the Primate of Hungary, would deliver an address to the nation.

Calvinists or not, they all drew their seats nearer the wireless set and waited in anticipation for his frail and much-tortured voice. He did not disappoint them. Starting in a low key he analysed the problems and wanted to reassure his nation that '*We Magyars want to live and work as the flag-bearers of peace in the European family of nations*'. Aunt Rose started clapping. He continued in his saintly way that he wanted to reassure his enemy too. '... *We, the small nation, wish to be undisturbed in reciprocal honour with the great United States of America and the Russian Empire, equally.*' His mode of speech was convoluted and yet totally basic. He told his nation of ten million that in the forthcoming free election he did not intend to seek office and begged them to go back to work 'forthwith!' He ended his speech with '*We, who note and want to propagate the good of the whole nation, trust in the Almighty – and not in vain!*'

The Hungarian delegation got out of their cars in the large square in the Russian barracks and the commanding officer asked the party to 'be good enough to inspect the guard of honour'. Somewhat taken aback, Maléter stepped forward to oblige and the others followed him as he wove between the immaculate lines. The Russian captain, whose gently curved sword picked up the nearby electric light, reflecting it into Maléter's eyes, turned to face him.

'Tovarisch General, thank you for the honour of inspecting us!'

'Tovarisch Captain, the honour is mine. You have a fine bunch of soldiers there, be proud of them,' Maléter answered in perfect Russian.

The delegation was welcomed by General Malinin, who ushered his counterparts into the officers' mess, where the table in the corner was bending with the weight of ice under the Beluga caviar. Four champagne coolers were chilling the vodka to wash down the mountain of inviting black sturgeon eggs. The conviviality was tangible and the hospitality overwhelming. Nobody seemed to want to start the 'negotiation', but eventually Malinin turned to Maléter and said, 'Listen, Paul, the only way to stop us getting a neck-ache looking at you up there at near seven foot is for you to sit down.'

'I suppose we'll have to some time.' Maléter smiled as they started their walk to the room to the right of the caviar table.

The next two hours were spent agreeing with each other on every issue except that of why on earth there was a need for further Russian divisions to pour into Hungary if it was their intention to leave.

Malinin's sidestepping was plausible. He went on rambling about the necessity of a show of strength against the imperialists of the West just in case the Suez crisis got out of hand. This did not seem to quite fit in with the Hungarian neutrality declared only two days before, but Malinin continued about 'the tap having been turned on – it will take some time to turn it off'.

Maléter shook his head with a wry smile, trying to hide his disbelief and show acceptance of what he just heard. He picked up the direct-line phone in front of him to convey this latest message to General Király, Chief of the National Guard, as he had been doing all evening. It was dead. He fiddled with the contacts to no avail, and as he was about to ask for an engineer, the main door burst open. General Serov, dressed unusually for him in full dress uniform, filled the door frame, surprising the Russians and the Hungarians alike.

The head of the dreaded KGB walked up to Maléter, took off his white gloves and threw them on to the table in front of the still-seated general, a signal for his entourage to raise their submachine guns.

'You and your counter-revolutionary clique are under my personal arrest by the authority of … er, of … well, anyway, you are arrested and that's that.' Seeing the uncomfortable faces of the Russian delegation, he turned to them and shouted, 'And you lot can stop staring at me! Hear me? You will lock up these pigs somewhere. Now!'

The date was Sunday, 4 November 1956.

At 04.30 the heavy artillery bombardment of Brigadier General Grebennik signalled the attack against every important military and civil position in the country.

In the Parliament building, pandemonium replaced all normal activity. Király asked Nagy to allow the National Guard to fire back. His request was initially declined. In turn Nagy tried to talk to Andropov, who refused to pick up his telephone on the direct line. Then Lieutenant General Janza, who had been sacked two days before, reported 'in his official capacity' to Nagy that the Soviets had started an offensive against the capital. The prime minister lifted his hands and covered his ears for a few seconds, then picked up his pince-nez and clipped it on his nose. He twirled his grey moustache and took a plain sheet of paper and his black and gold Waterman.

***

The low-flying jet woke Aunt Rose's small family. The total silence that followed was soon broken by the low thud of the heavy guns. Her husband walked to the wireless set, turned it on and called out to Adam.

After the *Egmont* – once again – the female announcer, in a clearly shaken voice, announced the prime minister, who introduced himself in a casual but hurried voice:

'*This is Imre Nagy, Chairman of the Council of Ministers of the People's Republic of Hungary, speaking. In the early hours of the morning Soviet* units began an attack against our capital with the obvious intention of overthrowing the legitimate, democratic Hungarian government. Our troops are engaged in battle, the government is in its place. This is my message to the people of the country and to the public opinion of the world.'

The three occupants of the room looked at each other in stunned silence. The radio went on to play the national anthem, *'God bless the Hungarian ...'* It could not have been more appropriate. Aunt Rose started to sob quietly, her husband held his head in disbelief and Adam went to the window, thinking he had heard the grinding noise of tank chains on the cobblestones. He was right. He could clearly see the large T34s turning into Charles Ring Road on their way to take Parliament. It was all over.

～

Adam was stuck in Budapest for two more weeks. Totally disillusioned and utterly frustrated, he listened to Radio Free Europe and the BBC World Service for a glimmer of hope – a piece of news, anything that would sound vaguely like the UN doing something other than condemning the Soviet Union, time and again. Deep down he knew it would never come, so when the man from the flat next door told them that some trains had started to run, Adam collected his toothbrush, put on his grey raincoat and large-brimmed hat, said his goodbyes and headed for Southern Railway Station.

At the other end of his slow journey, some eight hours later, he put his key into the front door of his bedsit. His homely landlady, who had looked after him like one of her own, was quick to pounce on the young man.

'Adam, for God's sake, get in quick!' The rotund woman dragged him in.

'What's the matter, Aunt Liz?' He drew back.

'They were here – less than twenty minutes ago. You know, the police, in plain clothes!' She sounded exhausted.

Adam thought quickly; he knew he had to act fast. He telephoned László, who told his friend that Major Nemes's men were interested in him as well. He went on to explain that he had opened the door to the

SSA men and pretended to be his own elder brother to avoid arrest. His bravado had saved him for the time being, but he had to admit that he might not be so lucky next time. He agreed with Adam's suggestion that they had better go into hiding immediately. Adam readily offered the family cottage and got in touch with Nick.

The next afternoon they were on their way to the village of Jonk, where Nicholas and the family were absolutely delighted to let them stay. The girls were growing up nicely and the idea that three strange third-year medical students would be part of the family excited the Anna and Kathleen, twelve and sixteen years old respectively. The only trouble was that the whole thing was supposed to be a secret. After all, the police were after them, and it was only a matter of time before they were going to knock on the door. That is if they were in the mood to knock.

The village policeman was an old school friend of Adam's and promised to let the family know of any police activity relating to him or his friends, which happened exactly two weeks later. The telephone call from Pécs was luckily taken by him and, on hearing that three detectives would arrive the next morning, he duly relayed the news to the Zentas. Nicholas decided to hide the trio in the bottom of his wine cellar, deep under the hills, just as they had hidden Ruth in Budapest when the drunken Russian soldiers were looking for some feminine company. For the following week they were walled in, celebrating Adam's twenty-first birthday by drinking Nicholas' wine and appreciating it as a drier Riesling variety with a good earthy aftertaste.

This was followed by another two weeks of toing and froing between the cottage and the wine cellar until Nicholas decided to tackle the issue head-on and suggested that they should leave the country. Although the young men had thought of the idea whilst drinking the Riesling, the fact that the head of the family had now spelled out the inevitable came as a shock to them all. There was no time to waste. They had a quick family photograph taken and next morning the three got on the train to return to Pécs and plan their escape. The ingenuity of László, alias Spotty, became invaluable during the planning week. The basic problem was that they had left things a little too late in the day. All exposed people had escaped one way or another many weeks before, whilst the trio were drinking in the cellar. The authorities were reasserting themselves increasingly. ID checks were more common and retribution against those acting suspiciously was frequent. So, the size of the group and the provision of false IDs became paramount. For the group, they decided on five; the trio, naturally, plus László's brother Andrew, who had ended up in the notorious 'Star Prison' in the city of Szeged. As a student at the university, he was busy studying architecture, but in his free time he had also engaged in some anti-commie leaflet distribution which resulted in him being sent down and locked up, until he was let out by his friends during the second day of the revolution. A thoughtful, introspective chap, he would undoubtedly bring common sense to the group. His friend Dennis was a sixty-year-old actor, who also fell out with the commies and was given no more film or stage parts. The 'Errol Flynn' of the land, he now worked as a mental nurse and had a uniform, which, according to Spotty, 'would come in very handy'.

The planning had to be meticulous. It started with copying a road map of the area. They would want to cross the border just north of the confluence of the Hungarian, Yugoslav and Austrian frontiers. They picked this particular point for two main reasons. The mechanical Iron Curtain, removed during the uprising, was getting replaced rapidly from north to south, so it was safest from that point of view to cross at the southernmost tip. The other reason was more political. It had to do with the sensitivity of Tito's Yugoslavia, whose relationship with the Soviet Union was just improving after five years of hostility. The Russians were at great pains not to offend them with an accidental border crossing; consequently they were thinner on the ground in this vicinity.

Much more difficult was to make credible false IDs for the initial train journey from Pécs to as near to the frontier as possible.

László had pinched some Communist Party notepaper at the time of the arrest of the secretary, so he typed his own authorisation to transfer party funds to a more westerly town. He was to carry everyone's money in case he had to show those funds.

Dennis, the actor, donned his male-nurse uniform and had a form filled in authorising him to transfer a mental patient to another asylum farther west.

Andrew was to be the patient.

Nick was to be made up by Dennis to look like his own and recently deceased aunt. It wasn't too difficult to dress up like her. All he needed was plenty of peasant clothing and a shawl to cover as much of his face as possible. That left Adam. They just couldn't think of anything for him. Neither could he, but he reassured his friends that he would find something and disappeared to spend the last night in town with ZsaZsa. He turned up for supper at his girlfriend's home and she nearly fainted on seeing him.

'My God! Adam, what on earth are you doing here? Come in.' The surprised girl dragged her very part-time lover into the flat. 'They're looking for you everywhere. I thought you had escaped weeks ago.'

'No, darling, it's tomorrow morning actually, but I thought I'd invite myself to yours for dinner or something. You don't mind, do you?' Adam raised his hands to protect his head from the blow he considered certain.

'Do I mind!? Yes, I do, most certainly! I feel like screaming, but I can't, can I?' ZsaZsa held her face between her hands. 'I can't shout because that would attract the attention of someone who might spot you – and if I let you in I still can't shout, because Mum likes you, doesn't she? You know how much we all worried about you during the past few weeks? You could have sent a message of sorts, you're supposed to be ever so clever!' Her eyes were beginning to fill with tears.

'Sweetheart, please forgive me, and please let me in – someone will see me stood here.'

ZsaZsa stepped back. 'Oh, Adam I missed you so – what happened to you?'

'I'll tell you later, but are you sure your mother is not mad at me for propositioning her on the phone?' Adam asked, smiling, as ZsaZsa wiped her face with the back of her hands.

'That's one thing I'll never understand. You know, had it been anyone else, I would have become homeless, instantly. But the great Adam Zenta, well, that's different! You know something, I must be the only one who does not see this … this … difference! What is it?'

'Well, being classically handsome, superbly intelligent, utterly affable with a voice like Caruso does do something to mothers, you know, even if it leaves their spoilt daughters utterly cold.' By the time he had finished his banality Adam was kissing ZsaZsa's mother's hand.

'Oh, Adam, it's so nice to see you, you are such a romantic,' she sang his praises.

'Anachronistically so, Mrs Merő, but I do wish it impressed ZsaZsa somewhat too. You know, I virtually had to fight my way in.' Adam took her arm and the two started to walk to the living room she grandiosely called her salon.

'This sort of treatment is usually reserved for revolutionary poets.' ZsaZsa was still unimpressed.

'Or reactionary ones – see *Andrea Chenier*.'

'Yes, but you can forget about me going to the gallows with you,' she retorted.

'Enough of all this nonsense, you two. ZsaZsa, you'd better set an extra place.'

The extra setting was duly placed and ZsaZsa's elderly father came out of his study to join them.

'Good evening, sir.' Adam greeted him with a slight bow of his head and offered his hand.

'Nice to see you, young man, I hear you're in trouble.' They shook hands warmly.

'Yes, sir, in big enough trouble to leave the country tomorrow – luck permitting.'

'Intolerable. Rumours have it that over a hundred and eighty thousand people have already left, an insurmountable blow to a small nation of ten million, especially if most of them are youngsters, like yourself.' He shook his neatly combed, totally white head repeatedly.

'If there is a good side to this perhaps the commies won't be able to retaliate against the nation – I suppose every family will be affected, including most party members.' Adam tried to please him now.

'I suppose so, I suppose so,' the surgeon mumbled to himself. 'Do you like "Kaiser's meat"?'

'One of my very favourites.' Adam was delighted at the prospect of eating the glorified pork chop.

The pompous conversation continued throughout the tasty meal, right up until liqueurs were served. As Adam was sipping his Triple Sec, Mrs Merő told ZsaZsa to make up the spare bedroom for their guest, which she did hurriedly and with anticipation.

After the second liqueur Adam excused himself, blaming the early start, and said goodbye to the parents, receiving a hug from the mother and some back-patting from the surgeon.

He had hardly settled down when some shuffling on the corridor carpet alerted him to the impending arrival of ZsaZsa; no mean feat considering the awkward layout of the large flat. ZsaZsa had to get out on to the balcony of her bedroom, which faced the communal garden, walk along it past her parents' bedroom and return to the kitchen, only to cross the corridor to the front room, where Adam was waiting for her.

Within seconds the two naked bodies were clutched together in a firm embrace.

'You know, I want to pinch myself, this just can't be true.' ZsaZsa's eyes were brimming with tears again.

'It's true, sweetheart, but it's for the last time.' Adam tightened his embrace.

'I know it is. You'll forget me soon,' she whispered.

'You know I never will.' Adam kissed her tenderly, meaning every word.

~

Adam was woken at 6 am ZsaZsa delivered a mug of milky coffee amidst a lot of noise to make sure they all heard this, her 'official' visit. Her parents soon appeared in their dressing gowns to say farewell to the young man they were so fond of.

Adam did not want to prolong anyone's agony. At the front gate he kissed them all, turned on his heel and started his short walk towards the railway station, without looking back once.

The date was 4 January 1957.

20

Escape

Not wanting to see ZsaZsa's tears nor indeed to show his, Adam turned the corner and for the first time he felt a strange feeling of apprehension. His secret, the fact that he still had no false ID and could not even think of one, made him feel low enough to call himself a few choice names. Yet none of these included such words as conceited or inept, for he was quite convinced that he could handle the next few days as a shadow of the well-organised four. By the time he got to the very busy railway station, yet another ornamental classic of the last century, he was excited enough to have a go, come what may.

He positioned himself in a corner so that he could see the passengers and soon recognised Spotty. It was not too difficult as he was dressed as a commie party secretary of sorts, wearing a good suit and a decent coat with matching hat. A leather briefcase, containing the all-important letter of authorisation, completed the immaculate set-up. When László noticed Adam he realised what had happened and gave him an exceptionally dirty look, which Adam ignored. His saving grace was that they would all sit in different compartments or even coaches, and would not appear as part of a group, so talking to each other was out of the question. László passed his friend and murmured something to the effect that Adam would not die of old age and he would take personal charge of that. He then looked around and a slight smile appeared on his face before he climbed into the first-class compartment – where else would a party secretary travel?

Adam followed László's glance and noticed an old peasant woman with a wrinkled face, dressed in black from head to toe, carrying a basket full of shopping and a brand-new broom. From their plans he knew it was Nick, alias his aunt, and thought, Now that's what I call a good disguise. She struggled to the train, made sure that someone helped her up the steps of the third-class compartment and settled herself and her belongings on one of the hard wooden benches.

Soon the small and rusty windowless white van, which was euphemistically referred to as an ambulance, delivered the remaining two; Dennis in his mental-nurse uniform and a battered, dopey-looking younger patient dressed in a very heavy, featureless grey canvas suit with no pockets, lapels or belt. He was grabbed under the armpit by his escort and helped along the busy platform towards the second-class compartment, where the seating was slightly more comfortable.

There was not much else for Adam to do but to get on to the train, yet he was reluctant. It was a cold and grey January morning with the odd flake of snow drifting aimlessly through the air in the full expectation of dying as soon as it hit the ground. Adam wondered whether their haphazard journey might produce the same result at the border. He checked the ticket László had bought the day before – second class, which somewhat disappointed him. It would have been nice to make this departure in first class, and for a moment he considered paying the supplement on the train, but he soon told himself not to be so stupid as that would inevitably attract attention. With his best suit and the spotted tie he wore to put him into a good frame of mind, and carrying a borrowed plastic briefcase containing some dried sausage and the dissecting-room white coat - which distinguishes a medic from a mere mortal – there was just enough room left for a copy of their extraordinary edition to remind him of the reason he was leaving the country of the Zentas. He took a deep breath, stepped into the light and drifting snowflakes and walked towards the westbound 08.30 on Platform 2. When he finally boarded the train he was ready for anything.

Although this was no intercity express, the train left on time. Something of the old MÁV tradition must have lasted. The old commuter train stopped at every village along the line, or, as the passengers liked to say, at every tree. It was pulled by a Truman steam engine, affectionately named after President Harry, for giving the nation a bunch of them after the war to restart the system. The slow journey and the innumerable stops for shorter or longer periods gave the five plenty of opportunity to contemplate their future – or perhaps the lack of it.

Adam had a real problem. He was travelling with his own travel document, which was about as useful as a bullet in the back of his neck. He sat by a window in the penultimate compartment of the train, just in front of the coupling to the last third-class coach with wooden benches. From his seat he could check the platforms of the village stations if they were on his side. If not, he had to dash to the exit door just behind his seat on the other side to reconnoitre for any secret police embarking for ID checks. This kept him reasonably busy, but periodically he also had to keep look forward along the open carriage, just in case they got on without his seeing them. Noticing the 'gentlemen' would be no particular problem because of the way they would be dressed.

It all went well for a while. The first problem they ran into was the 'old lady with the shopping', Nick. An inebriated peasant sat down next to her, hell bent on conversation and on touching 'her' knee; a phenomenon not too uncommon in a land where the *pálinka* bars opened at 6 am so that workers could have a few tipples before facing the day's activities. Nick had worked out a sort of plan for such an event and replied with a forced whisper, complaining sotto voce of a sore throat and the ineffectiveness of Hungarian penicillin. The unshaven drunk was gallant in not expecting an answer but went on mumbling about the 'bloody Ruskies', which was the last thing Nick wanted to hear right now in case it drew unwanted attention.

Just after midday the train stopped yet again at a small station, where Adam, on looking out of his window, immediately spotted the two men wearing expensive leather coats, wide-brimmed hats and very good-quality gloves. Their collars upturned, they were very obvious. They might as well have whistled the *Internationale* as their signature tune. People began looking at each other nervously. Brainwashed and browbeaten over the years, even the totally innocent became shivering wrecks as soon as these men appeared.

They boarded in the guard's coach just behind the coal carrier and asked the guard whether he had noticed 'any unsavoury counter-revolutionary bastards' on his train. The engine driver's assistant looked towards them, the whites of his eyes appearing twice their normal size, framed in a face full of coal dust, and answered that he was too busy shovelling coal to look at the 'bloody passengers'. The SSA were used to this sort of reply from genuine workers, who had so little to lose that they couldn't care less and spoke their minds. The well-dressed men were anxious not to get their coats contaminated with coal, so they slipped away and entered the first-class compartment. Suddenly Spotty felt rather ill at ease.

'Comrade, any particular reason for your travel?' Asked the taller of the two.

'Bit of a nuisance, really, Comrade, but I have to take some money to Zalaegerszeg. The Party HQ was ransacked during the counter-revolution and they need some money t pay wages.' László handed over his fake letter. 'Do you want to see the cash?' He touched his briefcase on the seat next to him.

'That will not be necessary, Comrade, but do be careful when you alight, there seems to be a lot of thieving going on. I would not mention it to anyone – you never know. Good journey, Comrade.' The man touched the edge of his wide-brimmed hat and nodded towards his companion to move on.

Their progress along the train was slow as they wanted to drag the job out to the end of the journey, so it was some time before they reached Dennis the actor. Until now he and Andrew had sat next to each other, Andrew gazing vacantly into thin air or staring at some of the passengers, with Dennis patting his head once in a while in mock sympathy. As they were approached, Dennis delivered a gentle prod of the elbow into Andrew's side, which was the agreed signal for him to start slobbering. Within seconds, saliva was everywhere, down his chin, on his clothing, and if there was any left he blew bubbles with it; an unsavoury set-up that the leather-coated duo wanted to get away from – quickly.

'Taking him to Egerszeg asylum, the ambulance should be at the station,' Dennis reassured the two as they pulled back in disgust.

As one of them was about to take the document from the mental nurse, his 'charge' coughed up a generous amount of saliva, some of which landed on the leader's well-polished shoe. Dennis took the piece of towelling they had for the purpose.

'Comrade Officer, excuse my idiot. So sorry, so sorry.' He wiped Andrew's mouth, then bent down to do the same with the shoe, making a worse mess of it.

'Get the bloody hell away from me! Why the fuck you don't just shoot these good-for-nothing bastards, I'll never know. They just use up good fresh air! Good-for-nothing cretins!' He turned on his heel without looking at the piece of paper the actor turned male nurse was offering to him.

Two compartments back the drunken peasant had kept up his alcohol level with the occasional swig of pálinka from a litre bottle he had brought along, making sure he had enough firewater for his journey. He handed over his travel document and offered the pálinka. This was declined and number two asked the 'old woman' to produce her papers. She fumbled in her wicker basket, eventually finding the battered old ID, which the man gave a most cursory examination. He did, however, start to talk to her. 'Very good picture! Where are you going to, my old aunt?' This was not an unusual way to address a person in a country where everyone old was referred to as uncle or aunt.

'Egerszeg, my son, Egerszeg,' She whispered.

'What's wrong with your voice, Aunt?' He asked.

'She is not very well, you know,' intervened the drunken old peasant, putting his hand on her thigh protectively.

'Oh, you have a sore throat? I am sorry, Aunt. Put this away safely.' He handed back the document and walked on towards the last two coaches. Adam had been observing the activities of the police ever since they boarded the train. He knew he looked rather obvious in his compartment, and as the SSA walked into the last-but-one coach he tucked his borrowed briefcase into the back of the overhead rack and left his seat to start his retreat towards the end of the train. He was hoping against hope that the men might get off at the next station and ignore the last coach, but ultimately he knew it was not to be. He kept walking towards the end door and, to his great relief, found that instead of the customary padlock, only a twisted wire secured it.

When the two leather jackets appeared in the frame of the far door, Adam swung open the rear door and stepped out on to the narrow steel ladder leading to the top of the train, and with his left foot kicked the door closed. Standing on the ladder, he could still see into the corridor of the coach at a very narrow angle, so he decided to climb up to the roof. The chill of the early afternoon hit his face as he cleared the top of the ladder. The westerly wind blew the coal dust and the smoke straight at him, and Adam decided that the best way to lie on the roof was with his legs towards the engine and his face just at the edge of the coach. This way he would produce very little silhouette in the occasional sunshine breaking through the light cloud. He did not regard this as a fun thing to do on 4 January and cursed himself for not making the effort to falsify some ID. Then he pictured László in the warmth of the first-class coach and thought to himself, You idiot – you will not get far in the West with this sort of thinking and preparation.

The two plain clothes policemen duly arrived at the door and one of them opened it.

'Damned irresponsible to leave the door unlocked, anyone could fall out – hmm, must talk to the guard about this.'

What commendable decency, Adam thought.

~

Adam had to repeat the whole manoeuvre twice more before the two diligent albeit dilettante fellows got off the now very sparsely populated train. There was just one more stop before they reached their destination, Zalaegerszeg. By the time the train pulled in it was pitch dark, and after they alighted the four had a good giggle at Adam's expense. He looked filthy and his face was covered with soot. He maintained that it would give him better camouflage.

They could not believe their luck when the announcer declared that the train to Zalalövő would leave in five minutes. This was most significant for them because it took them some twenty miles farther along, so they ordered Spotty to get the tickets.

This time they all got into the same coach of an even slower train and, having convinced themselves that there was no police presence, dismantled their disguises and gathered together to organise their strategy, agreeing on three main points. The two with handguns, László and Andrew, would throw them away. The reasoning for this was that if the Russians patrolling the border district found anything like that on would-be escapees they would bump them off there and then. Without them one stood a chance of being deported somewhere extremely cold in Mother Russia. Their second point was no alcohol, however tempting in a temperature well below freezing, and finally they agreed on not stopping to help anyone injured. In case of sprains or fractures the person would be left behind.

Thirty-five minutes later the five got off the train and donned their white coats to camouflage themselves in the snow, which by now covered all the land. They started their long walk along the railway lines, which actually reached well into Austria in pre-war times. The lines led them into very heavy bush land, and although they were no longer used for passenger traffic, they soon encountered the odd shunting engine or inspection gang parking their self-propelled rolling platforms so they had to throw themselves on to the snow of the railway embankment to avoid being seen. After half an hour or so, they decided to leave the lines and use the small gravel road running parallel with them, on their right. It took them to the small village of Farkasfa. László suggested that as it was not late enough to walk through a well-populated place they should take to the field on the right. He got his self-drawn little map out and pinpointed an object in the distance. Checking his compass with the aid of his battery torch, he stepped into the ankle-deep snow. László was now leading the line of five, the last of whom was given the responsibility of constantly checking back, just in case someone was taking an interest in their walkabout.

The next problem they encountered was barking farmhouse dogs. It was their job to protect their masters and they did it most efficiently. The five wanted none of their attention, so they had to go farther into the open fields. In the total darkness such fields became hazardous, even dangerous in places. In daytime snow one could talk of a whiteout, but in the darkness and the blowing cold snow it became a black-whiteout, where objects became blurred and amorphous. Within an hour they were hallucinating, both visually and aurally. The flashing lights and weird noises were endless in their intensity and variety. They were throwing themselves to the ground, imagining danger where there was none, and ignoring the real ones, often sliding into ditches or tripping over snow-covered objects. By midnight they were totally exhausted.

Dennis the actor, just over sixty years old, could hardly keep up with them. He was protected in the middle of the five, whilst the others took turns in leading and being tail-ender. In order to keep up with the younger and fitter men, he decided to break rule number two and took to his hip flask. When he started to take more than the average number of tumbles, Nick halted the snowbound procession and, picking him up, noticed the sweet smell of dark rum.

Contrary to what they expected, the elderly and dog-tired man started to beg his friends, 'Lads, please, leave me here. I'll have a little sleep and in the morning I'll crawl back to the nearest farmhouse. Don't worry – you know, rule number three! Eh?'

A field conference followed. 'No way! Not you – any of us, but not you!' said Andrew. 'Let's regroup. One-three-one formation: László leads, Adam and I drag Dennis under his armpits and Nick stays tail-ender.'

They had to take a left turn into the middle of the field to avoid getting too far north. By now the snow was deeper and the night air very much crisper. Position change after position change slowed them down, and by first light they were completely exhausted and totally wet through. Having reached the outskirts of Kondorfa they knocked on the door of the nearest cottage.

The farmers were just about getting up for their morning's work and, after some initial apprehension, let them in. Adam asked for a day's shelter and a chance to sleep. The old folk could not have been more hospitable, and they climbed straight into their just-vacated, warm beds and slept like never before.

In the evening they got dressed. Their clothes were bone dry and warm, which made them feel good, at least momentarily. Dinner was dried sausages with milk, which they devoured in minutes. László paid their hosts a few florins, warning his friends that they were behind schedule to cross the frontier that night. As dusk fell, they set off for the next night's walking. They had a good break to start with, a well-concealed but straight road into the pine forest, due west. In a line of five, Adam leading, they set off into the total blackness of the road. The farther they got into the forest the worse the road became, and soon they were fighting the dense bush with all the disorientation the total darkness and the snowy ground could cause them. During a severe bout of hallucination, actor Dennis decided to take to Dutch courage again. He seemed to have an endless supply of rum and in no time he was drunk again. So they went back to the old and proven formation of one-three-one. The nearer they got to Austria the higher the ground became, which slowed them down even more. After a short conference they decided that the border crossing would have to be postponed again and they knocked at the door of another cottage just north of the hamlet of Apátistvánfalva.

After a promise to pay him well, the head of the household let them in and the wrinkled old peasant woman, feeling sorry for the frozen bunch, prepared them an omelette, which they devoured hungrily. Dennis was still in a daze and by now he had very little idea of what was happening around him. He picked up the earthenware water jug, turned to the rest of them and started to act out something from a film or play of his. He took a deep bow and in a voice trained to project to the back of a theatre he declared to László: 'I shall be serving tea now, Milady.'

His 'audience' found the statement amusing and disconcerting. This was no time to have with them a man who did not know where he was. Andrew, who had left the room earlier, walked in with a stranger. He quickly reassured the rest of them that everything was just fine. 'This gentleman will guide us to a safe spot on the border in return for the remainder of our money. He should know where it is, since he is, I'm told, the local smuggler cum poacher and assures me that he knows the terrain.'

They looked at each other – unsure. A moment later they all emptied their pockets and the man gave them their briefing. He would go with them to the edge of the woods, and when he peeled off they would head due west.

'First you will come to a small river, frozen over, then a very steep climb will take you to the top of the ridge and the old minefields. Then, a little farther along, the border will be marked. Then a very thick forest, which is actually in Austria, and when you reach the railway lines …'

'We will kiss them!!!' Shouted Adam.

'We will all kiss them!!!' They yelled, knowing from their map that they would be well inside Austria and out of danger.

'A word of warning, gentlemen.' The poacher raised his hand ominously. 'There is another group of twelve ahead of you with the same instructions and they are quite heavily armed.'

A few moments of quiet introspection were followed by great anticipation, and they put on their by now not-so-white coats, for the last time, whatever the outcome.

They crossed over a small hill into heavy bush land, and started to walk downhill into a valley. At the edge of the bush the poacher wished them good luck and turned back. They turned towards the west and, as he had said, came first to the river. Adam was on tail-end Charlie duty that night in a line of five. They started crawling over the ice on all fours, to show as little silhouette as possible, but by the time it came to his turn the thin ice under the snow cover had started to weaken. A yard or so before the west bank, Adam found himself shoulder deep in water. The others quickly dragged him out but his wet clothes froze on him instantly like a suit of armour, making walking extremeley difficult.

Nick quietly pointed ahead and slightly to the north, where the other group they had been warned about were approaching the ridge. They decided to take a more southerly route about 150 yards away.

A sudden and frightening short machine-gun burst broke the stillness of the past two nights with such violence that in a split second they found themselves flat on the ground, heads buried in the snow. The reply fire was a longer burst of a lighter calibre. One after the other they looked up to see that it was coming from the other group. The exchange of fire became fiercer, and looking at each other they realised that the commotion and the others' misfortune could bring them luck, by creating a diversion. Without much discussion László pointed towards the ridge, which reared up in front of them like a wall. They knew what they had to do, and in line they started to move towards it. They were exhausted by the time they reached the top, and now they faced their first obstacle: the minefield. The mines had been incompletely cleared during the uprising and were piled into heaps at regular intervals for collection, which, owing to the Soviet aggression, never happened. Consequently some of them were very much alive indeed.

Whilst the twelve ahead of them were busy with the Russians, the five slipped through the minefield one by one. A seemingly endless thirty yards took them to the actual frontier, an avenue cut out of the forest, marked by a succession of the long-awaited whitewashed stones, little pyramids about a foot high with the tips cut off. The gunfire was raging to their right. They stood at the edge of the cutting, totally frozen. Searchlights flashed as they scanned the terrain. All they needed was a quick dash, one at a time, to get through. At 11.15 pm Andrew went first, dragging Dennis. Then a pause, waiting for a lull in the lights. László set off, momentarily tripping on a barbed wire. Then Nick crawled on all fours. A little longer to wait – and Adam's head was bursting. The others were all through. Would his turn ever come? He wondered. He started to crawl, but about halfway along he impatiently got up and made a run for it. The white stones of the actual border were just about visible in the pitch dark. He patted one of them and three seconds later he found himself in the West! My God, he thought, even the trees look larger. The gunfight just north of them was still raging, and the next morning they learned that only two out of the twelve had made it through the frontier. Meanwhile the five were elated and clutched each other emotionally. It was now Adam's turn to lead, and a little later, by now deadly tired, they saw some lights in the forest, just outside Neumark. The first Austrian they met was a drunken forester. Joseph Patrick Dax gave them a very friendly measure of schnapps and they felt it warming the pits of their stomachs. Leaving the two exhausted ones, Dennis and Andrew, behind, the Stop Trio went ahead and threw themselves down to kiss the railway lines as promised, shouting and yelling, 'Thank you, God!! We have made it, we have bloody made it!!' Looking towards the border, the feeling of freedom overwhelming them, they cupped their hands around their mouths and screamed abuse at the Russians and the traitor Kádár.

A burst of wild machine-gun fire was the irrelevant answer.

The date was 6 January 1957. The time – midnight. It would remain engraved in their memories, for ever.

∽

Having walked on to Jennersdorf, where many press and radio reporters were in attendance, they gave interviews to newspapermen and Radio Free Europe and each received twenty-five schillings in return.

The broadcast was picked up by the elated Zenta family's battered radio back home and the news was soon all over Jonk and Pécs. The five felt – and acted – like heroes for a day, and when the pressmen disappeared they were shown to the refugee camp. It was an old and now hardly used school, where a cross-section of Hungary was packed in, in unholy alliance. They stood in the schoolyard and looked at each other – filthy from top to bottom, unshaven for three days, dressed in dirty white coats shredded to rags. Adam's soles were secured to the rest of the shoe by string. There was some bittersweet laughter, but they were all involved in private thoughts, contemplating their future.

When, two days later, the London Transport red double-decker bus, suitably converted into a mobile office for the National Coal Board, turned up to recruit coal miners for the Barnsley pits in England, László and Adam did not hesitate; they signed on the dotted line and became apprentice coal miners, at a stroke. Nick was whisked away by a contingency of Norwegians, Dennis and Andrew were to end up in America. The actor decided to act out – in real life – his best role on the screen or on the boards and became a celebrated butler to very rich American families. Andrew, the political prisoner, got a job as an animator for Walt Disney. Within two days they had all parted and gone their separate ways.

~

The large number of newly recruited coal miners filled three coaches outside the school in Jennersdorf and included both intellectuals and the dregs of society, criminals who had been liberated with the political prisoners in the early days of the uprising. Most reassuringly there were some genuine coal miners from Komló, just east of Pécs, who talked with pride of being miners and were looking forward to settling in the mother country of all coal mining, England. Adam soon immersed himself in the beautiful Austrian scenery as they drove through the imposing Brenner pass, surrounded by snowy peaks. The gleaming cars and well-kept petrol stations fascinated László, who, seeing yet another Italian mechanical wonder overtaking the buses rather recklessly, swore to have one himself soon, if not sooner!

By early afternoon they had arrived in the outskirts of Vienna and passed a monstrous statue of a soldier, the Soviet Liberation Monument, the sort of item Russians liked to leave behind wherever history took them. The verbal abuse from the refugees in the coaches was deafening and not unamusing: 'How many watches have you in your pockets, Iván?' Or 'Dishing out culture to the world from your "gimme guitar", Nikita?'

Having settled into the camp, yet another old school kitted out for the purpose, they were given some dubious-tasting soup with meatballs. With their bellies full, the duo headed straight to Stephansplatz to see the Dome and then to look at the Opera and the Ring with all its glorious baroque architecture. Back at the shops in Kartnerstrasse they gazed open mouthed at all the luxury before their eyes. With twenty-five schillings in their pockets they were not going to buy anything, but it was enough just to look, to absorb and to register what the West was all about. Then they spotted the Sacher Hotel, which was about to be invaded by a group of superbly dressed ladies and their escorts in evening attire. Adam was imagining he was similarly dressed and about to join them when László pulled him back and told him to look at his reflection in the glittering window. It was that of a well-proportioned six-footer with chestnut brown, gently waved hair combed back from a decent enough manly face. Perhaps a little on the pretty side, he would mature to handsome in a few years' time. All this dressed in a well-cut but filthy suit, dirty shirt and spotted navy tie. He didn't even dare to look at his shoes – the right one would have gaped at the front but for the string, which had to be replaced once in a while when it became too frayed. He knew he would have to wait before fitting in with that crowd and agreed with his friend that they were most unlikely to have many apprentice coal miners amongst them.

So it was back to the camp for the next day's journey. On the corner of the Ring his last image of Vienna was the girls, the women, the prostitutes. They lived up to their reputation of being the best-dressed professionals in the world, who would consider a ladder in their nylons the greatest disaster that had ever befallen them. Some were barely sixteen and many of them spoke their German with the rounded vowels of a Hungarian accent. They must have come with the first wave, Adam thought.

'How's business, ladies?' He shouted at them impishly.

'It would be a bloody sight better if you moved on, wearing that suit!' One dismissed Adam with a flick of her wrist in a perfectly fitting black leather glove.

'Come on, Zany, time to go.' László tried to sound sensible as they both turned back to take one more look at the beauties of the night.

'Ah, they are gorgeous,' Adam sighed.

In the early morning, with Germanic precision, the buses were ready to take the English quota to the Westbanhof. As they climbed aboard, some local ladies were handing out blue plastic bags of toiletries with US ESCAPEE PROGRAM written on them in good-sized letters, just to be sure that they would not be mistaken for tourists on the train. Adam in his dirty outfit did not care about anything. He was only too happy to have a toothbrush to call his own.

What followed as the train left the station and for the next day and a half was a triumphant march befitting any opera's second act. At station after station they were forced to stop, just to allow the local populace to pay their homage to the freedom fighters (and this was the first time some of them had ever heard the term) of a brave little land that had given such a bloody nose to the mighty Soviet Union. The onlookers brought clothing, warm winter clothes, chocolates and sausages, plenty of pork sausages that they devoured with fresh bread and mustard. As the train left the last station the men would stand in a queue to wash and shave and to change into clean shirts. By the time they had pulled into the German frontier station at Passau, they were beginning to look like the heroes that the people on the heaving platforms had come to see. Austrian, Hungarian and German flags flying in abundance made it clear that this was not the usual 07.15 express from Vienna.

The local press demanded interviews from one and all until the stationmaster intervened, shouting that the lines were getting clogged up behind, all the way back to Vienna. When the engine driver whistled and opened the steam valve just to push back the crowd they could still hear questions being fired at them: 'How many Russians did you kill,

Tibor? Was there any lynching? How many of your friends failed to make it?'

Next morning they arrived at Ostend to board the *Prinz Eugen* and, after some four hours of devastating seasickness, which affected every landlocked Magyar aboard, the imposing white cliffs of Dover towered above them.

The date was 13 January 1957.

21

ENGLAND

An overwhelming feeling of well-being hit Adam as soon as he put his right foot on the *terra firma* of England. He had to change step twice along the gangplank to make sure it was the right one that first touched the ground of the sceptred isle he called 'Anglia'.

The midday chill cut into his handsome face like a rusty razor. He shook his head and pulled up the collar of his coat, which had come from somewhere in Virginia. On production of his hastily issued entry visa the dour immigration officer looked at him and asked, 'What are you going to do in England?'

'Into university,' Adam answered, smiling, with his first words of bad English.

The officer looked at Adam's shoes, by now both soles safely secured to the uppers with pieces of string of various colours, and murmured, 'Fat chance.'

'Excuse, sir?' Adam looked questioningly at his first Englishman.

'It's slang for good luck – good luck!' He waved Adam on.

'Fat chance, fat chance, very good – I learn, I learn.' Adam kept repeating the words as he walked through the land of his dreams, heading for a coach marked NATIONAL COAL BOARD. The shiny black letters perhaps tried to match the black diamond of the Yorkshire pits, which he would now have the privilege to extract in his newly gained status of 'apprentice coal miner'. He secured the front two seats and László was soon sitting next to him. As they looked back into the coach to establish what sort of company they would be keeping in the future they realised that it was an extremely varied one – to say the least: a few youngsters of the Molotov-cocktail-throwing vintage, somewhat subdued, initially at least; a good-sized group of actual miners from the brown coalfields of Komló near Pécs, raring to get started on digging for England; and a similar bunch of lily-white-handed intellectuals, who would find the shovel a new and incomprehensible experience. And in the back row were four very dubious-looking men in their late twenties; unshaven and intimidating. László quietly remarked that perhaps it hadn't been such a good idea to open all the prisons during the heady days, to which Adam nodded his agreement without a word.

The gaunt-looking man from Jennersdorf was still leading the mixed bag to their unknown destination, extolling the Board's virtues of good working conditions and even better pay for one and all. 'Look at all the Italians who came before you. They all own chip shops now!' A young ex-tank-destroyer asked timidly: 'What is a chip shop?' 'Local delicacy, my lad – you'll find out, soon enough,' the man reassured his enquirer.

As the streamlined coach pulled out of the Dover harbour area it was one of the unsavoury specimens looking out of the rear window who remarked loudly, 'Look at those fucking idiots, they still drive on the left – what's up with them!?'

The duo winced.

The 'Garden of England' did not look at its best that morning, but whose garden does on a thirteenth of January! For the two sitting in the front seats there was much to absorb, so the greyness of the sky and the drizzle did not bother them in the slightest. The cars were the main subject of their discussion, and Adam counted seventeen different models in one minute. He took a particular liking to the Jaguar XKJ but he decided that the Austin A40 would more than do for the moment. László nearly jumped out of his seat on seeing a four-wheel variety of the BMW Bubble car. That was what he wanted, and he decided that he would not leave a chunk of coal – however small – unturned in order to get one. Then a giant Rolls approached on the other side of the road and they both immediately fell silent. Looking at his friend's expression, which was of surprise mixed with intimidation, Adam burst out laughing. Even he never thought he would ever get near to owning one of those.

Canterbury took their minds off the traffic and the cars. As the coach passed along St George's Place under the city walls towards High Street the magnificent cathedral suddenly appeared over the driver's head. Adam pleaded with the representative of the Coal Board to stop for a quick visit to Becket's tomb, but he refused to consider it and sadly Adam was in no position to argue. As the Gothic wonder disappeared from view he pondered his subordinate status, realising that he was not on a sightseeing tour but on the way to a new life, where he would have very little influence on matters; for a while anyway. So he patted the blue circular aluminium badge hanging on his lapel with NCB pressed on to it and tried to remind himself that although individualists, the English were a disciplined lot and he was only a refugee.

The rest of the journey up the A2 was uneventful and in any case it was soon dark. He was nevertheless pleased that the driver decided to cross the Thames by Tower Bridge, and he could just manage to see the outline of the Tower against the street lights. What a backdrop to the prison scene and the rattling of chains in Donizetti's *Roberto Devereux*, he thought.

The Lancaster Gate Hotel on Bayswater Road was already earmarked for demolition to make way for a towering replacement, but it was still more than suitable for the first-night stay of a bunch of tatty refugees. One of the receptionists was so pretty that Adam could not take his eyes off her, and he duly dropped his room key when she handed it to him. Her fresh, rosy face framed by cascading honey-blonde hair was a perfect setting for her large blue eyes, which paid less than a split second's attention to Adam before moving on to 'matters reception'. He knew he had been noticed by the beauty, who moved behind her reception desk with the ease of a super-fit snake, so he returned to the foyer after throwing his 'escapee' toilet bag on to his bed. The English beauty, the like of which he had never seen, was still busy, and Adam sat on an easy chair directly in her line of vision, should she ever look up. When she did there was a glint of recognition before she lowered her eyes to his shoes, turning her expression into a most compassionate smile. Adam extended his arms, trying to convey the message of 'what you see is what you get', but the girl's professionalism, which told her to have nothing to do with customers, won the day, and after another smile she disappeared from his life through the door leading away from the desk, only to be replaced by a burly cockney male. It was time for Adam to head for the room marked 'Television', which was already filled by the others, watching this marvel of the age.

The set with its twelve-inch screen was placed on a chest of drawers and was enlarged to something twice the size by a similar-shaped magnifying glass in a steel frame. John Wayne was chasing a bunch of baddies to the delight of everyone in the smoke-filled room. They all clapped at the end of the film and the screen was taken over by a newscaster dressed impeccably in a dinner jacket. The third item in the news was concerned with the arrival of a ferry-full of Hungarian refugees at Dover. The camera swept around the harbour first, then showed the *Prinz Eugen*.

'It's you, Adam – look!' László shouted across the room.

Adam stepped forward and saw himself walking down the gangway, changing his step. When he arrived at the bottom, the cameras zoomed in on his right foot so as to acquaint Britain with his string-tied shoes. The raucous laughter of the others just would not stop, and he soon had to defend himself from flying magazines being thrown at him for giving the proud Magyars a bad name in this, their new kingdom. The shoes – or what was left of them – had to go.

After a breakfast of bacon and eggs they were told by the Coal Board representative, yet again, that they were a lucky lot. They were to be taken to Blackpool, 'a beautiful and world-famous northern seaside resort town', for English language lessons, where they would be billeted out to empty boarding houses until Easter. Anything to stay out of the bowels of the earth, Adam thought, and it did sound exciting. The sea, eh? Until vomiting all over the English Channel he had had no previous knowledge of it, and they all looked forward to a more gentle acquaintance with the vast water. So it was back on the buses to Euston station for the five-hour train journey. There was a scramble for the first-class coaches but Adam and László lost out, so they used their cigarette rations to swap seats on the special to the north-west. Forty Marlboros did the trick, and they settled down to enjoy the English countryside, which fascinated them both. The winter green of the fields and meadows speckled with red-brick houses looked surprisingly different, and when the sun shone, creating long shadows, the whole thing looked like a beautiful, enchanted parkland.

Suddenly they felt an urge to declare affinity with their new country. Adam said that he now understood why the Zentas were such Anglophiles, to which László replied that on his mothers side there was a considerable English branch from Nantwich. They both felt better for finding some stepping stones into the new country.

From Blackpool Central a half-dozen coaches started to disperse the would-be coal miners to various boarding houses. The journey Adam and László had to endure was less than a mile, which made them think that if this was the sort of cosseting they were going to get from the Coal Board, mining might not be so intolerable after all. The Woodville Hotel, a standard Victorian boarding house in Albert Road, was very much like the rest of them – a parlour off the narrow hallway, a dining room in the basement and, to Adam's amazement, they were given two very small single rooms on the first floor, whilst the others had to settle into twins, including a father and his son, who had both been badly shot up some months before by the visiting liberators from Omsk Tomsk and Novosibirsk.

In the morning John Brightman, the herald of the National Coal Board whom they had met on the London Transport bus in Jennersdorf, arrived to distribute the first week's wages at apprentice grade. The princely sum of £7 13*s* 6*d* astonished them all. Whichever way they converted it, into Deutschmarks, dollars or, especially, Hungarian florins, it was a fortune. So, after a hearty breakfast which they considered the best meal of the day, it was off to the nearest shoe shop as far as Adam was concerned. At Timpson's he found what he was looking for: shiny, semi-patent slip-ons with nearly one-inch crêpe soles – an up-to-the-minute item, which impressed him if no one else. After he had glanced at the shoes he had just taken off for the fitting, it did not take him too long to explain to the salesman, whose hair was slicked back into a very short back-and-sides, that he wanted to leave them on. The man picked up his old shoes by the strings with his fingertips and before Adam could say his farewell they disappeared behind the counter, a thin metallic noise indicating their ultimate fate in the bin.

Right next door reigned 'Jackson the Tailor', the gentlemen's outfitters of the day, he was told. Twenty minutes later Adam walked out in a grey-blue checked sports jacket and navy blue drainpipes, with more than adequate turn-ups. The Double 2 white shirt was crowned by his old and lucky dark blue tie with white polka dots. With his old suit now in the Jackson bag he walked back to the Woodville, where he was immediately interrogated by the others as to the origin of his new-found 'elegance'. He succumbed easily and became the self-appointed expert on the shops of Church Street.

László and several of the others could hardly wait for lunch to be over to partake in a similar shopping spree. By mid-afternoon some three hundred Magyars were buying up everything in sight to the obvious delight of the shop owners and managers of the inner area around the Winter Gardens, Blackpool's gem of a Victorian entertainment complex. Some hours later signs appeared in shop windows welcoming Hungarians and assuring them of the best attention, some even offering discounts to them. Not understanding the principle, many of them thought they were threatened with some sort of second-class quality but Adam managed to convince them that John Brightman was right after all and they were just plain 'lucky'. John was a superbly interesting character. A Hungarian who had ended up in Pontefract after the Second World War as a POW, he had fought on the Eastern Front as corporal in the Royal Hungarian Army against the vast Soviet forces (whom he simply referred to as the 'Bolshie hordes') with sufficient bravery to be given several high decorations in the field by the Hungarians and an Iron Cross (second class) by the Germans. Eventually transferred to the Western Front, he was captured by Monty's army. His shrewdness had Transylvanian roots, and on arrival in England he realised he had to do something about his surname: Tóthfalusy. His girlfriend and soon-to-be wife Olive, a Yorkshire girl, once happened to say to John that he was a very bright man. He liked that, and by virtue of a short poll, Brightman he became. Small in stature but with sparkling friendly eyes and teeth the size of spades revealed by his ever-frequent smile, he created a good enough impression on the Coal Board for him to be put in charge of recruiting the Hungarian miners.

He spent the afternoon running from one shop to another, helping with translation where necessary and performing the conversion from centimetres to inches. On their way back a group of them were passing the Coronation Street entrance to the Winter Gardens just as the evening paper hit the news-stands. Adam noticed that one of the main features included the word 'Hungarians'. He bought a copy and took it to John, who flashed his spade-like teeth in laughter yet again. The article referred to some less fortunate refugees, stranded in London and by now more than a little hungry, who had caught some of the mallards in Hyde Park and roasted them on twig fires by the lakeside, a rustic scene not particularly appreciated by the Metropolitan Police. 'Hungarians eat Queen's Ducks', read the headline.

'Now, I said you were lucky – didn't I!'

'No argument, John.' Adam held both his hands up, smiling. 'See you!' He patted the interpreter on his back and turned into the optician's, where he had seen a pair of sunglasses he fancied.

Within a day the NCB's Hungarians were the best-dressed bunch of men in Blackpool, at least for once in their lives.

From midweek they had to attend language courses arranged for them by the Coal Board's management. The courses were organised in a nearby Methodist church hall and they were to last until Easter. The men were grouped by age, on the principle of the younger the brain the better its absorption power, thus the quicker the progress, so Adam and László, with a number of under-twenties, found themselves in Room A. In charge was a Miss James, a retired schoolteacher on the wrong side of forty, a spinster left unmolested by men who had never managed to come to terms with her inch-thick spectacles, which enlarged the windows of her mind to the size of small eggs. An utter darling of a lady, she was more than willing to give extra lessons in her Fleetwood bungalow to willing students like these two, at no extra charge. She took it upon herself to bear the collective guilt of the West for not giving any military help to the uprising by repeating the words 'Sorry we didn't help you' whenever there was a break in the lesson.

Her major problem was the sad fact that in the north of England in 1957 no one could muster up an English–Hungarian or Hungarian–English dictionary. Thus she had to resort to direct teaching methods and make her students work out the meanings of the words. Idiosyncrasies like 'quite a few', which meant 'very few indeed' in every other language in the world, held up progress occasionally, and the language of Shakespeare and Milton was accused of being illogical by a bunch of Hungarian mining students. The English vowels are the basic and immediate curse of the student and are the basis of any decent foreign pronunciation. Adam was to find this out for himself – soon.

Friday was payday again and the two decided that the new outfits were to be put to the test. Two tests to be precise: a good dinner and a serious attempt at romance.

Blackpool reflected well the new post-Second World War and post-Labour Britain; there had been a general upturn in the economy since rationing had been abolished a few years before. The years of Harold Macmillan's 'you never had it so good' were about to begin at home, whilst the 'winds of change' were just a meteorological 'low' as far as the imperial past was concerned.

The town was generally ready to do its own thing, to regain its pre-war eminence. Shops and boarding houses were in great competition to smarten up and give themselves a lick of paint. Cinemas on every street corner were full to bursting and the dance halls were just a sea of moving couples throughout the week. This activity was also reflected in the way people dressed, especially the girls, with colourful underskirts displaying the carnation look to show off perfect calves, which could not be resisted for too long by the hot-blooded Magyars, most of whom had been too long involved in things other than matters of the opposite sex.

Adam and László decided that the priority of their second Friday in this new land, which they had had adopted so readily, was to celebrate with a good dinner in a good restaurant.

A short walk from the Woodville, the Clifton Hotel was to be their venue, and with the recommendation of its three stars it would do nicely for the moment, thank you! Now this was the England they recognised from so many films. Style and elegance and, most important, the palm court band! The head waiter did not quite approve of their attire and he used his usual discretion with foreigners by ushering them to a corner table, just a little out of the way, close to the kitchen.

With their one-week-old English and no French at all the menu became an indecipherable challenge. After an initial hesitation, which to them felt like eternity, they decided on the expediency of random picking in the time-honoured way of the 'lucky dip', after settling on the soup of the day, which turned out to be a delicious leek and potato. László did well; having not so long ago landed in Dover, he opted for a Dover sole. It was somewhat different for Adam; his finger ended up pointing to cauliflower in the vegetable section.

The head waiter did his best to convince his guest that the item was just a vegetable, but Adam would not have it. With a beautiful name like cauliflower, how could he go wrong? He thought. The man in the striped trousers and somewhat shiny black jacket eventually gave up and accepted the choice of the 'vegetarian foreigner'.

After an appropriate lapse of time the Dover sole arrived, looking tempting enough. And then Adam – and the rest of the guests – saw the cocky head waiter walking towards him beside a trolley on which rested a silver dome, all being pushed along by a junior waiter. This was worth fighting for, waiting for and leaving one's country for – he thought.

When the silver dome was retracted and the full-size steaming cauliflower was revealed, it captured the attention of everyone in the busy restaurant. The maître d' did not want his charge go short and had decided to produce the largest one they could find in the vegetable cupboard. Adam, having insisted so vehemently, had to do the decent thing and proceeded to eat the giant item before him, murmuring quietly to László, 'You know, Spotty, I hate cauliflower more than anything else in the world.'

'Tough, Adam, you had better get it eaten,' László answered, adding, 'This "Dover fish" is the best I ever had,' and he placed a sliver on top of his friend's mound of a vegetable, which by now had started to steam up the window next to him.

Adam could hardly wait to get to the pudding to get the taste of the cauliflower out of his mouth. Later there would be dancing in the Winter Gardens. Now that would be fun, he thought.

Having paid the bill, they walked along the promenade and Victoria Street to the side door of the large and still-beautiful Victorian entertainment centre. Once inside they heard the strains of the music of the Victor Sylvester Dance Band pouring out of the ornate ballroom. They headed towards the sound and soon found themselves at the top of the stairs. Below them the large hall appeared full of dancing couples, rather like a large pot of colourful stew being stirred anticlockwise. A shade regimented, Adam considered, but almost hypnotic. For a moment he did worry about the speed of the slow foxtrot, which was considerably faster than in his lessons of years before, but he dismissed it as an incidental and insignificant problem. They shouldered their way along the wall facing the orchestra, looking over the sea of dancers at the little man conducting his band, bobbing rhythmically up and down, facing the dance floor. The diminutive Mr Sylvester was brilliantly turned out; his immaculate tails and superbly ironed trousers were complemented by his blinding-white evening shirt and waistcoat, starched like a suit of armour. The picture of this epitome of an Englishman was suitably completed by his perfectly parted hair, flattened by a generous application of Brylcreem. It was difficult to say whether the well-seasoned orchestra needed him at all, but there he was, baton in hand, smiling away at his numerous followers, who rightly considered him the greatest.

The garish elegance of the superlative room overwhelmed the two. Spotty declared the magnificent chandeliers and the ornate balconies typical of English lack of taste, but Adam wasn't so negative.

'Spotty, this nation spends more time indoors than any other. They decorate their houses in a style that would look ridiculous anywhere on the Continent, even as near as Holland. Their sunshine has to be generated from within, so the Victorians splashed on the colours freely, especially yellow or gold.'

'I didn't know you'd studied these things, Zenta! So it's to do with lack of sun, eh? That's why they are so pale,' László egged him on.

'Precisely, the men become pale and pasty, but look at their women; the world-renowned strawberries and cream! They are gorgeous!' Adam could hardly wait to make his first approach.

It didn't take him too long to take stock and soon he found a bunch of girls giggling in the far left corner, very near the bar. A glance at himself in the mirror on the left, a few deep breaths just to chase away his innate shyness, and he was off, leaving his friend, who was still staring at the ornate balconies.

Ten steps and he was standing opposite his choice, a fairly short-haired blonde with a waist he was sure he could hold in his two hands, thumbs and fingers touching. That impression was clearly created by the wide white belt holding the very flared dancing dress of white chiffon with large pink polka dots. Above the belt the dress fitted the youthful body like a second skin, but below all sorts of things happened, as it covered a multitude of coloured underskirts cut to various lengths centring on the knees to allow the passing viewer to think he was looking at a carnation held upside down. She must have noticed Adam heading for her because she pushed her hands downwards on the bodice to ensure that there were no wrinkles on it – not one. Her head tilted back a shade to reveal an extremely pretty face, pale with just the right amount of make-up, large blue eyes and full pink lips. She looked at Adam challengingly. He bowed deeply.

'May I have the pleasure of this dance, please?' Adam offered the well-rehearsed line, heavily accented but with a broad smile. It was the best he could do.

'You may,' she answered, raising her arms.

Adam slipped his right arm around her waist and took her tiny hand in his left. A few tentative shuffles and they were off – anticlockwise.

Victor Sylvester and his band played loudly enough for them not to have to worry too much about conversation, which suited Adam. They were soon engulfed by all the others. Mr Sylvester set a brisk enough tempo, and Adam had to concentrate on not leaving the gap before them too large as he noticed a little traffic jam building up behind.

The next number was a lot slower so the lights were dimmed and the spinning mirror-ball above became illuminated. Now, this is different, Adam thought as they passed the bandleader, who smiled at them.

Adam tightened his right arm around the girl's wasp waist and gently squeezed her right hand in his. She looked up to catch his eye and drew a little nearer. In seconds he was intoxicated. The reflections of the globe were playing on her hair and in her eyes, which sparkled every time the light hit them. He was about to fall in love when the number ended, and after the applause Mr Sylvester announced a 'short break during which Mr Reginald Dixon will entertain you'. The applause now greeted the emerging organ, with Mr Dixon hitting a G minor chord to start yet another slow foxtrot. Adam's partner's face showed clear displeasure which he – quite rightly – took to mean that she no longer cared to dance. He held her left hand to walk her back to the still-giggling girls, but stopped short.

'Drink?' He gestured with his right hand.

'Yeah, please,' she answered in an accent as broad as the ballroom.

At the bar area they sat at a small Britannia table and Adam continued.

'What drink you?'

'Brandy and Babycham.' Adam heard it quite clearly and repeated it to himself just to get used to saying it to the barman.

It took the barman three attempts to make out what his customer wanted and Adam returned with a beer for him and a glass of brandy and a small bottle of something looking like champagne with a Bambi on the label, which she proceeded to pour into the brandy.

They sipped a little of their drinks and then came the longest pause in Adam's life, to date at least. Something had to be said, but what? Adam was desperate.

'Hungarian.' He pointed to his chest.

The pretty girl murmured something about 'bad reputations', the meaning of which Adam would have to figure out with Miss James during the coming week, but she carried on drinking.

Adam looked at her legs as she crossed them. They were perfect. Like some porcelain structures emanating from the pink frills with dainty feet, which were totally inadequately covered by the gold backless stiletto-heeled slippers, matching her handbag. Utterly sexy, but how on earth would she go home in them? After all, it was a cold January night, thought Adam.

He had to say something. Looking at her sculpted feet provided the inspiration. He wanted to compliment them by saying, 'Your feet – small.' He repeated it twice in his head and touched her hand. When her eyes met his he smiled and said, 'Your feet – smell!'

'Pardon?' She asked incredulously.

'Your feet – smell!' Adam repeated more loudly and confidently.

She looked at him, once, twice, then picked up her brandy and Babycham and walked away, out of Adam's life for ever.

∼

Adam decided that there was only one thing to do and that was to learn to speak the language, properly. He talked his friend into a pact that they would not speak to each other in Hungarian any more, however hard that would be. They went to see every film in Blackpool's half a dozen cinemas every night to try to relate the action to what was said. Thus they covered the whole range from *The King and I* to *The Incredible Shrinking Man*. They pronounced every new word they learned the way they last heard in on the screen and ended up with a mixture of several accents. The following day poor Miss James would have to listen to a sentence beginning with a little David Niven and ending with a mouthful of John Wayne.

The Woodville Hotel in Albert Road gave them a wonderful opportunity to share in what the town had to offer. The Golden Mile and the profusion of entertainment made them realise that there could have been no better place to start their new lives. Adam's letters to just about everyone he knew in Hungary were full of praise for the opportunities and the spectacles England had provided so far, and he never mentioned the price he would have to pay for all this around Easter, when they were to become real coal miners.

One evening trip to the nearby Rossall's School was a great treat for the culturally minded, as the Royal Liverpool Philharmonic Orchestra was giving a full symphony concert, which included Beethoven's Violin Concerto, for the privileged boarding pupils. Campoli, the ageing violinist, gave such a remarkable rendering of the solo part that the members of the orchestra were applauding him as hard as the students and the few miners-to-be. Adam was equally impressed by the beauty of the English spring and the surrounding countryside, with its winding roads and all those Austins and Morris Minors.

A few weeks before the Easter holidays, at László's suggestion, they decided to put on a show of sorts. They went to the actual Opera House, a most beautiful Victorian grand theatre, and rented it for Friday night. A troupe of reasonable talent spent every evening rehearsing and, much to their own surprise, managed to stage a two-hour show, including the twenty-minute interval. The stage was draped with the Union flag and the Hungarian red, white and green tricolour with a hole cut into the middle of the white stripe to denote its revolutionary origin. László, by now fairly adept in English, made the welcoming speeches in both languages. The packed house then heard choral works, instrumental solos and a collection of opera arias, the latter by courtesy of AZ himself. At the end the mayor of the town thanked the Hungarians for the entertainment and a collection was made for his own charity, which produced the princely sum of £325. Next morning the local daily mentioned the event as 'Hungarians say thank you with music … which included some very well-sung operatic arias'.

They all now felt that perhaps they were accepted, and this spurred on the two to try to integrate into their new life, quickly.

∼

During his last few weeks in Blackpool Adam met Patricia Harris in the brilliant ballroom that had become his second home. Coming from Preston's Watling Street Road, she first had to explain to him the origin of her somewhat convoluted address. Adam knew little about the Romans in Britain so Pat had her job cut out, but at the end Adam got the point as to how an ancient and very straight 'street' also became a new road, in Preston. She would talk with great understanding about the seasonal unemployment rate of the resort town during the winter. So the Hungarians in the boarding houses were good news in the short term, but not quite so good in the long term. Each time they met their conversations tended to veer towards more serious subjects, which was important for Adam's ever-developing English. Pat was a lovely, slender brunette in her mid-twenties (a few years older than he), with chestnut-brown hair cut into a fashionable bob. She dressed elegantly, perhaps in a way that was a little too old fashioned, considering her years, making her look older than she was. She would interrupt their cuddling or his attempt at some sweet talk with, 'Adam, that's wrong, you don't say "be mine", it's too dramatic – operatic. You say, "I want you, darling" or "Let's make love" or better still say nothing at all, I'll know what you want.'

Their separation prevented the relationship developing much further, yet Pat turned up to see Adam getting on to the coach rented by the NCB, which proudly declared the destination BARNSLEY on the front. Adam ran to take a place on the back seat to see Patricia standing in her beige mac and white chiffon scarf in front of the Woodville, waving tearfully. After the coaches had turned left at the bottom of Albert Road, Adam kept repeating her parting words: 'Adam, you will go a long way – make sure you get out of Barnsley as soon as you can! Promise!'

The date was 5 April 1957.

The journey across the Pennines gave Adam and László their second chance to see the English countryside after their initial January train journey from London. The early spring brought clear air and good visibility, and they were now travelling across barren but magnificent moorland. They had a perfect view from the back seats and wondered how on earth (and for what reason) the British built all those dry-stone walls. Some way before Pennistone the traditional grey stone buildings took over from the brick ones of Lancashire and they knew they were well into the White Rose county. Far too soon, after clearing the romantic leafy bends of the road, the coaches suddenly turned right and they found themselves in a sort of a compound which they immediately recognised as an ex-prisoner-of-war camp. They were asked to get off and were ushered by NCB officials to the main hall to receive their allocation details.

The low-ceilinged unrendered brick hall was large enough to take a brigade of POWs. The six busloads of Magyars were asked to take their seats on the backless wooden benches, and suddenly two well-dressed gentlemen arrived to address them. The first was the local manager of the Coal Board, who was followed quickly by the familiar figure of the interpreter, Brightman.

'Gentlemen, welcome to the South Yorkshire area of the NCB.' The man opened his arms as if it to signal that this was his very own land. 'In the past this place has been the cradle of many foreign coal miners who have settled in this part of the country, happily. After the Poles and the Italians, it is now your turn to make this place your home. Go on, John, translate it for them.' He turned to his interpreter.

'Mr Wright says you are welcome to this dump. Everybody who stayed here before was very happy …' He was about to say something else, but one wit interrupted.

'Why did all the Jerries piss off home, then?'

John Brightman went for him. 'Don't mess me about. Even some of those didn't – look at Fritzy Kohler, happily married to Mavis. And Heinz – now Henry – what's-his-name, he lives around the corner, and not forgetting Bert Troutman, the Manchester City goalie. You see, you're just plain stupid and you don't know what you're talking about, so why don't you just shut up!' The official was a little surprised by the tone of his few welcoming words rendered into Hungarian, but he thought anything was possible with that crazy language, so he continued.

'You will soon receive your dormitory details and you will see that we went to great lengths to keep friends and families together. Tomorrow is Good Friday, so you will all receive your wages tonight. That certainly went down well. 'On Tuesday we will group you together. Experienced miners will be taken to Dodworth Colliery, the apprentice section will receive further practical training here and will be attached to Silkstone Hall for underground demonstrations and further tuition.'

Whilst Brightman translated, the odd 'oooh' and 'aaah' was vaguely audible. This made him wag the occasional finger, but when he announced that he would take personal charge of distributing the wages, they suddenly became very quiet.

A large trolley brought in the big wooden box full of brown paper envelopes containing the wages. Princely sums made up of crisp pound and ten-shilling notes and gigantic, incomprehensible coins were accompanied by a paper strip, denoting the deductions for NHS/Social Security, income tax and a new item: lodging. They were soon to find out what that meant.

The former Methodist church hall group found themselves in Dormitory D. The thirty-yard-long Nissen hut, a half-tube covered with rusting corrugated iron, had two rows of steel beds with thin mattresses and clean bedding. Beside each bed a small wooden cupboard contained a drawer and a small space below it. The shelf above the headboard completed the allocation. After every fifth bed there was a larger gap to accommodate a small window, and there was a communal shower room between each dormitory.

The long weekend gave them a chance to get acquainted with Barnsley, which turned out to be much more pleasant than they had been led to believe by the Lancashire folk of Blackpool. To their approval they noted that there were half a dozen cinemas, so their continuing education in the language of Byron could at least go on, thanks to the screen efforts of Richard Todd and Gary Cooper. Getting to understand what 'ta, luv' meant was their first hurdle in terms of the unfamiliar accent, but there were many others to follow. 'Thee' and 'thou' were not too difficult to accept, considering what a friendly lot these Yorkshire folks were. 'Cup o' cha' in the canteen took a little longer to sort out. The greatest impression on the two was made by the decency and honesty of the simple folk of the town, especially the women.

Easter Sunday started lazily. After lunch they watched a little television on the small twelve-inch screen, once again magnified by a larger glass lens, which kept dropping out of its metal frame. No matter, it was useful to pick up a few new words. In the afternoon the two walked into town again for some window-shopping and ended up in the Odeon to see *Anastasia* with Ingrid Bergmann and Yul Brynner. They decided that the murderous commies executing the last tsar and his captured family in Yekaterinburg would have done a consummate job; there was no way for the little princess to escape from that room with guns blazing, just no way. Then fancy her walking all the way to the West. 'The amnesia was a good ploy, though,' Adam added. Climbing the hill on their way back to camp, they had their first chance to introduce themselves to the culinary delights of fish and chips. Now that was something. Eating glorious cod in light batter out of the famous newspaper, the *News of the World*, whilst standing outside the shop, was something neither of them ever wanted to forget. Having finished the whale-sized, steaming-hot fish seasoned with salt and vinegar, with chips fried to perfection, they looked at each other, thought of what Brightman had said back in Blackpool and immediately rejoined the queue for a second helping.

By the time they had strolled back to camp the sky was full of exceptionally angry, virtually black clouds. Adam decided on an early night and walked to his dormitory, which they had affectionately named Gulag D. He put on his brand-new pyjamas and settled under his blankets, which had seen better times, probably during the war. Soon he was sleeping the proverbial 'sleep of the just'. But just after midnight the Yorkshire heavens opened. The black clouds discharged their large droplets heavily laden with soot, as if they wanted to paint the town jet black. Some of the sleeping Magyars were awakened by the sound of the heavy drops of rain on the corrugated roof, but it took a while for Adam to notice anything. Then what he did notice was most unpleasant. The first drop landed square on his forehead, and soon there were more to follow – in fact a straight line of them hitting him along the length of his army-issue blanket. Within minutes the droplets had become a steady flow, and he looked for the reason for the deluge. He noticed a gash along the corrugation. Bit of a nuisance, he thought, but it shouldn't be a problem for an ex-revolutionary who, not so long ago, had to be fished out of a river by his friends. All that was needed was to move the bed a couple of feet to the left. Alas, all his shoving and pushing were to no avail. Bending down to see the reason why, he was rewarded by the revelation that the army, not wanting the Jerries of El Alamein to pinch any beds, had screwed them firmly to the cement floor. When he asked László whether he could sleep with him head to toe he was told to 'get lost'. The others he managed to wake up told him to 'take a walk and be quiet about it', and some even suggested that he should 'go and serenade someone; after all, he liked singing'.

If it's singing they want, he thought, well, that's exactly what they will get. He dragged his by now sodden mattress and blanket into the passage between the two rows of beds, yelling out, '*Nessum dorma*' or 'None shall sleep now', from *Turandot*, which he had never liked so he didn't mind making a mess of it, transposing it a tone to avoid tackling the high C at the end. He need not have bothered as after the second line flying shoes and cardboard boxes were arriving from all directions. There was no question of ever getting to '*vincera*' – and he was not going to 'win' anything except further abuse until he lay on his repositioned mattress, very quietly. It took him the best part of an hour to contemplate his newly achieved status in the middle of the dormitory, and his last thought, before mercifully shivering himself to sleep, was that Pat Harris was right. He must get out of his predicament – and soon.

~

On the Tuesday after Easter the experienced miners were bussed to their place of work in Dudworth Colliery, leaving the camp fairly depopulated. The tuition of the apprentices began, which László and Adam considered quite fun. Within a week, alas, they had begun to notice that trouble was brewing. The indigenous Yorkshire miners did not mix too well with 'The Huns', as they started to refer to them affectionately. When a section walked out on the Magyars it was time for another chat, so along came not-so-happy Mr Wright in the company of John the interpreter to address them in the hall.

The NCB official started quietly but Mr Brightman whispered something in his ear to the effect that he should leave it to him and he took over in earnest.

'For Christ's sake, what's the matter with you all!?' The thin chap shouted. The Englishman in the pinstriped suit looked at him in total surprise.

'Haven't I told you not to work so hard, you bloody Stakhanovites? The bloody English are bloody fed up with the lot of you. Now cut it out and slow down, for Christ's sake! You are causing mayhem in the pits!'

He had not quite finished when grey-haired Mr Kovács from Komló stood up. Much respected by all fellow miners, Mr Kovács, an experienced foreman in his old pit, started off hardly audible.

'John, please calm down and tell Mr Wright that we are hardly doing anything, yet we still seem to be working too fast for the English. We just don't know how little to do for all these wages they are paying us. I have already sent five pounds home to my wife. We have never seen equipment like they have here, there is hardly any real work involved, not like back home.'

'Mr Kovács,' John's voice became quieter, 'I understand what you're saying, but please tell them to slow down, for Christ's sake.'

~

Two weeks later the pits involved announced a strike against the Hungarian miners who were working against 'agreed practices'. The man from the NCB announced that all Hungarians would be transferred to a pit where the chief safety supervision would be by the local management only.

John Brightman declared, 'You'll be getting your own bloody pit, which is so over-mined that there's hardly any coal left in it, so you won't be able to work so bloody hard – if that's what you want!'

'So much for *"Workers of All Lands Unite"*, then,' a young miner shouted, knowing his Communist Manifesto.

'Where is their socialist internationalism?' Another wanted to know. It was to no avail – they were separated and the half-dead pit soon outproduced all the others in the district.

~

Adam and László attended their classes and were about to be sent to Silkstone for a week's practical when László announced that a lady who worked in the canteen was looking for lodgers in Park Road North, by all accounts a nice Victorian area south-west of the town centre. The two did not hesitate. By the following Monday they had moved into their shared room, which was luxurious compared to what they had before. The large bedsit was complemented by a very small but perfectly adequate kitchen and they had their own bathroom. Neither of them could believe their luck. László took charge of culinary matters and stated that he would need one pound from each for them eat adequately, though for extras and treats he would need a few shillings more, 'only once in a while, mind you!'

Midweek he announced that his Nantwich aunt (until then Adam had not believed he had one) had invited him to go and meet her and an acquaintance of hers in Oxford, so he would sadly have to miss the week's underground tuition. 'Ever so sorry,' he kept repeating, 'you'll have to cook for yourself.'

Friday afternoon Adam presented himself for his medical prior to the underground work and met Dr J J Danaher, a consultant chest physician of obvious Irish ancestry. He glanced at the good-looking, chestnut-haired and very well-dressed young man. After he had taken his past medical history, he said, in a rolling Irish accent, 'My boy, you have the best English amongst all of you here. What, if I may ask, were you doing back home before those dreadful days?'

'Well, sir, I was a third-year medical student at Pécs University,' Adam answered.

Dr Danaher interrupted his percussion of Adam's chest. 'A medic, eh? And what would you be doing here, then?' He asked innocently.

'Sir, I am just trying to make a living.' Adam's answer was a little cheeky, although his smile attenuated his impertinence.

'Well, my boy, this won't do. Won't do at all. We must find you a place in a medical school somewhere. It won't do at all.' He whispered the last few words to himself. He looked at Adam as he put his shirt on. 'What is your name, my boy?'

'Adam Zenta, sir.'

'Well, Adam, here's my card. Tomorrow is Saturday, a good day for us to do a little work on your problem. Can you be at my house by four thirty?'

'Certainly, sir.' Adam looked at the card. 'It's just behind the town hall. I will be there at four thirty,' he added without hesitation.

༄

At 4.25 pm Adam, dressed in his Blackpool 'Jackson the Tailor' outfit and wearing his navy spotted tie, pressed the doorbell.

The round-faced, stockily built man in a tweed jacket opened the door. Smiling, he said, 'Hello, Adam, come on in, my boy.' He ushered his young guest into the Victorian living room. 'Meet Mrs Danaher.'

'How do you do, Mrs Danaher?' Adam took the lady's outstretched hand.

'Pleased to meet you. It's Adam, isn't it.' She smiled. 'Isn't it a lovely warm day?'

'Yes, madam, it is warm, I never expected such a warm summer in England.'

'Well, they say 1957 is to be the best summer on record for many decades – we haven't had a drop of rain since Easter, I believe.' The lady, whose hair was gently greying, smiled again.

'Yes, I remember the rain at Easter,' Adam said. And will I ever forget it? He thought.

'A cup of tea?' She asked.

'Very kind of you, madam – just a little milk, no sugar, thank you,' Adam answered with a gentle bow of his head.

'Now, my boy, let's get down to business.' The doctor took over the conversation. 'I have not been idle since we last talked,' he started enthusiastically, and proceeded to tell Adam that he had been speaking to his friend and near-neighbour, the newly elected Labour Member of

Parliament, Roy Mason, who was due to finish his surgery and would see them at his house.

Adam could hardly finish his tea. To see an MP in his own home was something he could hardly have expected, even in his wildest dreams. He replaced the empty porcelain teacup on the coffee table before the doctor and his still-smiling wife were halfway through theirs. The next few minutes seemed to last for ever, but then suddenly the convivial physician stood up and looked at his watch.

'It's time to go, darling.' He turned to his wife.

'Best of luck, both of you, I'll keep my fingers crossed.' Her smile became even brighter.

The two men walked along the leafy street and halfway along on the left-hand side, at a well-kept Victorian house, the doctor pressed the doorbell.

The young MP opened the door and welcomed his friend Jim. Turning to Adam, he offered his hand.

'I'm Roy Mason; you are the young man from Hungary, aren't you?'

'Adam Zenta, a former medical student,' said Dr Danaher, introducing him before Adam could even say a word.

They moved into the living room, a carbon copy of the one he had left a few minutes previously, except that this one had a small semicircular bar in the corner by the bay window.

'You know,' said the rather, small rotund parliamentarian, turning to them both, brushing his fingers through his curly brown hair, 'I'm dying for a proper drink. I have just had a very hard surgery and an even harder meeting with my constituency executive. You will join me?'

'Sorry to hear that, Roy,' the doctor said, looking at his friend questioningly. 'Why is that?'

'I just gave them a piece of my mind for the way they're treating all these Hungarian miners.' He turned to Adam. 'It's a bloody disgrace, if you don't mind me saying so. Now, what will you have, Adam?'

'Whatever you drink, sir, will be fine,' Adam answered with not a little hesitation.

'Mine's a whisky with a little ice and water.' Mr Mason certainly did not hesitate.

'Same for me.' The doctor smiled.

'Well done, gentlemen. Scotch all around!' The MP went over to his bar.

They settled on the comfortable easy chairs and Mr Mason turned to his young guest.

'Well now, Adam, let's hear your story.'

It was the first chance Adam had had to relate his involvement in the uprising and his subsequent escape. It was certainly not to be the last. He coped well with his brand-new English, which he tried to keep as simple as possible, and this impressed both men. They were ready to help.

'Well now, we might have a little luck here,' the MP started. 'We are having an education debate next week. I'll bring up your problem, I might even embarrass the Secretary for Education with it.' He laughed.

They continued chatting until they had finished the whisky, which became an instant hit with Adam, and said their goodbyes. During the short walk back, Dr Danaher, not wanting to be outdone by his politician friend, suggested that he might try to find some sort of hospital work for Adam. It all seemed too good to be true.

Mrs Danaher insisted that Adam stay for dinner and her husband made Adam tell his tale again. This time he didn't need to be concise, which pleased the lady of the house, and she listened with a smile. They both agreed that he was very brave, which Adam accepted with the most modest expression he could muster up.

After Adam's first dinner in an English home, which consisted of smoked salmon, braised oxtail, followed by apple pie with delicious custard, they said their goodbyes and Adam set off for the walk back to his digs. Deep in thought, he paused for a moment to admire the huge white limestone town hall with the clock tower, questioning the necessity of such a large, monumental edifice in such small a town.

As his friend was not supposed to return until Sunday afternoon, he was surprised to see László's shadow at the first-floor window of their room. As he entered it was to see him packing his small suitcase.

'Adam, you won't believe this,' László spluttered. 'Please understand, but I've got a place at Keble College in Oxford – into the second year, but who the hell cares. I have to sign in on Monday or I'll lose my place.' He hardly looked up as he threw his spare shirt into the battered case.

'Well done, old fellow, of course I understand. Can I help?' The tremble in Adam's voice revealed more than a little surprise.

Adam said nothing until he had heard the full story of László's few days in the 'World Capital of Learning', as he put it, and after all it was quite an incredible tale.

Auntie knew someone who was acquainted with someone else whose friend happened to be one of the dons at the college. They had a place left for a refugee student, so why not him? It was as simple as that.

Not to be outdone, Adam made his friend listen to the story of his Saturday afternoon and evening, which made László feel considerably better. They both realised that it was the parting of the ways and knew that they had to take it in their stride. After all, the loss of the close proximity of their friendship compared most insignificantly to the loss of their careers, families and country. They were both astonished, though, that it had happened so quickly.

Adam saw his friend off at Sheffield bus station first thing on Sunday morning, as László had been warned to expect a pretty awful rail service from the South Yorkshire town on a Sunday. He walked back to his digs disconsolate but determined. First things first, he informed the landlady about László; she kindly reduced the rent by a third, because of 'less washing of the bedclothes'.

On Monday Adam appeared in the apprentice classes and spent the day explaining to everyone, English and Hungarian, what had happened to his friend. In the evening he stayed behind to watch a little television in the communal hall, which was also used by some of the local girls. They knew that they would be well entertained by the foreign miners, who had money in their pockets and not much in the way of commitments. He noticed a very pretty girl with short-cropped brown hair and the most delicate features, in the company of a rather large one who, with the best of intentions, could not have been described as other than plain. Well, one thing does not change much in this world, Adam though; the pretty and the plain, as the former faces no possible competition and the latter might pick up some crumbs. He invited them both for a drink – Jean, the petite one, and the other, whose name he did not bother to remember.

As they were about to start their beer, Pete, one of the young and fully trained miners, turned up and seemed to know them both. Pete's surname was Uhrin. P Uhrin had no particular Magyar connotation but had he known how the English would pronounce his surname, surely he would have chosen Finland for his second home.

'I rather fancy the little one,' Pete whispered. 'But I'm sure the other one will be a dead cert. OK?'

'Piss off, Urine,' Adam replied. 'No bloody way! She's all yours.'

'I'm not taking any more of that from anybody!' Uhrin grabbed Adam's collar, raising his fist.

'Get off him!' Little Jean tried to get between the two men and burst into laughter. 'Piss off, Urine, that's very good.' She turned to Adam. 'What's your name, then? Judging by the width of your shoulders it must be Adonis, eh?'

'No, it's just plain Adam.' He was still shaking off Pete.

'All right, plain Adam, are you going to take us out, then?'

'Sure! You and I are a team. Pete is dying to get closer to your friend – look, he's stepping all over me here,' Adam said, pushing his fellow coal miner away.

They had a few drinks and the beer obviously did the trick for Pete because he dragged the large girl away under the pretext of her helping him to fill in his deed poll application to change his surname.

After two more beers Adam offered to walk Jean home. She lived on a council estate just opposite the camp on the other side of the road. She told Adam that the following Friday there was going to be a pop concert in Sheffield City Hall. The American Frankie Lymon and his group the Teenagers were to be the stars, with a good supporting cast. When Adam agreed to take her, her goodnight kiss was of such intensity that he was looking around for a suitable place to walk her whilst still in a clinch. When she slid away, promising heaven, she smiled at Adam and ran into her brick-built council semi-detached. 'And I'll bring some nice photos of me for you to see.' She waved, blowing another kiss.

~

Adam spent the following week contemplating his proverbial navel. The mining lessons hardly interested him. In his plastic briefcase he carried Rideout's *English Today* and the dictionary *Words*, which he had received from Pat Harris. When they were taken down to Silkstone for the midweek practical demonstration he would carry them and disappear into a defunct side branch of the mine and read by his tin and brass Davy lamp.

Back at his digs in Park Road North, he was writing letters to his old friends and ZsaZsa. He was full of the 'New World' he had found in England. Having described the outward manifestations, obviously new to everyone when arriving from the Continent, he now concentrated on personal and social attitudes. His repeated description of fair play, helpfulness and total tolerance of the opposing attitude occasionally gave way to presenting some of the less attractive side of 'Englishness'. He considered the generally available education worse than dismal, and believed it to be behind the 'them and us' attitude so deeply carved into everybody's soul. He was accepted by Dr Danaher because he was a medic and by Jean because he was a coal miner, yet he accepted Pete just because he was a friend. There was a difference. A noticeable difference, which he would meet only too often in the years to come. But above all he liked the 'minding one's own business' stance, because it gave him the latitude he never had back home, which he knew he could use to his advantage.

To Kiss and Rácz he had to write about the women he had met so far. There was a vast difference here, which he considered more positive. In the late fifties the girls in England already had a different basic attitude to boys which was far ahead of that of any other nations. In total contrast to the Continental girls, who insisted, 'I'm not that sort, but keep asking,' they'd turn their eyes away and would declare, 'Of course I will, but perhaps not tonight,' looking straight into one's eyes and assessing the response.

∽

Soon after lunch, Adam, dressed in his light grey sports jacket and blue drainpipes, but still wearing his 'lucky tie', crossed the main road to Jean's house. On his hair he wore just a trace of Brylcreem. He was cutting a dashing figure; well, certainly he thought he was. Pretty little Jean was wearing what Adam considered to be an expensive light summer dress. The abstract pattern, based on a very modern interaction of pink and light grey, fitting around every curve she possessed, complemented his outfit perfectly. That's always a good start, he thought. They walked to the bus station to pick up the half-hourly to Sheffield.

During the mile and a half to the town centre, Jean brought up the ice-breaking subject of the 1957 weather, the best summer since 'God knows when'. Adam agreed that it could not be better and, judging by the letters he was receiving from home, it wasn't better even in landlocked Hungary. He naturally took credit for 'bringing it' and 'promised' that it would stay the same whilst he was living on these shores. He 'could stay as long as he liked in that case', she said with a mischievous wink.

They settled in his favourite place in the last row upstairs, and the bus left only five minutes late, which was a 'miracle', according to Jean.

'Did you bring the photos you promised?' Adam asked, hoping that there would be some bathing-costumed snaps amongst them.

'I certainly did, and I hope you don't mind them.' Jean smiled with ever-widening eyes.

She fumbled in her grey leather handbag and pulled out a small magazine called *Health and Efficiency*, which Adam naturally had never heard of. She opened it at the appropriate page and there she stood against a barn door, illuminated by perfect midday sunshine, in absolutely naked glory. Adam gulped, and his eyes came to the point where all her perfect curves met in loving harmony; her pubes were shaved. Well, that's no matter, he thought. A further four pages followed in which 'Jean from Barnsley' was shown off from every conceivable angle. In one, her shapely breasts were held together by her upper arms to enlarge her cleavage, which needed no help from the photographer anyway. Her legs, either crossed or simply placed parallel in seated-sideways poses, were exquisitely shaped. Adam checked them immediately, glancing at her knees. Yes, they were the same, and moreover, they were tantalisingly right next to his. He drew nearer. Adam tried to show as much nonchalance as he could muster to express that he was 'laissez-faire' about such modern manifestations of his New World as eighteen-year-olds posing in the nude by barn doors.

The pop concert in the superbly modern City Hall was great fun and Frankie brought the house down with his current hit, reassuring the multitude of his fans that 'No, no, I'm not a juvenile delinquent'. Jean suggested a good pub after the concert and Adam was not disposed in any way to turn that down. Draught Barnsley bitter was a well-established favourite of his by then; he had, unlike his countrymen, taken easily to the proverbial 'warm beer'. They missed the eleven o'clock to Barnsley by a whisker and Jean suggested that they should walk out of the city and hitch-hike home. Adam wasn't too keen, explaining that he had done enough walking in January to last him at least for this year. He felt his more-or-less intact wage pocket in his trouser pocket and waved to a black cab.

The astonished Jean stepped into the taxi and Adam, mesmerised by her shapely bottom, followed her as closely as he could. Once they were settled on the black plastic seats the close proximity did what it was supposed to do and they cuddled up to each other. The petting became heavier and heavier, and by the time they hit the A61 they knew what was going to happen on the ever-darkening road ahead. After they had passed the last sodium lamp-post Adam gently pulled Jean to him. Their eyes met for a moment. Adam saw her large open eyes in another passing light. They were very happy eyes of gentle submission. Adam held her waist and twisted her on to his lap.

～

The question Roy Mason, MP, asked the Secretary of State for Education during the debate Adam heard at second or third hand was: 'What is the Secretary of State going to do about the two Hungarian medical students working in the Barnsley pits?' Dr Danaher did mention to Adam later that he was 'now famous, being written up in Hansard'. It certainly did the trick, because the following week a large package of application forms arrived to his digs; one for each medical school in the kingdom. And off they went. He completed five of them every night before going to see Jean, more often than not for a trip to the cinema, sometimes for a walk, which was usually followed by careless and easy-going fornication. The replies came back virtually by return post. The registrars of the universities were sympathetic but frank. The responses varied between 'full for this year, try next' to 'full for the next three years, try after'. He was down to the last three uncompleted forms when, in June, he opened the letter from Liverpool. The notepaper bore a crest on a dark blue base and three very peculiar-looking birds surrounding a book, which declared that there should be light, *'Fiat lux'*. It very much resembled the one László had at Oxford. The motto in the ribbon was to the effect that leisure should facilitate studies, *'Haec otia studia fovent'*. It didn't make too much sense, but the contents certainly did. The gist of the short letter was that there was one place left for a foreign undergraduate, which had not been taken up by the Nigerian to whom it had been allocated. Would Mr Zenta come for an interview on the first Friday of June, at 2.30 pm. presenting himself at the dean's office. It was signed by the dean himself, J M Leggate. Now it was up to Adam.

He got up very early on Friday. He had to get to Sheffield by bus and take the train to Liverpool Central, changing at Manchester Piccadilly. Dressed in his Jackson the Tailor suit and wearing his spotted tie, he carried his brand-new raincoat, thinking rainless 1957 or no rainless 1957, who knew what was going on on the west coast. He walked to the bus station, easy in spirit and full of confidence.

Things went well and he arrived at his destination by midday, so deep in thought that he hardly remembered any detail of the journey. He had time to kill, but as he couldn't face food owing to a swarm of butterflies having a lively party in his stomach, he decided on a coffee. Looking around, to his left he saw a beautiful classical building, jet black owing to the years of soot covering the exquisite architecture, which proudly declared its name: 'Lyceum'. Facing Church Street, its basement housed a café of the same name, and much later he learned that, above it, the building housed a highly respected gentlemen's club.

The café was elegant but the coffee awful, and after paying, and including a very generous tip, he decided on a walk. It took him to Lime Street, and suddenly he could not believe his eyes. The glorious edifices built in the best tradition of the English classical style housed the county court, the Walker Art Gallery and the circular Picton Library next to the museum, all of them facing the square's crowning glory, the uniquely overpowering St George's Hall. The long line of perfectly proportioned

Corinthian columns proudly looked down at the mass of people using the street, demanding their unlimited admiration; ignoring the sad fact that soot had turned them all 'Lyceum black'. What a city, Adam thought. I've got to get in here!

Just as in Pécs, only three years before, he jumped into a taxi and asked to be taken to the medical school. The driver, surprised by the short distance involved, murmured something to the effect that it was quicker to walk, but his accent totally floored Adam, so he just leaned back on the seat.

After receiving his tip, the driver showed the more affable side of his complex personality and murmured a 'good luck, mate'. That Adam understood, though he was a bit surprised by the sudden familararity of the driver in electing him his 'mate'. The 'good luck' part was certainly welcome.

After briefly admiring the Victoria Building, with its Big Ben-like clock tower built with two-toned bricks, he walked into the perfectly glazed brown-tiled Victorian hall, displaying the white marble statue of Christopher Bushell in the centre. The uniformed usher soon told him that he was in the wrong place, and through the back door he pointed across the freshly cut lawn of the quadrangle to an even older Victorian building. Adam walked over to the main entrance, where a similarly uniformed man told him to sit down on the built-in glazed yellow-and-red-brick bench. He had waited for half an hour or so when a group of well-dressed middle-aged men walked past him talking animatedly to each other, following an obviously good lunch. They disappeared through a door marked in Gothic capitals SURGICAL LECTURE THEATRE. Fifteen minutes later, the uniformed man tapped Adam on the shoulder and told him he could go in now.

He found himself in the nineteenth-century wooden lecture theatre, whose steeply raked benches had narrow ledges for books. They were carved with the names of a hundred years of students. It was at the same time a well-functioning masterpiece and an admirable museum item. The air reeked of surgical spirit and ether, which made Adam feel immediately at home. He sat facing the large table of well-dressed men. The thin one in the middle smiled most benevolently and asked him whether he was Adam Zenta from Barnsley, which Adam confirmed with a 'Yes, sir'. He then went on to introduce himself as 'Jack Leggate, the dean of the Faculty of Medicine', and, still smiling, he said that the 'gentlemen around him' were Professors Morton, Gregory and Harrison. They each nodded as he called their names.

'Mr Zenta, you state on your application form that you were a third-year medic at the time of the uprising and you would like to continue your studies in Liverpool. As I am sure you will agree, our two systems might vary, so could you put us in the picture as to how far you covered each basic subject? Take your time, there is no hurry.'

'Well, sir, I passed my professional examinations in physics, chemistry and biology after my first year and physiology and anatomy after my second year. We had started our clinical subjects in the third year when the revolution came,' Adam stated simply and concisely, worrying about his past tenses as he spoke.

'Well now, there is the difference we spoke about,' interjected Professor Gregory, smoothing the few hairs left on his balding head. 'You see, the professional examinations you mention you had passed at the end of your second year, which we refer to as "Second MB", do not take place here until the end of the first term of the third year. Hmm, so you are technically ahead of our starting third-year students. Interesting.'

Adam just about managed to follow all that.

'Do you have any written proof of your passes? Please don't misunderstand me, but it would help,' Professor Morton said, looking at his colleagues for approval.

'I have my "Index" here.' Adam put his hand into the battered brown vinyl briefcase he had been carrying his dry sausages in during his escape. It still smelled of smoked pork. He pulled out the little black handbook full of the signatures of his examiners and handed it over to the dean.

'I've heard about these.' The Dean smiled. 'Let me have a look. Good photograph. Who signed your physiology?' He asked.

'Professor Lissák, sir.'

'I know Kálmán Lissáak well!' Professor Gregory volunteered. 'A good man and a great oarsman at Oxford.'

'And your anatomy?'

'That was Professor Szentágothai.'

'John Szentágothai has my admiration,' the surprised Professor Harrison said. 'One of the greatest neuroanatomists alive. By the way, what nomenclature does he teach, the Jena one still?'

'No, sir, after the war we switched to the Basle one.'

'Pure Latin, eh? Now that's interesting!' He looked at Adam. 'We use our bastardised English Latin here. Shame, but there you are. Would you demonstrate for us a little?' He asked Adam, his eyes open with excitement.

'I would be pleased to have the interview in Latin,' Adam offered.

The four of them looked at each other. This was a chance to test their rusty Latin, they thought. So in turn Latin questions appeared from them, especially from Professor Harrison, who then disappeared for a moment, returning from his department next door with the weighty and much feared *Gray's Anatomy* textbook.

'What would you call this muscle in your nomenclature?'

'Would that be the *musculus flexor carpi radialis*, sir?'

'Certainly would. How about this one?'

'That is the *musculus flexor longus digitorum*, a deep muscle of the leg, I think.' Adam was growing more confident.

The others on the panel, not to be outdone, each asked a question relevant to their subjects and nodded their heads when Adam answered them decently enough. Then the dean took over.

'Mr Zenta, we would like to deliberate a little, so if you would be kind enough to wait outside for a few minutes I am sure we will come to a conclusion.' Then he turned to the uniformed man at the door, who had been quietly observing the procedure. 'Joe, please take Mr Zenta downstairs and give him a cup of tea.'

Adam was not quite sure what 'deliberate' meant, but he was happy to hear the word 'conclusion'. As they walked downstairs to the equally ancient students' cafeteria, Joe patted him on the back.

'You did well there, Mr Zenta, very well, you deserve yer cuppa.' He handed the pale brown liquid to Adam in a mug.

'Thank you, sir,' Adam responded.

'You call me Joe here, Mr Zenta. Just Joe.' He smiled.

Adam suddenly remembered Pécs and the dreadful Stumpy, and decided that he was suddenly where he was always meant to be; a million miles away from his previous life and all that it involved.

He had hardly finished the weak brew when Joe asked him to go back to the lecture theatre. When he entered the room there was only the dean sitting at the middle of the table. He was smiling even more widely.

'I am happy to say that we are in a position to offer you a place at this faculty, subject to certain conditions, which are detailed in this note. I am sure you will want to read it, and as you will have to produce it to others I did not bother to seal the envelope. Let us hope we will see you in the autumn. It was very nice to meet you.'

They shook hands and Adam turned towards Joe, who was reaching out to usher him out of the room. 'Well done, sir, see you in October.' He was more precise.

They also shook hands and Adam was left alone in the quadrangle to read the brief note. The notepaper proudly bore the crest with the peculiar-looking birds. Across its top in block capitals it stated: 'TO WHOM IT MAY CONCERN', then it went on to inform all that Mr Adam Zenta was to be permitted to enrol in the third year of his medical studies provided that he was able to fund all his fees and living expenses. It was signed once again by 'J M Leggate, Dean of the Faculty of Medicine'. My God, the battle has just begun, he thought. He looked at his watch and realised that there was enough time for some more sightseeing.

With plenty of food for thought he looked up and saw the top of a very large red tower. Ah, that must be their famous and still-unfinished cathedral. That's the one, he thought. He headed straight towards it. At the corner of Mount Pleasant and Hope Street he admired the curving colonnade of the Liverpool Medical Institution, Est: 1779. Goodness, that is old, it must be around the same time as Mozart's *Idomeneo*, he thought. Halfway along he saw the impressive art nouveau of the Philharmonic Hall, which was advertising the coming season under the directorship of a good-looking chap called John Pritchard. The magnificent setting and the cathedral itself suddenly loomed before him at the end of the street. The unfinished end came into view first, but as he walked along Gambier Terrace he realised that there was something unusual happening, which was not quite in keeping with the time he lived in. The red sandstone English Gothic, albeit simplified during the building process, was overpowering, perhaps even threatening. He walked in for a cursory look and was much taken by the delicate Lady Chapel. He did not bargain for the sight that confronted him when he walked out into the mid-afternoon sunshine. After his eyes had adjusted he saw a different Liverpool. The area just in front of the awesome palace of God was the worst dereliction he had ever imagined. Decaying Georgian terraces presented such filth that it was difficult to comprehend it. How could the city fathers tolerate such slums forty yards from the main entrance of a world-famous object of admiration? He wondered, as he looked at the dirty people looking after the even dirtier children playing in rags in the utterly unkempt Nile Street. All this in the geographic centre of a university city was too much for him, and he decided to walk away from it. To his utter amazement, within two minutes he was back in the civilisation of A. J. Cronin. Rodney Street, with its perfectly kept late Georgian buildings, was a different world only a hundred yards away. Some of the brass plates were polished to indecipherable oblivion, such as that at number 43, where Thurstan-Holland proudly announced the names of the physicians and surgeons consulting within. He stopped counting them when he passed two hundred and thought one more would not hurt.

He arrived at yet another architectural gem, the Scottish Presbyterian St Andrew's church, set in a graveyard that even contained a twelve-foot pyramid, Lyceum black, naturally. The architect, whose name was already acknowledged with his own plaque, must have been truly proud of the classical building. Adam looked at his watch again and decided that he had been wandering around long enough and it was time to get back to Central Station. He turned left at Mount Pleasant and started his walk downhill, feeling proud and fulfilled, and extremely content.

~

When Dr Danaher read the Liverpool note he became most excited and told Adam that it was time to get to work on finding financial backing for the next three years. He explained that there were no, or exceptionally few, rich old widows in Barnsley with that sort of money, so they might as well make an appointment to see the Education Officer at the town hall. The next day they walked out of the great white stone municipal building with an offer to fund half of Adam's fees, payable directly to the University of Liverpool. Midweek, the benevolent doctor pulled up in his black Rover saloon at Adam's digs and told the surprised young man coming down to meet him that after his Friday pay packet he would cease to be a coal miner and the following Monday he would start as a ward orderly at the Wath Wood Chest Hospital in Wath-on-Dearne, near Doncaster. He went on to explain that the word 'hospital' in this instance was something of a euphemism as it was more or less a terminal care unit, full of pneumoconiosis and tuberculosis sufferers, products of the surrounding pits, and as he was its medical director he could take a lenient attitude when Adam needed time off to chase the rest of his funding. Such was the goodwill of the day.

The hospital was a most agreeable place, situated in a leafy area just outside the small town. He had his own room and, although only an orderly, he was allowed to eat with the nurses next to the doctors' own dining room, because of his status as a medical student, but even the former often invited him in for a chat.

The patients were, in the main, men who were reduced by their ever-advancing respiratory disability to coughing skeletons, waiting peacefully for their inevitable cachexic end.

The medical staff of the hospital all wanted to contribute to Adam's future. Dr Wright had an aunt in Crosby, north Liverpool, who was willing to provide him with digs on a bed and breakfast cum high tea basis. Dr Martin offered his sister's house in Richmond for overnight stops when in London. Though Adam had no particular reason to visit the capital just yet, he was to take up the offer within a week. A lady member of the hospital board who was aware of Adam's predicament spotted something in the *Times Educational Supplement* to the effect that the American cultural attaché was organising financial support for refugee students and told Adam to be down there for Monday morning, before it was all snatched up.

~

Sir Paul and Lady Battersby-Smyth lived in grand style in a huge early Victorian mansion in Richmond. Melanie, their pride and joy, was just seventeen. She was their only child. Melanie developed an instant crush on the 'Hero from Hungary', as Adam was modestly introduced by her uncle on the telephone from Doncaster. During dinner they talked about Adam's very early morning appointment at the American Embassy. Melanie offered to be Adam's guide, which he certainly appreciated as he had never used the Underground before.

Early the next morning they were off. Living up to its reputation, 1957 continued to provide superb sunshine, which dominated everyone's conversation, even on the Underground, where there was not much of it to be seen. The English like to talk about the weather, Adam thought. Even Melanie went on about it as they resurfaced at Green Park station. A short walk took them to the American Embassy, and as they passed Roosevelt's statue Adam looked at it and put his hands together in mock prayer.

In the commotion inside it took some time for them to locate the third secretary he was supposed to see, and when they were ushered into his office Adam faced a young man with very short-cropped blond hair and thick glasses. He looked totally out of place; he had probably tried for the Marines and failed because of his sight and got shoved into diplomatic service as the next best way to serve Uncle Sam, Adam speculated.

On the invitation of the official Adam gave a short résumé of his problem and the young man listened intently.

'Well, if it is only a question of money, I will probably be able to channel you in the right direction,' he said, looking through his glasses, which magnified his eyes to twice their size. He picked up his telephone and dialled a number. After the usual pleasantries he told the person at the other end of the wire that he had an Hungarian freedom fighter with him whom he would like to send along. He took a piece of scrap paper and scribbled an address on it.

'Well, Mr Zenta, I want you to go along to the World University Service, at 59 Gloucester Place. It is a granting outlet for the Ford and Rockefeller foundations and it's not too far away – you could stroll along. You have such lovely company and it is such a beautiful day.' He looked at Melanie. 'I wish you the best of luck.'

They shook hands and in minutes the two were back in the brilliant sunshine. Adam, wanting to see as much of London as possible, had to talk Melanie out of 'the Tube'. London fascinated him instantly. With its mixture of tasteful Georgian terraces and ebullient Victorian porticoes, notwithstanding the dreadful modern structures filling in the gaps created courtesy of the Luftwaffe, it looked a sight in some places, but he felt there was a grand soul behind it all. Melanie took a liberty with their route and ushered Adam to all the places she wanted to see, so they ended up walking along New Bond Street, where Adam had his first culture shock as he became mesmerised by the wealth displayed in the jewellery shop windows and the creations of the many dress designers.

Adam was a little worried about the detours but Melanie would just take his hand once in a while and drag him along to cross over the street to see yet another wonderful shop window. In spite of this she rang the doorbell at their destination five minutes before the allocated time. Gloucester Place was undamaged by the war and presented confident Victoriana in its terraced houses. Once the homes of the wealthy, some of the houses were serving as offices, as in the case of number 59.

Adam was interviewed by a middle-aged spinster, very much in the mould of his Blackpool teacher, Miss James. Once again he explained his position and the lady smiled.

'It is so nice to see someone with a ready package. Most refugee students walk in here and say, "Can I be a dentist or can I be an engineer?" Now let us see.' She looked down into a large manila folder. 'I see, so Barnsley Education Authority is committed, therefore you need the rest of your fees and your living expenses. The former directly to the University of Liverpool annually in advance and the latter, say, by monthly cheque in arrears to you.' She looked at a set of tabled figures, then at Adam. 'Your personal monthly figure would work out at twenty-nine pounds, three and sixpence – would that suit?' She smiled faintly. Adam was a little confused with all the 'advances' and 'arrears' but he understood enough to know that he was going to get the money. He certainly wasn't going to ask her to continue the interview in Latin, so he just nodded and quietly thanked her.

The lady gave Adam a two-page form to fill out in the waiting room. They got on with completing it, Melanie prompting Adam here and there, hurrying him, presumably in order to get back to the shop windows more speedily. As instructed, they left the form with the secretary, who reminded Adam to let her have his Liverpool address as soon as possible for the first cheque, due for October.

Outside, Melanie took charge again, and she hailed a taxi to the West End. They got out at the bottom of Regent Street and decided to have lunch.

'To the Guinea-a-Piggy!' She said. Adam just followed.

At the first fast-food outlet in London at Leicester Square, Melanie paid the £2 2s flat tariff and they walked downstairs. Paradise on earth, Adam thought, as they filled their plates with as much roast chicken as they wanted. Having gone back twice more, they were so full that they could hardly walk upstairs. Adam did his mental arithmetic and told Melanie that with his new-found wealth from November he would be able to eat like this six times a week, provided he didn't have to pay for anything else.

'You're crazy,' she said. 'Do you want to see Soho?'

'Oh yes, Melanie, I have read so much about it in cheap and even not so cheap novels. Is it very far?'

Three minutes later they were standing outside the Windmill Theatre, which proudly declared that 'they never closed'. Adam ogled the publicity photos of some of the most beautiful naked girls he had ever seen. He looked for Jean amongst them. Ah, these are much taller, he thought, and, turning back to look at Melanie, he saw her heading towards the bowels of Soho. One of the first things he noticed was the presence of the two famous Hungarian salamis, Pick and Hertz, hanging in delicatessen shop windows. Had he not been so full he might even had bought some, but Melanie dragged him off. In early afternoon Soho was hardly in full swing but it still promised just about every type of sexual and culinary activity. A strange basic combination, but a realistic and honest one, he thought.

'And they say the English are not interested in languages!' He turned to his energetic guide.

'What do you mean? Of course we're not.' Melanie looked at him.

'So far I've seen French, Swedish, Italian and even Filipino lessons advertised near the small doorbells and they all have arrows pointing upstairs.' He smiled.

'Be your age, Adam,' Melanie reprimanded him, with a twinkle in her eyes. 'Hey, wait a minute! There is a Hungarian one for you.' She pointed at a small notice in Greek Street advertising 'Mariska's advanced Hungarian lessons'. 'Are you happy now?'

'Here, look at this! *Budapest-Hungarian* cuisine.' Adam was a little surprised to see the large sign.

'There is a more famous one across the road,' Melanie said, pointing to the green-painted woodwork of the *The Gay Hussar*. 'They say it is excellent.' Adam insisted on inspecting the menu and declared it 'absolutely genuine'.

'I wish we hadn't eaten all that chicken, I would have brought you here.'

'You will have your chance,' she teased, 'but I would prefer the *Hungaria* in Haymarket. It is rather posh and has Gypsy music – Princess Margaret goes there a lot, it is said.'

'Dear?'

'Very, but in England we would call it expensive!'

'Is this Melanie's English lesson?' Adam asked.

'Yes, but not quite like Mariska's Hungarian ones, so forget it.' Melanie turned on her heels and convinced Adam that it was time for Trafalgar Square, Buckingham Palace and home.

On their way back to Richmond on the Underground, which must be referred to as the 'Tube', she said, Adam asked Melanie about her father's title. She carefully explained that there were two kinds of 'Sirs', those who got the title for doing something extremely grand for the nation, on the recommendation of the prime minister, and then the baronets, and her father was one of those. His ancestors received it way back for something extremely dubious, which was never discussed.

'So you're aristocrats, then?' Adam asked.

'Well, on the lowest possible level, sort of …' Melanie shrugged her shoulders.

'So are we, you know! I have a de Lemhény after my name to signify something in 1604. Anyway, how am I to address your father, then?'

'Oh, you must call him Sir Paul, he is very particular about that.'

'And your mother?'

'She is Lady Felicity in her own right, daughter of Lord Beckenridge. He was very rich, let me tell you, but he died recently and Mother inherited his estate in North Wales.'

'And you?' He asked, raising his eyebrows.

'Melanie darling will do. Considering you are the hero of the moment, I'll let you …' She laughed.

⁓

During the dinner Sir Paul congratulated Adam on getting on so well during the day, echoed by Lady Felicity, who added that now Adam was definitely a medical student at Liverpool University he would be most welcome at Sudley Hall in Flintshire, whenever they were in residence. Melanie glanced at the ceiling in mock despair at hearing her mother's pretentious and totally ambiguous invitation, and she decided to add that next time they were due to go up was during the half-term break from her Shugborough College. Adam thought a week getting to know a little of Wales would be just wonderful. He thanked Lady Felicity for the invitation and said that he would be 'much honoured' to join them.

Lady Felicity started to giggle.

The meal was brought in by their young maid. Adam hardly understood a word she uttered in response to Lady Felicity's commands except the occasional 'yes, ma'am'.

The starting dish was smoked trout, which was a new thing for Adam, although he remembered that in his childhood Nicholas used to grill them in the open air. The stuffed roast pork was delicious and, once again, he wondered why English cooking got such awful an press on the Continent. After dinner Sir Paul decided to withdraw to his study, the lady of the house busied herself somewhere else and Melanie suggested a stroll in the garden. Adam needed no persuading.

The well-kept sloping garden had a small pond at the far end which was visited by some ducks. They sat on a wooden bench and held hands. Melanie was dressed fashionably in a very flared light brown summer dress with a tight bodice, topped by white lace. Her brown hair was perhaps just a shade too short for Adam's liking but it certainly complemented her assured personality in a tomboyish way. He put his arm around her slender waist and she put her head against his shoulder.

'You can kiss me if you want to, but I know Mother is watching, so be careful,' she whispered.

'Melanie, you are just like a spring flower, so small and delicate,' Adam said rather clumsily.

'Small! I'm just over five foot two, but they say good things come in small parcels – and I have great legs too. Do you want to see them?'

'Oh, yes please!' He said a little awkwardly

Melanie straightened her legs and, kicking off her shoes, pointed her toes and pulled up her multitude of skirt to mid-thigh. 'What do you think?'

He gulped. 'As you say, great legs.' He spread his arms in mock surrender.

'Adam, do you want to be my boyfriend? I don't have one right now.' She was totally matter of fact.

'Yes, I would like that, but I have to go back to Yorkshire tomorrow.'

'No matter, I can wait until I see you again – in Flintshire. It will be something to look forward to.' She tossed back her hair. 'I'm not a virgin, you know! I've had a boyfriend and we made love, on six occasions.' Adam could hardly believe his ears. 'They don't know,' she said, pointing towards the house. She looked up at him with her large brown eyes. 'Hold me, Adam.' She moved closer.

They kissed and fumbled but Adam could hardly take his eyes off the large house looming behind Melanie's dainty shoulders. His apprehension worsened as the lights began to go on and off in the house and he suggested that it was time to end their 'stroll'.

On their return Melanie advised her family of Adam's new status of 'boyfriend', which made him blush. Her mother gave a little sigh and her father grunted something incomprehensible.

The next morning Melanie, dressed to perfection for riding, accompanied Adam to Victoria coach station. She gave him far too passionate a kiss for her age and status and waved him goodbye. Adam waved back, smiled – more to himself than to her -– and settled down for the long journey to Liverpool.

22

LIVERPOOL

Adam settled into his digs in Crosby on the first Wednesday of October 1957 and went to see *The Great Caruso*, showing at the local Regent cinema, just around the corner from Belvedere Road, his new and rather elegant-sounding address. He found the Hollywoodisation of the life of his idol trivial, but he certainly liked the voice of Mario Lanza. The perfect timbre and the extra little individual twist to his tone made the voice fresh and exciting. He suddenly realised that not a note of singing had passed his lips since the concert in Blackpool. He would have to do something about it – and pretty soon, he thought.

The weekend gave him enough time to look around Waterloo and Blundellsands, the more genteel end of the sprawling city and port of Liverpool. He liked what he saw, and could not understand the occasional misgivings of others when he had mentioned the name of his new city. In any event he was too busy finding out what he had to do in his Freshers' Week, not that he was looking forward to yet another initiation. Knowing that this experience was going to be very different from those in Pécs three years before, he realised that he would be an outsider for a while, and that the length of the while depended largely on himself. The idea went against the grain for him, and on the green double-decker bus to Lime Street, deep in thought, he realised that he had but one way out, which was to integrate. The quicker the better.

In the Students' Union, where fresh-faced youngsters were finding out all about the extracurricular activities, he was asked to join the Communist Students' Society. He looked at the bespectacled bearded student who had approached him and said: 'You are an idiot, but I will come and talk to you one day,' mustering his best possible English. After two days he had had enough of being a fresher – after all, he was a third-year student and not a newcomer to university life – so he walked out of the Union building and went to see the dean.

Jack Leggate, as everyone referred to the retired surgeon, who had spent many years working in China, smiled at Adam as he walked through his door.

'How nice to see you, Zenta, how are you settling in?' The great mentor of many hundreds of Liverpool medical students asked, looking over his heavily rimmed spectacles.

'Very well, sir, I just came to say hello and register.' Adam felt totally relaxed.

'Very good, Zenta, I am glad you came early, I managed to get you a set of second-hand textbooks. You will find them with the main porter.'

'I never expected that, sir, I will collect them on them way out. Thank you, sir.' His words were slow and measured, as he tried not to make any grammatical blunder.

He signed a few forms presented by the middle-aged secretary and she enquired whether he needed any help.

He declined, but asked the secretary where he could find his yearmates of the following week. She told him that some came early and a few hung around the cafeteria below the Surgical Lecture Theatre, but if he had no luck there 'Mrs Macks' was a safe enough bet. Finding Adam looking bemused, she explained that it was an established café for medics to frequent when there wasn't anything better to do.

Adam found the revered dump of a café near the corner of Brownlow Hill and Crown Street. The black-glossed walls of the smoky groundfloor 'caff' were decorated with oversized playing cards, as if Mrs Mack's punters needed any invitation to play three-card stud. Mrs Mack took her position very seriously and considered her place as much a part of the university as any other 'faculty'. She kept strict discipline and if anyone stepped out of line by doing something like taking a drag of pot she would bar the unfortunate fool for a full term. People very seldom did.

Adam walked in and asked for a large black coffee, receiving a cupful of what might be best described as dark brown, lukewarm coffee-flavoured soup, and a weak one at that. Not at all the stuff he was used to in Pécs, where the thickness of the saturated black velvet liquid could nearly hold the coffee spoon upright. But this was the shape of things to come and he was sure there would be compensations, plenty of them. He settled into a corner, contemplating what to do with the thing in the cup, when a bunch of noisy students walked in. His luck was complete when he overheard one saying that the coming third year was a 'bugger of a hard one'. He picked up his cup and walked over to them. Dave, Geoff, Clive, Jim and a slightly older one, Bill, obviously knew each other well.

'Adam Zenta, new to third year.' He smiled.

'Where do you come from?' Asked Dave indifferently.

'Hungary.'

'Great stuff!' Bill was a little more positive.

'You have an awful accent, man.' Clive did not look up.

'It will go down well with the women.' Geoff smiled.

'Sit down, for Christ's sake!' Jim added, in an accent new to Adam. It turned out to be Irish. 'Everton, home to Spurs on Saturday, lads, anyone interested?' He added, looking at his friends in turn.

There was no response from the others.

'I would like much to see Everton.' Adam looked at him.

'Discerning chap, you will see the best in the world.'

'As good as Hidegkuti or Puskás?' Adam asked.

'If not as good as the Magyar Marvels, they will soon be, mark my words. Vernon and Young will amaze even you,' Jim said with the certainty of a real fan. 'Anyway, I always considered Kocsis to be the best of the execution squad you lot sent to Wembley in 1953.

'I think so too.' Adam started to drink his coffee, by now totally cold, but he did not care, he had made contact and he seemed to fit in.

Jim explained how to find Goodison Park and the chip shop right opposite the entrance to the Paddock. They would meet there at ten to three.

Bill, the smaller student, was watching the two finalising their arrangements. He turned to Adam.

'Listen to me for a moment. In the med school here we have our quarterly magazine called *Sphincter* and I have just taken over as editor. It's due out in a couple of weeks' time. Would you write me an article of about two thousand words for the first anniversary of your uprising? Don't worry about your back-to-front English, I'll slap it about for you.'

Adam could hardly believe his ears. 'That would be real good. I will start this evening, when I get back to Great Crosby. It will be completed by Monday.' So his short career as a newspaperman was not finished after all, he thought. He was itching to get home to start to write and quickly slurped the last drop of the brown liquid in his cup.

He considered a football match and writing a newspaper article during his first meeting with his impending year-mates quite a coup and got on the red 'Ribble' bus with a smile on his face. On the way back to his room he worked out what he was going to say. 'Just one year past …'was to be the title. He soon realised the onerous task he had agreed to. If I only had a dictionary, he kept thinking. It's no use, I will have to ask the ever-helpful landlady, Mrs Blair. She was never short of a word, he thought. With exercise book in hand he asked his landlady to let him use the dining-room table and set to work. The exuberant words, in very basic English, poured out without too much difficulty;

> *Just one year past since, in the middle of Europe, the freedom fight of ten million people was quelled by Marshal Zhukov's tanks. Just one year past since almost two hundred thousand Hungarian freedom- fighters became homeless. Just one year past since a state with her fifteen hundred years' long history was suppressed again by unscrupulous Bolshevik hordes.*

There would be no punches pulled, it would be straight from the heart, he decided, and what followed gave a brief potted history and a good description of the preliminaries of the revolution, the ensuing main events, both in Budapest and in Pécs, and his part in it, as well as accounts of his fellow refugees now in the West. Twenty-four hours later he optimistically ended it with:

> *History repeats itself, and this itself gives hope in a hopeless situation. Dictatorships always fall after the death of the Dictator. Later or sooner, the way of the empires of Julius Caesar, Napoleon, Tsar Michael (sic) and Hitler will be followed by Stalin's empire too.*

Poor English, Bill thought, but he wouldn't correct a word.

Adam turned up at the Goodison Road chippy on time to meet Jim for the game and told him straight away that the article was ready for Bill.

'You mean all two thousand words of it?' He asked incredulously.

'I think, two thousand five hundred,' Adam answered.

'Clever dick,' Jim said, and smiled.

'Pardon?'

'Never mind, I'll explain. Get in there.' Jim pointed towards the small gate, through which thousands wanted to pass in the next few minutes. It seemed an impossibility.

Inside, Adam was introduced to a spectacle he would never forget, an aspect of his new city which would make a lifelong impression on him, although the future would take him to the other local club, which was at this stage still lingering in the second division: Liverpool FC.

The game itself was totally different from what he was used to in Hungary. Fast, uncompromising football, blending stamina and determination and producing sheer entertainment. He found a new phenomenon in the interaction between the crowd and the players, as if there was some ESP emanating from the terraces, willing the Royal Blues on. Yes, Vernon and Young were good, very good – but different, very different, he thought. 'It's a different game,' he kept saying. He looked forward to getting used to it.

Bill was delighted with the article. He wisely decided not to over-correct it and left the poor punctuation alone, intentionally. He also left the phrase 'later or sooner' in the last paragraph, which annoyed Adam. He never knew why he had written it like that, since it was 'sooner or later' even in Hungarian. He had to put up with it for a long while, as his new friends kept quoting it to him. When enquiring about something he would be told that 'later or sooner' he would understand it.

The article turned out to be an excellent introduction for him, as everyone had read it and he did not have to spend too much time introducing himself to students and the staff, or in explaining how on earth he had got to Liverpool. Bill, in turn, also made him join the MSS, the Medical Students' Society, an august body of medics, also known as 'Jack Leggate's boys' after the much-respected, even beloved dean. He was in quickly and as far as he was concerned that was what mattered most.

The first week brought another surprise for Adam. He was told by one of the junior lecturers that there was 'another Hungarian' in the second year, who, having read the article in *Sphincter*, wanted to meet him. Thus he met Gabor Racz, another Racz, he thought, minus the accents, and his bunch of extremely likable friends.

Gabor had been very prominent in the uprising in Budapest and fought in it with gun in hand. A stocky, strong chap, slightly shorter than Adam, his shoulders reflected his prowess at water polo, which he had played for the University of Budapest. Good looking, with flaxen hair parted at the side, he blended into the British scene more easily than Adam, who had high cheekbones and curly auburn hair combed straight back in Continental fashion. Gabor had another distinction – he had an established girlfriend. When he had no choice but to escape to the West, he went to say goodbye to his childhood sweetheart, Enid, a budding ballerina. She decided that if he was going to leave, she would pack her bag too, and go with him. Their arduous escape bonded the two in early commitment to each other, and it was easy to see why. Enid was a stunning beauty. With a perfect figure that was perhaps a shade too tall and femininely proportioned for her ever to have made it as a ballerina, she had a face that was olive shaped with full lips and almond-shaped eyes – Hungarian to perfection. They were a most impressive young couple.

When Gabor recognised Adam among the third-year bunch in the cafeteria, he walked up to him.

'Gabor Racz, from second year, hi! You're Adam Zenta, aren't you?' He asked with a broad smile.

'Hello, Gabor, yes, I am Adam, how are you?'

'Adam is a rather an infrequent name back home, I don't like it,' Gabor said.

'I'm not too keen on it either, but it's the only one my parents gave me, so I'm a little stuck with it.' He paused. 'But you know, "Gabor Racz" sounds like a bloody car crash to me. Why don't you anglicise it to, say, Ramsbottom – it would suit. Apparently the custom is to keep the first letter, for the sake of the initials on your shirts, if you have any.' They shook hands warmly, still sizing each other up.

Gabor turned around. 'Hey, Dave, come here, let me introduce you to a fellow Hun. His name is "A-dam Z-enta",' he emphasised the initials, 'the Alpha and the Omega from Transylvania, a direct descendant of the Count himself, who – by the way – can be seen this week in the Gaumont for two and eightpence.' He turned to Adam and continued his monologue: 'As you can see and will soon hear, David Ahmed is from Pakistan. His father is Minister of Veterinary Services there, so he is made of money. His full name is Daud Shafiq Ahmed, Dave to you.' He gave a curt bow, indicating that his performance was over.

'Shut up you, Magyar peasant.' Dave shoved him aside. 'I hope you have more sense than your fellow countryman, he's been a pain ever since he arrived.' The lanky, dark Gregory Peck look-alike shook hands with Adam. 'Mind you, he had already made an impression.'

'He could have made a better one: on the pavement, by jumping off the top of the Victoria Building tower.' Adam smiled at them.

'Can we cut out this thrust-and-parry-type repartee, chaps? I am John Busby, just arrived, an intelligent lad from Warwick who's here for a course in cranial expansion.'

'Enough to fill your bearskin hat, Busby?' Gabor ventured.

'Listen, matey, it would take a couple of dozen brains of your size to come anywhere near the brim.' He grabbed him mockingly by his crumpled tie. Mercifully the ever-popular porter who had given Adam his cup of tea before his interview and knew most of the pre-clinical students by name interrupted the light-hearted students' fun by ringing the bell and yelling, 'Back to the lecture theatres, please, gentlemen,' and pointing towards them. 'That includes the "Foreign Legion" over there. C'mon now, Mr Busby. Could you move on please, Mr Thompson!'

Quick arrangements were made to have a pint at six in the Royal, the students' pub just opposite the world-renowned red-brick Liverpool Royal Infirmary, and Adam could not stop himself thinking how different their conversation would have been in Hungary. The easy-going attitude so quickly adopted by Gabor here would have taken months to develop over there, and only after careful evaluation of every aspect of the newcomer, simply to ascertain that he was not a secret police plant. He decided that student life was going to be fun.

He went back to the lecture theatre where he had had his interview in June and struggled with the thought that a year before he had been sitting in a similar place next to László at a communist show trial. Then he partook in world-shaping events and after a spot of bother, including escaping in a hail of bullets and the slight hiccup of a little coal mining, he was carrying on with his studies of human anatomy – alas, in English. It sure had been an eventful year. Professor Ronald Harrison, head of the Department of Anatomy, like his counterpart, Szentágothai, in Pécs, was a brilliant lecturer, who could hold his unruly audience spellbound. He certainly stopped Adam's mind wandering, with the logic of his argument and the eloquence of his delivery. How he wanted to speak English like that. The forty minutes on the 'Nerve supply to the upper limb' seemed more like ten, and then it was time for Adam to present himself to his 'personal tutor' (something he could hardly translate into Hungarian), Dr Macmillan, for a practical session amongst the mutilated corpses in the basement. Now, this was no different. The pungent smell, a mixture of carbolic, ether, formaldehyde and decomposing flesh, with naked bodies of all shapes and sizes lying on marble slabs surrounded by eager yet anxious young faces, must be the same the world over.

This wonderfully eccentric elderly man – who had travelled the world extensively and kept reiterating that it was the Japanese POW camps which came bottom of his list of personal camping sites – got more and more enthusiastic the longer he talked about the physical intricacies of the dead human body. He would have been quite happy to spend the rest of his days in the DR, as the dissecting room was simply known to all medics. The evolutionary development of the human skeleton from that of the chimpanzee made a particular impression on him and he found it impossible to understand anyone not wanting to know the transition from knuckle-walking to being a fully fledged, upstanding *Homo erectus*. Most of his students were more interested in another connotation of the word.

The 'demonstrators', who were newly qualified doctors, spending a year or two 'demonstrating' anatomy to students before specialising in surgery, were targeted by the female section of the third year, and more so as the much-feared second MB examination came nearer.

There was one who blended flamboyant sex appeal with single-minded teaching of the subject to perfection. Dr David Bowsher, with his piercing eyes, large volume of dark brown curly hair surging skyward and his white coat flying wide open behind him as he charged across the room, scalpel in hand, was the epitome of a latter-day knight on a charger. The women loved it. Any other man in the room paled into total insignificance when he walked in.

They were all Characters with a capital 'C'. Certainly not the withdrawn or taciturn Englishmen Adam knew from the novels he had read.

The evening in the Royal showed Adam how cliques formed within the medical students' fraternity. Groups appeared around the tables and after a little shuffling from one to another they settle down, and that was it for the duration. Adam was dragged to Bill Thompson and Jimmy Burns's group, which was also his designated study group 'K' for the next four years, but he decided to spend some time with the second-year lot of Racz, Ahmed and Busby too. They seemed such fun.

The happy social life of a medical student combined with the most difficult academic course yet designed by man usually produces the 'work hard, play hard' effect, but in Adam's case the 'work hard' part had to be the dominant one. Still without a decent dictionary his reading rate was abysmal – two to three pages of the physiology textbook per hour. And that was reading only. Chewing, digesting and absorbing it was another matter. This way, he worked out, it would take him a full year to read one book of that size, and there were three of them on the table before him. He often had to drag poor old Mrs Blair from her sitting room to explain simple words like pregnancy. She would blush as she tucked a cushion from the settee under her skirt.

The small saving grace of his career was that basically he knew the subjects for the end-of-year exams, but still there was the matter of presenting them with confidence and, worse, writing in an acceptable way. So it was with great delight that he overheard Gabor saying that he had just received new dictionaries from a Catholic monk. Adam pounced on his friend's old ones, which were hardly more than a travelling set. Nevertheless they made all the difference. Even if a word was missing he found some connotation from the neighbouring ones enabling him to carry on reading. He did this religiously Monday to Friday afternoon. Friday evening he would team up with some girl for the cinema and Saturday he would meet the others for football or a drink. Saturday evening was regularly spent in the Students' Union, where he did well on the dance floor. The girls liked his looks and his broad shoulders and he was also a decent enough dancer; a good enough combination to keep the odd girl staying with him for a chat or a drink after the dance. His English improved in leaps and bounds.

Shughborough College

1 November 1957

My Darling Adam,

I am sorry I have not sent the dates of my half-term break to you before but this does not mean I haven't thought of you every day. I knew you were busy settling in, in Liverpool, and it must have been very hard for you, darling. By all accounts it's an awful place and I wish I could have been there to help and look after you in your first few days.

You'll remember mother's vague invitation to spend a week with us at Sudley Hall. Well, I have now fixed it and the date is 13 Nov. We will be there for a week and North Wales is beautiful, even in early winter. It will give us a great chance to get to know each other even better. I get embarrassed when it is my turn to brag about my boyfriend to the girls at the college because I know so little about you. They even say you're just a figment of my imagination, but I know you're not. You are my Hero, mine, all mine, and I'm dying to see you again. Please say yes, you can come, and anyway, I will not take no for an answer.

Yours for ever,

Melanie. XXXXX

Adam smiled as he read the short letter from Melanie, and although he had nearly forgotten the stroll in the Richmond Park garden he felt good because he was wanted so positively. Sudley Hall was less than an hour's drive from the bus station he arrived at from Crosby every morning. It couldn't be easier. He sat down to write his first personal English letter, badly.

5 Belvedere Road, Liverpool, 23

Darling Melanie,

I was very pleased to get your letter of inviting me to spend a week with your kind Parents and you. I will be so glad to come to Sudley Hall.

> *I have so much to tell you about this wonderful city and all my friends at the University. There is even another Hungarian, a great fellow. Student life is so much more fun here and there is always a lot to do. I have even been to some football games with an Irish friend and another one is about to take me to a rugby one at Waterloo. It sounds like somebody will be beaten there doesn't it? Studying is very hard but now that I have a dictionary it is not such a big problem.*
>
> *I think of you very often with love,*
>
> *Adam*
>
>
> *PS. I am going to hear the Royal Liverpool Philharmonic Orchestra next Tuesday, an Hungarian pianist, Bela Siki is playing with them.*

~

It was all set. Adam was genuinely looking forward to see Melanie again, but when he bought his ticket to Flintshire he felt a little apprehensive.

The coach hurtled through the Mersey Tunnel and the dreadful industrial slums of Birkenhead. It was scarcely able to pass the crowd of striking shipyard workers holding shabbily made banners declaring 'Striking workers – 8th week' under the proud sign CAMMELL LAIRDS SHIPBUILDERS. Oh, how the Japanese or even the Polish shipbuilders must be laughing, Adam thought. As the coach drove farther south on the Old Chester Road the picture became more pleasing. Better-quality houses replaced the narrow brick terraces, and when the coach turned right to pick up the road to Queensferry, the scenery of the Wirral peninsula lived up to its reputation of having little to do with its giant neighbouring city and a lot more to do with rural England.

To Adam's amazement only the smallest possible road sign announced their arrival in the Principality of Wales, in English, with a small red dragon painted on it for good measure. Seeing the RAF station on the left, Adam thought, Where the hell were you last year when the MiG 19s were raining havoc over Hungary? It was reassuring to know that the great air force was still in good shape. After a couple of bridges the coach turned northwards again on the left bank of the River Dee, and the picture changed to undulating Welsh scenery, with still only a hint of the beauty that was to follow. With suitcase in hand, he alighted at the Northop bus stop and the silver Mark 3 Jaguar was by the stone cross as arranged. Gareth, the driver, was sitting in the gleaming car and Melanie was standing next to the open passenger door, waving frantically. Adam quickened his pace, and when he dropped his suitcase to greet Melanie he suddenly found her arms wrapped around his neck.

'Hello, my darling!' Melanie said excitedly, and kissed him on the mouth, keeping her lips closed. 'I have missed you so much!'

Adam was somewhat taken aback by the open display of Melanie's affection in front of the driver.

'Lovely to see you again, Melanie, what a welcome! Thank you.' It's another country, Adam, he said to himself – different customs, the women are much more open. He returned her kiss, his way, and she responded, a little. The car was soon off, turning left off the main road on to a narrow lane towards Mount Halkyn. Then another left turn and they were on a long straight drive with oak trees on each side, sadly bereft of leaves but still looking majestic. In the distance, but coming ever closer, was a two-storey sandstone Jacobean mansion. Sudley Hall was most elegant if slightly overpowering. The driver, dressed in a dark suit, white shirt and black tie, could just as easily have been driving a hearse. He got out and opened the large wrought-iron gates with some difficulty.

'You see, we don't use the gates too often. Normally we just park to the left of the wall and walk through the side entrance, but for you …' Melanie squeezed Adam's hand in the back seat.

Adam was too amazed to say anything. Gareth got back behind the wheel and drove another twenty-five yards to the main door. By the time Adam had retrieved his case from the boot, Sir Paul and Lady Felicity had appeared through the large light oak doors and greeted Adam very cordially.

Adam returned Sir Paul's handshake and kissed Lady Felicity's hand – much to her surprise – saying, 'Forgive me, I know this is not much of a custom in England.'

'Please don't ever stop it. Our men don't often do it but we like it, it's a very nice custom.'

'It's just that my father told me "you kiss ladies' hands and that's all there is to it" – so I do it automatically.' Adam was acting a little too shy for his age.

Gareth picked up Adam's case, but he reached out and took it from him.

'Now my father would be annoyed if I didn't carry my own suitcase.'

'Follow me, Mr Adam.' Gareth's heavily accented request sounded more like a command.

Adam was shown to his bedroom on the left side of the top landing, facing the front of the house. It was a fairly spartan room, obviously designed for an undemanding man. What it lacked in embellishments was compensated by the glorious view along the drive towards Halkyn way off behind the trees, with a light shroud of mist around it.

He freshened up and came back to the lounge, where Melanie was sitting on a sofa, watching television. She invited Adam to sit next to her and watch the early afternoon show *Double Your Money*, ably hosted by the very popular Hughie Green. A contestant was doing well, answering questions on opera, and had just been asked to account for what was going to be unusual about the aria he was about to hear. An obviously pre-electric recording of Colline's 'Greatcoat' aria from Act 4 of *La Bohème* was then played. The throaty voice started gently with *'Vecchia zimarra, senti'*, and the man immediately announced that it was: 'Listen, my venerable coat'. Mr Green agreed with him, but he wanted to know what was unusual about it. It gave Adam a chance to show off.

'The fact that it is a bass aria, but sung by the great tenor Caruso – he recorded it for fun and all royalties were given to charities.'

Melanie looked at him, then at the poor man sweating on the TV.

The gong went and Mr Green placed an understanding hand on the contestant's shoulder. 'Sorry, my friend, very sorry – aren't we, folks?' He spread his arms wide. 'My friend, you have just lost four thousand pounds. The answer is that it was a bass aria sung by a tenor. A round of applause, ladies and gentlemen, for a great contestant. Please!!!' The applause duly came and Melanie jumped up.

'Terrific. Mother, Poppa, listen to this ...' She ran out of the room to tell them whilst Adam held his head. He was embarrassed by Melanie's admiration, and at the same time it occurred to him again that he had not sung one note since Blackpool, just before Easter. He had to do something about that.

Melanie was still talking about her 'clever boyfriend' after the appetiser was served at dinner in the well-appointed first-floor dining room. Lady Felicity was hanging on to every word her adored daughter said. Sir Paul was more interested in what Adam thought of Liverpool, so the conversation was a little disjointed. Eventually Melanie prevailed and once again declared that hers must be the cleverest boyfriend amongst those of all her school mates.

After dinner Sir Paul, just as in Richmond Park, 'retired' to his study, Lady Felicity busied herself somewhere in the grand house and Melanie said that normally she would show the guest around the house before retiring but as they were in something of a musical mood, they could go to her room and listen to Tommy Steele, Shirley Bassey and Frankie Vaughan, adding that 'Frankie is from Liverpool, you know!' Adam did not, but agreed with her about the idea of going to her room.

Her large record collection more than represented the current top twenty. It was well organised and she certainly knew what might appeal to Adam. The young Shirley Bassey did indeed; good voice, he thought, virtually operatic.

They settled on her sofa, gently cuddling and pecking. Adam was totally unsure of himself. He wanted to make love yet worried about the possible consequences. He was sure of one thing – Melanie would tell him what she wanted to do.

'Melanie, can I stay with you here for the night?' Adam asked impassively.

'Good God no! They would kill me.'

'Well, yes, but it would be nice to …' Adam started to unbutton her tight bodice.

'No, Adam, I can't let you. Perhaps tomorrow. Yes, how about tomorrow?'

'All right, tomorrow, then, I can wait – just. Play Shirley Bassey again, please?' For a moment he thought, Oh to be with Jean, in Barnsley.

Adam was fascinated by Melanie's positive attitude to everything. It undoubtedly came from the fact that she was the only and very precious child of an ageing couple who doted on her. She was intelligent with a quick brain and definite views on most subjects, whether she knew much about them or not. With her thick brown hair cropped even shorter than at their first meeting in London, she looked younger than her age.

'Good morning, Adam, hello. Poppa, hello, Mother.' She skipped around the large simple oak table to be next to Adam, who was by now on his feet.

'Good morning, Melanie,' Adam answered first.

'Hello, darling,' Sir Paul murmured from behind his *Financial Times*.

'You look sweet in that skirt, darling, but don't you think you should wear something a little warmer on top, it's cold out there.' Lady Felicity's eyes were shining with admiration as she went to the Aga for another portion of delicious-smelling bacon and egg.

'Don't fuss, Mother, I have my jumper and the duffel coat. That will be plenty.'

'Slept well, Adam?'

'Very well, thank you, it must be the clear air.'

They all seemed keen to devour the breakfast, during which Melanie managed to kit Adam out for the impending walk, with clothes from Sir Paul's shooting wardrobe. He looked most countrified by the time he put on the oilskin shooting jacket.

'Melanie, where are you going to drag this poor man?' Sir Paul put his paper down.

'I thought of walking up to Pant-y-mwyn or perhaps to Cilcain. What do you think?'

'I have a better idea. Why don't we get Gareth to drive you to Tafarngelyn and you could walk along the straight road through the edge of Clwyd Forest, and after lunch he could bring you back from Ruthin? Much prettier.'

'And it will tire us out totally.' Melanie smiled.

'Well, you will have time to recover in the Castle Restaurant whilst you have a bite. I'll ask Gareth to get the shooting brake.' He got up. Melanie nodded and a few minutes later they were sitting in the back of the dark green wood-framed Morris.

It was a grey morning, about ten degrees Fahrenheit, but in the moist air it felt colder. They were both suitably dressed and raring to go. Adam welcomed the chance to be alone with Melanie. He wanted to talk to her, especially about sex, so when they got out of the car for the trek along the secluded road he put his arm around her; she seemed even smaller out of the high heels she normally wore.

'I missed you last night, Melanie, I could not stop thinking about how nice it would be to make love to you.' He squeezed her shoulder tenderly.

'Oh, me too, Adam, don't you think I wanted it too?' She moved closer. 'Never mind, darling, maybe one day …'

'Don't say that. You know, your "tomorrow" is today … now!' Adam stopped and held her by both shoulders.

'Well, in that case, thank God we are overdressed and that it's freezing. Anyway, really, I'm not that sort of person.'

'That wasn't what you said in London, Melanie, you said that …'

'I know what I said,' Melanie interrupted. 'I didn't really mean it.'

'So you're a virgin, then?'

'No, I'm not – but that was on holiday in Ireland and it doesn't count.'

'Why shouldn't it count? Of course it does!' Adam loosened his hold on her shoulder.

'It doesn't, I just wanted to get rid of my virginity, that's all. It didn't mean anything.'

'It doesn't take six times to get rid of one virginity, you know!'

'To be honest, I don't really know what happened, it was so awful, and I don't know if I am a virgin or not.' Her voice started to tremble.

'I could be useful to you! I know my anatomy, you know!'

'Stop it, Adam, that's a horrible thing to say, now I'll never let you touch me, never.' Melanie started crying. 'And anyway, I hated it … afterwards …'

'What do you mean, afterwards?'

'Stop it, Adam, it's too difficult to talk about it … he used to hit me … afterwards … for letting him … do it,' she sobbed.

'Oh my God, Melanie, but that's awful. Why, if it had been me, I would have just put my arms around you and loved you for it, for ever!' Adam embraced her and kissed her tearful face again and again. She composed herself and stared into Adam's caring eyes. 'As you say, we could not do it here anyway. It is freezing.' He looked at Melanie and smiled as he wiped her tears away.

'Thank you for being so understanding, darling, thank you.' She squeezed his hand. 'Let's go.'

The rest of the walk was just that. A walk in the woods in near-winter. Melanie explained the scenery and Adam was impressed by the peak of the mountain Moel Famau, which could occasionally be glimpsed between the leafless branches of the trees.

By the time they arrived in Ruthin the two were quite exhausted. Melanie told Adam that there were three choices. 'The large pub in the square, the castle, where we could look at the beautiful but noisy peacocks, or the little pub on the Derwen Road.' Adam preferred the last, saying that he would like to look at her rather than at those overrated turkeys. They walked downhill and on the right-hand side of the road they found the Eagle, a most convivial old-fashioned pub. Neither of them was too hungry after the large breakfast so it was simply a round of sandwiches, prawn for her and ham for him, to be washed down with a glass of lager and a pint of bitter. Sitting in the corner by the open fire they warmed up and Adam took Melanie's hands.

'I am sorry, but I must ask you again, about that man who hit you. What happened?'

Melanie explained that the family was on a visit to Brae and they were staying in a hotel there. She was attracted to the Italian head waiter in the restaurant, who kept watching her. He was around thirty years old, very mature and handsome. She bumped into him the next morning in the corridor and noticed his piercing look as he passed her. He whispered to her to meet him in the garden at three o'clock. She was there and soon so was he and before too long they were in a secluded clearing where he stared at her longingly. They kissed. She decided not to stop him, whatever might follow.

'Adam, you have no idea how awful it was for me to still be a virgin. I just wanted to do away with it. I didn't care who it was. But after he had me, instead of caressing me he raised his hand and slapped me across the face. My face stung and as I turned away he hit me again on my other cheek, calling me a "little whore" and "filthy cow", and asked me if I had no shame. During meals he would stare at me with his piercing eyes and afterwards he would wait to see me in the corridor and whisper the time he wanted to see me the next day. He had such power over me ... It went on for a week, he beat me every time ... afterwards. It was awful.'

'But you're such a strong person.' Adam was surprised.

'Strong now because I vowed that nobody would ever dominate me like that again ... nobody.' The tears were flowing down her delicate face.

Adam placed his palm over her lips and said, 'Enough, little one, enough. We will never talk about it again – look at me darling, look me in the eye. We will never mention it again, never – right?'

Melanie quietly nodded several times, holding Adam's hand tighter and tighter as she did.

Adam kissed her.

～

After they had changed, Adam arrived in the lounge first and Melanie soon appeared looking wonderful in a figure-hugging royal blue chiffon cocktail dress whose style owed more to the twenties than the present day.

'I am sure a wolf whistle would be out of place in a house like this.' He thought he would break the ice.

'Adam, darling, it's Saturday night, and I thought that if I didn't put it on now you'd never see it and that would have been a shame, don't you think?' There was no need to worry, she was back to her old self.

'Certainly would have, but when will I get the promised grand tour?'

'Right now, sir, follow me. Papa said we could start in the wine cellar.' Adam was astonished to see the well-stocked and most professionally kept wine cellar. There was not one bottle that did not come from France, and most of them dated from just after the Great War, a point he was eager to make. Melanie explained that Great-Uncle Broderick had owned a small chateau east of Bordeaux and on his death Sir Paul, who was the only drinking relative left, inherited the lot. Sadly the chateau had to be sold but no matter, the money had helped to buy Sudley Hall.

The large kitchen and breakfast area was on the ground floor with a good view of the grounds, which included herb and kitchen gardens. Next to the Aga there was an enormous working surface and kitchen utensils hung from the ceiling, like bats in a Transylvanian cave. The rest of the ground floor contained the old servants' quarters, which had recently been converted into a self-contained flat for Gareth and Blodwen, who looked after the house when the family stayed in Richmond Park.

The 'fun rooms', as Sir Paul referred to them, contained his study cum library, a large drawing room, the cosier lounge and the billiard room. Most featuring much wood panelling and tapestry, except on the walls around the fireplaces, which had oil paintings. All were furnished exquisitely with period furniture, 'most of it Georgian', Melanie said, which frankly did not mean an awful lot to Adam, but he liked it, and the total effect of the combination of style and luxury overwhelmed him. He had to be dragged out of the billiard room by Melanie, who promised to ask Sir Paul to give Adam a game after dinner.

During the dinner, ably cooked and served by Blodwen and Gareth, everyone talked about what they had done during the afternoon.

Sir Paul had apparently lost a sizeable sum backing horses at the Chester races, including one of his own. This had irritated him somewhat and he had decided that he would have to look for a new trainer.

Lady Felicity had met her friend Penny for shopping in Chester and had had a lovely talk over tea in the Grosvenor. She was happier about her finances as 'the prices in Chester were so much lower than in Knightsbridge'.

Adam had been impressed by 'the natural beauty of the Welsh hills, especially Moel Famau'.

When they all looked at Melanie, she put her palms in a praying position, placed them on her left cheek, tilted her head and quietly whispered that she had 'fallen in love with the most wonderful and handsome man – ever'.

Sir Paul looked at the ceiling in despair, Lady Felicity once again let out a satisfied sigh and Adam blushed. Melanie was back, in charge.

With a mixture of simple innocence and challenging bravado Melanie went on to say that the two of them were 'in love and committed to each other'. She leaned over the table to reach out towards Adam. He, still blushing, took her hand. It felt totally cold.

∼

After dinner, Sir Paul duly invited Adam for a game of snooker and offered him a drink. Adam asked for whisky with water. Sir Paul poured himself a large Armagnac and they removed their jackets.

'Adam, we like you very much and Melanie is the most important thing in our lives. This is all very sudden, and before the girls join us here I thought I would have a word with you.' He started to chalk his cue.

'Sir Paul, what Melanie said, what I hope she meant was that she and I are girlfriend and boyfriend. That is really all, hardly even that. Melanie amuses me with the way she puts it. I am also new in this country, finding my way, and the last thing I can think of is a commitment, but it is most pleasant to be her boyfriend.'

'Adam, Melanie is a very difficult girl, very headstrong and for some reason even more so since last summer, I think. That is why Felicity and I agreed to you coming here, we thought you would have a calming influence on her. Heads or tails?'

Adam chose tails. The half a crown on the back of Sir Paul's hand showed the lovely profile of the young Queen.

'Can I start just the same?' Adam asked, to Sir Paul's surprise.

'Well, you can break if you really want to. Have you played snooker in Hungary?'

'No, Sir Paul, the party regarded snooker a decadent game, but I had a few games in the Students' Union, in Liverpool.'

'Silly of them, the party, that is. Every working men's club in this country has a couple of tables – in fact all the best players in the land are working-class chaps. That policy wouldn't go down too well here.'

'Not many would, I fear.' Adam took his opening shot, whacking the cue ball to the right side of the triangle of red balls to blast them wide open in the hope that one would end up in a pocket, but promptly potting the cue ball in the top right.

'Well now, that's all wrong, I'd better give you a twenty-five start.' He scored his four for the foul and moved the indicator to twenty-five on the top line of the scoreboard.

Adam was not a match for the experienced snooker player, but with some coaching from Sir Paul, he picked up some good points as the game progressed. The two women arrived and Melanie insisted on taking some of Adam's shots. She was a good player and his score improved immediately, but Adam still lost. Sir Paul promised him another game and 'withdrew'; Lady Felicity soon realised that she 'had forgotten to do something' and left the room just after him.

'Adam, I love you so' Melanie ran to him with wide-open arms.

Adam put his arms around her minuscule waist and they kissed. 'You are beautiful, Melanie, I can hardly wait ...' Adam kissed her again. Her kisses were still those of a child. He put his hand on her chiffon dress over her small, firm breasts.

'Wait, Adam, wait, they might come back yet, let's play a frame, I'll teach you.' She wriggled away like a snake.

'I'll break!'

Melanie hardly touched the right side of the triangle, but a red on the left seemed to peel away from its fellows to the top left pocket, leaving the cue ball perfectly poised for the black, which soon followed the red ball.

'How's that?' She smiled, tilting her head, arms wide open, still holding the cue.

Adam grabbed her waist again, this time with no intention of letting her go.

'You are too good, that's how, but I'm better at this game.' He kissed her again. She seemed to respond better for a moment but as Adam relaxed his grip, once again she did the perfect wriggle, proving that the previous one hadn't been an accident.

They played a little more, but Adam's mind was on other things. As Melanie was taking a shot from the middle of the table the petite girl had to bend over the table considerably. Adam pinned her to it from behind.

'I knew you would do that, Adam, you're disgusting.' She turned around but stayed at the edge of the table, bending backwards with equal ease.

'I cannot imagine anything more provocative than a girl with bottom like yours bending over the snooker table – it's too much, you know.' Adam bent over, trying to kiss her. 'Come on, let's do it, darling, I want you so much.'

'Tomorrow, Adam … tomorrow, definitely.'

'What do you mean, tomorrow? I am going back to Liverpool tomorrow afternoon and I won't see you for months. It is really not fair.' Adam pulled away.

'Adam, I don't know how to make love, I'm only seventeen and I've had a bad experience.'

'We won't talk about that again, we agreed,' Adam interrupted.

'OK, we won't, but you must understand, it must be when it's right for me and it is no way right … now. But I will smuggle you into my room tonight. Come, now teach me to love first, not to make love.'

They walked along the top-floor corridor and as they passed the master bedroom Melanie knocked on the door and put her head in. 'Mother, we are going to play some records … yes, quietly. Goodnight.'

After three more doors they entered Melanie's room, which was a mess really. Her walking clothes were thrown on the bed and the turntable of her radiogram was spinning away dizzily. She made a vague attempt at tidying up and picked up a record.

'I think you'll like this.' She threw the cover with a smiling young man on it to Adam.

'Pat Boone. Looks American with the short-cropped hair, like yours.' Adam started to read the cover: '*Love Letters in the Sand* sounds very romantic.' He turned off the two larger lights, leaving only one on near the turntable. 'Let's have a cuddle, little one,' he whispered, 'let me take your clothes off.'

'Oh, no – not all – my knickers are staying on,' she objected.

'Very well, but mine aren't.'

They lay on the bed. Adam decided that he wasn't going to hurry, the cherry might drop in his lap that way. Melanie thought she might satisfy him some other way. Her fellow sixth-formers were good on advising each other on matters of heavy petting.

The contortional activity on her bed would have made an unsuspecting voyeur think that he was looking at a sexual act of the most athletic variety after Adam gently removed her panties. Alas, things did not go much past Graeco-Roman wrestling between two different sexes. Whatever way Adam approached taking her, he failed. She was an expert in sliding away or wriggling into another position, without making it feel like outright frank refusal. It was time for Adam to change tactics.

He started with the gentlest caresses on her back, arms, tummy and the outside of her thighs. Then he moved his hands to her breasts, hardly touching them. She relaxed.

'Well, what's the verdict, then. Am I a virgin?' She kissed him again.

'Well, you might well ask.' He turned her over to look at her eyes in the semi-darkness. 'Anatomically no, you're not. It's gone – for ever. Physiologically, as you have not experienced an orgasm, in a way you are a virgin, but psychologically I fear you will stay a virgin for a long, long time.'

'What do you mean?'

'What I mean is you are detaching yourself from sex. There is a word for that.'

'It's frigid, isn't it?' She pulled her head back.

'Yes, darling, it is. But I'll help you.'

'Not now, Adam – next time, I promise – I promise.'

Adam, exhausted, soon drifted into a deep sleep. In his last thought he promised himself a weekend trip to Barnsley to visit Jean.

~

On his return to Liverpool he immersed himself in the books the dean had so kindly given him and got ready for the end-of-term examinations, which he passed comfortably. It reassured him from the point of view of his future, and in his letters home he sounded more optimistic than ever. Emilia and Nicholas were delighted. They wrote to him regularly and they smuggled into their letters cryptic lines about the way the retributions were being carried out by the ever more vicious commies. 'Charleypeter went to Kistarcsa' meant that the enthusiastic reader of the demands on the fateful day was interned in a prison camp in that small town. 'Your noble friends were looking for you' was intended to convey that the secret police were looking for Adam. The connection was the name of the man. Major Nemes in English translation would be Major Noble. Then suddenly another letter arrived, stating that 'your noble friends told us to let you know that they did not at all like your article in the *Sphincter*'. Adam was shocked and wondered how on earth they had got hold of a copy of what was after all only a students' magazine. Then he remembered the bearded member of the Communist Students' Society. Surely he hadn't sent a copy to the Hungarian Embassy? It was time to keep his promise and take them on.

As other Hungarian refugee students were turning up in other faculties, such as engineering, veterinary science and architecture, Liverpool University finally had thirteen of them. Adam got them all to meet in a quiet corner of Mrs Mack's, where it was decided that he and the politically more liberal Paul Sigmond, a third-year architect student, should go to the next meeting of the communists to address them. The CSS president, a diminutive sort of fellow with a thin red goatee beard appropriately in Trotsky's style, accepted their offer and advertised the meeting as *'Crushed Counter-Revolution in Hungary – A Victory for the Working Classes'*.

Adam could hardly contain his feelings and had to remind himself that this was England and he had better keep his rhetoric measured. Just the same, he pitched in.

First, he went for the definition of the word 'revolution' by their very own Karl Marx, which stated that it was a *'spontaneous and forceful overthrow of an established political and social system by the people, when the ruling classes are no longer able to govern and the masses are no longer willing to be oppressed by them'*.

'Well, ladies and gentlemen, like it or not this clumsy definition certainly applied to us!' He went on to describe the desperate conditions of all working people in Hungary in the early 1950s. How the quislings like Kádár had brought back the Russians, who had initiated the current wave of trials, retributions and hangings. 'Ours was the true revolution – the fight for freedom – what is happening in Hungary now is the oppressive counter-revolution!' Then he concluded his allocated five minutes by saying: 'Have nothing to do with that half-baked ism which declares itself the fundamental principle of the people. Communism has never once been voted for by the people of Hungary, nor anywhere else for that matter. They instinctively know that it is a foreign import and that, the world over, blood is on their hands!'

There was considerable stirring amongst the members of the society as Paul stood up. He was much calmer and more circumspect.

'You say you're fighting to end the exploitation of the working classes. Well, where is that exploitation? Here, where there is collective bargaining for workers and, if they are unsatisfied with their lot, they can just walk out on strike. Or there' – he pointed eastwards – 'where they are bullied to work to unattainable norms for an unimaginable pittance. And all this in the name of building socialism. They have nothing. They own nothing. And yet they are daily told that the nation belongs to them. I have tried hard to find one aspect of everyday life in which the East leads; health, education, welfare benefits. But I cannot. Yet I know they lead in the arms race, in the space race and the Olympic bobsleigh race, for they spend every penny raised by their workers on showpiece projects with which they claim superiority for their system.

Please don't be duped by your leaders here, who are frankly either intentionally duplicitous liars or ignorantly naive.

'Adam and I will leave this room now and ask you, members of this society, to follow us. It will be a big step for you, but a step that you will never forget.' His voice was hardly audible at the end but he had planned it so and it worked. Paul and Adam stood up and some members followed them immediately. A few more walked out a minute later, heading for the bar; the remaining half a dozen stayed for a further five minutes and discussed a proposal presented by one of them. A few minutes later a handwritten note was pinned on the noticeboard. It simply stated: *'The Liverpool University Communist Students' Society wishes it to be known that the Secretary's resolution to disband the Society was passed by a majority of 5 to 1. All members will be reimbursed their current membership fees less 10 per cent administrative cost pertaining to the winding up the affairs of the Society.'*

Paul and Adam were on free drinks that evening.

~

Christmas found Adam once again in North Wales, which, in the winter, reminded him more and more of Transylvania. The Battersby-Smyths were good to him and wanted to ensure that his first Christmas in Britain would be a memorable one.

'Adam, my darling, oh, I have missed you so!' Melanie ran to Adam as he got off the bus.

'I've missed you too, Melanie. I love your outfit and the black beret is positively with it – Liverpool is full of them.' Adam held her tight and released her to kiss her cheeks.

'Never mind Liverpool, this is from Carnaby Street, if you don't mind. And they say you Continentals are supposed to know how to pay compliments!' Melanie was pulling a face at Adam.

'Well, sorry about that, you must tell me all about Carvery Street, is it in London?'

'Carnaby Street, yes, it is in London, I'll tell you all about it later, let me get you home.'

'Where is Gareth, Melanie?' Adam asked, looking around.

'There's no need for Gareth any more, dear boy, I have just passed my driving test. They teach us that too in the sixth form.' Melanie started to smile.

'That's not fair.' Adam was taken aback. 'Mind you, I can drive a tank,' he added.

They settled into the silver Jaguar for the short drive and Adam leaned over to kiss her.

'Can I interfere with the driver?' He pretended to pull up her skirt.

'As much as you like, Adam, I'm all yours.' It sounded very promising.

~

Two weeks later, back in Liverpool, Adam recollected the Boxing Day pheasant shoot as a pleasurable interlude during a boring Christmas. The comings and goings of the friends and relatives were initially interesting and Adam enjoyed some of them, but when he had to give the account of his escape yet again, to yet another aunt, he became tired of it. For the first time he realised that he was missing the family back home, his sisters and their friendly racket. With the arrival of so many guests he was removed to the end of the corridor and, other than on formal occasions, he hardly managed to get near Melanie. After a couple of whispered 'tomorrows' he gave up chasing her and was resigned to being her 'very serious boyfriend', as he was always introduced.

After the *'Auld Lang Syne'*, when Melanie kissed him for the second time with a passion that he could hardly countenance and declared that 'this will be our year, darling', he took her to one of the quieter corners of the house.

'I am not given to having a scene here on such a happy occasion when your parents have been so nice to me, but can you just tell me in what way is this year going to be "ours", darling!?'

'We will get engaged, it will be wonderful!'

'Just a moment, Melanie, don't you think in order to get engaged I would need to propose to you first? Get down on my knees or stand on my head, or something?' Adam's eyes were flashing. 'And as I have no intention of proposing to anybody whom I haven't screwed first, you'd better understand that. I am going back to Liverpool first thing in the morning. If you ever want to see me again, you had better visit me! I've had enough of your "tomorrows"! Goodnight – no – goodbye!' Adam stormed off towards his bedroom, which seemed to be at the other end of the world.

⁓

As it took well over half an hour to travel from Crosby to the medical school on the bus Adam decided to find himself a flat or bedsit somewhere nearer. Confident of his ability to do so, when he got back from Wales he gave a week's notice to Mrs Blair and took the bus into town to look for new accommodation. The lady welfare officer provided him with a dozen addresses and a city centre map. There were no lectures to attend for another week so he had plenty of time to find something, he thought.

The first few he discarded without even knocking on the door. The litter on the paths through the small gardens leading to the front doors offended his tidy mind. He could not live in such squalor and was surprised that anyone else could. He imagined having to clean up the front garden himself every night, so he went along to the next one and the next one. In Ducie Street he found a very young mother and a screaming baby in the room next to the one he was shown, and in Bentley Road he would have to share a bathroom with three others, although the bedsit itself was very well appointed. He went on. Mid-afternoon found him heading towards Princes Avenue, the once grand Victorian boulevard, now with most houses in various stages of neglect. Walking from the once genteel Princes Park, whose magnificent wrought-iron gates were still a work of great beauty and craftsmanship, he passed the statue of a bearded gentlemen who was simply declared to be Hugh Stowell Brown on his plinth. Must find out something about him, he thought. He was immersed in glorious Victorian buildings, where one block of houses in yellow brick was relieved by another in red. Imposing façades were all around him, but none appearing on his list.

When he passed number 12, he saw a notice in the first-floor window, written in haste: 'Flat to Let'. He knocked on the door.

A distinctly Mediterranean-looking middle-aged man answered Adam's call.

'You wanna see the flat, yes?' He asked Adam.

'Yes please, sir.' Adam thought he might as well be polite.

'Follow me.' The man turned around.

The corridor was a little dark, but clean. In the middle of the hall there was a large carved chest, with a padlock but prised open, ruining the pattern of the carving. They walked upstairs on the vinyl covered steps and the man opened the door. The two went through a small bedroom first, which Adam thought was an unusual arrangement, and entered the bright lounge, smelling of fresh wallpaper; more than adequately furnished. Next to the main room was a small kitchen with half a window, the other half serving another kitchenette. There was a smell of oriental herbs seeping through.

'Bathroom other side of corridor, sharing with a man. OK?'

'Yes, OK. How much is the rent?' Adam was interested.

'Two pounds a week, little less, eight pounds if you pay monthly, advance. Very good flat, will be let fast.' The man sounded confident.

'OK, I'll take it, do you want me to pay now for this month?'

'Certainly do.' The man did not hesitate.

Adam handed over eight pounds and his new landlord gave him the keys.

'I am Meester Polimeni from Italy. You see me first Monday each month. If you no see me, I see you, yeah? What are you?' He pocketed the money.

'Medical student from Hungary.'

'Oh, Hungrian, very good, very good, I like Hungrians, brave, very brave – very good, see you next month.' He disappeared into the corridor and knocked on the next door, shouting 'Meester Chandra, are you in?' Mr Polimeni was obviously collecting his January rents.

Adam looked around his flat and was most pleased with himself. He would move a few things around and it would be perfect for him – and only fifteen minutes to walk to the lecture theatre, what luxury.

He went back to Lime Street, caught the bus to Crosby and told Mrs Blair that he would pack that night and leave the next morning. She said she was sorry to lose him because he was a good lad who never tried to bring back girls, like some of the others before, but she understood the distance was a bit of a waste of time for him.

There wasn't much for Adam to pack but the books would be a problem, he thought, until Mrs Blair, reading his mind, turned up with a battered suitcase.

The next morning, after his usual bacon-and-egg breakfast, he said farewell and thanked Mrs Blair by kissing her hands, which brought a tear to her eyes.

~

Adam happily unlocked the door of his flat and then left it to spend the rest of the day in Church Street, at Woolworths, which proudly declared itself the first one opened in Britain. He bought crockery and cutlery for four as he had four chairs around his dining table in the window bay; pots, pans and two changes of bedding wiped out his savings from the first term. Such was the price of independence.

He had hardly settled in when he heard a knock on his door and when he answered it he was surprised to see a large Hindu standing there. Greying at the temples, pockmarked in the face, sporting a fair size handlebar moustache above the friendly smile, he appeared to be a convivial sort of chap.

'My name is Sushil Chandra, I am your neighbour and we share bathrooms, not to mention the kitchen window.' He spoke excellent English without the accent of first-generation Indians. He offered a handshake, which Adam was keen to accept.

'I am Adam Zenta, from Hungary, a third-year medic.' Adam smiled.

'Have you anything to eat, my boy?'

'No, not really, I was going to go over to the Students' Union for a bite, I'll be all right.'

'I am sure you will, but let me invite you to be my guest tonight, just simple fare, curried beans and sausages.'

'Very kind of you, Mr Chandra, it will be nice to get to know you. When do you want me?'

'Please call me Sushil. I'll see you in half an hour, Adam.'

The kitchen partition was no match for the smell of the frying onions and the curry powder as Sushil Chandra prepared his meal. Judging by the odours, Adam knew what to expect. More or less. Being basically the punctual sort, he knocked on Sushil's door at the appointed time. The big man welcomed him with a beaming smile. Adam stepped in and he could hardly believe his eyes. The untidiness was engulfing, if not monumental. The books were about two feet deep on the floor. Dante, the Bible, the Koran and the *Kama Sutra* featured amongst Hemingway, Steinbeck, Durrell and even a well-thumbed *Mein Kampf*, most in some stage of opening with crumpled backs or containing three or four torn pieces of papers as markers. The smell of curry, which over the years had tinged the once white wallpaper deep yellow, gave the whole room the ambience of an enchanted oriental cave in a total mess.

Over the tasty, simple meal, which Adam consumed at the table whilst Sushil sat on the floor eating with his chapatti instead of cutlery, they exchanged the stories of their origins. The Indian turned out to be a Brahmin, an former naval officer on the run from something awfully serious. He intimated that it was the murder of a fellow officer. Adam naturally did not press the point further, but the subject of murder was brought up by the host just the same when the large man from India asked him whether he knew who had been the previous occupant of his flat. Adam answered that he had no idea. He was told that she had been a very pretty prostitute who was gruesomely murdered three weeks earlier, her body was dumped in the large wooden chest in the hall, which explained why it was forcibly opened by the police some ten days later. It also explained why Adam's main room had brand-new wallpaper and why the rent was relatively low.

The young lady's brisk trade in the house was known by all the others and she was apparently very much liked by them. Sushil said that there was something very 'honourable' about a prostitute who was decent to everyone, which Western society could not acknowledge. This girl with the golden heart came to grief when a client of hers cut her throat instead of paying her. He then proceeded to wrap a towel around her neck and for some reason dragged her downstairs and placed her much-abused body in the carved wooden chest. When Polimeni turned up for the rent and got no answer at her door for the third time he opened it himself, only to find blood splattered all over the walls. The police were called and the chest was the first thing they went for.

Adam was speechless. Although he realised that there was some reason for his good luck in finding such a good flat, he had never imagined that he owed it to a young and most unfortunate prostitute's early and bloody demise. Sushil explained that he believed that some good would come from all this because the whole thing was predestined anyway.

Adam was very keen to get back to his room and to write about his new experience. He made an excuse, invited Sushil for some Hungarian food the following week and mentioned stuffed green peppers. He went back to his flat, took his Woolworths stationery from his briefcase, sat down at his bay window table and wrote to Nicholas and the family, to ZsaZsa and even to Jean in Barnsley, bringing them up to date with the new twists and turns of his life. He enjoyed telling them his good fortune of now being a student at a 'great medical school', and having very acceptable inner-city accommodation near the university, but he naturally omitted to mention Sudley Hall and especially Melanie to anyone outside the family. He then let the World University Service know his new address for the monthly cheque and wrote to Sir Paul and Lady Battersby-Smyth, thanking them for his last stay in North Wales. He did not mention Melanie to them and did not write to her separately.

The next week he continued setting up his flat, which he envisaged using until he qualified. By the time he considered it done he was virtually penniless. The end result looked good and, what mattered, it felt good to Adam. He was most surprised when his stipend arrived from London and contained an extra ten pounds for a 'one-off relocation'. This was a magic land, he thought.

The following Monday the post left on the carved chest included a lavender envelope bearing a Barnsley postmark addressed to Adam. The letter on matching notepaper with some violets in the top left-hand corner came from Jean, who informed Adam that her sister had got a receptionist's job in the Queens Hotel, in Barnsley, which meant that she could get him a really cheap room there for a weekend. For good measure she had torn out the page from *Health and Efficiency* showing her naked by a farm gate, and included it amongst the scented lavender leaves. He wasted no time and wrote back telling her to arrange everything for Friday; he would hitch-hike over in the morning and come back on Saturday afternoon, as he was playing in goal for the medics in a football game against the engineers on Sunday morning. Only one night with Jean, but it was better than nothing.

Early Friday morning Adam caught the bus to Kirkby and got off at the Cherry Tree pub on the East Lancashire Road, intentionally well dressed, as he considered that he would get lifts more easily that way. He was right. The second car passing stopped and a man in his early thirties asked him where he was heading. 'Barnsley,' Adam said with a smile, and the man told him he was going to Sheffield, so he could take him well past Manchester. He settled down next to the driver, who exuded the pleasant smell of an expensive aftershave. It certainly wasn't Old Spice, the one Adam had taken to wearing.

After enquiring about the geographic origin of Adam's accent, a recurring facet of his life which he knew he would have to deal with for the rest of his days, the driver expressed his admiration for Bartók's string quartets and the plays of Ferenc Molnár. Adam knew he had an intellectual to contend with, so he decided to play along as best he could. It did not take him too long to realise that the driver was a homosexual, who seemed quite taken by him. With the next question he probed Adam as to the reason for his trip, asking him whether it was a visit to a girlfriend. Adam, without flinching, declared that girls did not interest him in the slightest and he was only paying a visit to the doctor who had helped him to get his place in Liverpool. The driver's eyes lit up. They must get together for lunch some time when they were both back in town, he declared. They most certainly must, there was so much to talk about, Adam agreed. And people to meet, like John Pritchard – did Adam know him? The driver continued. No, but he most definitely liked his conducting at the Phil. Having got on the road towards Glossop the driver suddenly offered to take Adam to Barnsley; after all, it was not going to be such a long detour. Adam was grateful for the offer and to reciprocate suggested a Hungarian supper, if his benefactor didn't mind having it in a small flat on Princes Avenue. It would be a delightful experience, he had heard so much about Hungarian cuisine but had never had the chance to sample it. Certainly not the authentic variety.

Outside the Queen's the driver opened his immaculate briefcase and took out an immaculate calling card, apologised for it being a business one and offered to write his private telephone number on its reverse. Carefully leaning over on the bench seat he placed it on Adam's right thigh and with a gold fountain pen with the broadest of nibs scrolled GRE 5676 on it. A gentle but definite tightening of his fingers was followed by a smile and he placed the card in Adam's hand, folding his fingers around it. Adam said thank you, goodbye, and opened the door. The driver whispered don't forget and waved, more than once. Adam screwed the card up and put it in his pocket.

Jean was waiting in the small lobby, and on seeing Adam she ran to him, dangling a key in her hand.

'Come on, darling, let me take you to your room, Jane has booked you in already.' She pointed towards the well-used and once smart reception desk where her very ordinary-looking elder sister was smiling in their direction.

'I'll be your personal porter and before you say anything I want more than just the tip.' She dragged Adam along the corridor.

The room was clean, with sun-bleached curtains, worn carpets and a distinct smell of mothballs. But it had a three-quarter-size bed and within seconds the two of them were romping on it, which resulted in both of them being sexually relaxed but totally ravenous. Jean suggested the newly opened Italian restaurant named after ample research and consideration 'Antonio's Pit'. The Italian miner who had married well locally obviously did not want to severe his connections with the industry.

Well, it was just that, a pit, but the spaghetti bolognese was tasty enough and Jean giggled away merrily about people they knew, especially the refugees, who were still mining in the surrounding pits, English comrades allowing. The big news was that Uhrin had got fed up with the piss being taken out of him and changed his name by deed poll to Urding. After that there was not much else to talk about and they decided to go back to bed, until the last possible moment before breakfast.

Adam settled the account and Jean offered to walk with him towards the old POW camp on the hill on the A628, which still housed a few older refugees. They said their goodbyes, both knowing that, sex or no sex, their fling was over. Adam realised that whilst Jean was an expert on the practice of biology or even physiology there was little he could say to her that did not bring an instant lack of concentration to her eyes. To Jean, Adam was just a pretty boy who one day would make a very good lover, if he would only stop talking about boring things like actually liking being a student. Well, the fourth car, a Morris Minor stopped and Adam got his first lift to Penistone, where he had to wait nearly two hours for a van to take him to the untidy outskirts of Manchester. He lumbered into the city centre and, reaching Central Station, he decided to take the next train to Liverpool Central, to hell with the expense. It was a bad decision.

The hourly commuter train was the old-fashioned type, with coaches divided into compartments, each with its doors on opposite sides of the bench seats. Each was isolated with no connecting corridor. Adam was alone, happily admiring the intricacies of the warehouse architecture of Manchester and the surrounding countryside and even managing to have a short sleep, only to wake up at Warrington when two young and very drunk Scousers got into his compartment. One of them was still swigging from of a bottle of brown ale and sat down next to him, whilst his friend took the seat opposite. They were engaged in a conversation that Adam, however hard he concentrated, could hardly follow. Their broad Liverpool accent was totally incomprehensible to him, although he soon realised that they had but one adjective, 'fuckin''. They used the word with such virtuosity in so many contexts that eventually it made Adam smile, which was angrily noted by the one sitting on the bench opposite him.

'And what the fuckin' hell are you fuckin' laughin' at, mate?' He looked at Adam, raising his chin aggressively.

'Nothing, nothing at all, gents, no offence, I'm just enjoying your conversation, that's all, no offence.' Adam smiled. 'No offence.'

'You's a fuckin' foreigner, aren't ya?' The one next to him finished his ale and threw the bottle on the floor.

'Yes, friends, I'm a student, from Hungary,' Adam replied.

'A fuckin' student, eh, from 'ungary.' The younger one, about eighteen years old, tried to mock Adam's accent. 'We don't fuckin' like fuckin' students, do we, Joey?'

'No we fuckin' don't, Pete, no fuckin' way,' the one about Adam's age reassured his friend.

Adam turned away and looked out through the dirty window, trying to defuse the situation. It seemed to work.

The two talked a little while longer, until the one opposite Adam decided that it was time to sleep and lay down along the bench seat. The one next to Adam slouched a little to follow suit, but soon became jealous of his friend's comfort and turned around, placing his heavy and rather dirty winter boots on Adam's lap. Adam instantly knew that trouble was only seconds away. He gently pushed the boots away; they immediately swung back with an even heavier impact.

By now the train was hurtling at its maximum speed towards Liverpool and Adam was wretchedly trapped. He once again pushed the feet away and stood up.

'Stop this nonsense, what is the matter with you?' Adam's voice trembled.

'Vat is the matter vit you?' The Scouser mocked Adam and threw himself at him with his right fist leading the way. As it passed Adam's right ear he caught the flying forearm, twisting it around. The young man screamed out and woke up his fellow thug, who rubbed his eyes.

'Wot the fuckin' 'ell's goin' on?' He asked.

'This fuckin' bastard 'it me, Joey.'

Adam realised that it was no use offering protestations and wedged himself against the edge of the seat and the door.

'Oh, did 'e now? We'll see about tha'!' His every word became more menacing as he stood up and stretched himself.

Pete was still rubbing his forearm when Joe shoved him aside and lunged out with a punch which was well enough telegraphed for Adam to be able to pull his head aside. The fist hit the angle of the door and the window at the level Adam's head should have been, and the drunk slipped, mumbling another 'fuckin' 'ell'. Adam jumped into the middle portion of the compartment, hit Joey square on his nose and stood against the locked door, ending up facing both of them.

Looking at the two disoriented yobs, Adam thanked God they were drunk, but he sadly realised that they were not drunk enough. They waited for a few seconds, rubbing their wrists and trying to get a better foothold on the linoleum floor, staring at Adam. Joe moved a step forward and beckoned Adam, flexing his fingers in invitation repeatedly. 'Com' on, you fuckin' git, com' on.' Without taking his eyes off Adam, he sneered to his friend, 'Open the fuckin' door – get rid of the bastard!'

Pete pulled the window down and reached out, trying to get at the door handle. Adam knew from the time he had spent on top of the much slower Hungarian train during his escape that he would not survive if they pushed him out. So, it's fight for one's life, he thought. Looking at Joe, he jammed his right foot against the door on his side and, like a swimmer on the turn, pushed himself away using all his power. Flying past Joe, Adam elbowed him in the chest to push him aside and he fell on to the bench, grunting. With plenty of velocity behind him Adam kicked the back of Pete's knee; he, with his arm twisted, was still busying himself with the door handle. With his instep jamming the knee against the door, Adam heard the cruciate ligaments audibly snap – well, at least the posterior one. The young drunk yelled out and fell back as Adam felt a massive blow just below the back of his neck. It was, no doubt, aimed for his nape, but landed on his spine. As he turned around the much stronger and heavier Joe grabbed Adam by the scruff of his neck and butted him in the face.

'Here's ya first Liverpool kiss, la'.'

Adam's nose was instantly broken and his blood jetted out, covering his assailant as well as his own best white shirt. With Pete in a heap by the door, nursing his excruciatingly painful knee and much-twisted arm, the fight was becoming fairer. Adam kicked back with his heel at the crouching Pete. He didn't much care where he caught him, which happened to be on the left side of his face. There was another bony crunch; this time his cheekbone was crushed inwards. He was out of the fight but Joe certainly wasn't, raising both his fists in boxing style.

'Ye know wha', la', I'm gonna take you for twelve rounds an' I'll knock you fuckin' out in the last one!' He started jabbing the air, leading with his right arm.

Southpaw, Adam thought, I must go for his left shoulder somehow, but the narrow compartment did not present him with many options. He soon received a flurry of punches on both sides of his face, without ever knowing where they came from. Joe was sobering up fast and felt he was back in the gym, shuffling his feet as he stepped back just to start another attack, this time directed at Adam's body. They were not particularly hard punches, more intimidating ones, forecasting the final outcome of the twelfth round. Adam's efforts to defend himself were totally ineffectual against the much stronger, trained man. He managed to kick him in the shin once, which made Joe angry.

'I'm fuckin' gonna get you for tha'!' Another and much heavier punch landed square on Adam's left eye. That one really hurt.

The train's juddering from side to side made standing difficult, and as Pete stood up behind his pal, still rubbing his knee, it buckled under his weight and he fell forward on to Joe's back, pushing him towards Adam a shade too soon for him to be able to keep his balance. Joe staggered a little, fell forward and received a well-aimed kick in his groin. He crouched and for the first time he yelled out in agony too. Adam knew this was a chance not to be missed. He stepped up on to both bench seats and held on to the luggage racks. As Joe was straightening up he lifted his face only to see Adam's Timpson winter shoes hurtling towards him. Even his boxing reflexes were not expecting that, and when they made contact with his much-battered face the impact, owing to both men moving towards each other, was of double strength. His neck jerked back and then forward again. Adam landed on the floor and punched Joe on the left cheek, which probably hurt his wrist more than his adversary. Joe fell back and crashed on top of his mate, oblivious to the world.

The stop at Garston on the outskirts of Liverpool was the best thing that could have happened as far as Adam was concerned. He picked his small overnight case off the rack and caught a glimpse of himself in the mirror below it. A massive, swollen, blood-splattered face looked back at him. He staggered on to the platform, turning up the collar of his mac, gave his ticket to the collector, who did not bat an eyelid, and headed towards the bus stop in a very fogbound street. Mercifully the double-decker number 80 from Speke was on time. The front destination indicator declared PIER HEAD. It was the one that passed along Princes Avenue and the stop was just opposite number 12, his proud new Liverpool address. He got on and started cleaning up his face with his handkerchief. By the time the bus got to the bottom of Brodie Avenue the visibility had become hopeless, but the driver battled on until the narrower Rose Lane, where he had to turn right. He pulled up and a short chat ensued, with the conductor bending over to him.

'Everybody off, please. It's thick smog out there, too dangerous to drive in. Everyone off – please.' He emphasised the last word.

Adam got off first and disappeared into the by now totally thick 'pea souper'. No wonder, he thought, that all buildings are 'Lyceum black', as he still liked to refer to the colouring of Liverpool's classical architecture. He had a vague idea where he was as the university halls were not too far from where he was stranded. He decided on as brisk a walk as circumstances allowed, often resorting to feeling the walls ahead and noticing that occasionally he could see as far as his outstretched hand. It took him an hour to get to Ullet Road and another to his flat. Suddenly his nose started to bleed again and he mopped it up with his mangled handkerchief. He walked upstairs and, as he was about to find the keyhole in the badly lit corridor, his neighbour stepped out. Adam turned towards Sushil, who took some time to recognise his co-tenant.

Adam's mac was filthy all over. Where it was not covered with blood it was soot stained from the walls of houses along his long walk. Sushil helped Adam into his flat and sat him on his easy chair, which he used for casual reading.

'Have you been involved in an accident? Oh, this bloody smog,' Sushil said.

'No, Sushil, I have just been beaten senseless.' Adam placed his head in his hands and started sobbing.

He had rather a bad day on 11 January 1958.

23

M̲EDIC TWO

When Adam turned up for the game on Sunday morning, Jim and the others recognised him only because he was wearing his well-known mac. Looking at his swollen and discoloured face, they glanced at each other and Jim, the captain, quickly gave him one of the linemen's flags and pointed to the left-hand side of the pitch. Adam did not argue; his headache was too bad for that. He went through the motions of being a linesman instead of goalie and later could not remember one moment of the game, which, in any event, ended in a 2–0 win for the medics. Nor did he remember the drinks in the Rose. In fact he could hardly recollect anything of the whole episode on the train or later. He would say only that the whole thing was due to a 'bad design fault by the English coach builders' for leaving him with no escape route.

It came as little surprise to Adam when the following Thursday at 5.15 pm at the Medical Students' Society meeting in the old Surgery Lecture Theatre, as they came to what they called the Private Business Section, the last sketch performed was entitled 'Welcome to your first "Liverpool kiss"'. The scene in the railway carriage was so mercilessly re-enacted by the president and the honorary treasurer, with a large rag doll dressed in a mac similar to his, that, for a moment, Adam shivered. Nothing being sacred – and, quite rightly, nothing is to this day in that society – he received an even bigger hiding, with the nearly one hundred members yelling, 'Give him the Liverpool kiss!' The president duly obliged, picking up the doll and butting it in the face. He then raised the doll and shouted, 'Welcome to Liverpool, you are truly one of us now!' The juxtaposition of sheer violence and genuine friendship overwhelmed Adam. He stood up to take the doll and received the kind of applause he used to get after the top C at the end of Verdi's '*Stretta*'. But this was a far cry from the entertainment he used to dish out at another medical school some fifteen hundred miles away.

Back in the Royal he was placed in a corner and the pints were on the others. The lads were patting him on the back and the girls were looking at the varying shades of blue so artistically covering his once sculpted face. As Adam still found it difficult to talk, the friendly moments gave him a chance to contemplate the contradictions of England, where genteel behaviour contrasted with such low pursuits of the underclasses, unimaginable to a Continental. He shook his head in quiet disbelief. When 'time was up', the crowd of students, including Dave, Gabor and John, all in dark grey of sorts, burst into the pitch dark of Pembroke Place opposite the much-famed bricks of the Liverpool Royal Infirmary. Adam's light mac was the only visible item in the smog, which had returned with insidious vengeance. He was ordered to get to the front of those whose digs were in the direction of the Rialto Cinema and Ballroom.

'You lead the way, you're good at walking in the dark,' said John.

'Yes, but that wasn't this bloody difficult and at least I had a compass,' Adam protested.

'Get a move on, Zenta, you Transylvanians do everything better in the black of the night,' Gabor added for good measure.

'Why don't you just shut up, ZsaZsa,' said Adam, reaching out to grab the corner of the building to orient himself.

∼

When the third pale blue envelope bearing a Shugborough postmark arrived via Mrs Blair Adam decided that it was time to open one of them. Naturally he picked the last one and almost jumped through the roof when he started to read the last paragraph of the familiar writing. He could not help noticing that Melanie's lettering looked more spiky and much larger than usual.

The fact that you wrote to my mother without as much as a word about me and now that my second letter remains unanswered gives me no option but to come to see you! Our wonderful relationship must not falter at the first obstacle, which was of your creation in any event. I am your faithful fiancée, whose heart you're breaking with each day you ignore me. I'll knock on the door of your digs and I am sure Mrs Blair will give me a room. God knows what I'll say to the head, here at the college, but don't worry, I'll invent something. See you on Friday.

Your ever loving Melanie. XXX

But Friday is tomorrow. Adam was struggling with his thoughts. He could not figure out whether or not she was coming by car or train, but in any event Melanie did not even know Adam's new address, so the poor thing would be knocking on Mrs Blair's door. He went downstairs to the pay phone and dialled WAT 6328. On the other end of the wire Mrs Blair's pedantic voice declared with monotonous clarity that the caller was now in touch with the Waterloo number. When she realised who the caller was, she became a little more excited.

'But Adam, Miss Battersby-Smyth is already here, waiting for your call. I installed her in your old room, she says she is very comfortable there.' Adam was speechless.

'Well, er, could I speak with her for a moment?'

Melanie soon came to the phone with a 'Hello, darling, Mrs Blair has just told me about your new digs, how exciting! I'm dying to see them. Are you well?' Adam reassured Melanie that all was well with him, but as it was too late now for either of them to travel in the smog, he told her he would come to see her tomorrow after his physiology lecture. Then he held his head in his hands for a moment of quiet contemplation and walked upstairs to his room. His headache returned with a vengeance and he drifted in and out of sleep all night, waking up rather early and utterly tired. His face was very tender to shave and gravity was playing its tricks with his bruises, which now extended to the bottom of his neck into areas where there had been no contact with the fists of Joe or Pete. He looked an utter mess.

As he walked into the lecture theatre, Gabor welcomed 'The Transylvanian Elephant Man'. Adam answered with a loud whisper that he should 'go and put some more lipstick on – who knows, you might find a new husband today'. After the lecture Adam sneaked out and went to Lime Street to catch the red Ribble bus to Crosby, getting off half an hour later at the Myers Road West bus stop. He walked a short distance before turning left into Belvedere Road and knocking at the dark blue front door of number 5. Mrs Blair opened it and stepped back aghast. A moment later a most smartly dressed Melanie cried out, 'What has happened to you, my darling!?'

Over the ensuing cup of tea Adam tried to give a concise account of his trip and of being trapped. He injected as much humour as possible into the story and kept saying that they should see the 'other two', without avail. The mothering instinct and nursing talents of the mature woman and the young girl soon came to the surface, with all sorts of weird ideas as to how to alleviate the latent effects of bruising. To escape the potions, never mind the various cuts of steak for his face, Adam had to play his last card of being a medic and made up statements like *'in the third stage of resolving ecchymoses the only thing that has to be avoided is direct ultraviolet light, and as there is precious little chance of that in the current filthy weather, no transdermal treatment is required'*. That shut them up for a while.

Mrs Blair left the front room and Melanie soon declared her undying love for Adam, even if his face stayed in its current state for ever. Adam melted at the sight of her pretty oval face and dark olive eyes and in turn said that he loved her too, very much indeed, and he was dying to be alone with her again. He also added that there were, however, practical things to be considered, such as how to extricate Melanie from Crosby without Mrs Blair raising an eyebrow. She was ahead of Adam on that one and said that after his telephone call the previous night she had told

Mrs Blair that she had to go back to college on the afternoon train for the weekend's hockey finals. Brilliant, Adam thought.

After saying their goodbyes the young couple started their walk back to the bus stop, leaving Mrs Blair wondering whether Adam was right about not having a piece of Aberdeen Angus stuck on his eyes.

Back in Adam's living room he had to divert Melanie's attention from her two still-unopened letters on the cupboard, which he quickly swept into the drawer. He turned to her with a broad and painful smile.

'Well, what do you think? Isn't it a find?' He swept his hand around his domain.

'Far too big for one. Can I move in?' Melanie teased, but she immediately turned more serious. 'Adam, you nearly destroyed me by not answering my letters. I couldn't have hurt you so much, what was the matter?' She opened her eyes even wider.

'You know, Melanie, I did try to forget you. I wanted to have nothing to do with you and your "tomorrows". It was such one-way traffic with me doing all the wanting and you responding with all the rejections. It had to stop – no, it will stop, tonight! Won't it?'

'Tonight is millions of seconds away, what are we going to do this evening?'

'We are going to go to the cinema to see *South Pacific* – it's supposed to be very good. Opposite the cinema we can have a Chinese meal in the *Eurasia* Restaurant. Then ... then the rest is yet to be decided. As you can see, I'm picking dimly lit places – the way I look. I know! I'll take you to the Cavern, a new club not long opened, they say it's really great, all the best bands play there – mainly jazz, mind you!'

'Absolutely wonderful – what a plan!' She spun herself around the room. 'But it's early yet, what about this afternoon?'

'It's bedtime this afternoon, Melanie.' Adam pointed towards his bedroom. 'Come on, darling.' He pulled her hand gently.

'Well, OK, you have a one-track mind, Adam, but just for a cuddle, OK?'

'OK, just for a cuddle.' They walked to the bedroom and started to undress each other.

Later, when he rolled beside her, Melanie sobbed for a little while and with tears in her eyes she whispered, 'Adam do you know, you … you've raped me.'

'I am sorry, darling, there was no other way. I love you, though, and a rapist wouldn't, would he? Shall I rape you again?'

'Tomorrow, you bastard.'

⁓

A much more relaxed couple took the bus a lot later than planned. The conductor, a typical Scouser, gave them the tickets and, looking at Adam's face, he turned to Melanie, saying, 'You mustn't be so 'ard on the lad, luv.' They chuckled and Adam explained to Melanie that all Liverpudlians had considered themselves great comedians ever since they gave the world Arthur Askey. Because of the lateness of the hour, *South Pacific* was given a miss and instead they went straight to the Eurasia Restaurant, next to the Victorian and beautifully ornate Crown pub, the once favourite watering hole of the rich and famous staying in the Adelphi Hotel before their transatlantic voyages. They arrived in the narrow Mathew Street after their hearty Chinese meal and could hardly walk for the crowd. The attraction was a new band called the *Merseybeats*.

As they entered the Cavern club their coats were taken by a pretty girl with a round face and short-cropped hair, who liked to be called Cilla. According to some, she had a wonderful voice. She joked away at the door and when those who knew her asked when she would make her debut, her answer was usually 'A lot sooner than you think, luv'.

On their way down into the depths of the club they found everyone perfectly dressed in the current fashion of navy blue or black drainpipe trousers, matching jackets and very thin ties under the collars of their white shirts. The girls broke the monotony with colourful dresses, still supported by several layers of net underskirts, making progress rather difficult on the narrow staircase. In the whitewashed domed catacombs all the chairs facing the bandstand were occupied, with people already lining up behind them. The only illumination was a few sixty-watt light bulbs strung out across the cellar ceiling, shielded by old-fashioned tinplate lampshades. The whole thing looked extremely basic, yet they somehow knew that they were privileged to be there.

The two, Cokes in hand, were lucky to see a couple leaving the third row and jumped forward to sit on the chairs; Adam put on his sunglasses instantly. Melanie followed at the speed her dress would allow and settled down next to Adam, giving an approving look at the sunglasses that helped to cover some of his bruises. The band burst on to the stage dressed in matching light blue suits with black edging and struck up with one of the more traditional numbers. The more knowledgeable among the crowd, probably knowing what was to come, started clapping right away, and there were some early screams from the girls. Band and audience knew that they were in for a good night's entertainment. Once into their stride with well-known hits, the leader announced one of their own compositions. The crowd went silent in expectation and the new tune emerged. Less of the hustle and a lot more soul, Adam thought. Melanie was simply amazed by the sound she had never heard before. Perhaps it was not absolutely right but she was sure a smaller group could make a lot of it. At the end the noise of the appreciative crowd was so overwhelming that Adam had to lip-read Melanie repeating 'fabulous' time and again. On the way home she told Adam that it was like being present at the birth of a new sound, totally unique in popular music. Back in the flat they sat down and listened for a while to a few of Radio Luxembourg's offerings by special request of Melanie, and whilst Adam was very keen to put on his first small extended-play record of Bach's *'Toccata and Fugue in D minor'*, he had to concede to himself that it was better to play it Melanie's way.

'Adam, what about our engagement?' She turned to him, without any preamble.

'Melanie, darling, you are mad, aren't you?' Adam laughed. 'How? I have nothing to my name, you come from a wealthy family and a great background. What sort of a match is that? Your family's friends will look at you as if you have gone crazy and will dismiss me as a fortune hunter.'

'An engagement just means that you are committed to one another. Lots of girls at college have fiancés, one of them has had two already. And anyway, didn't you say that we could … after we made love?'

'You know full well that wasn't what I meant. Anyway, we didn't make love, I raped you, remember?' Adam pulled away.

'Why, Adam, was I so bad?'

'Melanie, the question of what you were like doesn't arise.' He was tempted to add that she was certainly no Jean, but just smiled to himself instead.

'All right, so no rape this time, let's go to bed, Adam!' She pulled him towards her.

Her verbal acquiescence did not ascend to her mind or indeed help to make her body in any way receptive to harmonious love, and once again Adam left her without a climax. He knew this but dismissed it, telling himself that it would happen one day.

It did not happen the next morning either, but when Adam murmured to her that he would start saving for the smallest possible diamond Melanie was overjoyed.

'You don't have to save for a diamond. Grandmother left me a huge rock, all we need is a piece of gold – but I would love it to be Welsh gold, is that all right? Oh, I love you, Adam, love you so much, you have no idea how happy I am.' She danced around the room naked, as Adam applaused her almost perfect figure.

∽

Having made his peace with Melanie, Adam threw himself into his studies once again, with Second MB, the great hurdle and curse of many a drop-out, being around the corner. He had a lot more difficulty with the subjects than he had bargained for and, as his reading rate was still rather poor, it had to be sheer swotting, night and day, with the help of over-roasted Kenyan or Brazilian coffee percolated to poison strength. The time he allocated for socialising with his friends was after the MSS meetings on Thursdays, to the maximum of two pints. He disciplined himself to perfection, and the only breaks in his mammoth studying sessions he allowed himself were the occasional letter to his family and once a week to Melanie. Thus he got through his exams with reasonable grades and started his pre-clinical studies.

⁓

The news came of awful communist retributions amongst his friends in Pécs, where scores of his contemporaries were. They usually involved imprisonment or deportation, and culminated in the executions of his personal heroes, Imre Nagy and Paul Maléter. Adam read the bulletin in *The Times* on 18 June 1958 and was totally devastated. Notwithstanding the press, even he could not understand the purpose of vengeance so long after the uprising. The communists had nothing to prove by then, except to themselves, and they proved once again that the greatest enemy of a commie is another type of commie, especially one who has changed his allegiance.

⁓

With the help of Dr Danaher, Adam got a vacation job as ward orderly in Barnsley Becket Hospital. For a while he did all the bedpan-carrying and trolley-pushing, like all the other orderlies, but the sister in charge soon singled him out for rota-organising in her office on the principle that if he 'talked the doctors' language he must be too good for carrying muck'. The work lasted for the duration of the summer vacation, which gave him ample opportunity to see Jean.

They visited the atmospheric but rather seedy local pubs, but on Fridays they ate at the small but elegant Queens Hotel. During the week, after an evening at the cinema, Adam looked forward to the walk around town with fish and chips in hand – a dish that would always be one of his favourites. Theirs was very much an affair of demanding young bodies. Jean was naively happy with Adam's status – after all, his white coat was exactly the same as Dr Danaher's – and through her father even offered him 'a good job, down t'pit'. Adam knew he was there only for the vacation.

Melanie invited Adam to join the family for a month in Juan-les-Pins in the South of France, but he wriggled out of it, saying that he had to save up for the Welsh gold. It was no lie.

~

Returning to Liverpool at the end of September, he visited the Battersby-Smyths at Sudley Hall for a week before the planned resumption of his fourth-year studies. The family welcomed him, realising that now there was a vague possibility of Melanie's boyfriend becoming a doctor. This was given great emphasis every time there was a stranger around, as there usually was. Adam, on the other hand, demanded that Melanie should not introduce him as her fiancé until it was an actual fact. The engagement was planned for Christmas and although Adam had already saved up enough money for the precious metal, he held back, or at least he tried to, but having had no decent family life for more than a decade, he was tempted to settle into the safe, if rather boring, life of an English gentleman's family. Yet he knew that his relationship with the lovely Melanie was, to say the least, unbalanced. They were all amazed when at dinner Melanie announced that she was not going to go to a Swiss finishing school as planned and Adam was astonished that neither Sir Paul nor Lady Felicity raised any objections to her becoming a full-time fiancée. Adam tried to make it as clear as possible that marriage was out of the question until he had got at least a semi-permanent job, and he still had no idea what he was going to specialise in, although thinking of his mother's terrible death from cancer, radiotherapy appealed to him.

Not wanting to disrupt the dinner, Adam waited until Sir Paul had withdrawn and Lady Felicity was busying herself as she did after each meal, then he turned to Melanie and brought up the question of the school in Switzerland. What he wanted to know was what on earth was she going to do with her time for the next two years until he qualified? He was not too pleased to hear that Melanie was going to spend some of it in his flat and the rest 'helping Mother to run Sudley Hall'. He was flabbergasted. He took great pains to explain that his upbringing told him that no chance of further education should be just dismissed, even if it was only out of snobbery, but she retorted that the culture in England did not demand grabbing every chance of sitting behind a 'bloody school desk' to learn how to catch a wealthy husband – especially if a girl had got her man already. And in any event, one day she was going to inherit the estate and the Hall and there was a lot to be learned about how to manage it.

Adam realised that there was no sense in arguing further, especially as Melanie had a point. She might as well learn the ins and outs of the Hall. The rest of the conversation centred on the ring. Adam had the money for the gold band and Granny's rock was, as Melanie said, enormous – almost three carats. They planned a trip on Saturday afternoon to Llandudno, where the family knew a jeweller. Melanie would drive as Adam obviously couldn't, but he insisted on being in full charge of the purchase.

The next morning Melanie was already in the hall, smartly dressed in a knee-length slim-fitting light beige suit and a small white pillbox hat, raring to go, when Adam arrived from the other end of the house. After a very quick breakfast served up by Blodwen, they walked towards the garage next to the stables and sat in the Jaguar, which had already been driven out by Gareth, who had been most concerned about Melanie's clearance of the metal door frames.

'I suppose he will want to see my bloody driving licence next!' Melanie whispered.

'Do you blame him? Are you sure you can handle this thing?' Asked Adam.

'Sure I'm sure!' Melanie put her foot on the accelerator and the gravel flew all over the yard.

In the wing mirror Adam saw poor Gareth shaking his head disapprovingly.

Melanie drove to Flint to join the narrow coastal road, at Adam's request. He wasn't to be denied today, not this of all days. He was astonished to see the tower of Liverpool Cathedral so clearly in the distance. The journey was boring until the noisy holidaymakers of Prestatyn and Rhyl livened it up a little. They joined the A55 at Abergele and Adam's head spun from Gwrych Castle on the left to the white limestone spire of Llanddulais church, which looked like pure marble in the early morning sunshine. The peninsula and the rocky top of the

Great Orme soon came into view. Llandudno must be at the bottom of all this, Adam thought, while Melanie sped away between the Austin A40s and Morris Minors, humming the current hit of '*Oh yes, we will make love*', helping out Alma Cogan on the radio.

'Dafydd Robertson & Son, High Class Jeweller' was tucked comfortably between two small hotels on the seafront facing the golden sand of the resort, which was still packed with people enjoying the late summer sunshine. 'At least half of them, if not more, are from Liverpool,' Melanie said.

Old Mr Robertson was expecting Melanie and he was soon showing her a small ingot with the distinctive Welsh hallmark. She produced the large diamond wrapped carefully in chamois leather and the old man's face lit up as he murmured something appreciative in Welsh. He estimated that the workmanship involved in mounting it in the simplest way, which was Melanie's request, and the price of the actual gold, which had to be substantial because of the size of the stone, would come to forty-eight to fifty guineas. Adam had only forty pounds for the purpose – not even the extra four shillings to make it up to guineas.

'Mr Robertson. That is all I have, I worked all summer as a ward orderly to save it.' Adam put down all the large white five-pound bills, printed the old-fashioned way, just on one side, to look internationally unique.

'I can't do it for less than forty-four guineas – perhaps forty-three, but definitely no less.' The Welshman threw his hands up.

'Please, Mr Robertson, we will come to you for the eternity ring too next year,' Melanie pleaded, with an exaggerated wink over Adam's shoulder.

'Forty-two pounds and I was robbed! Did you say your fiancé lives in Liverpool? Hah, he learned fast, didn't he?'

'I just cannot pay more than forty pounds. We'd better go.' Adam started to take the money from the spotlessly clean glass counter which covered all sorts of beautiful pieces. He did not notice the further exaggerated winking emanating from Melanie's large brown eyes when the old man's hand touched his.

'OK, Mr Zenta, you've got a deal.' The old man sighed, nodding his head repeatedly.

Adam was relieved to get the bargain and left the money in full payment. Melanie asked Mr Robertson whether she could be shown to the ladies' room. He walked along the corridor, closely followed by her, whilst Adam stayed looking at the shining miracles of the jeweller's craft.

Mr Robertson opened a side door for Melanie. Melanie slipped two pounds into his expectant hand.

And Adam smugly thought what a clever lad he was.

During a short walk on the promenade Adam excitedly explained to Melanie how resourceful the Zentas were when it came to bargaining and added that he thought he had lost the deal at forty-two pounds. Melanie said that he had won the deal when he started to take the beautiful crisp notes away. She did not mention her knowing winks at Mr Robertson.

Melanie chose the picturesque route on the way back. She knew what Adam liked so she turned left off the main road to the imposing bridge leading to Conwy Castle, already spelled the Welsh way. It was a wonderful surprise for Adam and he was speechless looking at the ancient fortifications and the perfect proportions of the medieval architecture.

'I have never seen a castle like that, what is it?' He asked excitedly.

'It's Conwy Castle, darling. Wales is littered with this sort of thing, I must take you to Harlech one day! You would love that, but we have no time for that today, I'm dying to get back to tell Mummy all about the wonderful ring – the most beautiful engagement ring ever, ever.'

Adam laughed as she turned the car around with ease and took the right turn onto the A470, signposted to Llanrwst. The luscious pastures of Wales on each bank of the River Conwy made Adam dizzy as he looked left and right. By the time she got to the T junction at Betws-y-Coed he was totally taken by the scenery and realised that he could love Wales, just as he had loved Transylvania as a child.

'Let me take you to a lovely and most romantic spot.' She smiled.

Adam needed no persuading for romance and the two walked uphill on a narrow path. He soon heard the lashing of falling water and was taken aback by the sheer beauty of the whole area. He put his arm around his unofficial fiancée and squeezed her tight. They kissed again and again.

'I love you, Melanie,' Adam whispered.

'I'm all yours, darling,' she whispered back, and her head slumped on his chest.

～

Once back at the medical school and in the all-important fourth year, Adam once again stopped all social frivolities except for the pint or two after the MSS meetings on Thursdays. He did not want to mess up his clinical studies, and the textbooks, even with his improving English, were becoming ever harder reading, especially pathology. Dead bodies were bad enough in the post-mortem room, but having to go back to his flat and to continue reading about them ad infinitum became a depressing chore. He counted the days to February and the Third MB, but, of course, Christmas had to come first; the Engagement. He had promised it and there was no going back, although he well knew the academic implications of Melanie popping up to Liverpool once in a while.

Melanie's visits gave Adam a chance to show her the ever-changing face and importance of the city. He was, normally, cocooned in his flat on Princes Avenue, studying the mounting pages of mindless pathology, so did not have much chance to partake of the ever-growing delights of Liverpool nightlife. On Thursdays he would hear enough from the others about the Jacaranda in Slater Street or the Picasso Club in a derelict building on Upper Duke Street, just around the corner from Sir Giles Gilbert Scott's monumental neo-Gothic cathedral, by now just past its halfway stage of building. Adam had plenty to show Melanie.

Naturally, she enjoyed the bustling nightlife, which always made a good dent in Adam's finances. During the week before Melanie's visits he would spend a couple of evenings at the speedway ground, which, when not used for greyhound racing, was one of the much-frequented venues for the fast-moving, small-engined motorbikes. Wearing his multipurpose white coat, which also had to double up for the next morning's ward rounds at Stanley Hospital, his job was to rake back the sand to the middle of the bends after the riders passed. With his smart appearance, he looked totally out of place amongst the Scousers, but the pay was good and his need for pounds, shillings and pence was always on the increase.

The clinical years' total exposure to medicine do provide their funny moments which form the basis of reunion dinners conversations even decades later. Year-mate David Davies – on a day none of them would forget – described a Grade IV murmur of mitral stenosis of the heart to perfection, after the most careful use of his stethoscope over the exposed chest, only to be told by the consultant that it was a superb achievement considering that his earpieces were loosely dangling around his neck. The very popular physician added that in this case there was precious little to gain by using the 'guessing tube'.

A few weeks later, at Mill Road Maternity, Group K, as the bunch was known, was to experience a great moment of medical training, observing their first delivery of a child. Carefully lined up along the back wall of the labour ward, they listened intently to Mr Pereira, the consultant in charge, taking them through the stages from the current lie of the baby about to be born to the last rotation, which would bring about the perfect delivery. As he turned back towards the young mother-to-be, the head appeared, and at the moment known as the 'crowning', Clive, number three in the students' line-up, fainted forward on to the cement floor, gashing his head in the process. As the staff now suddenly found themselves tending to the bleeding forehead, the woman – left unattended – completed the birth herself by sheer instinct. Then, trying to sit up to see, she yelled out in a strong Liverpool accent – to the obvious amusement of the others – 'Would somebody bloody well tell me what's the colour of me bloody kid!?'

Emergency work was learned during periods of living in at the various hospitals, all sharing one established tradition, the medics-and-nurses parties, usually held on Fridays. Adam knew he was going to like those! They were famous!

The pretty nurses, out of uniform, turned up in droves, some having already worked out who was to be the target of their attention for the night of beer, cheap wine and fun. The age of permissiveness was about to dawn.

The Christmas engagement was looming and, according to Melanie, the solitaire looked 'magnificent'. Adam proudly agreed. On arrival at Richmond Park, which the family preferred as a venue for the engagement party because some of the older members found it easier to get to London, he became the centre of attention.

Christmas Eve dinner was earmarked for the official announcement, and it was to be a formal occasion. Adam was wearing Sushil's dinner jacket, which fitted him splendidly. Dinner was to be served in the long dining room, which comfortably seated the seventeen members of the family. Having concluded the cocktail stage around the bar by the main hall, they were led in by Sir Paul and Melanie, closely followed by Adam and Lady Felicity.

The staff of three served the smoked trout, which had been brought down from Wales, with perfectly chilled Pouilly-Fumé. This was followed by a steaming rib of Scottish venison, cooked to perfection. The choice was a surprise on the part of Lady Felicity, who remembered Adam's description of how the family used to eat venison at Christmas in Transylvania. The Gevrey Chambertain further consolidated the success of the evening until the Hennessy XO arrived in the company of some awful black slurp, euphemistically called coffee. Adam thought to himself that the English had never really mastered the art of making what Suleiman the Magnificent called 'the black soup', in spite of owning most of the coffee plantations of Kenya. He nervously stood up to face the silence of the family, hoping they would all be comfortable with his accent.

'When I asked Sir Paul for Melanie's hand in marriage, he gracefully' – Adam meant graciously, and thanked God later that he didn't say gratefully – 'answered yes, provided Lady Felicity also agreed. When she kindly did, I felt I had a secure enough base to approach Melanie, but I needed just a little more courage. The right moment came when, in Liverpool, she remarked on how many good-looking friends I had. I realised it was time to make a move. Over a bowl of Char Sui chow mein I popped the question. When she threw her chopsticks in the air shouting "yippee", I took that to mean "maybe, if you are a good boy". I had not yet been two years in England.' Lady Felicity wiped a tear away with an Irish linen handkerchief she had pulled out from her sleeve. 'And I have already been lucky enough to be a part of a wonderful family, through my beloved. I thank every member for the hospitality I've received. During those two dreary years I had been a refugee' – more tears from Lady Felicity – 'then I became a coal miner and now I stand before you in a dinner jacket – borrowed, mind you – to declare my love and affection for Melanie. Now, I would just like to conclude by saying that my Melanie and I are engaged to be married.' The ripple of applause around the table and the shouts of 'well done' from Uncle Bill were still ringing in Adam's ears when he eventually found the ring in his pocket and placed it on Melanie's finger. Sir Paul made a short reply, taking up Adam's point by welcoming him into the family. He concluded by congratulating him on an 'excellent speech' and forecast a future for Adam in after-dinner speaking. 'No mean feat for a man who had no English two years ago and comes from a country where the speech is made with the first drink of the evening. I suppose more difficult in a way when everyone is sober.'

Lady Felicity was wiping yet another tear when Melanie stood up and said that it was the happiest day of her life, she was engaged to 'the most handsome man in the world', and proceeded to walk around the dinner table to show the ring to everyone.

The date was 24th December 1958.

～

Years can pass fast in the life of a student, and Adam's case was no exception. The grinding days of clinical studies were followed by several hours of daily reading in the Harold Cohen Library until closing time. After it had closed Adam worked late into the night or even into the early hours of the morning in his flat, and his studies were only rarely interrupted by the occasional visit to the Unicorn, hospital parties or visits from Melanie. When, much later, he tried to remember and make some sense of these years, he saw not an orderly pattern of life, but a strange distortion of it. A Chagall-like mess with vague figures resembling nobody – and textbooks, everywhere.

During the high summer of 1958 the proud green double-decker fleet of Liverpool Transport buses once again needed extra conductors to cover the holidaying staff happily settled on the deckchairs of Blackpool, or the more adventurous on Scarborough's beaches. Larry Maxwell, a dental hopeful, had already done the job during the previous year and Dave Ahmed and Adam decided to join him in what was by all accounts a well-paid job.

They signed up at the Speke depot and were duly kitted out with freshly cleaned uniforms, peaked caps and, most importantly, the ticket machines. Now, if there was ever a complicated contraption, this was surely it. Loaded with endless rolls of different-coloured papers, so coded by the shuttle printing head as to immediately indicate the grade and the length of the journey, it also had a holder for the different-sized coins for easy dispensing of change. The whole engineering miracle was placed in a leather satchel, with a pouch or two for the occasional paper money.

They received the shortest indoctrination, and the chief inspector placed the gismo around Adam's neck.

'Don't worry, la', I know it looks bloody 'ard, but you'll soon get the 'ang of it,' was the only thing he could remember later.

'Now, la', gi' us one and two halves from Pier Head to the Cricket Club.' Adam looked down, pulled the lever once, another one twice, tore off the crisp-coloured paper ribbons and said, 'Two shillings and seven pence please.'

To his great amazement he was correct and passed his test.

'Now a few bits of advice, la'! Always pack 'em into the front, smokers on top – then hook your chain across quick, like, after the last passanjeh. At night, in case of trouble, like, stay near your bell whenever you can. Gorrit? One ring for stop, two rings for go and loadza rings for drive to the nearest police station.'

Adam thought he understood it all right and next morning, smart in his dark navy uniform, he caught the 86 to Pier Head, the glorious extension of the city to the River Mersey. The three main buildings, the Mersey Docks and Harbour Board, the Cunard and the world-famous Royal Liver Building, which housed the huge Liver birds on its twin towers – sooted to Lyceum black – enticed ships and liners to the home the city would provide for their tired sailors. Below the shadow of the latter were the sheds and offices of Liverpool City Transport.

Adam was allocated number 97 to Page Moss, one of the less salubrious suburbs of the city, to be sure. At eight in the morning there weren't many people going that way, so he had a fairly easy start. A few to Scotland Road. Interesting, he thought, never forgetting that Karl Marx and his minder Engels had forecast that very spot for the beginning of the English proletarian revolution, a little bit overdue now.

Just as he was allowing himself a wry smile a matriarchal and grossly overweight mother with a half a dozen children of every imaginable size got on. Adam carefully ushered them to the front and asked her what she wanted.

'One, two halves and three quarters to Orrell Lane, son,' she answered. 'Now didn't I just bloody well tell you not to do that Jimmy!' She went on as she delivered a considerable clout to the head of the little lad who was pulling the worst-ever plaited hair of a pretty girl with a chocolate-smudged face.

'She stood on me toe!' He yelled, trying to justify his action.

'I never!' The girl yelled back, sticking her tongue out, displaying a semi-masticated piece of Mars bar.

Adam added the fares up fast as he could and turned to the large lady.

'That will be twenty-four pence, please,' he declared.

The woman thought for a minute. 'One and two halves and three quarters – what bloody school did you go to, la'? That's exactly twenty-eight pence, ya daft bugger. Yer doin' yourself in, la'.' She laughed, handing over the right money. Adam sighed.

By the time they got to Rice Lane the bus was full to bursting. Adam was dishing out the tickets as best he could, but the large amount of accumulated heavy change in the bag around his neck was making him stoop. At Walton Hospital the night-shift nurses were ready to go home for some rest and Adam hoped that a fair number would be due to alight. He held on to the platform bar and shouted.

'Let the folks get off first, please! Just hold it for the moment, you'll all get on!' The uniformed nurses were piling on and with two to go he was full. 'Get farther in, please, move along, move along.' He gave them a push in the back, and with his other hand he hooked his chain on and, standing right at the edge of his platform, managed to pull his bell, indicating to the driver that he should start. Just as he did, a running man jumped on next to him. 'Ta, mate,' he said, and tried to push past Adam, who felt his authority challenged.

He pulled the bell chain, ringing it twice, and the bus stopped, shaking everybody forward.

'I am full, and you're not on.' He pushed the man off the platform and pulled the chain again. The man fell back and yelled a few obscenities, doubting Adam's parentage and promising to see him at the depot. In spite of all this Adam liked his job. He felt in command.

He straightened his peak cap and turned to the nurses, the second of whom recognised him

'Girls, look, it's Adam Zeny, look, doesn't he look great in his uni!' one shouted.

'Come on now, girls, let's get you some tickets,' Adam answered in a mock-serious tone as he started to distribute the white tickets, indicating a short ride.

Their bantering went on for a while, all of them asking him for a date at the top of their voices, and by the time the bus pulled up at the Aintree depot he was exhausted. After a mug of tea he added up his takings and to his amazement he was 4s 8d over. He went up to one of the inspectors.

'Well, la', you'll just have to make it right on the way back, won't you?' He winked.

Adam was confused.

On the ride back to 'town' (as all Liverpudlians refer to their city in spite of King John's Charter) he had an easier time, but when he added up he was twopence more up, totalling 4s 10d. He walked up to the cashier and admitted his miscalculation, offering her the extra money.

'Don't be daft, me boy, just go over there into a quiet corner and get your money right.' She smiled at him.

Adam did what he was told and went through the ticket machine again and again, but whichever way he counted he was 4s 10d over. He returned to the window.

'Now, you're dead-on right, aren't you, me boy?' The lady smiled.

'No, I'm really sorry, but I'm honestly four shillings and ten pence over.' He scratched his head.

'Well, you must have mixed your own money with it somehow.' The lady winked.

'No, honestly, my money is all in my left-hand trouser pocket,' Adam said in a virtual whisper.

The woman had had enough of teaching Adam a more profitable accounting technique and with a face that bore no smile or wink she beckoned another inspector.

'Mr Zenta overcharged the public and he should be put on "report".' Adam accepted that it was a serious charge and was told that two reports and he was out – those were the rules. He said he would be more careful.

He struggled on as best he could to avoid the second report and after a short chat with the other two decided to carry his own money as an 'emergency float'. There were definite lessons to be learned here, he thought.

~

Before his final year Adam spent a short week with Melanie, this time in London, where the question of the wedding kept cropping up, only to be swept aside by him. His plans clearly scheduled the event of his marriage for some time after his pre-registration year, the time when all young doctors feel ready to be let loose on the world and all its patients.

Melanie integrated well into the social life of undergraduates and particularly with Adam's closer friends. She was praised for her emerging beauty, which matured to her advantage over the years, and for her stylish dressing, which separated her from the girlfriends of the others, who had more restricted budgets.

At each annual medical ball, which was already one of the most significant and easily the best organised social events in the city, the two always cut the image of an exceptionally handsome couple. Melanie showed off her waif-like waist, topped with her favourite low-cut décolletage and skirts always shorter than the strict fashion of the day, to display as much of her perfect legs as possible. Adam looked tall, dark and just a little different in Sushil's dinner jacket. That year he used the occasion for his last outing, as he was about to lock himself up for the next six months before final examinations. So the table of Group K pushed the boat out on this, their last ball as undergraduates. Champagne flowed, or at least to start with, before the men reverted to beer and the jackets came off for some more energetic dancing to the sound of the Merseysippi Jazz Band.

Adam was as drunk as the rest when the band struck up one of the current favourites, *'Midnight In Moscow'*. The rhythm was perfect as he broke away from the others and began to dance the Russian *kopak*, whilst the others looked on in amazement. The furious dance demands the kicking of legs from a squatting position with arms swinging away from the chest and back to it, with a fair amount of spinning around on one's axis; a dance needing much exertion and which encourages the onlookers to clap rhythmically. The few who tried to imitate him were soon on their backsides, whilst he would just walk away from the circle still squatting, holding his folded arms elevated in front of his chest.

Melanie, having been as surprised as the others, got a table napkin to cool Adam down as he sat back on his chair. He gasped for air and declared that this was his passing-out parade, as he was going to be *'ex circulatio'* until the final results.

What followed was twelve to fourteen hours a day in front of three or four textbooks and a mountain of lecture notes piled up on his dining table in the bay window of 12 Princes Avenue. The percolator kept pumping out the strong black coffee, which kept him awake during the hours earmarked for the purpose of work. Only when it came to revision did he use an easy chair or the sofa, and in the early hours of the morning he read himself to sleep with the more peripheral subjects like public health or psychiatry.

At the end of it all he felt quite prepared for the final assault in the early summer of 1961. The day before his first written paper he walked down to Lewis's department store and asked the engraver to mark his favourite Parker fountain pen – a Christmas present from Lady Felicity – with the words DR ADAM ZENTA.

Four weeks later he became exactly that, with lower-than-average passes in most subjects, but a distinction in the psychiatry question, in which he discussed the early diagnosis of schizophrenia over the past hundred years to such effect that the reader in the subject told him that with a little extra work in the coming years he had enough there to present it as an MD thesis. Adam was delighted.

24

Doctor

Adam took up his pre-registration post at Clatterbridge Hospital on the Wirral peninsula between Birkenhead and North Wales. It was a sprawling old brick-built general hospital offering just about every speciality to a young doctor, as well as excellent living-in accommodation and the liveliest of doctors' messes. He had to do six months' internal medicine and the same length of time in general surgery to obtain his full registration, and he thought he might as well do it in a place where he would have fun.

He certainly did not bargain for having to work a hundred and thirty hours or more a week, much of that in the front line in the Casualty Department. This is the year when most young doctors learn their medicine the hard way, the only way, handling the ill child with an anxious mother as well as a drunken father, in the biggest melting pot in the world. In 'Cas', as they preferred to call it, there were no class or financial distinctions. The learning process was so fast that they were soon able to handle a vagabond with Münchausen's Syndrome coming in for a shot of pethidine, or the confused Jehovah's Witness trying to prevent his child receiving a blood transfusion after a nasty accident. Adam was in his element on such occasions and dealt with the situation confidently and uncompromisingly. For this he received much respect from the sisters in charge of the wards and the lingering eyes of the staff nurses, and he mentally recorded the latter for use at the weekend parties, which were as regular as the overwork that soon followed them. Pranks were part of their release mechanisms and they often had to pay for them, as once when, following a particularly noisy party, they embarked on an internal ambulance race. The battery-driven gurneys used for taking patients from one ward to another were not much more than glorified milk floats. When a colleague suggested that they should have a race at three o'clock in the morning, Adam accepted the challenge and they played dodgems along the road to the Radiotherapy Department. At the breakneck speed of fifteen miles per hour they approached the bridge over the Clatter. As the bridge was extremely narrow, one had to give way and Adam, once again, found himself waist deep in cold water next to his gurney. The bill for the repair cost them dear.

The Austin Mini was the sensation of the decade and when Sister Jones bought one for herself she found it extremely difficult not to bring it into conversation after every third or fourth sentence. She checked its presence in the car park every lunchtime and often changed her hours, just to be on her way home in it an hour earlier. His friend Allan worked out a scheme that would divert her attention to something time consuming, then they could drive the car into the building, into the elevator, which was long enough for a stretcher, up to her third-floor office and park it in front of her door.

When Jonesey looked out of her office window and saw her parking spot empty, she almost fainted. When she opened her door to rush out to find out what had happened and saw her car, she did. It took the best attention of the junior doctors and a patient's handy brandy to get her composure back. It was one of their pranks that was always recalled with great amusement by those involved.

The better weekend parties usually had some vague excuses attached to them. Adam had recently been introduced to the first horn of the Royal Liverpool Philharmonic Orchestra, Michael Ogonovsky, a delightful half-Hungarian and, like himself, a football fanatic. They decided to organise a game between 'The Band' and the medics. The silly season was at its height, so even the *Liverpool Echo*, the local evening paper, declared its interest. Johnny Connell, a first-class rugby player, took it upon himself to captain the medics and with wives and sweethearts looking on the two teams took to the field behind the surgery block and the game started.

Adam stood proudly in goal, and with three extremely pretty nurses watching he made sure he got noticed. Spectacular-looking saves were frequent, Adam diving for the most innocent balls to make the saves look as difficult as possible. Then he would turn around to acknowledge the applause with a wink, which each of the three took to be directed at her. Johnny and Oggo, as Michael was called by the players, worked hard up front, but it became clear that the medics were about to establish themselves in no uncertain way. By the time the final whistle was blown by a senior registrar acting as referee, the score stood at the unbelievable 10–1 in their favour. Johnny, taking the game very seriously, told him that he was a typical Continental show-off-type goalie and he should never have let in the 'softest ball' of the game.

Adam's strip stood out, being totally filthy, from the leaping dives and energetic rolls after catching the ball, but he knew he was established for tonight's party. By the time it started in the mess, the *Liverpool Echo*'s back page was announcing that 'Medics Play Tune to Philharmonic'.

What followed was one of the best parties of the year, with new input from the Phil boys, plenty of beer and curling sandwiches. The girls knew of the extra men taking part in the event and turned up in droves. Their mingling was furious, their drinking was serious and their determination to bed each other was single minded. By eleven o'clock couples were disappearing in the direction of the staircases, with zombified looks on their faces and a bottle of something in the men's hands just in case some sudden drought might break out at bedroom altitude.

Adam was still undecided as to which of the three to fall in love with and the dilemma weighed heavily on him. He knew the decision would dominate his life for the next few hours, and after a couple of extra drinks, he went for the soft option, the bustiest one. He was not going to regret it.

Wendy was a most voluptuous sixteen-year-old student nurse, who wondered whether there was life beyond being a good Catholic girl, and the time to find out was now. Adam was very willing to give her guidance, the best he could, along the agonising road, so long as it ended in his bed. He grabbed a large bottle of pale ale to assuage the thirst that was sure to come and placed his spare arm around the girl's silky shoulders with such tenderness that it bought a tear to his eye.

He knew he had the ultimate responsibility in shaping the beautiful creature's first encounter in bed.

Wendy belonged to the largest category of virgins, those who are dying to lose it but keep postponing the great event. She had not, so far, taken into account the persuasive properties of alcohol imbibed in large quantities over a relatively short period of time in the company of a hunk whose only remaining thought was to flatten her. It was sure to be her night.

Three hours later, complying with previous instructions, the switchboard woke Adam and reminded him that he had a driving test at 9.30 am in Birkenhead. He mumbled something not too sophisticated in Hungarian and decided that there was no time to waste on shaving. He dressed, planted a kiss on Wendy's huge left breast, the one on which he could see a red impression of his profile, and covered her up.

He squeezed a quarter-tube of toothpaste into his mouth, started to chew it and ran to the car park. He spat out most of the Colgate and got into the Volkswagen Beetle lent him by his friend Allan to drive to the town centre driving-test establishment. Parking around the corner, he tied his 'L' plates on the gleaming nickel bumper, ran into the building and presented himself to a very officious man who looked at his papers and said, 'Dr Zenta, would you be good enough to read the number plate of the white Ford Popular over there.'

'Where, sir?'

'Right over there, on the left.' The man pointed.

Right on the left, Adam thought, what sort of language is this, especially when your head is about to burst.

'7079 KB.'

'Let us proceed.'

The owner of the VW was an excellent casualty officer and a good friend of Adam's. Allan was a lover of music with a large record collection and they listened to a lot of opera together when they were on call. He had given Adam a few lessons in his Beetle and let him loose in it on the internal roads of the hospital grounds. In due course Adam was allowed to drive out to the main road and negotiate a couple of roundabouts and traffic lights and thought he was doing well. Being on the list, he was sent a notice of cancellations of tests and, after a total of some three hours of driving, he had presented himself the first time on the principle of 'let's just see what's it like, I'm bound to fail'. After hitting the kerb a few times, he did just that.

This time, thanks to the party and Wendy, he just plain forgot all about it. Adam started off reasonably well and he was pleased with his performance as they chugged along the road. No problem with the emergency stop and the reversing into a side road was perfect. It's a doddle, he thought, as the examiner turned gently towards him and took a couple of deep sniffs. Adam could not believe the man's nose. He continued perfectly, using every ounce of his power of concentration. No mistakes at all. Good, he thought again, but then he suddenly coughed. A small tracheal cough, not much more than a tiny grunt, but he immediately knew he was in trouble. The anti-peristalsis began, and the contents of his stomach started to travel in the wrong direction. He pulled up at the red lights just behind a Ford Anglia and turned to the examiner.

'I am very sorry about this, sir.'

He just managed the last word, opened the car door and with jet-like projectile vomiting placed the previous night's food and beer on to the tarmac of Argyle Street.

The lights soon changed but he was in no position to start off, to the obvious anger of a few drivers behind him. He knew there were to be two more spasms to offload at least.

'Dr Zenta, you're drunk! What a disgrace! In fifteen years of examining I have never seen ...'

'Sorry, sir,' Adam interrupted, and vomited once more.

The indignant examiner demanded to change places. Adam got out and puked once more, to an ever-increasing and non- appreciative audience. He was walking around to the passenger door when he heard the examiner scream.

'Hell, I say, hellfire! Look at my shoes, they are covered.' He started to jump up and down to shake off the vomitus.

'Sorry, sir,' Adam mumbled, holding his handkerchief in front of his mouth, trying to suppress the hiccups indicating the end of his gastrointestinal episode.

'I should think you are sorry! Well, I am delighted to say that you have failed.' The man drove back to the office and gave him the slip indicating the fact. Adam waited for a few minutes and took off the

'L' plates for the drive back to the hospital. He turned into a side road to take him back to Borough Road and was halfway along when he realised that he was the only one driving in his direction. One-way street, eh, he thought. God, Zeny, you are a failure, aren't you. And he masterfully executed a three-point turn.

※

'Mr Woodcock's office here, Dr Zenta, I am his secretary, you know, the registrar's office at the university.' There was a smile in the voice.

'Yes, of course, what can I do for you?' Adam was surprised.

'Mr Woodcock would like to speak with you if it's not inconvenient.' Well, it wasn't really, so Adam hung on for a while.

'Dr Zenta, according to our records you speak Russian, is that correct?'

'Well, sir, I used to be able to, but I had to bribe my stepmother to give me the right grade at matriculation and with learning English all the time since then I'm sure I've lost it. What is this about?'

In perfect Queen's English the man went on to explain that the university was to host a group of engineers and metallurgists from the Soviet Union and needed someone to escort them socially for a few days. He had mentioned it to the chairman of the Area Hospital Authority (a friend of his), who was delighted to let Adam be seconded for the purpose.

Adam did not take long to agree – it beat the seventy-two-hour shifts at the Casualty Department and he knew he might even be able to have a few good arguments with them. 'Hm,' he thought, 'I'll enjoy that.' Having confirmed the whole thing with his Administration Office he packed a spare suit and took the bus to Hamilton Square. He crossed the River Mersey on the ferry to the Pier Head and took a taxi to the Swan Hotel, opposite the art deco Royal Court Theatre and just across from Liverpool's bustling vegetable market. The manager was expecting him.

'Dr Zenta, they are all in the small lounge along the corridor. They are waiting for you.'

He entered the room, where three women and four men were puffing away at some indescribably smelly Russian cigarettes with long empty paper filters. They were all smartly dressed, in new and well-cut clothes.

Western visit issue, Adam thought, knowing that the way Russians were kitted out depended on the direction of their travel. An even better-dressed one, who seemed to command the attention of the rest, walked up to Adam and smiled. Like a hyena.

'My name is Vasily Alexandrovich Kazan, let me introduce you to our group.' He turned to the eldest. 'This is Academician Vladimir Vladimirovich Shokolyov, Professor of Metallurgy at the Second Engineering University of Moscow. This is' – he turned to a very attractive woman in her early twenties – 'Rimma Kabalyevska, from Kiev University ...' and he rolled off the other names in very quick succession, as if he had done this on many occasions. Adam wanted to confirm only one thing. He turned to Kazan.

'Gospodin Kazan, are you a metallurgist too?' He asked, using the deferential term 'mister'.

'Well, no, Doctor, I am an – how shall I say? An administrator, an arranger of this tour for our illustrious scientists. I look after all their needs, it would be correct to say.'

'You look after them! I understand, don't you worry about it. I will look after them too! They will be very well looked after!' Adam smiled and the others joined in, laughing.

'Doctor, you are not English, I am right?'

'Well spotted, Mr Kazan. I am Vengriy, as you call us, a Hungarian. I am going to be your host for the next few days, just to help you with the social things you want to do. I understand you have a very busy scientific programme.'

'Yes, a visit to English Electric tomorrow and Jodrell Bank the following day. Saturday we have a free day and we go to London on Sunday. What do you suggest for Saturday?'

'I suggest I take you up to Blackpool, to see the illuminations, the best in the world.'

'I believe in Sotchi on Black Sea we have the best,' Kazan murmured.

'Just you wait and see, gospodin.' Adam insisted on calling him 'mister'.

'My *tovarishchi* would be very pleased if you called us comrades for the next few days instead of mister, would you mind?'

'Well, now here we do have a problem. You see, that would break my tongue off, Mr Kazan. But I am your host and we must be friends. My father's name is Nicholas, so you may call me Adam Nicholaievich if you like. Is that all right, Vladimir Vladimirovich?'

'Very much all right. If you like it is OK.'

'Now that is settled, would you like a drink?'

In the order vodka was not mentioned at all, but they all had a good go at the hotel's gin and whisky supply. When Kazan was called away to the telephone they took it in turns to say how sorry they were for the way Hungary was treated in 1956. Adam was quite taken aback at this spontaneous apology, and whilst he hoped that many more and bigger ones were to follow, he felt genuinely sorry for them. In his thoughts he thanked Mr Woodcock for getting him involved – only an Englishman would think this way, and he enjoyed the irony of it all. By the time they were ready to retire they were even discussing the first signs of the Sino-Soviet rift, though Kazan tried his best to play it down as a little quarrel amongst bosom friends. When at last they said *'Do svidania'* in the corridor Adam received a very strong handshake from the quiet, bespectacled scientist Iosif Timoseyevich Alexandrov. He then reached out to Rimma and hung on to her hand as long as he could. In return he received from her darkest of eyes a lingering, smouldering look. Heading to his room, he realised exactly why the famed Russian lyricist wrote *'Ochi chornaya'* – Oh, darkest of eyes.

Even though some awfully dull chaps from the Faculty of Engineering joined them the group was still rather small for the large bus taking the party to the English Electric factory on East Lancashire Road, so they spread themselves out a bit. Adam moved around to speak to everyone a little, leaving Rimma to last.

Adam made sure that as he sat down their knees touched, just sufficiently for her to look at him for a split second. She did not move away. They conversed lightly about how a 'beautiful young lady became an engineer in Kiev'. Adam was interested to learn that there was no such thing as the *'Great Gate of Kiev'*, and it was just a figment of

Mussorgsky's imagination for the closing scenes of his *'Pictures at an Exhibition'*. Adam told her that he had a recording of a live performance by the greatest of pianists, Sviatoslav Richter, and guess what?

'Yes, I know what, he makes a mistake in one of the "Promenades".' She looked at him admiringly. 'He is famous for that! When he recorded it again he made the same mistake, so he left it in.' They laughed as their shoulders touched.

The visit to the factory was, Adam thought, interesting for those who found the making of modern electrical appliances, well, 'interesting'. At the lunch break Kazan decided it was time to introduce a little controversy. He asked one of the local women, who had been invited by the shop steward of the Electrical Engineering Union to join the comrades in the canteen, whether it was true that in England women were paid less than men, which she confirmed. When she was asked how much she was paid she told him to mind his own business. Adam tried to explain to the commissar that the British were most reticent in talking about the money they made. Condescendingly, Kazan said he understood that, the way they were exploited by the capitalist system, they were naturally too ashamed to say.

Kazan then kept pressing his point about equal pay, saying that in the Soviet Union men and women got the same wages. 'But here – no! Yes?' The woman, being a little annoyed by now having lost her chance to have her usual tea break, told the comrade that 'the wages are different because we never actually do the same jobs! See?'

In the afternoon they were shown around the planning and drawing rooms and the note-taking of the Russians was furious. At the end Kazan proudly declared that in Omsk there was a factory that was far more advanced than this. The others looked at the ceiling and shook their heads in disbelief. After the evening drinks in their hotel lounge Adam's attention was taken by the way the studious-looking Iosif kept staring at him. At ten o'clock precisely, when Kazan was once again called to the telephone (from Russia, to save foreign exchange), to make his daily report, Iosif walked over to Adam and asked whether he could talk to him.

'Dr Zenta,' he spoke in a whisper, 'I am a top-rated atomic scientist working in the Voronezh branch of the Soviet Nuclear Energy Establishment and I want you to help me defect to the United States.'

Adam could not believe his ears as the man walked back to his seat. He looked at him across the room and saw him nodding twice. His appetite for seducing Rimma disappeared instantly. 'I don't need this,' he murmured to himself, and looked again in the direction of Iosif, whose eyes were still fixed on him. On Kazan's return he chatted a little about the trip to Jodrell Bank the next morning. Some of the others were excited about meeting the famous Professor Bernard Lovell. He felt the same way – exactly, he added – and said *Do svidania* to each in turn. Rimma didn't look at him this time.

Adam took two steps at a time to get to his room. He threw his jacket on to the small easy chair, lay on his back and picked up the telephone.

'Operator, can you get me the police, please,' he asked in a virtual whisper.

'The police, did you say, luv? What's the matter, can we not help?' A chirpy voice asked.

'Please, dear, do as I ask. It's nothing to do with the hotel.'

'Good evening, sir, Desk Sergeant Jones here. What can I do for you?'

'Sergeant, I need to speak to someone from the Special Branch or the Aliens Department or something like that.' Adam was still whispering.

'That's not as easy as all that, especially this time of the night. Can we get back to you, sir?'

Adam gave the name of the hotel and his room number as the extension number had been scratched off the handset. He waited for an eternal twenty minutes before his phone rang.

He gave the shortest description of his problem to the quiet-sounding man on the other end of the line, who seemed to be fully informed about the visiting Russians and offered to come and see him.

Another twenty minutes passed before there was a knock on his door. Adam let in a tall, thin man in a rather shabby navy suit. He introduced himself as Sergeant Hopkins, Aliens Department.

Sergeant Hopkins listened to Adam's story without saying a word. He picked up the phone and asked the operator for a number.

'Hopkins here, sir. I am with a Dr Zenta at the Swan Hotel, Liverpool. You know about the bunch of Russians that we have in town? Well, the doctor is acting host, he says he has a defector for us – correction, for the Yanks, sir.' Adam could not hear the answer as he sat in the easy chair. The sergeant turned round.

'It wouldn't be a Doctor Alexandrov, would it, Doctor?'

'Yes, his name is Iosif Timoseyevich Alexandrov. I suppose he is a PhD.'

After a few more minutes on the telephone Hopkins turned to Adam and said, 'Inspector Brown of the Special Branch is on his way. He said never mind the Yanks, we want him for ourselves.'

'Shit,' said Adam, thinking of the tug of war to come.

Half an hour later, an affable short, bald man walked into Adam's room, which was beginning to be too small for the purpose of international intrigue.

Two hours later Inspector Brown was delighted with the result of their discussion. In the morning he would set up the whole operation. He reassured Adam that they considered him perfect for helping with the job.

Shit, Adam thought.

The following morning the coach turned right in front of Lime Street station and headed towards Widnes. Joe, the driver, suggested they use the old iron contraption known as the Transporter to cross over the River Mersey. This much-revered Victorian dangling device was just about large enough to take the bus. They drove on to it and after a few tentative shakes the large cage started to move towards the small village of Runcorn. Creaking along next to the magnificent railway bridge, they were soon enveloped in steam and smoke as the 7.05 am from Euston, pulled by the magnificent Pegasus steam engine, proudly crossed it. Noisy and totally outdated, it seemed to be a player in a bygone age just about to visit something of the future.

Adam manoeuvred himself next to Rimma. As the huge engine passed them the driver whistled in salute to the bone-shaking Transporter. They became invisible for a moment and Adam squeezed her hand. Rimma moved an inch closer. After the train had passed them the clatter and rattle continued whilst the professor from Moscow talked to his Liverpool counterpart, Professor Richardson. Meanwhile Iosif looked at Adam sternly. He nodded back, which produced the faintest of smiles on the Russian's face. In the front next to Joe, Comrade Kazan was reassuring the driver that in the Soviet Union no such engineering dinosaur existed. Joe told him that sadly it would not exist here much longer either as they were planning a modern bridge, but it would surely be missed once it was gone.

Having driven through the pretty Cheshire town of Knutsford, the Russians sat quietly marvelling at the autumnal English countryside and perfectly kept agricultural land. These were things, the land as nature provides it and its cultivation by man, that were ingrained on the Russian soul, whether that of a muzhik peasant or a cultivated professor.

Joe drove along the A537 sedately and took a sharp right at the hamlet of Chelford. Suddenly they all gasped. Individual worries and ideological handicaps forgotten, they looked to the right in awe. The gigantic dish, tilting slightly backwards, listened intently to the sky. Another turn to the right and they were in the compound. A few seconds later, outside the main brick-built entrance, they saw a small man in a striped grey suit. His tie just a little off centre, he was trying to brush back a few long strands of hair across his bald dome of a head.

'Vladimir, how nice to see you again!' Professor Lovell moved towards his guest.

'Nice to see you too, Bernard, but what a dish you have got here!' Professor Shokolyov extended his arms, gesticulating towards it.

They shook hands and embraced, leaving the others behind.

Kazan was last off the bus and remarked to Joe, quite seriously, that there were no guards to be seen.

With a smile he was told that nobody was able to pinch that big thing, not even a Scouser.

After the formalities were over the party was allowed to see the radio telescope without any hindrance. In the control room they were shown how they were tracking the latest Sputnik and relaying the information back to Lvov in the Ukraine. Iosif, not too interested, took a few notes. The youngest man in the party, having asked permission to take some pictures, even to Adam's surprise was told, 'Why not?' With the help of the women they photographed and filmed every nut and bolt of the enormous structure. The Leika cameras, copied from the plans of Zeiss Ikon when the Red Army took Dresden, worked overtime and the six-millimetre film camera, under the direction of Comrade Kazan, had to be loaded several times to cope with the work at hand. The Soviet Union was sure to have something very similar, very soon. Work done, they were invited for lunch, where Kazan was visibly overjoyed with his achievement. He was sure to receive a promotion for what he had in the bag, even if it was with permission. Perhaps he would get a medal too. His mind was bursting with his own importance.

After the lunch of fresh salmon and salad Professor Lovell once again assured his friend Vladimir that they would continue their cooperation in space research and that he was looking forward to receiving data from the current Sputnik. In reply Professor Shokolyov reassured his host that he would make as much information available as was expedient. The whole thing was a little one sided, Adam thought, but he didn't care too much. He had other things on his mind.

When the Russians were told that life got a little lazy in Britain from Friday lunchtime onwards, Kazan dismissed the idea as decadent, but nevertheless even he did not object to doing some shopping back in Liverpool.

'Some souvenirs at least,' he said.

Adam, back in his job as the social commissar on their return to Liverpool, took them around the shops of Bold Street, then Church Street and down to Lord Street, the main shopping areas of the city. He soon realised that the Soviet Union was a shade behind the West in the production, distribution and exchange of hard currency, so Woolworths emerged as the clear favourite. Still, the professor also wanted to call into the nearby Littlewoods after seeing some underwear in the display windows. Adam used the stroll to ask Rimma for her room number and found out that the three women were placed in a twin and a single and, yes, she was in the twin with Olga. With her jet-black eyes wide open she was virtually apologising for his bad luck. Kazan approached Adam and asked whether he would help Iosif find a bookshop selling scientific publications.

'There is the University Bookshop on Brownlow Hill some distance away – that might fit the bill,' said Adam, puzzled as to why a man with plans to defect would now want to buy books of all things. He suggested they take a taxi whilst the others went back to the hotel. Kazan agreed.

Once in the cab Iosif told Adam that he had no intention of buying anything. He would think of a title that they were bound not to have. But he did want to know whether anything was happening for him.

'That's the very reason I don't spend too much time with you, Iosif, I don't want Kazan to smell a rat. I have spent half the night in the company of people whose business is defection and will, no doubt, have to do the same tonight if you are to be sprung tomorrow. The whole thing has to go like clockwork. In the morning, at breakfast or on the bus, I will nod to you if all is well. Please be patient. How, in the name of God, did I get mixed up in all this?'

'I am sorry if I am trouble to you, but I am sure the Americans will be pleased with what I have to tell them.'

If you ever get farther than MI5, Adam thought.

'Seeing we are here alone I'll give you your basic instructions. If anything changes I will update you at breakfast or on the bus tomorrow, as I said. If not, I'll just nod. Now listen carefully.'

It took only five minutes for the instructions to be repeated twice, as they were simple and clear enough.

Kazan was waiting outside the entrance of the hotel when the taxi brought the two back. He could not help noticing the same registration plate on the taxi and thinking it too much of a coincidence.

After dinner Adam explained to the visitors that tomorrow would be a day of rest and that if anybody had any film left after Jodrell Bank they would be able to put them to good use. They were going to make a trip to Blackpool, a most interesting town dedicated to pleasure and fun. It was up to them to enjoy it. He had a drink with them in the bar and whispered to Rimma that it was a shame her not having the single room. 'What is wrong with your single room?' she flirted. He looked at her in embarrassment, knowing that there was company waiting for him there.

∽

'Doctor, can we just say, when you think he is isolated enough from the others, we will take him from you and your job is over.' Inspector Brown looked for Adam's reaction.

'Well, not quite, I will have the most unenviable task of telling Kazan that I have lost one of his scientists. I know what his reply will be!'

'Yes, quite, Doctor.'

~

The bus was doing as well as it could as it travelled through Ormskirk but it was September and the heavy traffic on the way to the spectacular Blackpool illuminations brought every vehicle to a near-standstill. The jammed roads exhibited every possible make of car, which fascinated the visitors, used to their Zils or Ladas.

'The fact that there are many cars on the road was always known by us, but I never realised there were so many different types of them,' Olga remarked. 'I have just counted thirty-two different makes or models, I can't believe it.'

'What do you have to achieve at work to be sent for a holiday to a place like Blackpool?' Oleg, the quiet one, enquired.

While Adam was busying himself with the answers he managed to give Iosif the all-important nod – this made the Russian most introspective. The bus finally arrived at the outskirts of the resort and turned on to the ring road, passing the large white windmill. They parked outside the Hippodrome cinema, which was showing the Douglas Bader film *Reach for the Sky*, starring Kenneth More. When Adam explained the story of the famed legless pilot Kazan remarked that they too had such a pilot during the war, a Hero of the Soviet Union.

'Yes, I think you are right on that one, wasn't his name Captain Medvedyev?' Adam asked.

'It's true! We made a film of his life also.'

'I know, I saw it back in Hungary. It was better than the one about Kirov,' said Adam provocatively.

'Yes, but Kirov was a more important comrade.'

'I suppose as a provincial party secretary he must have been,' Adam replied sarcastically.

Kazan did not deem Adam's comment worthy of a reply.

The hustle of a busy and dry weekend during the Blackpool illuminations is extraordinary by any standards, and the Russians soon got caught up in the carefree atmosphere of the place. They visited Madame Tussaud's waxworks, where Kazan was quite happy with the likeness of the newly installed Khrushchev. Outside, despite herself, Olga joined in the laughter of the large mechanical laughing man. Adam bought them candyfloss to eat and rock with the name Blackpool miraculously written through it, to take home. As they crossed over to the Promenade at the Tower, the small iron structure in the shape of the Eiffel in Paris, the policeman on duty in the middle of the road was directing the traffic and, like a good orchestral conductor, he was dignified but understated.

'Can I take a picture of him? I just love his helmet,' Rimma said.

'Of course you can, why not?' Adam reassured her.

The others wanted to take the same picture but Kazan interrupted, throwing his hands up.

'This could lead to a provocation, stop immediately! If Adam Nicholaievich asks permission and the policeman agrees then I agree too.' Adam stared in disbelief, but knowing the people's fear of the police only too well he was willing to play along for the moment. He walked over to the officer on duty.

'Officer, Officer! Please excuse me, but there are some Russian visitors over there.' He pointed over to the grey-suited bunch, each with the identical Leicas around their necks. 'They would like to take a photo of you, would you mind?'

'Not at all, not at all. So long as they don't blind me with the flashguns, tell 'em to shoot.'

Adam came back to the group. 'There is no problem – take your pictures.'

'Absolutely no!' Kazan yelled. 'This is sure to be a provocation! If you want photos, give your cameras to Adam Nicholaievich. He will take them.' Adam obliged, contemptuous of the man's innate stupidity, as he clicked away with one after another camera, thinking that his efforts would end up in several Russian family albums. When it came to Rimma's turn Adam insisted that she go across and stand by the policeman, who smoothed down his moustache and stuck his chest out, flattered by this attention from the lovely Russian girl.

As the early autumn dusk arrived, one by one the multicoloured illuminations came on, revealing characters from fairy tales. The connecting lights and small tableaux appeared on lamp-posts. In a few minutes the Golden Mile was ablaze.

'How many light bulbs are used for a display such as this?' Professor Shakalyov asked.

'Well, as an ex-Blackpoolian, or is it Blackpooler, I can tell you that. In excess of three hundred and fifty thousand, sir,' Adam answered with pride, as if the whole idea of the lights had been his alone.

They walked along the Promenade to catch a tram from the Blackpool Hydro Hotel on the north end. This way they could see everything. The coloured lights decorating the ordinary tram transformed it into a magic boat captained by a man dressed as Popeye. Olive Oyl was selling the tickets, which were once in a while inspected by Pluto, causing all sorts of commotion.

By the time they arrived at the South Promenade at the end of the ride the group were quiet and overawed. The vast, pulsating spectacle was an innocent piece of fun for all, especially the Russians, who could not fathom how the town council and the Chamber of Commerce together could finance such a show and financially benefit from it. It was now time to take a slow walk back to the bus.

As they walked along the pavement, Adam became tense and, brushing past Iosif, gently squeezed his upper arm. When their eyes met Adam nodded and whispered, 'Any moment now.' Outside the Tunnel of Love young couples, arms wrapped tightly around each other, were queuing along the pavement.

A large black Rover deluxe saloon with the engine running, facing south, was the only car at the end of the line of youngsters. As the group drew nearer the passenger door opened and at the same time a tall man on the blind side of the car started his six-millimetre camera running. The lamp-post above gave him more than adequate light. Adam gently elbowed Iosif from behind. He raised his arms and started his run towards the opening rear door.

'I request political asylum from the British government!' He yelled twice, closely followed by Adam, who was trying to hide his own face. He jumped in and slammed the door quickly. Not too far behind him Kazan was about to take off after them, but he was grabbed by an extremely powerful fellow, who very gently said: 'Come along now, sir. You could have had a serious accident running across the road like that.'

The black car turned left and disappeared towards Wharton aerodrome.

'Now, ladies and gentlemen, let me escort you back to your bus,' the big man said to the stunned group.

'This is kidnapping! Plain kidnapping!' Yelled Kazan.

'I am sure the film evidence will clear that up, sir,' the man said quietly.

'I demand to talk to the Embassy of the Union of Soviet Socialist Republics!'

'I am sure you do, sir, I am sure you do. I will arrange that for you, sir. Soon.'

∽

Adam was separated from Iosif at Wharton aerodrome and taken back to Clatterbridge Hospital in a police car. Fearing retribution against his family in Hungary, he was promised that his name would not appear when the news broke. The next day his belongings were delivered from the hotel. He found that they included a long-playing record of Prokofiev's 7th and 9th sonatas on the CCCP label, played by Richter. The dedication on the label said: *'Thank you for all your help. Come and visit us in my country. Love: Rimma.'*

Oh yes, Adam thought. I bet I would get a helluva welcome there right now!

∽

'Adam, what on earth were you doing on the nine o'clock news with that Russian defector last night?' Melanie asked on the telephone without saying hello.

'Oh my God, was I so recognisable?'

'Not really, with your face half covered, but you were obvious enough for someone who knows you. Mind you, I doubt if I do,' said Melanie coyly.

'Now you didn't really expect me to call you and say, I'll be assisting the defection of a Russian scientist, did you?'

'I suppose not. It was that mac of yours I first noticed as you and those Russians turned the corner. Anyway, I want to know all about it.'

'Melanie, I can't say more than what you saw. It's part of the deal.'

'God! You sound like a bloody spy! Adam, stop it.'

'Well, I might just tell you a little if you are a good girl,' Adam teased. 'So when are you coming to visit me? Because after this little escapade I doubt if I'll get any time off for quite a while.'

'I'll be there Friday afternoon, my darling, and I will be a good girl, promise.'

Adam put the receiver down and felt lonely lying in his room. He was pleased that Melanie was coming to see him. He didn't even mind discussing the wedding, if he had to. It came to him that after ten years it would be no bad idea to be in a home of his own, even if that meant marriage.

The following Friday Melanie duly arrived and booked herself in at a hotel near the hospital. As Adam could take only one evening off work a week he could not even get as far as Sudley Hall. The Thornton Hall Hotel was the pride of the picturesque village of Thornton Hough, in the middle of the leafy Wirral peninsula. A converted manor house with a good bar and even better kitchen, it was often frequented by the Clatterbridge doctors, especially after paydays.

Adam arrived first and decided to wait for Melanie at the bar, having a quiet drink with Allan Lewis, his friend and proud owner of the car Adam had used for his ill-fated driving test. Although Allan was quite a few years younger than Adam, he had a senior appointment as a second-year house officer in the Casualty Department. Coming as he did from an established and stable English family, there had been no need for him to change countries a couple of times or take up a brand-new language. With such advantage and not inconsiderable cerebration he had become a fully qualified doctor at the age of twenty-two. He also happened to have the best collection of classical and opera long-playing records, which he willingly lent to Adam to listen to while he waited for the next call from the wards.

The owner of Thornton Hall, Mr Wilbert Wright, a great friend of the doctors and a descendant of the flying ace of the same name, was on duty, and he knew the importance of the arrival. Adam did not have to wait long for the beckoning hand. By the time he got to the car Wilbert was carrying Melanie's suitcases across the car park, which was thick with multicoloured autumn leaves.

Melanie was busying herself with the front boot of her VW Beetle. She looked utterly up to date in her travelling outfit. The brown suede headband was virtually superfluous for her short bobbed hair. Her large olive eyes were exaggerated with heavy eye make-up, which contrasted with her pale face and lips coloured pale pink. The camel-hair half-belted coat, brown bell-bottomed trousers and platform-soled boots completed her outfit. The Age of Aquarius had obviously arrived at the Battersby-Smyths'.

She settled into Room 9 and Adam helped take her jacket off. The multicoloured blouse densely printed with white margaritas was skin tight.

'Mel, you look terrific. What is all this "mod" stuff?' The abbreviation passed his lips for the first time.

'Zeny, darling, one must move with the times.' She spun herself around. Adam put his arms around the slenderest of waists and gently pulled her to him. Their kiss was passionate enough, but it also reflected the inhibition of young lovers meeting after a prolonged break. They kissed again in a more relaxed way and Adam's hands moved downwards, following Melanie's perfect curves. He pushed her towards the bed.

'No chance, Adam, not until you've fed me.' She wriggled away. 'After eight hours on the road from Richmond Park, I need to have a shower first.'

'As I don't, can I help you with yours?' Adam wasn't giving up.

'All right, you can come and towel me down when I call you.'

From her tone Adam knew that there was no point in pushing the matter further, but he also knew that his time would come.

At dinner Adam told Melanie the story of his latest unfortunate attempt at gaining his driver's licence. Naturally, the part of the large-breasted Wendy was written out of the story. What did remain was just the game of football and an awful lot of drinking. He knew that the story lost something with his self-censorship, but there was no need to make cuts in the next one with the Russians, so he let loose.

Melanie could not, at first, understand why Adam accepted even the idea of helping a bunch of Russians. Adam spoke of the irony of it all and wanting to see their apologetic faces. He never thought there would be a defector, but when Iosif told him what he wanted to do, he just knew he had to help, 'just to rub a little salt in'.

'You should have heard Kazan's scared shouting when Iosif ran to the car.'

'I have, on TV. His face was a picture of utter fright.' She opened her eyes wide to give an impression. 'And you there, grinning with half of your face covered. It wasn't too difficult to know what was going through your mind. What happened to him?'

'That's classified!' Adam said in mock seriousness to camouflage the truth, which was exactly that.

'Nothing is "classified" from me, Adam!'

'Well, he wanted to get to America, but the way the big lads were talking he would never get there. The man has a vast knowledge of the Soviet Union's present nuclear capacity and what I think will happen to him is that he will be told that he will need to be debriefed before they will let him go and they will use the process to brainwash him to stay here.'

'That's disgusting!'

'Well, it may be, but by the time they've finished with him, he will be happy to have a new identity and a spacious office with a decent salary.'

'And the girl you mentioned on the phone? The one who left you the record.'

'Ah, Rimma, I don't know why she didn't jump – probably for some family reason. For a while she'll think she will be allowed to join him one day, then along will come an Oleg or an Ivan and it will be bye-bye, Iosif.'

'That's cruel, Adam, very cruel!'

'The Russians are the softest, nicest people on earth as individuals, but collectively all Slavs are vindictive and barbarous,' Adam answered with some exaggeration.

Melanie's concentration wandered for a moment, but when it returned it went straight to the point, changing the subject.

'Adam, darling, I thought we would also touch on the subject of us for a moment.'

'You are right, but you shouldn't have let me take off on the Russians, you know what I'm like. Well, I finish my job here soon and have a crack at part one of my psychiatry membership. That will take us to March two years hence. Then I'll get a job as a registrar, so would you like to be an April bride – in two years' time?'

'I couldn't imagine liking anything better, darling. Oh, to be an April bride – any April!' She grabbed Adam's legs with hers under the table.

⁓

After another Christmas at Sudley Hall Adam decided to apply for British naturalisation. He didn't even want to countenance the idea of travelling on his honeymoon on a refugee document. His security clearance was to be at the Hope Street police station in Liverpool. He was told to allow himself three hours for the interview.

He was relieved to see that next to a distinctly London-accented, tall, thin fellow sat Sergeant Hopkins of the Russian escapade.

After Adama was politely seated opposite the two and with the niceties over, the man from the capital pulled out his desk drawer and placed a four-inch-thick file marked Dr Adam Zenta in front of himself, which made Adam wonder what on earth could fill such a thick package.

The officer in charge went through Adam's life with ease. His only problems were the lengthy Transylvanian and Hungarian place names. On a couple of occasions, Adam did offer to read them for him, leaning over the table, but the plainclothes officer pulled the folder towards himself. Clearly Adam was not meant to read a word in the buff-coloured file, so he let the man struggle with such tongue-twisters as Nyárádszentlaszlo or Székesfehérvár. The officer thought that his life would be easier with the short ones like Pécs, but after Adam had corrected his pronunciation from Pecks to Pech a couple of times, the senior officer gave in and pushed the file over to Adam, carefully covering the rest of the page with blank papers. Having gone through Adam's life with a fine enough tooth comb, two hours later the man from London smiled as he picked up the final pages.

'Sergeant Hopkins. You did not mention Dr Zenta's help with the defection of the Russian scientist.'

'I was going to, sir, when you got to it, sir,' the sergeant replied.

'Well, go on, what happened?'

Having been quiet so far the sergeant took his chance with gusto and retold the Blackpool story so that Adam's participation was most favourably exaggerated. He even gave him full credit for the idea of filming the moment of the defection in order to have immediate visual evidence against a possible charge of kidnapping. The Londoner was impressed this time. He declared a ten-minute break and Adam was given a cup of tea, which was considerably superior to the hospital brews.

The lanky London officer left the room, taking his file with him, and the sergeant and Adam discussed the importance of the arrival of the new manager for Liverpool Football Club from Huddersfield. It was time for their team to regain its rightful place in the First Division and Mr Bill Shankly seemed to be the right man for the task.

The officer did not, in fact, return for half an hour, but when he did he was most serious.

'Dr Zenta, I have just spoken to my superiors and we will make a clear recommendation for an early and positive resolution of your application. And what I am about to say now is off the record. Would you, from time to time, do some favours for the Home Office?' He looked Adam straight in his face.

'Do you mean the secret services?' Adam asked outright, and saw his interviewer wince.

'You ask a plain question, Doctor. Yes, that is what I meant really.'

'Yes, I will do that,' Adam answered quietly.

The man from MI6 explained to Adam that he was not being asked to do any spying, for the moment, but rather to act as a very occasional 'go-between', and anyway probably nothing would come of it. He added that after Adam had taken his oath of allegiance and had received his naturalisation papers, he would have to learn the Official Secrets Act and sign it. Needless to say, he added, not one word of this was to be mentioned to László or Melanie or anyone at all.

'Even the sergeant hasn't heard a word of all this, have you, Sarge?' He smiled at Hopkins.

'Not a word, sir, not a word.'

Adam left the run-down police station at seven. He crossed Hope Street and looked at the board to see what was going on at the Phil, as it was affectionately known in the city. John Pritchard was about to conduct Wagner's *Tannhauser* overture, something from Albinoni he had never heard of and Debussy's *La Mer*. Sounds good enough for some contemplation, he thought. He bought himself a ticket for the upper circle.

~

Adam was pleased with the way he passed part one of the membership examination within the year he allocated for the purpose, and with his MD already behind him he was ready to try to get a job, perhaps out of the Liverpool area. He did love the city, which had been so good to him and where he had spent the fun years of his student days and later as a young and carefree doctor. He certainly wasn't going to miss the foul language and the dirty underclothes at the Casualty Department, nor the litter, nor the majority of Scousers, who were so adept at masking their ignorance with arrogance or aggression.

The recent decline of the port and the constant strikes in the car industry had produced a situation that also brought about the sudden decline of the once legendary airport at Speke. The picture was a far cry from the booming early sixties. Leaving the once great city like many others, Adam became an early member of the exodus, which later numbered over half of its population. This left a political void for the opportunist left, the Trotskyite Militant Tendency, which they gradually filled with ease.

When the letter came Adam did not need any persuading to accept the offer of the post of registrar at the Kent Mental Hospital, in spite of two similar jobs in Liverpool. One thing was certain; he knew he would miss his football at Anfield on alternate Saturdays.

When he broke the news to his best friends he found he was not alone. David Ahmed was going to get married to little Vi and take a surgical post in Canada. Gabor Racz, having already married his childhood sweetheart Enid, was to leave for America, and John Busby, wedded to Ann, was going back to his birthplace, Warwick. He already had a general-practice post lined up for him in his picturesque town. 'The Leaving of Liverpool' of an earlier generation was once again well under way.

Adam, having passed his driving test in due course, finished his period of notice, bought himself a second-hand yellow Ford Consul coupé with black vinyl top for £85, packed his belongings in the boot and the seats around him and slipped quietly out of the city for south London.

Melanie prepared a small top-floor flat in Half Moon Street in Mayfair for him, which was to be his home for the shortest period of time. Until the wedding.

~

The junior registrar's post in psychiatry at the Kent Mental Hospital was a hard job to fill for the inexperienced appointee. He was third in line after the consultant and the senior registrar. His boss, Dr Albert Porter, was a giant of a man. Built like the proverbial brick outhouse, bold, with a Karl Marx beard, he looked anachronistic and overwhelming. Attentive to patients as if his time with them was unlimited, he had the patience of a sliding elevator door for his long-suffering staff, seeming hell bent on turning them all into new patients of his units.

'You, with your bloody accent, and they with their advanced lunacy have no chance of getting on together, which is probably just as well,' was his welcome to Adam on Monday morning.

But Adam soon saw through him. The old 'alternate hot and cold water treatment' was nothing new to him, after the commie headmaster of his later teens. One thing was for sure, he thought – the harder they appeared, the more easily they bent. Adam was willing to play along, knowing that his time was certain to come.

'Zenta, you are a central European, coming from the cradle of psychiatry. Are you a Freud or an Adler man?' Porter interrogated him, looking him in the eye.

'Both of them and many others, but my favourite is Viktor Frankl. After all, we Hungarians should stick together.'

'I suppose he was a good exponent of logotherapeutics but he dragged in irrelevancies. Have you read his *Man's Search for Meaning?*'

'I used it for my MD thesis and in my primary too, sir. I am a believer in his theory that life holds a potential meaning under any conditions, even the most miserable ones.'

'Not much relevance to a bunch of teenagers locked up permanently, screwing each other, but you might find something useful in it for Unit Q. You will be in charge. I hope it will change your life. You seem to be good at theorising. Well, we will see.' He turned away.

Adam, having thought 'theorising' was an essential part of his vocation, was a little surprised at the remark, but decided to bide his time on the principle that those who are given to should not ask for a choice.

Unit Q comprised two old-fashioned hospital wards leading off each side of a central corridor. Designed in the days of unenlightened psychiatric practices, they were pure bedlam. The two long rooms of young male and female patients, some thirty-six in each, included totally uncontrollable epileptics, spastics and pathetic little autistics, and were regarded by all with general disdain.

On his first overnight duty Adam realised what Dr Porter had meant about the miserable and the unfortunate in constant battle with the ever-increasing output of their hormones. Unable to comprehend what was happening in their circulation, the fit and the strong would find their way to the flat roof for sex.

The most active groups were the phenobarbitone-resistant epileptics, who appeared to have the most insatiable appetite for copulation, whenever they were not having a fit.

Night Sister Appleby was an understanding and, in her private life, puritanical Welsh woman who took it upon herself to explain to Adam the rules and regulations of the wards. What he had to face in clinical practice had, of course, nothing to do with the fashionable fundamentals of psychoanalysis, but he was at the sharp end of learning the art of his new vocation. Doctors accepted that this was their baptism of fire.

No self-respecting junior would call out his off-duty superiors, especially if he had the shortest of all fuses, like Dr Porter. So Adam learned, like all good juniors do, from the sisters and staff nurses. Their pragmatic if not always sympathetic approach to patient care was based on sheer practicality, a product of their ever-shrinking funding.

Adam's first object was to get to know his new patients; most difficult because they either could not or would not talk much. Having no insight into their conditions, they were of little help to themselves. He dealt with the medical manifestations of their basic condition and worked out a schedule of assessing each of them individually and regularly. He planned this to take place weekly; the deeper he got involved the longer it took, which inevitably slowed him down.

By the end of the year Adam had published two papers in the *Journal of Psychiatry*, which gave his name an airing in the profession, to the delight of all the staff, with the exception of Dr Porter. The consultant considered Adam's unconventional approach meddling in things he knew little about. Adam had virtually no private life outside the hospital. One weekend in six he spent in his dingy flat in Half Moon Street, usually writing, but he did insist one Friday night on a recital in the Royal Festival Hall, when his hero, the pianist Gyorgy Cziffra, paid one of his infrequent visits to England. The abused artist of pre-1956 Hungary had the all lights lowered in the renowned hall except for a spotlight on the Steinway and himself.

He opened robustly with Liszt's *'Hungarian Rhapsody No. 2'*, which received prolonged applause. His interpretation of Chopin was perhaps not as sensitive as Rubinstein's but it was idiosyncratic enough for a few eyes to open in surprise. His Debussy was well thought out, reflecting his wish to become a naturalised citizen of the Fourth Republic of France. Saving the best for last was obviously the artist's wish for the evening as he concluded with Liszt's *Grand Gallop Chromatique*, which was considered virtually unplayable by the average concert pianist. The whole concert was a triumph for both artist and audience, but not for the newspaper critics, who kept on worrying about the subdued lights and considered the whole thing more suitable for a piano bar. Adam knew of Cziffra's wilderness days when he had been forbidden by the

SSA to play in concert halls and been forced to earn his living as a nightclub pianist in a dive called the Poppy in Budapest. He wondered about the critics' self-proclaimed professionalism.

~

Sir Paul and Lady Felicity Battersby-Smyth request the pleasure of your company for the Wedding of their only daughter Melanie to Doctor Adam Zenta de Lemhény, in Bodelwyddan Church at 11 a.m. on Saturday, 2nd April 1966, and afterwards to a Reception and Grand Ball at Sudley Hall.

Dress Formal. Carriages after Breakfast. RSVP Sudley Hall.

The invitation went out to two hundred and thirteen people. Two hundred to friends of the bride, nine to Adam's friends and their wives. The rest were sent to the Zenta family in Hungary, as a memento.

These invitations for Hungary were the usual courtesy ones that kept flowing into that unhappy land from the West as the young refugees started to marry in their new countries. There were seldom any acceptances.

Adam was given a long weekend off for the wedding and a week for his honeymoon in Nice. Off-season, he could just about afford the hotel. As Melanie didn't want Adam to see her preparations for the big day, the Thornton Hall Hotel once again became the staging post. Adam arrived late Friday afternoon. Some guests were already booked in.

He joined his friends for dinner, where they reminisced about the past few years they had spent together, and in order 'to look their best for tomorrow' the wives left the dining table after coffee, leaving the men to go to the bar to have a drink in lieu of Adam's stag night. The whole thing was most orderly and by one o'clock Adam found himself in bed – alone.

⁓

The hired morning suits fitted Adam and his best man John perfectly. The two friends sat patiently in the front pew of the white stone church. Through the pretty stained-glass windows the sun made several good attempts to illuminate them. With twenty minutes to go the small church was full to capacity. The various groups were clearly distinguishable. The Battersby-Smyths, right of the aisle, in conservative dark morning suits, and their ladies, equally subdued, in dresses with matching hats. The other first row comfortably contained Adam's nine remaining friends after John's elevation to best man. There was an empty row behind them, just in case – the ushers thought – anyone else turned up for him. From the third row onward the bride's side's overspills occupied the rest of the church. Their ever-enlarging group contained Melanie's school friends and their partners. With millinery creations befitting Ladies' Day at Ascot and flowers on their short dresses and skirts, some of which were clearly in the micro league, the girls were a reflection of the new age. Most lower legs having disappeared into knee-length shiny plastic boots, some with enormous platform soles, there remained acres of pleasing thigh to delight their escorts, who were turned out in the lightest of grey morning suits. It was as if a part of the Southport Flower Show had been recreated in one corner of God's house, Adam thought.

For the next fifteen minutes or so he was the centre of female attention as he stood before them, occasionally turning around to see some of the arrivals and so displaying a virtually perfect profile and a playful smile. The women's appreciative looks were undisguised as they sized up the shapely, mature man whose gently curving chestnut-brown hair was fashionably cut, slightly longer than usual. His broad shoulders were well displayed by the Moss Bros. suit, whose tails made him look taller than his six foot. For a few more minutes the show belonged to him.

The black Rolls-Royce carrying the bride and her baronet father was only three minutes late, but it took Melanie some time to get out of the rear seat of the vintage car. Another minute or so was taken up by arranging her six-yard train. She looked in a small hand mirror held for her by one of the four bridesmaids, then nodded. Sir Paul, in his well-worn morning suit, sporting an extra-large pink carnation, looked handsome, proud and relieved. He extended his right arm and Melanie placed her left hand on his. They both looked up, Sir Paul whispered something reassuring to his daughter, a steward gave a thumbs-up sign and the organist hit the keyboard with the first chord of Mendelssohn's Wedding March, the most enduring offering to marital bliss for everyone. Heads turned as one. The two men at the altar looked straight ahead.

Melanie was dressed in pure white. The traditionally cut dress had a high neck, long sleeves and a simple, perfectly fitted bodice. Plain in the front, the skirt at the back of the pure silk dress was supported by a number of gathered petticoats extending well under the lace train. The veil was held firmly by a small tiara and, falling in front of Melanie's face, it accentuated the intentional paleness of her make-up, which had taken over an hour to achieve. The bridesmaids and her young nephew, Alastair, the only pageboy, were dressed in cream-coloured Victorian period costumes. The procession walked slowly and elegantly along the aisle. When it reached the halfway point Adam nudged an elbow into John's side and told him it was time they turned around.

Adam could hardly believe his eyes. He was treated to a vision of total beauty walking in his direction. The picture had a dreamlike lightness, and when their eyes met he was enchanted and wanted to reach out, but by then she was standing next to him. That moment he felt he was in heaven.

From then on Adam remembered nothing but the perfect oval face covered by lace. His next conscious recollection was receiving a congratulatory handshake from John outside. He suddenly realised he was a married man.

The fleet of four Rolls-Royces carrying the family was followed by a cavalcade of cars. Triumphs, Jaguars, an Alvis, a couple of Aston Martins, a Cobra and dozens of Morrises and Austins took to the road for the short ride back to Sudley Hall.

The marquee on the main lawn to the left of the oak-lined driveway looked almost as impressive as the Hall itself. Sir Paul, Lady Felicity and Dr and Mrs Zenta lined up at the entrance to receive their guests. It began quite seriously, but as the colourful miniskirted bunch arrived to offer their congratulations the tone of the proceedings changed. There were shouts of 'Melanie, where did you find him?' and 'Has he got a brother?' One micro-skirted friend told Adam that she wanted to be psychoanalysed by him – immediately. Melanie's frustrated jealousy was masked by a constant smile. She looked at her classmate. 'I am sorry and I know you could do with it, but Adam's appointments are all with me – for ever.'

The wedding breakfast of smoked salmon followed by guinea fowl was served with Pouilly Montrachet and Gevrey Chambertin. When it came to the toast the 1956 vintage Lanson was equally palatable. Sir Paul, toasting the couple, declared that it was his and Felicity's pleasure to give the couple their wedding present now: the deeds to a flat in Ovington Square in London. Adam was astonished. He knew the family was reasonably well off but he considered it awesome to receive so generous a present. He looked at Melanie questioningly; she leaned over to him and whispered, 'Poppa just received a huge cheque from Lloyds.'

Melanie did not change for the evening. She returned in her magnificent gown with the train detached, and when the reduced section of the Welsh Guards Band struck up, it gave Adam, by now in white tie and tails, a good chance to show how a real Viennese waltz was spun. The evening activities continued into the night. Adam danced with the bridesmaids and with some of Melanie's friends. As he returned one of them to her seat, she asked Adam whether she could introduce him to a couple who were distantly related to her. Adam was, of course, delighted to make the acquaintance of Ian and Tracy Stuart.

25

Marriage

The celebrations went on into the early hours. By four o'clock the majority of relatives had disappeared, leaving the hard core of revellers to carry on until breakfast. After the delicious bacon and eggs had been devoured, Melanie and Adam changed into their travelling clothes. Adam turned up in his brand-new blazer, sporting his medical school badge; Melanie was in a fashionably short green suit and a matching pillbox hat. They received a round of applause. Gareth was ready with the Jaguar, fully kitted out with the 'Just Married' paraphernalia, to drive them to Speke Airport in Liverpool, to catch the Starways flight to Nice.

As they drove along the cobblestones they waved to their friends, who lined up along both sides of the driveway. Adam looked to the right and caught sight of a tall, elegant woman in a shocking-pink satin gown. Her perfectly shaped pale face was crowned with a cascade of wavy blond hair which fell to rest on her shoulder. He waved to Tracy Stuart and turned towards his new wife. His expression was drawn and serious. Melanie held his hand and said, 'Darling, you look so tired.' She placed her head on Adam's shoulder. 'Oh, I love you so!'

'Adam, Adam, Zany, darling, yes, yes, yes, I just had my first orgasm!!! Oh, I just had sex for the first time, isn't it unbelievable!? Oh, Adam, thank you for that, I'm a woman at last, I can't believe it.' Melanie jumped out of bed on the last day of their honeymoon. It was early afternoon and the sun threw shadows over her breasts as she jumped up and down in the small bedroom.

'Well then, you should come back for more,' Adam pleaded as he stretched out in the bed.

'Oh, I want to treasure this feeling for ever – Adam, it's like your whole body is churning inside you and you want to continue to quiver and shiver, it's fantastic!' She sat on the bed and took his hand. 'What does actually happen in your body when you "climax"?'

'Mel, the physiology of orgasm is usually glossed over in the textbooks, but principally your tensions are created by the arousal blood flow around the orgasmic crescent, which is between the clitoris and the urethral opening. They are released by my stimulating an area around the front wall of the vagina, the so-called G spot, and if I then can trap your clitoris with my pubic bone at the same time, you virtually shouldn't have to do anything. This combination should send a message to your brain to produce a parasympathetic response, creating a conflict in the plexus of nerves, which – in turn – produces a uterine contraction and a little of the isotonic fluid content of the uterus is expelled on to the posterior wall of the vagina – will that do?' Adam smiled, watching Melanie's reaction.

'That sounds like technical gobbledegook to me. It's so much nicer than all that – will it happen every time now?'

'I doubt it, Mel, it will depend on how relaxed you are and how much you concentrate – how much I concentrate, I suppose. We'll do our best, eh?'

'I am just delighted that it happened.'

'That's what honeymoons are for, no?'

'Yes, but you have no idea how much I had to listen to about it from the other girls at college, and I'm sure half of them faked it.' Melanie could hardly stop talking about her new-found experience, which – she considered – had changed her life for ever.

On return they moved into the superbly styled Ovington Square flat, which was the result of a judicious conversion of a Victorian house around the old drawing room. It gave them an elegant living room, a rather small kitchen, with access to the patio garden, and two bedrooms. It was a mere stone's throw from Harrods and the exciting eating houses of Beauchamp Place, and was perfectly situated for the young couple, who wanted to be part of the new London scene.

They had hardly settled in when the telephone rang.

'Dr Zenta?' The voice was curt.

'Yes, who is it, please?'

'I am about fifty, slightly balding with a little extra weight – well, perhaps forget the word "little". I will wear a camel coat and carry a black briefcase. Would you please meet me at seven in Tattersalls – you know, it's next to number one Knightsbridge. I'll be around the back end. I know what you look like.' He put the phone down before Adam could insist on a name.

'Who was that, Zeny?' Melanie asked.

'The hospital wants me to admit a new patient, Mel,' Adam lied. 'Albert Porter offered my services. Wasn't that nice of him?'

'That reminds me, we must invite him for dinner. Mother said it was important.'

'One day, Mel, we should have a few real friends in first.' He walked out of the flat.

Adam was amazed that in less than a year the SIS should want his services. He drove around the corner, parked his car and walked through the lounge, noticing his contact immediately.

The rotund man rose and beckoned Adam to an empty seat.

'For the sake of this conversation, Doctor, please call me *Arthur*. I am your case officer and naturally that is not my real name. I would have changed it if it were. The reason for my asking you to see me is to take you to an office to sign the Official Secrets Act. There you will be briefed about a situation which has suddenly cropped up. So let's have a quick Scotch and I'll drive you there. How long is your alibi with your wife good for?'

'Unfortunately long enough, I told her I had to admit a case from Bromley.'

'That's good, very good, Doctor.'

Arthur was quite an agreeable chap, Adam thought, so they drank their miserable measure of whisky and Adam was taken to the Embankment office of what he believed to be the Ministry of Defence. He was given a lengthy document to read and the clerk left the room. Adam paged through the flimsy leaves and a few seconds after he had read it completely, three people walked in. The clerk asked him whether he was happy with what he had read. When he agreed Adam was asked to sign it, which he did with the gold Parker pen he had used not so long ago for his membership exam. The two others witnessed the signature and left the room. Arthur walked in.

'Well done, Doctor. I will put you in the picture about something which, if my information about you is correct, you might even enjoy.'

'Yes?' Adam looked at him with interest.

Arthur started by explaining that basically all he had to do was to make a delivery of a psychiatric textbook and come back with a small package. 'Bit of a dead drop or brush contact, if you don't mind. You are familiar with our dreadful jargon? It means just a little "postman's job", that's all.'

'Yes, but you omitted to say where this great act of espionage would take place.' Adam was a shade sarcastic.

'Quite, Doctor – in Hungary, of course. Have we really not mentioned that?'

'No, you certainly have not and you can forget it. Do you really want me to walk into Hungary with my past? I wouldn't last five minutes.'

'That's where you are wrong!' Arthur went on to explain to the surprised Adam that he had a few more cards up his sleeve. He spoke of the recently announced amnesty for minor misdemeanours during the uprising and said that he considered Adam to qualify. Adam argued that arresting the county head of the secret police was hardly a minor act, but Arthur offered to call the Foreign Office to clarify the amnesty. When the third secretary confirmed its existence, he also added that it had not yet been tried out and the FO would love it if Adam would be a 'test case'. Adam was about to walk out on them when Arthur asked him to listen a little more.

'As you know, 1966 is football World Cup year. Hungary is in it and the authorities would not jeopardise anything. Besides, football itself would be your cover. Liverpool FC is about to play a European game, against Budapest Honvéd. It is all arranged for you to go as part of the staff, as official interpreter. The GCHQ ciphered the book you will be taking.' He was getting carried away.

'It is obviously for an asset. Are you sure you can trust him? I know you had most of them blown by Philby and Co. Over forty of them were liquidated. I can imagine half a dozen easier ways to get the book there, including the diplomatic bag.' Adam played hard to get, though he was getting excited by the idea of visiting home for the first time in ten years. It would be even better if he could cock a snook at the commies. 'I'll do it provided I am satisfied with the whole set-up.'

'You will be, I am sure of that.' Arthur smiled for the first time. 'Since we lost all of our operators, as you have just mentioned, we are keen to establish others. There's a fair crop of new dissidents there with wonderful samizdat publications. One of them is of particular interest to us. He is an architect, a good family man, much respected even by the communist government. We must recruit him.'

'What's his name?'

'Andre Tóth.'

'What? I don't believe it!' Adam was delighted. 'He was one of my best friends in college, we still correspond and I am godfather to his son. I don't believe it.'

'We picked the whole idea from your security clearance in Liverpool, when you mentioned him to Inspector Brown. You see, we did do our homework.'

'You certainly did. At least you can be sure he is no double agent, that man is as straight as a die. He works for a very large state architectural firm at the top end of Váci Street, in the centre of Budapest.'

'Precisely. It gives him great cover to meet people. What we want him to do is to collate and dispatch. It is most important for us to know what's going on there and how much is tolerated by the government. I am sure you see that, Doctor.'

'You know, I have really enjoyed coming here to talk to you people about my family and friends, it's so comforting. Can I bring my wife next time?'

'OK, Doctor, don't be sarcastic – but we will surprise you from time to time.'

'I am sure you will. What is the set-up?'

Arthur explained to Adam that one of the directors of Liverpool FC had Police Committee connections, had been approached by MI6 and had agreed to help. A letter of invitation would come soon, appearing as normal as possible, asking Adam to help with the interpreting. Dr Porter would agree so that he could take a long weekend off. That was also arranged. Needless to say, Melanie could not be involved in any way at all, as per the Official Secrets Act. Adam would take delivery of the coded book. He would, however, have to contact his friend himself and perhaps ask him to come to see the game, where it would be easy to arrange the swap. It sounded perfectly simple.

Adam insisted that the idea of a psychiatric book seemed ridiculous, and an architectural publication would be a much better proposition. Arthur picked up the phone and arranged it with GCHQ, just in time.

Arthur personally drove him back to his car, and when he got out of the Rover he wondered what on earth he'd let himself in for. Yet the potential excitement was too much, and anyway, there was no way of getting out of things honourably. He mumbled something about a headache and went to bed, missing his favourite TV programme, *That Was The Week That Was*. Within a week Adam's trip was fully prepared. Albert Porter, to his great surprise, was more or less affable when he agreed to his time off. By Wednesday he was reading a letter of invitation from the secretary of Liverpool Football Club, Paul Morrison, for a day trip 'to arrange the two legs' of the first ever eastern European trip of the famous club. The 'Anfield Machine' was, by now, under the management of Bill Shankly, the gritty Scot from Huddersfield, who, soon after his arrival, became an instant success in the city.

Adam did not mention the trip to Melanie, just kissed her goodbye. She said she was so happy just having Adam to herself, and in her contentment she decided to rearrange the furniture in the comfortable flat, for the third time in two weeks.

Having left his car in a side street by Euston, Adam boarded the 8.05 to Liverpool Lime Street and went straight to the restaurant coach for a hearty bacon-and-eggs breakfast. On the stroke of midday he got into a cab. As he was driven along Great Homer Street he felt delighted to see his old city, in spite of the riot of weeds along the kerbs and intersections.

Paul Morrison, a tall, slim, slightly balding man with good intelligent features and a friendly manner, was Adam's age. Urbane, in a very well-cut suit, he was not Adam's preconceived 'arranger of games' for the most obvious reason. Already considered the best of his ilk, he was destined for an illustrious career at the club. The men shook hands. Morrison wanted to waste no time.

'Let's join Mr Shankly and the team for lunch. They have just arrived from Melwood, our training ground.'

'Ah, Melwood, I used to go to watch them training in my student days.'

Morrison looked at Adam with a mixture of surprise and curiosity. 'So, you are a supporter?' He asked.

'As fanatical as any Koppite!' Adam smiled.

The team, which was about to make such an impact on the European scene, were settling down to their eight-ounce steaks, with all the usual embellishments. The men walked across to a corner table. Adam felt strange among all the players whom he knew so well without their having the slightest notion of his existence. He only wished he was coming here as a prospective signing for the number-one jersey, but that was the deserved property of Tommy Lawrence. None the less he gleefully noticed that some of the players were whispering to each other about his identity.

Mr Shankly welcomed Adam loudly enough for the others to hear and gave him a letter in Hungarian, from the director of Budapest Honvéd FC.

'Yer see, Doc, I can't understand their stupidity,' said Shanks, his eyes growing wider with each word. 'How do they expect a Scotsman to read a letter in Magyar? I could work out the two dates, and they are no good for us. I wish the UEFA would sort their mess out, once and for all.'

Adam glanced at the shortish letter.

Flames of Straw

'Well, Mr Shankly ...'

'Call me Boss, Doc,' the great man interrupted.

'Well, Boss, let me telephone them right away, let's see what I can do.' Adam's offer facilitated the consumption of their steaks and they were about to leave when the Boss stood up.

'Team, I want to introduce to you a doctor from Hungary, which once had the greatest team the world has ever known. My idols, Kocsis, Puskás and Hidegkúti, played in it. He is going to be our interpreter for the games. I want you to pay attention to this man, who was once a coal miner in Yorkshire. He doesn't mind if his hands get dirty, unlike some of you this morning. You will all get to know him on the trip, but meanwhile you'd better sort yourselves out or you will be annihilated by that no-good Leicester City tomorrow.'

Adam felt like shrinking into invisibility, but knowing the Boss's style from the press he smiled at the team as he followed the small man with the dark red shirt and the lighter red tie out of the room.

Two hours later Adam was still talking, by now to the third official of the Budapest club. At the other end decision-making was passed from one person to another, all suspecting some unknown advantage to Liverpool in the proposed dates. Another hour and a half produced agreement and Adam was congratulated by the secretary and the Boss.

'Well done, Doc! Paul, this is the sort of man we wanted for this trip, I am glad you found him.' Turning to Adam he said, 'I hope you will bring your father to the game, even he is a Honvéd supporter.' The Boss was out of the room before Adam could thank him for the idea.

The efficient Paul Morrison had a taxi waiting for Adam to take him back to the station. It was just past midnight when he slipped into bed next to Melanie. She murmured something and kissed Adam's forehead as he put his arm around her. It took him another hour to fall asleep.

～

'Melanie, darling, I want to tell you something.' Adam decided it was time to say something after the new BBC 2 programme, *Match of The Day*, classically commentated by Kenneth Wolstenholme.

'What, darling?' Melanie yawned.

Adam explained what had happened in the loosest possible way, saying that he had accepted the idea as it was only a short, three-day trip. Melanie looked up angrily.

'Adam, I don't understand why you want to leave me for three days! You've always told me that you never wanted to have anything to do with them, then you are helping some stupid Russians and now this. Is it safe, Adam?'

He admitted to himself that it was too close to call and took her face in his hands, going though the whole rigmarole of the arrangements to convince her. He told her everything except the bit about carrying the two copies of the *Architectural Review*. Within an hour Melanie had surrendered.

⁓

Leaving thousands of supporters behind in the terminal building at Liverpool's Speke Airport, the Liverpool Football Club party took off in the Aer Lingus special. For every one of them Hungary was to be a new experience. The Iron Curtain, though a little rustier than before, was still a formidable barrier in every sense of the word, even to sportsmen and athletes. Basically nobody liked the idea of going but it was the manager's job to try to inject some enthusiasm into the dull flight.

The Boss went down the aisle to talk to the players about the two cities uniting into Budapest and how many great footballers they had produced, but he kept emphasising that those days had gone and they had nothing to fear. 'You'll marmalise 'em!'

Adam was seated in the window seat next to two experienced football journalists, Bob Azurdia and John Beith, who knew a lot about the conditions in Budapest, having covered many international games. Talking to Adam, John soon realised that there was another story on the plane beside the obvious footballing one and remarked, in jest, that he would keep a camera focused on Adam, 'just in case'. He also said that he considered him rather foolish to 'test the amnesty'. Adam carefully restrained himself and just waffled away about homesickness. John then asked him to be careful of what he said in his hotel room when talking to his father as – if one thing was sure – it would be bugged. Adam managed to fake a look of surprise and Bob proceeded to explain to him how easy it was to prove the presence of the tiny listening devices. Turning to John, a small man with the sharpest of pens, he asked him to play a part in the trick they had used before, just for the fun of it. He agreed.

When they landed, and as Adam walked down the steps of the flight to the waiting grey bus, which was flanked by two frontier guards in battle fatigues and carrying oversized Kalashnikovs, he was scared but reluctant to admit it to himself. As the spirited party was fooling about he felt totally lonely and started to question his own sanity. He managed a faint smile in the direction of the guard, which was not reciprocated. In the arrival area he collected the passports and beckoned the large group to a special gate situated next to the diplomatic channel. A young corporal, wearing the light green lapel of the Frontier Security Corps and sitting behind a high desk sheltered by inch-thick glass, called his superior. The major, a well-proportioned middle-aged woman in a white blouse with green epaulettes, looked at Adam.

'I am Dr Zenta, the interpreter for the party.'

'We know who you are, Doctor, and quite honestly don't understand the need for you, since we all speak English and have a number of official interpreters, one of whom will in any case be allocated to your group,' she said nonchalantly.

'I suppose they felt more comfortable with their standard practice,' Adam said, handing over the bunch of navy blue British passports, amongst them his, the only one without a stamp in it – always a cause of suspicion in countries that have a special fascination with rubber stamps. He was glad the major's emphasis was on the word 'official' and not on the 'we know'. They were ushered through immediately, which the club officials put down to Adam's efficiency. The 'Ikarusz' coach, the pride of the Hungarian automotive industry, was soon full of the confident team and their retinue. The journey to the hotel along Üllői Road created little interest for the team until Adam pointed to Ferencváros FC's new green-and-white-painted stadium. Roger Hunt – who had already been dubbed 'Sir Roger' by twelve thousand yelling voices at the Kop – quietly remarked that the rest of the city 'could also do with a lick of paint'.

The large wicker cases containing the team's kit and an ample supply of beefsteaks, milk and other basic cooking ingredients, just in case the local food caused some stomach upsets, were unloaded with great speed, and Adam stood by the reception desk of the Gellért Hotel – second to none in the group of 'grand hotels' of the world – to check in his charges. The receptionist was well briefed. Room allocation completed, they agreed to meet in half an hour for tea. Adam's room was on the end of the third-floor corridor, number 354.

By the time he had returned to the ornate foyer the two journalists were waiting for him. John asked Adam to watch what they were about to do.

'My name is Mr Azurdia, in Room 204 overlooking the road, and I am an insomniac. This is Mr Beith, in a very quiet room, of 274, at the back of the building. He wouldn't mind changing with me. Would you please alter things in your records?' He asked with a smile.

'Sure,' the receptionist answered with a slight American twang, and went ahead, scribbling a note of the changes with her sharply pointed pencil.

Bob and John both looked at Adam.

'Now you ask for the same. Colin Doors of the *Daily Mail* will oblige. He knows what we are doing'

Adam spoke to the receptionist.

'I have a problem with my room,' he said, in his obviously perfect Hungarian. 'I would like to be nearer to Mr Shankly, whose interpreter I am. My room seems too far away. Mr Doors does not mind an exchange.' .

'Certainly, sir.' She looked down at her ledger as Adam handed over his keys. Then she looked up at him; her face was a light shade of crimson.

'Er, well, there seems to be a problem. Your allocation designates Room 354 for your stay. Why is there a problem with it?' She tried to sound helpful.

'No problem at all, except I want the room next to Mr Shankly. Anyway, you just arranged an exchange for those two gentlemen a minute ago.' Adam pointed to the two chatting journalists. 'Can I speak with the manager, please?'

After a while the manager arrived, and first of all he too reassured Adam that he could have any room he fancied, until his attention was drawn to the red mark in the ledger. He took a deep breath.

'Dr Zenta, can I have a word with you, please.' He left the reception desk and took Adam's arm, ushering him to the far corner. 'Doctor, you have lived in Hungary,' he whispered. 'If I say your room must be 354, you know why, don't you.'

Adam nodded with a wry smile.

'And by the way, the man behind me, sitting by the yucca plant, is also yours, a part of your package.' The manager sounded as if he could not have cared less.

Adam turned around to see his shadow, who looked like somebody out of *The Third Man* – wide-brimmed hat, leather overcoat with collar turned up and a cigarette in his tobacco-stained fingers. He could not have been more obvious.

As Adam turned away to walk to Room 354 he noticed the smiling journalists. The room was at the very end of the third-floor corridor, next to the chambermaid's storage cupboard. It was more than adequate, but with a faint smell of staleness. He unpacked his suitcase and was about to make the two telephone calls to Nicholas and Andre Tóth to confirm his arrival. His sense of fun in full flow, he thought he ought to talk to the Counter Intelligence Department of the Ministry of the Interior first.

'Good afternoon, comrades! Microphone testing: one, two, three, four. I am Dr Adam Zenta, as you know, and this is just to tell you that I take this room to be under full surveillance and I will not engage in any duplicitous activity in or out of it. I will now make two telephone calls. One to my father on Jonk 44 and another one to my friend on Budapest 34 34 88 to invite them both to the football match tomorrow as my and Liverpool FC's guests. I take it that you do know about the game? When I have talked to them, you will find me right behind the manager, Mr Shankly. You see, I am here as his personal interpreter. I have no intention of causing any damage that might lead to the overthrow of the People's Republic. So you see, you might as well give your chap in the chambermaid's cupboard a day off, and if he makes himself known to me tomorrow, I'll get him a ticket too. A very good evening to you all, comrades. Over and out!' Adam was very careful not to mention the chap in the hotel lobby. That would have been too humiliating, he thought. Telephone calls completed with meetings arranged, he did go to see Bill Shankly, and in the company of some of his staff they addressed themselves to the sensitive problem of cooking dinner for the team. The manager's instructions were unequivocal. Medium-rare fillets, using the meat brought from England for the players. He could not care less what the officials were to eat from the menu. Local bread or cakes were all right but all the tea had to be made with English pasteurised milk. Bacon and eggs for breakfast were once again to be made from the club's stock of provisions, as was also the light lunch. Supper after the game was to be a free-for-all and a trip to a nightclub later was a possibility.

The all-important pre-match-day dinner with the leadership of Budapest Honvéd FC was the social highlight of the fixture. These events were hosted by the home club at their favourite restaurant. The bus delivered the directors of LFC to a most picturesque restaurant, the Golden Barrel, where the Gypsy Band of Lakatos Jr was fiddling away with great gusto. Pálinka was offered and taken, after Adam gave the OK with an affirmative nod, and they settled opposite each other along a long table covered with best Hungarian embroidery and plenty of wine in carafes. The jovial dinner of clear chicken soup, veal goulash with dumplings followed by the heaviest of all puddings, walnut-stuffed pancakes in chocolate sauce, was washed down with an unending supply of the best wines of the land. The chairman host addressed the directors of LFC and Adam standing next to him faithfully translated his enthusiastic welcome. He offered his toast to ever-developing international sporting links.

The very large Mr Roach, a senior director of Liverpool, sitting on the other side of Adam, stood up and gratefully accepted the 'fine words' of his counterpart. He then proceeded to tell a 'couple of stories', the first of which Adam just about managed to render into Magyar. When he started the next one, cigar still perched in his mouth, Adam realised that he was up against a pun, the double meaning of which would be totally lost in translation. Having had a few drinks himself, he quickly replaced the joke with one about the English, Scottish and Irish Foreign Legion officers to be executed by guillotine. The first two, having received the customary reprieve after the malfunction of the French gadget, were followed by the Irishman, who, looking upwards at the mighty blade, 'spotted the problem, sir' and advised them how to fix it; a new story for the Hungarians, who exploded in laughter. Mr Roach looked well pleased. Adam suddenly understood why he had had to spend all those indecisive hours on the telephone, and one of the party even confirmed it: 'Nobody opens his mouth out of turn here!'

Mr Roach ended his contribution to the evening by proposing the loyal toast, cigar still firmly perched in his mouth. After they had drunk to the health of the Queen, Adam asked the host chairman on his left if he would now like to toast the chairman of the Presidium of the People's Republic. By now totally drunk, the stocky chap performed the greatest act of bravery of his life in the Nomenklatura. 'No bloody way, Doc, he's just a drunken cowardly sod,' he whispered.

The evening was completed in a very dark bar in the Citadel, a bastion just behind the hotel, where after a few more pálinkas, and after one of them had fallen off his small bar stool, the LFC directors declared the evening a roaring success for international sport. It was time for them to get into the small bus for the two-minute ride back to the hotel. Adam, having drunk one for one with the rest, entered his bedroom and decided to make contact with the comrades again. In a loud and drunken voice he greeted them. 'Good evening, comrades, microphone testing, one, two, three. Are you receiving me loud and clear?' As he fell into bed smiling to himself, he had an idea.

Adam knew there was no chance of much sleep during the night. He kept thinking about seeing his father again, after ten years. Then his mind would drift to the passing on of the copies of the architectural magazines packed carefully int a plastic bag for his friend. He wondered how on earth Andre had been recruited by MI6 and what was the nature of his old school friend's information-gathering. It felt reassuring to him, even in the middle of the night, that he was not the only idiot to get involved in the mire. He fell asleep way after half past three, and it felt like only minutes later when he received his wake-up call.

After breakfast Adam went down to the lobby to find Nicholas standing by one of the sofas. He ran to his father, who still cut a fine figure with his tall but slightly gaunt appearance, and the two men embraced in tears. The man in the large-brimmed hat and overcoat sitting in the corner observed the scene and had to admit to himself that it seemed a genuine reunion of father and son with no danger to the people's state.

'Father, I have half an hour before we leave for the training ground; it's a nice day, let's go for a walk.' Adam, wiping his tears, took Nicholas' hand and virtually dragged him towards the revolving door, exchanging a brief look with his shadow.

'You look so well, son. What a man you have become, we are so proud of you.' It was Nicholas' turn to wipe his tears. 'But isn't this dangerous?'

'No, Father, this is as good a time as any – after all, there is this amnesty.' During the brief walk Adam kept telling him how much he missed the family, especially the girls, and how sorry he was that they could not come to Budapest. Nicholas explained that Mica was a very good stepmother to them and although money was short, they lived well in the village. He also added how much he wanted to meet Melanie, and Adam responded that he would arrange a car trip for a visit if all went well with this one. Turning on to Liberty Bridge, which had once borne the proud name of Franz-Joseph, Nicholas glanced back and whispered to his son that they were being followed. Adam commented, 'Once a policeman, always a policeman,' confirming that he knew he had a shadow, and shrugged his shoulders. They reminisced about their last meeting in 1956, at the food depot, not too far from where they were right now. There was no doubt they were both still just as committed to the ideals of the revolution.

Having suddenly turned to walk back to the hotel, they wrong-footed the leather-coated man, committing him to walk towards the pair. He could not hide his disappointment as they brushed shoulders on the narrow pavement at the Buda pillar of the bridge. Adam took a good look his face and laughed, thinking that this guy was an even bigger amateur than himself.

Adam introduced Nicholas to Bill Shankly, who shook his hand warmly and said in his grinding Scottish accent, 'Mr Zenta, I am pleased to make your acquaintance. You have a grand son – we don't know what we would have done without the doc here.'

The fitful way the team trained would result in a grand thrashing by the Hungarians, Adam thought, as he distributed a thousand florins to each member for incidental expenses on the way back from the training session on the coach. The sum, which of course had nothing to do with their wages, had considerable casual buying power. There was little chance to spend any of it until after the game, except for the purchasing of some postcards in the small hotel shop. Some of the directors were still nursing thick heads from their last pálinka or whisky of the night before, and went off for their afternoon nap.

Adam walked the short distance to the coffee bar, talking endlessly to Nicholas. He found his father in a good frame of mind. Farming was his only chance of earning a living. He had to do a lot of hard, manual work, which obviously helped him to keep his trim figure. Adam kept repeating how upset he was that he was not seeing the girls, as he still referred to his sisters, especially Kathleen, who was a fanatical supporter of tonight's opposition. There was much to say and neither of them cared about the leather-coated man, who kept walking past them once in a while. They just looked at each other with knowing smiles.

The English press appeared first and headed straight for the bar. The two Zentas joined them and received a fair amount of backslapping for no particular reason, except that they knew of Adam's not so successful key-swapping attempt when booking into the hotel. Some of the gentlemen of the press still insisted that 'there was an even bigger story here, somewhere'. Andre Tóth walked into the bar and mingled quietly with some of the Hungarian football writers. He removed his trilby, showing a balding head that gleamed in the corner light. Adam embraced his friend and passed the very plain-looking plastic bag containing the magazines to him. Tóth swapped it for a ten-by-fifteen-centimetre solidly packed grey paper package, which Adam inconspicuously placed in his mac pocket. The melee around the men in the bar was approaching mayhem, which gave the onlookers from the hall no chance to see the exchange taking place. Over a beer Andre told Adam that he would slip away when the team got on the coach. Now Adam had to do something with the incriminating package bulging in his pocket, but for the time being it just had to stay where it was.

∼

As the two teams slowly walked to the centre circle of the famous floodlit Népstadion pitch the uproar among the crowd was deafening. Introduced by the diminutive Mr Shankly to make the team look taller and more intimidating, Liverpool, in their new all-white away kit, were matched by the red and white of Honvéd. The two team managements – some more glassy eyed than others – were seated in the government box. Adam was at the end of the second row next to Nicholas, who was thrilled by the unfolding spectacle. The game itself started unsurprisingly with a number of furious attacks by the home side. Ron Yeats, whom the manager simply called Colossus, in the centre of the defence had to show both his footballing skills and prowess as team captain in marshalling the others around him. Tommy Lawrence, in goal, was certainly earning his keep as he threw himself around, stopping the best shots of the new Hungarian star Tichy. Mr Shankly kept bobbing up and down on the bench, unashamedly coaching from the sideline. To the uninitiated his gesticulating with both hands moving parallel would not mean too much, but the players seeing it knew that, having spotted some weaknesses in the turning abilities of the opposition full backs, he was demanding more action by the wingers.

He obviously made his point more forcefully during the half-time interval, because Liverpool came back in a much more fiery mood. The attacks by the two wingers, Murphy and Thompson, increased and eventually culminated in a run by Ian Murphy. Proudly wearing the famed number-seven jersey – until recently the sole property of the legendary Billy Liddell – Ian won the ball in his own side and, sidestepping one and all along his intended route on the right wing, he firmly turned the full back the wrong way and delivered the perfect pass. The centre forward, Ian St John, netted the ball with a diving header, which was disallowed for a questionable offside. The final result of the goal less draw disappointed the Liverpudlians.

As the players took their communal bath, Mr Moran, one of the coaches, and his helpers collected the discarded sweaty kit, strewn all over the tiled floor. Adam walked in and saw his chance. Having spotted Ian's jersey, and pretending to help, he picked it up and wrapped it around the grey paper package. With a few other muddy items he placed it in the kit basket. After shaking a few hands in congratulation he went back to the main hall leading to the government box. The press from both sides were there in abundance, interviewing Mr Shankly, who responded with the expected lines about the pleasure of being there and the greater pleasure of 'going home with a result'.

After supper in the hotel Mr Shankly made the shortest of speeches in his distinct and hardly understandable Scottish brogue. 'Hey, lads, nil–nil or not, you have just beaten one of the greatest sides in the world. I'm proud of ye.' He turned to Adam and whispered in his ear that some of the lads might want to go to a nightclub and would he arrange it for them.

Although not arranged by the official party, throughout the whole trip Granada TV was quietly engaged in making a documentary about the historic visit, entitled *The Kop Flies East*. Restrictions on the players' activities being lifted, there was no reason for them not to join in the trip to the Moulin Rouge, which – for political correctness of the commie type – was most imaginatively called 'The Budapest' during this period. The show was the usual extravaganza of beautiful leggy and a few busty girls, intermingled with the odd juggler or ageing singer. It culminated in the current craze of dancing the twist. The boys were in raucous mood and their spirits were running high .To everyone's surprise the giant captain jumped on to the stage, towering over the six-foot girls. The bandleader was not going to miss his chance; he made a sign to the girls and they burst into the can-can. Ron Yeats didn't budge; he lined up amongst them and did the whole routine to great applause and to the absolute delight of the waiting TV cameramen, saying, 'It was a bet, after all.'

Adam stood drinking with Ian Murphy, reminiscing about the time when, as a young locum, he had treated Ian's family in south Liverpool, but knowing that sooner or later he had to discuss the matter of the small package wrapped in his jersey. Adam's eyes kept scanning the room, watching the goings-on. He suddenly noticed his shadow sitting a few tables away, drinking cheap sparkling wine in the company of a very pretty young woman. This was the moment to come clean. Adam beckoned the waitress in fishnet tights and the shortest of skirts and asked her to take two whiskies over to the couple. He leaned back in his chair in mischievous anticipation. The drinks were duly served, much to the consternation of the recipients. They questioned the waitress as to the source of such expensive tipples and she pointed towards Adam's table. Adam stood up with glass in hand and raised it in salute to them. The man walked over to Adam immediately.

'Sir, it is most kind of you to send us the drinks, but I cannot imagine why,' he said.

'Surely you know it is in gratitude for your diligent observation of all my movements during the past two days. You deserve it.' Adam's voice was a shade too mocking for the man to accept.

'A mistake sir, I have never seen you before. You must be drunk, sir.' He tried to sound indignant and placed his drink on the small table.

'Ah, I see, you can't drink on duty, eh? What a shame!'

The man mustered up a disdainful look and walked back to his female colleague, whose glass was empty by the time he returned.

Adam knew what he was doing. His actions sprang from the thoughts he had had as he fell asleep the night before. The idea was that the more noise you make the less likely it is that the onlooker will think you have anything to hide; the principle that he was to use often in the future. So he threw himself into the scene of chatting to the bevy of beauties and interpreting the wishes of the team members to them. The secret policeman looked disgusted and his companion became indifferent; they decided that he was just another loud-mouthed, drunken Western tourist.

Next morning Adam had to say goodbye to Nicholas. He handed over presents for the girls – some simple fashion items from 'the famous' Carnaby Street, as they forever afterwards referred to it in their letters. Nicholas laughed, as he was convinced that they would go wild when they saw them. He threw his arms around Adam and tearfully kissed him on both cheeks. Meanwhile the happy crowd of Liverpudlians mounted the coach, and there was no sign of the 'shadow' or his lady accomplice. Adam knew that should there be any problem leaving the country, it would happen when the flight was called, to put the management at a disadvantage. When the group walked into the centre hall of the terminal, with Adam leading, he saw two frontier guards with their ever-present submachine guns dangling around their necks walking straight towards him. His heart sank to titanic depths. A few seconds later they stood right in front of him and the senior of the two looked straight at him.

'Are you Dr Zenta, the Liverpool interpreter?' He asked in a very measured voice.

'Yes, I am,' replied Adam, his voice a shade shaky.

The man's voice was virtually apologetic. 'Would there be any chance that you could give us some club lapel badges for our kids?'

Adam breathed a sigh of relief and moved – fast. He took his own and a few badges off the surrounding players' blazers, telling them that he would explain why later. Mr Morrison helped with some from his personal supply; a couple of directors and the journalists had a few extra ones too. He went back with a handful of the precious little red brooches with the Liver Bird mounted on a shield over a small brown leather football and handed them over.

'There you are, plenty here for everybody. All right?'

'Thank you, Doctor, sorry for bothering you with a request like this, but we are football crazy here and Liverpool don't come this way often, do they?' He was virtually servile.

Adam's nerves were still on a knife-edge. 'I'll do my best to get them to return,' he reassured the two heavies, and walked towards the check-in desk with a pulse rate of well over a hundred. When his turn came, he had only one request for the ground staff. To seat him next to Ian.

As the Aer Lingus special started its take-off run on Runway 36, Adam's cheer filled the cabin. It would take a MIG 21 to get him now, he thought.

In the ensuing conversation it didn't take him long to beg the number-seven shirt off Ian Murphy. In a benevolent gesture he was delighted to donate it for a charity event in London in aid of aged Hungarian refugees who had fallen on hard times. Now all Adam had to do was to retrieve it from the giant basket that was on its way back in the aircraft hold, just beneath them.

∽

Adam walked into the small office that Arthur, his handler, had previously used for talking to him in the Ministry of Defence. To his surprise Arthur was flanked by a half a dozen others, who appeared to be most interested in what he was about to deliver.

'What the hell is this, Arthur? A fucking congress? You told me our set up was "one to one".'

'It is called a debriefing, Adam, nothing unusual.' Arthur smiled.

'Are you sure some of them don't belong to the Kim Philby fan club? Him, for example.' Adam pointed to a thin, suave-looking man, immaculately dressed with a fair wavy quiff on the top of his head and reeking of expensive aftershave. 'I suppose he is also ex-Cambridge, isn't he?'

'Now, Adam, no need to be like that, Mr Blunt is our expert on cement works. You will see in a minute. Have you got it?'

'Of course I've bloody got it. I still don't like all this audience.'

Adam took the grey paper parcel from his mac pocket and put it on the desk in front of the bay window. Arthur started to cut the string holding the wrapping paper together and unfolded it. Soon, the table was covered with a semi-transparent blueprint with the title 'Sárvár Cement Works' at the top, 'Architect: Andre Tóth' printed just below it. Adam was astounded. Until now he had been convinced that he was bringing back details of the intellectual opposition and a few Hungarian samizdat copies. This was big. As the pages unfolded even he realised that the 'cement works' was five storeys deep with six-to-ten-metre walls. It could only be a rocket silo or some nuclear storage establishment, or indeed both. He felt sick.

'Where is Sárvár?' Asked the sharply dressed man.

'About thirty kilometres from the Austrian border as the crow flies,' Adam answered suspiciously. 'Why?'

'Well, it's location, location and location, isn't it? Even with ICBMs you want to save every mile, don't you.'

'Adam, the evaluation of what you brought over will take many weeks. Let us talk about a few general points. Was there any problem with you passing on the coded magazines?'

Adam explained how the exchange of items took place in the crowded hotel bar and how Andre had disappeared in the mayhem created by the press attention. Even Arthur managed a smile when he got to the concealing of the package in the number-seven jersey. He patted Adam on the back somewhat patronisingly and handed him a package not too dissimilar in size to the one he had brought over from Budapest. 'Well deserved,' he added. Adam took it. Why not? he thought.

Dog tired, he walked into the hall and hung up his mac. He was happy to be back, and their reunion reflected that. Melanie kept rather quiet whilst he recounted the meeting with his father and every other detail that he could tell his wife. He even mentioned his shadow and their encounter in the nightclub and, of course, the lapel badge incident at the airport. She smiled, gave him a hug and whispered in his ear, 'Adam, darling, I am pregnant.' Adam's response came about five seconds later as he stared at her. It seemed like an eternity to both of them. He kissed her on the lips with a passion that surprised even him.

'Thank you, darling, I am really happy to hear that. Clever girl. You see what a decent orgasm can produce!' He smiled.

'Stop it, Adam – nothing to do with it.' She pushed him away.

'Want to bet?' He pulled her towards the bedroom.

The dizygotic – as the sister in charge snootily described the non-identical twin boys to the shocked Melanie – were born on the ides of March 1967 and christened Andrew and Richard. Adam was overjoyed, and decided that it was time to look for a consultancy. He was by now senior registrar to Albert Porter, who – since the football trip – had become quite a fan of Adam's. He drew the conclusion that his boss was obviously working for the SIS one way or the other. This was confirmed, to his mind, after the consultant received a knighthood in the New Year's Honours List. 'It was certainly not for the scientific papers he produced,' Adam said to Melanie. 'But now, we must invite him for dinner.'

Knowing his taste, roast beef was in the oven when the giant bachelor knocked on the door in Ovington Square. With no sign of his famous ill temper now he was socialising, he gave Melanie a peck on the cheek and shook hands with Adam. The conversation over gin and tonic and whisky was a little incongruous. As Albert had suggested his junior for the undercover job, and had been fully involved in the planning and knew the result, while Adam only suspected his superior's involvement, there was not much of a basis for straight speaking. Adam decided that there was no way he could mention the reasons for the trip so he changed the subject; after all, his boss was there to give him professional advice.

Adam asked him about available consultancies and Sir Albert liked to be asked to give advice. He started in high spirits, telling Adam to 'forget about the National Health Service consultancy posts in the journals'; he happened to know that one of the best private practices was about to come on to the market and Adam should consider buying it. Adam was naturally worried about the cost, as he had not been appointed a consultant in the NHS, and he did not know how he could afford it. He was reassured that as he had his membership of the Royal College of Psychiatry, this gave him a consultant's status and that was enough. The practice was the last purely private psychiatric one in Harley Street, and a chance like that in the current political climate would never come up again. 'Knowing your all-round ability, I do believe that your future would be best served with that move, if you could raise the funds. It's rather expensive at ten thousand guineas, but you will be in a position to charge almost anything you like. Most of your patients will be millionaires, from film stars to the aristocracy, not to mention the high-flyers of industry or commerce.' Adam knew he would find sleep difficult to come by that night.

As Sir Albert took another sip of his gin and tonic, Adam slipped into the small kitchen to check on the preparation of the dinner. Melanie was slicing the bread for the soup and Adam's enquiry was not appreciated. 'Out, I can't work if you watch over me!' She shouted. With a noticeable flash in her large oval eyes, she pointed the bread knife towards his stomach. Adam looked at her again and thoughtfully retreated. He walked upstairs to check on the boys, who were fast asleep in their separate cots. He felt uneasy about Melanie, who was just serving up the soup with a smile as he came downstairs.

Skilfully avoiding catching his white moustache or beard with the soup spoon, Sir Albert savoured the tasty tomato aux croutons and complimented Melanie on it. He once again mentioned the importance of independence in practice. 'You see, for example, you would not have to go around asking for permission as you did for your last Budapest trip – and I'm sure you will have more of that sort of thing in the future.'

A chill ran down Adam's spine – he was now sure that his boss was speaking for 'The Ministry'.

'It is the awful cost that bothers me, having recently become the father of two. I will have to look for a decent prep school soon.' He probed the new knight.

'That's no problem, I will point you towards the right finance house, which will amaze you with their low-interest loans.'

'Oh, Adam, you always worry about money, you know Mother will be able to help, she inherited such a lot,' Melanie interjected.

'Your mother has already helped enough with this place, darling.' Adam looked at his wife, who seemed totally calm now. 'I suppose at least I won't need to worry about having to buy a car for a while. That 'Littlewoods Pools win' after my Hungarian trip came in handy for the Humber Sceptre.' He had lied in explaining his sudden acquisition of money.

'Well, exactly. I will ring my merchant bankers first thing on Monday. Your contract will expire in Kent at the end of the month, if I'm not mistaken. Do you have any holiday left?'

'I think I have a week.'

'One more week in the rat race that you don't have to win any more, how nice.' Sir Albert smiled behind his full beard.

'Sir Albert, can I count on your advice from time to time?' Adam asked.

'I insist on it, dear boy.' Albert became introspective for a moment, then he smiled. His mission was accomplished. The cuckoo had laid the egg in the unsuspecting bird's nest.

~

Adam was amazed at the ease with which he obtained a loan from the special account of Hewitt, Adamson & Co., and with the scrolled grey-black banker's draft from a Bank of England account he walked into the ground-floor consulting room of 43a Harley Street. The ageing and rather hunched Dr Alfred Zuckerman, consultant psychiatrist, was delighted to see his well-known name featuring on the top of such a valuable piece of paper and remarked that he had never come across such an easy transaction in his long life, and 'how nice it is for the staff, who won't have to change the way they address the boss. AZ will do for Adam Zenta too'. The two men smiled and shook hands. The old man sighed once and walked out. Less than two weeks later one of Allah's less compassionate handymen put a bullet through the back of his head whilst he was walking his cocker spaniel in Regent's Park.

Adam sat in the antique chair behind the fine mahogany desk and looked around. All modern items and paintings would be disposed of and replaced by period pieces, even if they had to come from the cheaper antique shops of Fulham, he thought. The adjacent treatment room and the secretarial offices were in excellent condition and needed no particular attention. He addressed himself to the appointment book and was delighted to see that there were some new patients booked in over the next weeks and plenty of 'follow-ups'. The latter were, of course, euphemisms for the fact that his famous neurotics wanted to see their new doctor, or in the case of the few Americans, their new shrink.

Carnations in the lapel were sadly outdated by then, so Adam settled on wearing a rather loud, blood-red silk kerchief in his top pocket. It conveyed the same impression. He never attempted to match any of his spotted ties with it. He considered that utterly vulgar. The following week was spent on studying case notes and rearranging the furniture. The former proved the lesser problem.

Adam's staff consisted of two part-timers. Under the overall management of the unmarried thirty-something Hilary was the married, much more junior Claire. Claire had a family commitment of a couple of young and often screaming children, so she did not seem to mind being number two, so long as she was able to take the occasional extra day off. It seemed to be a sloppy arrangement to Adam but he soon realised that it worked. Monday was spent going over the routine. Chaired by Hilary, the meeting went smoothly enough until she asked Adam whether there were to be 'any preferential telephone callers'. Adam's blank expression lasted only a few seconds. He thought of Arthur for a moment, then of Melanie, and dismissed the idea. 'Certainly not' was his curt answer. 'I cannot think why anyone should butt in whilst I'm seeing my patients.'

On Tuesday morning Adam arrived early, a nervous wreck himself, entering a new world of which he knew little, but he felt good, very good. To be his own boss at thirty-nine in a very well-known practice, in the Mecca of private medicine, was something he had never imagined for himself, even with a 'little help from his friends'.

The first patient announced by Hilary was followed by several others. All of them were women, dressed in the highest of fashion, each wanting to spend a little more time than their allocated thirty minutes with Adam. It seemed to be a fair game. Clinically he was hardly challenged. A few prescription changes to introduce the new generation of tranquillisers were followed by one session of what could vaguely be described as psychoanalysis – a prolonged chat with a very rich middle-aged American lady whose husband, a second secretary at the Embassy, was paying less attention to her, which she was convinced was her fault, given her unstable childhood in Boston, which still caused her to be uncommunicative. She did not want to be convinced to the contrary in less than a dozen sessions.

One of the patients in the afternoon session was a young opera singer who was due to have a decisive audition at Covent Garden. She said that she hardly ever suffered with stage fright but was a nervous wreck at auditions. Adam quickly mentioned his operatic past to show sympathy and suggested a short and light hypno-analysis, followed by another, slightly deeper one just before the end of the day, as there was no time for more radical adjustment of any intrinsic mental distortion, which in her case was simple immaturity. She quickly passed into a light hypnotic state and was told that she should be confident that she could relax, which she had not been able to do at auditions for some time. At the second session a slightly deeper state was achieved and Adam suggested, 'When you walk into the room you will feel confident and sure of yourself, perfectly at ease.' He repeated this several times, then he asked her to relax on the couch. He told her that when she went to bed that night she would feel a heavy, sinking feeling but would have a good night's sleep.

Wednesday late afternoon Adam received a telephone call.

'Doctor Z, guess what, I have got the part of Oscar in the new production of *The Masked Ball*! It was very strange!' The opera singer sounded on top of the world.

'Yes?'

'I slept very deeply last night, yet during the day I was as nervous as could be, but as soon as I walked into the room, I felt as cool as a cucumber, I just couldn't go wrong. I felt wonderful!'

'My mistake,' he replied. 'Perhaps I should have suggested that you would feel relaxed all day, not just "when you walk into the room …"'

'Oh, no, Doctor, it was better this way. My adrenalin was flowing, yet when I had to sing I just felt elated. Fantastic! I am so grateful to you, two tickets will be on their way as soon as they're printed. And more than that, I'm sending you all my friends – all of them! And I told them you had film-star looks! I am sorry, I hope I'm not embarrassing you!' She was about to lose her voice.

~

And send them she did. They came perhaps for no other reason than to 'just have a look'. Adam earned an inordinate amount of money from these 'initial consultations', as he called them, trying to give them a vaguely respectable name.

Determined as ever on having a good time too, he tried to drag Melanie to the Wigmore Hall for an occasional recital and the Festival Hall for the inevitable Tchaikovsky, but it became more and more difficult. Having joined the Friends of Covent Garden, they were at most of the first nights, and by the end of the season Adam realised that there were more and more 'hellos' to be said. This was even more common in the West End theatres, where the donors of complimentary tickets would also invite them backstage after the performance, or they would be asked to join them for a 'quick bite', usually neither quick and certainly not just a bite and very often ending in the early hours of the morning. A great delight to Adam, but an utter drag for Melanie. Within a year he was a minor celebrity.

After a year or so, Melanie started making the occasional excuse to forgo these jaunts. Andy and Rick were growing up fast and old Mrs Roberts, the babysitter, who lived a few doors away, became less and less available. Adam, though, wasn't to be deprived of his nocturnal activities and decided to go to the *Sunday Night at the Palladium* shows alone. Joan, a regular patient for minor depressive episodes, left the odd ticket for him at the box office. A not entirely confirmed lesbian, who lived in Chiswick with another dancer from the chorus line, was no threat, and occasional arrangements were made for Adam to go backstage. The long room seemed to be full of the six-foot beauties in various stages of undress. He offered to withdraw but was dragged in and told that males walking about did not bother them. And in fact, some of them were about to go to the Café Royal, so 'why not join the girls?'

Sitting in their usual basement corner, the girls started their round of gossip – the latest assessment of who was with whom, and for what. Adam was ignored, which suited him as he continued to pour the Chablis, feasting on the sight of the beauties of theatreland. Eating their lettuce sandwiches, the girls often turned to Adam for free medical advice, on subjects ranging from the new contraceptive pill to the much-used aversion therapy for the 'treatment' of homosexuality. Adam was most supportive of the former, which he thought now put women on an equal sexual footing with men for the first time, but he was dismissive of the latter, commenting that no homosexual had ever been 'cured' by having been made to vomit.

He became aware that the eyes of Joan's live-in friend were watching him. Sharon was a six-foot 'body perfect'. With her high heels and the honey-blonde bun on her head, she towered over Adam, who liked to give his height as 'six foot in shoes'.

By the time Adam had dropped the four at their digs, it was once again early morning. He had enjoyed a great and very innocent time, though he felt a terrific temptation to return to his old ways. Things had not been going well with Melanie and this evening had been such fun.

On Monday morning Adam asked for Joan's file, and without hesitation dialled her telephone number. He had a story ready about some change of tablets, but luckily Sharon answered.

'Hello, Sharon, I'm glad it's you. Adam Zenta here. Can you talk or is Joan in earshot?'

'Oh, how nice. By the way, thanks for all that wine. Boy, have I got a headache!'

'It was great fun. Sharon, do you mind if I come straight to the point?'

'Not at all, Adam, is something wrong?'

'No, nothing's wrong, Sharon – it's just that I know you are Joan's girlfriend, but I wondered if you'd join me one evening, for dinner.'

The silence was longer than Adam expected. 'Adam, as you will know from Joan, we have been having a relationship for over two years …'

'Please, Sharon, sorry for interrupting – yes, I know it all, but I'm still asking you. One condition, mind you, could you wear flat shoes – please?'

'Well, OK, a "dinner is a dinner", as they say, but flat shoes? No way! I'm getting my six-inchers out and wearing my hair piled up. Pushing seven feet in total. Do you still want to take me out?' She giggled.

'Yep, I'll meet you on my stilts. Which day?'

'Gosh, I've just used my best line to put off fellows with dates in mind. Friday, please.'

'Friday it is, then, see you at the stage door.'

Adam replaced the receiver and told himself that it was he who needed a shrink, if after two years of fidelity the best he could do was to make a date with a lesbian.

~

The Villa dei Cesari on the Embankment was a most lively, genuine Italian restaurant with good music. Adam chose it because it would offer an opportunity for a little physical proximity on the dance floor at a time when it was conversationally needed. He was delighted to see that Sharon was wearing modest three-inch heels and her honey-blonde hair was loose and allowed to play with gravity, covering the deep cut-out on the back of her full-length green chiffon dress. She still had two inches on Adam as they walked to their table on the river side. When they took their seats she shrank to an inch below Adam's height.

'You see, I'm all legs, I'm shorter than you now.'

'So in bed, I would need to bend down to kiss you, right?'

'Wrong! No bed, no kissing. A dinner is a dinner. Where is it, I'm starving.'

'I was only theorising,' Adam laughed as the head waiter turned up.

The piping-hot fettuccine relaxed Sharon, who began to talk of her love affair with Joan. The Tiller girls all knew of it, but it was the first time she had explained her feelings to a male. The tenderness and open intimacy of female homosexuality were simply exquisite to her.

'If you men could make love like girls do, all would be well, but from what I hear from the others with men it's all crash, bang, wallop. It's all a power game for you men, especially when someone is taller.'

'Are you implying that you've never had straight sex?'

'Never! Ever since I was nine years old I've preferred the female shape. Mind you, I was only a pair of very thin legs. The boys never looked at me anyway. I've had two girlfriends before and now I'm happily settled with Joan. I love her dearly.'

Sharon was a delightful dinner partner whose adoring looks at Adam would have fooled anyone in the room, including him, had he not been forewarned. The more she talked about her homosexuality the more it bothered Adam, and perhaps excited him.

The band started the current hit from Italy, 'Volare', and Adam asked Sharon to dance. There were no other couples on the floor and he went for the closest possible clinch. The diners around the other tables looked at the striking couple – the males with envy of Adam and the females with envy of Sharon's legs, the right one of which made a frequent and full appearance through her split with every backward step she took. Adam felt comfortable with her and she with him. There was hope, Adam thought. He pulled her even nearer.

The Saltimbucca alla Romana went down well with the Valpolicella Reserva, and during the third dance Adam kissed her very gently on the cheek. She did not pull away.

'Oh, Adam, you are such a lovely man, a hunk if I were only straight. What am I going to do with you?' They walked back to the table shoulder to shoulder.

'Can I just ask you to relax, then I will suggest something. Just relax, relax. Look at the light of the candle. Have a glass of wine.' His voice was softening and she was clearly going under.

'Do you want to make love?' Adam whispered.

'Oh yes, Adam. I do!' She answered hungrily.

'All right, when you hear me using the word "waiter", you forget all about this.' He leaned back in his chair, absorbed the joyous scene before him and put his arm up. 'Waiter! Two large Italian brandies, please.'

Sharon shook her head and yawned. 'I'm sorry, Adam, I just dropped off for a moment, how rude of me. It's so relaxing being with you – where were we?'

'I think you were asking what you were going to do with me.'

'Oh yes, I know what, let's have another dance. It's so nice to dance without having to throw your legs about in the air.'

As they danced ever closer, and paying very little attention to the music or anything else, for that matter, Adam admitted to the amazed Sharon that he had hypnotised her for a few seconds, but he carefully omitted her answer to his question. She said that she had been hypnotised once on the stage by the famous Alberto and ended up 'swimming across the Channel'. He reassured her that hypnosis would not make anyone do anything they would normally not do, so she must be a frustrated Channel swimmer, yet with her long legs she could just paddle over, anyway.

'Adam, please take me away from here, anywhere.' She turned on her heel and walked back to their table.

He hurriedly paid the bill and they got into a black cab and told the driver to take them to the Cumberland Hotel at Marble Arch. There was always an available room in that giant establishment.

Within minutes they were in bed. It seemed Sharon did not want to give herself time to change her mind. As they lay in bed she looked Adam in the eye and said in a little girl's voice, 'You see, I'm shorter than you when lying down'. Some time later, after her first and last heterosexual climax, she stopped kissing and turned away. 'Oh, please, forgive me, Joan! Forgive me, Joan,' she whimpered, before starting to quietly sob.

When Adam woke in the morning Sharon was gone and it was his turn to remonstrate with himself. He knew this first step was to be reinforced by more of the same; he could no longer stop himself, and he didn't really want to. Never mind, he thought, I'd better get some story sorted.

Not all of Adam's escapades – during what he liked to describe later as his 'wild years' – concluded in easy success. A particular peccadillo proved rather difficult to handle.

Vivienne, the beautiful wife of a City merchant banker who preferred Caribbean fishing to her company, was a casual acquaintance from a dinner party given by a fellow psychiatrist. Carefully noting her splendid dark features, Adam stored them in his mind, but his chance came some time later when they accidentally met as she was looking for a taxi in Harley Street, following a consultation with her favourite gynaecologist, Simon Marks, who happened to be a good friend of Adam's.

Having been – once more – reassured that 'everything was in perfect working order', and thus her ongoing hypochondria allayed for the moment, she was eager to put things to the test. Adam was the softest target she had ever aimed at and she decided to aim well.

'I've heard that you and Melanie are parting and I must say, Adam, it hasn't surprised me at all.' She smiled, showing off the crowning achievements of the Street's best dental surgeons.

'Neither am I, Vivienne. Providence prevailed – I never deserved her and I am losing her for my sins, which are innumerable.' Adam, overstating reality, pitched in, sensing adventure.

'You're bad, Adam. You shouldn't say things like that – a girl would want to know more!' There was a gentle tremble in her voice, which Adam instantly recognised as unmistakable interest.

'Dinner on Saturday?' He asked, raising his eyebrows.

'Well, yes, I wouldn't mind.' She lowered her head. 'Somewhere safe, Adam, my husband is deep-sea fishing with his chums, but as you know, the whole of Highgate knows me and they are all out on Saturdays.'

'Naturally, Vivienne. How about Manchester?' He smiled.

'Perfect! I can visit my mother in Prestbury,' she responded, surprising Adam.

'Well, Vivienne, I didn't mean that literally, but I will come up, if you are serious. I can always arrange a meeting of sorts. Would you ring me at my rooms next week and we'll make arrangements? What sort of food do you like?'

'Italian,' she answered, smiling.

'Italian it will be.' They shook hands and parted.

Adam walked to his consulting room, took his Egon Ronay guide from his main drawer, looked up under Manchester and decided on La Terrazza, aka Mario's and Franco's, in Nicholas Street, in a narrow alleyway behind the giant Piccadilly complex.

He was sitting on the bar stool facing the full restaurant when a taxi pulled up. It was just visible through the window on the left, which also had a full view of the car park on a derelict piece of land.

A vision of overemphasised elegance was soon walking upstairs towards him. She turned all heads in the restaurant as they observed her utter perfection, from diamond hairclip to golden toecap. Adam, not known by anyone, could make as much fuss of her as he wanted. Vivienne responded with equal enthusiasm and settled next to him, swirling her yellow ostrich feathers around her pearl-covered neck. She took his elbow.

The margarita was placed in front of her by the ogling Italian barman and the head waiter presented the oversized menus. They were not studied long by either of them, but dinner was ordered just the same. They enjoyed each other's eyes as they sipped their drinks.

Looking over Adam's shoulder, Vivienne's eyes inadvertently caught the headlights of another car making its way into the car park. She looked again and drew her head back in utter fear.

'Adam, get me out of here, please get me out,' she pleaded in a loud whisper.

Adam followed her line of vision, to see a gleaming white Rolls-Royce pull up with four passengers. 'What's the matter, Viv?' He asked.

'Adam, it's just too bad to be true. The people in that car are my husband's ex-partner, his cousin and their wives, all friends of ours. Look, they're getting out! Please do something, they mustn't see me with you! What the hell are they doing here anyway!? Adam, hurry!' She was becoming hysterical.

Adam observed the well-dressed bunch as they started to walk towards the entrance. He called for the head waiter and threw a ten-pound note in front of the barman. Another twenty cancelled the meal with Franco and Adam asked to be taken out by the rear door.

'There is no back door, here, sir, it is on the other side,' he answered as the group were greeted in the hall, downstairs.

Adam explained to the sympathetic and rather excited Franco that his help would be much appreciated. He nodded and disappeared for a moment, returning with a large white damask tablecloth in his hands and an over-satisfied look on his Latin face.

'We do what they did to the Kray brothers – cover her! Nobody to know who is under! Yes?'

'Yes!' Adam and Vivienne yelled in unison, to the utter delight of the surrounding customers, who were getting more and more involved in the proceedings, which were rapidly turning into a farce.

The elegant group were getting ever nearer as Vivienne's head was eventually covered. The nearest table started a ripple of applause, which was taken up by the others. At the top of the stairs the newly arrived guests were astonished by the unusual spectacle and all eyes focused on the perfect legs and the delicate Italian shoes.

Adam on one side and Franco on the other, walked Vivienne to the top of the staircase to the sound of the clapping hands. Holding her under her arm, Adam felt Vivienne's body quiver. He tightened his grip in reassurance and she responded by placing her head on his shoulder. Coiffure ruined, she whispered a thank you.

A further donation from Adam secured a quick taxi and Vivienne was unceremoniously pushed into the black cab. Adam followed her and handed back the tablecloth.

Situation and reputation saved, Adam asked the driver to take them to the Midland Hotel.

Adam's practice was growing busier and busier as visitors and wives of nearby embassies were delivering parcels and papers under the guise of psychiatric consultations. All to be collected by Arthur.

MI6 were so pleased with the 'cement works' result, now over two years ago, that whenever Liverpool FC had Budapest games, like that against Ferencváros, twice during the ensuing years, Adam had to devise ways of bringing back the packages, which had become mercifully smaller and more important as time went on. His last 'football trip' was in fact with Bob Stokoe's Sunderland side against Vasas in the Cup Winners' Cup, after they had beaten Leeds United with the brilliant Ian Porterfield goal. The microfilm was built into the heels of a pair of riding boots he had bought at a cobbler's near Váci Street. He carried them out, slung over his shoulder, and complimented the duty guard, saying that 'they don't make them this well anywhere else in the world'.

Adam received regular cash payments from Arthur for his troubles, and the first five thousand pounds he invested in Lloyds, becoming a 'name'. The requirement to own a minimum of two properties was duly fudged with his father-in-law. Adam's finances were in good enough shape as Lady Felicity showered money on Melanie and the twins, making his professional earnings available for luxuries. The Battersby-Smyths also established trust funds, ensuring money for the higher education of the boys and good lump sums when they became of age.

Professionally, his colleagues held him in high regard as an analyst, and his paper 'Varying Depths in the Hypnotic State' received much recognition. His flamboyant ways were, however, not appreciated by all. Some complained about his way of life and forecast the fate of Dr Ward of the Christine Keeler/Mandy Rice-Davies episode for him too. Adam naturally dismissed any similarity. He could not explain to anyone that his was a special situation created by the SIS, and his lifestyle was, to some degree at least, a smokescreen.

At Ovington Square, Melanie became increasingly reclusive. Having got what she wanted, which was Adam and more importantly 'the boys', she was convinced that he was hers for keeps, and often said that she knew 'he would always come home – after all, nobody could love him more'. Her days consisted of driving the twins to kindergarten and later to school, then shopping at Harrods or Harvey-Nicks. For the latter she didn't even need her car, thus her 'territory' became reduced to less than half a square mile. In the evening, waiting for Adam, who was often called in for a hospital opinion after his consultations were over, or when he was out with a singer from the latest musical offering in the West End, she would pour herself an extra-large gin and tonic. Adam, being a 'straight whisky, wine or beer drinker', as he described himself, and having nothing but contempt for both ingredients – and the combination of the two positively repelled him – would pour scorn on her. Melanie's reaction was to withdraw into herself and sit around most of the day just waiting for his return. The developing agoraphobia soon presented Adam with a challenge. He had written a paper about the subject some time back and knew that the condition was hardly ever an isolated symptom, but more part of a greater insecurity. He also knew that much of it was being caused by his deplorable behaviour. The question before him was whether or not he was willing, or indeed able, to change his lifestyle of hard work followed by even harder play; the most common of many doctors' dilemmas.

Walking through his waiting room the following Monday he was astonished to see a most beautiful oval porcelain face with cascading blonde hair staring at him from the front page of *Vogue*. He bent down to the coffee table, picked up the glossy magazine and took it into his consulting room. Claire, at reception, thought it most odd. AZ was not the female-magazine-ogling type, not unless one of his patients appeared in it, when she usually brought it to his attention. She knew there was no patient in that particular issue.

Adam looked for the legend inside the third page. It was short. 'Tracy Stuart, wife of City banker Ian, relaunches her modelling career after the birth of her son. She says she has also been offered a part in a new play, specially written for the small screen.' He closed the magazine, placing it in front of him on his well-laid-out mahogany desk, and asked Claire to bring him a strong espresso. He could hardly take his eyes off the perfect face as he leaned back in his chair with his arms clasped behind his head. He got himself home early that evening, not bothering to comment on the whiff of gin on Melanie's breath.

'Melanie, dear, I've been thinking. We haven't done much entertaining lately and you hardly see any of your old friends now. Do you recognise this picture?' He placed the magazine in front of his wife.

'Oh yes, Tracy Stu', let me see what she is up to. No good, I wager.' She picked it up. 'She's going on the box, eh? That's interesting.'

'I vaguely remember her from our wedding, that's why I brought the mag home. Why don't you get in touch with her? Get them here for dinner, or perhaps we could go out with them.'

'Adam, you know how I hate leaving the boys with babysitters!' She glanced towards the playroom.

'I notice that Ian – that is the right name, isn't it? – is a City banker. I could pick his brain on money matters.' Adam tried to sound nonchalant.

'Well, all right, I can try, that's if they haven't moved. The phone number I have is ages old – seven years, to be precise.'

'OK, Mel, it's just a thought.' Adam finished his meal and walked over to the boys' room.

The two six-year-olds were as good as any of their age, but very different in personality. Andy, who regarded himself as senior by having been born twenty minutes before his brother Rick, was 'messing around' with his toy guitar. He was clearly musical and could easily recognise most Beethoven symphonies. Rick was a more playful little fellow who preferred guns and cars. They both, however, had a fascination for aeroplanes, and often complained that Adam could not fly one, like their prep-school friend's father, who was a private pilot instructor at Biggin Hill Flying Club.

They looked quizzically at Adam. 'We're not going to have a Hungarian lesson, Dad, are we?' Andy asked.

'*Ma este, nem,*' Adam answered.

'Not tonight!' Rick translated quickly. 'Oh, goody.' He took off around the room, his model Spitfire in his hand, buzzing away with engine noise as he ran.

Adam had to break the eternal bad news of it being 'bedtime', which was one of the many fatherly duties left to him, but which did not endear him to 'the sprogs', as he called them.

The boys most skilfully negotiated another half an hour out of Adam and he returned to the spacious lounge. Melanie was on the phone.

'Well, that's fine, Tracy – oh, I am looking forward to seeing you both. I have been so lazy about this sort of thing lately. So, we will meet you there – yes, I know the place, I had my eighteenth there, just before I met Adam – eight o'clock, then. 'Bye.' She turned around.

'Well, are you impressed? I have spoken to Tracy Stu'. Firstly I invited them, then she invited us, but we finally agreed to go out together. Ian's society of sorts is having a small but very expensive May Ball at the Hamilton Place ballroom. Do you know it?'

'No, but I heard that you did, and that will do. Hamilton Place is very near, we could virtually walk it.'

'Certainly not, Adam, my hair would be such a mess by the time we got there. But if it's a nice night we could walk back home. I would like that very much.' She sounded happier.

'Of course, darling.' Adam glanced at the magazine. He could hardly wait for the rest of April to pass.

~

When the Zentas first walked into the small, busy place, Adam thought that only the English would think of putting a ballroom in a basement. He soon had to admit that it had charm and character in its Georgian setting. They picked up the glass of Lanson offered by the waitress and walked into the area just left of the dance floor, near the bar. Their hosts had not yet arrived and Adam turned to Melanie and complimented her on the new full-length figure-hugging black dress. She was wearing her dark brown hair combed straight back, which made her look very elegant but a shade severe. Adam was dressed in his fairly new dinner jacket with the 'in' scarf lapel. The three-quarter-inch platform soles pushed him comfortably over the six-foot mark. As the Stuarts walked down the curved staircase it was a pair of pale pink shoes and a matching dress which Adam first spotted. It was the same dress that Tracy had been wearing on the *Vogue* cover. He wondered whether he should mention it – after all, it had been three weeks ago. The snake-like motion of her figure as she walked down the steps in the silk dress did not seem to be contrived. It was just naturally sexy, Adam thought. What women call their crowning glory in Tracy's case was exactly that. Her bleached-blonde hair was everywhere, a cascading waterfall of it. She looked just as she had on the cover of *Vogue*.

Seven years before, when Adam had first seen her at his wedding and then on their departure for the airport, he had been impressed by her because what he saw was such a perfect picture. Now at twenty-nine Tracy was a mature beauty, handling herself with such confidence that she turned the heads of men and women alike.

The women embraced each other, cheeks hardly brushing, and then offered their cheeks to the men. Adam kissed Tracy on both sides of her face.

'Don't you dare say it.' Melanie wagged a friendly finger at Adam.

'Say what?' Adam said innocently.

'He's such a bore with his usual line that "we Continentals do it twice". I've heard it so often.'

'Well, that could be said of my showbiz lot too, the way they kiss, except I wouldn't believe most of them do it once.' Tracy's laugh was decidedly naughty.

Ice broken, they sat at a corner table. There was no dinner as such, but the small army of waiters were positively in overdrive with the canapés, which were different with each offering. And the offering was endless. The champagne was equally often replenished. This was to be a splendid night, even if the men, not knowing each other, were at some disadvantage. The two women had far too much to say and the men were definitely out of it until they had been through the whole Shugborough class of whatever year. The men started off slowly, and when Ian offered Adam a cigar – although he seldom smoked them – he took it. They exchanged basic information about their work and Adam was annoyed to find Ian such good company. He was about five foot ten, a former football player in the front line and now a Liverpool supporter. Adam was genuinely thrilled to meet someone with similar interests and told Ian the story of his football trips, not mentioning the 'parcels', naturally. He did mention the microphone-testing episode on the first trip. Ian interrupted.

'You know, Adam, I invest a lot for some of the Liverpool directors, a few of whom you obviously know, and I was up there recently. They all talk about the trip and that story of yours gets better with each telling.'

'Yes?' Adam asked.

'Well, the last version I heard was that you went into your room and said, "Good evening, comrades, microphone testing, one ... two ... three ...'

'Yes! I did.'

'But they go farther now, saying you decided to find the bug.'

'I never did; it's impossible without equipment.'

'Precisely, but just listen. The story goes, "He took up the carpet and right in the middle of the room he found a large brass plate."'

'Yes?'

'"Then he got his screwdriver and released the screws – and guess what, the chandelier fell off the ballroom ceiling, to the floor below."'

'Well done, LFC!' Adam laughed. 'Melanie, please remind me not to go anywhere without my screwdriver.'

Their laughter was relaxed and the two men seemed tuned in with each other. They were enjoying the light-hearted conversation.

Inevitably, the band struck up with a recognisable evergreen – this time it was the turn of 'I only have eyes for you' – and both men took their wives for a dance on the small but highly polished and newly sprung floor. Not sharing the tune's sentiments, glancing over his wife's shoulder, Adam noticed Tracy's posture as she leaned slightly back when dancing. It combined elegance and sexuality to a degree that led to his mind overflowing with fantasies. He knew that he had taken the first inevitable and perhaps irreversible step in pursuing her when he first recognised her picture on the magazine. No – before! When he was introduced to her at his wedding, he corrected himself.

But there was Ian! A man whom he had genuinely learned to like in just a few minutes. He is dispensable, he thought, then dismissed the idea immediately. It will have to be a genuine, all-round friendship of two men whose wives get on well. That was impossible, he thought. The deeper they got to know each other the more insurmountable the whole thing would become.

The music stopped and they both realised that they had not exchanged one word on the dance floor. Adam suggested a drink. Melanie looked at him piercingly and agreed, saying that Adam looked as if he needed one.

When Ian and Tracy rejoined them frivolity returned and light-hearted conversation and repartee took over between the two men.

'Do you play squash?' Ian asked.

'No, I think it's a game for idiots,' Adam answered without hesitation. 'I would like to take up private flying, though. Interested?'

'Look, no wings.' Ian spread his arms. 'And I cannot stand the smell of kerosene.'

'Well, not much there, but we appear to like good booze, so that will have to be our mutual interest.' Adam smiled. 'It's a lovely night – why don't you to come back to Ovington Square for a nightcap?'

'Good idea, let's do that. I've had enough these modern dances where you can't even get hold of the girl any more.'

They did have one more dance. Adam had the chance to put his arm around the perfect waist of Tracy for a few minutes. His slightly stronger-than-normal hold elicited no reaction from her. They were soon on the short trek back to Knightsbridge. The shop windows of Harrods accounted for about ten minutes' extra time before they settled down to some of Adam's specially percolated coffee and large Hennessy XOs. He stuck with his whiskies.

The session of old jokes produced a few of Tracy's 'dirty' chuckles, which – after a few more whiskies – Adam found totally irresistible. Ian, on the other hand, told her that 'she was irritating and should control her vulgar laugh'. Several attempts by Melanie to talk about 'her twins' elicited no response from anyone. Adam and Ian decided to meet for a drink the following Friday after work, and at three in the morning the Stuarts called a taxi.

As the Zentas walked upstairs to their bedroom Adam decided that he was in love with Tracy and thought that Ian was the greatest guy he had met for a long time. He also complimented himself for organising such a splendid night.

～

Adam and Ian regularly met for a drink, either in the West End or in the City, depending who finished later. They often dined in the local bistros, on Tuesdays mainly, which they decided to call their 'Monday Club'. It was on the principle that if it was good enough for Sheffield Wednesday to play football on Saturdays, it was good enough for them to call their Tuesday outing Monday – and to hell with the political version of it; if they wanted their name back, they could always sue.

Ian gave sound investment advice to Adam, which produced a good income for him, as well as enabling him to put more money into Lloyds. As Adam could not interest Ian in availing himself of the latest advances in psychotherapy, he decided to interest him in girls instead. His world was full of them, and when Ian found Adam drinking with a couple of showbiz beauties, the handsome Englishman pounced with a dinner invitation. At the start of the promiscuous seventies such arrangements would invariably end at the Cumberland, which the men would leave around two, having given money to the girls to pay the bills in the morning, after their lie-ins. The women often changed, but the system always worked.

Enjoying each other's company, the men would occasionally decide on no dates and 'just to have a chat', in which case they would go to the Savoy Grill for a 'proper meal'. It would be washed down with Ayala, which they did not consider a 'champagne rip-off'. The following week two new girls would grace their table at yet another well-known eatery. Jenny's Bistro was a frequent favourite. On Fridays or Saturdays even the wives were taken out, which became increasingly difficult for Adam. As his marriage was hitting rock bottom, Melanie was beginning to repel him. Oh, to be in the company of Tracy, he fantasised, but rules were rules – so he just stole a look when he could.

The two men had now become almost inseparable, so over a meal at Simpsons they cooked up the idea of a family holiday. They agreed on the Cambridge Beaches Hotel in Bermuda and announced the arrangements over a dinner at the Stuarts'. A picture of 'Windswept', a pink detached house within the hotel grounds, was produced. Melanie was the least excited about the trip as of late she didn't much 'like travelling'. Bermuda just seemed to her to be a little too far. But planning continued and in early September they were off.

The holiday went well. They all had a little of what they expected from it. The golden beach, snorkelling, the swimming pool and fishing trips were all lapped up in good fun. Adam just longed for the serpent-like body of Tracy to be next to his, yet he had to admit, for the first time, that she was a bit on the skinny side and her breasts were, well, a shade too small. He was usually attracted to more voluptuous women, but he was in love with her, even if he knew there was absolutely nothing he could do about it.

A typical hot and starry night took them to Hamilton, where the energetic and talented Roy Castle was playing his trumpet in the smoke-filled dining room, well supported by other acts. They dined well and three of them drank far too much, the exception being Tracy, who had little time for alcohol, but was seriously watching the changing expression on Adam's face. When his leg accidentally touched hers under the table he felt her returning the pressure. Adam swallowed. The moment he had waited for was there. He pressed against her again and, yes, she was rubbing her lower leg against his. There could be no mistake. As they danced he held her closer than ever before. On returning to the table, the childish game of footsy continued, and when Ian danced with Melanie, Adam used the opportunity and touched her knee. Their eyes met for a split second and she drew her thumb along his thigh from his knee to his hip.

Adam and Melanie had just said goodnight to the babysitter when they heard the row erupting through the thin separating wall. It went on for some time. Next morning at breakfast, Tracy was sporting a shiner of a black eye, which she got 'when she slipped on the wet bathroom floor'.

Ian waited for an opportune moment and dragged Adam away.

'Don't worry, Zeny, she won't play footsy with you again! I've made sure of that!'

'Ian, you didn't hit her? For God's sake, man!' Adam was struggling. 'We were drunk, we were very drunk, and anyway, it was my fault.'

'You were drunk, she wasn't! And anyway, I never blame the man, we all have a go. She should not have allowed it to happen.' Ian was adamant.

'Well, yes, but please, Ian, this time it was my fault. I had drunk too much. You should have hit me, seriously.'

'Forget it, Adam! The bitch has learned her lesson, you are my best and only friend.' His eyes were strangely aflame, looking at his wife some yards away.

He suddenly changed the subject. 'Let's have a beer.' Adam considered that the Stuarts' marriage was over.

On their return the 'Monday Club' continued its deplorable existence but the fun element had been lost. Ian had become increasingly aggressive in his womanising and heavier in his drinking. He complained of a headache. Adam just told him to 'drink less and take a couple of paracetamols'. So much for the early diagnosis.

New Year's Eve was always as important for Adam as it was for Ian, who liked to think of himself as a genuine Stuart, once of Scotland. He had even bought a large piece of Highland hill from the Forestry Commission as an investment.

It was his turn to throw the party. Tracy, in the guise of busying herself, could hardly hide the tension. Melanie looked at Adam questioningly. People were arriving in good numbers when Adam found Ian in his den with an extra-large whisky in hand. He approached him.

'What's the matter, Ian?' He enquired, pretending to be casual.

'That bitch gets on my nerves and I have a terrible headache.'

'C'mon now, Ian, let's find a couple of tablets – everyone's arriving.' Adam became concerned.

'All right. OK, let's.' Ian rubbed his eyes and stood up. He swayed, dropped his glass and crashed headlong on to the glass coffee table, foam pouring out of the corners of his mouth. Adam noticed that his right thumb and index finger were twitching and realised the danger. The fit soon became more generalised and he had to save his friend's tongue, but Ian was fighting him off. Adam yelled for Tracy and shouted to the guests that the den was out of bounds.

Jacket off, he went to work to save his friend's life on the floor of the small den. Broken glass covered the carpet. His first thought was late-onset epilepsy, but he soon remembered the twitching right hand and thought he was up against a Jacksonian type of attack. As he controlled the fit, Ian quietened down but became incontinent. Adam was hoping that the exhausted man might now fall asleep, but two further attacks followed. He managed to drag Ian into his bedroom, and when he was satisfied that his tongue and breathing were safe he called for an ambulance. Adam was officiously told that, being the day it was and because of a big pile-up at the bottom of the M1, it would be some time before they would be there, especially as there was a doctor already present.

Adam had his friend admitted to King Edward VII Hospital, where his well-known colleague, the neurosurgeon Sir Charles Little, agreed with him that a space-occupying lesion was the likely diagnosis. He went to the anteroom and gently told Tracy that Ian had a brain tumour which had possibly overgrown itself and burst. She started to shake, but there were no visible tears in the coveted green eyes.

A week later Ian Gordon Stuart, aged thirty-six, was buried in Highgate Cemetery. Tracy was 'too upset' to attend his funeral.

On 13 January 1975 Adam, with a transparent pretext, visited Tracy and they made love on the rug in front of the open fire.

26

Divorce

Adam quickly invented a new friend for the purpose of the 'Monday Club' so as to spend as much time as he could with Tracy in Highgate. For the first time in his life he felt he was with a woman he loved truly, and like many men in love before him he thought he could walk on water. In fact he was destined to sink in mud.

Twice a week they visited restaurants around the northern edge of London or more recklessly in the West End. The two were in love and nothing else seemed to matter to them. The showgirls soon realised that his interests now lay elsewhere. They all knew who Tracy Stu' was but she was never regarded as one of them, however much she wanted to be. Although her TV parts were good, she always managed just to miss the really big break, but as a model she was second to none. It all went well for her until she was told that it was all right to have hardly any breasts as a young model, but those in their thirties were expected to have something more to hang a bodice on.

⁓

'Zeny, do you think I am too flat chested?'
'Stu', darling, I love you as you are.' Adam didn't hesitate.
'That's an implicit statement that I am.'
'No, it is an explicit statement of my feelings.'

'OK, Doc, do you know a decent plastic surgeon, then?'

'Yes I do, I counsel for a dozen or so of them, why?'

'I want new breasts. Can you please help me? My job is on the line.'

'If you are sure that's what you want, of course I will, but there is no need for it on my account.'

'Zeny, it is not for you, it is not for me either. Every time I lose a few pounds I have to stuff more cotton wool into my bra. The clothes don't hang right on me. I am on my own with a child to support, I need to earn every penny there is. Ian changed his will a month before he died, everything is in trust for Joe, and that is controlled by his father, who vehemently objects to my way of life. All I've got is a small lump sum to tide me over and a very meagre monthly allowance. I must be able to earn.'

'All right, in principle I'm all for it, if the patient is committed, which I can see you are. Leave it with me.'

He poured a glass of Perrier for her and for himself a glass of Chablis *premier cru* and listened intently as she poured out her heart for the first time, describing how violent Ian had become even since their holiday in Bermuda.

'Ian's personality changed because of the growing tumour.' The realisation that he had missed something important was dawning on him. 'I can't believe that I didn't even consider it. The aggression when out with girls. It was all part of the disease process. It's so simple and I am a doctor, I should have spotted it.' Adam buried his face in his hands.

The dinner arrived and both of them pushed the food around the plate. After the main course Adam asked for the bill.

～

Stu' had her new breasts within a month and Adam was allowed to peep under the bandages at his first hospital visit.

'What do you think, Zeny?' She asked with a twinkle in her eye.

'No pun intended, Stu', promise, but I am hugely delighted.'

Adam visited her in the hospital at every opportunity and when Tracy was discharged he picked her up in his brand-new white convertible 4.2 E-type Jaguar, the motoring milestone of the seventies.

He took no appointments after four in order to be able to see her in Highgate before his trek back home to Knightsbridge. The inordinate amount of time he spent on the road gave him plenty of opportunity for soul-searching. For the first time in his life, and to his absolute delight, he was unselfishly in love and just as much in lust. He knew now that his marriage was over and it would only be a matter of time before he would need to leave home, and that would have to be engineered to suit all concerned. He realised that his attitude and actions were pathognomonic of male midlife crisis, but he shrugged his shoulders. He certainly was not going to hypnotise himself and suggest some weird and wonderful solution for his subconscious.

Melanie had long ago transferred her remaining affection to the twins, and once again she was happy to be in her square quarter of a mile. The once bubbly obsessive became a phobic recluse and Adam knew that he was the main cause of this. He argued with himself that as he was determined to leave and marry Tracy, the best thing was to remove the cause from Melanie's life and leave home as soon as possible.

Tracy's operation, as far as she was concerned, was nothing less than a miracle, and if a miracle is not shown off to the world – whether it is prepared for it or not – it's not worth having. She was ready for her first night out and Adam decided on the Savoy. On Saturday nights the restaurant was packed to bursting, but he managed to get a table on the upper level. Tracy worked out her entrance by an intricate scientific formula as to length of steps versus pace and rhythm, which worked to perfection. The heads moved in unison as she followed the maître d' and Adam to the corner table. With the fountain of her golden hair and her pure white chiffon dress with the deepest décolletage in town, designed to launch her brand-new breasts, she stopped several conversations. She took her seat against the wall to the delight of all those looking at her, and whilst Adam acknowledged a few smiles she tossed her head left to right and then back again, which ensured that her long hair would end up as nature had intended it.

During a not too remarkable dinner, which was washed down with a fine Pouilly Montrachet for Adam and the usual Perrier for Tracy, they were entertained by the wonderful miniature comedian, Ronnie Corbett, and his statuesque six-foot French wife. They had one dance. Adam still had to be a little careful not to bump too emphatically into the newest of all the superstructures in the capital. Neither of them wanted to end Tracy's wonderful social reappearance. At midnight they caught a taxi to La Valbonne nightclub, fashionably situated just around the corner from Carnaby Street, and settled down to a drink.

Adam took Tracy's hand and looked into her green eyes. 'Will you marry me?' He asked gently.

Her forehead was furrowed as she returned his stare. 'No, Adam, I won't.' Her answer was emphatic.

Adam was speechless in amazement. 'Why ever not?' Was all he could muster up, before Tracy took his arm and led him to the dance floor.

They danced for a while and returned to their table. Adam took her hands again. 'Tracy, was that your final answer, before?'

'Now look here, Zeny, you're a married man who lives with his wife and children. You're in no position to propose to me. I'm very fond of you, you make me very happy, I love being with you, but I don't know if I am ready to marry again. You know I married Ian when I was eighteen, and now, at long last, I am free, I want to stay exactly that for a while. I am truly sorry, because you and I are so good together. Ask me in a year, I may feel differently then.'

'It's a deal. I need a year to sort a few things out myself. Meanwhile I won't let you out of my sight.'

'At least not on Tuesdays and Fridays.' Tracy was more than a little sarcastic.

'I thought it was Saturday hours ago?' Adam smiled as he pulled her nearer. 'What's the matter, darling?'

'I feel very confused Adam, I'm a typical Pisces, just swimming in both directions, please forgive me.'

'You can't do anything I wouldn't forgive, you know that.'

'I know, Adam, I know, I love you too.' She started to cry. 'I am so sorry, being tough isn't one of my better traits.'

'Come on, sweetheart, let's go home.' He took her hand.

On the way towards Highgate, quietness prevailed in the Jaguar. It seemed to them there were more crossroads appearing in their lives than north London could provide.

For the first time since Ian's death Adam left his car in the driveway right in front of the solid oak front door. Tracy would normally ask him to park at the bottom of the garden and walk through the back gate. 'Just for the sake of appearances' – after all, she was supposed to be a widow in mourning. They went straight to bed. Adam made tender love to her, in spite of every bone in his body demanding passion, force and conquest.

～

Adam would try to call Tracy several times a day, not always successfully. His staff, knowing his aversion to the telephone, found this totally incredible. When he managed to contact her, she would chat away about anything. She seemed to adore the contraption, so be it gossip, work or sex she would burn the wires and titillate Adam to distraction. By four in the afternoon he could stand it no longer and he would drive to Highgate, like a maniac, for an hour of love, or just to be near her. The intensity of their physical relationship became all-consuming. It was certainly consuming Adam's mind, to such a degree that he was throwing caution to the winds, as if he were a mindless confetti-thrower at a wedding.

Adam took Tracy out twice a week. Tuesdays were bistro nights, mainly locally or just off into the countryside around the North Circular Road, and Fridays they would venture farther, staying the night in some picturesque small hotel. Although marriage was no longer mentioned by Adam – he was holding out for the year – there was little doubt in his mind that they were heading that way.

Within a month Adam received a thunderous reminder of his real position. He returned home early one Saturday morning to find Melanie standing angrily in his way, waving a well-enlarged photograph of Tracy and himself taken on their first night out in the La Valbonne. A most flattering picture that displayed their relationship perfectly. As he looked at it Melanie threw some more, of all shapes and sizes, in the air. One, taken in the Paris House Restaurant in Woburn, fell at his feet. He picked it up.

'Melanie, darling, you didn't need to go to this trouble, I was about to come clean with you anyway,' he started softly.

'Don't you "darling" me, you disgusting pig. And don't flatter yourself either. They came unsolicited from Mr Stuart, Ian's father. That whoring cow of yours is looking at another set of these photos right now, having to explain to the old man what sort of grieving widow she is and whether she would ever make a fit mother.' Melanie lurched to the left a little as she took a swig from her gin and tonic. 'What the hell is going on here? How can you subject me to this humiliation?'

'Enough, Melanie, you've made your point, there is no need for name-calling. I will leave in a few minutes. I want to talk to the boys.'

He walked into their room and they stopped playing and looked at him immediately. They were, naturally, well prepared.

'Look, boys, this is going to be very difficult. You understand that Mummy and I do not love each other any more.' Adam sat down on a bean-bag with tears in his eyes.

'But Mummy says she loves you!' Rick interrupted.

'And she also said that you have lots of girlfriends,' Andy said quietly.

'Did she? Well now, then it must be true. You must always believe your mother.' Adam slowly regained his composure.

'Is it Auntie Tracy you love now?'

'Yes, as a matter of fact it is.' Adam swallowed. 'Not that it matters much. I only called in to tell you both that I am leaving this house now and that your mother and I will come to some arrangement about when I can come and see you.'

'Couldn't you stay, Dad, and forget all about her?' Rick was pleading.

'No, Richard, I couldn't do that. One day you will understand and know why.' Adam kissed the boys, who held back resentfully, before they relaxed enough for a hug.

Adam left the room and went to pack an overnight bag. In great haste he threw a few things together and ran to his car.

Melanie walked into the boys' room to hear them making a pact never to call their father by that name again. She called them to her, saying, 'Well done, my boys – well done.' With that statement her affections were totally transferred to the twin boys.

~

Adam spent the next month at the Churchill Hotel, reorganising his life and renovating the flat above his rooms at 43a Harley Street.

Used as a dumping ground for several decades by doctors passing through the premises, it was full of disused medical equipment and out-of-date drugs. Old magazines and medical books with yellowing pages were scattered everywhere. On top of this mix was a liberal thickness of dust, enveloping everything as if it was guarding their secrets.

The interior designer worked miracles with the place and at the end of the month Adam had a very smart three-bedroom flat, which any newly created bachelor would have envied. The only things he took from Ovington Square were his books and gramophone records. The cheaper end of the antique market was about to enjoy his business all over again. The three bedrooms were furnished in the dark mahogany favoured by the Victorians. The master bedroom received a little more attention with lighting concealed in strategic places. The smallest of the bedrooms had two beds ready for a possible visit by the twins. These came from Selfridges, a short distance around the block, which was about to become his local shop. The rest of the flat was furnished in antiques, from the hallway through the narrow corridor to the small study and the drawing room. The dining-room furniture had to be Regency reproduction 'for the time being'. The kitchen was state-of-the-art Möben, from Germany.

Tracy asked Adam to leave the choice of curtains for the bedroom to her as her house-warming present. He hoped it wasn't going to be pink. The 'grand opening' of the top-floor flat was scheduled for Friday, exactly four weeks after he left Knightsbridge. There were to be no guests, only Tracy and Adam. Bollinger for him and Perrier for her.

On arrival Tracy brought in her package and disappeared into the bedroom to hang the curtains on the previously fixed rails. On completion of the job Adam was called to give his approval to the shocking-pink curtains. He winced to himself, drew her closer and told her that they were 'a perfect choice for a man in love'.

Dinner was delivered from the Mignon, a Hungarian restaurant on Bayswater Road. He knew the owner, who had connections with Hungary. Adam had helped him out in the past with some currency transfer. He delivered it himself, giving Adam some instructions as to the warming up, if necessary. Adam thanked him and shook him by the hand emphatically. Glancing back at Tracy, the man leaned forward and told him with a knowing wink and more than a little Hungarian accent to 'have a sukkcesffull eevening' and reassured him that 'breengin the food, it vas no problema'.

They tucked into the cold fish in aspic starter, a very special Hungarian delicacy using perch-pike, followed by roast goose with pan-fried red cabbage and paprika potatoes. Over an hour later the meal concluded with Gundel pancake, the invention of the famous restaurant in Budapest. Mr Gundel, the greatest culinary name over a century before, had thought it a good idea to stuff the thinnest pancakes he could make with a chocolate and walnut mixture. After the meal Tracey, clutching her stomach, declared that Adam was 'deliberately sabotaging her diet'.

During the dinner Adam spoke only in the plural, as if this arrangement was virtually permanent. Tracy riposted that having a bachelor flat was not synonymous with being one, and her career must come first 'for Joe's sake'. He realised that the best psychology was not to pursue the point any more at such an early stage of their relationship. The whole thing would fall into his lap eventually, of that he was convinced.

～

Adam and Tracy became inseparable once again and were to be found everywhere that mattered. From the crush bar of Covent Garden to the pub around the corner from Harley Street, or Highgate, they were soon known by the regulars and staff alike.

Summer came but there was still a long way for the year to run before Adam could propose to Tracy again. Over dinners Tracy would go into rhapsodies about how much she enjoyed life without ties, and when Adam told her that his life was already tied to her she would playfully remind him that his divorce would take at least another two to three years. This, of course, would not stop her suggesting that he should make love to her on the long white bonnet of the E-type or 'listen to the grass growing' on the pasture behind the cottage-hotel they stayed at. Theirs was – as far as she was concerned – a 'fun affair', and the more fun the better.

It was a hot summer evening as they arrived at the magnificent home of Douglas, a new friend of Tracy's, for a barbecue in Bray. The beautiful garden stretched down to the Thames, where the swans swam close to the shore for titbits.

Douglas was a short, podgy estate agent, who appeared to be no threat to the women who buzzed around him enthusiastically. The party was a great success. Adam and Tracy tormented each other as they danced their own crazed version of something between the twist and the tango. Their sensual attraction was evident to all comers. It was eventually released in the hot stillness of the open night in a secluded part of the scented garden.

On the way back to Harley Street the ecstatically happy Adam was still asking who was who and how long she had known them. It appeared that they were all new friends of hers, models and their friends whom she had got to know 'quite recently'.

She returned to Highgate on the Sunday morning, waving farewell and blowing kisses from her car window.

~

Adam was in the middle of his Monday morning consulting session when Hilary coldly announced 'Tracy Stu" on the telephone. He could always sense that she did not really like her, but today she sounded even more icy. It was most unusual for Tracy to call him at work.

'Adam, darling, I am sorry for disturbing you at work, are you with a patient?' Her voice was softer than usual.

'No, sweetheart. Is there something wrong? You sound troubled.'

'Well, yes. I suppose there is.' There was silence for an everlasting split second. 'Adam, we have always said that the strength of our relationship is the honesty we have with each other, so I feel the need to come clean with you.'

'Tracy, darling, what on earth has happened?' Adam asked, feeling somehow that he knew what she was going to say.

'Adam, yesterday Douglas brought back my things from the barbecue and … we made love.' Her voice was hardly audible.

Adam felt as if he had been hit by a bolt of lightning. He shivered and dropped the receiver on to his desk and held his head. 'My God, what have you done?' On the other end of the line Tracy heard Adam repeating the words over and over.

He came to, Tracy's voice shouting from the receiver, 'Adam, Adam, Zeny, listen to me, I didn't mean it, it just happened. I don't know what to do or what to say. I'm sorry, Zeny, I'm sorry.'

'What difference does that make?' He sounded as if in a haze. 'Oh my God.' Adam replaced the receiver and wept.

The light went out on Hilary's small switchboard and she waited for him to buzz her. There was nothing. After a few minutes she became concerned and knocked on the consulting-room door. Hearing no answer, she gently opened the door. She saw the distraught man with his head in his hands.

'AZ, what's the matter, what's happened?' She walked around to his chair and tried to pull him up from his slumping posture.

'It's all over, Hilary! Everything I ever wanted is … over.' He slumped again.

'There's no way you can work in this state, I am going to cancel the rest of your appointments, you'd better go upstairs to the flat, immediately. Don't worry, AZ, leave it to me.'

'No, Hilary, just give me five minutes. Oh, why, Tracy, why did you spoil what was so precious?' He virtually mumbled his words.

He got through the rest of the day as if on autopilot, like a robot. Walking up to his flat, he felt mentally and physically exhausted. He sat down, his thoughts a kaleidoscope of what might have been. He imagined himself in happy situations with Tracy and little Joe, the twins, all in pictures of friendly and loving togetherness without any interference from Melanie or this Douglas. They had no right to get anywhere near his montage. Her face would appear again, those green eyes and the cascading blonde hair. Surely a true angel, if there ever was one. His daydreaming was suddenly interrupted by the ringing of the telephone. He picked it up. There was a little silence.

'Adam, please talk to me.' The voice was hardly audible.

'Yes, Tracy, I will – if I can.'

'Can you please come over to see me? Please,' she sobbed quietly.

'No, Tracy, I can't – let me think about things and I'll call you.' He put the receiver down before she could continue and staggered to bed. Sleep did come – eventually.

Adam woke around two and reached out to see whether Tracy was there. It was all a nightmare. He soon realised it was not. His thoughts returned. No, he must not throw it all away. He picked up his bedside telephone and called Tracy. The phone was picked up after one ring.

'Adam, is it you?'

'It is, darling. I must see you once more.'

'Not "once more", darling, always, will you?'

'Let us think about all this. I'll see you Friday night, we'll go out and talk.'

'Friday's such a long way away. Adam, tomorrow, please,' Tracy pleaded.

'No, let's leave it until Friday.'

⁓

From Highgate on the M1 all the way to Bedfordshire the most sensitive subject they touched upon was the health of the children and that of Tracy's corgi. Other than the initial peck on the cheek, there was no physical contact between the two.

In the delightful half-timbered building of Peter Chandler's Paris House restaurant, they were seated at a small table just past the window, which looked on to the long driveway into the grounds of Woburn Abbey. Politeness was the order of the day, each of them hoping that the past few days had given them a chance to think, to weigh and balance the situation. It was all pretended sophistication.

Adam thought it prudent to start the evening with a decent-sized whisky – a little Dutch courage would be no bad idea. Tracy, with her large glass of mineral water, was ready for the discussion. Intentionally, Adam delayed until the main course, to avoid interruption.

The arrival of the *saumon en croûte* signalled the time for an opening gambit. Adam gathered some strength and, as in his youth, when confronted with situations like this, he took a deep breath, mentally counted to five and launched himself at the subject full on.

'Tracy, I feel that it is the proof of my love that I find it impossible to share you with anyone else, especially a nincompoop like that Douglas.' He suspected it was the wrong thing to have said as soon as it left his lips.

'Adam, Douglas happens to be very kind and gentle.' Now Tracy suddenly felt that she had somewhat over-defended him.

'Well, is that it? Kindness and gentleness versus my obsessive passion. Is that it?'

'I suppose it is. Adam, you move too fast for me. I have said it before, for the first time in my life I feel free and I am not in too much of a hurry to give up this freedom. It has even occurred to me to play the field a little. You have, why not me? It's only human nature. Am I honest enough?'

'You are that all right, Tracy, you're leaving nothing to the imagination. Perhaps I thought you were something which you are plainly not.'

'Adam, I have behaved in an exemplary fashion. In our business you get propositions every day. Damn it, I have been tempted several times, but I've never misbehaved until Sunday. I am fed up with being good and proper. Can't I just behave like you? That would be some meeting of the minds, wouldn't it?'

Adam did not answer, pretending to be busy pouring. He sipped a little of his wine. 'You mean to say you want to be like I *was*, don't you? I was about to turn myself inside out for you.'

'Adam, darling, I do know that. I couldn't believe the change in you, I loved it.' Her voice softened. 'I am just not ready to reciprocate.'

Adam looked at the golden face of the woman he loved; she looked distressed and he knew her tears were about to flow freely. He changed his approach.

'My love for you would not be worth tuppence if I could throw it away because of a fuck. All right. But no more! Agree?' He forced a smile.

'Adam, I feel you intentionally don't want to understand what I am saying. No deals until we both feel free, until we both decide, both of us at the same time.' There was a little anger in her voice. 'Adam, I will be frank. I obviously don't love you the way you love me. Yes, there will be more fucks, if you please – as a matter of fact I am joining a man this coming weekend.'

'May I ask whom? I have an idea that it's not Douglas.' Suddenly Adam had a strange feeling of relief.

'Why not? It is the American singer Sunshine Johnson. At long last I managed to catch his eye after one of his concerts. He asked me out and I've said yes.'

'Oh! The swinging, rocking, ever-moving, hand-jiving Sunny Johnson, eh? The black singer with the dyed-blond hair that matches yours? I understand it all! Thank you for your honesty, Tracy. You have given me the happiest three months of my life. I thank you for that. You have also broken my heart, I do not thank you for that. It is over, then. We have a long drive back, let's go.'

At her front door Adam gazed at Tracy. The moonlight behind her gave her hair a vibrant glow. The beauty he wanted, wanted so much and had had for such a short while, was slipping out of his hands. He could no longer do anything about it. Looking into her eyes, he saw the tears he had been expecting. He took her into his arms. She melted for a moment and he kissed her passionately, more passionately than ever before. He loosened his arms and Tracy slipped out of his grip. She turned away and he reached out. It was too late. The door closed behind her.

∾

Tracy had to be erased from his mind so Adam threw himself headlong into work. He spoke to Arthur about going on a mission somewhere in the Middle East, anywhere, but he was told that unless he wanted to retrain as a commando, there was no detail for him. He considered throwing himself into the whisky bottle or the river, but ended up with the mundane job of working out the details of his divorce.

After Tracy was no longer in his life he did not want her to feature in his divorce. He instructed his solicitors to make any concession Melanie wanted – just keep Tracy's name out of the petition. Eventually the formula agreed was that there would be 'several unnamed women' at various hotels in and around the capital, implying his unsuitability as a husband and father. Access to the boys was thus restricted to a monthly afternoon visit, which might increase to a fortnightly one after the decree absolute. Financially he fared somewhat better. Adam was to be responsible for all expenses relating to the twins' education at a boarding school, but Melanie asked for no financial support for herself. The Battersby-Smyths would take care of her, if she took over the running of Sudley Hall.

The expected loss of Melanie coupled with the totally unexpected loss of Tracy left a large void in Adam's life. Suddenly he had too much time on his hands. He couldn't even go home to stick a model Wellington bomber together for the ceiling of the boys' room. The last thing he wanted was to ask a woman out for dinner. The memory of Tracy haunted him and made sure of that. As if it was an act of conspiracy, her career took off meteorically. Off the catwalk she was to be found in the glossy gossip magazines, usually near Sunshine Johnson. Adam longed for the days of laughter with Ian on Fridays, but had to be content with opera and concerts, alone. There were, of course, a number of women who knew of his new-found loneliness, but he parried every hint at a possible date with them. Several months passed, and the only friendly support he enjoyed was from Hilary and the rest of the staff, who stayed loyal to him in every way. His workrate naturally increased and he published two original papers, lectured at the Royal Society of Medicine and wrote a chapter for a training compendium for young psychiatrists. In the evenings and during the nights he would think of Tracy and wonder whether she ever thought of him. The short encounter seemed a million years away, and as if it had happened to someone else, somewhere else.

The next three years passed like a dream too confusing to be recollected. The only tangible result was flying lessons at Biggin Hill Flying Club and the obtaining of his Private Pilot's Licence, much to the delight of the boys. The rest was irrelevant wilderness.

27

MESSENGER

Adam was hungry and decided to take advantage of the still, clear evening. Longing to taste something from his childhood made him head for the respected small Hungarian restaurant in Soho, and he walked to Greek Street, to the *Gay Hussar*. The superb menu offered the delights that brought back wonderful memories. Veal *pörkölt* with egg dumplings, lightly smoked breast of goose, stuffed cabbage à la Kolozsvár or the one and only Transylvanian mixed grill. Once again feeling that he could demolish the whole menu, he settled for a light chicken soup with vermicelli followed by the *pörkölt*, as suggested by Victor Sassie. The cubed veal cooked in pure pork lard was swirling around his taste buds when he noticed four elderly Hungarians discussing something in Magyar which they obviously regarded as most important. When Transylvania was mentioned several times in succession, he decided to listen more carefully. What he heard was enough for him to walk across and introduce himself.

'Gentlemen, my name is Dr Adam Zenta, I am one of you. Forgive me, but I couldn't help overhearing what you were talking about. Thank God I am not the Romanian military attaché out with his girlfriend. Though I suppose he wouldn't go to a Hungarian restaurant. No offence, gentlemen, but your security should be a shade tighter.'

The four faces turned to look at him. A portly, slightly balding man who was clearly their leader stood up.

'I am John Szabó – well, János, I suppose. I have heard of you, Doctor. Frankly you are a bit of a disappointment to us.' His voice was slow and deliberate, emphasising each word.

'I am sure you are going to tell me why, but meanwhile may I join you with my whisky?' Adam smiled disarmingly.

John introduced the others in quick succession and Adam pulled a chair over.

'Adam, what I meant was that there you are, perhaps the best-placed Hungarian in the land, and you have not once made an effort to join any of our organisations in the UK, you have never turned up for a celebration of any of our National Days. You would rather watch the Tiller girls than our folk dance groups. You know, our girls' legs are just as shapely.'

'Well, John, you're obviously a straight-talking man and I don't mind you admonishing me. In many ways you are right, but there is this thing called an "invitation", and I haven't had one of those. But I'm here now, will that do?' To his everlasting amazement Adam found that, yes, they did know a lot about him. They knew about the football trips, without their deeper implications – though they'd even guessed some of those anyway. On the other hand he knew nothing of them except that John Szábó had written an article in the *Daily Telegraph* criticising the Trianon protocol of the 1920 Treaty of Versailles.

They agreed with Adam and, Glenfiddichs in hand, accepted in principle that he would take part in their fight to ensure that the true Hungary would emerge from the changes they all knew were imminent. Over the next few weeks they met frequently, talking over the subject again and again. What they eventually decided on was called *'The Gay Hussar Plan'*. Implementation of this was dependent on further intelligence from Romania. It would take some time.

Britain was in the throes of political turmoil. A weak and unpopular Labour government led by James Callaghan struggled from one crisis to another. High inflation and weak currency meant that money had to be smuggled out of the country in knickers, bras and any other concealed places that could be found, and after all this trouble sterling was refused in several countries. There was a sense of insecurity that culminated in the second wave of the brain drain. Most of the stars of entertainment became tax exiles rather than part with ninety-eight per cent of their income. Adam steadfastly refused offers from Psychiatric Congress participants to move to lucrative Santa Monica Boulevard practices in Hollywood. He didn't want to lose his sons, who were reasonably happily settled at Harrow.

Social conversations were invariably focused on politics. How could they revitalise and modernise the country, which had become the prisoner of the Militant Tendency and the trade union barons? As a dedicated right-winger this irritated Adam intensely. This new wave of politics had little to do with the England he knew. Surely this, if any, was the country of progressive conservatism and values and not that of the rantings of some crackpot like the Midlands' Red Robbo or Liverpool's silk-suited new Trotsky, Derek Hatton. Adam decided to throw his lot in with Conservative Central Office and walked into 52 Smith Square.

'So you want to work for our party in the coming general election?' asked the greying chairman.

'Wholeheartedly, sir. I can no longer stand on the sidelines,' Adam answered as he sat opposite the new party chairman in his poorly furnished and rather poky office.

'In what capacity, may I ask?'

'I don't mind if it is delivering leaflets, canvassing or psychoanalysing every opponent in the coming election,' Adam answered, more or less taking charge of his interview.

'I am afraid it is too late to put you on our list of approved candidates, we have a full complement for that. Perhaps next time. I see you live and work in Harley Street. Would you like to work for the new party leader, Mrs Thatcher?'

'I would be delighted. She is the sort of politician this country needs. Finchley, isn't it?'

'Yes. I will get you the details of the constituency chairman and her agent.' He flicked a switch on his intercom. 'Gabrielle, could you please bring me the package on the Finchley constituency. No, the small details will do for the moment. OK, Dr Zenta will pick them up on his way out, then.' He turned back to Adam. 'You know, we have to work on a shoestring here. She can't come up, there's nobody to mind the phone. Would you believe it?' He shook his head.

Adam told him not to worry about it, stood up and shook hands with him. On the way down the most basic of party HQ staircases, he could not help remembering the last time he had walked down one, in Pécs. It was sumptuous and he had the secretary of the Communist Party in front of him, just a few inches away from the tip of the bayonet of his rifle.

In the office downstairs, the package was waiting for him. A very smart young woman, Gabrielle, dressed in a red suit that followed every curve of her stunning body, held it out in her hand. In her mid-twenties, he thought. She had lively blue eyes and her hair, in which Adam detected a reddish tinge, was cut in a bob to just below her ears. When he introduced himself she gave a smile that transformed her business like expression into the best dental advertisement any toothpaste manufacturer could wish for. Her captivating smile still in place, she handed the package to Adam.

'Everything you need is here for you, until you meet the chairman of the constituency, Doctor. I'm sure they will be delighted to gain such a famous helper.' The smile continued.

'It's all for the cause.' Adam was strangely embarrassed looking at the beautiful woman. 'Well, thank you, Gabrielle. Hope to see you again.' He waved his hand and walked out into the secluded, leafy square.

In the late afternoon sunshine Adam decided against a taxi and with a spring in his step and delight in his heart that he was about to rejoin the human race, he strolled along the Embankment towards the House of Commons. He admired the overwhelming magnificence of the Gothic edifice even if he wasn't in agreement with what the Labour government was doing inside it. Big Ben struck four o'clock.

Adam continued his walk along Whitehall and cut through to St James's Street, crossed Piccadilly and entered the Burlington Arcade. In his effort to start an economic upturn he bought an expensive navy blue tie with light blue spots. Spotted ties made him feel good. By the time he was climbing the stairs up to his flat in Harley Street, he felt that the long walk had physically rehabilitated him. He showered and looked in the mirror. A handsome man in his early middle age, greying at the temples but retaining his good features, looked back and winked at him. He pulled his stomach in and decided that things were still 'reasonably all right'.

~

Adam walked into the Royal Opera House and settled into the plush crimson velvet seat at the end of the first row of the dress circle. He looked around the glorious red-and-gilt theatre and then into the auditorium. Below him swayed a multitude of standing youngsters. Central Bank had had the good sense to remove all stall seats for a Promenade-style performance of Puccini's *Tosca*, with none other than the new wonder tenor, Luciano Pavarotti, in the role of Cavaradossi. The expectation of the audience was soon rewarded as the big bearded tenor lumbered down from the makeshift scaffolding surrounding the painting of the Madonna he was working on. He hardly seemed to take a breath and in a virtually throwaway manner he delivered the stage-setting short aria '*Recondita armonia*', strange harmony of diverse beauties, which was to set the standard for anyone who ever dared to sing it after him.

As Adam stood up at the beginning of the first interval and looked at the youthful crowd standing before him, he noticed two women together some ten yards ahead. The one on the left was wearing her red-tinged hair in a bob. He elbowed his way through the throng towards them, his effort much rewarded when he found himself standing in front of Gabrielle. Gabrielle's face burst into the smile of smiles. 'Dr Zenta, what are you doing here?'

'Well, I just popped in to buy you ladies a glass of champagne. I am Adam Zenta,' he introduced himself to the other.

They walked up to the crush bar and were soon standing drinking the house Lanson. The short and hurried interval conversation confirmed that the two women were Conservative Central Office agents out for a cheap night at the opera. Their talking established that one was single and Gabrielle was married. Hell, he thought.

During the second interval he learned that Gabrielle's husband was in Spain, in Marbella, buying a bar, which would take him 'some time'. Good, he thought. They ate some of the gelatine-glazed open sandwiches washed down with a little more of the Lanson.

By the time Cavaradossi met his firing squad and Tosca had jumped from the battlements of the Castle St Angelo, Gabrielle's friend had decided that Adam was going to be hers. All she had to do was to inform him. The opera over, Adam asked the two girls whether they would join him perhaps for another drink at La Valbonne.

The three of them settled around a circular table near the mini-fountain and rockery. Adam asked Gabrielle for a dance. She wore a loose long black printed linen skirt and a minuscule mustard-yellow bodice that hardly covered her front. He held her close and asked when she was expecting her husband back. The 'perhaps never' answer encouraged him, but he was soon told that her friend Louise really liked him and as she had absolutely no complications in her life, the stage was set. Adam, ignoring her recommendation, asked her whether he could call her at Smith Square The 'absolutely no, out of the question' put an end to that and he handed her a calling card. 'The second number is my private one, please call me,' he said as she placed the card in her tiny handbag.

Louise dragged Adam on to the dance floor, gyrating while the disc jockey let Mick Jagger yell out that for some reason he 'could get no satisfaction'. Adam told Louise that with a half a dozen hypnosis sessions he could virtually guarantee Mick's problems would be over. She whispered into his ear, sensually catching the edges with her teeth, that it wasn't a problem she had. Adam looked down at her ample bosom, and nodded in presumed agreement.

∼

It was some two months later when Hilary buzzed Adam on the intercom. 'A Mrs Windgate is on the line with a private call for you.' He wondered for a moment.

'It's Gabrielle, isn't it?' He answered with some anticipation.

'Yes, Adam, it is. I hope I'm not disturbing you,' she said. Her voice was very quiet.

'Well, I'm having a break between a paranoiac schizophrenic and a manic depressive, your call could not have come at a better time. How's Central Office, are we still on line to give Mr Callaghan a bloody nose?'

'Things are looking good for us. How is Finchley doing?'

'All I can say is that Mrs T. is slave-driver. I was out canvassing for two hours last night and when I returned, she wanted to know if I had met anyone disagreeing. I said that other than a young couple chasing me away in Camille Street shouting, "Thatcher, Thatcher, the milk snatcher" things seemed to be all right.'

'You didn't tell her, did you?'

'I certainly did. Mind you, she is a tough cookie, the best thing that ever happened to us. Well, how are you?'

'Oh, very well, thanks. I've just found your card and decided to let you know that I'm ready for that dinner.' Her voice trembled a little. 'Gosh, I've never done this before. I'm ringing up asking for a date, how awful.'

'Don't worry about it. I did ask you to ring, didn't I? So when, Gabrielle?' The date was settled. Adam was to pick Gabrielle up at her mother's house in Battersea.

When he arrived at the simple whitewashed semi-detached house in Hazelbeach Crescent, Gabrielle noticed the gleaming white E-type drawing up and came to open the door. With a perfect sense of up-to-the-minute fashion she wore a just-above-the-knee miniskirt with purple knee-length plastic boots. He gazed at her gorgeous face, surrounded by the bob that had drawn his attention to her at Smith Square. She was just about to close the door when a small child popped her head around it and grabbed Gabrielle by her left leg. Adam bent down and asked her name. The little girl, whose face was covered in chocolate, said that she was Victoria, and added pertly that she wanted her mummy back soon. Adam reassured her and watched while she disappeared into the house in the direction of her grandmother.

The journey on the A4 towards the west gave Gabrielle a chance to explain that her husband had not, after all, returned from Spain – well, not in good time anyway – and that she regarded her marriage as over, bar the legalities involved. She remembered their last meeting as a most pleasant one, and anyway, he seemed 'to fit the bill for the moment', she added cheekily. Adam chose the long drive to get to know Gabrielle as well as possible before dinner. They chatted freely as the gleaming white E-type sped towards the Thames Valley, passing Heathrow airport.

Gabrielle knew that little Victoria would remain in her charge and thus the job at Central Office was essential for them as an income, which she would need to supplement from time to time. To do that she had signed on with model agencies for some extra work.

'I don't think I'll ever be as successful as your last girlfriend.' She smiled. 'She seems to be doing rather well.'

'Well now, you seem to know a little about me, or is it a lot?' Adam asked.

'Don't forget, I am a researcher, and it wasn't too difficult. Tracy still keeps saying some complimentary things about you in her interviews!'

'You know, Gabrielle, those so-called loves of one's life are bad news and best kept in the past.' Adam tried to sound philosophical. 'Otherwise they just take you over.'

'Not having had one of those, I wouldn't know. Where are we going, Adam? I'm completely disoriented.'

An incisive way to change the subject, Adam thought. 'We are heading for the Waterside Inn at Bray, on the Thames. Fairly new, belongs to Michel Roux, the younger of the brothers, and it's having a very good press.'

'I'm sure it will be wonderful,' Gabrielle whispered and, looking around, gave Adam a chance to familiarise himself with her beautiful profile.

They stumbled out from under the black canvas top of the white sports car and the smartly dressed concierge raised his hand to his peaked cap. Adam handed over the keys and the two disappeared under the low lintel.

The intimate ante-area with bar concealed the immaculate kitchen and the large, elegant chintzy restaurant on the south bank of the River Thames; it was the most English of settings, where through the windows you could see swans swimming around the jetty. The leaves had just turned rusty red, some of them falling gently in the early autumn breeze. Inside, near the window on the left, the two were involved in a conversation that had even touched on the taboo of tentative first nights out.

Gabrielle had definite views which somewhat surprised Adam. She certainly belonged to the rising right wing of conservatism and was a great fan of Mrs Thatcher's, a clear manifestation of her working-class support, where political guts overrode entrenched class prejudice.

'Adam, you've had so many girlfriends, are you a latent homosexual trying to prove your manhood or something?' Once again she had veered through a subject change of a hundred and eighty degrees.

'Lead me to the nearest bed and I will give you the answer,' said Adam, somewhat taken aback. 'Anyway, I'm the psychiatrist, I should be asking the questions.'

'Adam, you're so nice, so easy to be with – nevertheless, I think we'll skip the test just the same.' She gave a smile that lit up the room.

'That's better. Gabrielle, you're very beautiful when you're serious, but when you smile, you're irresistible. You should be in films!'

'I did become Miss Colgate once.' She giggled.

The wine waiter interrupted them. 'Another bottle of Sancerre, sir?'

'Two at least,' Adam joked, 'we're having a great time!' He realised that the Perrier days were a thing of the past.

Two hours later they walked out to the narrow road where the smart concierge was waiting for them.

'Sir, you really shouldn't be driving your car,' the man whispered as he handed over the keys. 'Why don't you check into the hotel on Monkey Island, it's just around the corner.' He pointed to the left.

'Hmm, perhaps you're right.' Adam accepted the keys, climbed into the car and sat next to Gabrielle, who was curling comfortably into her seat. 'Did you hear that?' He asked, turning to her.

'Yes, I did – he's right, you know, we are rather drunk.'

'Well, in any event I have just given him a treble tip, for the idea alone,' Adam said, noticing Gabrielle's wide-eyed amazement at his nerve.

After the short drive Adam parked his precious E-type by the footbridge and they walked across the river to the secluded island nestled under the giant trees. The night porter rubbed his eyes, managed a faint smile and offered a room in the annexe. With the only luggage being Gabrielle's small handbag, Adam put his arm gently around her shoulder and they walked to the whitewashed building. As the door closed behind them he pushed her gently against the wall, his arms wrapped around her neck, and kissed her passionately. She didn't protest.

~

'Adam, hello, Adam!'
'Arthur?'
'Yes, it is. I must see you urgently!'
'Long time no hear – thank God. How are you?' Adam leaned back in his consulting-room chair.
'I need to talk to you, please. I'm on my way to you, Hilary said you'd just finished.'
'That's true,' said Adam 'I'll see you in twenty minutes.' He replaced the receiver and went over to his minibar, an antique globe in the far corner, and poured himself a Glenmorangie. Twenty minutes later the doorbell rang and an excited Arthur walked in, clutching his briefcase under his arm. Adam took it from him and put a large vodka and tonic in his hand.
'Adam, this one is right up your street. As you know we've had nothing important from Hungary lately – it seems to be the happiest barrack in the camp – but we have had word that they are building a VVER 440 nuclear reactor in Transdanubia, a rather old-fashioned type, and our chaps think it's dangerous. The plans are to start construction around 1980.'
'You want me to go and steal it for you?' Adam interrupted.
'Stop mocking, but yes, we want you to get your hands on the plans – you see, we must know what the repercussions might be if there is a major mishap.' Arthur tried to be serious. 'Apparently there is a discontented chap there who works as a design engineer. He's willing to sell. You see, it's not even political any more, it's a financial transaction.' Arthur rubbed his thumb and forefinger together and smiled.
'I suppose I am on a percentage this time?'

'Adam, stop fooling, you'll do rather well out of it, you always do. This is the set-up.'

For the next hour and a half Arthur talked incessantly, cursing the language of the Magyars as Adam corrected his pronunciation of names and places as usual. It was a little difficult for Adam to explain that Paks, the nuclear site, was not Pécs, Adam's university city. But he did compliment the work of the commercial attaché at the British Embassy, who had prepared the ground well for the operative. Sadly, he had no one in the field to pay the man and collect the microfilm and it would have been too dangerous for him to do it personally.

~

'Gabrielle, I have to go to a school reunion in Hungary – fancy a trip?' Adam popped the question as they were sipping their aperitifs in Le Gavroche, where Albert Roux, the godfather of all independent chefs, ruled.

'Adam, you always ask the sort of question that I cannot say no to. I've never been to the Continent – of course, I would love to join you, but I have to organise everything to make sure Vicky is all right. When do you plan to do this?'

'I haven't received details yet, but obviously some time after the general election. I'm leafleting a big chunk of Finchley next week, then I'll graduate to Mrs T's canvassing team; she's invited me, did you know that?'

'Of course I did, she has often mentioned the "dishy Hungarian psychiatrist", even in Smith Square. You know she has an eye for the boys,' she said, smiling.

'Yes, I can imagine that, but I'd hate to psychoanalyse her. I think she has an impenetrable mind. I might get something out of her under deep hypnosis, mind you, but it would need the deepest one possible.'

After a meal that was once described by fellow Hungarian Egon Ronay, now the world's leading culinary expert, as 'a gastronomic and pictorial achievement with no detail neglected', Gabrielle would have travelled to the moon.

Gabrielle and Adam were watching the general election results in the packed seminar room of Central Office with the other incumbents. Having worked in Finchley for the two weeks leading up to 3 May 1979, Adam decide to stay away from the constituency office, knowing that the party's party would really start in Smith Square. It wasn't as conclusive as he had predicted, but by the afternoon of next day the Conservative majority of forty-four was in the bag. With Mrs Thatcher amongst them, the long hours passed in anticipation. Adam, observing the Leader closely, detected some strange loneliness in her. She knew what she had to face; the others at best only guessed. After James Callaghan's dignified speech conceding victory, she managed a faint smile and returned to her thoughts.

At a quarter past two the telephone rang and Gabrielle lifted the receiver. Proudly, she walked up to Mrs Thatcher, who was sitting on a well-worn sofa.

'Mrs Thatcher, it's Buckingham Palace.' She would never forget uttering those words, which would change her county's history. Wearing a royal blue jacket and matching pleated skirt, Mrs Thatcher stood up. She straightened her clothes and walked to the telephone. There were few a 'yeses' then a 'certainly' and an 'of course', then she nodded to her husband. Denis stubbed out his cigar and the two left the room, which suddenly filled with spontaneous applause. Outside they walked through several hundred supporters and press to the waiting car, which sped off in the direction of the palace.

Turning to Gabrielle, Adam gave her a huge hug. Given the political significance of the evening, and thinking of the humiliating days of the International Monetary Fund having to bail the country out of its government-imposed doldrums in 1976, the best he could say was, 'At long last we will see the end of the IMF around here.'

Because of the large amount of money he was to carry out in Deutschmarks, which was the only currency the Hungarian atomic scientist was interested in, Adam waited until the week after Geoffrey Howe abolished the currency exchange controls. On 30 October he and the E-type were ready to drive off to Dover. Given that it was a convertible soft top and that the two suitcases tied to the boot would totally obliterate the rear view, Adam asked Arthur to get him two rear-view mirrors, carefully adapted for 'special use' – in this instance the black conical rear could be flicked open, providing enough space for bundles of large-denomination German currency on the outward trip and, hopefully, the microfilms on the way back. Gabrielle settled into her seat, oblivious to the real reason for the trip, and likely to be unforgiving if she were to learn of it.

The short journey across the English Channel brought memories flooding back of his crossing on the *Prinz Eugen* in the company of hundreds of vomiting Hungarians, twenty-two years before. Gabrielle told him 'not to tempt fate – it could happen again' as they settled down for a little food and the only wine available, Blue Nun Liebfraumilch. Adam agreed that drinking it might facilitate vomiting and left his glassful for Gabrielle, who put on a brave show as she polished it off.

With minimal interference from customs officials they were soon off in the direction of St Omer and outskirting Arras. Anxious to put distance behind them, they travelled as fast as the open Jaguar and the suitcases allowed them. After Cambrai they took to the N45. It was a good choice as Gabrielle was able to see and learn a little of the real French autumnal countryside. The inevitable penalty was having to slow down behind farming traffic. The planned lunch in Charleville-Mézières became the shortest afternoon tea in the smallest of bistros. They walked back to the parked car, Gabrielle declaring that she was still hungry, and why couldn't they spend a little more time in the charming town. Once back in the car, they swung up to pass Luxembourg, heading towards Saarbrücken, where they joined the A6, an immaculate German Autobahn enveloped in thick woodland. The Germans' love of the evergreen pine was as strong as ever. Recovering the time lost in France, they arrived in the early evening at their destination at the Europahof Hotel in Heidelberg, an establishment not to be scoffed at. They booked a table for dinner and went for a walk in the newly pedestrianised area just below the castle and drink a stein of Löwenbräu.

Wanting them both to enjoy the magnificent scenery, Adam asked for packed lunches the next day when he checked out. They stayed on the Autobahn until Rosenheim, where he took to the south, and at Kufstein he joined the 312. In the Tyrolean part of the Alps the real overwhelming magnificence of the majestic mountains enveloped the roads. This being a new part of the world for them both, in their minds they romantically claimed it as theirs. The slow road allowed them to enjoy the upward gradient to Bad Reichenhall and the steep climb to Berchtesgarten.

The Hotel Geiger, majestically situated on its own small hill in the mountains, looked commanding, very much a Germanic masterpiece – three separate units, all in pale yellow, with plentiful ornate rustic red wooden doors, balconies and windows. Adam parked his car near the large stone in the middle of the lawn and asked Gabrielle to clamber to the top of the rock. She carefully negotiated it and perched there. Adam's camera clicked and the result later became one of his most treasured photographs.

They planned to arrive in Budapest the next day, which involved a fairly early departure. Adam rubbed his eyes as the white sports car purred into action, indicating its desire to devour many more beautiful miles.

They bypassed Vienna to she South and took the road towards the airport. The Budapest sign to the left was soon followed by the village of Nickelsdorf. Adam told Gabrielle to brace herself. They were about to approach the infamous Iron Curtain; the crossing could be unpleasant.

The odd wooden control tower soon appeared, peering over the treetops, and then the frontier station building came into view. There was not much of a sinister quality about it, until one looked at the barriers at each end of the large reservation used for inspecting the vehicles. They were twelve-inch solid-steel bars operated by underground electrical motors, set in large reinforced slabs of concrete. Even the softening effect of the red, white and green paint in a maypole-like spiral could not disguise the fact that once between them one would need a tank to run them down – a far cry from the movie impressions of Aston Martins snapping them about the place like matchsticks in 007 films.

Adam received immediate attention as soon as he pulled up. The immaculately dressed young lieutenant with the Frontier Guard light green banding around his peaked cap and matching epaulets, proclaiming him to be an officer the uniformed branch of the Security Service, saluted Adam in the sports car and politely asked him for their passports. Adam complied.

'How much foreign currency do you have on you? You must declare it,' he said in excellent Hungarian.

'Oh, about three hundred pounds, whatever that's worth today – and my credit cards, of course.' Adam smiled.

'The cards don't matter. What about your companion?'

'Now I have no idea, Lieutenant, I am not in the habit of asking ladies how much they have on them.'

'I will see your passport, please, madam.' His English was acceptable.

He walked around the car and stopped at the rear-view mirror stuffed with Deutschmarks. 'This is a new fitting. Why?' He turned slowly and looked at Adam.

'Well, Officer, I have had to put them on as there was no rear vision because of the suitcases on the boot. You see, this is a disadvantage with a convertible.' Adam was anxiously watching the man's hand, which was less than a millimetre from the release button. The vision of the guard touching it and discharging the money all over the ground gave him the jitters.

The guard walked around the car again and hung on to the other mirror as he bent down to look under it. 'Bring me the mirror, Corporal!' he shouted to a young conscript.

The two men inspected the chassis and asked whether they could drive the car on to the ramp. It came back half an hour later and they were waved on, having been considered harmless. 'Enjoy yourselves in our country.'

Always suspicious, Adam thought there were two possibilities. They had either found the money and pocketed it, which he couldn't check whilst Gabrielle was in sight, or they had fitted the car with a bug or homing device, in which case he would be monitored. He had to wait and see.

Gabrielle was enchanted by the small picturesque villages as they sped on their way to the capital. Adam, on the other hand, just wanted to get there as soon as possible. He had to make a few checks.

Being stuck between tractors or horse-drawn carts on narrow roads with the extra handicap of the right-hand drive slowed him down, and it was not until late afternoon that they arrived in the outskirts of the Buda Hills. He drove along the west bank of the grey Danube and then on to Margaret Island.

The Grand Hotel was an old-fashioned one with a good restaurant and spa facilities. In the middle of the great river, under giant trees, it was a perfect romantic hideaway for the young couple. As they arrived in their room, the porter placed their luggage on the racks. As the door closed behind them, Adam took Gabrielle in his arms and gently pushed her towards the bed. Gabrielle protested, mumbling something about a shower, but the words were drowned in his kisses. He removed the little she had on for the afternoon drive and looked down at her mesmerising face. Her bright blue eyes were searching his. Later, flushed and clinging to each other, they entered the dining room. Adam pressed a hundred-florin note into the hand of the head waiter. He removed the '*Foglalt*' sign from the immaculate and colourfully embroidered linen, indicating their reservation of the best table, under a large and rather tattered indoor palm tree. As they sat down the Gypsy band struck up with the syrupy Hungarian ballad *'I Left My Beautiful Land, The Famous Land Of All The Magyars'*. With a psychology that Adam could not have bettered, they created an atmosphere that was supposed to make him guilty for leaving his country and happy to be back at the same time. He handed the lead violinist another hundred-florin note, which the musician promptly placed in his violin bow.

'I'm very impressed, Adam The service here is impeccable. Do they think we are someone important?'

'I don't know about that, but this was the very table that Prince Edward and Mrs. Simpson used on their many visits to this hotel.'

He took her hands in his, playing with her fingers.

'The waiter probably realises that we too are in love – as they were – and we are treated accordingly.'

Gabrielle's face lit up again with her huge smile. She reached over and kissed him gently on his lips.

As they were hungrily devouring the pork fillet in cream and mushroom sauce an American couple turned up, asking for 'the Prince of Wales's usual spot'. Adam wasn't surprised at all to hear the maître d' saying that the secluded table over in the corner was the one, since 'they always insisted on privacy'. He received another note from the couple, and Adam felt reassured that his countrymen's entrepreneurial skills had not been blunted by the regime.

'I've been looking at you two, you look just wonderful together,' the American lady said in a distinct Brooklyn accent, with her husband behind her, holding their wineglasses. 'We would just love to find out who you are.'

'Oh, Esther,' the man whispered in exasperation

Gabrielle and Adam looked at each other in horror. Bonnie and Clyde on the run, Adam nearly said when he looked again at the man, who was about his own age with thick, curly, slightly greying hair and black-rimmed glasses. Adam stood up, looked at the man again and offered his hand.

'Aaron Greenfield, what are you doing here? I don't believe it!' Adam grabbed his hand. 'I'm Adam Zenta, don't you remember me?'

'Well, what do you know!' Aaron stood back for a better view, then the two men embraced. Esther fell on Adam's chair, saving herself from fainting. With seats provided for the couple, the two men turned to each other and for the next two hours they reminisced whilst Gabrielle was shown the Greenfield children's photographs with an up-to-the-minute description of their activities. On learning about Adam and Gabrielle, Esther kept repeating that 'you just must get married – you look so perfect together'.

Adam learned that Aaron was a professor of history in Syracuse, New York, and he was in Hungary for his first visit, researching a book on Hungarian Jewry.

'Your father will be in it,' he reassured Adam.

'Will he just!' Esther butted in. 'I know all about you Zentas, we have even talked of visiting Nicholas and your sisters, for Aaron's sake.'

Adam felt the situation changing by the minute. He was pleased to see his little friend from the past. He had often thought of finding the Greenfields and suddenly here Aaron was, quiet and studious as he remembered him, happily married to an archetypal 'Jewish princess'. Adam had not intended to visit his father on this trip, but he felt now he was due for a 'big surprise'. He was only hoping that old Nicholas would survive it!

Two hours later Aaron and Esther decided to practise their 'only vice', a little blackjack in the Hilton Casino in the Buda Castle district. They asked for a taxi. Adam ordered another bottle of Debrői Hárslevelü, which arrived with the lead Gypsy.

He beckoned his band to play another, rather self-indulgent song, *'Graying at the temple'*, for him, followed by *'Lara's theme'* from *'Dr Zhivago'* for Gabrielle, which, naturally, earned him an even higher denomination of a florin note.

By the time they had drunk the last drop of Debrői their spirits had risen well above the hills of Buda. Adam suggested a walk around the island to clear their heads. Gabrielle was enthusiastic, saying that she 'had always wanted to walk on the shores of a strange island in a city where I have never been before, especially at well past one o'clock in the morning – there's just nothing like it'. 'It's a deal, then.' Adam headed for the door and she followed closely.

They found the eastern shore facing Pest. Enveloped in the scents of the park-island and in the warmth of the night they kissed. They kissed again and again. Adam gently lowered Gabrielle to the ground.

An hour later they staggered back to their bedroom in the centre section of the main building. Adam carried a bottle of Törley *sec*, the award-winning Hungarian *champenoise*, just in case either of them developed withdrawal symptoms during the next few minutes.

Adam was full of passion for this incredible woman, but inside he was burning with hatred for what this gruesome regime had done to his beloved country, virtually reducing it to a nation of waiters. While Gabrielle prepared herself for bed he staggered to the open French window leading to the balcony.

'Comrades! We are gathered here to start another revolution. With goulash in our bellies and Törley *sec* in our hands we fear no Russians, Brits nor Americans. The time has come! "If you're not against us you're for us,"' he inadvertently quoted the man whom he detested more than any other – János Kádár, who, with borrowed money, had just invented goulash communism.

'Or is it "if you're against us you're not with us" or "whoever the hell you are with, I'm not with any of you!"' Tottering precariously, he turned his head back to the room. 'Gabrielle, who are you? They want to know!'

Gabrielle dropped her towel in amazement. 'What are you doing there, Adam? This is so dangerous. Stop at once! You are terribly drunk, please get down immediately.'

'No, I won't. I'm addressing my people and calling those who are with us to be against us, or is it the other way around? I want to have the naked truth!' and with a jump he was standing on top of the stone balcony. 'This is what I think of commies and Russians!' He started to urinate on to the ground two floors below.

'Adam, for God's sake get off there.' She ran towards him, but seeing him sway she stopped short. 'Give me your hand, Adam,' she pleaded softly.

'Which one?' Adam asked, turning around, holding the bottle in one hand and his penis in the other.

'The right one, you fool, don't you dare drop the bottle.'

Adam jumped off the balcony and tottered towards Gabrielle, who dragged him to the bed.

'Look, darling, not a drop spilled.' Adam gave her the half-empty bottle and crashed out for the next five hours.

～

'Adam, Adam.' There was a knock on the bedroom door.

Adam wiped his eyes. His head was banging. He put on his bathrobe and looked at Gabrielle, who seemed fast asleep. As he opened the door his eyes tried to focus on Aaron's glasses. 'What are you doing here so early? Can't you sleep?'

'Get dressed, I want to talk to you. Hurry, please. I'll see you in the lobby.' Aaron turned around and disappeared.

Adam woke Gabrielle and asked her to order her own breakfast, as he didn't feel like eating just yet and he had to meet Aaron. Gabrielle murmured something to the effect that she wasn't surprised and turned over.

When he arrived in the lobby the night porter was just about to go home. He smiled at Adam and told him that he was delighted that he was 'still with us', and added that he hoped he 'did not get a chill'. Adam put his hand to his head and with a forced smile headed towards Aaron, who, on noticing him, walked through the revolving door. Adam followed him.

'I know I can trust you, Adam. I've spent all night talking in code to my father. He's still with the CIA and so am I. We all know of your footballing trips, naturally, and frankly regard it as rather amateurish, but we think the over-noisy attitude was a good invention. It comes to you naturally. I've heard of your escapade last night.'

'You're not giving me a telling-off, Aaron?'

'I should be, but I'm not. We know all about you, you seem to be effective, and that's what matters. Now let's talk about Paks, that's what we are both here for, right?'

They walked towards the Danube. Adam looked at the spot where only a few hours earlier he had lain with Gabrielle. Aaron explained that his history professorship, although it existed, was really a front. When his father returned after the American members of the Control Commissions had been unceremoniously chucked out by the Russians at the beginning of the cold war, he joined the CIA. Aaron followed in his father's footsteps as soon as he graduated in history from Yale, and became a liaison officer with Mossad. After helping to dispatch Eichmann back to Israel to face the music, he was exposed to some extent and was passed on to the 'odd jobs' department.

Aaron was at pains to explain that basically the USA was not against the Hungarians building the plant. He wanted to have the plans because there was some disquiet amongst the geologists in the CIA. They were about to prove that Paks was located on an earthquake faultline and this, coupled with the inherent problems of the VVER 440 Model V213's lack of containment and even an unreliable scram system, was bad news for all. The meltdown of one of the planned four reactors would result in enough neutron embrittlement to affect the East Coast of the United States. 'No wonder Britain was also interested,' Aaron added.

Adam realised that the conversation between the two of them summed up everything. There was Aaron, fully in the picture as to the reasons for what he was about to do, and he ... well, he felt like a delivery boy on an errand, with no knowledge of the problem whatsoever. Just 'go, get it, pay for it and fetch it'. Adam had the advantage of knowing the malcontent. His father was a master at his old grammar school so he would be visiting home whilst Adam attended his reunion. These events were open days with several similar luncheons going on in town, and in the melee it would not be too difficult to talk. Surveillance would be at the best fragmentary, with so many ex-students attending from all over the world.

Aaron had no particular plan except that he knew a Jewish physicist working on the site and would interview him for his book. He would take it from there, over months if necessary, thus Adam was God-sent with his snappier arrangements. One thing neither of them mentioned was the eventual ownership of the blueprint. They could hardly pop into a Xerox office and make one for each, Adam thought. He suggested that sentimentality should not interfere and the visit to Nicholas, who was living with sister Kati, should be scrapped. Aaron reluctantly agreed and they planned to leave next morning, leaving the women in Budapest to do the museums and the sad-looking shops of Váci Street. Adam stuffed enough money into Gabrielle's handbag to pay the bills and get back to England in an emergency. She could not understand his generosity, but neither did she suspect anything.

~

The white convertible E-type and the rented beige Fiat set off from the hotel car park in tandem and turned left on Árpád Bridge towards the hills of Buda. Another left turn put them on the road towards the south and on to the northern end of Road 4. Adam soon noticed that they were being followed by a black Czech-made Skoda with two similarly dressed men inside. He felt good about that. It was back to old-fashioned visual surveillance and he could monitor that.

As they had agreed, the two cars kept in close formation, which enabled them both to keep an eye on the Skoda behind them. Adam had the best advantage of this arrangement as he was leading and the other two had to keep up with whatever speed he chose. The majestic Danube kept appearing on the left through the acacia trees and the bushes. Within an hour the prefabricated offices of the power plant that was to be built were visible on the left. The road leading to it had a barrier across it similar to the one at the frontier. Aaron took a sudden swing towards it, leaving Adam to continue straight along the dusty main road. The Skoda stopped for a moment to reassess and decided to leave the Fiat and continue shadowing Adam. Aaron reported to the gate and produced a letter to show he had an appointment with Docent Hámori, the renowned physicist, who was just to be elevated to the rank of Member of the Scientific Academy, the greatest honour the small country could provide. He was taken to an unpretentious office and, whilst the guard stayed outside, the interview took place. Aaron soon realised that this approach would not get him anywhere. Whilst the scientist would politely answer questions about his own past and the way he had survived the Holocaust against all odds, he regarded himself as Hungarian through and through and parried any suggestion about private meetings, dinners or anything that might even vaguely compromise him.

~

Adam was speeding towards Jonk, village traffic allowing. The black car followed him from a respectable hundred metres. They obviously considered him the greater threat. He pulled up by the entrance of the main school building and walked through the heavy walnut doors, and along the corridors decorated with the formal photographs of previous graduates. He was told his meeting would be held upstairs in the large classroom above the gymnasium, where the incident of his plimsolls hitting Generalissimo Stalin square on his nose had taken place, so many years ago. He walked in.

~

When Aaron gave the physicist – his final ploy – the letter of invitation to address the Houston Technology Institute's Scientific Symposium, Hámori excused himself, blaming the heavy workload involved in the design stage of the plant, suggesting 'perhaps after completion'. Aaron realised that his approach had failed. He wondered whether the scientist had genuine loyalty to the state and did not want to be placed in an invidious position that he might regret later, or was he really innocent and totally oblivious to having been approached to become a 'traitor'. They talked a little longer about the apparent motive for Aaron's visit and agreed that non-violent anti-Semitism was part of the make-up of central and Eastern Europe, and although Hungarian Jewry was the most assimilated and patriotic, there was still a long way to go before clear understanding of each other could be attained.

～

The old housemaster held court as the ageing alumni sat, each in their accustomed seats, awaiting to be called in alphabetic order to account for the past five years of their lives. Adam Zenta was still used to these rituals. He had the longest time to wait, and when he was called as number 35, he received a round of applause, just for his patience. In his five-minute slot he brought his year-mates up to date, describing his day-to-day work and his divorce, and talked about the twins doing so well at Harrow. He presented a bottle of Johnny Walker to the headmaster, the housemaster and the old boy who had organised the event, and ended by telling them that he was looking forward to getting back to the beautiful brunette whom he had left in a Budapest hotel. 'Nothing changed with Zenta!' someone yelled.

Before lunch they stretched their legs in the packed playground and Adam, just in case the comrades in the Skoda were watching from a suitable vantage spot, had an animated conversation with a few ex-pupils from forms below and above his. He was engaged in yet another chat when a scrawny stranger walked up to him. He leaned towards him and whispered that he understood Adam had twenty thousand Deutschmarks for him. Pretending that he was a long-lost friend, Adam hugged the unkempt-looking man in the usual Continental manner and got a noseful of cheap aftershave for his trouble. He asked him where the blueprint was and they agreed to meet in Paks' Fishermen's Csárda at dusk. With a wide, friendly smile, which would have been visible from a mile, Adam told the man to show interest in his Jaguar and to ask him to show him its features. He patted him on the back and walked away to speak to someone else.

Docent Hámori asked Aaron whether he was interested in seeing the general layout of the plant, the non-sensitive areas, naturally. Then he passed on the invitation of the plant's party secretary to join him for a dinner in the local fish restaurant. Aaron agreed, and they went off to the planning hut.

After a superb peasant-style lunch, several bottles of wine and above all easy-going convivial chat with Kiss, Rácz and Co., they visited old stomping grounds. Out of earshot of the others they argued a little as to at which exact point the party motorbike had been dumped in the stream. They were all given an invitation to a late-night party in a local wine cellar. Adam told them that he would join them later. He had 'a small errand to run first'.

Aaron and the two Hungarians settled at their table and ordered a bowl of *halászlé*, a hearty fish soup dominated by the excellent Danube carp. With some warm soft bread and a little pickled gherkin, it was a dish on its own. A lightly chilled Riesling made it an unusual culinary surprise for the American. The party secretary, a large fat fellow with a rounded face, was dipping his bread into the thick soup, whilst the other two engaged in a conversation that was well above his head. This did not stop him pronouncing on matters nuclear, like the advanced state of the peaceful application of nuclear energy in the Soviet Union, especially at the new Chernobyl plant, which he had visited recently with a party delegation. He thought this most different to the imperialist approach of America, 'present company excepted, mind you', which he had not yet visited.

Adam pulled up at the Csárda and was a little surprised to see Aaron's Fiat in the car park. In spite of its dusty state the white Jaguar was soon encircled by admirers. The black Skoda with its two occupants arrived a few minutes later. A young teenager, well versed in things motoring, asked whether he could see the engine. Adam pulled the lever and the huge domed bonnet popped open. When he lifted the large one-piece structure the 4.2-litre engine became visible to the crowd and there were a few gasps of admiration. He turned to the young man and asked him to explain to the others what was going on around the mass of metal as he had to admit he didn't know much about it. The teenager obliged with great enthusiasm and Adam told him he was most impressed. He then suddenly saw the unkempt man coming towards him, introducing himself as the father of the motoring buff. The man asked Adam whether he would take his son for a ride on Road 6. 'It would be an experience he would never forget,' he added, and nodded his head twice.

Adam looked at him and agreed. The young man jumped in, satchel in hand, and Adam took the road north, towards Dunakomlód. Soon they were on the open highway where Adam could put his foot down. Some two kilometres later the passenger opened his satchel and told Adam that his father had said that they would swap some packages of stamps for his collection. Adam turned the car around in a secluded area, checked for other traffic and saw a black car in the distance heading towards them. He wound the window down and pressed the release button on the conical rear-view mirror. He removed the rolls of large-denomination Deutschmarks wrapped in a plastic bag secured with a rubber band and handed them to the now much more serious youngster, who took out a greaseproof paper parcel from his satchel. Adam took it and placed it under his seat. The Skoda became visible as he accelerated away, and they passed each other just on the outskirts of the town. After they returned to the Csárda the excited boy started to tell his friends about the wonderful drive he had had and only Adam noticed that his father took the satchel from his hand and walked away. Adam refused other requests for a drive, pulled up the soft top, started the engine and sped away into a small road on the right signposted to Nagydorog.

By the time the black Skoda arrived he was well out of town and its perplexed occupants decided to keep a watch on the rented Fiat instead. Within minutes Aaron walked out, thanked his hosts for their hospitality and started his engine, closely followed by the Skoda.

∼

When Adam arrived at the vineyards of Pincehely the party was well on its way. Some twenty-odd had taken up the invitation for a little late drinking and salami-eating. Fruit, pork crackling and *pogácsa*, a savoury cake delicacy, provided the fare, and the singing of old Gypsy songs was well under way. He joined in light-heartedly and tried to forget about the parcel under his car seat. It was a balmy evening, ideal for the friendly gathering, which continued until early morning, when they all crashed out on old army-issue blankets, or whatever they could find.

After the goodbyes the next morning Adam excused himself, declining further invitations to lunch, and got into his car to 'study the maps'. He opened the parcel and to his relief the man's promise had been kept. The whole thing looked similar to the 'cement works' material of many years before – not the microfilm he was expecting, but a much larger package. There were formulae in such abundance that he was persuaded that this was the genuine article. What worried him this time was the sheer size of the package, which would certainly not fit into Ian Murphy's number-seven Liverpool FC jersey. He had a problem which would give him food for thought on his way back to Budapest.

As he got to the middle of Erd on the outskirts of the capital he was immediately picked up by a large Russian Pobeda, and noticed that the passenger was filming him. The close attention he was getting made him change his strategy again, and by the time he walked into the Grand he had a new plan.

Aaron and the two women were enjoying some patisserie when he spotted them in the café. The aroma of the freshly ground coffee was filling the air as he joined them, trying to act as naturally as he could. The thirty-hour growth around his chin made it difficult to look suave amongst the elegant clientele. As they talked over the arrangements for the evening, Adam caught his friend's glance. He looked down at the parcel, then at Aaron and nodded. Aaron's amazement was total. Adam declared that after the drive back and the coffee he just had to 'pop into the loo'. Aaron followed.

In three minutes Adam managed to convince Aaron that there was no way he could smuggle out 'the thing' and to 'never mind the next two weeks' vacation', he should get himself back to America immediately. Aaron wrote a number on a piece of paper and gave it to Adam with his room key. He was to call the number and say 'B12' as soon as the receiver was lifted. That was all.

Adam said to the ladies that he must go and get shaved and would see them 'in a tick'. He ran upstairs to Room 112 and made his call, leaving the parcel by the telephone. He dashed to his own room, showered and returned to the others. They were making plans for the evening when the pageboy turned up with 'a telegram for Mr Greenfield'. Aaron looked suitably surprised and took the folded paper from the silver-plated salver. He read it whilst the others looked on quietly and went even more suitably ashen faced.

'Father has had a heart attack,' he said quietly. 'Mother wants us to return immediately.'

'Oh my God, poor Daddy,' Esther exclaimed, and turned to Adam. 'You know, it's amazing, he's never smoked or eaten to excess, looks as fit as a Yiddish fiddler, and here he goes with his second heart attack. Interestingly we were abroad for his last one too – Beirut, wasn't it, honey?' She looked at Aaron.

'It sure was, darling, very unfortunate. Thank God he had made a full recovery by the time we got back.' Aaron talked softly, keeping his eyes down.

'He must have a genetic predisposition, probably familial hypercholesterolaemia,' Adam offered by way of explanation. 'How can we help?' Aaron was already on his way to reception, where the lady 'regretted what had happened' and told him the best she could do was to get two seats to Frankfurt on Lufthansa at 18.20 hours. They would advise regarding an ongoing flight. He had to move fast.

After the most hasty packing they checked out and got into the taxi, whose driver was quickly paid and well tipped by Adam in advance and told to 'put his foot down', an invitation all Hungarian cab drivers cherished. Five minutes later the two detectives walked in and, on seeing Adam and Gabrielle drinking at the bar, settled into a corner with a beer. Adam kept looking at his watch to give the impression of waiting for someone. At 6.30 he said to the waiter in a loud voice not to forget to give him Mr Greenfield's earlier bill too. The men jumped up hastily and went to reception. One of them checked the time and hit the desk with his fist. In the ensuing silence the noise of a large jet heading north-west could be heard right overhead.

'What on earth was that all about with Aaron?' Gabrielle asked with a puzzled smile.

'Probably his girlfriend wanted him back quickly,' Adam quipped.

'No, Adam, he's not that sort of person. It's something more sinister. What I don't understand is that you were so relieved that he had gone. Strange.'

'Never mind all that, what do you fancy doing tonight?' Adam put his arm around Gabrielle's shoulder. 'Let's discuss it upstairs, in the room.'

'I'm not sure, you make a suggestion.'

She put her arm around his waist and let her head fall on his shoulder.

∽

The early dispatch of the parcel by the unexpected route enabled Adam to stop worrying about it, at least until his debriefing by Arthur. The rest of their planned stay became a real holiday for them, starting with Lake Balaton and taking in the wonderful countryside surrounding it. 'A touring honeymoon if there ever was one,' Adam teased Gabrielle.

The Skoda, never too far from them, was a constant reminder for Adam that interest was still being taken in him, and after another day he decided to cut the trip short. His fear was that the unkempt fellow could trip himself up with his small fortune in Deutschmarks, bringing a multitude of problems for them both. They checked out of the Annabella Hotel at Füred and headed through the Transdanubean hills towards Vienna. The faithful Skoda was right behind them as they passed the giant Benedictine monastery high on the top of a hill to their right, so Adam decided it was time for a Jaguar performance demonstration for his followers. Gabrielle was terrified and berated him for his selfish driving, so after a few close shaves with slow tractors pulling out of farm entrances, he had to slow down anyway. They were getting near the frontier. He dropped his speed to twenty miles per hour. The black car had no choice but to overtake them.

When Adam drove into the border control area the two occupants of the Skoda were engaged in deep conversation with the captain in charge of the station. Gabrielle was ushered into the waiting room and Adam into the captain's small office, with six telephones displayed on his desk, signifying his importance. Adam was asked to surrender his keys as the Jaguar was about to be searched. He watched as the two shadows were instructing two young mechanics to search for something that might have come from the Paks area, which, other than its excellent Danube fish, was famous only for the nuclear station soon to be built on the shore of the sprawling river. The captain received a number of calls from the garage, grunting in response a few times. He examined the passports once again and asked Adam to go and join Gabrielle in the waiting room. An hour later the Jaguar was driven back to them and Adam looked at Gabrielle. Her expression was clearly indicating to him not to make any smart remarks. Adam complied. They walked to the car, which had even been given a wash to remove the hundreds of oily fingerprints left during the search, and drove away, due west, towards the luxury of the Hotel Sacher in Vienna.

'What do you mean "it's in America"?' Arthur jumped to his feet in Adam's plush consulting room.

'Well, my dear fellow, on this occasion I was little more than a messenger. It's with the Eastern Europe Section of the CIA.' Adam leaned back in the olive-green leather swivel chair.

'You might feel relaxed about that, Adam, but I'm sure not. It was, after all, our money!'

'Take it easy, Arthur. I'll get it back for you, just get them on the phone for me, you must have some access to them, because I haven't.'

'OK, Adam, you be at my office in the Ministry of Defence at 15.00 hours, we'll get your friend as soon as he arrives at work. See you then.' The irritated old spy left Adam still sitting in his chair, in a pose of careless relaxation.

Adam negotiated a copy of the plan from Aaron, which would be sent over in the next diplomatic bag, and a seventy-five per cent reimbursement of the Deutschmark payment. Arthur was happy with that as the money would be useful given his ever-tighter budget. Adam also received a small extra payment, which he decided to blow on more private flying at Biggin Hill.

Totally in keeping with his character, he decided that the thing he wanted to pursue was low flying, the taboo of the Civil Aviation Authority and CAP 85 Aviation Law for Private Pilots. Whilst Gabrielle appreciated the sheer excitement of flying six feet off the southern shores of England, with the aircraft's nose pitched up so that if a sneeze loosened his grip on the controls the plane would gain height, she preferred chasing cumulonimbus clouds in the clear blue sky.

They attended fly-ins in Jurby on the Isle of Man. On a Canadian visit they flew over the top of the world from Thompson, Manitoba, and on a holiday in Cyprus, just before partition, Adam flew around the whole island, including the 'panhandle', dangerously at six feet above the water, three hundred feet away from the shore. He would never forget the experience.

Appreciating the problems of the turn of the decade, Adam spent many hours researching and treating eating disorders, which were affecting over one per cent of young females. He became an early advocate of his own specialist therapy – support by psycho-dynamic and cognitive-behavioural means both in group and individual settings. His paper on this subject was much praised and brought him acclaim from the Royal College.

As a consequence Adam was invited to be guest speaker at the Royal Society of Medicine and chose the theme 'The Search for Safer Antidepressants', highlighting the severity of the side effects of the available treatments. He called for a quest for the 'Holy Grail' of antidepressant development to produce a more speedy onset of effect and demanded better drugs. He accepted that the pharmaceutical industry had made memorable progress in the side-effect profile and toxicity in overdose of antidepressants and concluded that 'much has been achieved in the past thirty years, since the recognition of the antidepressant effects of imipramine and iproniazid, but nothing as dramatic as their discovery. Perhaps more serendipity is needed to achieve the next breakthrough'.

The pleased expressions on the faces of the Council members of the College were outshone only by the delight of Gabrielle amongst the audience. At the reception afterwards she told Adam that her hands were still sore with clapping and that he looked very impressive behind the lectern. 'Ever thought of standing for Parliament?' She giggled. 'Perhaps I shouldn't tell you this but sitting next to me was a very attractive lady who was totally knocked out by you. She asked if you did house calls.'

'What did you say?'

'Not any more – only to me.'

'Is that right? Then you will have to marry me for that, Gabs,' he smiled, inventing the new diminutive.

'Is this a proposal, then, Adam?'

'Yes it is. Please say yes, Gabs.'

'Adam, I'm not sure I am truly in love with you. I love being with you, that's for sure, but in love – for ever? …'

He stared at her in disbelief. 'Look, Gabrielle, I love you desperately – in fact you needn't worry your pretty head about this. I will love you enough for both of us.' He took hold of her tightly.

Gabrielle looked up at him thoughtfully. 'How can a girl say no to such a proposal? Yes, I will marry you!'

'Sixth of October?'

'The date we first met? What a romantic idea!'

28

L̲LOYDS

The small wedding ceremony in one of the upstairs rooms in Marylebone Road Register Office was attended by Adam's friends, the surgeon David and his petite wife Violet Ahmed, now residing in Canada, as best man and witness, and, of course, the twins, who were most happy with the choice of the bride to be and got on very well with Gabrielle. Little Victoria and visiting niece Erika from Hungary completed the wedding posse. The short ceremony was to be followed by a reception in the evening at their home in Adam's Harley Street house, befitting his new, homely status.

Wedding day clothes were exchanged for black ties as the invitations stipulated and a few hours later Gabrielle had the chance to amaze all with her exceptional looks. Her dark hair styled to her shoulders in rococo curls was an interesting departure from her straight bob. Her dress was a full-length off-white Jersey crêpe creation by Bruce Oldfield of Beauchamp Place, making her look like a Greek goddess. She easily outshone the many stars of show business that Adam had kept as friends after he and Tracy, whose face still looked at him from every magazine stand, had split up.

Adam, not to be outdone, had chosen a tuxedo matching Gabrielle's dress, with waistcoat, emphasising that early middle age had not yet reached his girth. He cut a handsome figure with well-preserved good looks, and the only visible effect of passing time was the ever-greying temples.

At seven in the morning, after a very quick change, the couple presented themselves at Heathrow for the British Airways flight to St Lucia.

~

As he had promised the Hungarian grandees in *The Gay Hussar*, Adam took an increasing interest in affairs Magyar. He attended a few meetings quietly just to find out who was who and what political spectrum they represented. Not surprisingly he found all shades. From the ultra-right ex- Arrow Cross Party members through Horthy's traditionalists to Liberals, Social Democrats and even a few old-fashioned communists to whom none would talk much, and who would not want to return to their 'socialism-building comrades' – they were picking up all the benefits British capitalism could provide for them, thank you very much.

There was a significant intellectual strand – Cs. Szabó at the BBC Hungarian Service, established authors George Mikes, Paul Tábori and the suddenly famous Stepen Vizinczey, whose first novel *In Praise of Older Women* was already being transferred to celluloid.

The musical world was represented by the pianists Béla Siki, Géza Anda, Tamás Vásári, the violinist George Pauk and the cellist János Stárker. István Kertész was in charge of the London Symphony Orchestra and rumours abounded that George Solti was about to take over at Covent Garden. The Zentas would never miss one of their concerts.

The two leftist lords, Káldor and Balogh, were already adorned with ermine and were snoozing away in the House of Lords, as a reward for pumping outdated economic advice to the Labour prime minister, Harold Wilson.

They all thought that the psychiatrist was an interesting addition and Gabrielle was the icing on the cake.

A long procession of dinner parties was required to get to know them and Gabrielle became an excellent exponent of 'Hunglish' cooking, acceptable to both nationalities. It was particularly praised by Dr Peter Meisner, who was a year-mate of Adam in Pécs and qualified via Budapest and Newcastle. He had just become the rising star of gerontology at St Thomas's Hospital. Adam soon realised that this powerful group, some of whom had Hungarian Embassy connections via the numerous receptions held there, had tentacles in every echelon of London society. He was not surprised when he received the whisper that he would now be 'most welcome in the Hungarian Embassy – after all, everything was changing, in the main, and in his direction, so why all this fuss?' Adam's answer was to let them know that he was 'not interested in cherry-picking with commies – and if I want a posh drink I feel much more at home in the Carlton Club'. The matter was settled until 1989.

Among all these people Adam felt most at home with John Szábó, a dedicated man of the right leading the Association of Hungarian Freedom Fighters of the UK. With no obvious access to official intelligence, he astonished Adam with the information he was able to produce. They often met at each other's homes to evaluate the latest data from Romania. The picture emerging was that the plans of their Western Defence Board, which comprised most of the Romanian defence structure, were to be made available by one of their officers. John and Adam were desperate to obtain this information, which was after all an invasion plan in case of a Transylvanian conflict between Romania and Hungary. As far as Adam was concerned it was not to fall into any other hands but his and, through his, into NATO's.

It would be the crowning glory of his spying career to walk into his controller's office with the package.

All was ready – he was waiting for John to turn up and say that '*The Gay Hussar Plan*' was go. It was, like all waiting, boring, sometimes to the extent that he was actually beginning to question John's contact's existence, thinking him to be just a figment of someone's patriotic imagination.

∼

Adam's practice was getting busier year after year and this produced the financial rewards that enabled him to buy some property abroad. Gabrielle chose Marbella, and they decided to have a holiday at the flashy Spanish resort. They booked into the elegant Marbella Club Hotel. The easy-going Spanish way of life appealed to them both, and they found the bustling Puerto Banus yacht port complex fascinating. Within a week, two very energetic and rather pretty sales girls from the Promosol agency had sold them a villa in the El Rosario development, which they named 'Zenyblanca'.

Gabrielle stayed behind for two weeks to furnish the large white villa with its view over Gibraltar (on a mist-less day) and Adam returned home to catch up with work. He arranged a meeting with his financial advisers and was told his portfolio was right. He signed on and felt he had arrived.

Adam thought it was not inappropriate for him to feel content. There he was, in his fiftieth year, still buying the same size clothes from Savile Row, at the top of his profession with a good performance on the Council; there was even talk of his becoming president of the Royal Society of Medicine. He golfed at Hendon and skied at the top of the best mountains. His very successful second marriage with a beautiful woman was much appreciated by all, including his ever-growing twins.

Did he really want to go on being a spy, now that he was off the hook? He posed himself this question repeatedly in his private thoughts. Was it the Calvinist work ethic or misguided patriotism, and was it for Hungary or for Britain? He couldn't answer his own questions, even at their most gently probing, but he knew he was going to continue exactly as he was. 'Schizoid, self-delusional obsessive disorder,' he murmured to himself, and poured a large whisky.

One thing was sure. He wasn't going to drive the convertible E-type to the depths of Transylvania, so he presented himself to Henleys in Mayfair and bought a light-grey/navy XJS-HE, with full and original TWR conversion. A most noticeable performance car. He drove around in the West End for a while and went for lunch at his club, the Carlton. Life was very agreeable.

29

Moles

Adam could not countenance the fact that his grandparents, Titus and Kathleen, had just been forgotten.

Gabrielle wrestled with the intricacies of her new camera and Adam finished listening to cousin Andrew explaining how his grandparents had ended up in an unmarked and unhallowed grave. He was stunned. He had never much cared about what his ancestors had got up to, but the snippet of a story about adultery and excommunication left him feeling curious and he wanted to know more. The old physician was only too happy to oblige, feeling secure in the company of the erudite Adam from Great Britain. After all, this was only family chit-chat and not of much interest to the Securitate, the dreaded secret service of Romania. At least the three of them had something to talk about, knowing that the bug, hidden somewhere behind the glove compartment of the Jaguar, was recording their every utterance. Adam had to be alert, since according to John Szábó's final intelligence, he could be approached at any time by a contact, even by the slightest of 'brush contacts', and could be in sudden possession of something, most likely a microfilm or two. He decided to keep a very high profile, the ploy that had always served him best in the past.

Having left behind the small graves on the hill opposite the ancient church, whose graveyard contained several generations of Zentas, he pulled back on to the main road and started to drive back to Vásárhely. A dark grey Dacia saloon, which the Romanians built in abundance under licence from Renault, soon joined them on the twisting road.

The young couple in it tried to be as nonchalant as possible about their 'detail'. Whenever they caught up in the traffic, the dark-haired girl's arm would go around the driver's neck in a sudden show of affection. Adam smiled at them and continued asking his cousin more questions about the family's past. He had an idea.

When they arrived back in town at just past two o'clock in the afternoon with not much to do, he asked his cousin to take him to police headquarters. The old man shuddered and directed him to the modern building behind the town hall.

The car received the usual admiring looks from the on-duty staff as Adam pulled into the rear car park. These oversize thugs were professional accident arrangers. Various heavily loaded lorries would occasionally mount pavements, owing to a well-rehearsed brake failure. Thus they disposed of people from poets to trade union organisers who had even slightly offended the sensitive soul of the Conducador, Nicolae Ceauşescu or, even worse, his wife Helena. They shook their heads in disbelief, feeling virtually sorry for even thinking of having to flatten this car into a pancake.

Adam asked to see the man in charge, who turned out to be the chief of police, Colonel Constantin Popescu. He had enough gold braiding on him to be mistaken for a field marshal anywhere else in the world. The officer pointed to a comfortable chair opposite his desk. His adjutant pulled one up for Gabrielle too.

'Colonel, thank you for seeing me without an appointment. My wife and I are here as a fiftieth birthday present to myself, searching for roots and all that and doing a little research for a book. Now, I couldn't help but notice that a Dacia was following me and I understood that, if I gave them the slip – which I could easily do with my car – that would look very suspicious, wouldn't it? And as I have already had to threaten an old lady with a listening device that I would throw her out of the hotel window, I decided to come to you and explain everything and see if you could put your chaps to better use.'

'Well, to show good faith, I will speak with you in Magyar as my English is not very good and you seem to have forgotten your Romanian,' the man said with a wry smile and in a heavy Latin accent. 'I speak your language, because I had to learn it in elementary school when Hungary was in charge around here. As you know, we didn't have much choice about that. Yes, you are under surveillance, mainly because of your family background, which has always been hostile to the great Romanian people. We also happen to know that you have undesirable associates in London, especially of late.'

'You don't mean the president of the Royal College of Psychiatrists, do you?' Adam smiled.

'You know I don't, Doctor. I mean Mr Szabó and his cohorts, but let us suppose for a moment that you are just keeping in touch for old time's sake. Whom exactly do you want to see?'

'I came prepared – here they are.' Adam handed over a list of names and a few other notes with diary dates.

'I see. There are bishops, artists, theatre and opera dates here, quite a few of them. You will be very busy. Do you mind if I copy this?' He handed it over to his adjutant without waiting for a reply. The man saluted smartly and left the room with it. 'You know, I have been in the police business for a long time, and you're giving me all the wrong vibes. I just know you're a spy.'

'In your country there are more counter-espionage agents than there are solicitors in America. If I am a spy I must be the worst kind; getting everybody's attention wherever one goes isn't mentioned in any manual,' Adam answered readily.

'So you agree to reading them, huh?'

'I am a psychiatrist and not a bad one at that – I read everything. We are all fascinated by them, otherwise the publishing industry would fold, so don't let us be silly. John le Carré says that in England every family boasts to having had a spy at some time or other. Here every family knows they have one or more, probably mine included. Perhaps my old cousin shivering in fear outside in my car is one of your minions.'

'No he isn't, that's why we had to put him in jail for six years.' Popescu smiled benevolently.

'Be that as it may, Colonel, why don't you and your lady wife join us for dinner tonight so that we can get to know each other better and for you to see that we are just a regular couple – not spies. You will be a great asset for my book on the *New Intellectual Trends of Rumania*.'

'Romania, please – we find that spelling so insulting.'

'Romania is fine with me. Well?'

'You are a most persuasive man, Doctor.'

'I believe the Continental Hotel has a good kitchen?'

'Yes, but I have a better idea. I am already committed to going somewhere else and I see no reason why you shouldn't join me. It is an about an hour's drive to one of our party recreational centres, in an old hunting lodge. I am sure the Conservative or even the Labour Party has something similar in Britain, to relax the leadership for the class war ahead. Sadly it is for men only, madam.' He turned towards Gabrielle.

'Fine with me! I could do with an early night, if you men want to go and play snooker.' Gabrielle forced a poor smile. 'That's how they relax in our Conservative Club, you see.'

'Well, it's all arranged, then!' The colonel ignored Gabrielle's remark. 'I'll send my driver along to the hotel at six and you will be delivered back for lunch tomorrow. I am sure you will enjoy it.' He closed an open folder, indicating that the unscheduled interview was over. 'Oh, by the way, Doctor, why don't you leave your car here tonight – it's safer than the hotel car park,' he added in haste.

'Good idea. I'll pick it up tomorrow on our return,' Adam agreed.

The stiff-postured adjutant saw them to the front door and saluted as they turned away for the short walk back to the hotel, across Roses Square. They were soon followed by Adam's exhausted cousin, Andrew, who didn't really like the idea of Adam taking off with the chief of police, but realised that it was not an invitation to refuse. 'He's a very powerful man, you know,' he kept repeating quietly. 'He's taking you to the lodge our grandfather used to go to, for his wild-boar shoots.'

∼

When Adam climbed into the back seat of the well-kept black Mercedes, he was surprised to find the police chief in a smart sporty tweed-and-corduroy outfit. There was a faint smell of quality aftershave swirling around the car and the man was clearly in a convivial mood. He shook Adam's hand again and told him that the best invention the English had ever produced was the 'veekend'. The saloon obeyed every instruction from the sergeant driver along Highway 13 to perfection, and when it turned left into the much narrower 13A towards the north-east it swallowed up the kilometres with equal ease, leaving the odd ruffled-feathered or dead chicken in its wake. Soon after they had passed the still-beautiful resort of Sovata the Carpathian mountains loomed high in front of them; a ninety degree turn to the left at Parajd signalled their impending arrival. Adam admired the scenery, telling his host how astonished he was that he could recollect so many details of his childhood. His host was philosophical, saying that certain stimuli could set off such reactions in a man.

The lodge, the size of a small hotel, at first glance looked as good as new, still displaying the very ornate Magyar woodcarving of tulips and nightingales, so fashionable during the dual monarchy of Austria and Hungary. A closer inspection would have revealed several important modern changes and additions.

The place was teeming with women of all ages and sizes, going about their chores. Adam's overnight bag was snatched from him by a large but well-proportioned woman with a heaving chest dressed in Romanian folk wear. He was allocated Room 29, but followed his host straight into the bar, where the colonel was subjected to much hugging and shoulder-slapping from his fellow aficionados. The policeman introduced him as Sir Doctor Adam Zenta, who used to be a '*banden*', meaning 'scum', a derogatory term used especially for Hungarians, but who was a famous 'Englisher' now.

The men, all smartly dressed as if they were on a mission to prove that they were different from the poverty-stricken multitudes outside the compound, forced a smile at Adam. Some walked up to shake hands, whilst others were contented to look down into their beer glasses.

After a few drinks they walked into the well-laid dining room and sat around a long rectangular oak table. The cutlery, with its deer-horn handles, was complemented by the Bohemian crystal glasses. At nine prompt, a small retinue of maidens in colourful peasant dresses began serving the piping-hot game soup with dumplings, which was followed by venison stew. The whole scene was that of a comradely men's mess dinner, with very tasty offerings. There were no formal speeches and no toast was proposed to the beloved Conducador, whose large photograph loomed over the fireplace, keeping a close eye on the proceedings. The wine flowed in abundance and the odd comrade decided that enough restraint was enough and started to indulge in a little bottom-pinching as the maidens passed by. The recipients put on a show of annoyance and wagged the occasional finger in friendly acknowledgement.

From the entertainment area the strains of Gypsy music became audible, and a few of the men picked up their wineglasses and walked towards the connecting door. Adam followed his host, and as they settled on the comfortable sofas the girls dressed in brilliant folk costumes rushed in and gave an impromptu performance of a furious Romanian folk dance. They concluded by dragging up the fat comrades for a little long-overdue exercise. Half an hour or so later, the band was dismissed and a well-known singing starlet walked in to much applause. A Yamaha music centre was placed behind her; she set the rhythm to a soulful, moody number and began to sing. She had a wonderful voice which would not have been out of place in a good West End musical, and with her figure-hugging blue chiffon dress, held up by an intricate arrangement of narrow strips, criss-crossing all over her beautiful torso, she left little to the numbing imaginations of the Nomenklatura. There was no doubt she was a star in the making.

As she finished her last song the door was flung open and the girls, now changed into very small, slinky, Western dresses, ran in with well-rehearsed spontaneity. They started to dance in disco style with each other and called the men to join them. The good comrades obliged in strict pecking order. The colonel was number two after the county party secretary and the local mayor and the others followed him one by one. By the end of a slower number they were all looking admiringly at each other and settled on the sofas to give some physical expression to their ever-increasing desire.

Adam walked to the bar, ordered another whisky and sat on a bar stool. A rather attractive, tall, slender woman came to sit next to him and smiled. She reached towards him, having decided that his hair needed a little adjusting, and obligingly ran her fingers through his greying locks. Pulling her bar stool nearer, she leaned closer, her lips almost brushing his. Adam felt more than a little uncomfortable and moved his face away from hers. Thanking her for her company most profusely, he walked back to his chair, sensing that he was in a predicament. His host pushed his own nymphet off his knees and came over.

'Adam, we are all friends here, it's just a little innocent fun. Don't you like any of them?'

'Colonel, I ...'

'Constantin, please,' he interrupted.

'Constantin, I have only been married two years,' he subtracted three from the actual figure, 'and my wife and I are happy. You know I've done all this,' he waved his hand around, pointing to the girls, 'in my day. Now I'm quite happy just to get drunk.'

'You don't like our girls? They are picked from all over the country!' The colonel looked Adam straight in the eye.

'No! I think they're gorgeous, absolutely gorgeous!'

'I know, you want one of your own kind, a Magyar girl, eh?'

'I suppose that would be nice – it's been a long time since I've known one.'

'Hey, Rozi! Here!' The officer beckoned to a pretty blonde girl, who was about to settle on a settee next to a comrade with a good-size belly. 'You are to look after Sir Doctor – understand?'

The girl walked across the dance floor with a wiggle that went on for ever and put her arm around Adam's neck, withdrawing it like lightning when Adam asked her in Hungarian what she wanted to drink.

Adam whispered to her to act naturally and put his arm around her waist. She pulled the pins from her hair and let it roll to her shoulders as they walked to an empty sofa. Around them the friendliness of the couples was reaching new heights, making Adam think that, after all, there might have been something in the legend that they were the Dacian descendants of decadent Rome.

With their heads touching in a tender gesture, Adam managed to convey to Rozi that he had no intention of laying her, but they might as well pretend to be bed-bound for both their sakes. The look on her face displayed both incredulity and disappointment. Rozi's advances had never been rebutted before.

The colonel was called to the telephone by one of the elderly minders of the girls and hurried to the office. On returning he flicked his brandy glass with his large gold signet ring several times. Hands were withdrawn from breasts, dresses and trouser flies as he picked up the microphone.

'Comrades, I have just received some wonderful news from North-West Air Traffic Control in Turda. In a few minutes you will all hear the noise of a helicopter landing in front of the building. The son of our redeeming Leader, Comrade Nicu Ceauşescu, is joining us from

Sibiu for a few hours. We will be honoured to receive him and delighted that he wants to spend some recreational hours with us,' he ad libbed, making up his announcement as he went on.

The air traffic control man's information was correct because the colonel had hardly completed his garbled sentence when the approaching aircraft's noise became audible. Protocol demanded that the son of the comrade dictator should receive just a little less organised enthusiasm than the ex-cobbler himself. So, clothes adjusted, they were ready in a line-up on the veranda for a few minutes of rhythmic clapping – Adam included.

The handsome, tall young man with Romanesque features was helped off the helicopter and his head was pushed down by an aide to avoid the idly swerving blades. It became fairly obvious that the man was more drunk than his reception party. He leaned heavily on his underling as he passed the clapping revellers, mustering up all his concentration to manage a smile and a lazy wave.

Back in the entertaining room the First Secretary of the district Communist Party, dressed immaculately in Yves Saint Laurent specially flown in from Paris, slumped on to sofa number one and smiled at the pretty singer, who was once again standing in front of her Yamaha. She realised that this was an important moment in her career and loosened her long straight black hair.

'I'm not going to drink piss. Get me some Black Label!' He yelled crudely, demanding his favoured Johnny Walker. 'And some oysters, you bastards, oysters! Do you hear me?!'

The staff suddenly burst into unprecedented activity, skirts rustling, trying to find the items requested by the loathsome drunk, who was being groomed to take over the presidency from his father – his liver allowing.

'Who's that man with the little blonde? I haven't met him before.' He pointed aggressively at Adam.

'My guest, esteemed comrade. A doctor from England researching a book, sir.' The colonel jumped to attention.

Nicu got up and staggered over to Adam. 'Are you a fucking spy, then?' He asked.

'No, sir, I was born near here and came over to study my family's lost roots.' Adam stood up, answering him fairly firmly.

'If you were born around here, why are you better looking than all these ugly shits?'

'You and I were just lucky, sir – they are pretty average, aren't they, except for the colonel, he's not bad looking.' Adam tried to make light of it.

'Are you gonna fuck this chick, Doctor?' His speech was almost unintelligible as he spat out the words.

'Well, probably, but I don't think we should be so discourteous.' Adam tried to sound gentlemanly, but Rozi just smiled.

'I want her, but as you're a guest, you go first.' He looked around and caught the friendly glance of the singer. He staggered over to her and took the mike out of her hand. 'This is the one I'm going to fuck tonight! C'mon, you little whore.' He pulled the narrow straps of her dress from her shoulders and peeled the rest off as she wriggled in mock-apprehension. He pushed her on to the table as her delicate underwear fell to the floor. 'Right here, I'm going to fuck you right here, on the table,' and unzipping his trousers, the handsome beast mounted his prey, who went most willingly to her public slaughter. A few minutes later she received her best applause of the evening.

Adam thought discretion was the better part of valour and declared that he was going to bed. Rozi followed him.

'Now listen, Rozi. I'm saying this once again, I have no intention of screwing you, to become a porno star for the titillation of Mrs Ceaușescu or for blackmail, so why don't you just settle down on the bed, in sight of the camera, right over there.' He pointed to the middle of a chunky wall clock as soon as he entered the room. 'I'll sleep on the sofa.' It was positioned just below the clock, out of range of the spying lens.

Obedience to their original orders was obviously well drilled into the party girls of the recreation centre. Rozi twice tried to slip out of her dress and seduce him, but on both occasions she was suitably rebuffed by Adam, if for no other reason than to impress the bugging devices of the bedroom.

~

Adam decided not to go into details with Gabrielle about the previous night's activities, except to say that it was all rather boring and he felt it was less suspicious if he was friendly with the enemy. For the next two days Gabrielle and Adam called on the rest of the Zenta family, all impoverished or downtrodden, victimised by the state in the name of the dictatorship of the proletariat. To their astonishment they found that, be it for breakfast, lunch or dinner, they always ended up sitting with nine people around a table. They were entertained way above the meagre rations allowed each family owing to fairly active bartering of produce or the black market. He considered his cousins most ingenious. On enquiring gently about the reasons why nine was the preferred number, suspecting some old superstition, Adam was told that ten or more in a room constituted a public meeting and a police licence was required, and anyway, as they were always being watched, they toed the party line. Once again in his thoughts he thanked Nicholas for his decision of September 1944 and for removing his family from this unfortunate land, even if the train journey did take four weeks.

The news of their presence had spread around town, yet there was absolutely no evidence of anybody wanting to pass anything on to him. Adam decided on raising his profile a little higher. He gave an interview to a communist journalist about the researching of his book, which was printed on page eight in the national party daily, *Scienteia*. Following the publishing of his reasons for being there – and having thanked the Romanians for their 'wonderful cooperation' – he and Gabrielle presented themselves at every public event or opportunity, hoping for some contact. None came, but he noticed that the Jaguar was no longer tailed by the men of Securitate. He knew why. During its overnight stay in the police compound, whilst he was in the company of Colonel Popescu at the 'recreation centre', in addition to the recording facility, it had been fitted with a homing device. This manifested itself in the reading on the battery charge gauge, which was slightly lower than usual.

Gabrielle was quietly wondering what on earth was going on. Adam was not a good enough actor to disguise his expectation during, or disappointment at the end of, the day. The following morning he would become interested in yet another visit and in the evening in another opera performance. 'We must see this particular *Samson and Delilah*, darling, it has a damned good Hungarian tenor singing the leading part.' By the evening Samson had had his hair cut and Adam had received nothing for his trouble. After two more unproductive days thinking that his brush contact had been well swept away by the Securitate, he decided it was time to leave. Empty handed.

Having dropped cousin Andrew back at his flat they said their final goodbyes, promising the earliest possible reunion. The men embraced each other fondly and posed for the final photo of the trip, arms around shoulders. Leaving Vásárhely behind, Adam headed for Road 15, passing Torda. The Jaguar purred away along the mountain road, with the battery charge gauge still showing the slight deficit.

Adam decided that if he wasn't fated to take away the secrets of the mountain, then at least then he would get one more glimpse of it. He took a lesser road and eventually the bean-shaped, very artificial, smooth-looking mountain near the Gorge of Torda came into view. The wear and tear on the roads showed that they had been used recently by heavy-duty traffic, totally out of harmony with the peaceful nature of the surrounding countryside. Deep cuts and the occasional dried mud marks of tank caterpillar tracks were obvious signs of recent military activity. It was a quiet day, except for some carts, tractors and people going lazily about their chores. Or that was what he first thought. He decided to pull up at the roadside.

'You know, Gabs, we are about to leave Transylvania, who knows for how long. With all the family visiting we have done, we have not bought a single souvenir. Would you pick some of those lovely wild flowers for me to press?' He asked her, loudly enough for the listening device to note.

Gabrielle immediately understood what he wanted. 'Of course, darling! Over there are some gorgeous ones by the roadside,' she agreed, equally loudly.

Ahead of him in the low autumn sunshine a number of people were in clear view through the windscreen.

Gabrielle walked over to the roadside ditch, whilst Adam concentrated on his view. All activity seemed to stop and most people turned nonchalantly towards the car. Three different objects, from a tattered briefcase to a food box, suddenly reflected a flash of the sun hitting lenses. The micro-cameras were obviously rolling and he knew he was in the right place, but he felt totally ineffectual.

Gabrielle returned with a bunch of glorious flowers and placed them on her lap. As they set off they discussed the colours in easily understandable, slow English, and Adam, still concentrating on the scenery to his right, turned off the road at the picturesque village of Mészkő, heading north on a virtual dirt track. Just past the chapel on the left, curious activity became evident. Young men of roughly the same age with similarly cropped haircuts, denoting military origin, were engaged in well-organised idle activities. A slightly older man was talking to the lapel of his jacket as Adam took a sharp left-hand turn. He had only a few seconds in which to pull up. The mud road was blocked by an overturned lorry, which, judging by its rusty state, must have been there for some time. The road was clearly not wide enough for a U-turn and he decided to reverse back. At the junction the man, still talking into his lapel, was waiting for him.

The conversation that followed was a masterpiece of international communication where the parties don't share a common language. With a little Romanian and German, spiced by some French from Gabrielle and, whenever totally stuck, reluctantly rescued by a little Hungarian, Adam and the man argued over the tourist map as to his supposed route. Whenever Adam pointed anywhere near the green oval shape in the distance, the man started to wave his hands, indicating the 'no-go' nature of the place. Eventually, running out of patience, he traced his finger along Road 75 and back to Torda. Adam reluctantly agreed to return to the Torda–Kolozsvár road, which would take him back to the point where he had entered the country some two weeks before.

The hopes he had of seeing some of the most spectacular parts of the old Principality of Transylvania and crossing over to Hungary at Gyula were now out of the question. He knew he would save a lot of time on the old road. He changed his plans and decided that the prudent thing was to get out of Romania as soon as possible. He told Gabrielle what he was about to do, which met with her total and grateful acceptance.

'Do you want to listen to an opera, darling?' She grappled for a cassette.

'Yes please, it seems like a thousand years since we listened to *Lakmé* on the way in.' Adam sounded apprehensive.

'I was thinking of something more cheerful, like *Die Entführung*. She pushed in a cassette of the old Josef Krisp recording and the splendid, upbeat introduction suddenly commenced.

'An escape, or is it an abduction, from the seraglio – how appropriate, you're right. Herr Mozart is bound to change my mood. Oh God, what a depressing place this has become, and not only by bad fortune, but bad intention too. Let's get the hell out of here.' He pressed the accelerator down and tapped the battery gauge, which still showed a reduced reading. Gabrielle nodded in understanding. 'We will have a slow crossing at the border,' Adam added, knowing the Securitate 'recording studio' had to be removed from somewhere behind the glove compartment.

For the last time they passed the huge oval, artificial mountain on the left. Although the entrance was on the other side, the activity around it was reminiscent of moles coming and going in the middle of the night. He was annoyed with himself for not having been able to collect its secrets, whatever they might have been. He drove on, knowing that there were only three sad hours left in Romania.

Next to it they saw another small wonder of the world; the legend of the Crevasse of Torda, created by God to save the life of St László. The knightly King of Hungary was trying to escape from his ungodly foes when, in response to his prayer, the Almighty opened up the ground behind him to swallow up his enemies in its horrendous depths.

After Mozart, Adam requested the carefully selected highlights of *Der Ring* that he had painfully put together from the famed recording of the Vienna Opera with Solti. He thought Wagner suited the dramatic scenery. In spite of the poor road the car covered the mileage with consummate ease. He drove through Nagyvárad, a truly Hungarian city trapped in Romania, where Karl Dittersdorf had spent many productive years as the Kapellmeister of the Catholic bishop in the eighteenth century. The large impersonal frontier station soon came into view.

Adam drove straight into the 'special lane', where he was stopped by a frontier guard. He gave the uniformed man their two passports. The officer leafed through all the pages and was about to hand them back when the lieutenant, whom Adam recognised from when they had entered two weeks before, appeared from the office, fastening his tunic. He was running towards the Jaguar.

'I'll have those!' He snatched the passports out of the hands of his NCO.

'Dr Zenta, there are a few other formalities to be done, like an extensive customs search of your car. There has been such a lot of drug smuggling going on, mainly from Turkey, mind you. You don't happen to be carrying anything given to you by strangers, do you?' He managed a faint, rather surly smile and gave a lazy salute. Meanwhile the surveillance cameras were recording their every movement.

Adam reassured him that he wasn't a drug smuggler and handed the keys to the lieutenant, knowing that on the car's return the battery gauge would show a normal reading. The lieutenant got into the vacated seat and drove enthusiastically to the concrete building, where the blue-overalled mechanics were waiting. Adam and Gabrielle entered the drab waiting room.

'Gabs, I'll be so very pleased to be a hundred and fifty yards farther away from here.' He pointed towards the just-visible Hungarian sentry along the road.

'Me too, darling, me too.' She moved closer and kissed him.

'I hate the Romanians, they are the most incompetent, bombastic lot, with their pseudo-Latin reinvention of themselves. Whatever they do is a caricature of the real thing, they're so bloody obvious. The country is full of natural wealth and even with the theft of this perfectly run province they have managed to become the paupers of Europe.' Adam was letting off steam.

'Stop it, darling. I know you're upset but the walls have ears – you told me so.'

'I don't care any more, they can't pin anything on me. Anyway, to hell with them!' He felt frustrated, knowing that he was about to leave empty handed.

~

To Adam's amazement it was the sergeant who drove his car back from the concrete garage in a most competent way, as if he had never driven anything but Jaguars all his life. Not so stupid, Adam thought. He pulled up smartly and got out and, ushering the two into the car, hurried into the office. As Adam and Gabrielle settled in, the lieutenant ran across the tarmac in some hurry to push the red button on the panel of the stand to open the massive, electrically controlled barrier. As the large armoured car-proof structure slowly started its journey upwards, he bent down to Gabrielle's open window.

'There they are!' He said in a whisper, and threw a small transparent plastic bag secured with simple rubber bands, containing three black microfilms, on to her lap, once again mistaking her position as the driver's.

He had hardly finished the sentence when the sirens started to scream from the four corners of the compound. Everyone turned towards the sergeant, who was now running out of the TV monitor room, having spotted his superior's action on one of the screens. He was fumbling to unbuckle his gun holster. The lieutenant, realising he was exposed, swung on to the boot, wedging his knee against the spoiler and holding on to the base of the small aerial on top of the rear window. He too was searching for his gun as the sergeant got nearer to the panel with the red button. His face was frenzied. Baring his teeth, he pounded on it several times, but it was too late, and the blue-, yellow- and red-painted barrier continued to rise. Its electronics could not accept another command until it had reached its uppermost position. There was still some distance between it and the car. Adam kicked down fully and the long engine housing of the car lifted upwards in response to the acceleration. The barrier reached its top position and a second later it started to descend. The sergeant held his gun and took aim into the blinding sun, but by then the lieutenant was comfortably ready for the shoot-out. There was a split-second difference between the timing of the two shots, just about enough of a difference to ensure that the NCO fell holding his shoulder, his bullet ricocheting off the descending barrier. The nought-to-sixty acceleration of 5.1 seconds was enough for Adam to slip underneath it, tyres screeching, gravel flying as he continued to gather speed. The poor lieutenant just about managed to hold on to the spoiler as they now suddenly had to pull up at the much smaller Hungarian control post, spinning to the left to get behind the building. A submachine gun fired towards them as the two men leaped out of and off the car and took cover behind the concrete wall of the small office, leaving the bewildered Gabrielle to her own devices. They were totally exhausted by their few seconds' journey, which had hardly taken them the length of a football pitch.

'Lieutenant Georghe Lupu, but from this moment on George Farkas, of the Romanian State Security Directorate; I request political asylum and demand high-level debriefing on the matter of a breach of the Warsaw Treaty.' He even managed a smart salute this time, staking his future on the fact that although the two communist governments were supposedly friendly, there was enough entrenched animosity between them to dream up some reason to refuse his extradition.

The exhausted lieutenant did not mention the microfilms Adam had last seen on Gabrielle's lap. Adam just added that he was delighted to help an ex-countryman in his escape and indicated his desire for an early onward departure. He presented their passports, which were duly stamped, and for the first time he shook hands with the burly lieutenant as they smiled at each other. Adam waved back to him as he turned away at the door and started to walk back to the car, where the cool Gabrielle was waiting for him.

'Where are they?' He asked impatiently as he turned the ignition key.

Gabrielle looked at him, shaken. 'Oh, darling, I don't know how to tell you this, but they are back there.' She pointed towards the Romanian frontier station.

'What happened, for God's sake? I saw them on your lap!' he shouted, nearly hitting a bulky lorry.

'Adam ... I thought ... well, I really thought that you would never make it under the barrier and I threw them out. They only looked like some small film containers and I knew they were stolen so I thought if you had to stop, they shouldn't find them on you. Don't you think ...?' Her eyes grew larger and larger as she went on explaining the inexplicable.

'No, I don't bloody think! They were the real purpose of this journey, for God's sake, and you just threw them out!'

'I didn't understand their purpose, that's all, and those people were so terrifying, I just didn't want any trouble for you.' She pulled away. 'You know the Romanian lieutenant on the boot, he threw his gun into the car when the two of you went to the Hungarian checkpoint.

Here it is.' She handed over the revolver, still smelling of cordite from the shooting.

'Give it to me!' He snatched it from her hand. 'I might even shoot you with it!' Adam placed the gun under his seat.

'Adam, what were you going to do with those films?' Gabrielle asked, with more than a little interest in her voice.

'Look here, Gabs,' his voice turned somewhat sarcastic, 'I was going to take them home with us and give them to a nice little man called Arthur and forget all about them.' He calmed down. 'But obviously I was never meant to have them,' he added sadly. 'I was just going to be a good delivery boy.'

'Sounds like spying to me.'

'Gabs, don't ever use that word to anyone! Never!! Promise!!! I just wanted to do someone a favour.' His voice was at breaking point as he thought of his signature on the Official Secrets Act. 'I suppose I was never meant to have them,' he whispered to himself, pressing his foot down on the accelerator. Ahead of them the Great Hungarian Plain, which he knew as the Puszta, suddenly expanded like a friendly, grand invitation.

～

Adam sat down on the chair behind his desk, facing the usual mounds of correspondence before him. Gabrielle came in with a whisky and handed it to him. The clinking of the ice against the glass meant home, comfort and pleasure, all things one should treasure, he thought. He picked up the telephone to make his last-ever call to Arthur.

'Who are you calling – can't it wait?' Gabrielle asked.

'Just want to let Arthur know that I have absolutely nothing for him. I want to get it over with.' He started to dial one of the few numbers he knew by heart, having always considered it too banal to learn telephone numbers.

'No, don't do that, darling! Wait a minute.' Gabrielle took the receiver out of her husband's hand and replaced it. Adam looked at her with consternation. 'I have something here for you.' She smiled and fumbled in her Louis Vuitton shoulder bag.

Adam stared at her face, which burst into her captivating smile as she placed the small transparent plastic bag, secured with criss-crossed rubber bands, on his desk. In the cheap-looking package the black microfilm containers were just visible. 'Howzat!?'

Adam looked at the miserable package, then the beaming Gabrielle, then the plastic package again. 'For goodness' sake, Gabs, what sort of game is this?' I could have a coronary, he thought, but realising his good fortune he relaxed.

'Gabs, you will suffer for this!' He stood up.

She ran out of the consulting room and headed upstairs, towards the flat, Adam close behind her, two stairs at a time. She tried to slam the bedroom door shut, but Adam was too fast. She threw herself on to the bed.

'What are you going to do to me?' she asked, laughing. 'I'm ready for my punishment.'

He pulled off his spotted tie and started to unbutton his shirt.

∽

Adam took advantage of Saturday morning to take his 'detail' to the MoD office and Arthur, who was beaming as he walked through the door into his small room, which resembled a corporation paper recycling tip. They shook hands and without any further ado Adam put the films on his controller's desk.

'Adam, if these contain what they are supposed to contain – and I have no reason to doubt that they do – you have given us a trump card at the START 2 negotiating table. This is an unbelievable coup,' he started off in a staccato voice. Adam knew the old spy was excited. 'Are you ready for a formal debrief?'

Adam nodded.

They walked along the long corridor running parallel to the Thames and turned left into one of the oak-panelled boardrooms. There were only a few unoccupied chairs left, one of them at the very end of the large table, obviously earmarked for Adam. He sat down, feeling a little more excited than usual. Arthur took the chair next to his. There was another one, empty, on his right.

The chairman, a new face for Adam, said he was from Naval Intelligence. This brought a smile to Adam's face, as the whole thing was about a landlocked matter, but that's the way the Brits work, he thought. The chairman began by saying that the first word from the laboratory was that the films were up to expectations, both in content and quality. He said he was much indebted to Mr Szábó for the initial tip-off and to both operators. Adam looked up and smiled; he was glad that Lieutenant Lupu, aka Farkas, also got a mention.

Adam was invited to give his account, which was mercifully short. 'Two weeks of expectation and getting absolutely nothing but Romanian aggravation, followed by less than a minute's high activity, which made me more exhausted than sidestepping a hundred yards in Courchevel's powdery new snow.' He carefully omitted any reference to Gabrielle's clandestine activity.

'I must interrupt.' The commodore raised his hand. 'I don't think we should continue without the other operator.'

Adam smiled at the chance to meet the burly and brave lieutenant for the third time He turned around as he heard the door open behind him. He threw his hands to his head in frustration and utter surprise as he saw Gabrielle walk in, wearing a smart business suit and a smile. Around her shoulder was her favoured Louis Vuitton bag.

'How stupid of me!' Adam yelled, and banged on the heavy oak table. 'It was there for me to see and I was blind. Bloody blind!' He sat down, still holding his head, as his wife placed a reassuring hand on his shoulder. He looked up at her and she smiled the smile he had fallen in love with. Her blue eyes were full of tears.

They all looked at the emotional couple at the bottom end of the table and the young naval chairman of the debriefing committee stood up.

'The evaluation of the films will take some three weeks. There is no need to continue now. Can I just say thank you to Dr and Mrs Zenta for their valuable work and adjourn this meeting until such time as we can meet in less emotional circumstances. Meanwhile can I just say to you both that you will not be used operationally in the future.' He started clapping and the others followed. Arthur even stood up for a moment to show his own appreciation.

Andrew Zsigmond

Gabrielle and Adam left the room and hurried down the long corridor into the lazy autumn sunshine of the Embankment. He put his arm around his wife's shoulder. She drew nearer. 'We have a lot to talk about, Gabs. Let's find a pub, I'm dying for a pint.'

'Tattersalls?' She asked cheekily.

30

Epilogue

It took them a lot longer than the time of 'a pint' in the 'Haymarket' to disentangle all the whens, wheres and hows of their involvement with each other's activities. To spy on a spy wasn't all that unusual, and although the rule book was quite clear that one should not fall in love with one's subject, Gabrielle did eventually get clearance from Arthur and Co. to marry Adam, provided always that she continued her surveillance of him during *The Gay Hussar Plan*.

Gabrielle had felt immensely sorry for Adam when she slipped the films into her handbag, but she could not even countenance the possibility of Adam – as a chance result of an acute attack of misplaced sentimentality for his old land and hatred for the oppressors of his birthplace – letting the details fall into the hands of the Hungarian government, however much they regarded themselves as 'reform communists' by then. After all, the Warsaw Treaty was still in existence, even if only on paper.

Adam felt deeply hurt – for a while at least – at not being fully trusted, but that too he considered 'was part of the game'. He wondered whether his beloved Britain would ever trust him, but then, putting it the other way around, he asked himself would a Briton ever be trusted even in the most democratic Hungary. His own answer was an unequivocal 'no', and that made him feel a little better.

They were more at ease between themselves now that they could disregard the Official Secrets Act and Adam had to laugh when Gabrielle told him that, as an SIS agent at Central Office, she had had to pick up political snippets. The farthest she ever got was finding out that the odd 'promising' young Tory MP was a well-closeted queer. The Service loved that sort of information and she was encouraged to unearth more of it.

⁓

After due deliberation, Adam came to the inevitable conclusion that for him it was back to mainstream psychiatry, spiced with a little golf at Hendon, skiing whenever possible and the odd flutter on the financial markets. And Covent Garden, of course, for a little 'real fun'! With the exception of golf, Gabrielle was only too happy to be involved.

Having left the world of 'dead-letter boxes', 'brush contacts' and being a 'messenger boy', their happy, if not ordinary, life continued around family events. The boys and Vicky were happy to partake in such activities, when it suited, and their attitude was summed up in the way they addressed Adam.

'The Controller' became the pseudonym that he was never allowed to shed. A latecomer to the family was Erika from Hungary. The pretty blonde daughter of Adam's younger sister Anna came to study at RADA 'to become a star'. She reminded Adam of himself all those years ago when he had arrived in Dover so full of expectation and he was convinced that she, too, would make it.

⁓

Less than ten years were left of the old century when, during an afternoon consultation period, Hilary announced with noticeable displeasure in her voice that 'a Ms Tracy Stuart' was on the telephone. It was a voice from the past, one that he wanted to forget – for good. Yet somehow he felt he wanted to see her.

He was amazed. They met a few hours later when she entered his consulting room. Tracy was what she has always been – a cool beauty who had remained in a time warp. It was all still there, the flowing blonde hair cascading to her shoulders and surrounding a pale face, and oh, those evergreen eyes! Their momentary embrace was that of old friends, but Adam prolonged it, old memories returning with the force of an avalanche for at least a second, when it became whatever they each wanted it to be. He ignored the vague reason for the consultation and by the end of their conversation he could think of nothing but not letting her leave. The invitation for dinner left his lips with the ease it used to more than a decade before. The acceptance was equally quick. The arrangement was to meet at Giovanni's, the best-hidden restaurant in the West End.

Adam buzzed through to Gabrielle in the lounge upstairs and said that he had been suddenly called to the College and, the way things sounded, he would be late coming home.

At the intimate Italian restaurant in Goodwin's Court, awkward at first, they had hardly started to eat when their feet accidentally touched and he realised that their old feelings had risen like a menacing phoenix.

Tracy's flat, granted to her in her recent divorce settlement from James, a sort of theatrical agent, was in the grandiose Chesterfield House in South Andley Street. There was no question of not inviting Adam back; he just followed her straight to the pink-and-white bedroom and it took him less than a split second to justify to himself his wayward presence there.

Their doomed second affair was a very short one. Reminiscing over the past invariably brought tears to Tracy's eyes but, strangely, not to Adam's any more. He found her more emotional than all those years ago, more easily upset, more tender and responsive. What annoyed him was that she seemed totally undemanding as far as his time and affection were concerned, which he should have considered welcome, but found irrational. The affair, he knew, could not last. He thought he was under Tracy's spell again but felt he had to keep delaying the inevitable break. When it arrived, it came with the suddenness of a bolt from the blue.

Adam noticed that something was dreadfully wrong with Tracy's short-term memory. During a dinner at the fashionable Langan's Brasserie, a question from her alerted the dormant physician in him. He spent the next hour probing and testing her surreptitiously. It became apparent to him that she was facing an enormous problem when she started to relate a story she had only just completed a few minutes before. Stuck in the middle of a sentence, talking about a close friend, she looked at Adam across the table in total desperation and whispered that she could not remember what 'she' was called. Seeing the tears of confusion appearing in her eyes, he gently offered the missing name, which helped for a while. A few sentences later she failed again. Staring into the distance and then looking at him she cried out, 'Adam, what's the matter with me?'

Adam hurriedly took her back to her flat, kissed her and arranged for her to see him first thing in the morning. He spent a sleepless night lying next to Gabrielle.

Next morning Tracy walked in two hours late.

He showed to her to the patient's chair and with that gesture he realised that their second affair was also over. He questioned her about things he knew she should know and found that she gave several inaccurate answers. He picked up the telephone and dialled the Middlesex Hospital Neurology Department and talked to Sir Desmond Bark-Jones, who immediately offered 'to run a few tests'.

Their parting kiss was once again that of two friends.

Within a year Dr Alois Alzheimer's sclerosis claimed a beautiful and far-too-young-a victim.

Gabrielle was once again a step ahead of her husband. On Friday morning, the day of the funeral, she told Adam that she had arranged the cancellation of all his morning appointments and handed him his black necktie. 'I understand you have a funeral to go to – spots will not do today,' she said, turning on her heel. Putting it on, Adam looked at himself in the mirror and met the steely glance of his own reflection, offering him a vision of moral blindness which was not prepared to be kind to him.

~

The coming decade saw the now totally grey, steadily ageing but still very upright Adam discharging a tremendous amount of work. He completed the presidency of the Royal Society of Medicine in great style, in no little part thanks to Gabrielle's skilful help with its important social dimension.

With the 'outbreak of democracy in Hungary', as he referred to the changes of 1989, he was made a very welcome guest there and presidential honours followed in abundance. Knighted for his part in the revolution and his uncompromising stance against communism, he was made the new republic's honorary consul in the United Kingdom and received the honorary rank of brigadier general in the oldest regiment of the country, the National Guard.

Back in Hungary Nicholas died at the ripe old age of eighty-five, having already buried his much younger second wife, Emilia. Gabrielle and Adam, with the twins, attended the simple Calvinist funeral in Jonk, and on lowering the lid of the coffin just before the ceremony, Adam's thumb caught the unburied edge of a nail, causing him to bleed from the spot he had injured with the scythe at Titus' grave many years before. He showed it to Gabrielle, who whispered what the peasant had said to him: 'There is a blood bond between the three of you.' Adam's lips twisted into an inappropriate smile.

～

The European storms of 1987, the worst in two hundred years, were followed by various hurricanes, notably Alicia, Gilbert and Hugo – then came the destruction of the Piper Alpha oil rig in the North Sea and the Exxon Valdez oil spillage in Alaska. This catalogue of disasters was topped by the San Francisco earthquake of 1989, and there were the ongoing and by now non-newsworthy settlements of the asbestosis claims in America. Thus 1990 had already announced itself in rather poor form when Adam – instead of his regular cheque from Lloyds – received a letter from Mr Anthony Gooda announcing his first loss of some £15,000, wiping out his previous year's gain at a stroke. He sought advice from his agent, who told him to increase his premium limit to half a million pounds. By the following summer there was another demand from the same pen for £200,000. The commiserating Mr Gooda added that the amount should be paid in full within six weeks, otherwise it would 'attract interest'.

Cursing – in three languages – every asbestos fibre ever invented, Adam prescribed himself a Zantac for his self-diagnosed 'oesophageal reflux' and wrote out the large cheque, having been reassured that he could not possibly lose more than another hundred thousand. The following year he lost another £400,000 and joined the largest and fastest-growing club in the country. He became a deficit millionaire and his name was mentioned in the press with other victims from the Establishment, such as the Duchess of Kent, Frederick Forsyth, Edward Heath and Camilla Parker Bowles. It was time to 'mortgage the cat', as the current saying amongst the Lloyds 'names' ran. As the ever-larger claims continued, he inadvertently found himself amongst those who were convinced that underpinning these financial disasters was the possibility of mismanagement of the syndicates, which had now started to claim more than just the victims' money.

The ever-sensitive and supportive Gabrielle soon spotted Adam's increasing anxiety and characteristically offered to help, suggesting that they should liquidate their assets. Pension policies were cashed in en masse and Gabrielle parted with some of her inherited jewellery. By the end of the year they had to decide the fate of their holiday home in Spain.

The setting of some of their best times together, and those of their extended family, 'Zenyblanca' was put on the market. The sale affected Adam far worse than he was prepared to admit, and the continuing dismantling of his financial base, to avoid bankruptcy and the usual consequence of being struck off the Medical Register, took its toll. His indigestion worsened, his sleep pattern suffered with the unending stress and his sudden ageing became noticeable. He reacted the only way he could, by working all the hours God sent. This helped him in the short term, but he knew well enough that he was stretched to the limit and however valiant his efforts, he could not possibly win the battle against that most English of all institutions, Lloyds.

They remortgaged the last possession they had, the house in Harley Street, and he appeared in front of Dr Mary Archer, the wife of the celebrated author, who was heading the Hardship Committee of the once proud monolith. After being reminded of the nature of 'unlimited liability', he made his case to her that although he personally 'could live on top of a tree' the only way he could continue paying was to be allowed to work in the fully mortgaged house. He had to pretend to be 'in control', as 'a failed psychiatrist would not be able to attract one depressed or even deluded patient'. Dr Archer was sympathetic and he was allowed to continue to work, provided he continued to make regular payments. His 'dyspepsia' was becoming an increasing problem for him and taking Zantac became a regular habit.

He also considered spying again, but with the political changes in post-Berlin-Wall Europe, he was of no further use to the SIS. Detente had put an end to picking up packages or carrying microfilms and the Service was now committed to undermining the IRA to such a degree that it would have to negotiate from weakness. There were, of course, 'jobs' working against the drug-supplying countries of the Third World, but he knew his face did not fit for that. Gabrielle became his strength simply by force of her sheer presence – she could substantially alter his mood, but she needed to be in the know. Adam was still too proud to put all before her. He still considered that everything was 'his fault' and that he – alone – had to find the answers. And above all she had to be protected.

Retirement permanently postponed, Adam carried on working with Gabrielle in search of further potential cost-cutting. Their partnership worked well, and she found the secrets of the stars who were still coming to be treated by the handsome, white-haired psychiatrist, tremendous fun. It was a new world for her, and she soon became fascinated by the variety of the work – and especially Adam's holistic approach to eating disorders and above all the way he introduced hypnotherapy into the much-debated neurolinguistic programming in psychosomatic illnesses.

The swingeing regular repayments over the years rendered him virtually penniless.

At sixty-five he still cut a handsome, if ageing, figure. Gabrielle, some twelve years his junior, on the other hand, was a beautiful middle-aged woman with a future. In moments of contemplative self-doubt he wondered whether he had anything to offer anybody – especially her.

The last year of the century was passing them by and like everyone else they were involved in planning some sort of celebration. The Zentas decided to keep it simple. Through his consular contact, Adam stocked up with Törley *sec* to beat the spiralling champagne prices and invited the family and friends to an open house in Harley Street. They were 'going to have some fun!'

Gabrielle, always anxious to ensure that Adam was 'eating the right things', told him that he looked as if he had lost weight once again. Adam reassured her – patting his tummy – that it was time to do exactly that and he was feeling extremely well. And as he had never lost a day of study or work in his life through illness, he was not about to start now. He would explain that the odd episode of indigestion he suffered after late-night eating was well controlled, 'with Zantac – the new wonder drug'. And anyway, all men of his age suffered with that.

Gabrielle pointed out that she was well aware of that but she didn't like to see him take so many of them.

In December Adam had just returned from Christmas shopping with his granddaughters Emma and Ilana when he suddenly felt rather ill. He walked to his consulting room and looked into the mirror hanging over his washbasin. The reflection of a pale and sunken face shocked him, but he couldn't dwell on it too long because of the bout of vomiting that followed. When it was over he took another Zantac and decided that it was time to examine himself. He lay on his much-loved Victorian examination couch and opened his shirt. Placing his right fingers over his left hand he decided to palpate the pit of his stomach. Yes, there was a definite hard swelling extending from below the ribcage. He dug in deeper and felt tenderness over the enlarged liver area.

Adam fastened his clothes and walked back to the mirror, this time feeling the sides of his neck. There was a small painless swelling on the left side. He looked at his image again and was utterly shocked when he saw the gap between his collar and his neck. He allowed himself a short sardonic smile, straightened his tie (spotted as always) and walked back to his desk. The two-minute telephone conversation that followed set up a consultation with Sir Douglas Green, whom he had got to know when he presided over the Royal Society of Medicine. He was told to 'pop over' in the morning. All Adam had to do was to cross the street.

The fearful Gabrielle, waiting at the bottom end of the scanning room of the King Edward VII Hospital, was looking at the gloomy expressions on the faces of the radiologist and the surgeon. She knew the profession well – every gesture and innuendo was engraved on her mind from the RSM lectures she had so regularly attended during Adam's presidency. She realised that the news was going to be bad.

The four of them met a few minutes later in the small office of Sir Douglas. There was no need for pretence.

The word 'inoperable' would remain in the haze of the following day, but Gabrielle would not give up reminding Adam about the 'many new advances in chemotherapy' – and demanding 'other opinions, damn it!!!' Adam was determined that he was not going to let them start him on chemotherapy until January: 'I'm not having the family here and me wearing a bloody wig,' adding that in any event he had no inspiring belief in it.

During the week leading up to the millennial day he had to succumb to administering morphine to himself, which gave him enough respite from the pain to examine his options. There was but one. He headed for the safe and picked up the insurance policy lying next to the gun of the 'burly' Romanian lieutenant, brought back under his Jaguar seat. It was the only policy he had managed to keep away from Lloyds' claws. Medical & Mercantile Life Assurance Co. Ltd was proudly displayed on the plastic policy cover as he opened up the document. Definitely valid, £500,000 assigned to Mrs Gabrielle Zenta – not much, he thought, but it would give her an income. Then his eyes focused on paragraph 7. It all came back. To save on the premiums, so many years before, he had initialled the permanent suicide clause. He hit the desk with his fist in anger. 'I can't even blow my bloody brains out!! Well, we'll see about that!' He replaced everything in the safe and started to think. There did not seem to be an answer. In suicide, both the method and the substance are detectable with ease. He remembered how the Bulgarian Secret Service used to bump off their dissidents with minute pellets fired from an umbrella. That was until a London biochemist found that the inexplicable 'coronaries' were due to a ricin resin. If only I'd kept up with my pharmacology better, he thought. He walked to his bookshelf and took his old Stedman's compendium from the top row. He flicked it open at succinylcholine chloride.

Andrew Zsigmond

⁓

December 31st in 1999 was a horrible hazy sort of day. A good way to leave the century behind in the hope a better future. Adam had gone to get his hair cut the preceding week and had even endured a couple of sessions in front of the ultraviolet lamp to get rid of the dreadful ashen-grey hue of his face. The night would have to pass in style; 43a Harley Street was full of an expectant buzz. The whole family was present, compleminting Adam on how well he looked. The two granddaughters were already giving the piano in the drawing room a very hard time. Adam gave himself another dose of morphine and started to pour the champagne for the Puszta cocktail, which contained just that little extra touch of the Hungarian firewater, pálinka. He wanted them to be in an extravagant, convivial mood. He managed to hide the one episode of vomiting in the patients' toilet in which he saw a little fresh arterial blood. He continued with the festivities, putting his arms around Gabrielle's shoulders whenever he could.

Gabrielle's fare was befitting. She produced a buffet that Claridges would have proudly displayed. The established post-Lloyds Zenta house wine, the Hungarian Tokay Oremus from Disznókő – the nearest thing from the old country, resembling a Chablis *premier cru* – went down well.

A few minutes before midnight Adam opened the front windows of the drawing room and put on the television set. The noise in the streets of the capital was overwhelming. A few seconds before the hour the face of Big Ben came on to the screen and the countdown began throughout the nation. Flashes already showed that the celebrations were over in some of the main centres of the world. The streets of Budapest, Berlin and Paris were already becoming deserted, but London was about to explode in frenzy. David Dimbleby was counting down and the room went suddenly quiet. Five – four – three – two – one – zero. The cannon of the Household Artillery opened their twenty-one-gun salute in Hyde Park. The cameras flashed between the new capitals of the UK – Belfast, Edinburgh, Cardiff and then back to London. Happy faces, drunks, young lovers and old wrinklies were interposed in a grand collage. Happy new century to you all! Adam raised his glass for the last time. The Törley was poured by the twins and the kissing began. It was all so convenient for Adam. Without fuss and bother he could go around for a farewell embrace and a kiss. When, at last, he got to Gabrielle he kissed her with passion that reminded them both of the first time. They kissed again and again. Gabrielle remarked that it was the best night of her life. Adam knew it was to be his last.

The melee continued as Adam walked out of the room for the last time. The excruciating pain had returned by the time he got to his study. The syringe was ready in his main drawer. He knew the substance was still undetectable and that there must be no easily noticeable needle mark for the post-mortem that would be demanded by the insurance company. The extra-thin thirty-gauge needle would help. He rolled his tongue up against his hard palate. The two sublingual veins were easy to see. The left one looked a shade larger. He took the syringe in his right hand and aimed carefully. The two millilitres of crystal-clear liquid emptied into the tortuous blue vein with ease. He had just enough time to drop the plastic syringe into the open fire and drag himself to his chair.

Knowing the inevitable end was near, Adam felt taken over by a strange feeling. Yes, he thought again, your life does flash past you, but it was more than that. He also saw Titus' proud moustachioed face, followed by that of the handsome Nicholas, then his own. He tried to think of a common denominator, and there it was: the three of them totally obsessed with the love of their women. From darkness emerged a glorious kaleidoscope made by the beautiful faces of the women in their lives, like shooting stars, only to pass him by. The experience was most agreeable. Suddenly, a magnificent flurry of incandescent red and yellow flames of burning straw framed an image of Gabrielle's face, from the time they had first met. Then it all disappeared in a split second, a momentary image, just like the lives of the three Zentas.

Adam rubbed his eyes and reached out for the photograph of Gabrielle he had taken during their first trip to Budapest, which he always kept on his desk. Holding it in his hands, longing to kiss it for the last time, he gasped for air, then pressed the picture against his chest and fell on top of it, suffering a massive heart attack.

Hearing the noise of shattering glass in the study Gabrielle started to walk towards the closed oak doors.

She opened them with some apprehension. From the famed street ever louder drunken strains of *'Auld Lang Syne'* filled the elegant study through the large open windows.

THE END

Andrew Zsigmond is a doctor in Liverpool. He was born in Transylvania of Sekler-Magyar stock into a family ennobled in 1604. His parents moved to Hungary in 1944, where he was educated, studying medicine at the University of Pécs, where he became involved in the Hungarian Revolution. The uprising was brutally crashed in 1956 and with his friends he escaped into Austria, where he was recruited to work as an apprentice coal miner in Yorkshire. He soon gained a place as a medical student at Liverpool University, qualifying as a doctor in 1961. He has worked as a physician since and now has a private practice in the city.

In 1963 he became a British subject and for a few years was involved in politics, standing for Parliament in 1992 as a Conservative candidate. In 1993 he was made Honorary Consul for the Republic of Hungary and was decorated for his part in the uprising by the President.

He has been president of the Liverpool Medical Institution and chairman of the Association of Aviation Medical Examiners. Knighted by several international orders of chivalry, he was made a chivalric baron in 1998. He is multilingual, and lists among his hobbies opera, classical music, the arts, golf (badly) and skiing (better). Clubs: Liverpool Artists Club, the Liverpool Athenaeum and the London RAF Club.

Flames of Straw is his first novel.

Lightning Source UK Ltd.
Milton Keynes UK
UKOW04f0125121113

220862UK00002B/53/P

9 781438 949086